THE EMPTY CROWN

THE EMPTY CROWN

The Sword of Maiden's Tears
The Cup of Morning Shadows
The Cloak of Night and Daggers

ROSEMARY EDGHILL

GuildAmerica
Books

THE SWORD OF MAIDEN'S TEARS
Copyright © 1994 by Rosemary Edghill
THE CUP OF MORNING SHADOWS
Copyright © 1995 by Rosemary Edghill
THE CLOAK OF NIGHT AND DAGGERS
Copyright © 1997 by Rosemary Edghill

Published by arrangement with
DAW Books, Inc.
375 Hudson Street
New York, New York 10014

ISBN 1-56865-342-5

PRINTED IN THE UNITED STATES OF AMERICA

CONTENTS

The Sword of Maiden's Tears

AUTHOR'S NOTES

Many things can happen in the time it takes to write a book. For example, when I began this one, the Columbia Library School was still open and the underground sections of the World Trade Center were still intact. If I had to try to revise these sections to reflect the Real World of Now, this book would have been set somewhere else.

And so I beg your readerly indulgence. The heart has its raisins which the kumquats know not of, as the French don't say.

Special thanks to:

Neil Christiansen

Kate Elliott

Bonya Far-Rider

Esther Friesner

Nicole Jordan

Daniel Sifrit

and the Ladies' Proofreading
and Cookery Consumption Society
(you know who you are)
without whom this book
would have more commas.

CONTENTS

CONTENTS

· 1 ·

Never Trust Anyone
Over 30

IT WAS APRIL 30TH and it was raining. Naomi was at kendo, Michael was at the gym, Philip was (probably) torturing small animals, and Jane was at New York Public doing passionate in-depth research on a subject of which nobody'd ever heard, and about which she would insist on telling all of them the next time Naomi made dinner. Which would be, now that Ruth came to think about it, tomorrow.

As for Ruth, Ruth was alone.

Ruth was tall and blue-eyed, brown-haired and sensible, with a face, as Naomi often said, which made her look like the better class of Flemish Madonna; oval and even, with regular unexciting features and a small pink mouth. Ruth was rather vain of that mouth, and bought it lipstick far in excess of that which is deemed needful by proto-Librarians.

People had told Ruth she was sensible from the moment she had first fallen into the toils of the educational system; so much so that by now Ruth was ready for actions senseless and insensible.

Unfortunately, she didn't seem to have any talent for them at all. After all, wasn't she on her way toward a Master's in library science—*library science,* for God's sweet sake, was there anything more sensible than that?

Sensible Ruth.

Sensible Ruth was out walking in the rain. Today was her birthday, and Ruth was thirty. Thirty. All alone, and on the threshold of the rest of her entire life, which would be spent solitary, virginal, and depressed in some minuscule upstate New York library where the book was on view between the hours of three and three-fifteen every other Wednesday.

Such a depressing future called for ice cream at the very least, and there was a Häagen-Dazs shop on Broadway.

Ruth's Columbia-sponsored housing was on 116th Street between Broadway and Riverside Drive, but the streets were fairly safe this close to the college, even at night. Marooned by the changing demographic currents of New York City, Columbia University stood like a last bastion of Gilded Age Gotham in a sea of late-twentieth century chaos surrounded by a moat of chichi restaurants and donut shops.

Ruth hesitated between ice cream and going to the Hunan Balcony and really pigging out, but when Naomi got back from her martial arts class she sometimes liked to cook. So Ruth contented herself (sensibly!) with a pint of something that ought by rights to be called Death by Chocolate and turned back toward the apartment.

The fine spring rain haloed everything and dampened her skin and clothes like heavy dew. It made the slope of 116th Street slippery as glass, and Ruth's attention was divided neatly between her footing and the ice cream as she wended along.

But a New York pedestrian is nobody's fool. She had enough attention left over to spot the body.

Ruth Marlowe, after some practice, was a good New Yorker. She'd lived in New York since she'd come to Columbia three years ago with a fistful of equivalency credits that let her collect a shatteringly inconsequential BA in History on her way to the Master's of Library Science that might actually let her earn a living. She knew the rules: If you see a supine-or-prone body, run—or at least walk fast—in the opposite direction. Never interfere. James T. Kirk would not have found a lot of sympathy here in New York City for his darling habit of breaking the Prime Directive.

But this body was different.

For one thing, it didn't look like your average muggee. Even from here, in the rain-misted streetlamp light, Ruth could see he (he?) was dressed in a bright-colored tunic and boots—maybe a medievalist wandered over from St. John the Unfinished, and thus more likely to respond favorably to an offer of help.

Unless he was dead.

Ruth tried not to think about what she'd do if he were dead, but as she minced closer she saw that he was breathing. He'd crawled out of—or into?—the narrow alley that ran between her building and the one behind it. If he hadn't been so fair, she might not have seen him.

So fair—and dressed in linen and cramoisie, though the linen was stained and there was blood in the long silver-blond hair. She crouched and leaned forward, shying away from touching him for fear of hurting him further. Her heart hammered with near-exposure to violence. But at least he was alive.

He rolled over on his back then, moaning, and with the improved angle and visibility Ruth could see that his skin was not only fair, but albino-fair. He wore a belt and baldric of silver-studded leather, luxurious and theatrical.

His ears were pointed.

Good makeup, but not period costume, Ruth was thinking, when he opened his eyes.

They were bright leaf green, and when the pupils contracted in the streetlamp's glare she could see that the pupils were slitted. They flashed in the dark like a cat's.

Ohboyohboyohboyohboy. Jane is going to kill me for being here instead of her, Ruth thought automatically.

His hands roved over his body, obviously in search of something. Ruth repressed a wince of sympathy—they looked like they'd been stepped on.

Mugged. Definitely.

Whatever he was looking for, he didn't find. His eyes focused on her and he moved, painfully, to sit up.

"My sword," the stranger said. "Where is it?"

Ruth stared into his eyes and couldn't think of a single thing to say.

Mistaking her silence for a number of things it probably wasn't, the stranger-elf began the laborious process of attempting to get to his feet. Ruth backed away and looked wildly around for someone, anyone, even Philip, to enlist in the solution of her peculiar problems. Finding none, she looked for the sword.

Ruth's experience with swords was not as limited as that of other women her age. She'd never joined the Society for Creative Anachronism (though Naomi, who cooked for the local revels, had suggested it often) but Ruth had been a medievalist by inclination all her life—and she'd practically lived in the Hall of Arms and Armor at the Met.

So Ruth looked around for a two- to four-foot piece of metal with a handle, with X- or cross- or basket-shaped hilt, in a scabbard or without one, covered with gold and jewels and enamel or just very plain.

She saw nothing fitting the description.

When she looked back at him, the elf was standing. He was taller than she was but not as tall as Michael, which was a good height to be.

Standing, his clothes were covered with a long dark cloak, making his face seem to float unsupported in the shadows. He met her eyes.

Fair, that face; fair as a flower despite the puffiness around the jaw, the split and still bleeding lip. Fair, and ageless as a nun's.

"It isn't here, is it, human girl?" The elf brushed back his hair and winced. A large plain ring on his finger flashed mirror-bright. His hand came away wet with blood, black under the streetlamps.

"Are you hurt?" Ruth asked, since one must say something, no matter how stupid. The elf sighed.

"I am hurt; I am slain; I am— Where am I, precisely?"

Reality, Ruth kept herself from saying. "New York."

"Ah."

Plainly this meant nothing to him. He looked around again—looking up, as no native-or-acculturated New Yorker would think to, and his mouth settled itself into harsh lines having little to do with the drubbing he'd received. For a moment Ruth saw the world through his eyes: a perfidious Albion of dark satanic mills, frighteningly alien.

"It seems a large place," he said. He tried to keep his voice even, but the sound of it made Ruth revise her estimate of his age downward. Younger than she, and therefore less threatening.

"Eleven million plus people—as of the last census."

He looked quickly at her, as if hoping to catch her in a lie, and she saw the quick cat-in-darkness flash of his eyes.

It was the eyes, perhaps, that decided her, with the backward wistful logic of *"If a mad ax-murderer pretending to be an elf has gone to all the trouble of getting mirrored tinted contact lenses, why don't I let him get away with it?"*

That, and the fact that it was her birthday, and she was thirty, and all her hopeful attempts to climb up to the imagined sanity and perks of the adult world didn't seem to be worth the trouble. Like Oakland, California; when you got there, there was no there there. Or so Gertrude Stein had said.

"Look," said Ruth, with firm calmness. "Why don't you come back to my apartment? You can at least get cleaned up. I'll make you a cup of tea."

"I thank you, mortal girl." He looked pleased, but not surprised— and more relieved than pleased, as if good manners would have kept him from asking for what he desperately hoped for.

"Ruth," said Ruth steadily. And besides, she could always hit him with one of Naomi's *shinai.*

"I am . . . Melior." He hesitated over the name, as if there had been going to be more. "Melior," he repeated firmly. He shook his head and winced.

"Come on." Ruth, belatedly awakening to the fact that where there had been muggers there could still be muggers, glanced up and down the hill. She took a few steps toward home and sanity, meaningfully. Melior followed.

He had long since lost track of how long he had sought the Sword, for the time changed with each Borderland he crossed, but he thought it had been long indeed. But never yet, in all his years of war and wandering, had Rohannan Melior of the House of the Silver Silences been so caught between joy and despair.

Despair, because the Sword was lost to him again. For a brief moment he had held it in his hands, and even though it had been spellbound to carry him into this city of dreadful night, Melior had found and passed many Gates, and with the Sword's aid he could win free of even the Last World itself.

But through foolishness, through inattention, through the cursed luck that had dogged every step of his quest, the Sword was ravished away, stolen by a brace of common footpads.

If that were all, despair would be his only companion. But there was Ruth.

He had never known her name until this moment, but it seemed to him that he had always known her face. It had been his companion on the blood-soaked battlefields of his homeland; a promise that he had once been too young to understand. Her image had burned in his heart like the brief bright lives of humans, only awaiting her presence to kindle itself past all extinction.

But to find her here, in this world, human and mortal and with no idea of the greater worlds that held her own in nested embrace—

It was difficult at times, Melior reflected, to know when you were well off. Was it better to search for his heart's-ease forever, or to find her like this?

And the worst of it was, she did not know him.

The lobby of the building that held Ruth and Naomi's shared apartment was one of those typical New York glass air locks, requiring for its navigation two different keys and the agility required to ski through a revolving door. Melior acted as if he'd never seen one before, which made things difficult. He watched Ruth's every movement with a grave courtesy, as though he expected to be quizzed on them later.

The building's elevator alternated between dysfunctional and homicidal, and the apartment was only on the seventh floor. Ruth opted for the stairs. Melior followed her, limping slightly, the authentic signs of a recent beating turning flushed and red.

Deliberately she did not think. Why borrow trouble when the universe gave so much of it away free? She achieved her door (7A), unlocked two more locks, and was in.

One carpet, indifferent khaki. The entryway was a clutter of inadequate mismatched bookshelves covered with trinkets, souvenirs, and just plain junk. The living room was an antiseptic horror of "furniture-provided-by-the-college"; vinyl-covered and mended in tape. She and Naomi had put throws on the couch and chairs; fake fur and patchwork, tie-dye and corduroy. Melior stepped into the middle of it like an insulted cat, senses straining at normalcy.

In the overhead light of her own living room, Ruth got her first good look at her rescue project. Forced herself to look; confronting the unwelcome head-on with iron determination, just as she had every day for the last four years. Beyond which point lay that undiscovered country from which no traveler returneth, thank you very much, and this was a hell of a time for her thoughts to lead her down *that* particular primrose path. She turned her attention back to her guest.

This was nothing ordinary in the way of Upper Manhattan mugging victims. Where it wasn't bruised, Melior's skin was as smooth and blemishless as a child's; pale as the lily. He looked foreign to this place, but whether his own place was Graustark or Elfland Ruth wasn't prepared to say.

It began to seem even less likely that this was a long, careful entrapment, a way to gain access to a woman alone, and Ruth felt herself begin to relax.

"Make yourself comfortable," Ruth said. Belatedly she became aware of half a pint of Häagen-Dazs, unconsumed, slowly melting in her hand. "I'll put on tea," she said, retreating.

The kitchen, bereft of elves, was soothing. She put the ice cream carton into the tiny freezer compartment of the antique refrigerator and put the kettle on the stove, then sluiced one tea towel to sopping and filled another with ice cubes. She put both into a bowl and returned, reluctantly, to the living room.

Melior was standing in the middle of the living room, his back to her. He'd removed his cloak and belt, and had pulled up his shirt to inspect reddened ribs that would probably be gloriously black by morning. When he heard her come in, he smoothed his clothes down and turned to greet her.

"Ah," he said, eyes on the bowl. "Probably more than I deserve."

"You're lucky you weren't stabbed," Ruth said. The words came out more harshly than she intended. She skirted around him and put the bowl on the table.

Now that he'd removed his cloak, Ruth could see him better. Melior looked gaudily medieval in red tunic and white undertunic and high leather boots, but slender rather than broad; a dancer's body. He picked up the towel full of ice and pressed it gingerly to his jaw.

"I'll get the tea," Ruth said, and fled.

Back in the safety of her kitchen—*Oh, Ruth, this is NOT a good idea*—Ruth concentrated on providing tea. Besides, she was safe, Naomi would be home soon, and Naomi was authentically dangerous with hockey stick or frying pan.

And Melior *was* hurt. You couldn't spend your entire life not helping people out of stark raving cowardice—

But was it cowardice or common sense?

Tea. Probably-still-okay milk and Demerara sugar. Big stoneware mugs. The kitchen supplies were Naomi's: if Ruth was sensible, Naomi was competent. Perhaps Naomi and Michael should get together and beget a master race of tidiers; perfect secretaries and chiefs of staff.

Ruth found half a Zabar's cake and sliced it. She puttered desperately in the kitchen, unwilling to go back to the living room and Cope once more.

Who was he? What did he want? How much of her scant time, money, and emotional energy was he going to need—and how guilty would she feel if she didn't provide them?

The teakettle shrilled. Ruth dumped loose Russian Caravan into the pot and poured water over it. Anonymous white stoneware, safe to drop.

But that meant the tray was loaded and the Minotaur must be faced. Ruth went back into the living room.

Melior was sitting at the table by the window now—the one she and Naomi used both as dining table and desk-by-courtesy. His skin was reddened from the application of ice packs, but he looked better. He looked up as she entered with the tray, and not the shadow of a suspicion crossed his face that he should leap across the room and take the tray from her. She set it down on the table. Melior looked at it.

"I guess you'd better tell me what you were doing just before you got jumped," Ruth said grudgingly.

"Gladly. But first—forgive me if I offend—is it possible, in this establishment, to bathe?"

Ruth poured out tea, black and fugitively iridescent.

"You want to take a shower?"

"Yes, if— If that is traditional," Melior said hesitantly.

Ruth spooned two heaping servings of Demerara rock into Melior's tea—*for treatment of shock, give sweetened hot liquids and wrap up warm*—and pushed it toward him. He took it and sniffed at it cautiously, then sipped.

"If it is an imposition—" he began.

"Oh, sure. I mean, no. Go ahead—I'll get you some fresh towels and stuff." Ruth fled once more.

Why does he make you so nervous? You're the one who invited him in. Ruth rummaged through the closets to find something he could wear when he came out of the shower. After some thought, she sacrificed Naomi's black kimono to the Cause. Naomi was tall, and the kimono was wide. It should do.

Because he's going to be trouble. I know he is. And my capacity for handling other people's trouble is somewhat overextended just now.

Ruth took the kimono and towels into the bathroom and piled them precariously on the edge of the sink. She made one quick tidying swipe and caught a snapshot glimpse of her reflection in the mirror: long brown hair worn in a fashion ten years out of date hanging sheepdog over her eyes; blue eyes the only vivid thing in her face, which was pleasant, sensible, and unexciting.

You're the one who was tired of being sensible, her mind maliciously reminded her.

But that was before she'd met elves, or persons purporting to be elves.

When she went back to the living room, the cake, the milk, and most of the sugar was gone. Melior was standing, looking out the window, through which could be seen Riverside Drive, the Hudson River, and (in daylight) Fort Lee, New Jersey.

"I have to find it," he said without turning around.

"Your shower's ready," Ruth said. She pointed. He walked past her into the bedroom, picking up his cloak and swordbelt as he went. There was a suitable interval, and then Ruth heard the sound of the shower. Apparently he'd figured out how to work it—assuming he didn't really know how.

She tiptoed to the bedroom door. Ruth might know armor in passing, but her real passion was clothes. She would have embraced far more socially risky acts than inviting a strange elf in for a shower, just to be alone with his clothes.

His clothes—*garb,* the SCA always called it—was laid out neatly on one of the twin beds: cloak, tunic, pants, and boots (on the floor nearby), all from the later TSR period. Gloves—well, one glove anyway; the other must have been lost. For undergarments there were a pair of knee-length drawers knitted out of a soft shiny beige yarn, knee socks and muscle shirt of the same material, and a long-sleeved shirt with a shorter hemline than the tunic. The shirt was the pale beige color of real linen and embroidered around the sleeves with an entire wildflower garden in silk floss; the front was smocked to narrowness with a thousand tiny tucks.

She turned all three pieces of knitted underwear inside out and found neither seam nor maker's mark: apparently it had been knitted all of a piece, and to size. She set them aside.

The smocked shirt yielded more clues: hand-sewing, and of a sort that ought by rights to have driven an entire convent blind. Nothing storebought or modern about this.

The pants were—it took her a moment to make up her mind— leather. Buckskin, she thought, and soaking wet, but buckskin was famous for retaining its flexibility no matter what you did to it. They'd still been making men's trousers out of it as late as the English Regency—those snow-white inexpressibles so beloved of Beau Brummell. This particular pair was flapped at the front and closed with four sterling silver buttons set with small sapphires.

Ruth sat back, aware of the chilly buzzing in her head that she associated with late nights and too much coffee—a dizzy dazzled vacation from common sense. Silver jeweled buttons?

Pointed ears?

Maybe they'd wash off while he was in the shower.

Speaking of which, she'd better hurry up.

The scarlet tunic was wool—that was an easy one—with appliqués of felt and leather on the breast and at the elbow-length sleeves. The front laced shut, the vexed grommet question having been settled by interleaving a thin piece of punched leather between the two layers of wool so that the rawhide thong wouldn't cause the wool to stretch. Once more the fabric was sumptuous, the workmanship superb. As in "several thousand dollars of custom tailoring" superb, and even if you could afford to buy it, who could you find to do it?

It was too much money to spend playing dress-up for a joke.

She turned her attention to the cape.

It was a dull blotchy thing, green and gray and brown, contemptible until you realized that pure white wool had been carefully painted with these very colors, because a man wearing such a cape—no matter how scarlet his tunic—would not be visible in a woods or from any great distance. It was half-lined with sheepskins and fastened shut halfway down its length by a system of horn buttons and leather loops sewn to the inside face. It was thick as a blanket in her hands; she could not imagine how Melior could have stood up in it, especially once it had gotten wet. Carefully she spread it over the back of a chair to dry and turned to the boots. High soft Errol Flynn style boots, reaching above the knee and notched so they could be folded over to cuff in proper buccaneer style. Soft and silky as a well-oiled Coach bag.

And strapped to instep and heel, spurs of bronze and jeweled gold. She was sure about that. Ruth had haunted enough craft fairs to know the look of handmade jewelry. She set the boots down carefully, soberly, heels together.

That left, for her delectation, a baldric and swordbelt, both top-grade harness leather. The belt was at least six inches wide and riveted with small silver roundels, each of which supported a silver ring. The for-soothly equivalent of the sadly-defunct Banana Republic photojournalist's vest: a ring for everything, and everything on its ring. A regular utility belt.

Still attached to rings were a knife in a metal scabbard and a small pouch. Reluctantly forsaking the knife—which looked to be lovely with enamel work and rock crystal—Ruth opened the pouch.

"Were you afraid I couldn't pay for my lodging?" Melior said behind her.

Ruth jumped back, agonized. "I was just—"

"Searching my possessions," Melior finished.

Naomi's black kimono came very close to not meeting in front at all. Wearing it, Melior looked like some perilously exotic Kabuki dancer; a paragraph from the lost language of cranes.

"Let me help you."

He took the pouch from her nerveless fingers and upended it on the bed.

"Signet ring—useless—sixteen *taels* in copper for chummage—useless—a useless earring, a map of no place I'm ever likely to see again, flint and steel, tinderbox, perfume, dice—useless."

"All useless. Have it if you like," he said in a deadly tired voice.

Ruth was saved from having to answer by the jingle of keys in the lock.

"Ruth?" Naomi called.

Naomi Nasmyth was about Ruth's age, but then, Naomi was deep in the toils of acquiring a Doctorate in Library Science and had been at Columbia, woman and girl, since the age of eighteen: BA in English, Master's in Library Science, Teaching Certificate, and now back to the erebean regions of the Library School's Doctoral Program.

As was often the case with roommates thrown together by fate, Naomi was all that Ruth wished to be: tall and vivid and poised and serene and organized. Black hair and hazel eyes and sangfroid that Emma Peel would envy—not to mention good at games. Ruth could have easily hated her, if not for the fact that Naomi had looked her up and down on the day she moved in and decided Ruth was in need of tidying, thereby smoothing Ruth's way enormously through the freshman maze. If there were two kinds of people in the world—Teflon and Velcro—then Naomi was definitely a Teflon person, the sort to whom trouble never stuck.

Ruth hoped it wouldn't stick now.

"She's back from the dead and ready to party! Ruth! You here?" Naomi called cheerfully.

Ruth could see the reflection of Naomi's voice in Melior's eyes. And to their mutual surprise it was Melior who moved, sliding away from one confrontation into another. Ruth barely had time to register his absence before she was moving herself, following him. She looked past his shoulder into Naomi's eyes.

Naomi's face was utterly still, entirely calm.

"Are you all right, Ruth?" she said.

Ruth stared at her, as dumbstruck as if she hadn't been hoping all night that Naomi would come back. Melior stepped aside so that Naomi could see her clearly.

"Speak, Ruth. Your friend desires to know if I have harmed you."

"He's an elf," Ruth blurted out, and the rest of her strange stasis was swamped in a burning sea of humiliation. "I mean, he was mugged, Naomi."

"Right the first time," Naomi said.

"And the second," Melior said. "I was 'mugged,' if that is the word for being assaulted by priggers and cutpurse varlets."

And that was why you decided to take up cross-dressing. Ruth could almost hear the words, but Naomi didn't say them.

"Well," said Naomi, "maybe we can help. Right, Ruth?"

Ruth swallowed hard. "Right."

Naomi heard the story of how Ruth had found him. She heard Melior's story—which, now that Ruth had a chance to hear it over a second time and while being told to someone else, consisted of little more than his name and the statement that he had been mugged and his sword stolen. After he had told Naomi that much, Melior retreated into the bedroom and emerged a few minutes later in his white undertunic, buckskins, and boots. Naomi looked at his clothes, and at Ruth's face. She did not ask any further questions.

"Looks like the first thing you need is some more inconspicuous clothes," Naomi said. "And anyway, I'm making ginger stir-fry chicken; you'll have to stay for that, so why don't I see if Michael's home and can loan you a sweatsuit or something?"

It was Ruth's personal belief that if the Creature from the Black Lagoon itself showed up in the living room gnashing its gills and dripping slime, Naomi would hand it a towel. Ruth had seen her outface most of the forms of street weirdness that New York had to offer, as well as a number of the more offensive forms of college bureaucracy, and had yet to see Naomi flapped—if that was what you called the opposite of being unflappable. Melior gave Naomi a smile that instantly made Ruth unreasonably jealous and inclined his head.

"I would indeed be churlish did I despise such well-captained hospitality," Melior said gravely. "I pray you, Lady, be aware that I only bring peace to this house."

"That's fine, then," Naomi said. "Kitchen's too small for three, so why don't you make yourself comfortable in the living room—and get ready to tell your life story once more with feeling."

"I am utterly at your disposal," said Melior, with only the faintest hint of mockery. Ruth, absorbed in their interplay, actually jumped when Naomi took her arm in a firm grip and pulled her toward the kitchen.

Once there, Ruth was occupied—in the same sense that an enemy city in wartime is occupied—with the task of chopping fresh ginger root into even, coin-thick slices. Naomi took the wok from the top of the refrigerator and set it on the stove. Formidable cleaver in hand (and incidentally barring Ruth's escape), Naomi set about reducing an entire helpless chicken to raw boneless gobbets suitable for stir-frying.

"So," Naomi said over the metronomic thud of the cleaver on the chopping block, "what is it this time?"

You would think to hear her talk, Ruth thought with a flash of unreasonable irritation, *that I was forever getting into predicaments that Nai was getting me out of!* She allowed several slices of ginger to elapse before she answered:

"I was up to the Häagen-Dazs on Broadway, and when I came back I found him lying in that alley behind the building."

"Dressed like that?"

"No," Ruth snapped, "I took him shopping before I brought him home."

Naomi's only comment to that was a faint snort and a raised eyebrow that made Ruth unreasonably cross with herself. "And?" Naomi prompted.

"He said his name was Melior, he said he'd been mugged, he said they'd taken his sword." *And he asked where he was, just as if he didn't know, and his ears are pointed, and his eyes glow in the dark.* "So I brought him back here," Ruth said, beginning to feel that this course of action was hardly defensible. "And he asked if he could take a shower. He really *was* mugged, Nai—he's all over bruises."

"And he's got genuine Mr. Spock ears that don't come off with water," Naomi said flatly. She took a double handful of chicken gobbets and dropped them into the wok, then scooped the remaining debris into a plastic bag and knotted it shut before dropping it into the trash can. Plop-whick-thump-bang. "And you're usually more careful than that. So what do *you* think is going on, Ruth?" Naomi turned back to the refrigerator and began divesting it of scallions, garlic, bok choy. She pulled out a bottle of peanut oil and sprinkled it generously over the chicken, and then lit the gas stove.

"Ready for the ginger in a minute," Naomi warned.

Ruth continued her careful cutting. "I don't know what's going on," she finally said. "If I said I thought he was a Tolkien elf, you'd say I was crazy. There isn't any such thing as an elf," Ruth added, carefully grammatical.

"There are more things in Heaven and Earth, Horatio—as the actress said to the bishop," Naomi said cheerfully. She swiped the pile of ginger from beneath Ruth's knife and dumped it on top of the chicken. "Watch that for a minute, will you? I'm going to go call Michael."

Michael Harrison Peacock—to give him his full name, rank, and title—was not the sort of person who would be called "Mike," even if you knew him very well. He sometimes reminded Ruth of an enormous friendly dog—a black-haired, green-eyed, friendly dog with eyelashes much longer than hers, far too ebullient to be contained by anything less than a full two-syllable "Michael" (or, as was often the case, "Oh, MI-chael, HON-estly").

Michael was somewhere around Ruth's age, which was oldish for a Master's program, and stood out by being one of the few men in her Lib Sci classes, but Michael would have stood out in any lineup—except, perhaps, a Chippendale's revue. Michael was six feet, two inches tall, had a body purchased by extended work at the gym several nights a week (and in fact Michael worked there four mornings a week as one of the instructors), and a face so flawlessly gorgeous that it was always a surprise that he could speak intelligible English. He was far too imposing for any normal woman to entertain thoughts of having a romantic relationship with him, and if Naomi hadn't been assigned as his Student Adviser, Ruth could easily have gone through her entire two years at Columbia without ever speaking to him—which would have been her loss, as Michael was genuinely, uncomplicatedly nice.

As for why he was in library school instead of working as a model, gigolo, or exotic dancer, Ruth couldn't imagine—nor why he was studying for an M. L. S. at the age when he ought by rights to have been clawing his way up the corporate ladder somewhere.

She'd even asked him once, and only days later realized that "I'm trying a number of different things and this one was next," was hardly an informative answer. But Michael managed to make even mysteriousness seem wholesome, and once Ruth had managed to stop being dazzled by his wholesale gorgeousness, she found that Michael made a perfectly nice friend and study partner.

If he had any flaws at all, Ruth reflected, it was only that he was a little *too* nice and accommodating. There was, after all, the fact that Michael let Philip hang around with him.

"Got him!" Naomi announced triumphantly. "He'll be over here in about— Ruth! I told you to watch that!" She deftly elbowed Ruth out of the way and began stirring furiously at the smoking wok. "Well. Not *too* much harm done. But honestly, Ruth—"

"If God had meant me to cook, She would not have invented the telephone," Ruth said solemnly. "I could start the rice," she added, knowing what the answer would be.

"Oh, no you can't. *You* can go out and be nice to our guest. *I* will preserve my remaining pots from Grievous Bodily Harm. Go."

Thus dismissed, Ruth went back to the living room. And the elf.

Melior was sitting at the table by the window, his back to her and his attention concentrated on the window. Ruth knew that he must know she was there, but he didn't move a muscle in acknowledgment.

"Ahem," Ruth said. Melior turned his head.

"What a wonderful place your new York city is," he said disparagingly. His voice stressed the name in odd places. "Come, sit, and peruse it with me, mortal maid."

"Naomi wants to know who you really are," Ruth said, sitting down opposite him.

"And you do not? It must be wonderful to be incurious—I wish I had been born so."

"If you're going to be nasty, you can leave," Ruth said sharply.

Melior turned and looked at her. As his head moved, Ruth saw the iridescent flash of cat's eyes, and watched, fascinated, as the pupils contracted to vertical ovals in the lamp's glare.

"I am sorry, mortal maid—Ruth. My temper is not good—through my own stupidity I have lost so much more than belongs to me alone that I am sick with it. But you are not my enemy."

"Who is? What have you lost? If you tell me, maybe I can help," Ruth said.

Melior smiled. "I owe you the round tale—I do not see where the harm in the telling lies, only the urgent need. But that may wait until this "Michael" the warrior-maid Naomi has summoned comes to us. It is not in me, I think, to tell this tale twice."

Ruth smiled, a little distantly, wishing someone would call *her* a "warrior-maid." But Melior, apparently, called them as he saw them, and Ruth knew perfectly well that she was nobody's idea of an Amazon. The conversation flagged. Melior went back to gazing out the window. From the kitchen Ruth could hear the incomprehensible sounds of culinary sorcery.

Just about the time Ruth suspected she'd been dismissed, Melior swung around sharply to stare in the direction of the hallway. As Ruth gazed at him blankly, there was a familiar banging on the door.

Michael. Someone must have left the street door open again—that's why he didn't buzz. Melior must've heard him. Ears like a cat, too.

But even convinced it was Michael, Ruth looked out through the peephole first. And saw what she had subconsciously expected to see. And sighed. And opened the door.

"Come on in, guys. Nai! Michael's here—and with Philip." *Quelle surprise.*

Michael came in, smiling at Ruth and looking around until he saw Melior. Tucked under one arm, football-wise, Michael held a brown plastic trash bag, undoubtedly full of clothes.

Philip scuttled past Michael and flung himself onto the couch, from which he surveyed the room through white-reflecting round glasses—bifocals, in fact, and only one of the many surprises Philip held in store for the uninitiated. Ruth looked at Philip, who gazed blandly back before devoting himself to the portable computer that he usually—and tonight was no exception—carried with him.

Ruth didn't much care for him and they both knew it, but Philip LeStrange was a de facto part of their group, grandfathered in under the umbrella of Michael's indiscriminate good will and Naomi's optimistic tolerance.

"Hi, Ruth," Michael said. "You must be Melior," he added, looking past her. He held out his hand.

Melior stood, and gazed at Michael's outstretched hand in the blankly helpless fashion with which polite people greet the unfamiliar. As Ruth had originally estimated, he was not quite as tall as Michael, and the sight of the two of them together—dark and fair, fantastic and mundane—made Ruth imagine a weird sort of mirror that reflected opposites. After a pause too slight to be insulting, Melior stepped forward and grasped Michael's hand above the wrist in an oddly formal gesture.

"And you are Michael, whom Naomi has summoned," Melior said.

"And this is Philip." *Whom Naomi has NOT summoned,* added Ruth with mental uncharity. "Philip, this is Melior."

"Okay," said Philip. He glanced up and then away, the flash-flash of the overhead light on his steel-rimmed glasses making a jarring cross-reference to Melior's cat-glowing eyes. Oblivious to the social graces, Philip went back to tap-tap-tapping on his computer, a true wannabe-cyberpunk, poised to leap right into the future.

"Naomi says you got pretty beat up. I know a little bit about sports medicine—I can at least tell you if you're going to need to make a trip to the emergency room," Michael, all shining rational competence, said. "And I brought some street clothes for you to try." Michael jerked his head toward the bedroom, whole body language indicating that Melior should accompany him. After another socially-baffled pause, Melior acquiesced gracefully and was led away.

Which left Ruth alone with Philip—which was the same as alone, unless Philip was in one of his chatty moods. Well, worse, actually. Ruth liked being alone, which was more than she could say for being with Philip.

Ruth Marlowe was a charter member of the sane, reasonable, people-can-get-along-if-they'll-just-try contingent of the Silent Majority, and having never been really popular in her life, saw no reason to disparage people simply because they weren't cool enough to hang with. But there were, she felt, limits to that kind of social tolerance.

Putting up with Philip, in Ruth's opinion, was carrying tolerance to self-destructive extremes.

Philip LeStrange (Jane had told her—and God alone knew how Jane had found out—that his middle name was Leslie, and Ruth hoarded this information against a day of great need) was weedy, blond, short, twenty-two, and the product of respectable (and, Ruth felt, overindulgent) parents who were sure that his health was too delicate for anything more than a quiet respectable career as a librarian. It was something to do with a heart murmur, Michael had told her once, and if she had been Philip's parents and in possession of this knowledge she would have encouraged her only chick and child to take up lumberjacking.

Philip LeStrange had pale blue eyes and no mercy and if he did not idolize Michael he would have been impossible to tolerate. As it was, he was merely difficult. Philip was wonderfully ill-suited to the library field, having no particular interest in any writing that did not appear on a computer screen, and was already planning to specialize in the electronic databases that were encroaching (like mold) on the traditional library resources—for in his own small and illegal way Philip was brilliant.

At least, amended Ruth, Philip was illegally brilliant if you believed half of what he said about his computer hacking and other anarchic activities, but since she had no talent in that realm herself and did not take any particular vicarious delight in random lawbreaking, she had no idea how much of what he said he did Philip actually did and how much was just retold urban folklore with himself cast in the starring role: an amoral Robin Hood of cyberspace, unfailingly successful.

It was a pity he was so unprepossessing. Perhaps that was why Michael put up with him—and why Ruth herself did. Philip rapped the rap of a darkling prince of the city, soigné and dangerous, when what he resembled was a pink-eyed laboratory rat, sickly, hopeful, and fatally out of synch with true hipness. Clothes that would look gloriously macho on Michael—blue jeans, black high-tops, white T-shirt, and red (James Dean) Lands End windcheater (not that Philip had ever heard of James Dean)—made Philip resemble some alien life-form unconvincingly impersonating a Real Human Being. But Philip's utter inhumanity did not breed compassion in Ruth's bosom—which was odd, considering what she put up with from Jane.

"Somebody want to set the table?" Naomi called from the kitchen.

"I don't suppose you want to help?" Ruth said punctiliously to Philip.

"No," said Philip, smiling his most irritating smile.

Naomi, on the whole, handled Philip better. She was perfectly willing and able to make him look ridiculous—a talent Ruth lacked, and the only thing Philip hated enough to mind. When Ruth went into the kitchen to collect five plates, Naomi sailed out the other way, and when Ruth came back into the living room, Philip had just finished dragging the table into the middle of the room and was flipping the tablecloth over it.

"Hi, Ruth," he said, as if he'd just now seen her for the first time.

Ruth set the plates on the table and dealt them like a poker hand. "Hello, Philip; suborned any good governments lately?" The trouble was, she *ought* to like Philip; she never had to define the words she used for him.

"Nope. Been down at the dump, shooting rats." Philip smiled, nasty-sweet.

"That's not original," Ruth said. The trouble was, she didn't like Philip. Plain and simple, and somewhere underneath it all she felt it was her social duty to *try,* as if anything she did or didn't do could change the future course of Philip LeStrange's theatric self-referential life.

"But it's good."

"The trouble is," Ruth observed to the ceiling, "that the good parts aren't original and the original parts aren't good."

Philip walked off into the kitchen. He came out again with a large bowl of rice, following Naomi who bore a large bowl of ginger stir-fry chicken that smelled wonderful at eleven o'clock at night and far too many hours after a supper Ruth hadn't eaten anyway. The table service was assembled with the ease of long practice; Naomi liked to cook and the rest of them liked to eat, and that—as much as any mysterious agenda—was what held the five of them together.

That, and, perhaps, the fact that all of them were equally unsuited, somehow, for the space and time they were in now. Even Jane. Or maybe especially Jane.

"*Michael!*" Naomi called. "Food!" ("Slop the hogs," Philip muttered. "Oh, shut up, wetbrain," snapped Ruth.) The bedroom door opened, and Melior emerged, the gorgeous embroidered linen shirt replaced by one of Michael's navy and khaki striped rugby shirts, making Melior look even more exotic, if possible. Michael followed, no sign of unease visible.

"Ribs cracked, maybe, but the rest is just bruises," Michael announced to the room at large with a charming lack of self-consciousness. "Ro here was real lucky." Ruth saw Melior's mouth curve in on itself, ever so slightly. Melior didn't think he was lucky.

And no one among these lunatics she called her friends had said anything about cat's eyes, pointed ears, or any elvish thing whatever. Ruth began, ever-so-slightly, to doubt her personal grip upon sanity.

Seating five at the table meant using the two chairs, the step stool from the kitchen, the high stool with the straw seat from the living room, and arranging the table so that someone could perch precariously on the arm of the couch. Out of consideration for Melior's ribs, he was given one of the chairs. Ruth had the other.

"Just a minute," said Michael, before they were all settled. He got up, went into the bedroom, and came back bearing a bottle. "Happy birthday, Ruth," he said, grinning.

Ruth felt her eyes begin to tear; she forced her mouth into a smile before it could bend in another direction.

"Bet you thought we'd forgot," crowed Naomi.

"I didn't," Ruth protested. "But I didn't tell anyone."

"I hacked into your records," Philip explained. "*Thirty* . . ." he let his voice trail off, as if unable to imagine such senescence.

"Someday, my son, you, too, will be thirty—maybe," Michael said to Philip.

"Well, open it and let's eat," Naomi said briskly. "And for dessert, there's birthday cake. I hid it behind the real food in the freezer because you and the roaches never look there."

The wine was poured—even Philip took a little, and Philip disliked alcohol in all its forms.

"A toast," Michael said, when the glasses were ready, but it was Melior who stood and raised his glass.

"To the Beltaine child," Melior said. "May she find what she seeks."

Ruth felt rather as though she had been given a very great gift—and one that she didn't know how to unwrap. *That's right,* Ruth thought. *It's Beltaine. May Eve—the 30th of April. Walpurgisnacht. But if he's from Elfland, how did HE know?*

Then Melior drank, and the moment of strangeness passed.

"Now the story," Naomi said to Melior, once the dishes were scraped and the cake was sitting on the table thawing.

"Lose the ears," Philip suggested. Melior raised an eyebrow in Philip's direction but said nothing. He looked around at the other three.

"Is it your will that this tale be told?" he asked. "For know ye this: Rohannan Melior of the House of the Silver Silences is a prince and a king's son, and the son of a prince and a king's son and so on to the beginning of time, and the words that he speaks are not without power in whichever of the worlds he speaks them."

Philip smirked, caught Naomi's eye, and didn't say anything.

"I think we all appreciate that, uh, Melior," Michael said courteously. "Why don't you tell us what happened, and maybe we can do something to help."

Melior stretched—and winced—and smiled ruefully. "Very well, Friend Michael. But this is not a tale for high words, as it is not a tale of high deeds, merely of stupidity, overconfidence, and pride."

"That we can handle," Naomi said.

Philip leaned forward—really paying attention, Ruth realized, and not out of a desire to help, but more because if he were asked to help it would give him a chance to do what Philip loved to do best—meddle with permission.

"Well, then," Melior said. "First the tale, then you may ask what you will—for as strange as you are to me, I warrant you have never seen my like as well."

"Not since *Star Trek* was canceled," Philip said. Ruth kicked him.

Melior began to speak. He spoke as clearly and as fluently as if he were reciting an old and familiar story. The others became as still and silent as an audience spellbound by a play, and soon, listening, Ruth lost all sense of anything beyond the tale he told.

· 2 ·

The Elf-Lord's Tale

"MY NAME IS Rohannan Melior of the House of the Silver Silences, and that House is one of the seven Great Houses of the Twilight which rule a land so far from this land that the World of Iron in which you dwell is barely a myth for our scholars. As we rule over the Men of our land, so does a High King rule over us, and that he shall have died is the cause of tragedy both in my world and your own.

"Yet it is not the death of the one who is known now in death as Rainouart the Beautiful, High King of Chandrakar, which is the tragedy, though the Sons of the Morning and the Daughters of the Evening Star do not die in the time and season of Men. The tragedy came once the funeral games were ended, and Rainouart's funeral boat was set upon the bosom of the wave, and it was time to say who from among the Seven Houses would be High King thereafter, for Rainouart had ruled long and left no son or daughter behind him, and of the Lords Temporal, our Barons, there was none among them whose puissance and courtois was greater than his fellows'."

("I saw the miniseries," Philip said under his breath. Ruth put her foot on top of his and pressed.)

"At first it seemed that all might be settled with reasoned council—that it was not, you may know when I tell you the High King died when my mother was but a child, and from that time until I grew to manhood his successor was not chosen.

"The way of it was this:

"There was a lady among the Houses whose name was Hermonicet, who was the most beautiful lady born to the Houses of the Twilight in the memory of the Morning Lords or the reckoning of bards. To the sorrow of all and the envy of some, her father had betrothed her when only a child to the Lord of the Western Marches, who lived in wild solitude at the very edge of the sea.

"That her father was wise and kind the barons only knew later. Then, they knew that the Marchlord her husband had lately died, and so the Lady Hermonicet was free to remarry how she would.

"Many hopes were pinned upon her choice—for I have seen her, and I tell you truly she is all they said she was; as beautiful as the stars, and as cold. And when it seemed that the Barons—among them my father— might come to agreement on who now would rule them, the Lady spoke from her sea-tower and said she would take no one to spouse save he who would now be High King, and open the gates of her tower never, save to that one lord.

"The lords who were met in council at the place of the High King's death tarried not one moment more over their deliberations but went forth to arm and to raise their troops, and there was thereafter in that time such a war and travail that it set brother against brother and father against son—aye, and sister against brother, and cast-out Lady against her once-loved Lord—and none of this for the High Kingship, nor any reward more lasting than the sea-cool kisses of a heartless elphen jade with nothing in her save trouble and despite."

("So there was a war," Philip said.

"How long did it last—and what happened next?" asked Michael.)

"At last, and this an undertaking of years, and with many good men slain, Lord Baligant, a younger son from an undistinguished house, and not even of the line of one of the Treasurekeepers, took the High King-ship—by force and by guile, and partly, so I believe, because all who might depose him were sick and weary with war, and took good care that they should not come again to the sea-tower and there become en-glamoured of Hermonicet's beauty once more. So Eirdois Baligant of (by courtesy) the House of Vermilion Shadows became High King-Elect over the Houses of the Twilight and future husband to Hermonicet the Fair.

"But the wounds of that long war were not healed, nor was Baligant a forgiving suzerain, and despite the fact that law and custom compels that the High King may not go to war with any of the Great Houses, nor condemn a Son of the Morning without a trial before all his peers, I fear me that Eirdois Baligant has found a way to punish those he will not forgive."

(Here Melior paused for a long moment, and refilled his glass, and drank. Ruth, roused by the silence, glanced quickly to right and left, but the others were merely listening, as nonjudgmental as a movie audience.)

"And the way of that is this: In our land are Twelve Treasures: Sword and Cup; Lance and Shield; Harp; Mirror; Cauldron; Comb; Cloak; Horse; Book; and Crown. Each is a talisman of surpassing magical power; all conjoined defend us from our enemies and ensure the peace and fertility of the land. Each one of these Treasures is separately entrusted to one of the noble families of Chandrakar for safekeeping, lest, possessing them all beneath his own hand, the High King's power grow too great and his spirit too haughty. No one of the Great Houses may have more than two in its keeping for the same cause; should such a thing fall out through death or wedding, the present guardian of the Treasure must find someone willing to guard that which he has guarded.

"Line Rohannan is guardian to the Sword, called the Sword of Maiden's Tears, which renders its possessor infallible in battle, with an insight into his enemy's heart as keen as a sword's edge."

("Excuse me, Melior, but that really doesn't explain how you came to be mugged on 116th Street," Naomi said. Melior nodded. "Forgive me, Mistress Naomi, but I had rather tell too much than not enough—and this is not a tale I care to tell twice.")

"Be such things as they will—the Treasures are twelve and in the wardship of the Seven Houses of the Twilight, and the particular care of Line Rohannan of the House of the Silver Silences is the Sword.

"But never had I seen the Sword, though I was much past the age when its secrets ought to have been entrusted to me. Our land had been at war, and lest any be tempted to bring the Treasures to the field of battle and use them, brother against brother, they were hidden away in various wise, and only a few knew their hiding.

"So Baligant was proclaimed, and the date for his wedding and accession set, and those with Treasures in their care set themselves to retrieve them, as my father set me.

"And thus was Baligant's subtlety and guile made patent, and the way to his revenge made clear, because the Kingmaking is a ritual that requires all the Twelve Treasures to be present, and the lineage that does not come before the High Seat upon that day with the Treasure entrusted into its care may never come before it again: all rank and seizin are forfeit, and that line is forever banished from the Twilight Lands."

("And when you got to the wherever-it-was, your sword wasn't there, right?" Michael said. Melior nodded.

"I could write this turkey by mail," Philip said.

"Get a new scriptwriter, Philip," Ruth said.

"Now, children," Naomi said.)

"The Sword of Maiden's Tears was not where my father had left it. I sought it within and without the land, always aware that the time draws near that Line Rohannan will be called upon to present it to the High King, and aware of what will befall us do we not.

"And thus, in the end, such fear made me overhasty. I achieved the Sword at last, but in my haste allowed myself to be whelmed by magic and cut loose from the worlds; so loosed, I fell, as I must, down through the worlds until I reached the World of Iron, than which there is none lower that we know of.

"The Sword fell with me; such is its magic that even then all was not lost—though the way be filled with hazard, it was not impossible that in the end I would regain my own fair Chandrakar."

("But you were mugged," said Ruth, speaking out for the first time.)

"But I was mugged, as you say, when I was not above half-an-hour in this world, and the villains, charmed by what ill stars I know not, took from me the one thing I would not willingly have given them.

"And here, in the ruin of all my hopes and the destruction of my Line, begins your own horror, my mortal friends.

"The Sword of Maiden's Tears is forged with a great magic, that no one save the Morning Lords can wield it. Yet it has been taken from me by a man of mortal kind, and so I tell you that soon he will begin to prey upon his former kindred, shunning the light, and unslayable save by that very sword which shall be until his death his dearest treasure.

"There are no others of my kind in this world, I fear, yet only my blood may wield the Sword safely. I do not speak of the disaster fallen upon Line Rohannan, for its weaving none of the Seven Houses had a hand in and that weaving may even now be past all unraveling. I speak only of the evil to fall upon your kind, here and now in this new York city, should the Sword remain in those hands which have stolen it, and do I fail to recover it.

"Do I not regain the Sword of Maiden's Tears, my friends, your race is doomed."

· 3 ·

Ruth Amid
the Alien Corn

"GREAT GOING, GUY—and I bet Ruthie here believes every word," Philip said, with a wholly spurious enthusiasm. "So you're an elf with a magic sword, huh?" he added, smiling patronizingly.

Ruth prepared to leap to Melior's defense, but she needn't have bothered.

"Were I an elf *with* a magic sword, young Philip, I would have no despite save that my visit to your pleasant realm was to be so short. And do you choose to call Rohannan Melior liar and *warlock,* pray do so openly, lest he call you coward."

"Hey, nothing personal, Elfie," Philip said, holding his hands up in a mocking gesture of surrender.

"Get a life, Philip," Naomi said without heat. "Now, Melior, as far as I understand it, you aren't here by choice. You ran into a booby trap of some kind that dropped you in the middle of New York, and then you got mugged, and when you were mugged you lost this ceremonial sword which, according to you, will do something pretty awful to whoever has it."

"That is the essence of my tale, Mistress Naomi. I must regain the Sword, before it is too late. And then I must try to return to my own place—before it is too late."

"I think the cake's defrosted," said Philip ingenuously. He bounded to his feet, the image of helpfulness, and sprang off to the kitchen in search of plates and forks.

"Have you any ideas about how to, uh, regain this sword?" Michael said carefully. Ruth, looking at him, had no idea how much he believed of Melior's story—but *she* believed, defiantly determined to hold Melior to it no matter what mundane apostasy he contemplated.

"In the lands I know I would seek aid at the nearest castle. Were I within the boundaries of a town, there would be magistrates to inquire of—as well as taverns, and receivers of stolen goods who might inform upon their patrons. Here—" Melior sighed, and bowed his head, suddenly looking very tired. "Here every building is a castle, and I know not where to begin."

"There is also the possibility that the magic doesn't work here, Melior," said Naomi, very gently.

The elf-lord looked up at her through ice-crystal lashes. "And perhaps I am no prince of Chandrakar, but a mad mountebank trying your charity," he finished. "But no."

He slipped off his ring and set it on the table. Ruth picked it up. Instead of the carved intaglio suitable for sealing letters that she had expected to see, all she saw was a round-edged rectangle of some mirror-black stone.

Hematite? "Signet ring?"

"Here." Melior ran his thumb over the stone. For a moment colored lights sparkled just beneath the surface, then faded away again. All of them had seen it. Melior turned back to Naomi.

"There is too much iron in the air for this small a magic to work. But the Sword was enchanted with a greater magic than any living thing can wield; if the ring works even so much as this, the Sword will work well indeed."

Michael picked up the ring next, and when Philip came back with plates and forks, Michael flipped it at him. Philip looked inquiring.

"It lights up," Michael said.

Philip tapped with a thumbnail; weighed it in his hand.

"No, it doesn't," he said positively.

"It's magic," said Naomi helpfully.

There was a knock at the door.

"I'll get it," said Ruth to no one in particular.

"It's the Thought Police," said the door when she approached it. Ruth took a quick peek through the peephole, then opened the door.

"Hi, Jane."

"I hope it isn't too late. I know it's one in the morning, but I saw your lights, and anyway, it's May Day and I forgot your birthday, so I thought

I'd bring you some flowers," Jane said, still hovering on the doorstep, daffodils outstretched rather in the manner of one offering a poisonous snake.

"Come on in. Everyone's here—Naomi made me a cake—and there's someone here I'd like you to meet," Ruth said, quasi-mendaciously, falling back full-length on trite, timeworn, hackneyed clichés. She accepted the flowers with an overpowering sense of *cusp;* she'd thought no one remembered her birthday and it seemed that everyone had, and if she'd known in advance that they would, would she have gone out at all—and if she hadn't gone out, would Melior even have been there?

Flowers in hand, Ruth went off to the kitchen. There must be a carafe somewhere in there that she could use for the daffies. *Daffies, daffodils, daffy-down dillies. . . .* She saw the container she sought, high on the topmost shelf, and strained, tiptoe, to reach it.

"Let me." Melior, behind her. He reached past her, over her shoulder, and plucked the vase down deftly. She turned. He held it out to her, brows quirking.

"And are you sorry, now, that you rescued me? And do you think me, as the others claim to, mad, or misled, or larcenous?" Melior said softly.

Ruth took the vase. "I think you're a long way from home. And I think the first thing to do is get back your sword." She filled the vase and put the daffodils in it, and stared firmly at Melior until he moved and let her go back out into the living room.

Michael and Philip, heads together, were conferring over the mysterious signet ring. Jane was sitting in the chair Ruth had occupied, back perfectly straight (rather as if she were auditioning for a role as one of the better class of Egyptian hieratic statues) while Naomi, draped over the couch, filled her in on the evening's events with swooping theatrical gestures.

Melior brushed past Ruth and walked out to join Philip and Michael. Jane looked up as he approached, face carefully neutral, and Ruth was seized by a sudden, heart-clutching, irrational panic—a panic that somehow this was the last good moment they would all have together, that, irrespective of normal fears of madmen and con artists, somehow an evil angel was watching over everyone here, marking them for his own.

Honestly, Ruth, you'd think the lights were going out all over Europe or something. It's late, that's all.

Shrugging her shoulders at her own silliness, Ruth walked over to the table.

"Oh, good," Naomi said, "Michael, go get another plate, there's a good lad, and then we can cut the cake and decide what we're going to do with Ro, here." Naomi, unflappably competent.

"Melior is my name," Melior corrected her gently. "My Line is Rohannan."

"Chinese," Jane said cryptically.

Another plate was brought, and another glass, and the more-chocolate-than-thou cake was scrupulously divided into six enormous pieces—which might not go with red wine in anybody else's opinion, but Ruth found nothing to complain of.

"What were you doing out so late, Jane?" Naomi asked around a mouthful of cake.

"Whatever it was, you shouldn't do it." Michael said firmly. "And don't the dorms have curfews? You could get mugged, you know."

Jane elevated one shoulder, face studiously blank. It didn't matter what you said to Jane: if she listened, it was because she already intended to do what you were telling her anyway; if she did not have such an intention, it was a waste of time. Ruth had found that out a long time ago; she saved her breath.

"I was mugged," Melior offered with wary pride. "And I a blooded warrior of Line Rohannan."

Jane gazed at him for a moment, thinking it over.

"Yeah," she finally said. "But you're from out of town."

Philip whooped with laughter, spraying crumbs.

"Anyway," Michael said with firm persistence, "Ro—*Mel* and I will walk you back to the dorm. I thought he could stay with me; I've got the most room."

And are of the right gender, Ruth added mentally. Michael lived alone in off-campus student housing; Ruth wasn't sure where Philip lived, but she knew it was with several other people. She and Naomi were overcrowded as it was, and Jane lived in the dorm, expensive and cramped though it was, because with one thing and another, at nineteen to Philip's twenty-two, she was the youngest of them, the result of skipped levels in grade school.

From the vantage point of eleven years' seniority Ruth was not sure that all that skipping had been a good idea, no matter how gifted and accelerated Jane was. Jane was glib, Jane was verbal, Jane was never at a loss for a witty rejoinder, but Ruth suspected that the child Jane had been had suffered from being forced into adulthood too soon. Emotionally she lagged far behind the people with whom she had been thrust, willy-nilly, into peerdom, and coped with this estrangement by permitting herself no emotions at all, lest they turn out (incomprehensibly) to be the wrong ones.

Jane, in short, had perfected the fine art of glib superficiality. Bring on what elves you chose, they would not faze Jane Treasure Greyson of

Patroon County, New York. She'd be too certain it was some form of
extended malicious practical joke. And Jane, so far as Ruth could tell,
had wit but no real sense of humor. Which made her a refreshing change
from Philip, in case anyone was interested.

One would think, all things taken into account, that Jane and Philip
would consider themselves soulmates. One would be wrong. If there was
one person in her circle of acquaintance whom Jane bestirred herself to
have open feelings about, it was Philip. And the feeling was murderous
revulsion, which was too bad as everyone else thought they would be
perfect for each other.

They were, after all, both short and blond with bad eyesight, Jane
slightly plump and moon-faced to Philip's thin and weedy, but with nice
gray eyes behind the ghastly horn-rimmed thick-lensed glasses. And,
Ruth thought wearily, if she would wear clothes fashionable or even suitable she would look very well.

But either she didn't care or she didn't notice: Jane was still wearing
the shetland sweaters, plaid pleated skirts, and poly-cotton blouses with
Peter Pan collars that her mother had picked out for her in high school,
and she would probably still be wearing them when she went for her first
job interview. Jane came from a family that could (and did) trace its
lineage back to the Signers (of the Declaration of Independence) on both
sides and who (Ruth gathered, mostly by omission) felt that a library
degree was the height of intellectual attainment for womankind; their
collective psychic feet firmly mired in a past where the two professional
tracks for nonmarrying daughters were nurse and librarian.

So here Jane was, massively unready to cope with Real Life in any
form, and being hustled neatly down a greased chute to neuterhood and
intellectual stagnation.

Ruth looked at her wineglass suspiciously. Surely she hadn't had *that*
much to drink?

It's turning thirty. That's what it is. Oh, Ruth, you ARE a goon.

"—and then tomorrow after class we can roust some of the local
pawnshops," Michael was saying, "and I'll ask the Scadians on campus—
not making out like it was stolen, you understand, just misplaced."

"Your kindness does you much honor, Michael Peacock, but I fear
you draw that covert in vain. Who takes the Sword will not relinquish it,
did his dearest kinsman beg him for it," Melior said sadly.

"Yeah, well, you don't know earthlings very well, Elfie. Probably he
ditched it in the trash somewhere after he pried all the jewels out of it.
But if you want to offer a reward or something like that for it, I could post
it on the Internet and some of the local BBSs."

BBS stood for Bulletin Board System, and there Ruth's knowledge of cyberspace ended.

"He hasn't got any money, Philip," Ruth said, all the while calculating how much cash she could divert from her overtaxed savings account to cover reward, and food, and the dozen hundred things Melior would need.

"But if there are pawnbrokers in this city, I can get money, Ruth," Melior said. "If your world still trades in gold and precious gems, I have that which I can sell."

Ruth thought of that exquisite earring; the spurs; the delicate wicked crystal and enamel knife. "I'll buy them," she began.

"Get together what you want to hock," Michael said, interrupting her. "I'll take it and get it valued—then Ruth gets first crack at it. Philip, you can post a reward of twenty for information leading to, and fifty for the thing itself."

"That's too low!" wailed Philip, rather as if he were hoping to claim the reward himself.

"Yeah, well, if you offer more than twenty you're going to have to chase down a lot of false leads, and if you offer fifty for the return you'll at least get people negotiating," said Michael, as if he did this all the time.

"Settled, then," said Naomi briskly. Briskly was the way Naomi did things, keeping meetings and discussions and planning committees moving steadily forward, never getting mired in attitude and argument. "Today's Friday, right?"

"Six more weeks of class," Jane said, as if announcing the weather. "But none tomorrow. So I'll see everybody here for dinner."

And that was that.

It was about two o'clock Saturday morning when Michael, in the company of Rohannan Melior, left Naomi's apartment for his own. He carried all of Melior's wordly possessions bundled under one arm in the bag he'd brought his own clothes to Naomi's in. Their study might prove something. Then again, it might not. Michael was prepared to withhold judgment indefinitely in default of cold hard proof. *Just the facts, ma'am.* And meanwhile, the guy *had* been beaten and *did* have to sleep somewhere.

Michael wasn't worried about trouble from his chance-met houseguest; Michael knew his own worth; the worth of 200 pounds of well-sculpted beef on the hoof. A big impressive body, so that nobody, ever, would try to start up something with him. And so nobody would ever get hurt.

Michael not only abhorred violence, he dreaded it, with the fey certainty of all his Irish blood that the thing which had already destroyed his life once beyond all recovering must certainly come again.

But not tonight. And not for him. And not from some wimp elf-wannabe that talked like a cross between Alistair Cook and the *Lais* of Marie de France.

But Ruth, now. . . .

Michael liked Ruth. Michael had always liked Ruth, from the moment Naomi had first introduced them, banging them together repeatedly like half-spheres of plutonium which refused, stubbornly, to react. There was something about Ruth that was less-than-right, but it did not affect any of the fundamental Ruth-qualities that Michael liked, and everyone, God knew, was entitled to his own secrets. But maybe not now.

Michael regarded his companion. Melior walked unselfconsciously beside him, eyes flicking left and right, scanning the territory before him as if he thought that at any moment it might burst out into violence. There was something familiar about that, and after a moment Michael identified what it was.

The cop look. Melior had it. Whoever he was. *Whatever* he was.

And that made things, if possible, worse. Ruth had it bad for this guy; Michael could see that even if nobody else could. Had it bad for Mel the Elf, who, bad actor or no, had blown into town like some sort of con man, telling them there was trouble right here in River City, roping them all in and stringing them along in the name of some kind of obscure payoff.

A psychic payoff, maybe. Contracts signed in blood.

Michael shivered.

It didn't matter—or, maybe, the worst of it was—that Mel the Elf really was authentically strange. Pointed ears and glowing eyes, maybe he was just a space alien who thought he was an elf. (As if that were a more sensible approach to the problem.)

"There are more things in heaven and earth, Horatio, than are dreamt of in your philosophy," Michael quoted to himself. "We're here," he said aloud.

Michael's apartment was small (which is to say, large by New York standards) and neat, paid for by scrupulous saving and a number of rotating part-time jobs (including one summer that had indeed been spent dancing in an all-male revue) that—along with his life in New York City—would be over by graduation. In six weeks' time (without elvish intervention) he would be a new-made Master of Library Science with a major in children's literature, ready to take some library somewhere by storm.

There were few enough men in the field—and the bad old sexist bias so strong—that even in today's "recovering" economy Michael Harrison Peacock, Male Librarian, could very nearly take his pick of jobs. He had six interviews scheduled for the last two weeks of June, and after that he'd know.

It wasn't the future he'd wanted, but it was the future he was going to get. And Michael had seen enough of real life to be grateful rather than disappointed.

He stood back as Melior entered the apartment, watching for some clue that would tell him more about Melior. Crazy or just lying?

Or, worse, real?

Melior walked to the center of the living room and looked around himself, then back at Michael. Michael closed the door and locked it three ways: chain, snap-bolt, and the deadbolt he'd bought after the first week because the other two wouldn't stop a professional housebreaker more than ninety seconds.

"And?" Melior asked, when Michael turned back. Michael raised an eyebrow.

"There must be more, Michael-my-friend. You have said so little before opening your home to me." Melior watched him narrowly, and Michael found himself looking for the iridescent flare of light reflecting silver-green off the retina, scientific cause for the folk belief that cat's eyes glowed in the dark.

But human eyes didn't.

"I think your story's bunk," Michael said bluntly.

"Ah." Melior might not understand the word, but the tone was clear enough. Nevertheless, he did not seem to be particularly hurt by Michael's disbelief. "Would that I could string a convincing warp of fancy for you. I cannot."

"What is it you really want?" Michael asked.

"I want the Sword," Melior said simply. "I want to take it to my own hall. And I should like a private word with he who stands as High King," he added mildly.

"Violence never solved anything," Michael said, and regretted it as Melior turned and stared right into his eyes.

Green and silver, flickering like flames. Like flames . . . Like FLAMES—

"You know better, warrior," Melior said flatly. Michael, released from whatever spell Melior had cast, looked away, shaking with reaction.

Lucky guess. Lucky question. Gypsy tricks. Leave it. "You can have the couch; I'll get out the extra blankets. Tomorrow we can see about getting you some clothes that fit a little better—" Michael talked on, filling the air with words, putting space between himself and the ancient scar that Melior had so casually ripped open.

And somewhere inside himself, Michael Peacock began to believe.

Ruth lay awake after everyone was gone, gazing out of westward windows while the sky slowly paled toward dawn. Saturday. May Day. And maybe Melior had already vanished with the dawn. Maybe the whole evening had been some bizarre form of hallucination caused by turning thirty.

Because if it hadn't been—if the world had suddenly turned into the sort of place that could encompass both war in the Balkans and war in Elphame; pipe bombs and fairy knights with gilded spurs—Ruth wasn't sure she really wanted to have anything to do with it.

At last she gave up trying to sleep at all. Rising quietly, tiptoeing past the other bed where Naomi slept as sweetly as if she had not been hostess just last night to an elf-lord from nowhere, Ruth gathered up skirt and sweater and sensible walking shoes and slipped into the living room to dress.

The living room window shades were half-drawn, and the early morning light sliding beneath them made the room mauve and chilly. Michael had taken away Melior and all his possessions; there was nothing here to prove either that he existed or didn't. *"And I awoke and found me here on the cold hill side."*

Ruth struggled quickly into her clothes; thrift shop and antique store finds, they saved her from the need to confront the twentieth century head-on. Wearing secondhand cashmere and heirloom lace, she was saved from defining herself by this retreat into others' definitions and others' selves. And—sensible Ruth!—a cashmere twin-set was undeniably warm, warm enough, even, for a chilly, early-morning May.

Soft blue sweaters and retro kiltie skirts; sometimes Ruth wondered if there was as much difference between her and Jane as she thought. But she had chosen her own clothes, piece by piece, out of her own needs for her own purposes, and the clothes Jane was wearing were not her own; new in themselves, but fostering a secondhand image—sense of other, not of self.

Selfness was very important. To be yourself. Even if, as it turned out, you didn't like who that was, you just couldn't live your life to suit someone else's definition of who you were.

And if that meant coming down four-square in favor of reckless insanity, then that was what it meant. Ruth slung her purse over her shoulder and took her keys firmly in hand. She closed the door very quietly as she went out.

Michael lived twenty blocks south, on Riverside at 96th. It was not, Ruth insisted to herself, that she was going there—who'd be up, at quarter to six in the morning?—but rather that it made a convenient destination. Down to 96th, back up on Broadway, coffee and a bagel somewhere along the way as reward for the early morning walkabout. And besides, the walk would clear her head.

Elf or not? The morning air was sharply cold, with only the faint promise of later warmth to make it bearable. Regretting her absence of coat, Ruth walked faster. Elf or not?

Magic or not? Ruth amended conscientiously, thinking of Edward Eager, of children's books fame, whose characters always seemed to be getting into situations just like this. Only Eager's creations were fictional children, not real adults, and their imaginary garden of bright images had no room for the thousand razor-edged horrors of contemporary urban life.

But Melior seemed so reasonable, so radiantly sane. . . .

Ruth walked faster.

This section of Riverside Drive still echoed some of New York City's lost gentility. Across the road there was a grassy berm sloping toward the fence which guarded balls and small children from the precipitous drop to the river; where they hadn't been vandalized into oblivion, park benches stood, facing the water. Some were occupied by sleeping homeless, some by early joggers doing stretches.

A fifteen minute walk brought Ruth to the block that Michael's apartment was on. She looked up but wasn't sure which windows were his. Time to cut over to Broadway, in search of that bagel that was her ostensible reason for coming out.

Melior was sitting on one of the park benches.

At first she wasn't sure it was him. In New York such brilliantly silver hair was not uncommon, even if achieved by unnatural means. But she felt compelled to make sure, and by the time she crossed the street he had turned to look at her and she knew it was him.

"Michael kick you out?" she asked, sitting down. Melior smiled. He was wearing black sweatpants, ill-fitting canvas Chinese slippers, and a heavy wool sweater that Ruth recalled being a favorite of Michael's. Its oatmeal color made Melior's skin and hair seem even paler and it could have accommodated an additional person without any particular strain.

"No." Melior smiled. "But I am not so fond of being perched in such a hot and sealed height. The door locks of itself if you pull it shut. I came out here to think."

"About what?" Ruth asked.

Melior hesitated, then sighed, leaning forward to rest his hands on his knees. His long hair spilled forward, hiding his face.

"He speaks, does this Michael who means me no harm in all the world, of what money my small goods will fetch, of purchasing for me suitable raiment at some gap. He speaks of what use I may be, and of what employment my hand may be turned to—in short, Ruth, he speaks of how I may fit myself to this world! And I cannot stay here! I *will* not!"

Melior took both of Ruth's hands in his, holding them strongly as if her belief could make some difference to him.

"I must find the sword—I must! And once I have—"

"You'll go home?" Ruth said.

"I will try. It is not as easy as that—if it were, I would leave now and return with an army to help me in my search. It is—" he stopped and shook his head, amused at himself. "And here I sit, trapped perhaps forever in the Last World, arguing magical geography with a mortal maid who is quite certain that I am plain and simply mad."

"You're not mad," Ruth said resolutely. She was conscious of his hands on hers, strong and warm and firm. "Maybe you aren't an elf, but I don't think you're mad."

"And your companions? Michael and Naomi and Philip and Jane? Do they grant any truth to the full-moon tale I have told them? It does not matter—they will have proof soon enough."

"Proof?" said Ruth, suddenly wary.

"Ruth, do they think I prate of cursed swords for simple pride alone? The Sword of Maiden's Tears is *cursed*. The human who wields it will become *grendel*—losing all humanity, he will become a monster that lives to slay, and subsists upon the flesh of what once were his fellow men."

"So all we have to do is wait for the bodies to start turning up—and follow them back to your sword?" Ruth said.

Melior stared at her as if she were suddenly mad. "I had not thought to find in you such a stony heart, Ruth. Do we but wait, it is true, the monster's predations will lead us to our prize—but what of the innocents who must die for such convenience?"

"These are the nineties. No one's innocent anymore. And people die all the time," Ruth said, nettled.

"Then I will be glad to leave here," Melior said flatly. "Even if I ride only to join my bloodline in disgrace and exile."

Ruth pulled her hands free abruptly.

" 'Welcome to New York—now go home,' " Ruth quoted harshly. Unreasonably, Melior's words hurt—and why should she value Melior's good opinion so much, only having known him half a day? "I'm sorry this place doesn't fit your fairy tale notions of good behavior—but then, you're a prince anyway; what would *you* know about real life?"

"I know about war, for I have seen it," Melior said somberly. "And I know that when war is over, and peace comes once more, then even soldiers put away the arts of war and live as peacefully as they may."

"Then you don't know very much." Ruth thought of the horrors she could rattle off without a pause, the catalog of poisoning, abuse, random shootings, bombings and mutilations, greed and madness.

And that without leaving the United States; worldwide she could add civil wars and famines, plague, treachery, and cruelty beyond the imagination of ancient tyrants. So much badness everywhere, and no one allowed to believe, even for a moment's respite, that things were better than they were or ever had been.

"I have abandoned my search for truth and am now looking for a good fantasy."

"No," said Melior, breaking into her thoughts, "perhaps I do not. But I know that I do not want to stay here, and I know that every life the *grendel* ends is a life *I* have ended. If not for me, those who may die—and may already have died—would not have done so."

"Wrong," said Ruth. "They'd just be killed by something else."

Melior laughed. "What an odd way you have of cheering me, Ruth! Come, before you have heartened me into a black melancholy, let us waken Michael and persuade him to feed us—and disclose to me what gap holds my future garb. The day is well advanced, and I am persuaded it will be a busy one."

Michael answered the door on the first knock, his worried look vanishing at once when he saw Melior and Ruth. Though not as skilled as Naomi, Michael was a better cook than Ruth—who wasn't?—and over scrambled eggs and toasted bagels he explained the mysterious "gap" in Melior's conversation.

"Since you're here, I figure you could take Mel here down to The Gap and get him some stuff. Shirts, toothbrushes, that kind of thing."

"They don't sell toothbrushes at The Gap," Ruth said, just to be difficult.

"Use your imagination. Just get him a few things so he won't look like an escapee from the Christmas Revels," Michael explained, naming the large, Medievalist, and largely amateur production put on every December to raise money for charity. "Sneakers. Jeans."

"Using what for money?" Ruth asked patiently. "You're talking about a couple of hundred dollars, Michael, even if I only get one of everything."

Michael squirmed around in his chair until he had freed his wallet. He pulled out a sheaf of twenties and handed them to Ruth.

"Oh, Michael, I can't!" she said.

"It's a loan. I'll get it back. Mel says it's okay to sell his other stuff; I'll get it back easy."

"Not his clothes," Ruth said dangerously.

"Well, sure," Michael said.

"Ruth," Melior began, "they are only clothes, and—"

"Fine. If you don't want them, *I'll* buy them. Shirt and tunic, two hundred dollars, fair price." She shoved the money back at Michael, who had the baffled look common to men when the subject of clothes was raised. "We can hit up a cash machine on the way down to Macy's," she added, looking fiercely at both of them as if they contemplated disputing her.

Neither one did.

"You can pick them up when you get back," Michael said meekly.

And so it was that, at ten of the clock on a bright sunny morning that was the first Saturday in May, Ruth, a list of Melior's probable sizes in one hand and Melior's wrist in the other, was leading her charge down the slippery narrow steps on the IND and into the New York Subway.

She had decided on Macy's 34th Street for this expedition partly because she could put Melior's clothes on her charge card (and pay on the never-never, as they said in England), and partly for the fun of showing Melior a bit of New York. Melior's existence was impossible to deny, but Ruth found the magic and the cursed sword he feared equally impossible to credit. Magic swords were for Saturday morning TV, not real life—and Melior had said himself that magic worked poorly here, if at all.

So the sword wouldn't work, and he wouldn't find it, and so he'd have to stay. It was such an unworthy selfish thought that it didn't even make its way entirely into Ruth's consciousness, but it was there just the same.

Melior didn't balk at the stairs, though he did wrinkle his nose eloquently once they had descended far enough to smell the ambient perfume of the subway system, composed in equal parts of urine, rotting garbage, and unwashed bodies. Ruth handed over money and received tokens, and carefully guided her charge through the turnstiles and onto the platform.

Melior's face was bland and expressionless. His hair was neatly bound back at the base of his neck, covering those ridiculous, impossible ears. He stood near the edge of the platform, head down and body relaxed, lost in his own thoughts, and if Ruth had seen him all unknowing she would have thought him a student perhaps, a dancer, something lithe and graceful and focused on his art.

The train came before she knew it. Melior heard it first; head up, face turning toward her to gauge her reaction to this new experience. Then he stepped prudently back from the platform as the train came rushing in to fill the entire platform space with battered silver cars that rocked and wheezed.

It was late morning on a Saturday and Ruth was not quick enough to gain them seats; all the way down to the 34th Street Station she and Melior stood, clutching the centerpole facing each other, Ruth's nose occasionally buried in the oatmeal wool of Melior's sweater as the rocking ride jammed them together.

She'd expected him to be irritated or upset; frightened, haughty, any of these were proper reactions if—as he said he was—Melior was an elf-lord from some feudal fantasyland who had never seen a Manhattan subway before. In intermittent glimpses of his face, Ruth saw nothing of that sort; Melior turned a countenance smooth and bland to all assaults and sensations.

And so Ruth had no clue to how angry he actually was becoming, until it was much too late.

The 34th Street Station was located in what the announcers liked to call "Lower Midtown" and realtors swore was the heart of the business district. Penn Station was a block away on Seventh Avenue, Macy's occupied an entire city block, and most of the letters and numbers of the New York subway system crossed below, in a sprawling multilevel madhouse of arcade shops and misleading signs and people, people, people.

Ruth, clutching Melior's wrist tightly, plunged into that chaos with the ease of long practice, towing Melior behind her because needs must and dodging creeps, panhandlers, and incense salesmen with the obliviousness of the habituated New Yorker.

Melior was not so habituated. He did not ignore any of these myriad new sensations—each was brand new, any might be a threat, and so all required investigation. Dazzled and exhausted and cross, he followed Ruth as best he could, but something was bound to happen, and it did.

Ruth automatically veered left to avoid the annoying and semi-dangerous gaggle of loitering teenagers with their bizarre hairdos and equally peculiar shoes. Never get involved was still Ruth's motto, and the kids—impossible to guess ages when she was working so hard at not making eye contact—were looking for trouble. Anyone could see that.

Melior couldn't. She felt the sharp yank on her arm as he jerked back, tripped by one of the kids; heard all of them start yelling at once, jabbering in a *patois* she couldn't make out over the echoes and the noise. Heart starting to hammer, she pulled harder on Melior's wrist, and found herself yanked sharply back, forced to confront the situation.

Melior was facing the leader, gazing challengingly into his eyes. The boy was poised on the balls of his feet, bouncing back and forth, poking at Melior's chest and talking very fast. Out of the corner of her eye Ruth saw hurrying pedestrians glance over and then look away, unwilling to be involved.

"You godda pro'lem? You godda pro'lem wit me? Hey? Hey? Hey, geek, you godda—" the leader of the Lost Boys said.

Melior moved, capturing the wrist of the trespassing hand and twitching it. Ruth heard the pop of dislocated bone as if there were no other sound in the world, then Melior tore his other hand free of her hold and shoved the leader in the chest, hard enough to send him sprawling into his fellows. The boy's wail of pain was high, supernaturally falsetto. No one stopped, or even looked his way.

"My problems are no concern of yours," Melior said clearly. "Is that understood?"

If they had been professional thugs, they would have finished him— rash defiance cows the hardened criminal only in bad fiction. Knuckling under was the only defense; the daily papers were full of the obituaries of those who tried to fight.

But probably they were, indeed, only schoolkids, and Melior terrified them as much as they frightened Ruth. They looked away, unwilling to face him, an animal submission as abject as a dog's. She could see tears running down the face of the boy whose wrist he'd broken; the flesh was already swollen and shiny.

"Good," said Melior, as if they had answered. He took Ruth's hand and allowed her to lead him away, but he never stopped looking back.

"What did you think you were doing?" Ruth demanded as soon as they reached the street. "You could have been killed!"

"They were not armed," Melior said dismissively.

Ruth grabbed a double handful of his sweater, and shook him, spent fear transmuted to anger. "And how do you know, Mister Elf-prince? Do you know what a gun is? Have you ever seen one? How about a switch-blade? How about being arrested for assault and sent to Bellevue for observation and never getting out?"

"I will not be handled by rabble," Melior said flatly. He looked down at Ruth, leaf-green eyes bright and sparkling now with fury. "Do you think I do not understand violence and imprisonment? Yet I will not truckle cowardly to gutterspawn such as they. The laws of your world are not mine and I will not grovel before them."

"I don't understand you!" Ruth wailed.

"No," said Melior, "you don't. But that is of no moment—come, we will—" he broke off suddenly and stepped backward, staggering as if his balance had deserted him.

"The Sword—" Melior whispered.

Ruth looked around wildly, but nowhere in the busy street and bright sunshine did she see the sword that Melior had described to them the night before.

"It is gone," Melior finally said, sighing. "Perhaps it was never here." Gently he unknotted her clutching hands from Michael's sweater.

"What do you mean? Did you see it?" Ruth demanded.

"I— Perhaps to say I *felt* it would be best. I have held it, remember, and all Great Magic has its own unmistakable aura." Melior shook his head, dispelling the last of his preoccupation. "But I don't know where. And it has passed out of range."

· 4 ·

In the Hall of the Mountain King

HE'D NEVER BEEN anyone worth being, and he wasn't now. His name was Kevin, and yesterday—April 30th—had been his birthday.

Yesterday was the day things had gotten bad—bad the way you read about in books, and always thought you could face better when it happened to you.

Last night, an hour after sundown, Kevin Shelby found he couldn't face it very well at all.

Be a man, Kevin. His mother's remembered voice echoed through his head. *Be a man, Kevin,* she'd always said, just as if there were alternatives.

He wished there were. He really did.

When he was just a kid—yesterday he'd turned thirty—his teachers always used to tell him that he was bright enough to go far. The higher education didn't matter if you were smart—or maybe higher education would somehow magically appear if you had brains and manners.

But it hadn't. People talked about scholarships, when what they meant was that you'd get some money, a little money, not even enough for a whole year's tuition and there might be other ways, better ways, full scholarship ways, but on his own he could no more locate them and unravel their mysteries than he could fly to the moon. And so all of a sudden he was out of high school, just another bright boy with good grades and potential and a shiny new diploma that didn't matter, and all of a sudden the higher education mattered very much and there was no hope of getting it.

Kevin was a bright boy. He knew what "slipping through the cracks" was, and that it happened in the educational system all the time, and that *he* had "slipped through the cracks" but there were ways around that.

There had to be.

From eighteen to twenty-five there were jobs—small jobs at first but getting better, only there wasn't any way to save much with the bills always mounting at home and his mother and his brothers always needing something.

But he had five thousand dollars in the bank and a catalog from Pace University in his underwear drawer on the day his mother decided his space was more valuable than his company, and it was time a big boy like him—*be a man, Kevin*—got a place of his own.

So he did. Somehow he thought it'd help. But the money melted away and then so did the nice clean upscale job; he scrabbled for work—*any* work—and took in roommates just so he could pay the rent. It had seemed such a low rent, such a manageable rent, when he moved in.

He thought his luck had turned when he went to work for the TA as a track worker. A job with the city was secure, the risks of working on the underground railroad didn't bother him, and the money could be good. Only now he was twenty-five, then -six, then -seven, and the money went . . . he wasn't exactly sure *where* the money went anymore. Beer and weekend movies, bets on sure horses, fine clothes to impress women he didn't see twice, and once even on a motorcycle, stolen before it was insured, and leaving nothing behind but eighteen months of payments.

And slowly Kevin Shelby came to realize that some vital turning point had been bypassed; the signpost to that deserved future of respect and higher learning had been changed from "soon" to "never" some night while he slept. "Got any college?" the interviewers always asked, and now, forever, the answer would be no.

And he was still smart: a reader of newspapers and magazines, of history and fiction. Smart enough to see now that he would never do anything lasting, anything important; never do something that no one else could do, or, even, touch the lives of those around him in any way that he could be proud of. And some day he would die, and he might as well never have been born.

And much as if it had been party to his inner deliberations and wished him to know it endorsed them, the TA in its fickle wisdom laid off a good ten percent of its loyal work force—which included him—and at thirty, when he searched for jobs, Kevin did not possess that aura of youth

and possibility that he now knew he once had worn like a cloak; that
potential for success that had gotten him hired.

It was one thing to contemplate the inevitable fall into welfare and
the gutter at three in the morning, safe and warm and well-fed in your
own bedroom. And it was quite another, Kevin learned as the weeks went
by and the unemployment benefits trickled down to nothing, it was indeed quite another thing to face a cold and hungry future on the streets
without money or food or even a place to sleep when a young and healthy
body and pampered sensibility insisted there *must* be another way.

There was. Kevin met Roy.

As the old joke goes, Roy was living with him at the time.

Roy Turpin was the latest in the series of roommates who seemed
constantly to come and go, one taking half the bedroom, one sleeping on
the couch and with rent and utilities split three ways the apartment was
possible—just.

But that was before the lost job and the tiny fractional unemployment checks and the scant savings dwindling. The stereo, the VCR, the
television itself, all the luxurious toys of past prosperity trickled away,
sold for too little cash, each sale shredding a little further the cloth of
hope.

And then there was Roy. Roy who never had any difficulty coming up
with his two bills for the monthly rent, Roy who worked various odd jobs
and odder hours, Roy who when the last roommate left had picked up the
slack without either comment or complaint, Roy who one day asked
Kevin if he wanted to pick up some money—not a lot, just a little—for a
few hours spent loading a truck up in Queens.

Roy offered a hundred dollars. If it had been more, Kevin probably
would not have taken it, would have done the right thing—

Be a man, Kevin.

—would have continued riding the downward economic spiral until
he fetched up against something, anything, that would give him salutary
shock enough to make him *look,* make him see and feel and *do* something.

But it was not to be. In a lifetime of luck just faintly sour, never good
enough to be heroic or bad enough to be romantic, Kevin took one more
fractional step down the wrong road entirely.

The truck's cargo was stolen, of course, and even when he believed
that absolutely, Kevin went on loading boxes, because if he didn't, if he
made a fuss, Roy was sure to get mad, and move out, and Kevin needed
the money desperately and besides, he didn't really know for sure. . . .

But that night, after the truck drove off and Roy clapped him on the
shoulder and steered him to the nearest bar, Kevin felt as if he had lost

something worth keeping, some talisman that, retained, would have shielded him from all the dark he saw ahead.

Be a man, Kevin.

That was only the beginning. There was more loading and unloading, daytime pickups and deliveries, all compensated in cash, and Kevin spent half his time worrying about how far he was in—dreaming fantastic Mafia dreams swagged in bloody tinsel—and the other half swearing he was in no trouble at all. Roy had never said they were breaking the law, had he? Well, then, they weren't.

And slowly the hope of an orderly real life dwindled. Kevin stopped looking for work at all. Roy always had some project he needed a little help on, and Roy became the center of Kevin's universe, replacing all other gods and ethics and futures, until Kevin Shelby *(be a man, Kevin)* measured every act not by legal and illegal, good and evil, but by whether Roy would like it, and whether he would be caught.

And then, in the end, it all came down to violence.

Yesterday had been Kevin's birthday. Thirty, the age you didn't trust anyone over. He would have liked to celebrate it—or mourn—but instead he and Roy had spent the evening with some of Roy's friends uptown.

Kevin didn't like them much, but what could you do? And besides, the casual talk was of dark knights and illegal acts, vicarious romance and self-determination, the refuge of the road. And a thousand dollars' worth of counterfeit subway tokens to take away, to package up and sell fifteen for ten dollars to a grateful public tired of fare increases.

They were almost heroes, Kevin told himself.

But then, on the way out, walking down Broadway, hungry for Chinese and beer and trying to think of nothing at all, it happened.

"Hey, Kev, wouldja lookit that?"

Kevin followed Roy's gaze without difficulty and saw a big blond in a red dress and a cape, holding something long and thin that glittered as if caught in a spotlight shining for it alone. Then the figure turned, rotating slowly as though determined to see everything at once, and Kevin realized it was a man, not a woman—a man with long silvery hair streaming over his shoulders, wearing strange clothes that had the insistent familiarity of something seen in a dream.

"Damned faggot," said Roy. "Hey, Kev, let's have some fun. Let's have some fun here, boy, whaddya say?" He put an arm around Kevin's shoulders and hurried him toward the man.

Accompanied by the staccato tocsin of outraged car horns, the man in the red dress and cape crossed Broadway. That the motorists stopped at all was perhaps a tribute to what he held in his hands—five feet of dangerous glittering metal and gem-studded hilt.

Less reckless, Kevin and Roy had to wait for the light. Roy bounced up and down, jittering as he waited.

"Oh, boy—oh, boy! Now there's a sword just like in that *Conan* movie. I know somebody'd give me a thousand bucks for a sword like that, custom-made and everything."

And Kevin knew suddenly just what Roy planned, and crossed the street with him anyway.

Possibly if Roy had been alone, he would have changed his mind; as they followed their dreamwalking quarry down the slope of 116th Street, it became clear that he was one of the body-building kinds of faggot and not the wimpy kind of faggot. But Kevin was there as witness, and so Roy went ahead.

"Hey—you! Girlieboy!" Roy said, and the faggot turned around and his eyes shone red and green and he looked like something you'd see in a nightmare of a movie but never in real life. And then Roy swung at him with one of the sweatsocks full of bootleg tokens—aiming not for the head, but for the wrist of the hand holding the sword. And the sword fell to the ground in a brassy tintinnabulation because the sock had burst and scattered bootleg largess everywhere and the faggot, girlieboy—

Be a man, Kevin.

—was reaching for the sword when Roy hit him again, knocking him to his knees.

"Get it, Kev!"

And Kevin grabbed the sword.

There in his hand was everything he'd ever wanted. The chance to make it right, to make amends, to take back the life he was supposed to have had. And the nightmare thing lying in the street reached for it, grabbed at Kevin's leg, and filled with revulsion and terror he struck out, bringing the sword down, the flat of the blade hitting the white-blond head with the sound of an ax on wood.

The man tried to get up one last time, and Roy kicked him down and went on kicking as if he wanted to be sure he'd done it right.

"Gimme that, Kev."

"I don't want—"

"You put him in with those trash cans—come on, hurry up." And Roy pulled the glorious renascent sword out of Kevin's shocked fingers and shoved him toward the body.

Kevin was strong. The health and strength that had first commended him to Roy's attention served now—he hauled their prey upright and slung it carelessly into an alleyway. The sound the body made when it fell made him smile. Some sort of balance had been regained, some eternal adjustment made.

The silken-swift/The gloriously fair . . . He'd read that in a book once and that guy/thing/creature/girlieboy they'd mugged made Kevin think of it now: beautiful in a dangerous inhuman way, but what right did that thing have to be beautiful when Kevin's world had all gone wrong? He turned back to his partner, and the sight of the sword in Roy's hands was jarring, unwelcome.

"Hey, Roy, give that here, okay?" Kevin said. Roy's face twisted in an ugly knowing grin.

"The hell, Kev. This's mine—I saw him first, didn't I? You wouldn't 'a hit on him without me. You want something, you go back and see what else he's got." Roy pulled off his jacket, began to wrap the naked blade. "Hey, Kev, you gimme your jacket, okay? Gotta get this covered up."

And Kevin, thinking and planning for the real world for the first time in his life, eyes and mind and heart fixed on a goal that was for the first time in his life something he could not bear even to think of not achieving, ready, willing to be-a-man and intent now with a will of a passionate intensity, that Kevin shrugged off his jacket and handed it to Roy.

To his good buddy, Roy.

For the sword.

For Being A Man.

They got out of there then, walking quickly up the sidestreet through the light April rain that had begun to fall, heading for home.

Kevin had always hoped for better things; each time he saw his apartment he winced a little inside, knowing he could have, ought to have had, better.

Be a man, Kevin.

But tonight he didn't waste a moment's mourning on the worn, the shabby, the walls overdue for painting and the ubiquitous roaches. Tonight he followed Roy in meekly, locking the three locks, the deadbolt, and the chain, and went off to his room to see if what he thought was there was still there.

It was. And when he came out, Roy had unwrapped the sword, had laid it out upon the once cheap and new and now worn and shabby couch.

It did not contrast with its surroundings, shaming them by its perfection. It simply dismissed them, as if in its presence nothing else could be important. It was a little over five feet long, with a yard of blade that tapered gradually from the hilt to the point, as if it had been drawn out so, taffy-soft in the child-time of its forging. The blade had a soft rich sheen, promising sharpness; not mirror-bright like the daggers in the Hoffritz window, rhodium-plated against tarnish, but softer somehow, soft and sharp at the same time, like gold. Precious as gold, with its soft white sheen.

Later Kevin would come to know the rest of it well: the crosspiece, an undulating wave of the same white metal, seeming to change form each time he looked at it, now serpent, now woman; the hilt, long enough for him to put both hands around, ornamented with tiny gold beads later revealed to be the pulls of drawers he could never open, set against a dark swirling richness that seemed now wood, now stone, now goldsmith's lacquer. And then the pommel, the counterweight that moved the center of gravity up the blade so that a man holding it as it was meant to be held would feel only its lightness, the pommel was a globe the size of an orange, an opal or a diamond or perhaps a sphere filled with swirling summer smoke, always changing.

"Hey, lookit this, huh, Kev? Lookit this—sure is something," Roy said prayerfully. His hands hovered above the blade, making might-be mystic passes, unwilling to touch it.

Wild for to hold. Other scraps of poetry came to the surface of Kevin's mind, relics of a time when he believed in the power of intellect. Now he had abandoned intellect, and all he had left to voice his feelings and his fears were borrowed words, clumsy of fit. *Wild for to hold. Wild for to hold.* Was the wildness in the sword, or in him—or in some New Wave mixture of objects and life history?

"You got to give me that, Roy," Kevin said, sweet reason forcing the words out through the expanding lightness in his chest. "You got to give me that sword right now, Roy," he said, as his lips pulled back in a smile that made his jaws ache.

Roy turned away from the sword.

"Right now, Roy!" Kevin shouted on an upskirl of laughter, of a fine joke, the best joke ever, or certainty and rightness like champagne bubbles in his blood as he brought the bat, his Louisville Slugger from childhood days, down, and down, and down again.

And then he laughed until the tears came, kneeling there on the floor beside Roy, waiting for the labored, concussed breathing to stop as if its silence were his permission to go on. And he thought that all his life had led him to this moment, that it had given him as little choice as it gave the bullet fired from the gun's barrel, and as he waited for the breathing to stop he filled his eyes with the sword, with the sight and fire and tainted certainty of it.

"Be a man, Roy. Be a man," Kevin said to his dying friend.

He was afraid, and he was alone. He had no choice, and he knew it. And worse. He knew what he was going to do next.

· 5 ·

Pard-Spirit on
34th Street

RUTH FINALLY CONVINCED Melior to go on into Macy's as, even if
he had sensed its presence (Ruth was inclined to doubt this), Melior's
magic sword was nowhere he could get at it just now.

Once she'd succeeded in getting him into the store she wished she
hadn't.

Ruth had lived in New York for three years, and had long since
forgotten the dazzling rush of sensory overload brought on by her first
exposure to The Big Apple. And even so, Ruth had come from another
city; a smaller city, but still a city, Urban America at its best, the twentieth
century.

Melior hadn't.

For a moment she saw it through his eyes: the golden marble, the
sixty-foot ceilings, the space filled with people all rushing at top speed to
no discernible place. The glittering piles of *Things,* all displayed to catch
the eye, and over all the roar of conversation, the pong-pong-pong of the
callbells, and the Muzak of some alien and unconsidered civilization.

Melior took a step back, pushing her into the influx of shoppers from
the street, dazzled and blinded and completely helpless.

Ruth clutched at him, too. She took a deep breath, forced the sense
of vertigo and helplessness away from her, and pulled him aside into a
quiet backwater of the eddying onward torrent of trade.

And this isn't even Christmas Rush, Ruth thought to herself. Macy's was a little crowded, sure, but not impossible to navigate this early on a Saturday.

But what must it look like to someone who came from a realm of knights and castles, forests and quiet green fields?

If he did. If this weren't all some long elaborate hoax. But how, otherwise, to explain those eyes, those ears, except by the tale that Melior himself told, of war, treachery, and elfin magic?

Beware, beware/His flashing eyes, his floating hair, Ruth thought sourly. But if he froze up like hell's own autism poster child at the sight of a department store, how in heaven's name was Melior of the Silver Silences going to be able to get enough of a grip to search for a demon-infested magic sword in New York City?

But it was less than five minutes later that Melior released his death grip upon Ruth's arm and sighed.

"This is a marketplace?" he asked, in even, if faintly disbelieving, tones.

"It's Macy's. The world's largest department store," Ruth added apologetically. "I know it's a zoo, but we can get everything we need here."

"Except the Sword," Melior said with a ghost of a smile.

"Except that."

Without Michael's checklist it would have been harder, since neither Ruth nor Melior had any idea of Melior's sizes. But socks and underwear were achieved without difficulty, and they went on to the next thing on Ruth's list.

"Shoes. You'll feel better once you've got proper shoes that fit." Ruth said hopefully. She consulted the store directory and headed them in the direction of the shoe department.

Melior's head was constantly in motion, turning to look at this and that, watchful, all of him moving with a kind of frantically-achieved stillness, a suppressed kinesthesia that made Ruth's jaw ache in sympathetic tension. He restricted himself to brief questions, all his will directed toward learning the parameters of this world he was trapped in. In the shoe department Melior was discouraged from his first choice—

"Not those."

"Why not, Ruth?"

"They're rain boots. For women."

—and became the proud owner of a pair of black leather high-tops (for which Ruth paid, wincing at the price, but this had been her idea, dammit). Michael's Chinese boxing slippers went into the bag; Melior wore the sneakers, looking somehow even less normal the closer he came to being properly clothed.

Next they recrossed the store to the men's clothing department. Ruth had been thinking of something casual, yet conservative: clothes, she vaguely thought, like Michael wore, bland and inoffensive. She headed for the display of blue jeans. *This won't take long,* she thought hopefully. Melior followed her.

"Here we are: Levis for It. We'd better try a few different sizes; Michael wasn't sure, but he thought a thirty-four inseam. . . ."

"No."

Ruth looked up. Melior ran his hand over the mound of folded clothing. He held up one pair—heavy folded cotton *de Nimes,* as it was once called, denim indigo-dyed, stiff and harsh—and shook his head.

"I cannot wear this, Ruth," Melior said.

"What's wrong with them?" she burst out. "They're *jeans,* dammit. I wear them, Michael wears them, everybody wears them!"

"Michael's are not like this." Melior reached out and stroked the fabric of her wool plaid skirt. "And you are not wearing them now." Melior tossed the jeans back in their pile, not appearing to notice Ruth's flustered retreat. The jeans hit with a thump like a book being tossed down—heavy and unyielding.

"They'll get like Michael's with time," Ruth said, half-stammering.

"I do not have time," Melior said flatly. He reached out and put a hand on Ruth's shoulder, pulling her toward him. "You say I must have clothing of this world so that I may move freely in it. I understand that— and believe me, Ruth, I am grateful for the time and silver you expend in my service."

"Plastic," muttered Ruth. The corner of Melior's mouth quirked upward.

"But I do not dress this way for my own joy, but to serve an end. And I cannot serve that end rasped bloody by peasants' canvas trousers."

"Well what do you want—silk?" Ruth snapped. It was true that jeans had begun as work clothes, cheap and long-wearing for ranchers and farmers, but they had long since become (with all inconvenience retained) the universal dress of the twentieth century. She knew Melior wasn't from here, but when faced with Levis, empathy faltered. If he would not wear jeans, what would he wear?

"I want suitable clothing for this time and place," Melior corrected her softly. "Everyone does not wear these—and there are so many things for sale here. Let us but search a little farther, my friend, and try if we may not find something that suits both our needs."

Melior gave her his most dazzling smile, and in the dim strange neon

light of the "Young Actives" department Ruth saw for the first time that
his teeth were pointed; curved canines a little longer than the rest, slant-
ing down to meet the upward thrust of pointed teeth in the lower jaw.
Great. Just what I need. A vampire elf.
"Okay. We'll keep looking."
Now it was Ruth who followed Melior as he prowled the aisles of the
"World's Largest Department Store." Suddenly he stopped, fairly quiver-
ing, taut as a bowstring. Ruth followed his gaze.
"Oh, no. Not that. Anything but that."
This particular department swore that it sold clothes for men 18-25.
Ruth imagined that those numbers must refer to their IQs, as she
couldn't imagine any sensible person shopping in a department lit pri-
marily by red, green, and amber key lights and the glare from a dozen
monitors all tuned to different music videos.
The mannequins were flat silvery cutouts, headless and ostentatiously
jointed and wearing clothing that Ruth had never seen on any living body
that wasn't on television. Melior went up to one mannequin and felt the
fabric of the baggy batik-printed rayon pants.
"Yes, Ruth, here. If you please," Melior said.
In the end it was jeans they settled on—but jeans as soft and pliant as
Melior's own buckskins; acid washed, frayed, and artistically patched.
Melior ran his fingers over them and then held them up to his narrow
hips, looking questioningly at Ruth.
"After all this you want jeans anyway?" Ruth gibed. The light made
her eyes hurt and the music made her teeth hurt; she wondered why the
management didn't just set off smoke pots if their aim was to drive customers out of the store.
"These are different," Melior said inarguably. "And I have seen
many here wearing garments such as these."
"Well, you'd better try them on," Ruth said grudgingly.
Armed with a range of sizes—as Michael's list contained approxima-
tions, nothing more—Melior vanished into the dressing room. Ruth took
advantage of his absence to collect for his future use a red snakeskin belt
with a *faux*-silver buckle. Thank God she'd talked him out of the pink-
and-turquoise baggies. Or the red, acid-washed, overdyed jumpsuit. Or
the tie-dyed spandex jodhpurs. Or—
*Honestly, Ruth, get a life. You're going on like you're dressing up a doll.
Buying clothes like this—spending all this money—and it isn't even for yourself. You'll be paying this off until the Last Trump, and for what?*
"It's worth it," Ruth muttered back at herself. "And he's worth it.
And I don't want clothes like this for me, I want—" She ran the sinuous
length of the supple leather through her hands, ran the ball of her thumb

over the cold hard sculpture of the buckle. *I want someone who dresses like this for me.*

"Is this suitable, Ruth?" Melior had come out of the dressing room while she daydreamed; he stood before her—*a ghost of rags and patches*—in artistically-frayed and very tight jeans that molded the entire swell and sweep of calves and thighs and anchored Melior firmly in the twentieth-century world. His hair had come loose of its tie and flowed over his shoulders. He looked like a particularly delectable rock star; silvery and shining and insulated from mortal touch.

"Ruth?" Melior said again.

"It's good, it's fine, let's go pay for it, okay?"

Melior regarded her closely. "What is wrong, Ruth? Is this so unsuitable? I admit that I find this *department store* very strange, but surely you should not?"

"Go on. Take them off so we can go pay for them, okay? After all, they don't matter—they're just part of your equipment for this impossible mission, right?" She looked away in frustration, and when she looked back, Melior had retreated to the dressing rooms again.

"I do not withdraw my question," Melior said, once this new purchase had been added to their growing store and he and Ruth were out in one of the main aisles again.

"I'm so glad to hear it. Why don't we go get lunch—my feet hurt."

"I will not be toyed with," Melior said, stopping dead. Shoppers detoured around him, giving him wary and resentful looks. A small child, towed away by its uninterested parent, cried: "Ears, Mommy!" pointing up at Melior.

Ruth stopped, too, and looked back at him.

"Fine. Nobody's toying with you. God knows I'm not stupid enough to do something like that, great big dangerous interdimensional vampire elf as you are, and there's nobody else here. Whatever the problem is, it isn't you, and you wouldn't be able to understand the explanation anyway, so why don't you get off my case and let's go get some lunch?"

Melior took the time to think this through, giving her entire speech his active consideration for possibly two minutes while Ruth stood, glaring and irritated all out of proportion to the offense, and waited.

"We have not finished our shopping yet," Melior offered.

Ruth took a deep breath. Other shoppers swirled around them, oblivious.

"Fine. We will finish our shopping. And then we will go get lunch. And so we can go get lunch before the next glacial age is on us, we are going to buy what *I* pick out and what *I* think you ought to be wearing and you are not going to argue with me. Is that clear?"

"Perfectly clear, Ruth," Melior said, with the corner of his mouth quirked in that maddening half-smile.

And that, of course, was how they wound up in possession of the black leather motorcycle jacket (on sale).

Ruth swept back through the menswear department like an avenging angel with a mission to shop and a tight deadline. She picked out a black turtleneck sweater, a white "river diver's" shirt with twelve tiny silvery buttons down the placket, and an orange-cotton T-shirt that said *"It's not my planet, monkey-boy"* in raised black paint-spatter letters. Along the way she collected a pair of Ray-Ban aviator sunglasses with a beetle wing mirrored finish, in the hope that they'd help to make him more *normal* looking. She thrust them at him as soon as they were paid for.

"Here! Put these on!"

Melior did, and was instantly transformed into an F.B.I. agent from Betelgeuse. But at least his eyes were hidden.

His flashing eyes, his floating hair—oh, stop it, Ruth!

And having filled out Michael's list and gotten Melior as much in the way of clothing as your average (male) freshman brings to college, she saw the jacket.

There were three of them left, hanging on one of those movable stands that retailers use to tempt the unwary. Ruth went closer and looked. "Sale," the sign said. "End of Season." Ruth ran her hand over the sleeve. Hard and slick, acrid with the chemicals of its tanning. Lined in a slick acrylic satin, almost as black. A thing of studs and buckles, zippers, flanges, pulls, and straps. Twentieth century armor for a real-world dark knight.

He'll need a jacket, Ruth argued to herself with insane practicality. *It'll be useful.* But that wasn't why she wanted to buy it and she knew it.

"Melior? Come over here; I want you to try something on."

He wore it so she wouldn't have to carry it. It meshed with the mirrorshades and clashed oddly with the dobby sweater. They were almost out of the store when Ruth remembered one last thing.

"Hat."

"I beg your pardon, Mistress?"

"Hat," said Ruth. "We'll get you a hat. Covers a multitude of sins—and ears," she added, remembering the little boy. They'd been lucky so far.

They retraced their steps. Macy's was always changing its ground-floor layout. All the impulse purchases were there—and the luxuries.

Jewels and perfume, silk scarves . . . and in this day and age, hats. Ruth led him toward the haberdashery display.

"It doesn't have to be much," she said. "This?" Ruth held up a watch cap, silky black cashmere, and looked at Melior hopefully. "No. That." Melior turned away and reached for the hat: black, fur-felt with a low crown and a wide, sweeping, oval brim. He picked it up.

"That's a woman's hat," Ruth pointed out.

"I don't care. I like it." He put it on, settled it on his head and looked in the mirror, gazing at his reflection, face half-hidden by the sweep of brim; a cipher in mirrorshades and leather. And he didn't look silly at all—he looked fine, better than fine, like a fey horseman riding out from the other world to claim—

What?

Not me, Ruth thought, firmly bundling her imaginings away. *I already know what he wants.*

"Okay. Fine. You want to look like Doctor Who? We'll take it."

"Do not bother to pack it," Melior said with his new command of idiom, "I shall wear it out of the store."

"Don't you think you'd better take the tag off first?"

And so they emerged, blinking and ravenous, from the underworld of the consumer-driven marketplace at about 2:30 of a fine Saturday afternoon. Ruth led them down Broadway until she found what she was looking for: a Blimpie's, chosen on this occasion because it had both seating and table service. She led Melior to a table in the back and handed him the menu. Melior stared at it for a moment, then handed it back.

"I cannot read this, Ruth."

She stared at him in surprise. She had just naturally assumed Melior could read—he seemed so *civilized,* that it was just ridiculous to think of him as illiterate.

"There was little time for scholarship during the War, but I can write a passable hand in Court and Common, read those and half-a-dozen more, and spell a passable *dweomer* in the alphabet of high sorcery," Melior offered in response to her blank look.

"But?" Ruth prompted, knowing there must be more.

"But here in the World of Iron I cannot read your sigils. Any of them."

"But you speak English!" Ruth protested.

"Do I? I imagine I would speak the common tongue of whatever land I found myself in. It is the way of things when one goes Gatewalking."

"Well this land hasn't *got* a common tongue! And everyone here can read. Mostly."

"So I gather. And so can I read, though not here. Perhaps you will teach me, if there is time." Melior took her hand across the table.

World enough and time. Had we but world enough, and time/Thy coyness, Lady, were no crime. . . .

"Hey, uh, excuse me. I saw you come in, and—could I have your autograph?"

Ruth jerked her hand away from Melior and looked up. The boy was standing in front of Melior, looking at him hopefully. He had on jeans and scuffed white sneakers and a sleeveless denim jacket open over an indeterminate heavy metal T-shirt. He thrust a copy of the restaurant's take-out menu at Melior.

"I really love you, man. I love you a lot," the boy said.

"Ah." Melior looked from the boy to Ruth and back. "Certainly. A pen, please, Ruth."

Ruth took the precaution of uncapping the pen before she handed it to him—no matter how sophisticated he was, Melior could never have seen a pen like her 89-cent Flair. But he took it without a bobble, and signed the menu in swooping curlicues of florid purple that matched no alphabet Ruth had ever seen.

"Hey, man, thanks—I saw you in concert last year. Got all your albums." The boy departed, still talking over his shoulder, and hit only one table and the trash can on the way out.

Ruth held out as long as she could and then burst out laughing.

"And what," asked Melior when she had subsided somewhat, "was that about?"

"Oh, wait till I tell Nai! He thought you were a *rock star,* Melior—it must be the jacket. And he— And you—" The thought was too much for her; the previous tension too great; Ruth began to laugh again. "What did you write?" she finally managed.

"My name. It was what he wanted, was it not? And now, will you read this ordinary to me so that we may be at meat?"

It was fortunate for Ruth that, lifelong anachronist that she was, she was aware that an ordinary was the bill of fare at an inn. After some consultation Melior chose a chicken sandwich and herb tea. Ruth had a tuna salad and coffee. The waiter who brought them smiled as if they were all in a conspiracy together.

Now that she was habituated to it she could see it: Melior acted like a rock star, a celebrity, and people treated him as one. Or perhaps it was the other way around, but now that she was looking it was impossible to miss the aura of anticipation, of charisma, of grand seigneur expectation that even New York roused itself to meet. Melior was famous, Melior was news—whoever they thought he was.

They dawdled over lunch. Ruth took the time to organize all the purchases into two large shopping bags; Melior removed Michael's borrowed wet-sheepdog sweater and put on the new orange T-shirt. Ruth saw herself reflected in his sunglasses as she read its printed slogan once more. *"It's not my planet." Right. And what if it isn't?*

If this were happening in a book or a movie, Ruth would have had her expectations ready. Whoever had tripped over this wonder should take it directly to the authorities. Fictional people rarely did, of course, and Ruth, reading or watching, was always vastly indignant with whoever allowed the strangeness to simply slip away unrecorded; to keep it selfishly and not add it to the universe's store of marvels.

But it wasn't as easy as that. *It never is.* . . . If she believed Melior was a lord out of Faery—*and I do,* Ruth promised herself fiercely—who could she tell? The Mayor? The President?

Faced with the personal task of making someone notice the unlikely truth about reality, Ruth realized she wasn't up to it.

And Melior was not some abstract cultural phenomenon; not an Elvis sighting in a 34th Street deli. Melior was a person, with things that he needed.

And she would rather give Melior what he needed than pay homage to some ideal of civic-mindedness that was as much a dead issue as the White Man's Burden.

In the end, what Melior was didn't matter. His existence made Ruth's world no wider.

"Come on. Let's go find a subway."

Melior held his tongue until they reached the street. Heads turned to look at him; Melior looked back.

"Subway's this way," Ruth said. "Come on. We've got to get back."

"I know. I will not go in those ways again. I will walk," Melior said. He looked up—taking his bearings from the sun, Ruth realized—and set off.

By the time they reached 42nd Street Ruth realized he was completely serious. He strode down the sidewalk perfectly possessed of both himself and it—*nobody would ever guess he'd been mugged flat last night,* Ruth thought admiringly—gazing openly around himself in a fashion no New Yorker would be caught dead doing, with the cold May sunlight glinting on the silvery spill of his unbound hair; flashing off the oil-slick surfaces of his sunglasses' lenses, and glinting upon the innumerable chrome widgets of his black leather jacket.

Jaded New York crowds parted for him as if they were the Red Sea. Ruth, soldiering on behind with two shopping bags full of underwear, was less fortunate.

She put up with this as far as 79th Street—Museum Row, and lovely and dangerous Central Park on her right hand. The pedestrian traffic was thinner here, and Melior had slowed down enough about an hour before for her to keep up with him.

"It's only a couple of stops on the subway to Michael's from here," she offered, having finally called a rest. She dumped the bags on one of the green wooden park benches that lined the sidewalk here and collapsed beside them, throwing a wary protective arm over them. Melior showed no sign of flagging.

"No. You may take the subterranean way, if you will. I shall walk."

"Walk? How are you going to walk? You can't find Michael's by yourself—you can't read the street signs!"

"I know the way lies north, and that the river is to the west of us. If I follow the river I will find it—and that I will do gladly, rather than venture into your underworld again."

Underworld is a good name for it, Ruth thought wryly. She did her best to remember that, no matter how frazzled she felt, she was at least in her right world, with no particular sins of omission hanging over her. Melior was not.

"All right. Okay." She rummaged in her purse and dragged out her wallet, scrabbling through it until she located the remains of her cash machine advance. She counted it carefully. "Fine. Let's take a taxi, then—I'm not going to walk another forty blocks carrying your underwear."

Hailing a cab was a difficult process—at least until Melior properly understood what a taxi was and why it was wanted. Then he simply stepped out into the traffic in front of one, bringing it to a horn-blaring stop.

"You could have gotten killed!" Ruth said once they were both inside.

"Yeah—you tell 'im, lady. Crazy foreigners. Where to?" the cab-driver agreed.

"One-sixteenth and Riverside, please." They might as well go all the way up to her and Naomi's place, so long as they were taking a taxi.

"But I was not killed, Ruth. And one can be killed in so many ways. Every exercise of skill is a risk," Melior pointed out as the taxi began to roll.

"You don't know how things work here—you can't just take it for granted—"

"That the hired car will stop?" Melior smiled. "Ruth, I do not. And though this is a ghastly place, it is not entirely different from some places I have seen. It is only more so."

Only more so. What a convenient and time-saving way of putting things.
The ride uptown was brisk and uneventful. They stopped right in front of Ruth's apartment; the fare was seven-fifty, and Ruth, unwilling to argue, gave the cabby a ten. This left precious little in her wallet, and she hesitated even to total the Macy's charge slips lying like a nest of vipers at the bottom of her purse. But it was worth it. By dressing Melior in earthly raiment she made him hers, sort of. Or maybe it was a way of giving him all the help she could in regaining his sword.

The Sword of Maiden's Tears. Every time she tried to think about it sensibly, her mind skittered away, as from something too God-knows-what to take seriously. But the Sword—and its absence—was the central problem that had to be faced.

He'll never find it. Never. This is New York. It's gone. And it would be a minor life triumph if Ruth could figure out whether that made her happy or sad—and why.

· 6 ·

My Dinner with Melior

RUTH COULD SMELL the powerful fragrance of baking bread and Something-with-Burgundy the moment she arrived on the seventh floor. Melior's nose twitched, too; he looked at her, eyebrows raised questioningly.

"Oh, God, I forgot. Saturday dinner," Ruth said. "Everybody will be here."

"With such an ornamental puzzle presented for their delectation, how could they not be?" Melior said.

"Don't flatter yourself. Naomi's cooking. Everybody'd be here anyway," Ruth said.

Saturday—or sometimes Sunday—dinner at Ruth and Naomi's (Naomi's, really) had become something of an institution. Even splitting the cost of the raw materials four ways (Naomi provided the kitchen and skill) it wasn't as expensive as a no-holds-barred dinner out, and it was light-years above the *cuisine de scholastique* available in the Columbia dining hall.

More important even than that, Naomi's dinners took hours to prepare, and anyone who wished could profitably spend the day in the apartment, mincing garlic and the reputation of absent friends in an atmosphere of togetherness.

And that, thought Ruth with a cool dispassionate intelligence, was something none of them could get anywhere else, wasn't it? The thing that drew them all together was that all of them, each of them, was alone. Alone, but not loners. Just people who didn't fit in anywhere, which by some merciful alchemy made them more tolerant of others who somehow didn't fit. *How unlike life,* Ruth thought cynically.

When she opened the front door, the first thing she saw was Jane—surrounded by books, of course. Jane's guitar in its case sat propped primly against the wall under the window. Jane looked up as Ruth entered—and looked wholly disapproving as she saw Melior.

I wonder what that's about, Ruth thought.

"They're ba-a-a-ack," Jane called toward the kitchen. She made one more entry in her notebook, closed it with a slam, and began stacking the books in a neat pile to one side of the table. Ruth glanced at the spine-labels: 398 and 291—Folklore and Mythology.

"Ruth? Is that you?" Naomi called from the kitchen.

"No, it's Jack the Ripper," Ruth called back. She thrust the bags at Melior. "Why don't you go put on your jeans so everyone can get the full effect?" Ruth said, and headed for the kitchen without looking back.

Naomi was there, bending over and peering into the oven, which gave forth its lovely scent. She looked up when Ruth entered.

"Beef with Burgundy. It's cheap, it's stupid, it'll feed fifty. And how was *your* day?"

"Vertical?" Philip added sweetly.

"You're not tall enough for that gesture, Mrs. Siddons." Ruth shot back. Philip was crouched gnomelike on the step stool shoved under the window. One of Naomi's mixing bowls was on his lap; he stirred the contents intermittently with a long wooden spoon. She wondered how Naomi had ever gotten him to help.

"Melior thinks he saw his sword."

Although, looking back on those crowded few minutes outside Macy's, she wasn't sure that "saw" was the word she wanted. Sensed?

"Fine," said Naomi. She peeled up the foil on the pan in the oven and prodded mystically beneath it. Satisfied, she closed the oven. "We can talk about that after dinner. Michael's going to be a little late; he called."

"Off hocking Elfie's stuff," Philip added, surprisingly helpful (for Philip). His glasses flashed as he looked down at the bowl and started stirring again.

"Faery gold vanishes in the light of the sun." Jane edged into the kitchen beside Ruth. Jane herself looked as though she might vanish in the light of the sun, assuming she ever saw it. For one still cursed with the puppyish roundness of unshed baby fat, Jane gave a surprising air of insubstantiality. Her mouse-blonde hair (indifferently long), straggled down over the shoulders of the "pretty in pink" shetland sweater she wore. She shoved her glasses up on her nose again.

"It's just a good thing that the sunlight never reaches street level, or Michael'd be in trouble. I wish he'd go away," she added under her breath. Ruth knew it wasn't Michael she meant, but Jane had barely met Melior. What could he possibly have done to tick off Jane?

"Okay, you guys, get out of my kitchen. Ruth, why don't you go see if Mel would like a cup of tea, or something? Dinner won't be ready for an hour or so. Michael said you went clothes shopping, so I dug out an old suitcase to donate to the cause; it's on my bed."

"What's that?" Ruth pointed to the bowl Philip was stirring.

"Wouldn't you like to know?" Philip said.

"Out," Naomi insisted.

Jane preceded Ruth into the living room. Ruth, blissfully unwary in the comfort of her own home, looked up to see Jane's back stiffen into silent, long-suffering disapproval.

Melior had taken Jane's guitar out of its case.

One would not necessarily think of Jane in connection with the guitar. Guitars seemed so frivolous, somehow. Jane's whole nature cried out for nothing less than a grand piano, funereal in black lacquer, but as Real Life is conducted without an art director, Jane had come among them with an entirely ordinary acoustic guitar that reposed, when not in use, in a black fiberboard case innocent of paint or decals.

In Melior's hands, the guitar became a different thing entirely.

He had slung the strap over his back, but held the instrument almost vertically, his long pale fingers wrapped about the neck. His free hand stroked the strings and the sound box as if the guitar's whole shape were faintly unfamiliar but one that he was learning fast. His head was lowered, his face turned toward the guitar. In jeans and T-shirt, sneakers and sunglasses and long silver hair, he could be taken for any normal student at Columbia—and that made him just as much an outsider in this room as being an elf-king did.

"You shouldn't take things that don't belong to you," Jane said in a tight voice.

Melior looked up and focused on her. "I beg your pardon, Mistress." He dipped his head to slip the strap over it and held out the guitar. "My reckless curiosity has ever been my sin." He looked at Ruth. "And does this habiliment meet with your approval?" He held out the guitar.

"You look just like all the other kids," Ruth said.

"But you don't wear sunglasses indoors unless you want people to think you're a junkie," Jane added. "Are there guitars in Elfland?"

The question could have been either offensive or ingenuous, but Jane's perfectly-controlled tone gave no clue as to which it should be.

"Things similar," said Melior, still holding the guitar toward Jane. "And do you play?"

"No," said Jane, "I just carry it around for fun." She plucked it out of his hands, giving the impression of a small field mouse skittering around a large lion, and went to replace it in its case.

Children, thought Ruth, from the vantage of a decade's seniority. "Naomi says that dinner won't be for at least an hour. Do you want some tea?"

"Yes, I thank you," Melior said. "And is there perhaps a map of this city?"

"I've got maps," Jane said surprisingly. "I'll get the tea." She flipped the locks of the guitar case shut and went off to the kitchen again. Ruth looked at Melior.

"I am strange here, as well as a stranger," he observed. "Is it true, Ruth, that of all the Five Races only humans abide in the World of Iron? I had heard that was true, but it is always desirable to have firsthand information." He removed the sunglasses carefully and set them on the table. The silvery lenses reflected back at Ruth like a second set of eyes.

Ruth sat down on the couch, and got the benefit of the westering sun full in the face. "And what are the Five Races?—by which you may understand that, yes, as far as I know nothing but humans live here. There are rumors, of course," she added darkly, "but they're only fairy tales—myths."

"I am put in my place," Melior observed. "The Five Races are those peoples able to use magic. They live in the World That Is, though not all live together in one Land. In my own, humans and my kind live—and perhaps the Sea People, although they are wild and canny and dislike to meddle in the affairs of landsmen unless they can do so to their own advantage."

"How like life," Ruth muttered. "So there are mermaids? With tails?"

Melior raised his eyebrows and looked amused. "I have not enquired. But to summarize," he went on, his tone of voice putting Ruth forcibly in mind of some of her duller professors, "the Five Races which abide in the lands of the World That Is are these: the Earth Born, which are called humans; the Sea Born, called merfolk and *ceildhe;* Night's Children, who have as many names and forms as the stars cast shadows; and my own kind."

"The elves," Ruth supplied. "And that's only four."

"Ah," said Melior, "but you are not a scholar of the mysteries, and I will not burden you with gossip you will never have a use for. And "elves" is only what the Earth Born call us."

"Elf. In German, *Erl*. From the Old Teutonic *Eorl*, meaning 'Lord,' which passed into English from Saxon as 'Earl,' " Jane said. She set down the tiny tray with the brown Rockingham teapot and the sugar and creamer.

"So you do remember," Melior said.

"Not personally," Jane said. "And that has to steep."

Melior withdrew his hand from the teapot.

"So what do you call yourselves?" Ruth asked. She half-suspected she was being made the butt of an elaborate joke, with all this highfalutin taxonomy of races and titles. Modern anthropology had proven that every society called itself Us, and everyone else it met, Them.

"The Folk of the Air," Melior said quietly. "The Sons of the Morning and the Daughters of Twilight. The Star-Begotten."

"Twinkle, twinkle," said Philip mockingly from the safety of the doorway.

If Melior had done what Ruth half expected—flayed Philip where he stood with a backlash of hauteur and pride—it would have been possible for Ruth to successfully dislike him (even though she, herself, frequently felt that Philip would have been a good deal better company if he had been drowned at birth). But instead, unexpectedly, he laughed.

"Perhaps all peoples—if they were honest—have too high an opinion of themselves! But I think it must be far stranger to think there are no other peoples in all the wide world—although this world is not so very wide," Melior said.

"What do you know about it?" Philip said aggressively. "You guys are still fighting with cavalry and swords—what do you know about guns and bombs—and airplanes? Or computers? Or spaceships?"

"Nothing," said Melior, in tones that suggested he did not grieve for his lack. "And what do you know, my fine mannikin, of horsemanship, or sorcery, or Gatewalking; of the treaties that bind the Five Races—"

"Of which there are four," Ruth muttered.

"Or cars—" said Philip, adding to his list.

" 'In the time twixt the dark and the twilight/When the night is beginning to lower/Comes a pause in the day's occupations/That is known as For God's Sake, Shut up, Philip,' " Jane misquoted strenuously. "We agreed; we could discuss this when Michael gets here."

Ruth realized that some agreement had been reached by the others while she and Melior were out; through a childish pang of hurt feelings at being excluded she wondered what exactly the agreement was.

The talk turned quickly and briefly to school; Ruth and Michael would graduate this June, but Philip and Jane both had another year to go. Ruth thought guiltily about her master's thesis, still unbegun. *"The*

Role of the Librarian in the Illiterate Society." She wondered if there were elf-librarians, and what sort of books they guarded.

Having settled that he and Jane were both behind in their coursework and that it was a waste of time anyway, Philip flipped on the TV. The late-afternoon sunlight bleached the picture to oblivion, but the sound worked fine.

"A Bronx man is being sought in connection with the death of Roy Turpin, 36, of North Queens Avenue. The body was discovered early this morning by—" Ruth tuned out the sound and the pastel image of a shrouded body being bundled into a waiting ambulance. Just another beautiful day in Fun City.

"Your tea, Ruth." Melior sat down beside her, pushing a teacup gently into her hand.

She took it, but when she looked up to thank him he was not looking toward her. Melior was staring out toward the setting sun, his mouth set in a grim line.

Michael arrived at a quarter of eight, when the brownies that Philip had been mixing were long since baked and only perilously preserved from the depredations of starving students (or persons purporting to be starving students), an entire loaf of French bread had been anointed with garlic butter, toasted, and devoured, Ruth had removed the tags and staples from every one of the day's clothing purchases and stowed the clothing itself in a green vinyl suitcase of surpassing hideousness (she did not, even now, total her charge slips), and Naomi had finally said "the hell with it" and set the table.

"Hello, all," said Michael.

"It's about time you got here," Philip said.

"Oh, honestly, Philip, don't you ever think about anything but food? Don't answer that," Jane added.

"Hi," said Ruth and Naomi in ragged chorus.

Michael flung his windbreaker through the bedroom door and advanced on Ruth. "Okay, how much did you spend?" he asked.

"Why?" Ruth demanded suspiciously. Melior made a sound that could be taken (by the suspicious nature that even such a *sensible* person might be supposed to have) as amusement.

"You may understand that it must be a very great deal, my friend, or else she would tell you," Melior suggested.

"It couldn't be," Michael said. "Ruth doesn't *have* a very great deal of money."

"Oh, thank you so much, Michael Peacock. *For* your information, I followed your list exactly—"

"Almost exactly," said Melior.

"She got him a leather jacket," said Jane.

"It was on sale!" Ruth pointed out. "And he'll need it. He'll be cold."

"No he won't," said Philip with a smirk.

"Philip, dear, if you ever do find out what the facts of life are—" Ruth began.

"A leather jacket?" Michael said in tones of pained disbelief. "What's he going to do with a leather jacket? It's *May*."

"Join the road show of Shakespeare's Punk Elves in Bondage Revue," Jane said, looking as if it were nothing to do with her. "You can wear a leather jacket in the summer."

"I beg you will all stop discussing me as if I weren't here," Melior said. He did not raise his voice, but it cut efficiently through the cross-chatter. "I now possess a leather jacket, which was purchased at my insistence. It remains for Ruth to be reimbursed for this and for the other items."

"Right." Michael's face assumed an expression of studied disinterest, which would have been believable if not for the quirk in his mouth and the slant of his eyebrows. He pulled his wallet out of his hip pocket and pulled out a sheaf of bills bound together with a paper tape. It was not a terribly impressive sheaf until you realized that the "one" on each of the bills was followed by two zeroes.

"Five thousand dollars," Michael said. "Cold, hard, legal tender."

"Who'd you mug?" Philip asked with interest.

"Sold the earrings and all the sterling. Except this—" Michael dug deep into a pocket and flipped Melior's signet ring at him. Melior plucked it deftly out of the air and slipped it onto his finger.

Michael dropped the sheaf of bills into Ruth's hands. She stared at it as if it were a book she didn't want to read.

"I took the spurs down to the Met," said Michael, referring to the Metropolitan Museum of Art. "I've got a friend down there. Stephen Mallison. He's Arms and Armor, but he knows something about forgeries."

"Like the Cellini salt cellar," Jane said.

"I don't see why they had to take it off display just because it was fake," Ruth said. "It was an *old* fake—and besides, it was pretty."

"Beauty our only criterion," Naomi said.

"Pretty is Truth and Truth is Pretty—" Jane began.

"But anyway," Michael said, heaving the conversation back on track by dint of main force, "I showed him the spurs and told him *I'd* been told they came from Ancient Atlantis."

"And he believed you?" said Naomi with interest.

"Patience, my child. *I* didn't believe me; I made that clear. What I asked him was what they were really; I hinted I thought they were stolen."

"As a deception only," Melior clarified firmly.

(Philip: "What do you care, Elfie?" Naomi: "Philip—")

"I had to give him some reason why I'd come to ask him about them. Museums know what's old, expensive, and stolen—they have to in order to keep from buying it and then losing what they paid when they turn it over to the rightful owner. Anyway—"

"Dinner's getting cold," Naomi said. There was a brief interruption as food was brought from the kitchen and distributed. Ruth offered the money to Melior; he shook his head. She set it on top of the television set as a last resort and hoped nobody would forget about it, although how you could forget about fifty one hundred dollar bills was something beyond her capacity. When plates were full and most of his audience occupied with beef burgundy instead of airy badinage, Michael resumed.

"So he told me they were no more Atlantean than my grandmother and didn't look offhand to be very old. The workmanship was top drawer and they'd cost somebody a brick to make—solid gold rowels and all that—but Ancient Atlantean or ancient anything else they were not. He begged me to remind whoever I'd gotten them from that only mounted cultures which had invented the stirrup would have any use for spurs."

"I had a horse," Melior said. "It died. And the spurs?"

"I left them there; he said he'd show them around. You said sell them, so I didn't think you'd mind."

"Indeed not. You may keep them for all of me."

"So leaving aside however much Ruth spent on clothes—"

"Six hundred and eighteen dollars and thirty-five cents," Melior said.

Everyone at the table stared at him. Ruth's cheeks flamed, as if she'd been caught in secret sin.

"You told me it was a decimal currency, Ruth. One hundred cents to the dollar. The lackey recited the total each time you paid. I added it up," Melior explained. "Part of that is tax," he added.

"And the jacket was necessary," Naomi said, poker-faced.

"It was only—" Melior began.

"It was on sale!" Ruth interrupted.

"And that leaves," said Michael, who intended to become a children's librarian when he graduated and so had a great deal of practice in being heard over other conversations, "about four thousand dollars and change."

"Is this a great deal of money?" Melior asked.

Michael shrugged. "Depends on what you try to do with it." He applied himself to his dinner.

Four thousand dollars. Ruth was old enough to know that this wasn't the enormous amount of money it seemed—not when her and Naomi's joint rent and household expenses were nearly a thousand a month—but surely it was enough to last Melior until he found his sword.

And if he doesn't find it? He doesn't have a birth certificate, or a high school diploma, or a Social Security card. Or a passport—and where could they deport him to, anyway?

Dinner, having been so long delayed, was a swift, brutal business, accomplished mostly in silence. Finally Naomi cleared the plates away.

"And now, for dessert," she said.

"Damn! I forgot the ice cream!" Michael burst out. "It's in the freezer at my place. Look, Mel, I'll give you the keys—could you go down and pick it up for me?"

"That was the most unconvincing con job I've ever seen in my life," Ruth said, once the door had shut and the sound of Melior's footsteps on the stairs had been heard. "Why didn't you just say, 'Melior, why don't you get out of here so we can talk about you behind your back'?"

"Because doing it this way is what is called manners, Ruth dear," Naomi said. She sat down at the table. "I hereby declare the first meeting of the New York Council on Elvish Affairs in session."

"Right," said Michael. "And the first question is, who is this guy Ruth rescued last night really?"

"What's the second question?" Jane asked helpfully.

"Do we believe his story?" Naomi said.

"But if he's an elf—" Ruth began, and stopped.

"Very good," Michael said to her. "He could be a real elf with a fake story."

"Or a fake elf with a fake story," said Philip, who was, in his own small way, a completest.

"Or a fake elf with a real story," said Jane, "although that means we still have to believe in *some* elves, just not *this* elf."

"Okay," said Naomi. "Reasons for believing he's an elf. Anyone? Ruth? You've spent the most time with him."

"Well," said Ruth. "He's got pointed ears."

"Plastic surgery," said Philip. "Makeup SFX."

"You'd see the line," Jane pointed out.

"Shut up, guys," said Michael. "Let Ruth think."

"And slit pupils, like a cat's," Ruth went on. "They reflect, too, like a cat's, and I've seen them change shape. People don't have eyes that green, and while that could be contact lenses, they don't reflect or make your pupil change shape like that. And his teeth are pointed," she rushed on, "like a—a wolf's. And it *could* be dental bonding, but *why?*"

" 'Why' comes later," Michael said. "Okay, he's got pointed ears and fangs and his eyes glow in the dark. And probably that isn't makeup; SFX makeup is meant to fool a camera, not a human eye; it just isn't that good. And something that isn't makeup is that beating he got last night. I looked him over then—it was pretty raw. But today his bruises are almost healed—and another thing. I looked him over pretty carefully twice. He's got a good set of muscles on him—and scars like you wouldn't believe. If you showed me that and told me this guy'd been off to a war where they fought with swords, I'd believe you."

"There's one other thing that isn't on your list," Jane said. "He could be a not-a-human-being and still not be an elf."

"Occam's razor," Naomi said.

"Or in English, cut to the chase," Philip added. "If he was a space alien, why say he's an elf?"

"Why not?" Jane shot back. "If he's a space alien, he doesn't think like an Earth person—and aliens are a lot more likely than *elves.*"

"Would you listen to yourself?" Philip said. "Space aliens are *likely?*"

"What reason do we have to *not* think Melior is an elf, after he's said he was one?" Naomi said pacifically. "Jane, you were looking through folklore today—what does it say about elves?"

Solicited in the area of her competence, Jane subsided.

"First, there are no reports of elves in America, only some unproven sixteenth century reports of 'weird black dwarves,' which lets our guy right out. Most of the folklore lumps elves right in with fairies, and it sort of boils down to: 'No force, there I was, out after dark and I saw this Real Weird Guy who took me home with him and we got to drinking and that's why I've been gone a week.' "

Jane shrugged. "Elves and UFO stories have a lot in common: time distortion, missing days, memory loss, and strange ailments suffered by those who've met them. In fact the descriptions of elves and of space aliens are almost identical, allowing for there being about seven hundred years between them, and this guy doesn't match any of them. What he really is, is a prime specimen of *genus Tolkienus,* the fictional elf. You know: tall, glowing, noble—"

"With a palantir strapped to his forehead and a long gray cape," supplied Naomi.

"He didn't say he was an elf. He said humans called his kind elves," Ruth pointed out, with a scrupulous regard for the facts.

"So we have a certain amount of physical evidence that Mel is Not

From Around Here," Naomi summarized. "Anything else? Or opinions
to the contrary?"

"The clothes and jewelry," Michael said. "It cost a lot to put that
outfit together. If this were a con job that would net him a couple million,
I could see a few thousand going to prime the pump. But it's *us* he's
working this on—if it's a sting. There's no way he could get back his initial
investment. So there's no reason to waste the money. And he was really
thumped. Don't forget that."

"It's more than a few thousand. All those clothes were hand-sewn.
Every stitch. They don't even do that for movie costumes anymore," Ruth
said. She flung out her hands helplessly. "I can't even imagine what it
would cost to make them."

"And don't forget the ring," Michael said. "It glowed. We all saw it.
No lights, no wires."

"Not a dream, not a hoax, not an imaginary tale," Ruth said.

"And besides, I was looking around in cyberspace today. He wasn't
there," Philip added. He dug around in the pack at his feet and laid
something out on the table.

Photographs. Four Polaroid shots of Melior, looking pale and interesting, his eyes glowing like red moons in the flash.

"Just in case we want to fake him up some ID," Philip said. Naomi
decided not to have heard him.

"Okay, show of hands: does everybody agree that Melior, who and
whatever he really is, all semantics aside, doesn't come from here?"
Naomi asked.

Ruth raised her hand, feeling a little ridiculous. Slowly, so did everyone else. Michael winked at her.

"Great. That subject's closed and isn't going to be debated any more.
Saves time. Now, what about his story?"

"Which story?" said Jane. "The one about the elf-war?"

"I don't think we need to worry about that," Ruth said, after a pause.
"I think the only thing we have to worry about is whether or not we
believe that he lost a sword that he has to get back."

"Never mind that he's got a hope in hell," Philip said sweetly.

"Yeah, right, never mind that," Michael said.

"I think the question is, what would he want us to do to go looking
for the sword?" Jane said. She fiddled with the hem of her sweater,
staring off into space. "And what would happen if he didn't get it back?
Really, I mean, and not just in elf-space. Here."

"He said," Ruth said, cudgeling her mind for scraps of a conversation
that had seemed less important at the time than her own feelings, "I think
he said that if a human had the sword, it was cursed—I mean, the sword

was cursed whether a human had it or not, but its curse was, if a human had it, it—the human—would turn into some kind of monster."

"Tolkien again," Jane sighed. "Gollum, gollum, what has it got in its pocketses—can't these people ever be original?"

"Tolkien did it because it was an archetypal theme," Michael said. "The cursed thingummy that turns its owner into a beast. They're pretty thick on the ground in folklore and mythology."

"We'll just have to wait and ask Melior about it," Ruth said.

"You will not have to wait," said Melior.

· 7 ·

Fractured Fairy Tales: Hansel and Grendel

NONE OF THEM had heard the door open. Melior stood there, with the bag containing the ice cream in one hand, and Ruth's keys on their brass ring keychain in the other.

He took those out of my purse! Ruth thought on a rising flare of indignation.

"You know," Naomi said with commendable calm, "you really shouldn't be back yet."

Melior smiled, wolf-teeth gleaming. "I ran," he said. "Both ways."

Ruth stared, with guilty complicity, at Melior's black high-topped leather sneakers.

"You spied on us," Jane said, as univolved as if she were reporting the weather.

"How did you get the door open without us hearing you?" Philip asked.

"Guile has its uses," said Melior, "and you were greatly involved. But since your councils were bound to affect me, I wished to know what their result was."

"You got back too soon," said Ruth. "We were just trying to figure out how you could possibly benefit by lying about the sword."

"We'd already decided you were an elf," said Naomi.

"I do not lie," Melior said. "Catch." He threw the bag, with fastball accuracy, straight at Michael.

He caught it with a thump. "I guess this means dessert."

"And then you can tell us all about your magic sword," Jane said. Philip sniggered. Ruth kicked at him but only succeeded in dislodging her precarious perch. She slid backward off the arm of the couch, but Melior was there to support her.

"You stole my keys!" she whispered to him in an accusing undertone.

Melior shrugged and released her. "I brought them back. I do not steal."

"Just like you don't lie?" Ruth shot back. Melior's eyebrows rose, a Mr. Spock gesture he could have no way of knowing was associationally hilarious.

"Exactly the way I do not lie, Ruth. I borrowed the keys."

"And would you borrow the truth?" Ruth shot back.

Something made her look sideways then, to meet Philip's china-blue gaze.

"Oh, go on," Philip said. "This is fascinating."

"Shut up, Philip," said Ruth and Melior in unwitting chorus. Philip made an obscure handsign and slithered off his chair to follow Michael and Naomi. Melior watched him go.

"Privacy," he said, "is a state devoutly to be wished for, and, like all wishes, unlikely to materialize."

"Look," Ruth began uneasily, "no one meant—"

Melior waved her to silence. "Of course you did. Who would not? Is that not true, Jane?"

"Sure." Jane was gazing aimlessly out the window, her lank mouse-blonde hair falling in snake-locks against the pink shetland sweater. To all intents and purposes she was paying no attention to Ruth and Melior. "We all voted you're an elf, so that's settled. But it doesn't mean you're a *nice* elf," she added, turning around.

"If he was nice, would he be hanging out with us?" Naomi said, coming back with brownies. "But seriously, Melior, none of us has any experience with sword-quests, or magic—"

"Or elves," interrupted Michael helpfully. He was carrying four dishes of ice cream, balanced perilously. Philip had the other two. Jane jumped up and went to unload Michael. "So naturally we're a bit curious," Michael went on.

Melior favored Michael with a crooked smile. "And you wonder how I twist my nets to lure you in. I cannot deny that I do, friend Michael. The stakes are too high; I need allies."

"Yes," said Michael carefully. "And we were sort of all wondering just what the high stakes are, you see."

"For myself, I lose all if I cannot present the sword when Baligant summons it. Myself, my kinfolk, all that I am or wish to be—gone." There was a pause, then Melior added, "I cannot imagine this tugs on human heartstrings greatly, and your charity in aiding me in this cause alone is rightly limited. Yet there is a matter that I would have—at least yesterday—held to be of your deepest self-interest."

"Why yesterday and not today?" Michael asked, getting his question in before Naomi elbowed him for interrupting.

"Because yesterday I believed you valued the life of your fellows— and today I see that this is simply not true. If hundreds, if thousands, if tens of thousands of your kind were to die, you are so many here you would not even notice."

"Way to go," breathed Philip.

"Why don't we just go back to pretending it's yesterday, then?" Ruth asked. She took a brownie and bit into it, distracted for a moment by pure chocolate ecstasy.

"Very well," said Melior. He prodded delicately at the mound of vanilla melting in the dish before him and obviously decided to leave well enough alone.

"If you don't want that, I'll eat it," Philip offered.

"Pig," said Jane.

"Slug."

"Louse."

"Maggot."

"Children," said Naomi.

"Wormhole," Jane said, getting in the last word. Philip took Melior's dish and dug in, oblivious.

"About the end of life as we know it?" Naomi prompted helpfully.

Melior looked around at them all—wondering, Ruth suspected, why a group of mere humans took so little interest in a real live elf and his enchanted passions. Little did he know how wondrously the real world concentrated the mind—after a go at page one of the *Times* no one had much emotional energy left for any one else's problems, no matter how exotic the anyone. Other people's problems were distractions. And distractions made you lose your place on the ladder—not even of success, that would be too venal, but of simple garden variety survival.

Of course, after an eon or two of being, well, *sensible,* you got the reckless urge to gamble. To trade on other people's good natures, as they had so long traded on yours.

In short, thought Ruth crossly and personally, *one day you decide to chuck it all and get stupid.*

"The end of life as you know it," Melior repeated. "Perhaps. Perhaps only the ending of a great many lives. You did not, either of you, find word of the Sword in your travels?" He looked hopefully at Michael and Philip.

"That's another reason I went down to the Museum with your spurs today. I'm guessing that if the sword is hocked, sold, restolen, or just sent off to be appraised, Stainless Steve'll get a hold of it at some point, or hear about it. As of today, he hadn't."

"Nothing on the boards," said Philip. "I posted the reward. Maybe something will turn up."

"No," Melior said sadly. "If this—" he gestured with his signet ring, "—has even a little magic, the Sword's wards will be in full effect. At least for a while, and this while is far too long for whoever has it."

"You keep saying that," Jane said, from the corner into which she was barricaded. The Coke-bottle lenses of her horn-rims turned to silver coins in the light as she tilted her head. "You keep saying that, but could you be a little more specific?"

"Very well, Mistress Jane, since you most particularly ask it. The Sword of Maiden's Tears is, from a human's point of view, cursed. One of the oldest and simplest spells—and most powerful. Powerful enough, I fear, to work even here.

"Once a human seizes upon the Sword, he will begin a transformation. A metamorphosis into a monster whose only food is the flesh of the humans who were once his own kind, and whose only desire is to retain possession of the Sword. A reasonable desire, that, as once the transformation takes place, the Sword is the only thing that can kill him."

"What about an atomic grenade?" asked Philip.

"Have you got an atomic grenade, Philip?" asked Jane.

"The only thing," Melior repeated. "Not fire, not sorcery, not boiling lead nor cold iron. The Sword alone will slay the grendel."

There was a pause. "Beowulf," said Jane.

"By the shore of Gitche Gumee/By the shining Big-Sea-Water?" quoted Michael inquiringly.

"Wrong poem," said Ruth. "That's Longfellow."

"Grendel is a proper name," said Jane. "The name of the monster who slew—and ate—King Hrothgar's warriors every night until Beowulf slew him. By ripping his arm off," Jane added, with gloomy relish. "It's an epic Olde English poem from around 1000."

"Grendels are bespelled humans," Melior said. "They are often used as guards. The transformation cannot be reversed, as it feeds upon a human's inmost heart to find the fuel for its work."

"Real scientific, Elfie," breathed Philip.

"Never mind the details," said Naomi just a little sharply. "So you're saying that whoever has that sword of yours will turn into a cannibal monster?"

"No. Only any human who seizes it. Against the Morning Lords this magic will have no effect. It was thought, at the time, to be a security measure," Melior said disgustedly.

"Okay, one monster. Height, weight, distinguishing marks? Last known address?" asked Michael.

Melior looked at him as if he suspected, for a moment, that Michael might be joking. Then he relaxed with a visible effort. "If I knew where it was, Friend Michael, I would go there and take the Sword back. Each hour it possesses the Sword renders it more powerful. And each kill. As it kills—and feeds—this hapless human will begin to grow, and change. A *grendel* never ceases to grow; some I have seen are enormous. The larger they are, the less human their form; they begin to go about on all fours. . . ."

Melior roused himself from what appeared to be a private memory. "You will know the *grendel* because it will not look elvish or human. And because it will be trying to kill you."

"Terrific," said Michael.

"Could you be a little more specific?" said Jane. "Like, how stupid is it? And if it walks around in broad daylight munching people, somebody's going to notice."

"The *grendel* is cunning, but is said to lack human reason. They shun the light; the older ones can stand it for short periods, but a man when he is first made *grendel* will instinctively retreat to a cave or other cover of darkness. As for the kills—" again Melior shrugged, and an expression of helpless frustration made a mask of his features, "—I had hoped they would be noticed, and reported to the magistrate or mayor of this town—"

Philip snorted.

"—but now I know they will not be." Melior put his head in his hands. After a moment's hesitation, Ruth put an arm about his shoulders.

"That isn't true." Everyone looked at Naomi. There was a frown line between her eyes, as if she were trying to reason something out. She ticked off the points on her fingers as she spoke. "We have a mugger who has your sword. Having it—you say—will turn him into a monster, a *grendel* that will murder—"

"And eat," said Philip helpfully.

"And eat people, hide during the day, and can't be killed by anything but your sword. What does that suggest to everybody? Come on: the category is Fairy Tales and Folklore."

"I'd like to buy a vowel, Vanna," Michael said. Naomi made a face at him.

"Werewolves?" said Ruth finally.

"Got it in one. And do you think werewolves won't make the six o'clock news? He'll turn up," Naomi said grimly.

Melior looked at her, suddenly hopeful. "One could wish," he said carefully, "that it did not require so many deaths to reveal his presence."

"It's okay," Jane said comfortingly. "If your werewolf didn't kill them, they'd probably die anyway."

"Almost certainly, given enough time," Ruth said editorially.

"But it would be nice to catch our elvish Godzilla before he started racking up a body count," Michael said, "if only for neatness' sake."

"How?" said Philip, in his best "imitation of someone being helpful" voice.

"Consider his airs and his graces/And the way he kicks over the traces/The shape of his head/And the width of his bed/And be sure that you cover all bases," singsonged Jane from some lost mine of doggerel.

"For the Snark *was* a boojum, so you see," added Naomi.

Melior looked from one to the next, baffled.

"Don't worry about it." Ruth squeezed his shoulder. "We're like this all the time."

"Except when we're worse," Philip said, grinning evilly.

"But we'll help," said Michael firmly. "Right, guys?"

There was a pause, during which no one disagreed.

"What else have we got to do with our time," said Philip. "Pursue higher learning?"

"Okay," said Naomi. "I declare the first official meeting of the New York Council on Elvish Affairs closed. We help Melior find his sword."

And what then? Ruth wondered, almost twenty-four hours later. The party the night before had broken up late; Melior departing with Michael and the maps of New York City that Jane had brought. Ten miles by two and home to eleven million people—how were they going to find one enchanted werewolf in all that?

Especially since it's so full of neighborhoods that I don't think even a werewolf would enter alone, Ruth thought. She stared at her textbook. She'd been staring at the same page for half an hour and had yet to make sense of it.

She had no real reason for believing that Melior would come to the apartment today. He'd gone home with Michael. Ruth fingered the bundle of currency on the table before her. And forgotten his money.

Why should Melior think anything more of her than he did of any of the others? So she'd taken him shopping, for God's sake. It wasn't as if it were the equivalent of a formal proposal. Just because he was the most exciting, exotic thing to happen to her ever. . . .

Didn't mean that the reverse was true.

The phone rang.

"Hello?"

"I wish to speak to Ruth." Melior's voice, sounding small and uncertain.

"Melior? It's me. Ruth. How are you?"

"I am arrested. They have said I may make one telephone call. I did not know who else to call, Ruth."

Ruth had never been any closer to a police station than an episode of *Hill Street Blues* and she didn't want to be here now. She had the wholly unfair superstitious feeling that she would be arrested, too; not for anything she had done or not done, but simply at some draconian whim. Ruth had been under the grindstone of the system; it was not an experience she cared to repeat.

"Excuse me," Ruth said carefully to the receptionist, "I'm here to pick up somebody." *I hope.*

And there civilized converse ended, because she had no idea what sort of name Melior might have given—if any—and she knew he didn't have any ID on him. But the receptionist, if not exactly gracious, was patient with Ruth's patent bewilderment, and soon Ruth found herself talking to a uniformed sergeant who was equally disinterested, and equally patient. What was her relation to the individual? When had he been arrested? Did she know the charge?

"I don't know," Ruth repeated helplessly, beginning to want to cry. She wished that she'd waited for Naomi, or called Michael, or even asked Jane to go with her. She'd never felt so helpless. "I don't know; he called me maybe an hour ago. Do I need a lawyer? Can I see him?"

There were none of the comfortable courtesies of Televisionland available here; when she saw Melior again, it was in the middle of a crowded hallway, and his hands were cuffed in front of him and he was sitting on a crowded bench with a number of other people, all under the watchful eye of a policeman. The black leather jacket that had made him look so trendy yesterday was scuffed now and only made him look hoodish; the mirrorshades lent his face an alien reptilian coldness.

"Ruth!" he exclaimed, and, to the uniformed patrolman, "There! I have sent for my hostage—now release me." He jumped to his feet and the handcuff chain jangled as Melior pulled on it. Ruth had a sudden snapshot vision of the links breaking outright. The cop put a hand on his baton—and who could blame him?, Ruth thought with a dash of desperate empathy.

"Nice to see you, too," she said, her voice shaking only slightly. "Good thing you remembered my number."

"Are you his sister, ma'am?" the policeman asked.

"Yes. Yes, I am. Please, what has he done?"

"Tried to beat the fare. Refused to take his summons. If you want to pay his fine now, you can both go home."

Ruth felt her knees go weak; the giddy relief was like half a bottle of Scotch. "Yes. Yes, thank you. I'll pay the fine."

The officer took a clipboard off the wall and sorted through the papers on it. He removed a sheet and handed it to Ruth. "Room 202, ma'am. The clerk will give you a receipt to bring back here."

Ruth took the paper. The policeman pointed off down the hall. Melior started to follow, and the policeman put a hand on his shoulder, warningly. Melior looked ready to explode.

"Sit down," snapped Ruth, as to an erring collie. "Wait here and mind your manners. I'll be back as soon as I can."

Luck; oh, blessed luck. *Oh, don't let the fine be more than I've got on me,* Ruth prayed to herself, but surely it couldn't be more than five thousand dollars if they were willing to let him go without booking him. She looked at the page in her hands, but all she could make out in that handwritten hash were the typeset words at the top of the form. "Arresting Officer's Report" it said.

But he hasn't been arrested. He HASN'T. And I can get him out of here. And then I'm going to kill him.

The fine, counting everything, came to seven hundred and sixty-eight dollars. Ruth received a computer-generated receipt that listed dollar amounts next to citations from the New York Civil Code. A few hours in the library tomorrow and she could find out everything that Melior had done.

She already knew the worst.

"Fare beating," the clerk said. She wasn't wearing any uniform, just a photo ID with a name Ruth couldn't make out; she looked freeze-dried into some eternal senescence, Ruth's own nightmare of what she herself would resemble in twenty years' time, brought to Madame Tussaud life. "Cheaper to pay the fare than the fine."

It's not his fault. He didn't know. He's from out-of-town, Ruth wanted to say and didn't. Even as she chose not to argue it, she wondered if there might be some mistake. Yesterday Melior had flatly refused to go back into the subway tunnels. Why, today, should he be trying to beat the fare?

Mutely Ruth handed over currency and received her change and receipt. She went back downstairs with her paperwork and handed it to the uniformed officer, who inspected it carefully before reaching for the key to Melior's cuffs.

"Tell him to behave himself—next time we might not be so backed up. This is in the computers, even if we didn't book him," the cop said in a weary voice.

"Thank you," Ruth repeated, her own words giving her a sense of inanity, as if she were some kind of celluloid puppet; one of those spring-loaded things with a head eternally nodding. "Thank you very much."

Finally they let her take Melior away.

It was Sunday, May second, a drizzly gray evening on 42nd Street—and probably the rest of Manhattan—when Ruth and Melior emerged from the Transit Police station. The sense of freedom was overpowering; even though Ruth had been in no danger, she was trembling with exhaustion and the aftereffects of stress.

And I've got a nine o'clock class tomorrow. Terrific.

"Would you like to tell me just what that was all about? It's a damn good thing you had my number—and just *how* did that happen, by the way?" Ruth asked.

"Michael told it to me. He said I might have need of it."

"He was right. And I'm still waiting for an explanation. If I hadn't had that cash from last night, you'd still be in there, you know—and if you had to go before a judge, I really don't think he'd be impressed with your More Tales From Elfland biography."

"I *saw* it, Ruth," Melior's voice vibrated with utter conviction. "I saw the *grendel*. I was this close." He measured a space in the air with his hands.

"So you jumped over the turnstile to follow him," Ruth said flatly. Melior nodded.

"There was shouting. There was a man on the platform—I know what your guardsmen's uniforms look like, now, but I did not then and he seized me. The *grendel* got into a subway car. And I did not," Melior said, rubbing the back of his head.

"And nobody noticed they were in the same car with a *grendel?*" Ruth asked.

"No. It does not look any different yet, but the stink of high sorcery is on it. It is a scent your human noses do not catch, I think, for no one else remarked him. Yet it was he. So close—I *sensed* it—!"

"I sense the presence of Bellevue if you're not more careful!" Ruth snapped. "What if I hadn't been home? What if you'd gotten hurt?"

"Hurt?" Melior cried, stopping to stare at her. "I am slain already!

Don't you understand? I'm lost—thwarted at every turn by the World of Iron, by the thousands who choke the streets of your city! He hunts where I am helpless, thwarted by his kindred! I'll never catch him—never! This beast hasn't a single throat—" Melior was shouting, now, and even in Times Square people were stopping to look.

"The people—that great beast!" Ruth tried to remember who'd said that. Alexander Hamilton? It was like him—the elitist of his day. Maybe Alexander Hamilton would have understood Rohannan Melior; God knew, Ruth didn't.

"Oh, will you shut up? Things can get worse—trust me," Ruth said with weary anger.

"How?" Melior turned on her savagely. "How worse than my failure?"

"Well," said Ruth viciously, "you might have to live with it. Here." And it was unholy what a shameless pleasure that thought gave her.

"Ah. Yes." Melior struggled with his surging emotions and won through to a white-lipped calm. "Very well. Walk with me, Ruth."

Bridled by guilt, she walked up Broadway with him as the day darkened. A mingy rain began to fall again; both of them ignored it. It sparkled on Melior's hair like crystal beading, too light yet to soak in. Late afternoon on a Sunday, and raining besides—the streets were almost empty (for New York). They jagged sideways, onto Fifth Avenue, and after a while Melior began to speak.

"I began where I had sensed him once. I spent all night studying the maps—I was certain I could find him, no matter his resort. It is only a handful of days since he and his fellow shamefully defeated me; he is weak yet. As weak as he will ever be. Perhaps, even, he has not fed yet. And he escaped me." Melior's voice was flat, uninflected. "And so he will continue to do, in this bizarre land where everything is out of joint. Whereas he, though a beast out of nightmare, knows what I do not, and can thereby twist the unjust laws of this insane realm to thwart me at every turn."

"Now just a minute, Hamlet," Ruth began.

"Tell me wherein I am in error, Ruth," Melior purred silkily. "Tell me how well I manage myself in this place. I am taken into custody for an offense I do not recognize as I commit it, children stare at me upon the streets, I cannot even read the handbills that are posted." Melior gestured at a passing bank window, filled with posters advertising its services.

"Okay," said Ruth. "You've convinced me. You're a failure. Give up. Go home."

They walked on in silence. Ruth wondered if she'd hurt him, or offended him, or if he'd even noticed what she'd said. The sky continued to darken. Twilight. Evening. Night, in an hour or two. Sunset was at 6:48, if she remembered rightly. Ruth Marlowe, compulsive memorizer of vital statistics. Today, unencumbered by packages or places to be, she was willing to walk, yea, even unto 96th Street, where Michael lived. They were passing 50th Street now. Rockefeller Center, Saks, Saint Patrick's Cathedral.

"How?" Melior said at last.

"What?" Ruth said.

"How shall I give up—and go home? Sorcery sent me here, to this place where sorcery goes awry. Without the Sword I cannot begin to hope of returning."

"And with the Sword?" Ruth asked.

"With the Sword, I may *hope*," Melior said, choosing his words precisely. He sighed. "I play with words and try your patience, Mistress Ruth. I cannot give up. I shall blunder on, hopeless, until I die."

" 'There's just no word to describe your behavior at times, Don Quixote,' " Ruth said, quoting the caption from a long-ago *New Yorker* cartoon. Melior shrugged. "You do have local help," Ruth said, trying again. Silence.

Ruth grabbed his sleeve and hauled Melior to a stop. "Look, just what is it that you want me to say? 'Give up'? You've already—"

Melior seized her in turn. And kissed her.

Ruth was not a cloistered nun. In her lifetime she had certainly been kissed and more than kissed on enough occasions that the act itself did not come as total surprise. On the majority of those occasions, however, Ruth's consent and cooperation had at least been solicited.

Melior solicited neither. With expert efficiency he pulled her close, pressing her body against him as if he were trying to drown in it. And for one moment Ruth was willing to help him. But—

"Not here!" She pushed him furiously away—Melior let her go—and uttered the first words that came to her. "Are you out of your mind?" She looked quickly around, but no one seemed to have taken advantage of this momentary lapse to pickpocket, mug, or worse, either of them. Madness, to become so distracted on a city street.

"Yes," said Melior. "No. If not here, Ruth, then where?" His intensity had no leavening gleam of mockery now, and Ruth's mind steadfastly refused to make any sense of the situation. Suddenly she felt as if New York was as alien to her as it surely must be to Melior. Why had he done it and what should she do?

Her mouth felt bruised, sensitized, tingling and tender and naked. That it was beyond silly—what would a lord of Faery want with Ruth Marlowe—did not, somehow, ameliorate the physical sensations one whit. It took nearly all of her fast-fading store of common sense to pull free from the remains of Melior's grip and start walking once more.

She ducked her head and strode as if her life's ambition were to outrace Melior. Unfortunately, he had no trouble at all keeping up.

"Do you reject me?" Melior asked, coming up beside her.

"You can't just go and kiss someone on a public street," Ruth countered. "Something could happen."

"I did not kiss 'someone.' I kissed you."

"Well, why don't we just forget about that, okay?" Ruth's cheeks burned; her heart rattled its ivory cage far faster than brisk walking could account for. Melior had added a fresh and unwelcome dimension to the puzzle he presented, and wide new vistas of ghastly humiliation opened before her.

"Why don't we not?" he said in her ear. "Hold yourself my guide and preceptress; do you not, who knows what harm I may get myself into? I might, perchance, kiss young Mistress Jane," he added lightly.

Despite everything, the mental image so conjured made Ruth giggle. "She'd kill you," Ruth said. And then, more soberly, "Don't. She wouldn't like it." Not quite against her will Ruth slowed to a normal walking pace. 59th Street. Columbus Circle. Central Park.

"Even I know that," Melior chided her. "The paladin for Mistress Jane has yet to win his spurs. While I—"

"You're just looking for a good time?" Ruth said. She'd meant it to be light, nonthreatening, but despite herself her voice skirled and flattened, exposing pain.

"No!" Melior protested. "I want—I meant—" he stopped. "I find you passing fair, Mistress Ruth."

The opening was too good to miss; without conscious volition her internal monologist took over. " 'Passing fair, passing strange—sorry, just passing through,' " Ruth quoted airily. " 'The same thing happened twice last week: O' heaven help the working elf.' "

"Do you reject me, Ruth?" Melior softly repeated.

Oh, heavens no; just what I need to round out my year; a one night stand with a passing elf-king. "I think," Ruth said carefully, "that we come from two different worlds—"

Melior was surprised into a bark of laughter; only then did Ruth realize what she had said. She laughed, too, the sound a little strained with tension.

"Right," she said. "Literally true. But you may be taking things for granted that we don't—here; and just maybe this isn't such a good time to rush into things? Besides, shouldn't you be thinking about how to off this *grendel?* You can do it; of course you can." She chattered on, hating the sound of her own voice and the way she was talking so he wouldn't, because she was more afraid of what Melior might say than of what he would leave unsaid, because, because, because. . . .

You wanted an adventure, Ruth told herself brutally. *You wanted things to be different; a chance to be . . . senseless? Insensible? Well, whatever the opposite of sensible is. You wanted it. You got it. Now quit whining.*

"And with you beside me my fortune is assured," Melior agreed ambiguously into the silence. "Is there ever a good time to rush into things?" he added rhetorically. "But there is no time, Ruth. There is no time left at all."

Sheer moral cowardice and the passionate desire to end this discussion kept Ruth silent; but even through her confusion a faint traitorous voice insisted that she, that Melior, that all of them were overlooking something vitally important.

· 8 ·

Gather, Darkness

IN SCATTERED MOMENTS of lucidity Kevin Shelby labeled Friday night the Last Good Time. Friday night—before. Before he had done what he did not have the strength to avoid doing, before he had firmly and irrevocably overstepped the line that separates the Okay People from those who have Really Bagged It.

Without knowing it, Kevin had always valued his self-esteem; his own good opinion of himself, the certainty that he'd always been right; justifiable. Now that sweet self-content was gone. It was as if some warm covering had been stripped from his ego, and something raw and red stood snarling in the chill.

But he had the sword.

The sword, and nothing else. He'd held it in his arms all that horrible Friday night, clutching at the hilt and staring into its jewels in order not to see Roy's body lying on the floor.

He'd thought it would be bloodier, somehow. More blood, and redder. The way it was in the movies. It wasn't like that, but Roy was still dead. Did it matter? Did it maybe not count because it had happened all wrong? Would the ever-present all-seeing *They* forgive it and forget it because he hadn't meant it to come out quite that way and besides it was all Roy's fault to begin with?

Would someone, anyone, please give him a second chance?

No. Bright, educated, admonished all his life to—

Be a man, Kevin.

—accept responsibility, Kevin Shelby knew the truth. No excuses. No second chances. Roy was dead and it was Kevin's fault. He'd killed him, and the weight of self-loathing, self-contempt, slid like a stone curtain between his life before and life after, cutting him off from contentment and filling his vision of the world with poison.

But he still had the sword. And to make all of this, any of this matter, to ensure that Roy Turpin had not died for nothing at all, Kevin had to keep it.

He could not stay here. Toward dawn that simple fact of self-preservation penetrated Kevin's consciousness. He became aware of what he had been smelling for some time—the thick organic scent of Roy.

The body on the floor. Nothing to do with me. Nothing!

Roy who was dead as a doornail, as last year's elections, as history. Roy was dead, dead, dead and decomposing, the blood on the floor pooled and drying to black jelly, the shards and gobbets dried and starting to look like any meat you'd accidentally left out of the fridge overnight, the smell of piss and shit transforming *the body on the floor* into just another Bowery bum. A disposable wreck. Human garbage. And eventually even the super in this building would bang on the door and then use his key, wanting to find out just what trouble his tenant was making for him now. Then there would be police.

And police would almost certainly want to know how Roy, how *the body on the floor* had come to be here. They would find Kevin's sword, and take it away, and then everything that had happened to Roy, that had happened to Kevin, would all be for nothing.

So Kevin got up. He pulled down the window shades because the glaring pink light gave him a headache. He turned back, and without thought the sword flickered in his hand like summer lightning, carving through . . . *it* as if it were hot butter, and when it had struck, Roy Turpin's head rolled free, gathering motion from the canted floor until it banged gently into the television set.

Kevin carefully wiped the blade of the sword on the couch and went into the kitchen, already forgetting what he had just done. He drank a glass of water, holding the sword point down like a dangerous walking stick. He threw up the water and everything else left in his stomach all over the dirty dishes in the sink and the clean ones in the drainer, and felt a certain cheap exultation because he didn't have to clean it up—he never had to clean anything up again. Then he drank some orange juice right from the bottle, and dropped the bottle to shatter on the kitchen floor as the juice came right back up in a pang of cramping nausea, still orange, in a vaulting arc that spattered the opposite wall. Kevin choked and spat, gagging, until his mouth was free of the rotten-sweet taste. Enough of this.

He went into the bathroom—carefully not looking in the mirror—

and turned on the shower. And when the hot water had come up and the roaches been put to flight, Kevin took off all his clothes, gleefully popping buttons, and stood under the hot water and scrubbed and scrubbed until no possible trace of Roy remained on his skin or in his hair.

Through all this the sword stood propped against the wall, glinting faint rainbows in the gelid dawn light.

Then Kevin stepped out of the tub—*not* bothering to mop up— toweled himself off, and went into his bedroom. He pulled the blinds in here, too, a faint pang of worry breaking through for the first time. It was so bright out there. He felt the pounding behind his eyes already, the foretaste of a really bad headache. What if going outside gave him so bad a headache that something happened to the sword?

But he wouldn't think about that now. He'd think about that when he was ready. He polished the sword clean on the bedsheets, but once that was done and the covers had been pulled straight to provide a suitable backdrop for it, only the sword's presence proved that anything strange had happened in Kevin's life at all.

That was when Kevin had his great idea.

Maybe it was the light, or the memory of the last hopeful point in his life before the slide down to the Last Good Time. Maybe it was that, down deep under it all, Kevin Shelby was no fool, and smart enough to know how much anonymity a uniform gives. And knew, too, a place where he could vanish, far away from the light of the sun.

Kevin took down his track worker's uniform; the steeltoed safety boots, the gray work pants, the long-sleeved gray shirt with its sewn-on patches. He found his photo-ID and clipped it to his pocket. The authorization was out-of-date, but he wouldn't be needing to show it. And when he finally stood and looked in the mirror, he looked—ordinary.

Kevin smiled. He picked up the sword and crossed the hall to Roy's room.

Probably if he'd known he wasn't coming back, he would have been neater.

The thought made Kevin smile; with a swift gesture he stabbed the sword down, two-handed, at the center of Roy's unmade bed. It slid smoothly through mattress and box spring, stopping as its point touched the floor. Kevin released it, and it wobbled gently back and forth, held upright in place by the mattress stuffing.

Kevin thought it looked just like Excalibur in all the movies. But this one was his. *He* was King Arthur.

"Awright. . . ." Kevin breathed to himself, momentarily distracted. Then he searched the room and the closet, and when he was done he had Roy's blue nylon bomber jacket, worn on those outings when Roy wanted to convince someone he was a police officer or at least a security guard. It had an American flag patch sewn on one shoulder and a Seal of New York patch sewn on the other, and neither of these easily-obtainable things by itself conferred legitimacy, although they looked very convincing.

Then there was Roy's secret store of cash—five hundred dollars, stuffed in an envelope taped to the back of the dresser. But Kevin hadn't grown up with five brothers without learning about hiding places like that. He put Roy's money into his wallet and looked for the last thing that must be here, because he knew Roy had a pair and because Roy hadn't been wearing them last night.

He found them at last, pushed to the back of a drawer he'd already checked twice. Ray-Ban sunglasses, just like the Terminator wore. Kevin put them on, and the light dimmed to a much more acceptable level.

His mouth was dry and cottony, and his stomach growled with unfulfilled hunger. But he was ready to leave.

Almost. With shaking hands, Kevin carefully withdrew the sword from its mattress anvil. It glowed, whispering promises to him alone.

If he carried it openly like this, they would take it from him. Kevin frowned. He rested the point of the sword on the floor. Upright, its length measured him to mid-chest; the pulsing jewel of the pommel resting over his heart. He had to disguise it somehow.

A guitar case might have concealed it—if there were guitar cases that were five foot long, and Kevin didn't think there were. A rifle case, maybe, only the crosspiece wouldn't fit inside and anyway, a rifle case was just as bad a thing to try to carry through the streets of New York. He thought about it very hard, and then sacrificed his record collection to sheathe the entire sword, blade tip to pommel, in album covers. He wrapped that in newspaper, and the newspaper in garbage bags, and strapped the resulting package in every conceivable direction with heavy silver duct tape. A friend of Kevin's had once said that duct tape was the force that held the universe together. Well, maybe it was.

He hefted the final package experimentally. It was clumsy, but no one would suspect it contained a sword—*his* sword. No one would suspect it and no one would take it and it would be safe, he would be safe. . . .

If he could only get to the subway.

Dressed and ready to go, the bundled sword balanced precariously under one arm, Kevin lifted one corner of the living-room shade and peered out. The sunlight made him hiss—even through the sunglasses the light was a blue-white hammer of pain.

He dropped the shade. He couldn't go out in that. He was hurt, he was sick— Kevin rested the sword gently against the wall and used both hands to clutch his temples. He whimpered, deep in the back of his throat. He had killed Roy—and Roy was his friend—and in that one irrevocable act he had wiped out all future content.

But he'd *had* to. Roy'd been going to take the sword away. They'd see that. They'd have to. And it was only Roy, and Roy (let's be honest) was just a cheap hood, a mugger; and compared to all that Kevin could achieve, *would* have achieved already if he'd only had the luck, just a little luck, a little. . . .

It took him an hour to convince himself to leave the apartment, and in his pumped-up desperate haste to go and be gone before he lost his nerve, he left the door unlocked.

Encouraged by the uneven slant of wall and floor in the ancient apartment building, the door drifted slowly open. When the super came upstairs to mop the hallway at nine o'clock, he found it open. He called out. Then he looked inside. Then he called the police, but by then Kevin Shelby was already far away, riding the underground railroad, his own private newly-renovated carousel, round and round and round.

His train passed through the 34th Street station for the umpteenth time a few hours later, and Kevin had no inkling how close he'd come to last night's victim.

Last night's *first* victim.

Kevin had other problems of a more pressing nature. Problems of hunger and thirst and guilt. And fear.

That he was losing his mind.

Or that he wasn't.

· 9 ·

Through a Glass
Menagerie, Darkly

IT WAS PITCH-DARK and her feet were tired by the time they reached
Michael's apartment, but even so Ruth hated to leave Melior here and
begin her lonely walk farther north.

From her sidewalk vantage point she could look up and see that the
lights were on in Michael's apartment. No fear of leaving Melior to a chill
and empty room in an alien land, then. The window was surrounded by
ornamental bands of molded concrete; old, gray, baroque, and prewar.
The shades were raised, giving Ruth an unimpeded view of the living-
room ceiling five stories away.

"He's in," Ruth announced.

"Come up," Melior urged. "Michael will have to know of this, and
undoubtedly you can tell him of that which I will omit."

For one paralyzed moment Ruth thought Melior meant the incident
of the kiss; then her mind unstuck itself from that broken record track
and she realized that he meant the arrest and what had preceded it. With
a charisma that undoubtedly commanded troops in Elfland, Melior led
Ruth through the front door and up the five flights of stairs to Michael's
apartment.

Swept along by the force of his personality, Ruth did not even stop to
wonder if Michael might not be alone. Fortunately Philip was in plain
sight as Michael swung open the door in answer to Melior's knock. Like
the bad fairy in the tale, one forgot about Philip LeStrange at one's peril.

"I am arrested," Melior announced, as one wanting to get the ill news out of the way at once.

Michael stood back to let them enter. Philip was lying at full length on the living-room rug and staring spellbound into the tiny screen of his laptop—or, tonight, carpet-top. Two wires led from it. One was a phone cord. In the background the television babbled self-referentially, volume turned down low.

"Way to go," said Philip, removing one fist from his chin to hammer one-fingered at the keyboard. It was impossible to tell whether he was addressing Melior or the computer.

"Arrested? Hi, Ruth. What happened?" Michael closed the door behind them. There was a rattle of locks.

"Hi. I'm dead. Melior was arrested." Ruth walked across the room on legs that suddenly felt like lead to collapse on Michael's couch. She carefully did not look at Philip's keyboard. Where Philip was concerned, total ignorance was the better part of valor, in Ruth's educated opinion. "Pepsi. Diet Pepsi, ere I die," she enunciated, closing her eyes dramatically.

"You're already dead," Philip reminded the ambient air punctiliously. Melior entered the room cautiously (Ruth could see from beneath lowered lashes) and perched on the edge of a chair, a hard-edged contemporary figure of black leather and mirrorshades. Only the sensuous curve of a pointed ear beneath the fall of platinum hair proclaimed him something else entirely.

Michael went off to the kitchen, returning with those two staples of modern life, Diet Pepsi and potato chips. He deposited both beside Ruth.

"Arrested, you said," Michael informed her inquiringly. "As in, police-arrested?" He sat down on the arm of the couch, which creaked but seemed resigned to such treatment.

"Fare-beating," Ruth said comprehensively. She grabbed the nearest ice-cold recyclable aluminum five cents deposit in the following states can, popped the top with expert fingernails, and quaffed nonnutritive sweeteners to the full. Thus refreshed, she was able to sit up. "The transit cops nicked him."

"Good going, Elfie," Philip said. Melior removed himself from his high seat to crouch beside Philip, watching whatever was going on in liquid-crystal cyberspace.

"It isn't as if he doesn't have the fare," Michael said off-handedly. "Plus about four thousand and several hundred more dollars."

"Not any more," Ruth said. "And besides, he'd left it at my house—which was lucky, since I was his one phone call."

Quickly, then, Ruth explained the rest: her trip down to the station, the good luck that let her ransom Melior without his ever really being booked, the ruinous cost of that one heedless turnstile vault.

"And he doesn't even *like* the subway. So we walked back," Ruth finished, leaving out great gobs of the story and hoping Michael wouldn't notice.

"If you are quite through with inessentials," Melior said crossly, "prove your teeth on this truth: if not for that guardsman's interference, I might have captured the *grendel.* So close to me it was, and still in the form of mortal man—and the Sword with it, though I saw it not."

"Yeah," said Philip in a meant-to-be-overheard aside, "but you didn't. You got caught. Close only counts in horseshoes and hand grenades."

Something must be going less than well for Philip; Ruth registered the fact clinically without having the slightest interest in finding out what it was. But for Philip to pick on Melior, who had a good six inches and a number of pounds on him, argued a more than usually complex death wish on Philip's part.

Ruth opened the potato chips with a loud snap and crunched a handful furiously, following this with a second Diet Pepsi from the six-pack Michael had brought out into the living room.

"And what," asked Melior with icy punctilio, "do you suggest I do?"

In the corner some sitcom Ruth had never heard of revolved around its sacred couch in living color. Philip tapped some key that seemed to signal an end to the evening's computer activities. He looked up into Melior's face, oddly anachronistic bifocals gleaming.

"Learn the rules. *Then* break them."

"Which brings us to something I guess we should have covered earlier," Michael said on a deep breath. "Tactics."

"As in 'How We Do What We've Already Made Up Our Minds To is Strategic,' " Philip said in an "aching-to-be-slapped" voice. Melior rocked back on his haunches and rose to his feet.

"Correct. You know 'What' but not 'How,' " Michael said to Melior.

Suddenly Ruth was aware of a sudden upswing of tension in the room. Had she and Melior wandered into the middle of a fight between Michael and Philip? But Michael never fought with *anyone;* he was a great big infinitely tolerant teddy bear who practically bent over backward to avoid confrontation. That was why he and Naomi were so much alike.

"Not so," Melior said evenly. "You forget, Friend Michael—I know precisely 'How.' I must track the *grendel* to his lair, claim the Sword, and kill him with it."

"Which you cannot do from Sing-Sing," Michael said.

"Or Bellevue," Ruth added. She was completely exhausted and she

hadn't studied and now there was going to be some kind of ugly scene—
she could taste it. Which meant she was going to feel like death on toast
in the morning. Good-bye, one third of the final grade.

"You see, Melior, the, uh, real world has rules," Michael was saying,
still with that charged politeness. "If you don't follow them, you're going
to attract a lot of attention. And that is something you can't beat, believe
me. They'll catch you, and if you're lucky they'll just think you're crazy
and lock you up."

"If I am lucky," Melior repeated in an inflectionless voice.

"And if you're not lucky," Michael said, "they'll believe you. And
then, my friend, you'll disappear into some five-sided room down in
Washington, while they try to find out who you really are and where you
come from."

"And how they can get there," Philip said unexpectedly, while Ruth
tried not to stare at Michael—or indeed, at anything at all. Was this
Michael spouting Oliver Stone conspiracy theories? *Michael?*

Philip folded up his computer and unhooked it from the phone. He
glanced at Ruth, then away, his shoulders hunched familiarly. "Just think
of all those taxpayers," he added obliquely.

"Aren't you both being a little pessimistic?" Ruth said. "Whatever
happened to *Klaatu barrada nicto?* Or *IDIC?*"

"*Star Trek,*" said Philip with the scorn of one who was born the year it
was canceled. Michael had the grace to look at least a little embarrassed.

"Well, maybe that wouldn't happen," he admitted. "But whatever
happens once you're discovered, you're here illegally, and you're not
human, Melior, so you've just got to be real careful—"

"That the soulless drones you call your landsmen do not know me for
what I am, lest I suffer the same unwelcome fate as any other intruder
into an ant's nest."

There was a brief silence.

"Yeah," said Philip, "something like that. So make up your mind,
Elfie, whether you want to do it your way—or do it."

On that note, Philip got to his feet and reached for his jacket. He
tucked his computer back into his knapsack and slung that over his shoulder. "This is going to be a stupid conversation. See you tomorrow, Michael. Coming, Ruth?"

Ruth was so surprised to be considered by Philip that she let the
moment pass her completely by. Not getting an answer he shrugged,
turned, and left, pulling the door shut with a jingle of hardware behind
him. Michael went to lock it. Melior sat down at the opposite end of the
couch from Ruth, taking Michael's place.

"What I like about Philip," observed Ruth after a moment, "is his

unstudied naturalness; his total freedom from the toils of worn, out-
moded, convention. For he is a child of Nature, and takes after his
mother." It wasn't quite fair; but on the other hand, Philip wasn't here
any more either.

"But is he right?" asked Melior.

"Yeah," said Michael, coming back. "He is. That's the problem." He
pulled up the stool to make the point of an invisible triangle halfway
between Melior and Ruth, and sat down on it.

"*Your* problem," Ruth added, with a mean-spiritedness that surprised
her.

But Melior did not seem to be able to understand that, Ruth realized
with a sinking feeling about half an hour later.

This was what the strange "before-a-storm" feeling was all about; this
particular argument must have been building since Michael took Melior
home with him on Friday night. Over and over again Michael explained
about how *big* the city was, how intolerant this particular civilization was
of error or transgression, how different from a land with elves in shining
armor where men made war on horseback. Melior was a stranger here;
his only hope of moving freely about the city—of moving freely *at all*—
was to not be noticed, not really.

Once he was seen for what he was, it would be all over, and the
possibilities after that ranged the Gothic gamut from guest appearances
on *Oprah* to being winkled down some Alphabet Agency rabbit-hole and
never being seen again. Along with all the rest of *them,* of course, just to
make things interesting.

Ruth believed him. Why not? Michael made perfect sense—and besides, he was right.

And over and over Melior patiently explained that these things did
not interest him—that all he wanted was the sword, and given that, he
would give them also his solemn word to trouble them no more.

"Look," Michael said finally, long after the time when Ruth would
have been reduced to interrogative screaming. "You've said you want our
help. That you need it. And, frankly, you owe Ruth here a helluva lot. So.
Bottom line. How reasonable are you going to be?"

"I *am* being reasonable, Friend Michael," Melior began once more.

"*You are not being reasonable!*"

Michael's full-throated bellow sent the adrenaline of shock rinsing
through Ruth's overtaxed veins. She stared at him in horror. He was on
his feet, and, as she watched, Melior got to his feet also. The two of them
faced one another like mirror images.

"You—are *not*—being reasonable!" Michael shouted. "You are saying we're all going to do it *your* way—and I am here to tell you, my

pointy-eared elf-boyo, as you seem to be a little hard of hearing, that your way *Will—! Not—! Work—!*"

Sheer volume flattened Ruth in her seat. She heard him, Melior heard him, probably everyone else in the building heard him.

"Now the question you have got to ask yourself is whether you believe me. Are you saying to yourself 'this mere human has an agenda of his own'? You're right. I don't want to be arrested or any other thing for having anything to do with you when you run right smack up against a system that's just too *alien* for you to understand. Because you do that and you're going down, my friend, and it just might be that you don't know how far down Down can be."

Michael was breathing very hard and talking very fast, low now and intense with his face flushed and his breathing ragged. Ruth watched him with the spellbound intensity of one who has seen a teddy bear turn into a wolverine right before her eyes. In the spaces between his words the television, unregarded, whispered its gibberish below the level of the senses.

"But there's another way. Our way. My way. You do it that way and it just might work. You might get what you want. But there's no more going off alone. There's no more plans that you try without clearing it with one of us. This is going to have to be a team effort, and if the way we do things looks silly to you, it's just going to have to look silly and you're just going to have to do it anyway, because our way— *my* way—is the only way things are going to get done."

Ruth continued to stare at Michael as if she'd never seen him before—and in some sense of the word, she hadn't. Not this Michael.

"And if I do not do things your way?" Melior asked.

"Then walk right out that door and keep on walking, elf-lord. None of us wants anything to do with you."

Ruth would have opened her mouth to protest, but some pang of self-preservation kept her silent. With clinical detachment she noted unconnected things. The beads of sweat rolling down Michael's face. The tightness of his clenched fists. The brilliant green of Melior's eyes, open very wide and fixed unblinkingly upon Michael, as if Melior were some strange cockatrice that could slay with a gaze. The moment stretched, until Ruth thought the tension of waiting to see how it would end would make her scream.

"Then, it seems, I must accede to your terms, Michael of the World of Iron. And I wish you joy of them."

Melior's voice was so even Ruth nearly missed the capitulation. When Michael turned away, she actually twitched; a jump dying stillborn.

"That's okay, then," Michael said in a voice that only shook slightly.

He ran a hand over his forehead. Ruth handed him a Diet Pepsi. He popped the top and poured the entire contents of the can down his throat; a masculine gesture Ruth envied even while wondering how it was that men could do things like that and she couldn't.

"The first thing you've got to do is, always pay your fare in the subway. And the second thing is, when you go out looking, you've always got to take a native guide."

"And the third thing is, when I see my lawful prey, I should turn away again and pretend I do not." Melior's voice was flat.

"Maybe." Michael's voice was equally uncompromising. "Because it might just be that if you jumped him just then, he'd get away. Or a bunch of people'd get killed. Or you'd get dead. *You don't know the rules, man,* and if anything you've said is true, you don't have time to learn them."

"It is you who do not have time, Michael. The *grendel* preys on manflesh. His appetite is as endless as the ocean, and as he feeds he grows. With so many tempting morsels for his plate, soon he will be immense. But his appetite will be greater."

It was too much tension; Ruth had to focus on anything other than them. And so she was staring at the television when the ten o'clock news came on, and the screen flashed red with the display graphic for the lead news story.

"Shut up!" Ruth hissed.

Michael looked where she was looking and lunged for the volume control. The newscaster's accentless midlantic diction filled the room.

"—arrant case of *cannibalism* in the New York Subway, Spokesman Dale Werther of the Transit Authority explained."

The screen jumped to the image of an anonymous bureaucrat in a suit standing on a vaguely familiar subway platform. He was the sort, Ruth thought, that you would automatically decide was lying, no matter what he said. Thirty years of selective nonstop disinformation in the form of high-pressure advertising had produced an American consumer so savvy that he wouldn't even believe the truth.

"Every year over two hundred riders expire while in the subway, for reasons having nothing to do with the subway services."

"Like being mugged," Ruth said.

"The tunnels are also home to a number of animals, one of which may have had access to the body before it was found. We are investigating—"

"But the witnesses who found the body tell a different story," the news reader intercut smoothly. The news clip this time was of an older woman, indignant tears streaming down her face. The images were bleached and grainy, not the careful PR lighting of the spokesman.

"I don't care what nobody says—somebody *ate* on him, and I don't think it's no rats, and he didn't just die there in the car!"

"This footage was taken by one of the witnesses," the news reader said. "Transit officials could not be reached for further comment."

Last image of all, and the strongest saved for last: the inside of the subway car, jiggly with a hand-held Minicam, the color grayed almost to black with poor light and bad film. The unaccustomed eye took a moment to adjust, then enhanced the images to lucidity: the black streaks on the walls were spattered blood. The horribly altered bundle on the floor of the car was a body.

"Authorities are continuing their investigation."

The screen went bright with the network logo.

"And in Queens, a dyslexic woman teaches her daughter to read, back after this."

Michael flipped off the television. Silently, he began to pace the length of the apartment, reminding Ruth of a caged leopard and making her wish she were somewhere else. The televised images—more vivid in retrospect—made Ruth's stomach churn in helpless fury. This was the dark side of the fairy tale: the monsters to match the princes.

"And now he has gone to ground, in the trackless caves that lie beneath your city, and you say I may not hunt him?" Melior said bitterly. "The World of Iron is only a fable for sorcerers, but even so I did not think its men were mad."

"Yeah, right," said Michael, who wasn't really listening.

"But it isn't trackless," Ruth said in the over-reasonable tones of shock. Both men stared at her. "It's got plenty of tracks. Michael, Melior's talking about the *subway*. The monster's in the subway. And the subways are *mapped.*"

But strangely now it was Melior who held back.

"The *grendel* has fed, and will be more dangerous with each passing hour. I must know its territory before I seek it out. I am no coward, but much rides upon my life: if I am slain, then the chance of the *grendel's* death dies with me."

"I thought you said the sword was what would kill it?" Ruth said.

"Aye, sweet Ruth, and who will wield it if I do not? For any mortal who takes it up will change as well, and another *grendel* will take the place of the first."

"You have a point," Michael said. "Do you have a plan?"

"I must go once more into the subterranean *way,*" Melior said seriously, "and travel its byways and turnings. Perhaps I will sense the

Sword's nearness again. In any event, I shall gain an understanding of the ground over which I must fight."

Michael thought about this. "Okay. Tomorrow you ride the subway. But one of us goes with you. Ruth?"

Ruth hesitated. It seemed vastly mean-spirited to protest that she had her final exam in Cataloging tomorrow—except that she *did,* and if she missed it she might as well blow off graduating in June. And that meant the summer to get through without a job—maybe more if the course weren't being repeated until spring—and all of that meant money, time, trouble. . . .

"No; I forgot; we've got the Cat final tomorrow. And Naomi's rehearsing for her orals. That leaves Philip or Jane to go with you," Michael said inarguably.

Just about then the phone rang. While Ruth was still looking around to try to find where it was *this* week, Michael grabbed it.

"Hello? . . . yeah, she's here." ("Naomi," he mouthed at Ruth.) ". . . yeah, we saw the news. Mel thinks it's his *grendel;* he wants to go check it out . . . of course not. I'm going to send Jane with him." After this last statement there was an extended pause, through which Michael listened with patient good humor.

Which had been the only emotion Ruth had thought him capable of, before tonight. What was happening to all of them—was it *Melior* who was making them all unravel like badly-rolled string?

"She can skip that," Michael said at last. More pausing, then: "Yeah, I know that, Nai, but do you think I ought to send Phil with him?"

Ruth grinned to herself, and in truth that seemed to be a clinching argument, because soon after that he hung up.

"Naomi says I'd better call you a cab. So okay; you're a cab," Michael said agreeably.

"Gee, thanks," said Ruth. She stood up; looked around for coat and purse. The day had been full of too many strong emotions for her to feel anything at all now. The thought of the additional distance she had to cover was daunting, but Ruth had that vague distrust of taxis which a certain class of New Yorker feels, as if traveling by some means other than the preordained paths of buses and trains is somehow fraudulent and dishonest.

"But seriously, folks," Michael said. He dialed another number and gave instructions to the dispatcher. "Be here in about fifteen minutes," he told Ruth.

"Which gives us more than enough time to call up Jane and tell her she's cutting classes tomorrow—and why."

Michael began again to dial.

*   *   *

Ruth and Melior stood on the sidewalk in front of Michael's apartment, waiting for the cab. The spring darkness had closed in entirely, but here it did not frighten, instead lending the riverside the charm of unclarity.

"Michael thinks my quest in vain; it angers him," Melior said.

"Something did," Ruth pointed out. Her figurative ears still rang; who would ever have thought *Michael* could lose his temper?

"He fears to know himself a coward, and twice fears to test the knowledge," Melior said simply.

Michael a coward? Ruth shook her head in bafflement. She didn't think he was, but then she didn't think he was especially brave, either. Cowardice and bravery, like honor, were not concepts that came up very often in daily conversation.

"And do you, Ruth, also think I ought not seek the Sword?"

Yes, thought Ruth before she could censor herself. "New York is an awfully big place," she began, hesitantly.

"And I should content myself with securing my own happiness," Melior suggested, looking sideways at her. "Though I admit I had never thought to find it here. But what use is happiness when one is dead?"

"Dead?" Ruth echoed. She stared at Melior.

"If I remain here in this World of Iron I will die, Ruth, whether I face this *grendel* or not."

"*When?* I mean—"

"In fifteen years. Perhaps twenty." Ruth's shoulders sagged as relief replaced tension, and Melior smiled bitterly. "You think it a sufficient time, but even you, Ruth, would outlast it. And it is not so very long a time to one who was not born to die."

Furious with her own transparency, Ruth turned away. She still had her back to Melior, staring at the river with every evidence of fixed interest, when the taxi arrived.

"Ruth, I want—" Melior began, but Ruth didn't wait to hear it. She leaped into the taxi as if pursued by devils. It pulled away, leaving Melior standing alone on the street.

"Where to, lady?" the question came, and numbly, automatically, Ruth told him.

Coward, coward, coward, Ruth thought bitterly. *Always afraid of what people will think. Always. Still. After everything.*

She didn't remember her last night on earth, but she'd seen pictures. Her prom dress had been pink: pale satin spaghetti-strapped bodice, the skirt yards and yards of pale-pink tulle tinted darker pink at the edge of each asymmetric layer. Mom had snapped her picture just before she and Jimmy'd left the house.

But she didn't remember that. She didn't remember buying the dress, or why she would have bought something that, in retrospect, made her look so much like a flamingo. She didn't remember going to the Senior Prom, nor Jimmy Ramirez getting drunk, and most of all she didn't remember *why* she'd gotten into the car with him again. He had to have been very drunk, drunk enough so anyone could tell. The coroner's report said so. So her father said.

June 7th, 1981. And early on the morning of June 8th Ruth Marlowe's world ended, as she and three other kids hit a tree at something in the vicinity of eighty miles per hour.

Ruth graduated in absentia while on total life-support in the County Hospital. She'd been thrown clear; broken arms, broken legs, broken collarbone, but nothing that wouldn't heal.

Except that Ruth wouldn't wake up. *Coma,* they said, and, as time passed, *irreversible.* They unhooked the respirator. Ruth slept on.

Time passed and the world went on. And then, eight years later, Ruth woke up.

Woke up five years ago to find her mother dead, her father dying, the house she'd grown up in sold long since to pay the medical bills and all the world changed. Not beyond recognition. That would have been kinder. But changed just enough that everything seemed like a reflection in some cruel looking glass. Her father died about the time Ruth learned to walk again; it was almost a release from those painful interviews, each of them in their respective wheelchairs, when he tried not to blame her too openly for destroying his life and Ruth searched vainly for her father in this ailing, bitter, widower.

Seventeen going on thirty, and the only thing left for her to do was cobble together some kind of adulthood and pretend she agreed when the nurses called her lucky. Lucky, with what people called "the best years of your life" vanished in a night. She hadn't even had to go into Elf Hill to lose them. All she'd had to do was . . . whatever she'd done, that night. Something stupid, something cowardly, something that cared more for what people—Jimmy—would think than for life itself.

No wonder she'd been ready, ripe, and reckless for the first stray elf-lord who came along. Who didn't treat her like the thirty-year-old she wasn't, or like a raree show, or a science project, or like someone who should be *grateful—!*

Oh, yes, Rohannan Melior was something worth having. But what did something that wonderful want with *her?*

· 10 ·

Bread and Roses

HE WAS HUNGRY. Hungry, and thirsty, and he knew the only thing that would ease him. Kevin Shelby rode the subway, a magic sword from Elfland concealed in the awkward bundle at his side, and planned.

The run through the sunlight had been bad, very bad. Bad enough that Kevin did not wish to contemplate a repetition of it. By the time he had reached the subway entrance three blocks away, tears of pain were streaming down his face beneath the Terminator sunglasses.

He'd retained enough presence of mind not to vault the turnstile into the subway: Transit cops lay in wait for fare-beaters and if they caught him they would take him back toward the sun.

No, even in his pain and hunger, Kevin made himself worthy of the sword. He flashed his out-of-date ID at the token booth clerk and was buzzed through the "Employees Only" gate. The gate clicked shut behind him and he moved down the platform. Then Kevin was free—free in the system.

Even though the subway system itself was lit up bright as night indoors, the light wasn't nearly as bad. The blue-white pain behind his eyes receded and the sense of impending doom left him. He was in the New York Subway System, with hundreds of miles of track. It ran twenty-four hours a day, and all he had to do was avoid the parts of the subway lines that ran above ground and he'd be fine. He could transfer across platforms from Uptown to Downtown lines; he could even buy food, hot dogs and stuff, without ever leaving the system.

At the thought of a hot dog, Kevin's stomach lurched. His mouth was dry and cottony, a torment of an entirely different order than the pain behind his eyes, and his midsection was occupied with a sick numb cramping that testified to a too-long emptiness. But a hot dog was not the answer.

The train came and he got on—a car near the middle; safest place to ride the train. The doors shut with their familiar two-note chime, and the train started to move. Kevin braced himself against the rocking with the ease of a lifelong New Yorker and headed for a seat.

This early in the morning he had his choice; he chose one of the corner side seats at the front of the car, near both the doors to the platform and the doors that led between cars. Carefully he propped the sword, sheathed in record jackets, against the fake woodgrain veneer of the car's bulkhead and leaned back on the gaudy orange plastic seat.

Safe.

But immediate physical safety only left Kevin with the leisure to think of all the ways in which he was not safe, and of all the things he lacked. He rode the subway hour after hour, up and down and around, while the thought of food came to obsess him even more than it nauseated him.

He had to eat. And that understanding became the anvil upon which his fear was hammered, because that which he desperately must do was that which he could not do.

He tried. He bought sodas, candy bars, potato chips, mustard pretzels, soft-serve ice cream, candied popcorn, gyros, falafel, and hot dogs.

He threw all of them away before taking even a bite.

He couldn't even drink *water*.

The hours passed. The cars filled up with weekend ridership, a seething mass of assorted humanity that remained constant throughout the day. The car filled, but somehow there was always an empty seat beside Kevin, huddled in his peculiar misery, guarding the sword and riding the subway.

He was there when Roy Turpin's body was discovered, though he didn't know it. The story broke in time for the evening editions; he could have picked up a copy of the *Post* or its sister papers at any number of newsstands on platforms serving the IND and the IRT lines. But his head hurt too much to read, and television and radio did not penetrate the layers of concrete, stone, and steel that separated Kevin Shelby from the light of the sun.

By eleven-thirty Saturday night the cars were empty once more. By that time all of Kevin's fear and guilt were distilled into the particular horror of *need*. His mouth watered constantly, though that did nothing to alleviate his thirst, and for the first time he began to understand how it was possible to go mad with hunger.

The worst part was, he didn't have to be hungry.

He didn't know when the knowledge came to him. Sometime during that long dim suffering day he had roused into brighter awareness and knew the solution. He knew what he could eat, what would soothe him and nourish him and not fill him with sickness, nausea, and pain. He *knew*.

In some dying corner of his mind the part of Kevin Shelby that had tried to be good rebelled. Frantically it built barriers of impossibility against the sweet seductive reasonableness of that inner knowledge.

It would be dangerous. It would be messy. He might get caught, or hurt, or it *might not work*. The only defense he did not use was that it was wrong, for Kevin had forfeited the right to that defense sometime late Friday night.

And eventually sheer privation wore him down.

It was very late. He didn't quite remember how long he'd been here, or what he'd done before that, but he knew it was late. The car he was riding in was empty. His entire body vibrated with an unwholesome dishonest energy imposed from without, as much destroying his body as enlivening it. His hands shook. The vivid images of his intention painted themselves against his eyes, offering heat but no warmth.

And then The Other One boarded the car.

The Other One was a person of the sort that Kevin, in better days, would have avoided out of an instinctive sense of self-preservation. For one thing, anybody riding the trains at this hour *had* to be crazy. For another thing, he looked like the sort of person that somebody riding the trains at this hour would naturally run into, which was why nobody who wanted to keep their wallet and their neck rode the trains at this hour.

The Other One wore a long green raincoat and high-topped sneakers and hummed to himself as he selected a seat at the opposite end of the train. Kevin watched with hungry fascination.

The train began to move, pulling out into the tunnels and the relative darkness. The Other One got up and moved to a seat in the middle of the car. Kevin was on the "A" Line now, and the Uptown stations were several minutes apart. He clutched at the Sword in its clumsy wrappings. Sometime during the day he had picked through the plastic and tape and newspaper sealing one end. If he reached inside he could touch the cool curve of the jewel in the Sword's pommel.

He had to be strong. That was the important thing, the most important thing. If he failed, if he died here, it would all have been for nothing. His *life* would have been for nothing—all the things he might be, all the things he could have been . . . gone.

His mind hurt in a muddled, painful way. There was something wrong with his reasoning, somewhere—but he felt so bad. The thirst was the worst, worse even than the hunger.

And there was only one food that would appease the hunger and thirst.

"Hey, man, you got any spare change?"

Kevin said nothing. Now The Other was close, very close; Kevin could see him, smell stale breath and stale sweat and beneath it all the living aroma of *food*.

"Hey, man, I'm talking to you. What's the matter with you?"

The Other was his chance for life. If he didn't take it, he would die. It was that simple. And so Kevin Shelby took the final step that made his own life more important than right or wrong.

He stood up, forcing The Other back, and thrust his fist through the hole he had made in the cardboard record cover. His hand closed over the roundness of the pommel and slid farther to the ridged hardness of the haft.

"Hey, man, you got a problem with me?"

"No problem," said Kevin, and yanked to pull the sword free.

But it slid out only a little way, and then tangled in the tape and newspapers that Kevin had so carefully wrapped around it. And The Other laughed, and pulled out something small and shiny.

A knife.

Roy had always said—when there was Roy—that a knife would scare people more than a gun up close. Because a gun really didn't look like much, if it wasn't one of the ones too big to hide, but a knife always looked like exactly what it was.

Something to cut.

"Give me that," Kevin said reasonably, and The Other laughed. His eyes were on the jeweled pommel and Kevin knew he had made a mistake.

"Give what you got there and I let you keep your money."

The Other reached for the Sword.

Kevin grabbed the knife.

The blade slid along the palm of his hand. It bit deep into his wrist. Kevin didn't care. He knew what he wanted. He clawed The Other's fingers open, getting at the knife, and now The Other was trying to get away, but that didn't matter; Kevin was pushing him back, and back; The Other's body hit one of the poles in the center of the car and he tripped with Kevin on top of him trying to get the knife right way round in his hand.

The train pulled into a station. After a moment the doors opened onto the empty station platform.

"Help! Help me! Help! I'm being mugged!"

Then Kevin found the right way around with the knife.

It slid in so easily at first it didn't seem that it could have worked, but The Other was suddenly silent, and lay quietly beneath Kevin as the doors shut and the train began to move again.

And then there was the cutting, which was good, and the eating, which was sweet relief. But even the eating wasn't enough somehow, so there was cutting and cutting and cutting. And when it was over, Kevin's skin felt stiff and hard, and with the new bright energy he felt he ripped the coverings from the Sword.

It was simple, then, to jam the switchbox so the doors of the car wouldn't open. And around five o'clock in the morning, when the train was on standby in a tunnel, it was simple to use the Sword to lever open the doors again, so that Kevin could step out of the train and into the tunnel.

· 11 ·

The Looking-Glass War

AS AN ELF he was a total washout. And as a way to spend Monday, it was comprehensively stupid.

Jane Greyson had few illusions about Life and was willing to get by with fewer. She had no idea why people insisted on making the best of things, as transformation was a concept unknown to her philosophy. Hers was a policy of Things As They Are, and if something wasn't best there was no point in trying to pretend that it was.

In that context, whether or not the person called Melior was an elf as defined in the Oxford Unabridged Dictionary New Revised Edition was of much less importance (as less subject to logical proof) than the fact that Ruth and Michael and Naomi had all agreed to treat him as an elf and to do what they could to help him. Once that was settled, Jane had something to work with, secure in the knowledge that her opinions would not be consulted.

Thus it was that Michael and Ruth had not really had to explain that Melior couldn't be trusted to run around loose. In Jane's opinion nobody could be. The world was too endlessly inventive; if your number was up, it would get you, and that was that.

But Ruth especially had insisted that Melior had to have somebody with him who knew the ways of the world, and though Jane knew that the others regarded her as an unworldly little incompetent whose sole recommendation lay in that she was *not* Philip Leslie LeStrange, she supposed they felt she had at least enough sophistication to guide a pointy-eared whatever-he-was around the subway system.

He wasn't an elf. Jane clutched that cockle-warming knowledge to herself with all the surety of one who has read several very good translations of several very elderly Eddas. The *Aelfvar* were a race of Norse demigods who lived in Aelfheim and stayed out of the affairs of Men. Furthermore they were dark-skinned and short, and probably didn't have pointed ears at all. And most of all, they didn't exist.

But nobody would have believed him if he'd said he was a Vulcan.

Jane considered this carefully and decided that probably Ruth would have believed him, but would never have admitted it to the others. And possibly it would have mortified her so much that she would even have tried to conceal *him* from them, too, so all in all it was just as well that he'd said he was an elf.

Even if he wasn't one.

But they'd all voted to let him be an elf, so Jane abandoned the ultimately fruitless question of what Melior *really* was, and concentrated on what they were doing.

Which, on this fine Monday morning in May, was almost precisely nothing.

The record time for traversing every last inch of the transit system is somewhere just under twenty hours; every year an impromptu "subway rally" is held to try to better that time. Today she and Melior weren't even trying to come close to it; they'd ride as much of the subway as they could cover until around three—when Michael and Ruth would be done with their exams—and then go back and try to figure out what to do about the creature that Melior said was down in the subway.

Personally, Jane couldn't see what the fuss was about. She understood that Melior wanted his sword back—Jane understood about wanting to retain ownership of one's own possessions—but she really couldn't see that one more crazed cannibal roaming New York could make a difference one way or the other. So what if he ate people? *Stone cold dead hath no fellow,* Jane quoted to herself. If they were dead, who cared what happened afterward? They didn't.

Still, taken all in all, the day was a wash.

After the phone call last night, Jane had spent some time planning out a suitable route. Fortunately, the book on subways that mentioned the subway rally also mentioned enough about the paths taken for her to reconstruct it. This morning, bright and early, at the ghastly hour of 7:00 a.m. she had presented herself at Michael's apartment and prepared to be bored.

Melior was living up to her expectations in that respect. At least he hadn't tried to talk to her. And she *had* brought a book.

*   *   *

Ruth chewed on the end of her regulation Number 2 lead pencil and wished she were somewhere else. Anywhere would do, but specifically she wished she were the one with Melior on the subway instead of Jane.

The room where she and thirty-five other bored and nearly-graduated student librarians were being tested to destruction did nothing to improve her mood. Vast, chalk-scented, dusty, scrupulously silent, and seemingly devoid of all human life, it seemed to be a dress rehearsal for the buildings in which she would spend the rest of her working life.

Ruth noticed the test proctor looking her way and quickly bent her head to the test paper again. She hated library school. She hated her *life*. No, worse, she was *bored* with her life, and being bored with your life before you'd really even started it led to chilling speculations on the whichness of what you would do for the rest of it.

No, not even bored. Dissatisfied.

The right word at last. Ruth stared at her paper and tried to summon up some interest. Cataloging: Dewey or don't we?

Back to work.

The questions were multiple choice, but that didn't make them any easier. All the answers were *almost* right, but in the eyes of God and Columbia there was only one really right answer.

Melior.

Not an answer, no, not even a question, and not a problem she could avoid, after last night. The defiant fact of his existence was an assault upon the fabric of her world, was a wound she would carry with her forever, and in all honesty and good conscience she still had to deal with his problem: the missing sword, and the monster that had been caused by it.

What if it was a coincidence? Ruth's logical mind insisted. *Murders are horrible, but they happen. None of us had inside information about that killing. What if it's just an ordinary lunatic and not a GRENDEL?*

Melior thought it was a *grendel*. But Melior, Ruth realized with a chill, standoffish clarity, wanted magic to work in this world. If magic didn't work here, he would remain here until he died.

But would that be so bad? He said his world was at war; here he'd have years of peace. WE'D have years—

Which was the root of the matter, really. She loved Melior—how could she not? And she thought, maybe, that he loved her, but if he found his sword, he was going back to Elfland.

If he could.

And Ruth, who wanted his happiness more than she wanted her own, suddenly wished he couldn't.

*   *   *

The Computer Department of Columbia University had, until quite recently, occupied the basements of several scattered buildings. Only last year, in a series of shuffles reminiscent of Three-Card Monte, had the Powers That Were consolidated their mainframes, their LAN-servers, their free-standing PCs in one location.

The students called it Hacker Heaven.

But, of course, nothing like that went on there. The Age of the Hacker was past: penalties were too high if you were caught, safeguards were too stringent. Cyberpunks existed only in the imagination of the media.

Right?

Michael knew better. And so, while Ruth, who was no morning person, slogged slowly through her Cat Final, Michael checked answers with the reckless abandon of one who only needs to graduate to become employed, and finished the three-hour exam in forty minutes flat.

And went looking for Philip, knowing where he'd be. Where they'd both, unknown to the others, agreed that Philip would be.

"You know that this is illegal?" Michael Peacock said, mostly because he knew it would give Philip such pleasure to hear it. And it had been his own personal wonderful idea, too.

"I know, I know," Philip muttered, not really listening. "Isn't it wonderful?"

His laptop reposed on the table beside the computer reserved for student database searching, connected to the bigger computer—and its modem—by arcane means. The big screen was currently welcoming them to Columbia's Electronic University Services. At intervals Philip hit a key on his laptop, to no apparent effect.

Suddenly the database computer screen went blank and the laptop emitted a small, self-satisfied beep. Philip sat back and looked at Michael.

"It's showtime," he said.

"Okay, kemo sabe, where do we go from here?" Michael asked.

"Anywhere," Philip said. "Okay," he added, in his voice for lecturing the mentally deficient. "What goes in here—" he indicated the laptop, "—goes up there—" the computer, "—but we can use the programs stored in here to modify there." He sat back, smug.

Michael had long since given up wondering what Philip was doing in library school. There was no point in asking, because Philip didn't seem to know either. There was going to be trouble there, ten-fifteen-twenty years down the line, sure as taxes. And there was more hope of avoiding taxes than of derailing the trouble for his friend.

Michael Peacock knew something about human nature and inevitability.

"Okay, Phil. The first one should be easy. Get us into the Department of Motor Vehicles database."

After five hours on the subway, Jane felt that lunch was in order. She mentioned this to her companion.

"How do you live like this?" Melior responded. He had been staring out the window almost the entire time—except when they changed trains—watching the interplay of light and shadow and the alternation of station and tunnel that were familiar-bordering-on-invisible for Jane.

"Consider the alternative," Jane said. "Do you want to stop for lunch? Because I do, and this *grendel*-thing is as likely to be in a McDonald's as anywhere else."

Now Melior looked at her. He'd taken off the mirrorshades that Ruth had bought him, and Jane stared into eyes of a green found only in coloring books, with slit pupils that waxed and waned in the light. Jane felt her stomach lurch with more than hunger; with an instinctive rejection of the unnatural. Of Melior.

"Come on," she said. Once she'd gotten him moving, they could find some place to eat. First things first.

"You do not believe, do you?" Melior said, showing no inclination to shift himself. He smiled, showing pointed teeth. "Were I in my proper place, I could show you magic to freeze your young blood; wonders to lift the heart. Then you would believe."

"You really don't get it, do you?" Jane said. *"It doesn't matter.* Magic or not—who cares?"

" 'Who cares'?" Melior echoed blankly. "But, child, it is *magic."*

"I don't care. Nobody cares. And I'm hungry," Jane said flatly.

"Then we shall eat, of course." Melior rose to his feet in a perfect motion that made Jane sharply aware of her own clumsiness. The comparison did not make her like him any better.

Since Melior had the window seat, she got up and moved to the center of the car. They were just coming in to a station now—someplace in Brooklyn she'd never heard of. But there had to be McDonald's even in Brooklyn, didn't there?

"But tell me, Mistress Jane," Melior said to her back. Jane stopped but didn't turn around. She knew what came next. Now he was going to say something witty and obscure that was supposed to make her feel like a jerk.

"If you do not believe in me, why are you helping me?"

There it came. Jane's view of the universe was reconfirmed.

"Because Ruth asked me to."

"And would you do anything for Ruth?" Melior asked, still in the tone of one who hopes to play verbal trumps.

"I'd do this," Jane said, conceding nothing.

The doors opened on yet another unfamiliar platform. Jane walked out through them without looking back to see if he followed.

In the computer room, the screen was filled with endlessly scrolling lines.

"Don't worry about it," Philip said. "I'm downloading everything to the capture buffer."

"Great," said Michael, who wasn't absolutely sure what all this meant but it *sounded* good.

From the DMV computer they had progressed by easy stages into the Coroner's Office computer for New York County (which is to say, for Manhattan and Brooklyn). If there were a *grendel,* and if it were killing, the resulting bodies would be entered here.

It hadn't been that hard to get in. Michael had been surprised.

"The thing is," Philip had said, "people lock up the information they think is valuable. Too bad they don't know what it is. How do they know what I'm going to want to know? Or they leave it unprotected but scattered, which really isn't going to slow anybody down. You can always put it back together. A librarian is a synthesist, isn't that what they're always saying in class? A specialist in general knowledge? People are such dorks," Philip added, on a sigh of pure disgust.

The screen scrolled up into darkness, leaving only a flashing square of cursor.

"What's wrong?" Michael asked.

"We're done. All the homicides since April thirtieth. Of course, we've only got Elfie's word for it that that's when he showed up—" Philip pointed out sneeringly.

"If this is a scam, it's a scam like I've never seen," Michael said. Philip looked at him curiously and shrugged. His bifocals went flash-flash in the light.

"Look, Michael—I don't care. Elfie's a moron and he's going to get us all killed. But who wants to live forever, especially at these prices?"

It was better away from the train. The train was too bright. Too . . . dry. It was better here, in the lay-bys and access tunnels of the underground railroad. There was rest. And there was food.

If only his skin didn't itch.

When he had been human, Kevin Shelby had been a track worker in his underworld kingdom, and perhaps some of the knowledge he had gained then remained to him, but it was more a matter of instinct now that led him to the deeper and less traveled sections of the line; to the storage cupboards, the equipment depots, the niches for a man to stand in as a train passed by.

The prey.

Only hours after that first, well-publicized kill, Kevin—who still, for a while longer, remembered that he had once had a name—found his second subterranean victim.

It was dark in the tunnel. The air they pushed ahead of them in their headlong flight warned him well in advance each time a train was due. There was plenty of time to find safety; to crouch in a niche designed for the purpose until the heedless glass-and-metal worm was gone. Eventually he reached a place in the system where the tunnels opened up: four, five, six sets of tracks running parallel for a few yards before diverging to their separate lines once more. And in the vaulting darkness on that quiet Sunday, Kevin could sense movement.

He could smell food.

He did not have to debate within himself for very long before killing; the maddening hunger that had left him so briefly had returned again, stronger than before; the hunger that was the Sword's true legacy to humankind: an unslakable and very specific appetite.

And about the time his last victim was discovered, Kevin killed again.

Somewhere between the subway car and here he had unsheathed the Sword from its makeshift scabbard. There was no need for concealment any longer; he carried the Sword naked in his hand. He heard a voice call out to him, and flinched momentarily away from the beam of a weak flashlight, but whether this new Other was track worker or fellow interloper Kevin did not choose to care. Between recognizing the prey and lashing out with that killing engine was no more than a heartbeat.

And then again there was food; warm glorious soft sweet fulfilling food.

He gorged until he could eat no more, crouched there between the pillars. He was safe; such trains as passed in the distance carried no one who would see him for what he was. At last, satiated, he stopped groping toward unfamiliar delicacies in the intermittent darkness. What he left behind would be finished by rats; it was unlikely that this body would ever be found, no matter who it had been. Kevin wandered on, with a vague certainty that his journey now led to some definite destination.

It was then that his skin began to itch.

The dark glasses had gone long since. Now the militaristic nylon bomber jacket was discarded; its heat and weight maddening to skin gone suddenly raw and sensitive. He paused again and again to scratch everywhere his hands could reach, until his nails drew fresh native blood to mingle with the dried blood that caked his clothes, and found no relief. Eventually shirt and undershirt were abandoned in the tunnels as well.

He folded them neatly and set them aside carefully, out of the damp. Perhaps, at the time, he even meant to come back for them. And some unreckonable time later, what was left of Kevin Shelby found the cure for the itch, just as it had for the hunger.

She'd known he wouldn't do something as sensible as go to McDonald's.

Melior caught up to Jane just as she was about to go through the antique yellow-painted wooden turnstile that led to Darkest Brooklyn.

"Wait," he said, and like an idiot, a worldling, a mundane, she did.

"Stay a moment," he said, just as if he thought he was Shakespeare and she was PBS, "there is something I wish to see."

And then he went back to the edge of the platform, to the sheer drop-off that led only to the tracks below—and jumped off.

"Hey," said Jane.

Her voice sounded weak and unconvincing, even to her. If not for the fact that she felt completely unequal to the task of explaining this to Ruth, she would have gone off and left Melior-the-elf right then, and if she had held out any hope that he would have stayed put she would at least have had lunch before she dealt with him.

But since she knew perfectly well he would not, and equally she knew that Ruth would not be satisfied by even the best and most reasonable explanation of events, Jane abandoned lunch and egress and went back to the edge of the platform and looked down.

Melior was nowhere in sight. Jane was methodical; she looked both ways. She even looked behind her, back toward daylight and sanity. Nothing.

"Hey!" she cried, a good deal louder this time.

Two glowing green orbs of the cat-in-darkness sort appeared out of the blackness. They flashed and vanished as Melior looked away.

"Mistress Jane?" Melior said. His voice, pitched low to carry, sounded weirdly as though he were standing just beside her and not several yards away. "It is just as I thought. Come and see for yourself."

Jane looked all around, but this station was not one of the ones with a manned token booth (or any sort of token booth at all, to be brutally accurate), and apparently this quarter of Brooklyn was not particularly well-traveled at 12:45 Monday afternoon.

She looked up the tracks. She didn't see an oncoming train, but uppermost in her mind was the fact that if Melior here was to get himself creamed by a train, she didn't even have to bother to go back to Ruth and the others. She could just jump in front of the next one.

"Where are you?" Jane called, trying very hard not to feel ridiculous.

Melior came out into the light of the platform, looking like a fifteen-second clip from the next thing in horror films. He'd taken off his mirror-shades, and in the shadows his eyes flared green-yellow and silver, reflecting all the light there was. His pale skin seemed to pluck up shadows from the surrounding air, making him look not only unearthly pale, but white in the way of mushrooms and fishbellies and things far better left unexamined. His leather jacket hung open, his shirt was smudged with tunnel grime—a thousand innocent things conspired bizarrely to form one snapshot image of horror.

Jane jumped backward, emitting a mouselike and inelegant squeak. She gritted her teeth. He'd done that on purpose, she was almost certain.

But either Melior was a very good actor (granted) or innocent of such subtle plottings as Jane assigned him. He walked up the railbed to the edge of the platform and heaved himself up.

"I could not be certain from inside the *cars*—" Melior's distaste gave the word a foreign and unfamiliar flavor, "—but now I am certain. This is such a place as a *grendel* would lair."

"*'Just the place for a Snark/I have said it thrice: /What I tell you three times is true.'* Lewis Carroll. Charles Dodgson, if you prefer. *He* saw fairies at the bottom of the garden," Jane added expansively. "Which doesn't mean there were any."

"But there is a *grendel*—and it has been here, at least recently," Melior said.

What did it do, leave graffiti? Jane thought, but did not say it. Offensively smartass remarks were Philip's speciality. All Jane did was state the obvious. They couldn't get you for reporting the facts.

"Or so I think," said Melior, with sudden suspicious humility, "but, as I have been told far too many times for my liking that I do not understand this World of Iron, I wish you to see what I have seen as well, and tell me, if you may, wherein lies my error."

"You mean I'm supposed to tell you if you've made a mistake. And I have to go down there to do it." *I can hardly contain my rapture.*

It was spring, so it had been raining recently, and, as after every rain, pools of water had collected at the bottom of the faintly-curving floor of the railbed. The tunnel was littered with garbage tossed from the windows of passing trains or flung from the platform itself, and from where Jane stood she could see the busy and entirely unworried—and large, and well-fed, and nothing-at-all like Stuart Little—rats saunter to and fro.

Melior vaulted down off the platform again and held up his hands, obviously ready to assist her.

"We're all gonna die," Jane muttered. Hissing curses between her clenched teeth, she sat down on the edge of the platform—wincing at the filth—and slid off into the unknown. Without help.

The drop was farther than she had expected, and jarring. The first sensation she registered was the soft but not treacherously moist squish of compacted litter beneath her sneakers.

The second was the wind that heralded an oncoming train.

She flattened herself against the platform, but without Melior's help she had no hope of climbing up it again. Jane was not particularly tall; the lip of the platform was a foot and more above her head. It was streaked with grease and soot and probably the entrails of a thousand rush-hour suicides.

And Melior stood there, oblivious.

"It's a *train*," Jane said, in a voice that refused to be either steady or audible. She knew she had to do something, but terror held her still. Movement was a surrender to fear.

And now Melior reacted, but slowly, slowly: where every instinct screamed at Jane to run, he had to reason out the danger with instincts honed to something entirely other.

The light was a faint spark in the distance now. The trainman had seen them, or seen something; the despairing wail of the seldom-used whistle echoed through the tunnel.

And Melior caught her by the arm and began to run.

They ran. Wet garbage slid beneath Jane's feet. They ran away from the lights of the platform and into the darkened tunnel where there was no light to see by, and despite this Jane's greatest fear was that she would lose her glasses and be blind in truth. They passed the end of the platform and ran on. The smooth close walls of the tunnel mocked their efforts, providing them no place to hide.

And even if there were a place for one, there would not be a place for two.

The train's klaxon was constant now, and with some unoccupied portion of her mind Jane recognized that it was not slowing as it neared the station: an express, or some other line running on the Double-L's tracks. The roadbed beneath her feet pitched sharply downward; she would have fallen if not for Melior's inflexible grip on her arm.

And then, miraculous—though also what Melior was running toward, having seen it in his previous explorations—the tunnel intersected with another, and in the safe hollow where the rails crossed, Melior dragged Jane to her knees and threw his arms around her.

The train thundered by instants later.

Sparks sprayed up from its wheels; there was a teeth-setting scream of metal on metal. The wind of its passage stank of burning oil and liquid rot. And it was *loud,* a rhythmic thunder that terrified by sheer disorienting volume, even while the reasonable mind insisted that the sound came from a machine that was bound by Man's laws, incapable of transgression.

It seemed to go on forever.

At last the train, with one last wailing tocsin, fishtailed its way to its next destination, and left them behind.

Slowly Jane became aware that Melior was holding her in an embrace so tight it hurt. His face was buried against her neck; the upraised collar of his leather jacket tickled her nose. He was shaking. She wondered if he was crying and desperately hoped not.

But of more immediate interest was the knowledge that she, Jane Treasure Greyson, had survived a genuine urban myth folk legendary experience and was now invested with bragging rights.

Melior raised his head. Jane saw with sincere relief that he was not crying. Maybe elves just didn't, but Jane was thankful for small favors, whatever the genesis.

"Have you taken hurt, Mistress Jane?" Melior said.

"No, I'm fine." Which, whether it was true or not, was one of those automatic dumb things people always said to prevent true communication from taking place.

Although on this occasion it was more true than not. Jane was more than fine. She was exalted.

She had won. She wasn't quite sure what game they were playing, but she knew she had won. She'd done it. She'd been competent. She *hadn't fucked up.*

Melior seemed a bit taken aback by her matter-of-factness. Slowly, stiffly, he unwound his arms from about her and got to his feet. Jane scrambled after, inelegant but unwilling to be assisted. She realized with dismay that she had been kneeling in something not only gross but *wet,* and the palms of her hands were greasily black from their contact with the tunnel walls. She wiped them defiantly on her powder-blue corduroy slacks.

"So," she said, with a dawning delight at how cool she sounded, "what was it you wanted to show me, before we were interrupted?"

"Forgiving me for my foolishness; it seems that Friend Michael was right, and I do in very truth need a keeper. I did not wish to place you in such mortal jeopardy, Mistress Jane, I did not realize—" Melior broke off in the manner of someone who realizes they're about to be less than politic. "I did not precisely understand the nature of these conveyances," he finished instead.

I wonder what he was going to say before he stopped? Jane thought with less than urgent curiosity.

"Well, now you know," she said equitably. Self-confidence swelled like a golden balloon in her chest. *She had done it.*

"Yes," said Melior, "now I know. And I fear that when Mistress Ruth discovers how I have used you, she will be less than kind." Melior sounded more upset by that than by his recent brush with trainicide.

And Philip will be sure to say something disgusting. At regular intervals. For years.

"I wouldn't, you know, *mind* if you didn't mention it," Jane suggested carefully. She looked up the tracks the way they had come. The platform was a surprising ways distant. There was no train in sight.

She looked back at Melior. He was smiling.

"Then we shall not trouble the mind of Mistress Ruth with inessentials, by your leave. And for this day's grace, Mistress Jane, know that you have some claim upon Rohannan Melior of the House of the Silver Silences, who has incurred a debt that he shall repay."

Yeah, right. That and a dollar-fifty'll get me a ride on the subway.

But Jane smiled back. "So what was it you wanted me to see?"

What Melior had wanted her to see lay some distance farther down the tunnel, where the light from the platform dwindled to inconsequence and only the red-and-green of the lights in the tunnel gave any illumination to see by. Now that she was habituated to them, the subway tunnels took on a weird beauty, almost as if they were caves instead of human creations. Every surface was covered with the furry flat blackness of greasy soot, and the signal lights did little to illuminate the space.

Once they had to pause for the passage of another train, but there was plenty of warning, and plenty of space to slide into. Jane estimated that they had walked the equivalent of about two city blocks when Melior stopped.

"Here," he said.

"Where?"

They were standing almost beneath one of the signal lights. It was green, indicating that a train might pass with impunity, but even in its ghastly viridian light the interior of the tunnel was only shadow-shapes.

"Here," Melior said again, and now Jane could see that he was pointing downward, at something wedged between two of the girders that held up the roof and divided the sets of tracks from each other.

"I can't see in the dark, you know," Jane pointed out.

"I do not want to touch it. The *grendel* has been here, and left this behind."

Jane took a step forward and poked at the bundle experimentally, then pulled it out before Melior could stop her. It wasn't that much of a gamble; the thing looked dry, and if it turned out to be stuffed full of human hearts she was already braced not to squeak.

But it wasn't, and she didn't.

"Mistress Jane!" Melior protested, but Jane was already holding it up. She felt cold zippers, nylon, and acrylic fur. A bomber jacket like the police wore.

"Get a life, will you?" she muttered under her breath. Something on the jacket flaked off as she ran her hands over it, but the darkness was too deep to see.

"Don't touch that. Put it from you; it reeks of evil."

"I don't smell anything."

But who could, down here? The mingled smells of urine and rotting garbage had long since put her nose on overload. Jane could no longer smell them, and *l'air du subway* was only a burnt-rubber taste in the back of her throat.

Or maybe Melior was feeling metaphorical?

"I said leave it!" To Jane's surprise, Melior grabbed the jacket and flung it away into the outer darkness. There was a squeaking and a scuttling that would have played havoc with Jane's delicate nerves if she'd happened to have any.

"If that was your proof, you've just thrown it away," Jane said after a pause.

" *'If'?* " Melior demanded. "The creature sheds its varied skins; I show you proof and you mock at it."

"Oh." Understanding came with a jolt, the way it often does when a companion's bizarre actions suddenly make luminous sense.

"But it wasn't proof, Melior. Not of anything. Not to me. Not even to Ruth." *It was only somebody's jacket.*

And there never would be proof, Jane realized suddenly, and there probably wasn't a *grendel,* either. Because whether Melior was an elf or not, he was also crazy.

"How can I make you see, before it is too late?" Melior groaned, and Jane, galvanized to honesty, answered.

"I don't know."

· 12 ·

When the Magic's Real

ALONE IN THE apartment after Ruth's hasty departure, Naomi pulled the notebook she was keeping out of its storage place and glanced through it. A cup of tea stood at her elbow, spiraling steam into the air.

Nothing had changed. Everything was just as it had been the last time she'd looked: what he'd told her, what they'd done. She'd even sketched pictures of his clothes and jewelry—the clothes and jewelry of a self-proclaimed Prince of Elfland. And hadn't Michael said there was just too much of it to fake? Those eyes, those ears, those *teeth*—

My, what big pointy teeth you've got, Grandma.

None of it helped. She'd seen the same news broadcast Ruth had. The murder in the subway.

Melior thought it was his *grendel*. And what else, after all, could it be? *Almost anything.*

Too real for me. Naomi shook her head in sad self-rebuke and closed the book again. In the children's books she loved things like this never happened. She believed Melior (with reservations) but what she'd really been expecting was for his sword to turn up in the window of Sotheby's. Or something, anything, just so long as it wasn't this cross between *The Taking Of Pelham One Two Three* and *Silence Of The Lambs.*

Naomi shuddered. Did the murder make this more real, or more fantastic? She didn't know. She only knew that she resented it deeply. *"A real toad in an imaginary garden."*

And she was worried about Ruth.

* * *

"Sensei, I have a problem."

Master Paul Robillard was Naomi's sensei, or teacher, in the gentle
art of kendo. His dojo was located on Broadway a few blocks south of her
apartment, in a bright corner space two flights up from a greengrocer's.
There, three evenings a week, Naomi and seven others took master
classes in the Way of the Sword.

"If you'd stop dropping your wrist when you attack, you'd be fine."

Mornings, no one was here, except Sensei.

"It's not that sort of a problem," Naomi said.

"Well, why don't you get dressed and we'll talk about it?"

There were windows in three walls of the dojo; the huge square space
with its white-painted walls and bare wood floor, was drenched in light.
The back wall was still mirrored, and a barre ran around all four walls,
legacy of its one-time use as a dance studio.

Naomi padded out onto the floor in her *hakama* and slippers, and
bowed to the altar with its photos, oranges, and lit candles. Then she
turned and regarded herself in the mirror.

She'd come to Sensei Paul for help, but what could she say? Ruth was
the one with the problem, not her.

Since the fall semester, with graduation suddenly on everybody's
mind, Ruth had been, well, looking for a way out. Advanced coursework
wasn't the answer—as it had been in her case, Naomi thought wryly—
since Ruth had to get out there and earn a living before the Student Loan
Officer decided to take the debt out in white slavery.

But if Ruth were using Melior as a form of escapism, it was going to
backfire, badly.

Sensei Paul came out onto the floor, holding two masks in one hand
and a pair of *bokken* in the other. Paul was tall and handsome, with skin
like polished teak. He looked like a poster boy for street crime and was
the gentlest soul Naomi knew. He even made Michael look aggressive.
He crossed the floor and handed her the mask. Like most of the senior
students, Naomi kept the bulkier items of her kendo costume here. She
put the mask on, settling its familiar contours against her face, then took
her sword. It was shaped like a rough sketch for a *katana;* light brown
wood and a plastic sword-guard. Almost harmless.

But even a toy sword could kill.

Paul Robillard put on his mask, and Naomi's friend vanished. All that
was left was Sensei, who would whack her severely if she made a mistake.

It settled the mind wonderfully.

Naomi bowed. Sensei bowed. And then she let the sword-mind flow
into her as Sensei slipped easily into position and began circling her. Part

of her mind watched, waiting for her own opening, but, flying high above the room, the other part considered Ruth.

Things could be worse than they were, of course. Ruth could have fallen for some guy and gotten married as an escape from reality. Only Ruth never dated. Naomi had known her for almost three years and would have been happy to make suitable introductions. For a while she'd thought Ruth and Michael might pair up, but Ruth had made friends with him instead.

But if Naomi were any judge of human nature, Ruth was falling for Melior. And that would not be a good thing at all.

Whack!

"You're not paying attention," Sensei said. Naomi wanted to rub the stinging welt on her hip where the blow had landed, but didn't dare. She raised her sword again, but Sensei did not raise his. After a moment he straightened, and pulled off his mask.

"It must be a very bad problem, to make you so stupid," he observed mildly.

Naomi sighed. She'd deserved that.

"It is a bad problem. It's not mine, you see, and that makes it worse."

"Ah. A friend?"

"Yes." And the only thing Naomi couldn't decide was whether it would be worse for Ruth to fall for Melior—or for her to be the sort of person who never fell in love at all.

"You cannot solve the problems of others. Each person is his own problem, and his own solution."

"Thank you, Master Po. If I want Zen, I can go to the library."

Sensei Paul smiled. "Well, if "no-mind" won't work, why don't we see if we can beat it out of you with a good workout? And after that, you can tell me what's wrong."

"I have this friend," Naomi said. She was wrapped in a terrycloth robe, hair still damp from her shower, sitting on a stool in Paul's tiny New York kitchen while he whisked a bowl of green tea into an opaque froth. "She's getting really attached to this guy, and I think he's going to be a lot of trouble."

"That isn't a very detailed outline of the problem," Paul observed.

"I think details would get in the way of the facts," Naomi said.

"And how much trouble can this guy be for your friend?" Paul said after a moment. He set a bowl of tea in front of her. Naomi sipped and thought about it.

"I suppose he's what you could call the "attractive nuisance" type. No job. No money. In fact, he's sleeping on Michael's couch at the moment. He's got a . . . problem he wants help with. The help could turn out to be pretty costly, in the long run, but he's so gosh-darned cute it's hard to remember that when he's asking for just one little thing. It's like chasing a dream. She could pour her whole life into him and it wouldn't be enough."

And wouldn't Melior's dream be preferable to anyone's reality? Who wouldn't rather live in a world of evil emperors and magic swords, of monsters and heroes? Everything clear-cut and obvious. The perfect escape, with a side order of moral rectitude.

"And how does this come to be your problem? You aren't your brother's keeper, as a great Zen master once said." Paul regarded her steadily, his hazel eyes allowing for no evasions.

Naomi studied her tea a while longer. "I think it's my problem because I'm not objecting to what he's doing," she said at last. "If I see something that I don't like, and I say nothing, then it's the same as endorsing the thing I don't like. Isn't it?"

"That could be a hard philosophical position to live with," Paul said, as if addressing the bonsai in the window.

Naomi sighed. "It could be a hard position to live without."

· 13 ·

The Dream You
Never Found

RUTH FINISHED HER exam, handed it in, and went off to check her mail. She stood in front of her mailbox in the Student Union with its contents in her hand.

A letter from Carol in Idaho. A Macy's bill. Her student discount rate copy of *Library Journal*. Five crisp, bland, and forbidding envelopes—the fruits of her most recent spasm of job searches. Pray that they were all at least invitations to interview. One of them would be her future.

Suddenly the sight of them revolted her utterly; she crumpled them in her hand and stuffed them into her purse, seeking for the bottom, knowing that her defiant gesture was only empty theatrics, that later she would open them and read them out.

But she *did* throw the *Library Journal* in the trash.

Safe, sensible, prudent Ruth. Who never did anything drastic. Who never made a gesture that mattered.

With the crumpled letters still at the bottom of her purse, Ruth walked out of the Student Union.

She was contemplating wildness—or at least another pint of Häagen-Dazs Double Chocolate—and blinking in the unexpected May sunlight when she was hailed from below. Squinting down the steps, she peered until she made out Michael and Philip.

Philip's backpack was crammed to even more overstuffed proportions, and his laptop was balanced (with an accompanying sheaf of papers) upon his hip. Michael stood beside him, towering over Philip as usual and looking faintly uneasy. He was not the one who'd shouted.

"Hey, yourself," Ruth said, descending the steps.

"Looking for another line of work, yet?" Philip asked.

"I'll leave that to you," she said which, if feeble, was at least something. "I understand that there are positions in license-plate technology opening up every day." And where was—

"Seen Jane?" Michael asked, and Ruth's nagging disquiet kindled into six-cylinder life, even though she had a close concept of where Jane must be; she'd gone off to the subway to be Melior's Keeper-For-A-Day at an hour when Ruth was still doing her best to prop her eyes open. They'd been supposed to be back by one or two, but it was only the *subway,* for heaven's sake, and if she wasn't here she had every reason to be late. Ruth looked at her watch. Two-thirty.

Not so very late, but the unfocused fear still cut through her like a knife. "No," she began.

"Lucky you," Philip said, but Michael quelled him with a glance.

"She's probably with Nai," Michael said. But if she was, Ruth worried on, then why had he asked?

"If she didn't get arrested," Philip said.

"That social refinement we leave to you," Ruth said with gracious poison.

"Would you guys cut it out? I want to talk to Melior," Michael said.

Philip produced an eloquent subvocal rumble but said nothing. Michael headed across the street and the other two followed.

"How did the exam go?" Michael asked her when he had them both in motion.

"How does any exam go? And yours? I hate cataloging, I hate cataloging exams; everybody buys LC cataloging nowadays which means that some gnome in the basement of the Library of Congress or probably his computer is making us all file *Outlaws of Sherwood* under Folklore and books on the Miss America pageant under Beauty Aids and what's the *point?*" Ruth finished in a rush.

"Take it easy," Michael said.

"The point is, there is no point." Philip spoke up surprisingly. "No one here gets out alive. And over a sufficient period of time, all choices tend to normalize on a curve of random distribution."

"You mean if you wait long enough, nothing happens?" Ruth said.

"In a hundred years, who will care?" Philip smiled a lopsided and not terribly happy smile.

But I don't even care now, Ruth thought forlornly, and wondered what evil she had committed in the lost hours of that long-gone summer's night that was enough to poison all the rest of her years.

Naomi turned out not to be home either, though in her case a scribbled note proclaimed her out of eggs for the cake and back in ten. Ruth, putting on the kettle for tea, saw the cramped utilitarian student housing as if for the first time; a clarity of sight she was unable to ameliorate. Vinyl couch patched with plastic tape and draped with a length of tattered fabric. Threadbare sage-green carpet. Age-yellowed, obscurely-stained shades; each object a blatant letter of an alphabet in an unfamiliar tongue. Shabby, threadbare, rock-bottom, bone-weary. . . .

Ruth stared blindly at the spotted paint behind the stove and realized, with horrified clarity, that she was going to cry. Over the *couch,* for God's sake? She must be losing her *mind.* . . .

And there was no one here but Michael and Philip.

Snuffling only a little, Ruth lit the stove, and in the soft bloom of blue gas flame set the kettle on the stove and turned around to the sink. She splashed water on her face, but the sense of despairing dread still hung over her, like foreshadowing in a bad novel.

Heavens. How perfectly Celtic, Ruth thought mockingly. *The next thing I'll do is sit down and howl at the moon.*

But that wouldn't be sensible, some ghostly interior counterpoint inserted. Ruth sighed sadly over her inability to carry off a really good dramatic interior monologue and turned away from the sink.

Michael was standing in the doorway. Things always tended to look too small around Michael; he was large enough to make even Ruth— were she so inclined—feel small and kittenish, which was no mean feat when you stood five foot eight in your stocking feet.

"Feel better?" Michael asked.

"No," said Ruth honestly. She waved the unspoken words—hers and his—away. "I don't know. Melior. What if—"

"What if there isn't a sword?" Michael finished. "Or what if we just don't find it? What if he's stuck here forever? What if he dies?"

Ruth stared, struck reasonably speechless.

"Why is it you women always think that guys don't ever talk about anything but sex and fast cars?" Michael smiled, to take the edge off it. It did, even if only a little. "He's been sleeping on my couch for—what?"

"Three days," Ruth supplied automatically. "Friday, Saturday, and Sunday."

"And if he stays here, he's dead. He said he told you."

"He did."

Michael shrugged, uncomfortable.

"What is it, Michael-mine, that you found out between breakfast and lunch and aren't telling?" Ruth, goaded, pounced.

Michael met her gaze squarely. Michael always looked everyone in the eye, no matter what he had to say.

"The people who're supposed to be being killed, aren't being killed," he said simply.

It took Ruth a moment to shift mental gears from interior monologues to homicide and figure this one out.

"Which means his *grendel* doesn't exist," she said flatly.

"If," said Michael, leaning back against the wall and blowing out a breath of pure exasperation, "*if* his *grendel* is a magical creature, and *if* this world is the World of Iron his mythology talks about, and *if* elf-magic works as badly here as Mel seems to think it does, then he might not be right about his sword working better than that."

Ruth took a moment to puzzle all that out.

"No *grendel*, no way to find the sword."

"The real question is," Philip said, pushing his way past Michael to enter the kitchen and the conversation, "how *long* are we going to look for it before we give up?"

Philip's hair was pulled back into the thin queue that always reminded Ruth of a white rat's tail. His steel-rimmed bifocals made his eyes alternately distant and flat featureless coin-mirrors in his narrow mustelid face. He stood with shoulders hunched and both hands jammed into the pockets of his red windbreaker and seemed to be addressing his remarks to the refrigerator. But for once he wasn't trying to score verbally off anybody.

"How long?" Philip repeated. "He's sleeping on your couch" —to Michael— "and you've spun major plastic on him" —to Ruth— "and ya-ta-da ya-ta-da and ill-met by moonlight proud Titania—"

Ruth stared in shock. She hadn't known Philip ever read anything but software manuals.

"But the bottom line is: how long?"

Silence.

"After a certain point, finding the sword is like finding the kidnap victim: impossible. At least with what we've got to work with," Michael observed.

"Six hundred bucks and a leather jacket," Philip footnoted. "So the question is, 'can he type?' "

"What?" Had Philip been out in the sun too long? (In *May?*) Was he trying a new designer drug? (He didn't even drink *coffee*.) Was he all there? (But in his own sweet sociopathic way, Philip LeStrange was always all there.)

Philip turned away and hunched his shoulders even higher, as if denying the existence of his ears. "After the ball is over, Cinderella. And we pack it in. You and Michael are graduating this year, y'know. After that."

"I don't think," Michael said slowly, "that he's going to give up."

Philip shrugged angrily and stalked back to the living room. After a moment Ruth heard the tap-tap-tap of his keyboard.

But the obvious last line remained, as clearly as if he'd said it.

So when are YOU giving up, Ruth?

It was a morose and disaffected party which greeted Naomi's return.

A brown Rockingham pot of infused but undrunk tea sat in the middle of the living room table. Michael was sprawled on the couch. Philip was sprawled on the floor. Ruth was curled, feet up, in a chair almost too small for the gesture, paging through an old exhibition catalog and pretending neither of the others was there.

Naomi put down one of the sacks and shifted the other one to her hip.

"Who died?" she asked. "Or is that remark not in the best of taste?"

"No one died," said Michael, "and *that* was the curious incident."

"I see," said Naomi. "Do I take it, then, that the customary trappings of the wake are in order?" She lifted the lid off the teapot and pulled out the tea ball. The liquid running from it was almost black.

"I think it's done," she commented, heading for the kitchen. She returned a moment later with four mugs strung on her fingers like useful rings and the remaining necessities for tea gripped precariously among remaining fingers. She extracted the tea ball and poured tea.

"We were trying to think of what kind of job Melior could get," Ruth volunteered, at last, into the silence.

"Male model?" Naomi suggested at last, which at least drew a snicker from Philip. "But seriously, folks—is Jane all right?"

Ruth kept herself from snarling with an effort, and as a result Naomi's question stood unanswered when the buzzer rang.

Michael uncoiled from the couch with surprising violence and lunged for the buzzer. "Yes?" he barked, and the hash of street noise he got back seemed to satisfy him, because he hit the unlock button and held it down for a long minute.

"They're back," he announced, looking at Naomi's startled expression.

"You kids lead such interesting lives," she commented, and went on into the kitchen with the bag.

It was Michael who held the door open, allowing the sounds of sneakers on stair treads to fill the apartment. Ruth stared at her hands, as if she were being paid good money not to look. And eventually they got there.

Jane came through the door first, and for a moment Ruth didn't recognize her. The white turtleneck with the blue flowers, the matching blue cardigan, the pale blue corduroy slacks which were the closest Jane ever got to jeans were streaked and barred with black grime. The knees of her pants were literally black, with a polished-cotton sheen of ground-in dirt. There were even smudges on her face, painting on a faint *faux* glamorie of *trompe l'oeil* cheekbones.

"What the *hell* happened to you?" Ruth demanded in a voice she hardly recognized as hers.

Melior entered behind Jane. The black leather jacket, the artistically-distressed jeans, showed the dirt far less than Jane's once painfully-neat ensemble, but when you looked for it, it was there. Ruth got up. Jane ducked past Michael and fled to the bathroom.

Melior ran a hand through his hair. "We have been in the subterranean ways, Ruth. And as I foretold you, the *grendel* is there. I have found proof." He set down the bag he'd been carrying; Ruth saw a familiar fast-food logo.

Michael shut the door behind him. "And did you, ah, bring this "proof" with you?"

Melior regarded him with schooled blandness, and once again Ruth felt that ghostly echo of clashing wills between the two men.

"And how does one bring the scent from the earth, or the track from the mud? Yet they are no less real for that. The *grendel* casts off its human seeming, and becomes more powerful with each passing hour." Melior advanced into the room, wrapping the leather jacket around himself as if he were cold. "And we are here."

"Everybody's gotta be someplace," Philip commented. He sat up and leaned back against the couch.

"And I and thou are here," Melior said. "And yet I am forced to wonder, Master Philip, why should this be so?"

"Come again?" Naomi said from the kitchen doorway.

Melior turned toward her and favored her with a smile of dazzling charm. "I would not forgo your company easily, Mistress Naomi, nor yet the table you set. But I have learned, as you wished me to, that this world is wide. And so I wonder: when I fell prey to the traps which bespelled the Sword of Maiden's Tears, why should my place in it be here, and not some other place?"

"Well," said Naomi slowly, "there's no place like this place anywhere around the place, so this must be the place."

"Why?" said Melior.

"Why not?" said Philip to his shoes.

"Because things do not happen save for reasons," Melior said patiently.

Naomi laughed. "Brother, are *you* a long way from home."

"Yes," said Melior seriously, and smiled. He walked across the room to Ruth, and looked down at her. "But as you see, I have gone and come back again, unimpeded by the city guard."

"On Earth we call them policemen," said Philip.

Jane came out of the bathroom, damp and hostile. Her face was scrubbed pink and her cotton cardigan buttoned up demurely over the worst of the grime. She glanced at Melior; Ruth saw her do it and felt a flash of reasonless jealousy. Melior's hand closed reassuringly over Ruth's shoulder and squeezed warmly.

"So exactly where in the subway were you?" Ruth asked.

Again Melior and Jane exchanged glances. "Somewhere in Brooklyn," Jane said finally.

"And that's where the *grendel* is?" Michael said, working very hard to keep his voice neutral. From the kitchen there was a momentary whine of an electric mixer and a clatter of pans.

"No," said Melior patiently. "That is where the *grendel* was. But, so I am told, the tunnels are all linked, and it will not venture forth into the light willingly again."

"So it's in the subway?" Michael repeated again, as if it were very important that this question be answered. There was a rattle and bang of the oven door, and Naomi came back into the living room.

"Forty minutes," she said cryptically. She sat down on the arm of a chair and swept the room with a glance, very much as if they were all books and she were about to catalog them. "So. Why don't we all tell each other what kind of a day we all had?"

There was a moment's silence. Ruth felt again that strong sense of *peril;* as if the words spoken here would serve as choices; would set paths that all of them here would have to follow.

She was almost spooked enough to warn the others; to suggest it, making it a joke, when Philip spoke.

"Well, Michael and me hacked into the Coroner's Office and found out that whatever else this *grendel*'s doing, it isn't leaving a bunch of bodies lying around. Guess it isn't very hungry, huh?" Philip shoved his glasses back up on the bridge of his nose.

Ruth felt Melior go very still behind her.

"This is Monday afternoon," Jane said, getting all of her facts straight. "We heard about the last kill Sunday night, but it had to have been killed Saturday night at the latest, because it was found Sunday afternoon. But this *grendel*'s supposed to be hungry," she added, looking half-challengingly toward Melior.

"It starves from what it battens upon," Melior agreed. "The hunger that was a man's in life for glory or fame is transmuted by the curse into unslakable appetite."

"Betcha can't eat just one," Philip muttered.

"So if there is a *grendel,* as you believe," Michael said, "there should be more victims."

"Should there?" said Melior. He stepped away from Ruth now, and all five of them watched him. "How do you know there are not?"

"We didn't find any," Michael said. He sounded as if he'd looked personally, but Ruth knew he meant that it hadn't turned up in Philip's, um, *hacking.*

Philip's hacking. Was Michael really taking Philip's word over Melior's?

Was she willing to take Melior's word over Philip's?

When was she going to "call it quits"?

Was she going to?

"With your machines," said Melior, as if it were a personal insult. "The machines see nothing, so you say there *is* nothing. But these machines know only what men have told them."

"In the nonexclusive sense of the word 'men,' " Naomi added.

"So you're telling us there's something we've missed," Michael said, carefully neutral.

"I am saying I beg your trust, Friend Michael. For a time—a *short* time—more. You say there is no magic—" Melior raised his voice and spread his arms. The sweeping gesture was meant for a cape but somehow did not look silly when performed in a leather jacket. *"I* say there is. And I say that the creature I seek is there. In the subterranean. It hardly matters if you believe, you know. You are not worldlings for me to beguile with tales of sorcery, nobility, and gold. I ask you now for one simple thing—"

"This is something more substantial than buying a ticket, isn't it?" Naomi said, cutting through the spell of Melior's words.

"Yes," said Melior. "I do not need the cars. I need to get into the tunnels. On foot. I need your aid for that."

Jane shifted where she sat, but only Ruth noticed. She thought Melior might have tried to go down into the tunnels today, but probably Jane had stopped him.

"Into the tunnels," said Naomi. "Just jump over the side of the platform. Sounds easy."

"And get creamed by an oncoming train," said Philip.

"I would need provisions. Lights. And weapons; a good club; a sword or a boar-spear."

Philip made a noise. "In the first place you can't do it. In the second place, they'll arrest you. And in the third place, there isn't anything down there to chase. Period."

Now it was out and all of them had to face it. Not disbelief in Melior-as-he-was; only disbelief in his goal.

"If there is nothing there, then no harm can come, can it?" Melior said.

"We could be arrested," said sensible Ruth. Sensible *traitorous* Ruth. "We could get killed—by the third rail, by rats, by passing muggers. And if we got caught down there they'd fine us to death. I mean—"

"Bye-bye Columbia," Michael finished.

"You got a better idea?" said Jane, surprisingly defensive of Melior.

"*Not* getting creamed by an oncoming train leaps instantly to mind," Philip said helpfully.

"I do not propose that you do," Melior said. "This is not your battle. Only provision me, and I shall go alone."

"That'd look great on the six o'clock news. '*Dead Elf Found In Subway, Pictures At Eleven.*'"

"If you can't say something helpful, Philip, would you please go home?" Jane asked long-sufferingly.

"I know that you do not believe," said Melior, "and this makes no difference—not to me, and certainly not to the creature I hunt. And I must hunt it—with your help or alone."

Melior looked beseechingly toward Naomi. She ran a hand through her short black hair. "With us or without us," she said. "But, Melior, you just don't understand—"

"I think you should let him do what he wants, even if it is stupid," Jane said flatly.

"It isn't that it's stupid," Ruth began.

"Although it is," Philip said.

"But there's the little matter of unlawful trespass, breaking and entering, little things like that. It's illegal," Michael said, a hint of truculence in his voice.

"Illegal?" Philip said. "I sure hope so." He laughed, then frowned. "Get down on the tracks. There's got to be ways. The subway guys do it all the time."

"The 'subway guys' are trained to do it," Naomi said. "They know all the nooks and crannies of the system. And the train schedules. And everything."

"The trains—and the schedules—are on computer," Philip said sweetly.

"No," said Naomi flatly. "Not without proof—*real* proof."

Everyone looked at her. "This is not a game. This is not 'for-fun.' And it sure isn't the steam tunnels at Michigan State University," Naomi said. Her face was set, determined, and her voice vibrated with conviction as she spoke. "Everything Ruth's said about the third rail and the trains and everything *is true*. And it isn't just a matter of Melior not getting hurt—what if he caused a train wreck? Hundreds of people killed or injured—and our fault?"

"You'd have to do it at night," Philip said. "There aren't as many trains then."

Ruth had always suspected Naomi of being soft on Philip, for some unbelievable reason, but the look she riveted him with now was filled with such contempt that even Philip noticed. He ducked his head quickly, ears red, and didn't say anything else.

"I'm sorry, Melior," Naomi said. "We can't just go off and play in the subway on your word that there's something down there. This is real life, and this is dangerous. There isn't enough proof. I'm sorry."

That was that, and they all knew it. Even Melior didn't bother to argue. "I thank you, then, for all the patience you have shown me, Mistress Naomi. In my own place, I do not think that such kindness would have been shown to strangers." He inclined his head, acknowledging his defeat.

And then he turned and walked out the door.

"Hey!" In the moment Ruth realized he was really gone she lunged up out of her chair and flung—she'd never realized the description could be correct before—herself out the door. She thought someone tried to stop her, but if that was so, they didn't try as hard to keep her as she did to go.

Melior was waiting for her just outside the street door—or, if not waiting, then at least not leaving very fast.

"Wait," Ruth gasped, clutching at the edge of the door for support.

"Isn't it amusing, in a quiet way, that a Prince of the House of the Silver Silences, whose blood is filled with silver and starlight, who has commanded men in the field, and broken the Successor Lords on the Field of Glass, cannot entreat a moment's fealty from humans? *Humans,* Ruth. Can you credit it?"

"I'm human," Ruth said.

"Then perhaps you can explain it to me." He took her arm and drew her onto the sidewalk. He put an arm around her shoulders, and she leaned into him. The late-afternoon sun was just warm enough, and no one looked at either of them as they walked south on Riverside Drive, with the glassy swell of the Hudson beside them.

"I'm right," Melior said softly after a while.

"So what?" said Ruth mournfully. "It doesn't matter. It's a big thing to ask, you know. It's dangerous down there."

"I asked no one to accompany me," Melior reminded her.

"That wouldn't stop them," Ruth said darkly. "But it's—I know it's important to you, Melior, but it—It's just another *chanson geste* to you, and for us it's real. It's our *lives.*"

"And when I am dead, and you are *grendel*-ridden; when the House of the Silver Silences is cast into the Outer Darkness forever and the balance of power in the Morning Lands slides inevitably toward Night, then, *then* you will say that you had no inkling of its import." His voice was quietly bitter.

"That isn't fair."

"I'm not in a mind to be fair."

"You want us to throw over everything—on your word alone—for something that probably isn't even there! *What's in it for us?*"

"Ah." They walked on for a few moments in silence, past skateboarders and a hot-dog stand, past frisbee-throwing kids and joggers. "But what if it is there?" Melior said.

Once again it was Ruth's turn to be silent. Because much as she wanted to believe in the *grendel,* even with Melior's technicolor presence to bolster her faith, she couldn't. Not when it was so much more likely to be the forlorn delusion of a dying exile. Not when cynical twentieth century probability said that was the way to bet—against monsters and heroes, bright promises and valorous deeds.

"If it is," Ruth said, coward compromise in her voice, "there'll be proof, won't there? More killings? Michael said there weren't any, and. . . ."

"He said the machines had recorded none, not that there were none. This city of yours is vast beyond imagining, and rich beyond the dreams of madmen, but it holds its poor who sleep in doorways. I have seen them. And I think, were I such a poor man and did I have the coin, I would choose to sleep in the subterranean where the rain and wind come not. If such a man dies, who mourns him? Tell me that, Ruth."

"Well, maybe," Ruth said irritably. "But it isn't *proof,* Melior. It's just another fairy tale."

"And you, Ruth? Will you do for love what they will not do for reason?" Melior stopped and pulled her gently around to face him.

Conflicting emotions spun through her panic-stricken brain, but topmost of all was the sick certainty that there was no *grendel,* and that if Melior went down into the tunnels the inevitable They would catch him and trap him and put him in a cage, and then even frustrated hope would be dead.

"Love?" said Ruth, through a choking throat. "Who said anything about love?"

Melior stared at her for a long moment, his pupils dark vertical flicks against the light of the setting sun.

"I did. But it seems that I misspoke myself."

He let her go and turned away, and left her with a long loping stride that she could not have matched, even if she'd cared to. She sat on a bench, and eventually the unwelcome and low-comic certainty came to her that she was going to have to go back home and tell them all *something,* and that undoubtedly by then there wouldn't be any chocolate cake left, either.

• 14 •

Darkness at Noon

THE LAND HE passed through had neither sun nor moon. Its voice was the roaring of the distant ocean, and the water through which he walked was as warm and fecund as blood. Kevin Shelby had come into his kingdom at last.

Only he didn't know it—or to be perfectly precise, the one who possessed all these fastnesses did not precisely remember that once he had been a man who dreamed of glory. The One who was now would have thought Kevin Shelby's ambitions laughable if it had been confronted with them. The One who was now wanted only two things: food and the continued safety of The Object.

It was always hungry. There was still plentiful food available here in its realm, but with the focused facility of extreme paranoia The One knew that this soft sweet comfortable food was—still and also—a source of danger to it. A time would come when to hunt would be to imperil the safety of The Object, and The One did not want that. It was making arrangements against that day. Provident arrangements.

And there was one other source of danger. An Other, unlike either The One or The Object, an Other who wanted The Object for himself.

But The One was making arrangements for that, too.

Determined to pretend that nothing had happened, Ruth went back up the hill, away from Melior, toward Broadway and the Columbia campus. There she spent most of the afternoon, until twilight and a rumbling stomach made her admit that what she was really doing was trying to avoid her friends.

And feeling as if she wanted to avoid them wasn't *fair,* dammit, it wasn't *Ruth* who'd done anything to blush for. It was Melior who'd been so unreasonable; in fact, all of this was All Melior's Fault.

She wished she believed that.

She wished she knew what to believe.

But Melior had asked them—all five of them, Ruth and Michael, Naomi and Jane and Philip—for something they couldn't give him. It was all of their futures on the line here, and this wasn't some convenient fairy tale where the price of their mistakes would be death. No, it was worse than that: any mistakes any of them made would be mistakes they'd have to live with, all down the gray cheerless years of quiet desperation that were shaped by those mistakes.

You're a bundle of cheer tonight, Ruth told herself.

But it was true. It was a lot easier to gamble when the stakes were Success or Death. Half a century of being an impoverished failure was a little harder to swallow cheerfully.

She didn't believe in the *grendel.* And she didn't believe Melior would ever stop looking for it. And sooner or later he was going to run splat into the power structure and they'd take him and lock him up and—

Her hands were shaking. And her mind was, as it always did when she was upset, trying to push into the gray space that lay between eighteen and twenty-six, trying to find reality in what was actually and always would be a long gray vast shapeless expanse of nothing.

And that was the real joke, if Melior only knew it. She had so little to lose that she would gladly have gone into the subway with Melior bearing only an arc lamp and a machine gun—if she'd been able to believe.

In anything. Anything at all.

Ruth swallowed hard and wondered what he was doing and where he'd gone. *Melior* believed; good God, he had enough belief for any three normal people; he'd believe in something at the drop of a hat; just watch him and you could get yourself convinced of anything from the Doctrine of Signatures to the Ninety-Five Theses of Luther to the importance of flossing after meals.

Melior had passion. *Passion.* And wasn't that what everyone thought was such a hands-down terrific lifestyle accessory? A sensibility that went for the gusto like a starved pit bull? Mind, it might not know enough to come in out of the rain, but. . . .

If it had hurt less, she might have cried.

Some time later she looked up, conscious that someone was watching her. Jane was standing about three feet away, wearing a pink denim jumper (she must have changed her clothes) and balancing a load of books on her hip.

"I thought you were probably here," Jane said, sitting down.

"Welcome to previews of my post-collegiate depression," Ruth said mockingly.

"There wasn't anything there," Jane said simply.

"In the subway?" Ruth guessed.

Jane nodded, and sighed. "And he's going to go look for it anyway." Their glances locked, in wry complicity over the utter predictability of none-too-bright Tyrant Man.

Ruth shrugged, weary to the bone. So much for reaching out to grasp at magic. All it left you with was a handful of ashes.

"So we've got to stop him," Jane said stubbornly.

"What do you suggest, a straitjacket?" Ruth shot back.

"The New York Subway System has twelve hundred and fifty-seven miles of track and over ten thousand units of rolling stock. And somewhere in there he thinks there's a *grendel* and a magic sword. The *grendel* guards the sword. The sword is the only thing that can slay the *grendel*," Jane said pedantically.

"Right so far," Ruth said.

Jane leaned both elbows on the table, her lank hair swinging forward over her cheeks.

"So the only thing the *grendel* (if it really did exist) has to do to not get killed is *hide* the sword, right?"

Ruth stared at Jane and tried to find some flaw in her reasoning. Unfortunately it was seamlessly logical, as Jane's reasoning always was. Ruth wondered if the (probably nonexistent) *grendel* was as smart as Jane Greyson.

"Right," she said hesitantly.

"And even if it's too stupid to think of something like that, strategy requires that you act as if it *will* think of it, in case you get caught flat-footed. So whether the *grendel* thinks of hiding the sword or not, Melior has to."

"And?" Ruth prompted.

"So Melior," said Jane with a sour expression, "has to make an *enormous pounce*. He can't give the *grendel* time to know he's hunting it, because that would give it time to hide the sword. He has to move fast."

Light dawned. "So he has to know exactly where he's going," said Ruth. "Right?"

Jane nodded. "And if he has a chance of getting accurate tactical intelligence, he won't move without it," she finished matter-of-factly.

If Melior had enough information to know where the *grendel* was, wouldn't that mean that there'd be enough information to constitute *proof* of its reality?

"But he isn't going to believe we'll do it! Not after—"

"He'll believe Philip will do it. Because Philip will do anything for money. And you've still got Melior's money," Jane said.

Ruth made a guilty grab at her handbag, but Jane was right: there it was, a little over thirty-six hundred dollars, all that was left after the shopping expedition at Macy's and the run-in with the Transit Police.

"I couldn't. . . ." Ruth began.

He doesn't care what you do with it. And I bet you can't get Philip to do it for free. And if you did, it wouldn't give you—" there was a pause while Jane hunted for *le mot juste,* "—plausible deniability."

Ruth made a face. Jane was undoubtedly right about that. Only Naomi—and sometimes Michael—could induce the spirit of cooperation to inhabit the breast of Philip Leslie LeStrange.

But it could work. It might work. Bribe Philip, and have him go to Melior, and—

"So it's a deal?" Jane prompted.

"Sure," said Ruth, recklessly promising. "But where are we going to find Philip?"

None of them had much interest in hanging around after Ruth and Melior had left, even with the promise of one of Naomi's cakes in the offing. Jane had left almost immediately, and Philip had lingered only long enough to repack his laptop and rucksack. He'd left the printouts behind, the printouts that proved that the killer that Melior said was loose, could not be loose.

So not very long after Philip left, Michael left, too.

Monday was one of his nights at Lundgren's Gym; he walked downtown a dozen blocks and spent a couple of hours that afternoon working out with the free weights. A healthy mind in a tired body.

But at last it was ten o'clock, the last of the customers gone and the last of the weights racked and machines reset and towels bagged and vacuum run and all the hundred and one little chores by which Michael paid for his gym time accomplished, and the only thing left to do was go home.

And hope he didn't dream.

"I could be bounded in a nutshell, and count myself a king of infinite space, were it not that I have bad dreams. . . ."

So he went home to his adequate apartment and opened the window for night air as fresh as New York's ever got, and he popped a beer and was flipping channels looking for something amusing on the public access channels when the door opened and Melior came in.

He wasn't wearing that stupid movie-star hat he and Ruth had been so pleased with, and the mirrorshade aviators dangled from one of the pockets of the S&M Biker Slut jacket. His hair stood out around his head like a movieland special effect, and he looked as if he and the clothes were only coincidentally in the same place.

"May I come in?" Melior said, although he was already in and the door shut.

Michael sat up and put both feet on the floor. He had four inches and at least thirty pounds on the elf-guy and ought not to feel this sense of *threat* every time he faced Melior. But most guys would back down from somebody Michael's size, or do their best to let him know they didn't have to. Melior just seemed to take it for granted that if there was a fight, he'd win it.

Except there'd been a fight today. And Melior had lost it. Badly.

"You're already in," Michael pointed out. "Two questions: Are there any hard feelings about today? And where's Ruth?"

"Mistress Ruth left me shortly after I left you. And as for your refusal of aid. . . ." Melior sighed and shook his head. "I do not understand, but I must accept it. You have sheltered, fed, and clothed me, even if only for Ruth's sake and the amusement of the thing. That alone is more generosity than I could rightfully lay claim to in these lands."

"Uh-huh." There were any number of half-insults in Melior's speech, if Michael wanted to take him up on them. Michael didn't. "So, what are you going to do now?"

Melior regarded him with an exasperation that was very near the end of its patience. "I am going to take such of my possessions as I require, and bid you farewell, and go to hunt the *grendel,* which lairs in the *subterranean way* and has stolen the Sword of Maiden's Tears. If, upon discovering it, I took the Sword and slew it, then I would take the Sword and go to my own place, and pray I was in time. That is what I am going to do now, Michael Peacock."

"And, ah, what if it isn't there?" Michael said, very carefully, ignoring the fact that Melior seemed to have lost his grasp on the concept of present tense.

"It *is* there," Melior said flatly.

"Look," Michael said, getting up. "I didn't want to say this before, in front of the others, but whether it's down there or not really isn't the issue. What matters is that you can't just play Peter Pan in the subway tunnels without getting caught. If you go down there, they're going to catch you and lock you up somewhere the sun don't shine, if you take my meaning, and that isn't going to do you a whole lot of good."

"And doing nothing at all is?" Melior demanded. "Michael, try to understand. I swore an oath upon my father's head that I would find the Sword and bring it back. I *swore.*"

"I swore an oath once," Michael said. Melior's attention sharpened, focused on Michael as if the words Michael was about to say were the words Melior had been waiting for since the moment they'd met.

And because of that, Michael swallowed hard, forcing all the words that might have been back into silence. "I broke it. End of story."

"No. Not the end, Friend Michael. And this oath I have sworn I will die in attempting. *I want to go home, Michael.*" The words were uttered in a tone very like a wail, and Melior threw himself into the chair that stood beside the door. "When Baligant is vested, and the Sword is not among the Treasures, Line Rohannan of the House of the Silver Silences will be cast out, wolfshead. Doomed, and it will be my fault, who could not see the trap or, having sprung it, retain possession of that which it was death to relinquish."

"If you go down into those tunnels, you are going to hit the wall, Mel, and then it isn't going to be a case of won't. There won't be anything in God's Creation we *can* do for you." *And you're going to break Ruth's heart either way, my friend, and there's nothing to do about that but watch.*

"There is nothing else I *can* do now," Melior said bitterly. "I cannot compel your aid, and it is little consolation to me to know that the *grendel* will fatten itself upon the bones of my failure, growing in power until all this land is in despair, and no hero will come from the Morning Lands to succor you."

"That's a chance we're going to have to take." Thus spoke Michael Peacock, child of his times, growing up with A-Bomb drills in school and calluses on his neglected soul from living beneath the shadow of Armageddon.

"And you could have stopped it," Melior said. "That knowledge you will carry with you into the next life: you could have stopped it."

Suddenly something occurred to Michael. "Why are we talking about this as if it's already happened?"

Melior stood up. "Because I will not kill the *grendel.* This much I know for truth," Melior said, and walked into the kitchen.

Michael gave the remark about three beats' worth of thought and followed him. Melior was hanging over the open refrigerator, gazing into its electric depths. He'd had several rude things to say about New York America Earth beer when Michael had introduced him to the stuff, and passed it by now in favor of the two-liter bottle of unfiltered apple juice.

"You aren't going to kill the *grendel,*" Michael said uninflectedly.

Melior removed the cap from the bottle with the innocent pride of a recently-learned skill and raised the bottle to his lips. "I am not going to kill the *grendel*," he agreed, and drank.

A powerful sensation of being the straight man in an old Abbot & Costello routine took strong possession of Michael. "Maybe you could explain why it was you decided not to share this little factoid with us this afternoon?"

"You already do not believe in the *grendel* when I have told you of it," Melior pointed out reasonably enough for an elf who was a few sandwiches shy of a picnic in the first place. He put the cap back on the apple juice. "Why should you give any more credence to any other facts I might relate?"

"In the first place they are *not* facts and in the second place would you mind explaining this new theory of yours?" He was actually going to lose his temper, Michael realized with a distant amazement. Again.

Melior replaced the apple juice and closed the refrigerator door. He waved his hand; the gesture of an elf-prince who is at a loss for words.

"It is not a 'new theory,' Michael. It is a fact; an ability of my kind. I was not certain at first that it would work in this world, even though I had found my heart twin here, but now I know that it does. The future is not fixed," Melior went on, launching well and truly into his explanation, "it spreads like the fingers of a hand, of a hundred hands, each finger growing from all the choices that precede it. And when there are so many branchings—when any thing is as possible as any other—our kind is as blind as any human to what Will Be.

"But there are times when the choices do not matter, when the branchings of the future are few, and the road we must take is inevitable. Then the Sons of the Morning can see farther into What Will Be than those of mortal blood. The branches of my future are narrow and few. And I do not see the *grendel's* death upon them."

Michael heard this speech out in a respectful silence, and then gave the silence a little more elbow-room while he thought about it.

"You aren't going to kill it."

"True."

"But you're going to go out and try to kill it anyway."

"Yes."

"That is the stupidest thing I've ever heard," Michael announced.

"Then you haven't heard much, Friend Michael," Melior told him.

A few hours earlier, but in much the same area, Ruth and Jane, soldiers of the same side, plotted their next move.

"First we've got to *find* him," Ruth said helplessly. She could not imagine where to begin. Michael might know, but Ruth did not feel like seeing Michael just now. Where *would* you go to hang out, if you were as strange as Philip LeStrange?

"Come on," said Jane, no indecision at all in her voice. She got up and strode off. Ruth shrugged and followed.

They drew cover first at Hacker Heaven and came up empty; Monday night and the first week in May, and the only people in the computer center were harried students engaged in legitimate pursuits.

"Maybe he's at Michael's," Ruth said reluctantly, but a quick resort to the pay phone in the hall outside the computer lab revealed that *no one* was at Michael's, or if they were, they weren't answering the phone.

Jane hung up the phone and turned to Ruth. "Maybe he's at home."

For a moment Ruth thought Jane meant her dorm room, but that wasn't possible. Then she realized Jane had to mean *Philip's* home, and the dazzling possibility that Philip actually had an apartment somewhere struck her speechless. What sort of an apartment would Philip LeStrange have—and how did Jane know where it was, anyway, when none of the rest of them did?

Ruth said something to that effect.

"It's on his ID," Jane explained simply, which left only the question (better unasked) of what Jane had been doing with Philip's wallet.

In an orderly universe (or even at a college in the Midwest) Philip would have been in on-campus housing, subject to the laws of the Dean and the watchful scrutiny of his more stable peers. But Columbia was a campus in a city where space was at a premium and the students were encouraged to find any other place to live than the campus.

"Here?" said Ruth doubtfully. They were up above 120th Street, east of Columbia, and Ruth felt as if she were wearing a large sign with the words "Mugger Bait" blazoned on it. The street was dark, and dirty even by New York standards, and the doorway was one of those deep cubby-holes in the shadows of which anything might be hiding.

Jane didn't even hesitate. Up the steps, yank the handle (the outer and supposedly-locking door's lock was permanently sprung), and into the New York Urban Airlock. There was a round hole in the doorframe of the inner door where the electric lock was supposed to be, but at least the lobby lights worked.

Nobody had attended to basic daintiness in the lobby for quite some time.

"Sixth floor," said Jane.

The journey was accompanied by the distinctive grace notes peculiar to an unloved New York apartment building: rotting garbage, urine, antique grease, cooking spices, disinfectant, multilingual quarreling, dogs barking, the insistent bass thump of an overcranked canned music source.

Poverty. Or as it was called these days, low-income housing. The economies of depleted resources. Ruth thought of coming home every night to a place like this and recoiled inwardly. But some people had no choice.

And for some it was only a way station.

"Here we are," said Jane. If she disliked this place as much as Ruth did, she didn't show it. Her face behind the heavy horn-rims was as stolid as a plaster saint's. She raised her hand, and banged on the door with a vigor that made Ruth jump.

The noises within that had been making their feeble reply to the backbeat ceased. Jane thumped again.

The door was finally opened—on the chain—by a black-haired boy with a haircut that couldn't make up its mind whether it was punk or unkempt. He had on a black-washed-to-gray T-shirt that seemed to be a homemade advertisement for necrophilia. He looked at Jane, then past her to Ruth, and his eyes widened in disbelief.

"Uh, you got the wrong address," he said finally, which made Ruth grin inwardly.

"Is Philip here?" she said, knowing that Jane would simply argue the question of was-this-or-was-this-not the right address for Jane's purposes.

"Uh," said the boy again. He slammed the door.

"Phil!" they heard him yell, "It's somebody's mother!"

"I resent that remark," Ruth muttered. If she were a character in a movie she'd spin around now and kick the door open. The chain would break, and—

The small peephole in the center of the door went dark as someone looked through it, then there was a rattle as the chain was taken off. Philip opened the door. He was, Ruth was relieved to see, not in the state of undress that the inhabitants of all-male housing usually were. Philip looked, as usual, clean, neat, composed, and nonnecrophilic.

"What do you guys want?" he asked.

"Ruth had an idea," Jane said.

"Would it be okay if I had this idea inside?" Ruth asked.

"Um," Philip seemed nonplussed by this suggestion. "Just a minute." The door closed again.

"I could have gone home," Ruth remarked to the ambient air. "I could have stared at my *own* front door in perfect comfort and safety."

"They're probably all naked," Jane said grimly.

Which was apparently pretty much the case, judging by the hurried retreats and slamming doors that followed once Philip came back and opened the door again. By then Ruth was interested enough in getting out of the hallway that her standards were appreciably lower than usual.

Which was just as well. This was a Never-Never Land without Wendy. *Sleep all day, party all night* . . . Ruth thought grimly, as Philip relocked a series of chains and deadbolts behind them. The (empty) living room seemed to be decorated in Early Cardboard Box. There was a mattress and a pile of drawers *sans* chest-of- over beneath the windows, which were obscured only by ancient roller blinds, some with posters taped to them. The floor was covered with a medley of newspapers, books, album covers, and rug scraps. Linoleum showed through in places.

The walls were their original color of utilitarian gray, except where someone had made the attempt to redecorate, apparently with a can of glitter-purple lacquer. There were the remains of a couch, without cushions, up against one wall, buttressed by two more stacks of boxes and an array of cognitively-dissonant high-end stereo equipment perched on a set of college-traditional books-and-bricks shelving.

Male student housing, as per the norm.

"What do you want?" asked Philip. He seemed nervous, and Ruth could imagine why. Personally, she expected troglodytes to come lurching out from behind the bundled heights of paper.

"It's about *him,"* Jane said.

"Oh." There was a pause, while Philip reluctantly made the ultimate concession. "Come on."

When this had been a prestigious address, this had been a luxury apartment; left over from that halcyon era was the room that you got to by going through the kitchen and pantry: the maid's room, where once upon a time before color TV, some (Irish) cook or maid had wiled away her leisure hours.

There was a combination lock on the door. Philip worked it quickly, without explanation or apology, and opened the door.

The long-ago maid had made do with a room about six feet by eight—and it had probably been spacious in those days, Ruth thought, or at least seemed that way. She squeezed in beside Jane to the eighteen-inch walkway which was all the free space she could find. Philip slid in beside her and shut the door.

The ululation-and-static of a police band scanner broke the silence. Ruth looked upward at piles of junk on racks of gray steel industrial shelving, and located the source, but barely.

Some of the junk was lit and humming, and some of it wasn't, and Ruth was certain on very little evidence that Philip had every form of semi-licit listening device known to Man jammed in here. There was another scanner, tuned to the car-phone frequency, and a CB that seemed to be putting out mostly static.

By then Jane had edged around the first redoubt of technology and into an open space fully three feet square. It contained half a door balanced on top of two buckling file cabinets and supported a computer whose monitor was scrolling lit lines of gibberish. In front of this *mesalliance* was what seemed to be the room's only chair. Ruth sidled into the open space and turned around. Jane moved down next to a tidy bookcase completely crammed with impersonal technology. Ruth glanced around from her new vantage point. There was no sign of a bed anywhere. She looked back at Philip.

Philip looked as embarrassed as if they were reading his personal love letters. "Well?" he said. "This had better be good."

"How much would you charge," Ruth said, choosing her words with care, "to track all the disturbances of the kind Melior is looking for in the subway?" On her right, various scanners warbled and blatted.

Philip looked suspicious and interested; which was to say, his face went completely blank.

"Why?" he said.

"Why not?" said Jane.

"There aren't any," Philip said.

"Did that ever stop you before?" Jane shot back.

"What's he going to do?" Philip asked. Dear Philip, with no sense of social responsibility anywhere in sight; he'd been one of the votes, Ruth remembered suddenly, in *favor* of the expedition to Downbelow Station.

"He's going to go get it." Jane shrugged. "But he'll wait until he knows where it is."

"If he thinks we're looking for it. If we *are* looking for it," Ruth amended.

"So you want me to look for something that isn't there?" Philip asked, with a certain air of exasperated superiority. Beside Ruth the computer finished doing whatever it was doing, emitted a satisfied *queep*, and covered the blanked monitor with a rotating starfield.

"Which word didn't you understand?" said Jane.

"The part about how you want me to do an illegal hack for money," Philip said, smirking.

"Oh, come on, Philip, would you do it for free?" Ruth snapped exasperatedly.

Philip fixed his gaze on a point three feet above her head and an indefinite distance away. "You want to string him. Okay. I can do that. I won't even charge you for it, much, just expenses. Because it isn't going to work for very long. And then he isn't going to pay any attention to anything any of us says."

"You mean like he does now?" Ruth said.

"How much for expenses?" Jane said.

Philip bit his lip and figured. "Two hundred. That's just for the connect time. That's the truth."

Ruth took out her wallet and started counting twenties. Philip took them and stuffed them in his pocket. "Done deal. So why don't we go get some Chinese? I'm starved. Mel can pay."

"What makes you think we want to buy *you* dinner?" Jane said.

Philip smiled, his typical nasty smile; techie in the catbird seat. "Because you want me to explain to Elfie what he just bought."

Michael Peacock stared at Mel the Elf across the kitchen, and running on through his mind like an idiot refrain was the phrase: *this changes things, this changes things* . . .

Melior not only believed there was a nonexistent *grendel* haunting the subway system, he believed he was foredoomed *not* to kill it.

This changes things, this changes things . . .

Michael came from a large and aggressively Irish family, and, besides the usual collection of bluff, no-nonsense uncles, he had an accumulation of long-haired bookish aunts who, in addition to collecting advanced degrees at European universities, knew the folklore of their own particular ethnic group rather well indeed. Even if he didn't believe in them, Michael was more than familiar with doomed heroes who could see the future.

Having one of them in his own kitchen changed things, though.

This changes things, this changes things. . . .

"Mel, that makes it even more stupid. If you *know* you can't kill the thing . . ."

"I swore I would retrieve the Sword. I will fulfill my oath or die," Melior said simply.

Which might make YOU sleep well at night, boyo, but doesn't do much for the rest of us, Michael reflected.

"There are—" he began.

There was a knock at the door. Michael looked at his watch.

"Christ, it's after eleven." The knock came again.

Melior flowed out of the kitchen like cats and rivers and any number of other apposite similes. He placed himself behind the door and looked at Michael.

A cold hackle of foreboding whispered down Michael's spine. Angry with himself, he shook his head and went to the door.

"You going to open up or am I going to stand here all night?" came Philip's voice, only slightly muffled, from the other side of the door. And Michael, who *always* had to know how the story came out, opened the door.

Philip wandered in, looking, as always, like a cat checking out a new accommodation that he might not choose to approve. He looked around. "Where's. . . ? Oh. Hi, Elfie. Slain any good orcs lately?"

Philip came the rest of the way in, gazing about himself like a visitor to the Prado, and only then did Michael realize that Ruth and Jane were with him.

"Hi," said Ruth uncomfortably.

"Oh, what the hell," said Michael, standing back to let them enter.

"I better call Nai," Ruth said as soon as she was in. Michael looked at Melior. The elf's face was scrupulously composed, as if he were a cat trying very hard not to laugh.

"I suppose you're wondering why I called you all here," Philip said.

"The suspense is nearly bearable," Jane commented. She glanced at Melior, then away. In the kitchen, Ruth's voice was a low expository mutter on the telephone.

"It's after eleven," Michael pointed out with a certain amount of sweet reasonability. "It's Monday."

"Yeah, well, first you weren't here and then if it waited until tomorrow *he* wouldn't be here and that's the whole point, isn't it?" Philip said.

"Is it?" Michael asked.

"Look," Philip continued, Sweet Reason at its most arch. "You don't believe in *grendels*. I don't believe in *grendels*. There *aren't* any *grendels.*"

Ruth came out of the kitchen at the end of this speech and looked rather stunned at this intelligence. But what else had she expected Philip to say?

"There are," Melior said. He did not look at Ruth.

"But what we *all-l-l-l-l-l* agree on is that if there *were* a *grendel*, it'd leave *tracks,*" Philip continued.

"Cut to the chase, wetbrain," Jane muttered.

"Thank you for sharing this with us," Michael said. "Phil, it's late, we all have things we'd like to do with our tomorrows, we *know* all this already."

"Fine. You can leave. Him I'm here to cut a deal with."

"It's his apartment," Melior explained to Philip.

"Everybody needs a straight man," Jane said in an aside.

Michael walked ostentatiously over to the couch—his *own* couch, if anyone was interested—and sat down. "Tea?" he said to Ruth.

"That would be lovely," Ruth said, and went to make it.

"You want to find that *grendel*, right?" Philip said to Melior.

"I *will* find the *grendel*," Melior corrected him.

"Right." Jane spoke up. "But you've got to find it without it knowing you're coming, otherwise it's got options and you don't."

Melior looked from Jane back to Philip, an expression of bland wariness settling over his face.

"So *you* say the *grendel's* going to start killing people. So when it does, someone'll notice," Philip said.

"It has already begun, and no one has noticed," Melior reminded him.

"Maybe," admitted Philip. "Maybe not. But if there's a Creature from the Black Budget in the subway eating people, there's all kinds of ways it can get noticed. Not just corpses, which, hey, you already know I didn't find. But ways."

"Name them," Melior said sternly.

Philip smiled, all cherubic innocence. "Transit police overtime. Changed train schedules. Missing persons reports. Thefts, burglaries, love letters to the Animal Control Officer. Everybody always wants to cover his tracks. And most of those tracks get stuck in some computer or other. And I can find them. All it takes is time, money, and knowing what you're looking for."

The teakettle began to whistle; a hoarse, off-key note. Jane went off in that direction, following Ruth.

"And you would do this for me?" Melior said tonelessly. "Even though you do not believe?"

And you are going to stand there and let him, Michael thought, *even though you're convinced it won't do you or any one else a damn bit of good.*

"Hey," said Philip, doing his best to look like a used-car salesman. "I'm a believer in free enterprise. Rent my time and I'm yours to play with."

Ruth came out of the kitchen holding two mugs. She handed one to Michael and, bracing herself only a little, crossed to Melior to hand him the other. Melior took it without removing his attention from Philip.

"I am to pay you to discover the *grendel's* lair?"

"Yeah, something like that," Philip said.

"With what?" Melior said.

One look at Ruth's face was enough to tell Michael whose idea this originally had been. And this was something she hadn't thought of, either.

"Well, that, for starters." Philip pointed at Melior's ring.

Jane came out of the kitchen and nudged Ruth hard, handing her a teacup. Michael watched her take it, and wondered if she was going to pour it over Philip.

Melior looked down at his hand. He spread the fingers wide, and the strange flat oval in its baroque silvery setting flashed in the living room lights. "This?" he said. Philip's grin widened.

There was an almost imperceptible pause, and then Melior drew it slowly off. "Done," he said, flipping the ring through the air to Philip. "Fair bargain, Child of Earth, and silver and gold to bind it."

"Philip LeStrange, how *could* you?"

Ruth advanced upon Philip where he stood upon the sidewalk in front of Michael's building. Twelve o'clock. Witching hour. And Ruth didn't intend to leave enough of Philip for a good broom to sweep up.

"I had to make it look convincing, didn't I?" Philip demanded. "I can always give it back later." He flipped Melior's ring up and caught it. Flash, went the stone in the streetlight.

All of the replies she wished to make were cut short by Melior's unexpected arrival. He turned a glowing basilisk gaze on Philip. "You will see Mistress Jane safely to her door. I will accompany Ruth."

Philip opened his mouth to comment but couldn't think of anything to say. He looked at Jane.

" 'Night," Jane said, and strode off dormward with an air that said Philip might follow if he liked. Philip shot one last look at Melior and scuttled after her. Melior looked at Ruth.

"And you will accompany Ruth," Ruth said.

"Yes," said Melior. They started north.

"It feels strange to go about unarmed," he commented after a while. "I cannot remember a time that I went unweaponed before."

"I'm sorry about today," Ruth said tightly. Even while she said it she hoped they weren't going to restart any conversation containing words that started with L and other discredited romantic notions.

"But you did not fail me, even though you do not trust me. Did you not bribe young Philip to discover the truth I require?"

It is a peculiar sensation to feel your jaw drop from shock; Ruth filed the sensation away for later cataloging. "You—!" she said. *You knew.*

"An idiot, perhaps, but not a fool. You have hired him—but *I* have sealed the bargain." Melior's mouth curved in a private amusement. "And while awaiting my vindication, I shall acquire those items which are most likely to amuse a *grendel.*"

Ruth glanced sideways. Melior's mouth was grim again.

"If you knew I'd put him up to it, why did you let him chouse you out of your ring?" Ruth finally said.

"It is of less value to me than his cooperation. It is, after all, as easy to lie to me as to actually seek the truth. But he has made a bargain with me, and will give me that which he has said he would give. Philip is an honest creature."

"*Philip?*"

"A poor servant, but mine for this while." He stopped, and took Ruth's hand. "And it is of some value to me to have . . . more time, Ruth."

"Time?" Ruth was baffled; flustered by his nearness. "Time for what?"

"For everything; for nothing. For you, my Lady Bright, my heart twin—but fear not, Ruth; I recall your dislike of being courted in the open," Melior said. He walked on, not releasing her hand.

"I have a dislike of being made fun of, too, if anyone is at all interested," Ruth said in a tight voice. She yanked on her hand, but it was not relinquished. Perforce she matched her pace to his. After a moment Melior slowed to accommodate her shorter stride.

"And do I have an interest, even at the best of times, which this is not, in making sport of mortal girls?" Melior shot back.

"That's 'mortal *women.*' 'Girls' is politically incorrect, you know." *Stop, I'm from the Language Police. Surrender all your adjectives and come out parsing—*

"My Line has never taken overmuch interest in politics. But how, my lady, shall I court you, if I may not speak you fair, and costly gifts are beyond my power?"

"Cut it out," said Ruth. This time she pulled so hard she pulled him to a stop. Such a common sight of urban New York; a lovers' quarrel, but they weren't lovers nor were ever likely to be.

"I do not care if your heart is given to another," Melior went on, "though I do not think it is. I ask only the chance to incline your thoughts to me; why should I not hope?"

"*Because you don't want me!*" This time Ruth managed to get her hand loose; she would have slapped him if she felt she had either the coordination or the moral authority to carry through the gesture. "It's just a *game* to you—"

She stopped when she saw the look on his face.

"Game?" Melior repeated dangerously. "*Do not want you,* mortal girl? You mock me at peril—" He lunged for her. Ruth didn't wait to discover his intentions. She ran.

It was New York. No one noticed. And it took him less than half a block to catch her. One moment she was running; the next he simply lifted her off her feet and yanked her into the shadows.

"Is everyone here blind and deaf as well as mad?" Melior demanded crossly. Ruth felt the poky parts of a building pressing against her back and hoped it looked as if she were being mugged.

"This is no game, Lady Bright," Melior said. For one mad instant she thought he was going to bite her, but no.

This time was not like the last time. For one thing, Melior knew she was likely to object to being kissed. For another, Ruth wasn't sure she wanted to object.

Melior kissed her.

She could feel the zipper on his jacket where it pressed against the back of her hand. She could feel Melior's body, warm beneath the T-shirt and every muscle tense. A faint scent of cinnamon and bergamot clung to him, making absurd cross-circuited ideas skitter across her preoccupied brain. Finally she was able to work one arm free and put it around him beneath the jacket. When he felt her touch, he broke the kiss and stared down at her.

"Necking in doorways," Ruth said breathlessly, "how juvenile." Her heart was a jarring staccato in her chest and she found it ridiculously hard to breathe.

"I no longer regard you as a reliable source of information," Melior informed her. He bent his head to kiss the side of her neck, and Ruth closed her eyes to the sensation of being in a rapidly-falling elevator. Fortunately, he wasn't likely to go any further than this in a doorway. She hoped. At least she thought she did.

"Ah, Ruth, were it not for the Sword, even exile and death at your side would be bearable," Melior groaned.

How sweet. I wish I believed it. Hesitantly, she raised her hand to stroke his hair, just as she'd wanted to from the moment she'd first seen him. It was soft and fine, dandelion silk beneath her fingers.

"You don't even know me," Ruth said, voice whisper-soft.

"I have always known you," Melior said quietly. "I saw your face in my dreams and sought for you in the Morning Lands all my days. I did not know I would find you here."

Which was lovely to hear, but what they never told you in the books was that Capital-L Love didn't solve any problems, it just added more to a life that already seemed more than ordinarily overfull of them.

And what did he mean by it? Not a long white dress and orange blossoms, 2.5 kids, a Volvo, and a house in the suburbs—or, probably, anything else she could instantly imagine.

"Well, here I am. And it— It's cold, okay? I want to get home." But she wasn't cold. Not even a little.

He pulled her away from the wall, but only to put both arms around her and hold her as if someone were trying to take her away. When Ruth began to feel that he really might not be planning to let go, he released her and looked away.

"I forget my manners," Melior commented. Ruth let that remark sail by. "If only there were more time," he said wistfully. He put an arm around her shoulders. Ruth looked around to see if there was anyone to notice. There wasn't.

"But Naomi waits," Melior added, looking up the curving slope of street.

"Yeah," said Ruth, sighing. *No time? Waiting for me?* It was hard to think with her thoughts skittering through her brain like self-willed butterflies. But butterflies or not, she and Melior were going to have to have more than a little talk.

Because if he meant half of what he said, maybe she could use it to keep him from being killed.

· 15 ·

The Ill-Made Knight

IN ADVENTURES, RUTH reflected sourly, there were not *longeurs* during which everyone stood around waiting for something to happen.

Not that Ruth was standing around, by any stretch of the imagination. The Country of Mundanity wouldn't leave her alone long enough. It was the *adventure* that was standing still.

And the real world was strangling her. Last night it had been Naomi: was she okay, how was she feeling, did she want to talk? Ruth, distracted by Melior's avowals on the walk home, had been safe in bed and halfway to sleep before the similarity of those questions to the ones the psychiatrist she'd quit seeing used to ask made the penny drop.

Naomi thought there was something *wrong* with her. For which (Ruth admitted with scrupulous honesty) she had some grounds; Naomi was her best friend, and Ruth couldn't remember a single conversation they'd had since Melior had shown up.

Nonetheless, it was unreasonably annoying. And since Ruth knew the questions that Naomi would ask were all the ones Ruth knew were unanswerable, she was going to continue to avoid her.

Or would have, except for the fact that Naomi's first and last words to her at 8:30 this morning were:

"Don't you have a nine o'clock class on Tuesdays?"

Heroines of fiction would have laughed off nine o'clock classes and gone on mapping their rich emotional landscape. Ruth leaped up like a galvanized frog and made it to her class only ten minutes late.

And this afternoon, when heroines of fiction would go off for *tristesse* trysts with their lovers, Ruth was pretty sure she was going to keep the appointment she'd made three weeks ago with the Placement Office and answer those letters she'd shoved to the bottom of her purse.

Why, why couldn't she ever do something random and wild and burn all bridges behind her without looking back?

Because the one thoughtless act she'd committed—*must* have committed, although she had no memory of it—half a lifetime ago had cost her everything she had.

The bell rang, the class was over, and for all her punctilio in attending it, Ruth could not remember what had been discussed. She stood up, grabbed her books and purse, looked up.

Melior was standing in the doorway. Curious students eddied around him, leaving; Ruth was glad to see his hair was loose, carefully covering those fatal Spockian ears. He saw her and smiled.

"Michael knew your schedule, Ruth. He said he thought you would be here."

"Yes." Simple mortification turned her words to monosyllables. She walked out of the classroom with Melior beside her.

"So I will company you," Melior said, his speech making one of its strange slides into an archaism that was mere precision for a society not hers. "And lend to Philip the hours to spin his webs. And he will divulge to me where the beast bides."

Only even with the best will in the world, nothing Philip did would do that. And then what would Melior do? And what would *she* do?

They walked down the hall together. The sunlight blinded her momentarily as Melior pushed the door to the outside world open. Ruth started to speak, found her throat was suddenly dry, and tried again.

"What if— He might not find anything, you know. For reasons."

"Then I must search without the aid of his malicious engines, much though I would joy to have it. But I expect him to find things, Ruth. The *grendel*'s appetite grows with what it feeds upon. How can its murders continue undetected?"

"And if they do? If he doesn't?" There it was, the hard question, the one she needed the answer to.

"Three days, Ruth," Melior said, answering the question she'd asked and all the ones she hadn't. "Today and tomorrow and the day next, and when the next day's sun dawns, I shall go."

Into the subways, chasing monsters. A giddiness that ought to have been strong emotion but was probably actually a missed breakfast made her lurch into him. His arm was steady, a welcome pressure about her shoulders.

Who are you, Melior, and who have you been? What's your favorite color and who did you want to be when you grew up? Tell me all about

*Elfland and the girls back home and why just because you're the most
beautiful thing that's ever walked into my life I should believe that you want
me as much as I want you?*

"Breakfast," said Melior firmly. "And then, perhaps, you will show
me, Ruth, where in this city I may purchase a weapon."

It was late afternoon when Ruth (who had canceled her Job Placement Counseling interview) got back to the apartment. She'd left Melior
with Michael, having exhausted all the (licit) avenues of weapon purchase
in The Big Apple. And Melior didn't even want a gun.

He wanted a sword.

Or, failing that, a stout spear, or even a crossbow and a quiver full of
bolts, as he had explained helpfully.

They had gone to sporting goods stores, antique stores, camping
supply stores, and any store Ruth could think of that might hold something that could be adapted to Melior's needs. The results were less than
encouraging.

And three days from tomorrow—win, lose, or draw—Melior was going off to the subway. And getting arrested, if he was very lucky.

She turned her key in her lock and went in—both actions overlaid
with a touch of strange, now, because her mind kept imagining these acts
as Melior would view them. She went through to the living room and
found Naomi waiting for her.

"Did it ever occur to you, Ruth, that we could all have been wrong?"
Naomi said.

Naomi was sitting in the comfy chair beside the window. She wore a
white polo shirt and khaki pants and looked as though she'd been sitting
there waiting to ask the question since Ruth had left that morning.

She hadn't been, of course. Ruth took comfort from that thought.

"Wrong about what?" Ruth asked. She heard the defensive edge in
her voice and hated it, and covered her feelings by turning away and
painstakingly making certain that all the locks on the door were, indeed,
locked.

"About. . . . Where's Mel, by the way?"

"At Michael's gym. He— There's some stuff he wants that maybe
Michael can get for him."

"Uh-hum." Naomi picked up a mug of tea and stared into as if it
were some form of caffeinated teleprompter. "You remember we all
agreed that Melior *had* to be an elf. Nobody could do makeup that
good. . . ." Her voice trailed off.

Slowly, unwillingly, Ruth advanced into the middle of the room. She
looked down at the top of Naomi's head, still bent over the tea.

"They can't. Seamless. Waterproof. Glows in the dark. And the stuff he came with: emeralds, rubies, fine hand-embroidering? Come on." Hesitantly Ruth pulled out a chair from the table and sat down next to Naomi. "He's *real*."

"Just how real is he?" Naomi looked up from her tea and turned to face Ruth. "Philip thinks he's a science project, Michael'll rescue any stray kitten that meows, I've never been able to figure out why Jane does anything, and I'm just waiting to see what happens. What about you?"

"Me?" The word was emitted as an inelegant squeak, and Ruth felt her cheeks go hot.

"Yesterday I told him we weren't going to play any more, and he took off—and you took off right after him. I suppose it isn't any of my business, but—"

"Oh, Naomi," Ruth said, half amused, half exasperated.

Naomi smiled. "Well, what if he turned out to be an escaped serial killer with plastic surgery? If I lost you, they'd make me buy a replacement before I could graduate, and after six years I'm just about out of money."

Ruth snorted. "And then you'd have to travel door-to-door, selling Chocolate Suicide Brownies and rum-orange butter cookies to make up the difference. For heaven's sake, it isn't like that, Naomi, it— It just isn't," Ruth finished lamely, and stared at her friend.

Naomi smiled sadly. "I know; one elf appears out of nowhere and I go all over Sigmund Freud on you. It's just that I've had too many friends who went and did the *damnedest* things when they should have been thinking."

"And you think I'm one?" Ruth said, striving for lightness.

"You're about to graduate. You've hit the Big Three-Oh. And you— Something happened to you before I met you, Ruth; I wish you'd tell me what it is. But don't let it push you into being in love with this guy just because you can't think of anything else to do with your time!" Naomi finished up in a burst. She looked away, cheeks flushed. "Now you tell me I'm a jealous, interfering jerk."

"You're a jealous, interfering jerk," Ruth said obligingly. Naomi swatted at her; Ruth laughed, then sobered. "No; you're right; I don't know what's been wrong with me lately; one birthday divisible by five and I go all to pieces. And I'll tell you about what happened someday, I promise—but that isn't it with Melior."

Ruth took Naomi's hand; for whose comfort, she wasn't certain. *Why is it so hard to say? "When I was eighteen I became a Movie of the Week." Simple. The word is "coma."*

It would be easier to confess to being Batman.

"With Melior, the thing is, he says he *loves* me, Naomi, and I'm not sure *what* I feel. He's like a book I'm reading; I don't know whether I like it or not, but I don't want to stop before the end." Even telling the bare truth made Ruth feel the blush-heat on her cheeks again.

The silence might have stretched if she had let it; but Ruth jumped up and fled to the kitchen. The teapot was still half full. She poured a cup and drizzled honey into it, and stood drinking the tepid brew while staring out the window at the twilight.

The Seven Houses of the Twilight, and if Melior doesn't bring the sword home there's going to be six, not seven, and it doesn't seem real at all. Of course, why should it. . . ?

"Have you considered, when you think about him like this, that the reason he's so fascinating is because he's crazy?" Naomi said from the kitchen doorway. She threw the rest of her cold tea into the sink, took Ruth's mug from her hands, made a face, and slid it into the tiny microwave perched precariously on top of the refrigerator.

"I'm a librarian, I know these things. 614.58: Mental Health, all you have to do is look it up. Melior's insisting that things are a particular way because he wants them to be that way, not because they are or aren't or are even *likely* to be or not. And leaving aside sanity, he's on a collision course with the real world and there isn't anything you can do . . . except decide whether to jump ship or crash with him."

The microwave pinged; Ruth's eyes filled with tears.

"Oh, Naomi, why isn't it that simple?"

Forty blocks south of Columbia (give or take the odd block) and across Central Park on the Upper East Side—Fifth Avenue in the Eighties, to be more precise—lies a district variously called Museum Row or Museum Mile. The Metropolitan Museum of Art, the Guggenheim, assorted foundations and *very* expensive galleries deck the tree-lined street; Museum Mile is the natural habitat of money: physicians, psychiatrists, expensive psychics. . . .

And of the largest collection of people with obscure knowledge outside of a college campus.

"And do you think your friend can help us?" Melior asked.

"If it was forged, Stainless Steve knows where. If you want a sword, go to an expert."

Michael Harrison Peacock and Rohannan Melior of the House of the Silver Silences walked up the steps of the Metropolitan Museum of Art.

His friend Michael walked over to a guardsman in uniform, seated at a podium which, Melior supposed, must indicate his purpose and allegiance. But if there were letters upon it, Melior could not read them. The sorcery that had given him command of the local tongue (a common enough magic, useful when one traveled between the Lands) had not taught him to read its letters. The others forgot that, often; as young scholars, their lives revolving around books, must.

Ruth was such a scholar. And if he brought her to his world and stripped her learning from her, would she hate him, or would she feel their love was worth that price?

Folly, to think of a future when his life ended here.

"Come on, Mel. Steve can see us."

Stephen Mallison's work area was behind and below and in back of any number of exhibits, and reaching it was made particularly difficult because half the floors of the museum were closed for reasons ranging from installing frescoes shipped halfway around the world to recreating an Egyptian temple. They had to go all the way up to the fourth floor before they could find an elevator that would take them down to the right side of the basement.

It was, Michael realized as the doors closed, the first elevator Melior had ever been in.

The doors shut. Melior, seeing nothing but a small empty room, turned to Michael for explanation. And the elevator began to descend.

Michael stared at him, mouth half open and several reasonable explanations jammed in his throat. Melior flung himself back against a wall, scrabbling for a dagger that wasn't there. His pupils dilated, flashing red; he snarled, and Michael could see the long canid teeth gleaming in the faint fluorescent elevator lights.

"Hey; it's just—" Michael began helplessly.

Melior saw him; saw Michael's ease and knew there was no danger; and worse, knew that he'd looked like a fool. His green gaze fixed on Michael, and for a moment Michael felt the fury that raged against the bars of Melior's will like a separate thing.

Then Melior looked away and pretended neither of them was there.

It was the longest four floors of Michael's life.

When the doors opened, it was on the unlovely subbasements of the Met, and before the doors were fully open Melior had reeled through them. He turned and faced Michael defiantly; a creature caught between two fables in a land undeniably mundane.

"It's an elevator," Michael said lamely. Melior said nothing. Michael sighed inwardly, knowing Melior would be especially difficult now. Well it only stood to reason, as the spaceman said of the alien computer. Michael didn't like looking like a fool, himself, and he guessed an elf-prince in exile didn't either. "Steve's this way."

Stephen Mallison's office was at the end of the narrow brown and yellow corridor. A tall narrow oak door marked "Properties" barred the way; Michael rapped on it twice and opened it.

The chamber the door opened onto was both vast and crowded. Smells of rust and iron, dust and paper and oil and myriad alien scents assailed Melior's nostrils. He followed Michael into the space.

There were glass cases filled with artifacts; standing armor, racks of long-unused weapons, wooden crates scribed with glyphs that Melior couldn't read. The space had the orderly disarray of an archivist's.

In the largest open space available was a broad white table. To one side was a glowing box of the type called *computer*. There was a man sitting at the table. His pale red hair was as long as Melior's own, held back with a scrap of leather. His back was to them.

On the table before him were Melior's spurs.

"Hi, Steve," Michael said. "Don't bother to get up."

The man addressed as Steve spun his chair around on its large shining wheels. Still seated, he wheeled his chair to where Michael stood.

"Took you long enough. This your friend from Ancient Atlantis who wants the sword? Hi, I'm Stephen Mallison. I'm a Cataloguer at the Met, which is to say I'm a glorified packrat and work mostly with the computer." He held out his hand.

Melior knew this custom. He extended his hand for Stephen to grasp. Stephen's grip was warm and dry; a little rough and much stronger than Melior had expected.

"I am Rohannan Melior," he answered only, for to be so brief was not rudeness, not among humans and not here.

"And those are your spurs. Terrific. You know they've been driving me nuts for *days*? My real specialty is Restoration and Re-Creation of period weapons, and I've even got a degree to that effect stashed around here somewhere, but they don't look like anything I've ever seen. Where'd you get them?" He turned his chair on its wheels again and went back to the table. Apparently he was not going to get up.

"They were my father's," Melior began, but Michael interrupted him.

"Steve, do you know of anywhere around here we could lay hands on a sword?"

"Or a boar-spear?" Melior added helpfully.

Stephen gestured to the crates and cases in their serried ranks. "We got fifteenth, sixteenth, seventeenth—*lots* of seventeenth; there was a war on practically everywhere in Europe—some eighteenth, mostly ceremonial. Take your pick. It's no trouble; it all belongs to the Museum, and they're never going to display *or* deaccession it. And if they were important pieces, they wouldn't be left down here to rot."

"You, uh, *are* joking, right? About giving away Museum property?" Michael said.

"Probably," Stephen said. "But on the other hand, if your friend's a collector, it is usually possible to pry something loose quasi-legally. I could kick it up to Doctor Bonner."

"No," said Melior. "These won't do." He touched the glass lid of a case and then wiped his fingers on his jeans, making a face.

"Well, what is it that you want them to do?" Stephen said obligingly.

"I wish to kill a *grendel,*" Melior said seriously, before Michael could stop him. "These would break."

Stephen looked at Michael.

"A reproduction," Michael said hastily. "He wants a *new* sword."

"I take it we are not talking SCA-hit-them-with-rattan-wrapped-in-duct-tape type sword here?" Stephen said.

"Live steel," Melior said, and Stephen smiled.

"Now you're talking my language. Let me consult my files; we should have a list of the smiths we use to do our Re-Creation work."

Stephen Mallison turned in his chair and wheeled over to a bank of two-drawer file cabinets that supported shelving stuffed with long, paper-wrapped parcels.

"Why does he not rise?" Melior said to Michael, in puzzled tones.

The chair stopped and turned around. Melior saw the look that passed from Stephen to Michael and knew that somehow he had made another strange World-of-Iron error.

"Steve, it's just that he—"

"A horse fell on me, spinal nerves don't grow back, the miracle cures you see on television are the exclusive province of people with good health insurance and money to burn, and there isn't much call for a blacksmith who can't stand up. I go to Therapy three times a week and that takes all my spare cash. Now can we change the subject?"

"Ah," said Melior as understanding dawned. "You are crippled."

Michael groaned. But, Melior's strange charisma worked even here, and amazingly, Stephen smiled.

"That's right. I am not *challenged.* I am not *differently able.* I'm a cripple. But at least I've got my health." Stephen smiled a crooked smile.

"I think you are very able," said Melior, as if he had given the matter considerable thought, and as if his opinion mattered.

"Yeah. Thanks." Stephen turned back to his file cabinets.

"You've got a big mouth," Michael said under his breath.

"Michael, if you had told me he was a cripple, I would not have asked," Melior said reasonably. "But it is wonderful, that chair with the wheels. I wish—" He stopped. "I wish I could tell my sister that such things exist. I think we could make one."

Now it was Michael's turn to stare. He'd never thought of Melior having a sister, let alone a sister who would be grateful for a wheelchair.

A sister who was going to die because Melior wasn't going to be able to bring The Sword of Maiden's Tears home.

"Here we are," said Stephen. He bent sideways awkwardly, and straightened up with a thick manila file folder in his hands. "Two guys in California, one in South Carolina, one in Maine. They all do custom work. Two grand and two years, and you can have a sword that Conan the Barbarian would be glad to call his own." He spun his chair around and wheeled over to Melior. Melior took the folder, and gazed down at glossy colored pictures of swords laid on velvet as if they were jewels.

"But I cannot wait two years," he said helplessly. "I must have it by tomorrow's dawn."

"Then you're out of luck," Stephen said flatly.

"Steve," said Michael. "There's got to be something."

"Fine. Go down to Acme Rent-a-Sword and give them your credit card. Nobody uses swords any more, Mike—this is all custom work for collectors. And it takes time."

"Well, what about secondhand?" Michael heard himself say. "Or someone willing to *loan* one?"

Stephen looked from Melior to Michael for a long moment. He wheeled backward until he reached the table. He reached around behind it and came up with a canvas-wrapped bundle about a yard long, bound in three places with twine. He picked up a knife and began sawing through the twine.

"Do you know what a *gladius* is?" he asked Melior.

"No."

"Roman short sword. Sword of the legions. They conquered half the world with an oversized pocket knife *cast* out of a metal so soft that iron can chop it right in half: bronze." The twine was gone. Stephen flipped the canvas open.

He'd called it an oversized pocket-knife. Michael estimated it at about thirty inches long. It had a wide straight blade that came to a spade-shaped point. The quillons were narrow. The haft seemed to be wrapped in braided horsehair.

Melior stepped forward and picked it up. Hefted it, testing its balance.

"It's the last thing I ever made. Beryllium in the bronze instead of tin—ain't *nothing* going to chop that baby in half. You take that. I'll keep the spurs. Deal?"

Melior looked down at Stephen, saying nothing. Michael, standing behind him, suddenly realized that Melior's pupils would have narrowed as he walked into the light.

"I will return this if I can. The spurs are yours."

"No biggie. And now why don't you guys get out of here, and leave me alone so I can get some work done before this place shuts up shop for the night, okay?" Stephen said.

Melior rewrapped the *gladius* in the canvas and tucked the bundle under one arm. He walked past Michael toward the door. Michael waved good-bye to Stephen and followed him.

Stephen's last words reached them at the open door.

"And I hope you get home safe, Rohannan Melior."

· 16 ·

Love Among the Ruins

TUESDAY AND WEDNESDAY were replays of Monday, with Ruth getting edgier by the hour. Melior's plans for Thursday morning hung between them like the Sword he was looking for, keeping them from talking about any of the things that really mattered. He bought a canteen and a flashlight to go with the sword he and Michael had come back from the Museum with, and now in a few short hours he would be gone, and Ruth would have to try to make sense of a world in which the book that was Melior would go forever unfinished.

And the two of them had no privacy at all.

Melior slept on Michael's couch. Ruth shared a one-bedroom apartment with Naomi. And the moments and half-hours of privacy they'd snatched had been enough to make Ruth heartily regret that fact and not enough for her to be able to do anything about it, even if she could manage to find the nerve.

And he said he loved her. Said that she, Ruth, was the woman he had searched for, to woo and win, all through the Morning Lands—whatever they were (but, thought Ruth wistfully, they sounded pretty).

"If," said Melior, drawing the word out lazily. They sat in perfect propriety and chaperonage in a forgotten inglenook of the big main library down on 42nd Street. Melior sat across the table from her; mirrorshades and leather jacket and an expression of faintly rueful longing that made Ruth want to. . . .

"If," Melior began again, reaching across the table and taking her hand, "If the Sword were mine, and you and I were set upon the high road to Chandrakar—"

" 'You and I'?" Ruth quoted back to him.

"Did I go, I would take you with me, would you come," Melior parsed carefully. "They say the lower world holds the memory of the higher; did you never dream of Chandrakar the fair?"

"And if I did?" Ruth bandied back.

"Then you would go, did you hold me in fond affection or not. But if you have never dreamed her green hills and silver rivers, I must assume that it is I alone who am the attraction."

"If I went," Ruth pointed out prosaically.

"Oh, Ruth, do!" Melior leaned across the table. "Say you would come to Chandrakar for Rohannan Melior's asking. He would do you all honor, and set you at his right hand. It is not true that no human blood runs in the Houses of the Twilight; such alliance is a thing done, aye, and done before; you will see—"

"If I come," Ruth said. "And when did you develop a twin brother?"

Melior smiled instead of answering, and Ruth felt her innards go custard-pudding weak. Go to Elfland, like the man was asking—it would sure as hell get her out of finals week, wouldn't it?

And Melior's Chandrakar could be no more strange to her than the modern world was now.

Eight years. Not quite a decade. But in that time there'd been another Star Wars movie, almost half a dozen Star Trek movies, something called AIDS, two terms of President Reagan. . . .

And somehow, as if Life were an exceptionally boring book, Ruth had lost her place. Lost her place and all desire to regain it. *I try to take things one day at a time, but lately several days have attacked me at once.* Eight years of days, served up in one moment of awakening that Ruth, honest now, realized she would never recover from.

Melior said he loved her. And Ruth knew she wanted him. And if both of them turned out later to have been mistaken, well, lots of people were.

"Okay, Rohannan Melior. Take me to Chandrakar." *If you can, if you go, if and if and if and IF. . . .*

Wednesday evening. Ruth supposed she'd missed classes. She didn't care. She'd spent the day with Melior at New York Public again, consulting all the maps her skill could find for him. Maps of New York, to be laboriously compared against the subway maps. Geo-survey maps of the island Manhattan, its stone and water-table, marl, schist, and aquifer.

Maps of such terrain as the place had left to it after four centuries of building.

But most of all, the subway. Where Melior was going to go. And die, in all probability, even if it was only through being hit by a train.

A proper heroine, Ruth supposed glumly, would have spent the time begging him not to go. But she'd known it wouldn't do the least bit of good, and so she'd—*sensibly!*—done what she could to help him and let the rest go unsaid.

Everyone knew he was going after the (unproven) *grendel* Thursday morning. Michael was particularly upset—twice she had caught him and Melior arguing in corners—and Ruth had cherished a traitorous hope that Michael would stop him; do something splendidly male and physical and knock Melior over the head, tie him up in the closet, do *something* until the fit passed and sweet reason prevailed.

But when they'd left the library and gone back to Michael's, all Michael had done was propose Chinese at Naomi's, and Melior had volunteered to pick up the order Michael had already phoned in.

And all her idiotic purchase of Philip's cyberstealth had gained her was these three days.

Ruth wasn't quite sure how she'd ended up going with Michael, but she had, and now she was back at her own apartment, and he and Naomi were watching her with close fond anxiety; her dear friends watching over her to make sure she didn't do something stupid.

Like go with Melior. Into the subway, if not to Elfland as he'd asked. She hadn't told anybody about that.

Only there wouldn't be much point to following him into the subway, now, would there? They probably wouldn't let them have connecting rooms at Bellevue.

Ruth fiddled with the glass in her hand. Red wine; a good bottling, a special treat; or was it just cheap and sleazy nepenthe? She swirled the liquid around in her glass and stared down into it. Red as blood. The language of fairy tales.

Naomi fidgeted. Michael fidgeted.

"What in God's name is taking him so long?" Ruth snarled as, with perfect timing, the downstairs buzzer buzzed.

"He was going to stop by Philip's tonight," Michael said. "Probably on the way."

He didn't tell me, Ruth thought, unreasonably jealous. Of their last hours together, even if spent in company. And maybe tonight . . .

"Then he's lucky he isn't stuffed and on display in an antique shop on East 57th by now. Michael, have you ever *been* to Philip's apartment?" Naomi said.

"I have denied myself that pleasure," Michael said gravely.

"*I* haven't," Ruth said sadly, her mind elsewhere. "It's probably cold," she added, meaning the Chinese food. She stood in the open doorway listening to the elevator rise, waiting to see Melior again.

And after tomorrow morning you won't see him any more. This is the way the world ends. . . .

You couldn't see the elevator from their corner apartment. Ruth heard the doors open, and waited.

They say it settles a man's mind wonderfully knowing he is to be hanged in the morning. If that's true, why am I so jittery?

Philip LeStrange came around the corner. He held a shopping bag from the Chinese take-away in each hand.

He wasn't Melior.

He saw Ruth and stopped, and some of the pleased expression vanished from his face. It probably hadn't occurred to him until that moment that he was going to have to face Ruth.

"Where is he?" Ruth said. Philip set down the bags and took a hesitant step backward.

"Philip?" Naomi brushed past Ruth and went out into the hall. Ruth felt a hand on her arm. Michael.

"Come and sit down," Michael said gently.

"But it's Philip," Ruth said with the bewilderment of someone who has taken a mortal wound and doesn't quite realize it yet.

"Come on, Ruth," Michael said.

It was at least five minutes before Philip and Naomi came into the apartment. Philip still hung back, glancing sideways at Ruth as if she were a houseplant unexpectedly turned carnivorous. For once he had neither backpack nor laptop with him.

"He's already gone, hasn't he?" Her voice was remarkably even, Ruth noted with a certain pleased vanity.

"That's right," Naomi said. "Come and have dinner, Ruth." Her voice had the careful tone one associated with speakers to the hysterical. Or the mad.

"No, thank you," Ruth said, equally carefully. With careful, measured steps she left the living room. She passed through the bedroom into the bathroom. There she shut the door tightly, and turned on the shower as, after all, the walls of even the best New York apartments are rather thin.

Ruth had been in there long enough to get over the worst of her tears and to begin to notice that the spray from the shower had soaked the left side of her skirt. The hammering on the door was enough to make her jump.

"Ruth!" Michael's voice, raised in a bellow to bring sinking ships to mind. "Get *out* here!"

She unlocked the door. He shoved it in on her. He grabbed her and yanked her out into the living room, without giving her the opportunity to make even the most elementary repairs to her tear-blotched complexion.

"—irst footage of the Subway Snatcher. The footage you saw was shot by a rush-hour passenger who had intended to tape his daughter's sixth birthday party. Transit officials still will not say whether this . . . amazing occurrence has any connection to the closing of six Lower Manhattan IND stops earlier this week."

The living room television was on. Half the screen was filled with a graphic of a red claw superimposed over a black silhouette of the front of a subway car. Beneath it in yellow, jagged letters screamed: "Subway Snatcher."

"Kelly Groen is standing by live at City Hall. Let's go to her now. Kelly?" the perky newsreader (male) said. He turned expectantly toward the graphic. Nothing.

"While we wait, Rob, why don't we run that clip again?" said the other perky newsreader (female).

"Ladies and gentlemen," said Rob, "we would like to remind you at this time that what you are about to see has not been authenticated. We prefer to let you judge for yourselves." He spoke in the hushed tones of a very expensive mortician.

The screen went dark and *cinema-verite* jiggly; the symptom of home movies through the ages. The watchers took it on faith that this was a subway station; it might as easily have been any of a dozen hundred other things.

Whatever was happening was already in progress. The people moved with frightened pointlessness. The image on the viewfinder of the invisible cameraman veered wildly; at one point the image bleached out as the camera pointed directly upward into a light.

Finally the picture stilled. The dark blobs resolved into bodies at the edge of the frame. At the center of the picture was a hand, grayish-black and far too large for any proper hand, splayed on the subway platform as it levered its possessor up onto the platform from the tracks.

Blackness, as someone got between the camera and the picture. A sharp discontinuity as the camera was dropped. The platform's surface filled most of the frame, but off at one edge a hominid figure could be seen, blurred as footage of Bigfoot, walking away holding an awkward pale burden.

Then the film stopped.

"The victim has been identified as twenty-six-year-old Theresa Scarlatti, a secretary for Burford, Foote, and Hoo. Relatives—"

"We're ready to go to Kelly now," said Perky Two, and the picture did another two-step dissolve to a windblown blonde against a late-afternoon backdrop of rescue equipment, holding a microphone beneath her chin and prepared to tell the world at great length that she knew nothing, nothing at all.

Ruth looked at Michael. His face was pale, stretched with shock; it seemed almost as if she could look down *into* his skin and see through it to the skull beneath.

"There's a monster in the subway," Naomi said.

She'd thought she was tired before, but now a weariness beyond bearing stole over Ruth. She leaned against Michael. He put his arms around her and held her.

"Yeah," Ruth said. "It's real. Too bad we didn't know when it would do any good."

Kelly-Groen-at-City-Hall spent two minutes explaining that nobody knew anything, including when subway service would be restored, before the inevitable cut to a commercial about Life on the Edge with your favorite soft drink.

Ruth pushed Michael away and walked over to a chair with lagging, ungraceful steps and dropped into it. The Chinese food still sat, virginal and untouched, in its bags. She reached in and extracted a fortune cookie. *"It is better to travel hopefully than to arrive,"* it said. Sure it was. *Welcome to the Outer Limits City Limits.*

"Philip," Naomi said in a voice of soft and dangerous gentleness, "what did you tell Melior when you saw him?"

Ruth looked up, curious-rapidly-becoming-appalled as inspiration struck. Philip was sitting in the big chair under the window with his arms wrapped around his knees. He looked like he'd been kicked in the stomach. He didn't look up.

"Philip." Naomi's voice, still soft, but demanding.

A mumbled response.

"Phil. You were checking the police reports to find the *grendel*," Michael prompted.

"What did you tell him?" Naomi repeated, and finally Philip raised his head.

He wasn't crying—that would be too much, even for Philip, Ruth observed with glassy detachment—but behind the silvery bifocals his eyes looked red and irritated. He pushed them up, rubbing his eyes, reminding Ruth once again of a white rat grooming.

"He paid me," Philip said, only slightly muffled this time. There was a hint of desperation in his voice; a trace of actual feeling that must be as stunning to Philip as it was unbelievable to his friends.

"Yeah," said Michael. "He paid you to find the *grendel*. Well, it was on the six o'clock news, so—"

"*I* paid you," Ruth's voice cut across Michael's; banked coals on the edge of flaming. "*I* paid you to find it out, so tell me what I paid for."

Philip stood up and dug in his pocket. After much digging he produced a crumpled wad of twenties and set them on the table. Melior's signet ring gleamed on his finger.

"He paid me," Philip said. His voice was rough, slightly hoarse. "He paid me to tell *him,* not anyone else." Philip's entire body vibrated with the tension of futile resistance. "He gets what he paid for."

Michael had a look on his face indicating he'd bitten into a peach, only to find it rotten inside. "You made a bargain to look for the information for him. But it isn't a secret, is it?" Michael said coaxingly.

Philip closed his eyes. Ruth had problems of her own; only behavior as *out of character* as this of Philip's could draw her notice now.

"We made a bargain," Philip said, his voice strained.

"What sort of bargain exactly, Philip?" Naomi asked gently.

Philip rubbed his eyes again, and stared at the television as if the sports and weather could save him. When he spoke, he chose his words as if they were footsteps through an invisible minefield.

"He came and got . . . what there was to get. And he told me to pick up the stuff from Hunan Balcony and bring it here. And he told me not to tell you anything else until tomorrow," Philip sounded exhausted at having told them this much.

"But he doesn't think he's going to kill it," Michael said.

Michael's words didn't quite sink in. "If anyone else makes a stunning revelation," Ruth announced, "I shall burst my bud of calm—"

"And blossom into a copyrighted quotation," Naomi agreed. "If Philip feels honor-bound to do what Melior said we can talk him out of it later. After Michael explains *who* isn't going to kill *what.*"

Michael didn't bother to tell them what he suspected; that it was magic, not honor, that motivated Philip's reticence. If they had doomed heroes, why not a *geas* as well? And speaking of which—

"Melior isn't going to kill the *grendel,*" Michael said. "He said so."

* * *

He hadn't been here before, but the passersby were glad enough to furnish the information. And he had memorized the workings of the telephone.

"I know where I must go now," he said when she arrived. "Will you accompany me, Mistress Jane?"

It took Michael a while to explain elvish precognition to the others—especially as, he suspected, he hadn't understood Melior's explanation very well himself. But what he did manage to make very clear was that Melior believed that he could see into the future, and that Melior couldn't see himself killing the *grendel* anywhere in the future he saw.

"But why would he go if he knew he wasn't going to kill it?" Philip said in frustration.

"Because nobody else would go with him," Ruth said bitterly. "None of us believed in him, none of us trusted him enough to—"

"Hold on, Ruth," Naomi said. "Just how detailed is this vision of Melior's, Michael? Does he see the *grendel* at all? Does he see someone else kill it? We *know* it's there."

"Now," Philip added.

"When I get my hands on him," Ruth said in a low voice of promise, "*I* am going to kill him. The *grendel* isn't going to have anything to worry about."

"I don't know," said Michael. "He just kept saying we'd all be sorry later that we'd missed this chance."

"But anybody who has Melior's sword can kill the *grendel,*" Ruth protested. Her head hurt, and thinking was an effort. Her *brain* hurt.

But underneath the exhaustion and pain was hope, because if Melior's *grendel* was real after all that meant there was a way for the hero to win.

"Not quite," Naomi said. "The Sword of—what was it?"

"Maiden's Tears," supplied Michael.

"—is what kills it, but any mere human who touches the sword is going to turn into another *grendel.* You might kill that one, but there it'll be to do all over again."

"A woman's work is never done," Ruth said, with a faint attempt at humor.

"So where is it?" Michael said. "The sword, the *grendel,* the whole tamale?"

All eyes turned to Philip.

"No." Philip's voice was quite determined. "And I wiped the disks and tapes and shredded the papers." He looked grimly unhappy, as anyone might who was in the process of alienating his only friends.

"But, Philip," Naomi said coaxingly, "You've got to tell us. We can't help him if we don't know where he's gone."

"We had a bargain," Philip said wearily.

"Leaving aside how we could help him if we knew where he'd gone," Michael said.

"Well, this has got to be the first time you ever did something because somebody asked you to," Ruth snapped Philip-ward. "It's just a stupid promise—he won't ever know and I don't care if he does. *Where is he?*"

"If promising is stupid, then so is going down there when he knows he won't kill it," Philip said with desperate logic.

"Granted," said Naomi. "It *was* stupid."

"No," said Philip. "It was a covenant. If you don't do what you say you're going to do, nobody can ever trust anybody."

The words were obviously Melior's, and Philip's look of anguish was proof of the indigestibility of the concept. Ruth would have been less surprised if he'd started spouting Classical Greek.

"You ought to know better than to make promises to elves," Michael said sternly to Philip. "Leave him alone, Nai. I don't think he *can* say. I hope Melior had a good reason for making him promise."

"To get himself killed," Ruth said miserably.

Naomi bounced to her feet. "We've got to do something."

"We are doing something," Michael said. "We're waiting for midnight. Twelve-oh-one. Tomorrow. So why don't we have dinner while we wait?"

Their train was stopped at 34th Street.

"What are we supposed to do now?" Jane said. The station was jammed with angry commuters, jammed as if it were peak rush hour. The PA system was repeating helpful information over and over again with its speakers turned to "High Distort". Useless.

"I must get to the Down Town," Melior said. "The *grendel* is there."

Stephen Mallison's sword was carefully wrapped in brown paper with a red-and-white mailing label on the front. Melior carried it, hoping it would be as inconspicuous as Jane thought. He wore a *nylon backpack* slung over one shoulder; it was heavy with trailbread and chocolate and a two-quart canteen filled with brandied water. He carried a small lantern, and in the *backpack* were a dozen candles to power it.

And behind him stood his squire.

It might have been Ruth. It ought to have been Ruth. But Ruth loved him and Jane did not. Jane could bear to watch him die.

In fact, thought Melior, she might even enjoy it. He looked at Jane.

Jane's head swiveled as she regarded stalled commuters, backed up trains, and the indefinable air of Great Events in the wind.

"The *grendel* is downtown," she said, wanting to be clear on this one point.

"Philip's scrying has told me so. There have been vanishments and tales of prowling beasts, and now I will seek it at the center of its web of destruction."

That was the information Philip had given Melior, the information that made this work. The pattern of the kills. Jane did not waste time wondering if the information was true or false; it didn't really matter to her. This was the data they were using, and the rules of the game were that it didn't matter if the data were true or not. It simply *was,* and on its basis Melior would go to a certain place and begin his hunt.

She had already been prepared when he called her—not hoping she would be asked, because hope was not a word in Jane's personal lexicon, but, rather, being ready if he did.

No one else had to know, after all.

And so Jane, always so neat and ladylike, had real denim jeans and waterproof boots, a military surplus pullover, and a black watchcap pulled down over her hair to hide its telltale gleam. No one had seen her leave her room dressed that way; there was no one to ask her what she meant by it and no one to laugh; Melior had no clothes-sense anyway.

And everything she had could simply disappear once this adventure was over, even the backpack, with its freight of food and water, flashlight and map. Disposable. Deniable.

Assuming they ever went anywhere at all.

"The trains aren't going downtown," Jane pointed out.

She did wonder why the trains had been stopped, but not very much. How to get to where Melior wanted to go, following the laws of this world, that was Jane's puzzle.

"There is a way. There must be a way. Find it for me!" Melior pled urgently.

Jane thought hard for a moment. The trains weren't going downtown. Fine.

"Come on. Let's get out of here. We're going to the World Trade Center."

"She isn't there," Naomi said. She set the telephone receiver back in its cradle.

"Quarter to ten. They shut the phones into the dorm down at ten," Michael said. "I could run over there."

"No, leave it. Why shouldn't she get a good night's sleep?" Naomi said.

"Even if we don't," Ruth said. "Twelve-oh-one," she said to Philip's hunched shoulders.

Philip shook his head and said nothing. He'd already told them that "tomorrow" meant dawn at the earliest—the start of day in a society with no clock but the sun. Ruth thought he was probably right, but had no intention of letting that stop her.

"And what then?" Naomi said. *"Think,* guys—Melior's in the subway chasing a monster. The monster's real. What do we do?"

"Call CNN," suggested Philip, but his heart wasn't in it.

"Where do we start?" said Michael to the air. "Even when we know where to start," he added. Philip winced, very slightly.

"I think you're making this too complicated," Ruth said slowly. "You're looking for a *grendel* in the subway. Okay. It's grabbing people in Lower Manhattan, fine. But where is it *living?* Not on the tracks. This *grendel's* supposed to be not-too-bright, right? But it's managed not to get hit by a train—and even if a head-on collision didn't kill it, it'd still do a number on the train, right?"

"And make the six o'clock news. And the pages of all the newspapers," said Michael. "And this hasn't happened."

"So the *grendel,"* said Ruth logically, "hasn't been hit by a train. Or seen by one, because that'd be on the news now, you'd better believe."

"Right," Naomi said. "But it hasn't been. And the first thing anybody's heard was the news tonight," Naomi said. "The first thing *most* people heard," she emended.

"Not quite," said Philip, and clammed up suddenly.

"So where in the subway system do the trains *not* run?" Ruth asked. "We can start looking there. Simple."

"Break into the New York Subway System and she calls it simple," Naomi said.

"It beats working for a living," said Michael.

"New information on the Subway Snatcher. Details after this," said the television.

He found he did not like the subterranean way any more this time than he had the last time he had been here. Rohannan Melior of the House of the Silver Silences stepped, with painstaking caution, onto the subway tracks.

Mistress Jane had been correct. Far south, in the World of the Trade Center, was the terminus for the Double-E line. Commuters, forewarned, had made other arrangements. They had reached that place by surface means. Once there, the unguarded platform there had been empty.

And he and Jane had descended.

Jane shone the light down along the tracks, careful not to blind Melior's dark-adapted eyes. And as she walked she thought, trying out Melior's plan for practicability. Walk down to Wall Street. Track the *grendel* to its lair. Grab the sword, which Melior was sure would be there. Cut the *grendel* into collops. Leave.

The difference between a plan like that and wishful thinking was small, if even extant. And it required luck of a staggering order of improbability to work.

But Melior wasn't asking for Jane's opinion. Only for her help. She could give that.

"If someone sees you, they're going to stop you," she offered at last.

Melior stopped and turned back to her. Jane flicked the beam of the flashlight away as he moved, shining it away from him. In the darkness his eyes were metallic changeant moons; the light flashing from dilated pupils. Melior waited.

"The platforms. You can't get near them without being seen. There could be someone up there. Subway cops," Jane said.

A map both accurate and representational of the subway system was hard to find, but Jane had one. She peered at it. Down here the intervals between the stations were shorter. The flashlight's beam turned her map into a paper lantern; lighting the paper and turning the lines to gray scrimshaw.

"Or commuters. If there are any. If they see you, you'll be in trouble," she added.

Melior saw no reason to doubt her. Jane was not lying, and he knew it. "These commuters," he said after a pause, "there is one time more than another when they are likely to be here?"

"Sure." Jane looked at her watch. "Gone by ten, maybe, especially this far downtown. But you still can't get *past* the platforms without being seen."

"When the time comes," Melior said, "you may leave that to me. For now, we must find a place to occupy the time until we may proceed."

It was twelve o'clock, and Philip hadn't told. He was neither triumphant nor defiant about it, and even through her anger Ruth sensed that Philip was as frustrated by his refusal as they were.

"We've gone about this all wrong," Naomi said. She cradled a large earthenware teacup in her hands. She wasn't looking at Philip.

"Red hot needles, maybe?" Michael said. It was hard to tell if he was making a joke. Maybe Michael wasn't sure himself.

"About Melior," Naomi said. "He came to us for help. We shouldn't have just said 'no.' "

"He wanted to go hunting space-alligators in the subway," Michael pointed out. "*Grendels.* Whatever. But—" he sighed and rubbed the back of his neck. "Too bad we didn't know then what we know now."

"We don't *know* anything," Ruth pointed out wearily.

"But that isn't the point," Naomi said. "Going down into the subway is a stupid idea, take it all in all. It doesn't matter whether what's there is fictional or real. And we should have found another way for him."

"But you didn't." It was Philip who spoke. For the last several hours he had been all but silent, as the strange game he had played with Melior went from being a joke, to a business proposition, to a tragedy, and on to a contest of wills.

"No," said Naomi. "We didn't."

"And what are you going to do now?" Philip asked her.

"What are *you* going to do, Phil?" Michael said.

Philip's mouth twisted mockingly. "Me? When did I ever do anything that mattered, Michael?" He shrugged angrily. "All you've got left to do is take up a collection for the funeral."

"It's May 5th. Sunrise is at five-oh-five a.m." Ruth blurted out. She put the newspaper down. "And at five-oh-six a.m. . . ." She paused.

"We have to figure out what to do," Naomi said. She regarded her companions. "*Think* about it, guys. There *really is* a monster in the subway. It's killing people. Melior's gone after it, but he doesn't think he's going to do very well. It's up to us. What do we do?"

Anything was better than thinking about where Melior might be and what *he* was doing. "He asked for a sword," Ruth began.

"But only *The* sword will kill it. So he says. But since we don't have anything better to go on, we might as well take Melior's word for it," Michael said.

"So we get *The* sword," Ruth said slowly. The rules. All magic had rules. A story where the magic didn't have rules was no fun for the reader. There were rules to everything if you could only find out what they were. "But the *grendel*'s guarding it—isn't it?"

"Well," said Naomi consideringly, *I* would be. It sounds like first we've got to get the *grendel.*"

The One no longer slept. The One guarded The Object; guarded and fed and waited the day that The Other foretold to it would come and be destroyed.

Insofar as it could be, in the grip of its monstrous and eternal hunger, The One was content. It had purpose; the thing which its human chrysalis had always lacked. It had a function to perform, and, as far as its truncated intellect could perceive those abstractions, a sense of achievement, of honor, of glory and struggle.

And triumph.

The Other could come as he chose. The Other could come down into The One's kingdom and search as he chose. The Object was secure. And The One could disappear at will.

But The One did not choose to. At this moment there were Men in The One's domain, and The One remembered Men.

Men meant *food.*

Jane had explained the third rail and its lethal properties to Melior very carefully twice—the second time once she realized that he didn't have the faintest idea what electricity was. She was pretty sure now that he knew that if he touched it he would die. She had not bothered to enumerate the scant exceptions to that rule; they were unlikely enough to occur, and since he probably thought the whole thing ran by magic anyway, there was no point in confusing him.

The tunnels weren't so bad once you got used to them.

They spent the waiting time sitting against the wall of the tunnel, near a cubbyhole they could retreat into if a train came. Jane had brought extra batteries for her flashlight; she spent the waiting time reading a book.

And no trains did come. It was strangely silent here in the tunnels beneath the bottom tip of Manhattan; only a faint suck and sough of wind from a place miles away where the tunnels broke out into moonlight. Even the ventilation grates which marked some of the older tunnels were absent here. A separate world, an underground dominion where there was neither sun nor moon—

Abruptly Jane sat up straighter. Neither sun nor moon. Sun nor moon. . . .

And there was neither sun nor moon/And all the roaring of the sea—" Suddenly Jane wished for her guitar, the words of the old ballad mocking her. Neither sun nor moon. A sound like the sea roaring, or what you heard when you put a seashell to your ear, or wind. Rivers of blood, or something at least as disgusting.

Fairyland. By all the laws of ballad-land, the New York subway tunnels were Fairyland.

Was this the actual answer, the unriddle that would solve Melior's quest? The knowledge that the Real World—Melior's World of Iron, possessed all the landmarks and appurtenances of Faery, if only you looked at it just right?

"Ill met by moonlight, proud Titania." "How many miles to Babylon?/ Threescore miles and ten." "Oh, where are you bound?/Said the false knight on the road" "The sedge is wither'd from the lake/And no birds sing."

A faery knight, a ravished sword, a monster monstrous through its own cupidity. What was there in that baggage of twice-told plain tales from the hollow hills that could help now?

"It is past midnight," Melior said suddenly, "and those who travel are safe within doors. It is time for us to travel, Mistress Jane."

She looked at her watch. Almost one o'clock in the morning, and a couple of miles of tunnels to cover before they got to the place where Melior wanted to be.

"Whassamatter you guys? Ya wanna live forever?" Jane quoted, getting to her feet.

Now that she had made the connection, new evidence kept presenting itself; images from the ballads Jane loved to play without reposing the least belief in them. For Jane, normally unfanciful, these associations clothed the prosaic ugliness of the subway tunnels in faery. Once, in a place where A and C crossed 4-5-6 and several sets of tracks ran parallel, there was a faint mournful wail in the distance, and Jane and Melior retreated into concealment to watch the passage of a yellow-and-black flatcar. It did not rely on the third rail to power it; the watchers in their hiding place heard and smelled the workings of a gasoline engine.

Three men stood on its open surface, peering out into the dark. One carried a rifle. A Border Patrol for the line between fact and fantasy. When it was gone, Jane and Melior went on.

They reached the first platform. Harsh blue incandescence like a special effect spilled out along the tracks. The pools in the center of the trackbed were silver footprints, and every soda can and discarded wrapper was an elphen horde.

It was at this point that the first faint disquieting sensation came upon Jane that things weren't precisely right. *The time is out of joint.* She had the sneaking suspicion of the teetotaler that there might have been whiskey in the whiskey, a feeling that the description "self-controlled" was no longer Truth in Advertising.

Melior stopped just short of the point where anyone standing behind the yellow line which passengers are urged not to cross when a train is not in the station could see him. He held two fingers to his lips in an almost-familiar gesture and motioned Jane closer. She put out her flashlight and came over. The soot on the wall was the black matte softness of velvet and the slick untrustworthiness of grease.

"First I will go, and mark you well how I do it. Then follow, and haply no one will reckon us," Melior said. He looked over his shoulder at the platform. "And should the alarm be raised, do you draw them off and I will make my way as best I might."

And leave me to take the rap. But from Melior's point of view it was reasonable. He was best equipped to kill the *grendel.* She was just the spear carrier. If Melior'd happened to have a spear.

And Jane was very well equipped to deal with any question that began with "why." *Why did you, why don't you, why will you, why won't you, why do you. . . .*

Tolerated everywhere she'd ever been. As opposed, perhaps, to being wanted, welcomed, valued. Not noticed enough to be disliked; in a world where isolation kills and science has shown that any attention is preferred to none, Jane Treasure Greyson was tolerated; not even noticed enough to get rejected. Tolerated. And what is there in that to connect with enough to fight it? Tolerated. Blandly unseen, glossed over, endured. Until any one who dared communicate was forced to pay the teind for all those who never tried to. And driven away, so that she could keep the one thing she had.

She knew exactly what she did. Pitiless insight isn't called that for no reason. Pity makes allowance and turns its face away. Intellect does not. And so the same thing that let her see their neglect, that caused their neglect, made certain that they would never simply leave her alone, because such a clever little thing, such an earnest, forever hopeful of being loved little thing, such a biddable little thing must surely be useful, some-how—

But Melior valued her, without ever trying to know her. Without using her, except in such a blatant and obvious fashion that it was almost as if she gave her help freely. And for that Jane would provide the one gift in her ken. Loyalty.

"You'll need the map," she whispered back, and transferred it, care-fully folded, to his waiting black-gloved hand.

But all was anticlimax, as after that Melior crossed the open space, crouched low and moving swiftly, crossing directly beneath the platform, hugging it closely to minimize the time when he would be visible. To discover whether there were watchers in truth would have revealed them; they could only go on as if there were and hope that there weren't. His silver hair was a bright flag in the darkness; the sword a golden sparkle at his hip.

And Magic was afoot in the world.

Melior crossed, safely, making his way into the other darkness, hidden again. It would not have surprised Jane if he had gone on and left her there; after all, he had almost warned her. But instead he stopped, turned back, and waited.

And now it was her turn. She hesitated. It had looked easy when he did it. There probably wasn't anyone up there anyway. All she had to do was walk, very fast and crouching optional, across the space that was the open front of the platform.

And still she wavered. What if she slipped, what if she fell, what if there was someone up there after all? *What if she looked stupid?*

Go. The demand was almost a spoken word; clear enough to have been heard. Jane let it galvanize her; push her forward without thought.

Her shoulder slid along the soot, a featherwhisper scraping that told her she was going rightly. She watched her feet, chary of the bottles, the wrappers, the noisy treacherous footing beneath.

A subway platform is at least the width of the street above, sometimes the length of a city block and more. A distance hardly thought of when choosing which car to enter or stairs to exit by. A tiny eternity to cross through the gloom of the railbed below. Her heart hammered; consciousness was suspended in the throbbing silver of the Eternal Now and for once Jane Greyson lived in the moment.

Melior faded back into the darkness as she advanced, preserving the distance between them until she was safely past the point where she might be seen. Then he allowed her to catch up to him.

They went on. After a few yards the darkness closed in again and Jane flicked on her flashlight. A few blocks to the next platform, and then a little beyond that the crossing of tracks where they changed from uptown to crosstown lines as they navigated this web of angles toward their goal.

"Can I get there by candlelight?
Yes, and back again."

· 17 ·

Judgment Day

DAWN WAS A white sheen over Fort Lee, New Jersey.

No one had slept. Not Michael, not Ruth, not Philip looking red-eyed and stubborn like a mutant Spartacus of laboratory rats. The excitement of plotting how best to go after Melior's *grendel* had foundered on the complete lack of information and—on Ruth's part—a worry for Melior that was literally, surprisingly, paralyzing. He was facing the *grendel*. The *grendel* was real. Melior was foredoomed to die and he'd cut out on her without giving her a chance to make a real nuisance of herself, just like a paperback hero.

And she knew, with sharp and annoyed certainty, that her life was in suspension and would hang fire forever if she could not see Melior again and ask him—

What?

"Wall Street," said Philip in a flat, tired voice. "The attacks all center around the City Hall Station, down by Wall Street."

"Attacks?" Michael seized on the word. The morning sun was shining on his face, lighting his eyes to a brilliant green. But not the impossible green of Melior's.

"Attacks," Philip said. "Six or seven people that they know of are missing-presumed-history and about a dozen more are incommunicado, a small town in New Jersey. Trackworkers, and like that. And the street people are avoiding the Lower Manhattan stations for sleeping and pan-handling."

"How did you find all this out?" Naomi asked, honestly curious.

Philip pushed up his bifocals. "Stats. Missing person reports. I cracked BlueNet, the cop BBS, and pulled the local gossip for the last week or so. Everybody's jumpy, but it could look like just a lot of coincidence, you know?"

"Until last night," Ruth said bleakly.

"Which brings us back to Topic A: what do we do?" Naomi said.

"We could, of course, let the trained professionals handle it," Michael said. "That *is* what they're there for. They've got manpower, resources, access to tools. They can get an animal control officer in there with a net and drag the thing out."

"You're no fun," Philip said under his breath.

"Before it kills how many more people?" Naomi asked.

"That's a cheap shot, Nai," Michael said. "They're doing what they can right now, and telling them what we know isn't going to change that. Every whack in New York and the five boroughs is already calling up and confessing to being the Subway Snatcher. We'll sound like just one more nutcase."

"So we just say "What is Truth?" and wash our hands of it?" Ruth said. "What about Melior?"

"Well, what do you think we could do to help him—walk up to the *grendel* and refuse to let it graduate?" Michael asked.

"If he isn't going to kill it, and if all your damned trained professionals are so hotshot, why don't we get him out of there?" Ruth snapped back.

"Getting Melior Down and Not Hurting Anybody," Naomi said, gazing at the ceiling. "Does it matter whether the *grendel*'s dead if it's captured and Melior has his sword back?" she asked.

"Not to me," Ruth said. Suddenly the gears were turning in her head again. "I think we've been going at this inside-out. We've been concentrating on the *grendel*, because that's what Melior thinks is important. But the *grendel* isn't as important as the sword—"

"So forget the *grendel*," Naomi finished for her. "Find Melior, hold him off until the police catch the *grendel*—"

"And then find the sword," Michael finished.

"Which will be one of two places," Naomi said.

"Either where the *grendel* hid it," Ruth added.

"Or somewhere in Washington crated up next to the Lost Ark from *Raiders*," Naomi finished, "which may be difficult to get to but not impossible—"

"And burglarizing the CIA or searching the MTA will be a lot easier without playing Bullets and Bracelets with the Thing from Forty-thousand Plotlines," Michael said. "So all we have to do is get our hands on Melior and convince *him*."

"That's Ruth's job," Naomi said.

Everybody looked at Ruth, and Ruth had the panicked feeling of having been asked to speak in public.

"He'll listen to her," Naomi added inexorably.

"He won't do it," Philip said, not about Ruth.

"He wants the sword, not the *grendel*," Michael pointed out. "This is a way to the sword. If he doesn't get picked up. We didn't turn Melior over to the cops in the first place because if we did, he'd disappear into a little underground room somewhere. Which he still could, if we can't get him out in time."

" 'The mistake was in not forbidding the serpent,' " Ruth quoted. " 'Then he would have eaten the serpent.' Mark Twain."

"So how do we find him?" Naomi said.

"Come home, Elfie, all is forgiven," Philip muttered.

"Go where he's gone," Michael said. "And there's no good time for that."

"Right," said Naomi. "Come on, Ruth, let's get dressed for a little nightcrawling. Michael, we'll meet you at your place in about forty minutes. Check the radio to see if they've started running the Lower Manhattan lines again. We'll have to figure out how to get onto the tracks somehow."

"Jane was," Ruth said suddenly. "Down on the tracks, I mean. The day she went on the subway trip with Melior and came back all over soot. They were down in the tunnels somewhere. They have to have been."

"Fine," said Naomi. "They turn on the dorm phones at six." She looked at her watch. "It's almost that now. We can call her. Get going," she added, as Michael stood up. "And you," she said to Philip, "had better get back to your computers. I think this time you're going to work for free."

It took them four hours of painstaking subway crawling, backtracking, and waiting, to reach the stalking ground. In the pauses Melior told Jane as much as he knew about the nature of *grendels*.

"Their food is the flesh of their kind, and their whole nature is to hoard beyond their use and spoil what they cannot take away. And their appetite grows with what it feeds upon, until at last their hunger lays waste to all that is near."

Jane had pondered this as a lifestyle choice and then asked: "Well, just how much area can they lay waste to?"

Melior had smiled. "Anything within their reach, and their reach grows with time. If they could ever bear to abandon their hoard, they would be even more dangerous. But it takes much to dislodge a *grendel* from its place, and then the creature only lairs again as soon as it may."

"If it can stand the sun," Jane had added, and Melior had agreed. "But this one may be strong enough to do that even now. And if it is not, there is so much darkness in your city that its choices are many."

But Melior had not spoken for the last half hour or so. At their last stop he had made Jane put away her flashlight, and handed her, in exchange, one of those small camping lanterns that is simply a candle enclosed by glass. *How many miles to Babylon?* Now she followed him by the light of the candle *Threescore miles and ten* and tried to ignore the words that circled round in her head *Can I get there by candlelight?* *Yes, and back again.*

"Hist," said Melior, and Jane was so keyed up that it was only much later that she registered that the archaism should have been funny. "It is very near."

The scent of evil that these Ironworlders refused to ken hung in the tunnel like sickly marsh mist. The beast was near, and Melior hoped without knowledge that Mistress Jane would run when he bid her, when the *grendel* turned first to him, ancient enemy, and he made his futile assault upon it. Twisted product of magic gone wrong—elphen magic—it was his responsibility as March-Lord of the Silver Silences to undo what his kind had wrought.

Perhaps the little magic he hoarded against this moment could harm it; cripple it so that those who came after would find the *grendel* easier prey. Stephen's sword hung naked at his hip; there had been no time or chance to contrive furniture for it, but the weight was welcome—oh, to hold a sword again; to die a clean death with it in his hand—!

But he was so very far from home.

And his failure loomed dark and tangled across all the leys of the future, strangling his Foresight in its single asseveration: that the *grendel* would not die by his hand.

So it must be that he would die, and when he died the Sword would be lost here forever, and Baligant who had plotted his Line's downfall would reign triumphant.

He could see no way to escape that. Ruth and her friends would accept no proof he could offer that this danger existed. And even when Philip spread out all his truths to them as he had to Melior, would they say any different?

He did not know. He had not dared wait to find out. Each time he had brought them proofs they had thought him mad. Perhaps this greatest proof would have seemed to them only the greatest madness, and then they, lovingly and with kindness, would imprison him to keep him from doing what he must.

Perhaps he *was* mad. But as the humans of this land said: even though you were paranoid, it did not mean you had no enemies.

Jane wasn't there. Naomi put down the phone and looked at Ruth, who was just pulling on her jacket of choice. Merrie Month of May or not, it was going to be cold down there.

Ruth had scoured her wardrobe, as Naomi had, for clothing she wouldn't mind throwing out as soon as she got back. She wore a sloppy long-sleeved singlet that was already the shade of gray it would otherwise turn, gray-green cargo pants, and an Army Surplus windcheater that had seemed like a much better idea in the store than it had when she'd got it home. The black canvas hi-tops on her feet were another such purchase; impulsive and impossible and too much like the ones Philip wore. She'd pinned and braided her hair up into a hard knot on the back of her head and covered it with a crocheted black bun-doily that Naomi had dug up from somewhere. When she looked in the mirror Ruth decided she looked like the Terminator's fashion-victim sister.

Naomi, of course, looked as if she'd been shopping for months with the aim of schlepping through subway tunnels. She had on tightly-laced green rubber duckblind halfboots into which were tucked crisp poplin suntans *(ironed. . . .)* over which was a no-nonsense bush jacket. She was even wearing gloves, and Ruth, thinking of what she'd have to touch down there, wished she weren't the sort who regularly lost her winter gloves every March.

"You look like an outtake from *King Solomon's Sewers,*" she'd said, as Naomi was dialing Jane.

"Just trying to bring a fashion sense to urban fantasy," Naomi had answered as she listened to the phone ring on unanswered. Now she looked at Ruth, hand still over the receiver.

"We can worry about her or about Melior," Naomi said to Ruth, as if she were offering her a choice between chocolate and vanilla. "And personally I think Jane could be lots of places in no trouble while we know exactly how much trouble Melior is in."

"Right." Ruth drew in a deep breath, which did her exactly as much good as the last one had; none.

"Come on," Naomi said. "Let's get Michael."

A long time afterward Jane decided that what the problem had been was that it was too easy.

THE SWORD OF MAIDEN'S TEARS

It was true that Melior behaved as if the situation was dangerous, but then, Melior behaved as if walking the streets of New York was High Adventure. And it had been hour on hour, and all they had done was walk, through an environment that lost all of its terror and much of its charm through long acquaintance.

Now that changed.

It was after four o'clock in the morning, an hour in which Jane's body was asleep even if she wasn't. The first candle had burnt down and she had changed it by flashlight. Melior had given her his pack and canteen to carry as well as her own and panthered forward on flexed joints like a dark and dangerous balletomane. And she wasn't paying attention to much of anything beyond following him and wondering if they could stop soon.

There was a hiss. A clang as the *gladius* rang off the subway wall. Melior sprang sideways, landing directly in the center of the railbed. The sword flashed in the light of Jane's lantern and Melior's every gesture spoke of fearful threat.

She backed away, icy with the uprush of fight-or-flight chemistry, and in that instant there was a "tok" sound like the Babe hitting one over the fence and the scunnering ring of the sword sliding away into the dark, both combined with the snapshot image of Melior flung boneless to the ground.

It had happened so fast.

Facts. Jane dealt with them, the momentary chemical alarm pushed back to unimportance. New information reached another of her senses. Jane looked up, beyond the silver flame of Melior's hair being slowly extinguished by blood and black water.

She raised the lantern higher, but even so the light barely reached what stood in the shadows, that had struck Melior down so casually.

Jane looked at the *grendel*. The *grendel* looked at Jane. Melior's body lay between them; vulnerable.

It was so much taller than she was that there was no point in assigning it a height. It smelled of excrement and rotting meat, thickly and insistently; as she stared, she saw it more clearly.

Its skin was the livid purple-gray of gangrene, wrinkled like a raisin and beginning to scale. Patches of what might have been mold spotted the skin here and there; exotic fauna known only to pathologists. The *grendel*'s eyes were small white globes set in an angry weeping expanse of scarlet flesh; abraded sockets swollen and peeling.

If she had screamed, if she had run, if she had shown any reaction to it at all, things might have gone differently. If it had not eaten, recently and well, it might have taken more interest. But she was not The Other, and she was not The Object, and soon The Other would not be able to hurt it at all.

Jane stared at the *grendel*. Her heartbeat did not race; it was possible she was not thinking of danger at all. She simply looked, and recorded what she saw, and waited for what she saw to change.

There was a blast of sound; an eerie, flatulent howl. Startled, she dropped the candle and could still see; Jane looked behind her. Far but not far enough she saw the flatcar they had seen earlier; but this time it was on the tracks behind her, sweeping the tunnel with its spotlight. The over-amplified yowp of an electronic bullhorn stunned her with pure noise, its message lost to distortion.

She looked back. The *grendel* was gone as if it had never been there. Melior raised one hand; a feeble gesture.

"Run," he whispered.

There was only one direction possible. Melior on the tracks would delay the flatcar, moving at its stately 35 mph. She could get away.

This time Jane did not pause to think. She threw away everything she carried and ran.

The bullhorn squawked. The spotlight drilled into her back, but it had not cost her much of her night vision. Down here the lines converged again, and in the underground cathedral vastness warning lights burned like the stars of an earthbound constellation. On her left, across a no-man's-land of third rails, she saw the pale gleaming refuge of a station platform.

She heard the change in engine pitch as the flatcar stopped at Melior's body. If she was quick, she could reach the platform and a state of plausible deniability.

She didn't think the *grendel* would follow her to the light; more precisely, she didn't think of the *grendel* at all; that was something for later, after she had performed the function for which she now knew Melior had chosen her, and brought back the truth of her own eyes to the only people left on earth who might be able to act upon it.

There was a monster loose in the New York Subway.

It was on a May morning, and just like in any ballad the day was determined to be beautiful enough to make Pollyanna suspicious. Ruth had the edged feeling of too much tea and too little sleep, and the air like wild silk and the light like raw honey did nothing to anchor her in reality.

Michael was waiting for them on the corner. Philip was nowhere in sight. Conversation was superfluous. They walked over and caught the A Train downtown.

New Yorkers are a blasé lot. Once, many years ago, for a bet, to prove a point, or on some esoteric scientific *raison* a man undertook to walk stark naked (except for shoes) the length of Fifth Avenue. Extant photos (snapped from behind) show him passing among New Yorkers who are neither looking nor not-looking, strenuously proving themselves sangfroidian even at the cost of common sense.

This, combined with Warhol's heart-held dictum that there is a fifteen-minute time limit on fame, assured that no matter who had been dragged by what off a subway platform at the height of the rush hour the night before, today the trains were running and nobody would be so *gauche* as to wonder whether making the morning commute was worth the personal hazard.

The only trouble the three of them had was finding standing room on the rush-hour trains.

It took them more than an hour to reach West Fourth Street from 116th, in between the profit and the loss, in the T.S. Eliot where the dreams cross. When they reached it, Michael gestured and they were borne onto the platform in a tide of Thursday morning lemming ballet.

"Now I know why I don't work for a living," Naomi panted as they fought their way to freedom. "Where now?"

"Phone call," said Michael. "Coffee. And maybe one of you professional geniuses can figure out how we're going to get down onto the tracks in the middle of all this without being either seen or creamed."

"Easy enough if Lower Manhattan's still stopped," Naomi said.

"There's only six or seven ways to find out," Ruth pointed out.

"Come on. Let's find a phone that's working."

On the way out, Ruth glanced at the clock overhead. The time was seven-twenty-eight.

It was eight-thirty-five when Jane let herself into Ruth and Naomi's apartment with her spare key. It had been a little before five wen she finally reached the surface of New York, at a station and line she'd never seen, somewhere in the depths of Wall Street.

She'd struck out first for Broadway, and had seen the red warning flashes of emergency lights before she'd seen anything more.

Paranoid as a lifestyle choice, Jane had not had to think twice about heading south, toward Battery Park and away from police vans, emergency vehicles, firetrucks, minicams, and anything else containing someone who might ask her questions. She had a pretty good idea that the *grendel* wasn't Melior's little secret any more—which would account for the fact that there'd been no subway traffic until the flatcar full of fuzz showed up—but she didn't know how much of what version anybody knew, and she didn't intend to be the one to lighten the load of their ignorance. Jane had other plans for her Thursday.

Having gone south as far as was safe she headed east, having no desire to be mugged, either at any time or before she'd delivered the news to the others. Melior'd been right all along, and that should just about fry Philip to the ultimate max.

Earliest morning broke about twenty minutes after Jane came above ground; bright and clear, one of those mornings that seem almost to be safety-sealed for your protection; too good to be true. Vintage season, and like the C.L. Moore story, only the overture to the most select form of apocalypse.

But up-and-coming Gotterdammerungs weren't Jane's affair, and frying Philip LeStrange was. Philip *Leslie* LeStrange.

At the hour and in the area she had chosen, Jane's tatterdemalion appearance was not too much noticed. Just another strange street person, this one young enough to be a runaway.

She knew what her few observers thought and it suited her fine; Manhattanites weren't a charitable people. It took her until about six a.m. to hoof it clear of the media circus pitch and find a phone that worked.

It did not occur to her that she was already missed, that there was already videotaped proof of the *grendel*'s existence and that the others were already trying to figure out how best to save Melior from himself. She thought there was all the time in the world, and that Ruth would hardly relish being awakened so soon after dawn.

And so, hesitating, trying to decide not only what Melior wanted her to do but what a reasonable person *would* do, Jane waited until six-thirty to phone Ruth and Naomi.

The phone rang. And rang, and rang, until Jane was quite certain no one would answer.

She phoned Philip's number. Whoever answered hung up the phone without speaking, and after the third time, Jane gave up. Served Philip right for not giving them any of his *private* phone numbers.

Michael was out, too. But that was reasonable; Michael liked jogging, and morning classes, and other masochistic pursuits.

She found a McDonald's and ordered breakfast, simply because it was the sort of thing that normal people did and Jane, perhaps, had new doubts about her ability to fake normalcy. She ate it walking back up the street, wondering whether she was going to have an attack of nerves about going down into the subway again. She decided she wouldn't, and caught the "A" Uptown at Canal.

She tried Ruth and Naomi once more, while waiting for the train. No one answered. Jane did not speculate; she went home.

It is entirely possible that Jane passed Ruth and the others at some fulcrum point on the A Line. It is certain that when she reached their apartment (a better place to go than the dorm, where there would be more of that tiresome tribe, nosy people with awkward questions) and buzzed for admittance, there was no answer.

There was nobody home. Without any particular sense of guilt, Jane investigated the apartment thoroughly, but the scribbled notes and lists in Ruth's and Naomi's handwriting conveyed very little.

Except that they were both gone, at a time when they ought not to be gone. She phoned Michael again, but after fifteen unanswered rings she gave it up. After much thought, she even phoned Philip again, but all she got for that was a shouted "Not here!" and the receiver slammed down.

Curiouser and curiouser.

The television only had late-morning happytalk news to offer, and Doubleyew-ten-ten-Wins News Radio was spending its time on things with "East" in the title, like the Near East and Eastern Europe.

She could, of course, dash off and try to rescue Melior. Only she had no idea how badly he'd been hurt, or whether he'd been arrested, and whether anyone claiming to be his friend might just be arrested in turn. She was pretty sure that rescuing Melior would require extensive and creative lying, a skill she knew she lacked, and if she were detained in any fashion Melior's message might not get delivered. Besides, people might call her parents, and then there'd *really* be trouble.

And she knew that Michael or Naomi would be much more efficient at dealing with the mundanes. And success was to be preferred over speed, if you had to choose just one.

Jane gave up and took a shower, scrubbing until the water ran clear. She borrowed a skirt and sweater of Ruth's and a garbage bag for her subway-crawling clothes. Then she headed back for her own dorm room, trying to form a criterion for deciding when she'd have to do what she could without the others.

And then, having walked nearly twelve miles and been up for more than twenty-four hours, she fell asleep on her dorm-room bed before she began to wonder precisely how trustworthy Philip's roommates were in the matter of phone messages at eight-forty-five in the morning.

"Nothing." Michael hung up the phone.

"What *kind* of nothing?" Ruth wanted to know.

"No police reports. Philip says Downtown subway lines are on a half-hour delay, but they're running. No sign of Jane," Michael elaborated.

"Is he sure?" Naomi said.

"He called her again while I was on his other line, and he's got the computer scanning continuously in several places I don't even want to think about. No Jane."

"Dear Philip," Ruth said. "Three phone lines, no waiting. I don't even want to think about how he does that."

"Illegally," Naomi said. "And if he weren't feeling so guilty right now, you still wouldn't have the phone numbers."

"Well I do have them," Michael pointed out unnecessarily, "so come on. I think I know a way to get to where Melior is."

"And then we can play Dodge 'Em cars with real subways. Cute," Naomi said.

"Especially when you pause to consider that there's no place to dodge to," Michael answered cheerfully.

Rohannan Melior of the House of the Silver Silences, firstborn of his Line, of the line of the sons of the Morning Stars, Marchlord and Sword-warden, had had better days.

Much better days.

As it was, he had luck of a sort on his side. The Guardsmen had not seized him armed, and much as he grieved over the loss of Stephen's sword, things that Ruth had said had convinced him it was a better thing in this land to be found unweaponed.

The second point in his favor was that he was injured. In fact, his captors had used him with much solicitous concern upon finding him hurt, and Melior had let them, knowing that every moment spent on him was one more in which his squire might win her freedom.

They asked a number of odd questions about his name and their fingers, about who took precedence and what state he was in. "Utter confusion," Melior had answered honestly to that last, and after that they left him alone with the throbbing pain and sickness in his head until a litter could be brought. Until it came they would not move him, Melior had discovered, and as he lay across the tracks their machine could not proceed.

He realized, listening to them speak among themselves, that some felt he might be a mere thrill-seeker, whatever that might be, but others that he might be victim to the creature that they hunted, which had taken human prey in sight of many only the previous day. Melior closed his eyes against the pain in his head. Now Ruth and the others would have their proof, but Melior was no longer certain it would do any good. These humans who seemed to place too much emphasis upon maintaining the surface illusion at any cost did not seem to have the knack of hunting *grendel.*

He did not think their race would survive.

But at the moment it was Melior who wanted to survive, and not to be taken away to rooms without windows by tribes with meaningless barbarian names like Seaheyah or Efbeyah and tortured there to give up the secrets of his Line.

It was not hard to seem hurt and wearied when the lackeys came to carry him off. When they shifted him onto the litter they had brought, a bright light seemed to dawn behind his eyes and he lay only faintly aware until the cool morning air washed over him. Straps held his body to the pallet; it steadied and jarred as its handlers shifted it, and then began to roll forward on wheels.

Melior opened his eyes once and closed them again. Lights in a spectrum of colors, some flashing, some not. Barking voices, men's and women's both, and a constant howling as of war-horns. So much strangeness, and no Ruth beside him to show by her example that things were proceeding in the normal fashion for the world.

They lifted him into a small hut of the sort that moved and he did not fight them. He did not think he could stand, much less break the straps and run, and innocence was his only defense now that he had fallen into the toils of those his young friends feared more than *grendel.*

A Guardsman got in behind him, and the hut began to roll forward. It increased the sickness in his head, and he only hoped he'd made the right choice and not once more done something that Ruth would think was foolish.

The Guardsman spoke to Melior, his voice hard and barking. A woman's voice interrupted his, telling Melior that this wouldn't hurt, and asked again the meaningless questions about names and fingers and precedence while she shone a light in his eyes.

His eyes. Ruth said they betrayed him. He stared at the white-clothed woman in alarm.

"Reflexes normal," the woman said. "Hi, my name is Holly Kendal, and I'm your EMT for the morning." She brushed his hair back, very carefully, regarding the ears which his lady Ruth had been pleased to call beautiful but entirely wrong. He watched Holly Kendal, who was his EMT, as she sank white teeth into her lower lip and hesitated the briefest instant, and it came to him that she would not betray him.

"How are you feeling?" she asked carefully. "Do you speak English?"

"Dizzy," Melior said, closing his eyes in relief. Holly pressed cool fingers to his wrist. She said she was taking his vitals, that he was being admitted to Bellevue, and a number of other things that Melior simply did not find worth the trouble of remaining conscious to hear.

* * *

Michael took them downtown. It was after nine by now; the great commuter crunch had eased, and they had the weekday morning subways almost (comparatively speaking) to themselves.

Ruth hadn't counted on the rubberneckers and licensed gawkers. The station that Therese Scarlatti had been taken from yesterday was locked, iron gates and all, and removed temporarily from the roster of subway stops. The train might be running, but half the Lower Manhattan IRT stops were closed.

"Worry not," Michael said, and proceeded to take them around a number of crisscrosses and shortcuts that made Ruth exceedingly glad that she was doing this in the company of a six-foot-two weightlifting student librarian.

"Here we are," said Michael finally.

It was a passageway of the sort that let you transfer between uptown, downtown, alphabets, and numbers without paying another fare—assuming, always, that you thought being mugged was worth the trouble. The walls were white tile, the ceiling was claustrophobicly low, and Ruth wouldn't have touched the paving beneath her feet with her bare hands for anything short of life-threatening incentive. The corridor smelled strongly of unpoliced bodily functions.

Interrupting the white tile was a green metal door with a padlock and hasp.

Michael pulled out something that was not quite a key and jiggled it in the lock. After a moment the padlock popped open.

"If anyone is going to break any more laws, I don't want to know about it," Ruth said faintly.

"This is next to last," Michael said reassuringly. "Ladies and, um, ladies, allow me to present to you the jewel in the TA's crown; a little-known access corridor to take you directly—do not pass 'Go', do not collect two hundred dollars—to IRT track-level. If we're caught in here or on the tracks, it's B&E—that's Breaking and Entering to you civilians—but we'll probably get off with a fine providing nobody mentions elves, which will get us a complementary seventy-two-hour commitment for observation in the nearest loony bin. Just keep your mouths shut, okay?"

"I love it when you go all macho," Naomi said. "But how did you know that was here?"

"A friend of mine in Transit told me about it," Michael said, which made Ruth wonder until his opening the door made her forget. He hustled them inside quickly, which made her think this might be even more illegal than it looked.

There was a deadbolt on the inside of the door, and Michael dead-bolted it. He hung the outside padlock on the inside lock and gestured theatrically.

This corridor was smaller than the last, marginally cleaner, and lit by 40-watt light bulbs placed at the longest possible intervals.

"After you," Michael said.

"Idiocy before beauty," Naomi answered, and Michael started down the corridor, ducking.

· 18 ·

One Flew Over the Basilisk's Nest

THAT PLACE WHICH mortals named *Bellevue Emergency* caused Melior to revise his opinions about this world's humans. If they maintained such places as this for their sport, surely the *grendel* could not seem so evil to them.

The sliding doors of the ambulance entryway opened for the lackeys who bore Melior's wheeled cot. Holly Kendal walked beside him, carrying the board and papers upon which she had written.

Within the citadel the light was uncharitably bright, and harsh mechanical stinks burned Melior's nose while doing but little to conceal the odors of pain, fear, sickness, and blood which lay beneath. There was a harsh wailing and the polyphonr of voice raised in a fashion which he had never heard outside of a battlefield.

Holly-his-EMT placed a clipboard carefully on his chest and patted his shoulder. "You'll be all right," she said, but Melior could hear the unsureness in her voice.

She stared at him a moment longer and then walked away. The last Melior saw of her was her waist-length russet braid bouncing as she strode.

Then he was brought to another place, with no more interest shown him than if he had been as inanimate as the bed he was bound to. The Guardsman stayed with him, and there was much incomprehensible talk of preserving his simple rights and of someone named Miranda, who seemed to be the matriarch whose name must be invoked to solemnize his detention. Lackeys in white lifted him onto a metal table and off again, his chest was prodded with cold instruments, and through it all he forced himself to wait, muscles limp and face impassive, lest they put him back into the iron cage from which Ruth might not rescue him twice.

They kept him bound upon the pallet, called *gurney* among them, lest he damage himself before they could see the damage done him, and asked him many questions. His name. His age. His address. His occupation. To all of these except his name he gave answers that were true for Michael. They asked about his assurance, which puzzled him, and when they asked for his assurance card he said he had lost it.

The Guardsman asked him again and again what he had been doing in the subterranean way and how he had gotten there, and Melior answered as Michael had coached him for some other long-ago occasion: "I do not know. I do not remember."

The white-robed ones came and went for an hour's time, though the Guardsman never left his side. They spoke, when they were present, much to one another of pictures coming back, and though this made no sense Melior did not question it. To expose his ignorance would be fatal.

At last a minion came, waving blackened sheets of flexible glass, and said things like "mild concussion" and "absence of subdural hermatoma" and called him lucky.

Melior did not feel lucky.

But they unstrapped him from the moving bed after that and let him stand for a moment, and though he thanked them for their help and said that he would go he was told that he might not. They gave him pills to swallow from a tiny cup of paper, and gave him water in a larger cup of the same material. The Guardsman stood by, watching.

And so Melior submitted tamely to the removal of his clothes, to their replacement with a smock he would have blushed to see the meanest of his servants wear, and permitted them to bind up the wounds which the *grendel* had made. One minion laved the blue-black place on his cheek where the *grendel* had struck with burning evil-odored lotions. Another came and bound the edges of the wound together with painful sorcery, and then covered his work with pads and ointments and a swathing of pale cloth.

His hearing was very keen, and he did not miss the whispering in corners about his physical differences. His ears, his eyes, the beat of his heart; they had sampled all of these and liked none of them.

At last Melior was let to stand, but only so long as it took for them to bring a wheeled chair such as Michael's friend Stephen possessed. To the mean smock they had granted him they added a tattered blue robe of the material called *terrycloth,* which served to cover him more acceptably. It was probable, Melior thought, that they meant to keep his own clothes as payment for their services, and he was sorry for Ruth's sake, but there was little there he valued. His backpack and Stephen's sword were still in the tunnel, and the sword he did miss, but just as well to lose it there if he were to keep it only to lose it to jackals such as these.

He wondered if they would loose him now, but thought there must be more, and in this much he was right. Frank wanted to talk to him, it was said, and so once more Melior marshaled all his patience and waited for Frank, though his head still ached.

But Frank was not to come to him. He was to go to Frank.

They would not let him walk, but pushed him in the wheeled chair and brought him to a room that smelled of bitter smoke and poisons. In it was a couch, much like Naomi's couch, and there they bid him wait for Frank.

Part of The Object was missing. The One had reasoned this out slowly, taking painful hours to reach that conclusion. Part of The Object was missing—some essence, some informing spark. At first The One had wailed its rage, hot and blinding, but The Object had not kindled. Then The One had mourned over Its loss, knowing It could never venture out into the hot bright Destruction to seek the missing part.

Even striking down The Enemy had not cheered it, for The Enemy was not Food and was not dead.

But surely The Enemy must have died soon thereafter, else why had such a great benison been granted? The One did not have to find a way to survive the great Destruction to seek the part of The Object which had been lost. It was coming here. The missing piece of The Object was coming to The One.

Coming here. Seeking its other self.

Coming within his reach.

"Yeuch." Ruth slid gingerly along the tunnel wall and wished with all her might that she possessed the transcendent nobility of spirit that would allow her to ignore the fact that it was absolutely *filthy.*

She had never held an ambition to schlep around in the subway tunnels. Vincent of *Beauty and the Beast* held no fascination for her. If sensibility was an aversion to cheap theatrics, well, then, let it be so; Ruth was sensible.

But her heart was a sick weight in her chest and she desperately wanted to find Melior. *All* of Melior—and soon.

"We're inside the target area," Michael said softly, ticking off their blessings. "*Grendel* country. The disappearances—allowing for the layout of the tunnels—form a rough circle. We're inside it."

"Wonderful," said Naomi. "But where exactly is the "target area"?"

"Somewhere near City Hall," Michael said. He pulled a flashlight out of his jacket and shone it around.

"What do we do if a train comes?" Ruth looked around nervously.

"See these?" Michael shone his flashlight into a nook built into the wall, a door-shaped alcove that Ruth had seen but thought just for decoration. "Duck into one."

"Oh, thanks," Ruth breathed.

"If the trains were running half an hour apart during rush hour, they may not be running at all now," Naomi pointed out. "Half an hour! Usually it's five minutes."

"Come on," said Michael. "And keep your voices down. Sound carries. We're looking for Melior, not trouble."

"Who writes your dialogue?" Ruth muttered under her breath. But she followed.

Naomi was the one who found the sword.

It was fifteen minutes later, long enough for Ruth, who brought up the rear, to become inured to walking through a cylindrical garbage heap filled with rats which might at any moment chose *not* to scurry the other way and not long enough for her to stop flinching every time she heard a sound that *might* be the herald of an oncoming train. The three of them walked in single-file along the rail-bed, spread out far enough that only two of them would have to crowd into any one-person niche.

Ruth was desperately trying to keep from asking Naomi, who might actually know, just how much wider the tunnels were than the trains that ran through them.

If at all, Ruth emended mentally.

For some reason her hands were shaking badly, making the beam of her flashlight jump in ragged Morse along the ground ahead. It was that, more than anything else, which her mind had chosen to fix on, insisting that it meant she would probably faint, fall down in the muck, contract hepatitis, and die. Melior might be dead already.

And everything he'd told them about the *grendel* was true.

She was concentrating on that bleak prospect so hard that Naomi's sharp indrawn breath of surprise hit Ruth with the violence of a shout.

"*Michael—Ruth—LOOK!*"

Ruth saw it then: the gold gleam of the *gladius,* lying neglected and unlooked-for directly beneath the third rail.

Melior's sword. Ruth felt sick.

Michael started across the tracks toward it.

For God's sake, Michael! Ruth thought but didn't say aloud.

Michael knelt on the tracks, shining his flashlight on the blade, carefully making certain the sword nowhere touched the rail that carried its multi-thousand-volt freight of raw power. Then, still kneeling, holding the flashlight in his left hand because there must be, could be, no mistake, Michael began, very slowly, reaching out for the sword.

Ruth felt the gentle puff of breeze on the back of her neck. Like the breath of time.

Like the wind from an oncoming train.

How trite, Ruth thought. She saw the white oval of Naomi's face as Nai turned toward her; knew that Naomi had felt it, too.

Michael went on reaching for the sword. Ruth had to force herself to see what was there, not the bright arc-welding halations that imagination conjured so vividly.

Oh, God, Michael, RUN.

But Michael didn't run, and Ruth herself stood paralyzed, sick with fear for him, and wondering with giddy self-contempt if a little thing like breaking into a subway tunnel to chase a cannibal theriomorph at the word of an elf-prince—now almost certainly dead—from Otherwhere and finding herself caught in the path of a subway train was enough to induce a nervous breakdown in her, frail vessel that she was.

Naomi reached her and grabbed her arm, pulling her toward one of the niches. Behind Naomi, Ruth could still see Michael. He had his hand around the sword-hilt and was carefully, painstakingly, pulling it free.

It's Melior's sword, the one that Stephen Mallison gave him. He wouldn't just go off and leave it.

The train's headlights were a glow around the curve of the tunnel. Its horn sounded, not that it could have seen them, and the sound boomed off the tunnel walls like a peal of thunder.

"Ruth!" Naomi shook her, pushed her, dug sharp nails into her arm, and finally Ruth broke free of the paralysis enough to move.

They reached the alcove with an eternity—ninety seconds at least— to wait before the train reached them, time enough for Ruth to invent and discard a dozen better plans for safety. Then the train began to pass.

Ruth stood with her face pressed into Naomi's shoulder, both of them huddled tightly into this technological priest's hole as the train thundered by, and for all her terrorized anticipation, all Ruth felt as its passage hammered her with sound was annoyance that it would not leave and let her deal with whatever new horror awaited. But when the train had gone, rocking and wailing as it retreated down the tunnel, what Ruth saw was Michael.

He was holding the replica Roman short-sword as if he didn't want to be anywhere near it.

"Steve'd want this back," he said simply.

"What about Melior?" For a moment Ruth was surprised that her voice sounded so steady, then realized it was Naomi who'd spoken.

"This doesn't prove he's dead," Michael said quickly, watching Ruth. "All it proves is that Melior dropped it and couldn't pick it up. There could be a lot of explanations for that. He could be back in jail."

"How do we find out?" Naomi asked calmly. Once more Ruth envied her friend that. Oh, to be one of those self-possessed people.

"Get out of here and call Philip. Call the police."

" 'Excuse me, have you arrested any elves lately?' " Naomi suggested, and Ruth, stifling a hoot of laughter, felt the tightness in her chest ease.

"Or something," Michael said. "Or he could still be down here with a busted ankle. I want to finish looking around."

And so they went on, faster now, knowing that their target must be blatantly obvious or absent altogether. Through the still-damp-from-last-week's-rains-but-drying tunnels Naomi, Ruth, and Michael hurried; interlopers by need but well-aware of their precarious legal position; flashlights flickering off things that gleamed, scurrying crouched past the empty prosceniums of deserted stations at a New Yorker's walking pace.

There was suddenly a curious absence of rats. And Ruth was about to mention this; was tormented afterward by the certainty that had she only mentioned it things would have been different, different altogether.

"I don't think—" Michael began, and his words overlaid the *slithering* sound Ruth heard behind her. She turned toward the sound.

Shock; her body understanding terror and filling her blood with nightmare cocktails long before her blinkered modern mind could react. Then realization, and—oh, God—the *smell!*

"Muh—*uh!*" Ruth stammered, skittering backward, flashlight falling from fingers numb, nerveless with an extremity of terror never felt before, not even in nightmares. And the *grendel,* it had to be the *grendel—oh, God, so that's what it looks like*—reached out for her; slack-jawed drool and yellow twisted teeth.

Ruth, pedaling backward, fell. The sudden unexpected slap of the ground at her back was baffling more than anything else; her eyes teared with the unfairness of it all as the *grendel* shambled toward her.

She saw Naomi vault over her as she lay on the ground; saw the upraised golden flash of Stephen's sword and heard Naomi grunt as she shoved it into the *grendel*'s unaffected flesh. The *grendel* shrugged Naomi off and Ruth heard her fall and roll; heard the low *hu!* of expended air and knew Naomi was attacking again. She saw the lights of the tunnel walls blotted out as the horror stooped over her, ignoring the attack. She felt the *grendel*'s hand upon the side of her face and then Ruth, with some relief, recorded nothing more.

Michael had turned back when he'd heard the noise. Still talking, he turned the flashlight automatically to follow his sight and saw Ruth. And saw the *grendel.*

It was nearly eight feet tall, and seeing it Michael knew that Melior must be dead. He could not believe that this was something that had ever been human. Its arms were ape-long, and wicked horn-colored claws gleamed at the end of short fingers on blunt pawlike hands. Its skin was blackish green and toxic, cracked and scaled and shredding, its head an insignificant neckless bump between shoulders broad to the point of parody. Nose was lost in the swelling thrust of muzzle, giving its blunt-featured earless face a vaguely saurian look; cartoon dinosaur until it opened its mouth, then frightening impossible extension and jutting yellow fangs. The stink wafted from it like a fog; morgue and mass burial, blood and murder.

How could anyone hope to kill it?

Michael wished—desperately, unreasonably—for a flamethrower, knowing that if he had it in his hands this instant he could not use it, because the *thing* was close to Ruth and coming closer, reaching out one moist unclean hand like all the parodies of Frankenstein that ever were, unfunny at last.

It seemed an eternity before Ruth began to move, backing away slowly when Michael knew that what she should do was turn and run.

And then she fell.

He started forward, slow underwater-seeming motion with every muscle protesting at the movement, knowing he would not be in time and could do nothing if he were. They'd come down here unarmed, knowing what they knew, and Michael hated himself suddenly for that stupidity.

Naomi moved faster.

She'd been standing a little behind Michael, now she ran to him, pulling Stephen's sword out of his hand while Ruth was still falling. Michael grabbed vainly at empty air where the sword had been and ran at last, but not as fast as Naomi.

She sprang over Ruth's body, sword in her right hand and her shouted *kiai* echoing in the tunnel like a sea-bird's cry. His last sight of her was of Naomi poised in midair, golden sword gleaming in the light of the flashlight that Michael had somehow managed not to drop. The *grendel* raised its head and looked at him, its eyes like cankers of burning phosphor.

And then, without transition, Michael was standing, not running, standing staring and wide-eyed off into space, as still and dazed as if he had just awakened from a deep sleep, and all three of them were gone.

"No—!"

He ran forward, waving his flashlight, but there was nothing there. Not Ruth. Not Naomi. Only Stephen's sword lying on the tracks, and Ruth's flashlight, and the broad wet footprints of something that never should have existed at all.

What had happened? One moment he'd been running toward it, the next—

I want to die. Oh, God, please let me die. Not again. NOT AGAIN.

There was silence in the tunnel. After a long hesitation, Michael picked up the sword, then turned away and slowly began to leave.

"How are you feeling?"

That inane question humans liked to ask each other, this time from the mouth of a man dressed as no man Melior had seen yet: gray his strange garb was, gray as all the colors of smoke and morning mist.

"I'm Detective Lieutenant Frank Catalpano, N.Y.P.D. I'd like to ask you a few questions about what you were doing down there on the tracks, if you don't mind."

Melior knew that tone. The courtesy of princes; empty words, as no one would dare to refuse their orders. And this man was a prince of a sort, Melior guessed; only a ruler would dare show such arrogance, even to a wounded foe.

The gray man sat down upon the cheap couch and brought out a notebook and stylus from his pocket.

"Am I arrested?" Melior asked.

The detective lieutenant regarded him gravely. "Let's say we aren't making any charges at this point. The subway's a dangerous place to go, you know."

"So I have been told." Melior's first instinct was to lie, and he would have followed it without compunction, save that a lie must always be convincing, and Melior did not know what words were plausible and what words would betray.

"Just how *did* you get down there?" The gray man asked.

Ah, this was simple enough. "I do not remember," Melior said. He touched his bandaged head and winced. "I was going home," he added, which was truth of a sort.

"And you don't remember anything other than that?" The gray man patently did not believe him.

Melior shook his head and winced; and that at least was no act. "I fell," he suggested, putting uncertainty and guessing into his voice. "And where is home, exactly?" the gray man asked. No prince, this, Melior realized now, but a prince's man; brutal with the trust his sovereign reposed in him; elegant with a simplicity that disdained courts. Not even a warrior, this, but that which was much more fearsome. A *manhunter.*

Melior gave him Michael's address once more.

"Lived there long?" was the next question.

"Only a short time. I am staying with a friend." Half-truths and simple statements. Melior began to hope they might let him go.

"We didn't find your wallet." Prompting, helpful and encouraging. Looking for him to reveal something—but what? Melior wondered.

The silence stretched, achingly. Melior thought of a hundred ways to fill it and spoke none of them.

"Your friend got a name?" the grey manhunter asked.

"He is Michael Peacock," Melior said. "And surely he will wonder at my absence. If you do not arrest me, you must let me go to him."

"Hold on just a minute," the manhunter said. "With a knock like the one you got, you shouldn't be wandering around alone. What were you doing riding the subway at that hour, anyway?"

"It was rush hour," Melior suggested. "It is later now."

"What were you doing for the last twelve hours?" Questions again and again, and now Melior knew they were merely a veil for a certainty he could not guess at.

"May I call Michael now?" Melior asked.

The manhunter to princes pushed the stylus and a sheet of paper over to Melior. "Write it down here and we can have one of the nurses notify him," he said. "I've got just a couple more questions."

Melior stared at the blank sheet of paper. The gate to this land had given him knowledge of its spoken tongue, but nothing more. He could neither read nor write.

But a good commander—and Melior had been one—must be able to draw a map, however crude. Carefully Melior rendered the twisting angular symbols that were on the buttons one must push to activate the spell that would reach Michael.

Detective Lieutenant Frank Catalpano looked at the paper, folded it carefully, and put it in his pocket.

"I'll be sure to have one of the nurses call your friend for you, but before that, maybe you could tell me what you were doing in the subway," he said with polite insistence.

· 19 ·

A Candle in the Wind

"HAVE YOU HEARD from Melior?" Michael's voice on the phone was harsh and abrupt.

"No." Philip did not bother to glance up at the endlessly-searching computer. He already knew the answer. No elf. And it wasn't his fault, but the girls weren't going to see it that way.

"I've seen the *grendel.* It's got Ruth and Naomi. Stay there till I get there."

The phone went dead in Philip's car before he could think of a reply. Above his head the police scanner continued to broadcast its cryptic shorthand of 10-codes and civil citations.

The *grendel* had Naomi and Ruth?

Philip had thought things were already as bad as they could be.

He'd been wrong.

They'd just gotten worse.

His name, as it happened, really *was* Frank (For Francis Marion) Catalpano, although he was not with the N.Y.P.D. He was, however, on the side of the angels, if you defined the side of the angels as the side of the law.

Laws, it must be noted, can be rewritten, from time to time, for expediency's sake.

Frank worked for a mostly-unknown agency with the curious distinction of being the only private-sector service provider in a field usually reserved for governments friendly and un-. This agency (which had a fine, vague-but-impressive-sounding name) leased its services to the United

States Government, which paid very well indeed for an exclusive lien on the agency's time. This was not to say that Frank's employers did not have other clients, only that they did not do for these other clients what they did for the United States Government.

At least in theory.

And, being an exclusive private-sector subcontractor to the biggest employer there was, it was easy for Frank's bosses to move mammal-fast around the ankles of the Federal dinosaurs, so that almost before the first report had come in, Frank had been on the scene, complete with convincing ID and plausible cover-story, appropriate warnings-off to appropriate bureaus, and people in every New York City department who would say that Frank Catalpano was exactly what he appeared to be.

And as for the man in the room Frank had just left. . . .

The flashing eyes, the floating hair (as Frank's former wife Denise, a space cadet who'd held a liberal arts degree from Vassar, would surely have characterized them), and even the pointed ears of his prisoner did not faze Frank. He had seen them before.

This was another one. And as soon as the right people and the right equipment arrived, this one would vanish, too. Maybe the killings in the subway would stop, then, but Frank Catalpano neither knew nor cared. His agency was paid well by its biggest account to remain very focused.

"Detective?"

Frank turned to face the doctor. He looked at the name-badge on the rumpled white coat. Jenkins. The admitting physician.

"Yes?" He pulled his *persona* around himself like a cloak; world-weary New York 'tec who'd seen it all, done a lot of it, and could never on any account be forced to explain.

"Are you going to charge him? This—" Jenkins squinted at his clipboard, "—Ronald Melon?"

Rohannan Melior, Frank corrected him silently. *Of one of the Seven Houses of the Twilight. I'll bet my quarterly bonus on it. He's got the look.*

"No," said Frank, as soft and heavy as a fall of graveyard dust. "We're not going to charge him. Yet. But your patient, Doctor, is very upset. He needs rest. He needs to stay here for the seventy-two-hour observation period permitted by law so we can see what it is he's going to do."

Jenkins opened and closed his mouth. Frank plucked the clipboard out of his hand. He glanced over the crabbed hieroglyphics, and then took a pen from his inside pocket and wrote "Violent. Delusional. Do Not Approach." diagonally across the page.

"You got that, Doctor?" Frank said.

"The man's got civil rights," Jenkins muttered. "We have to notify the family, let him telephone—"

"You're real busy here, Doctor Jenkins." Frank gave the name full weight. It was wonderful what you could do with a name. Say somebody's name in the right way, and all of a sudden they got nervous, just as if you might take their name away from them as a prelude to other horrors.

Frank smiled. "I'm sure you're too busy to pay too much attention to one violent whack. Just give us a break, Doctor. Let us do our job for once, okay? Seventy-two hours. Okay?"

Frank watched Jenkins, as he'd watched so many others, looking for the moment that Jenkins would choose the easy way over the right way. They almost always did, and Frank was waiting for them on the other side.

It would be incorrect to say that Frank Catalpano didn't know right from wrong. In fact, Frank had a highly-developed sensitivity to right and wrong, and could always tell them apart. What he was doing was wrong. What he was asking Jenkins to do was wrong.

But for Jenkins it was the easier way.

And for Frank, it was legal.

"I don't suppose it could do any real harm," Dr. Jenkins said.

Frank Catalpano smiled.

Jane awoke with the sudden start of one who has overslept, forgetting important business. Recent memory slammed into place with a nearly audible thud. Melior. The tunnels. The police. The *grendel.*

The police had Melior now, and Ruth and the others didn't know about the *grendel.* And even if they did, they could look forever and not find it.

But Jane knew where it was hiding. She threw on the first clothes that came to hand and ran across the campus and down the hill to Ruth and Naomi's apartment. She let herself in, panting only slightly with the exertion of her run. Late afternoon sunlight streamed through the window. Two p.m.

And Ruth wasn't here, nor Naomi, though by all the laws of all the odd gods at least one of them should be.

If they weren't here, where were they?

Jane sat down on the couch, an unaccustomed feeling of let-down washing over her. They weren't here. She'd been counting on them being here. Someone to tell. Someone to save Melior.

But there was no one.

They did not mean to let him go. Melior accepted this with a resignation he did not extend to his confinement; he had not expected his luck to change.

He was in a small room with a bed and an unopenable window. "Held for observation," the white-robed monk-physicians had said when he had asked, and "seventy-two hours."

But he would not wait seventy-two hours until they discovered more pretexts upon which to detain a lord of the House of the Silver Silences. He would escape this place and warn his companions, if Jane had not already done so.

Melior did wish he knew if Jane had escaped in truth and not merely in his hopes. He wished he knew how far news of the *grendel's* existence had spread.

He wished his head did not hurt, and that he had his clothes, and that he did not feel so helpless in the face of an evil that the humans of the World of Iron would scoff at until the last of them had been hunted down and made food for its endless appetite. This city held more humans than Melior had ever seen; soon, feeding upon them, the *grendel* would be strong enough to burgeon until in all the land there was nothing more to eat.

The *grendel* must be slain. The *grendel* could be slain only by The Sword of Maiden's Tears. Which could only be wielded by one of the Sons of the Morning, lest some human paladin's attempt make him *grendel* in his turn. And the only Morning Lord in all this world, to the best of Melior's knowledge, stood here in this room.

Ruth and Naomi were gone. Dead, probably, but Michael could not make himself believe it. People died in a thousand ways every day, but they did not die at the hands of monsters created by magic swords.

Melior must be dead, too. Michael could think of no other reason, now, for him to have dropped Stephen's sword. Melior dead, and Ruth and Naomi, too.

And he hadn't done a single thing to save them.

Failure and coward, and *safe,* now, which somehow hurt the worst. That, and the thought of having to explain to Jane and Philip how it was that he'd just stood there and watched Melior's *grendel* do . . . whatever it had done.

Michael had learned long since in the roughest school of all that true life was nothing like fiction. He'd believed it, and asked nothing more of life than never to be reminded of the truth again. But he hadn't gotten his wish.

He could think of nothing he could do, no course of action he could pursue, and retained enough presence of mind to know that he was shocky; his judgment was gone. All he'd do now was mess things up further—if that were possible.

He called Philip and took a taxi home.

He could hear the phone ringing from the floor below, and when he got to his own front door he could still hear it, only faintly muffled. *How like life,* Michael thought as he dropped his keys. The phone went on ringing. Michael swore, and fumbled with his key ring.

On the fourteenth ring the phone went silent. Michael, who had just gotten the door open, snarled and kicked the door shut. It slammed with the sound of a gunshot, flat and final.

Jane put down the phone. No Ruth, no Naomi, and now no Michael. And it was almost four, too, on a Thursday; *someone* should be home.

Philip. Her hand hovered over the receiver for a moment, then she drew back. It occurred to her that Philip, having double-crossed Ruth in the matter of finding out about the *grendel,* might be lying extremely low. *Maybe later,* she temporized, and went to see if there was any news.

The Subway Snatcher was the lead story on the four o'clock news broadcast. Jane listened with interest to the story of the "alleged" disappearance of Therese Scarlatti from the platform of the City Hall Station yesterday evening.

But if that had been yesterday, Michael and Ruth and Naomi already knew about it. They'd known there was a real live *grendel* since yesterday night.

Jane puzzled over what to do with this new information, trying to decide what they would have done with the knowledge. Then, resolutely, she picked up the phone and began to dial Philip.

Philip LeStrange was in a quandary—which, as he would be happy to tell you, was a small wheeled cart used to transport lepers. He'd even phoned the dorm, but no one had answered; which would be reasonable enough if people hadn't been trying to reach Jane-the-Pain since seven-thirty yesterday night. Philip's nature was paranoid, not suspicious. It did not occur to him that Melior had confided in Jane instead of, say, him.

And now Michael said that the *grendel,* which had been only intellectual exercise even while Philip had been gathering the positive proof of its existence, had taken Ruth and Naomi. Taken them how? Taken them where?

And how were they going to get them back?

They had to get them back. Of course they did. Naomi was tough; she could beat up just about anyone Philip could think of. Of course they'd get them back.

It would be an adventure.

But he'd feel a lot better, he really would, if he was absolutely *sure* of where they were now and that they were safe.

Someone hammered on his door.

"Phone!" Alex shouted.

Not Michael if he was calling on the communal line.

"Tell them I'm not here," Philip shouted back.

There was a pause while Alex retreated. And returned.

"She says you got her pregnant," Alex shouted through the door.

This was peculiar enough to investigate. Philip went and opened the door.

"Hello?" Philip said into the communal phone.

"Where are Michael and the guys?"

Jane.

"Michael's home. Probably by now. Where've you been?"

"Michael didn't answer his phone. Has Melior called?" Jane asked again, very cautious.

"Why would Melior call?" Carefully; there were people listening.

"He's been arrested, probably," Jane said with the lugubrious satisfaction of being right.

"Where *are* you?" Philip, defeated, asked.

"I'm at Ruth's. Where is *she?*"

Even if the watchers had not been there, Philip couldn't say, despite what Michael had told him. Some fastidious revulsion to saying the words, or perhaps merely simple self-preservation, to refrain from speaking the sentence that must come out either callous or maudlin.

And perhaps, after all, he'd only misheard what Michael'd said over the phone.

"I'll be over there in a few minutes. We've got to talk," Philip said instead.

He met Michael on his front steps.

"Where did you think you were going?" Michael demanded dangerously.

This was a new sensation for Philip, and he didn't like it. He annoyed people, he revolted them, he made them envious. He did not make them angry. Michael was angry, now, just as if this weren't an *adventure*.

He didn't think, though, that Michael would appreciate enlightenment just now. Philip chose diplomacy as the wiser course.

"Jane's at Ruth and Naomi's place. She just phoned. She knows something about Melior."

"Come on," Michael said.

*   *   *

There was nothing he could do to gain his freedom, save wait until that unbroachable door should open. Melior accepted this, just as he had accepted the foreknowing of his own helplessness to stop the *grendel,* and let his mind turn on the only thing left that mattered besides escape.

Why *here?* In the Art Magic there were no coincidences; if the spell-trapped Sword had delivered him to this spot, such delivery had been purposed. To kill him and put the Sword beyond his kindred's reach forever would have been a simple thing, did he only appear at the bottom of a lake or the bottom of the ocean or the furnace-maw of a volcano.

It had been the new York city that he came to for a reason. Find the reason, and find perhaps the knowledge that would arm his human friends in their fight.

What did he know of magic? Not so very much; the swords that Melior fought with were physical things. But he was a prince of the House of the Silver Silences and the Heir of Line Rohannan, and he knew more than nothing.

He had assumed all along that it was mere accident that landed him here in the World of Iron, but what if the spell-trap laid upon the Sword was the trap of pulling it *here?*

He had not fallen through all the other worlds on his way to the Last World. He had been brought here, as the spellbound Sword snapped back along its invisible tether, cleaving tightly to its other part.

The part that was native to this place.

But what was it, invisible and yet so tightly-binding, native to the World of Iron and yet capable of being drawn into the higher realms where magic worked?

Melior knew. A child's riddle, that, and in turn a child's answer, so simple that he was filled with momentary fury at having been blind so long. When fury gave way to hope, he crushed the dawning emotion savagely. To hope would only make him careless; he must set forth his theory as painstakingly as a rhetor his argument, and solve it for his truth as any alchemist. The mad logic of his enemy—vindictive, and clever merely—seemed to mock at him, and Melior knew now there were no puzzles left, only answers that he prayed he would be able to prove in time.

Souls.

Souls wander in sleep as every wizard knows; wander and return to their source, having gone only a little way in their own world. And death is the longest journey of all, to a land so distant the soul does not retrace its way.

But there are states between sleep and death, when the transmigrant soul of even a mortal from the World of Iron could journey outside its native land; could even, if the time were long enough, journey to be trapped in a soul-cage and used, by an evil and bloody-handed wizard, as an ingredient in a spell-trap.

A spell-trap to bring the Sword of Maiden's Tears to the World of Iron.

The mortal thus riven would be bound to seek his other part, the part that was bound up in the Sword. The mortal whose soul had been wizard-thieved would be *linked* to the Sword. Would be able to find it, as a compass needle finds True North.

One of his human friends must be the key; all Melior's knowledge of the rules of magic said it. The Law of Contagion, of Consanguinity, the Doctrine of Signatures . . . each in its own way assured him that he had already met the mortal whose life had been Sword-touched by some rogue artificer of Lord Baligant's. All Melior need do was find the one among them who had journeyed in the twilight land between Sleep and Death and set that one to following the faint soul-call of The Sword of Maiden's Tears.

And to do that, Melior must be free.

Something was exceptionally wrong. That much was perfectly clear. Because Ruth and Naomi were not here, and Philip wouldn't say where they were. Because Melior wasn't here either, and because Melior knew enough to make the one phone call they always had to give you, and would call Ruth or Michael. Because everybody in New York seemed to know about the *grendel* now, and that complicated the equation of its slaying in ways Jane had not yet had time to reason out.

Because Melior had faced the *grendel* armed only with a bronze sword, after telling them all time and again that only the Sword of Maiden's Tears could slay it.

That was stupid.

And Melior was not stupid.

The downstairs door buzzed.

"Who is it?" Jane demanded, punctilious no matter what temporal blandishments beguiled.

"Oh, come on," Philip said, at the same time Michael said, "Knock it off, Philip."

Jane buzzed them in.

She knew beyond question that something bad had happened as soon as she saw Michael's face, and, Janelike, demanded the worst at once. "Where are they?"

"They're down in the tunnels with the *grendel,*" Michael said.

Jane sat down, thinking about the creature she'd seen. She refused to think past that vision and on to the brutal horror Melior had dressed so grandly in iambic pentameter. Down there. *La bas.* But not dead. Michael had not said they were dead and Michael was generally reliable about telling you the whole truth.

"Melior's been arrested," she offered.

"How do you know?" Philip shot back.

"I was there." That was a little better. At least Michael was looking at her now.

"Melior and I went down in the tunnels last night and found *it.* It hit him. The cops showed up and he stalled them, so I came back here. *It* took off. I don't think they saw it."

"He's alive." Michael's voice wavered, its owner unable to settle on an emotion.

"He hasn't been arrested," Philip said positively. "You think I wasn't looking?"

"That isn't very useful information just now," Michael snarled, rounding on him.

Philip took a step backward.

"This is your fault," Michael went on. "If you'd told us what you knew, *when you knew it—*"

"It wouldn't have made any difference," Jane interrupted. She might dislike Philip, but the satisfaction of seeing Michael slam Philip was not worth the sight of Michael losing his temper.

Michael rounded on her, red-eyed and numb with a dangerous grief.

"It wouldn't," Jane insisted stubbornly. "The only thing that can kill it is Melior's magic sword. It wouldn't have mattered if Philip had told you. You wouldn't have had the sword. But I know where the *grendel* lives, Michael. And the sword has to be there, doesn't it?"

· 20 ·

The October Subway

THE ALFRED ELY Beach Tunnel (most recently immortalized, after a fashion, in *Ghostbusters II)* was constructed—no surprises here—by Alfred Ely, who built it in 1870 in strictest secrecy (having rented the basement of a nearby department store for his project headquarters), tunneling clandestinely beneath Broadway to prove so far beyond a shadow of a doubt that a subway was feasible, lucrative, and safe, that the violent and semi-legal opposition of Boss Tweed and the Tammany Tiger (one of the first and greatest of the political machines in the days when politics was a sport but not a regulated one) would have its interfering fangs pulled forever.

Mr. Ely tunneled nearly 360 feet beneath and along Broadway, and, since the idea of an Underground Railway was still new and frightening, did everything that Victorian sensibilities could to ease the public's mind about its safety. The waiting area of his tunnel—which led from nowhere to nowhere, being only a pilot project—was adorned with crystal chandeliers, fountains, and murals. There was even—for reasons known only to the post-Federalist mind—a tank full of fish. The single subway car was a miracle of plush velvet and rare woods, and everyone who rode the subway spoke admiringly of its comfort, pleasure, and safety.

It is almost unnecessary to add that Alfred died in obscure poverty: so obscure that when the tunnel was rediscovered in 1912 during excavations for the Broadway BMT line—New York having finally got its subway system a mere thirtysomething years later—no one remembered who had built the tunnel or how it had gotten there. When next you stand at the City Hall Station on the BMT line, spare a thought for Alfred, one of history's most organized, dynamic, visionary failures.

Ruth wished she could. But at the moment her mind was on other things.

She had come back to reality lying on the ground; or, rather, in a nest of Snapple bottles and Pepsi cans that scattered noisily when she moved.

It wasn't dark, not entirely; a faint reddish glow came from somewhere and convinced her, for some seconds, that she was still dreaming. Then everything came back; Melior dead and the *grendel*—

Ruth sat up with a jerk, gasping as one does out of nightmare. Chilled stiff muscles protested, but Ruth didn't care. She stared around wildly. The *grendel.*

And no merciful providence had chosen to intervene during the scene change, whisking her back safely to her own warm, dry, clean apartment to have the *denouement* explained to her by Michael and Naomi who would have seen everything but be, nevertheless, safe.

Ruth got stiffly to her feet and looked around. Scrapes and abrasions she didn't remember getting protested; her jacket was torn and her hair had long since come down out of its tight careful knot. It clung around her face, stiff and damp and foul as though it had been dipped in ink.

Ink would be a godsend.

Then she saw the sword.

It stood a few feet from her head, propped against the wall, pointdown in a pile of bizarre winnowings from some punk-twisted Borrower. Hazard lamps—the source of the light—pop cans; liquor bottles; lunch boxes; curled bits of subway posters; anything that was even slightly shiny. A magpie's midden.

The sword towered over all this, pristine and gleaming and fakelooking as a special effect. It had a jewel in its pommel the size of a baseball and seemed itself to shine with a faint light. And if it wasn't Melior's magic sword, Ruth had been grossly misled about magic swords in general and the Sword of Maiden's Tears in particular.

She wondered what it would be like to hold it. She reached for it—

"Don't touch that." Naomi's voice, behind her. Ruth squeaked, startled, and shot a confirming glance over her shoulder. But she withdrew her hand.

"Hi, stranger, how's tricks?" Naomi said.

Ruth stepped gingerly out of the trash. Naomi smiled, a little crookedly.

"Long time no see, and all that."

"Naomi!" Ruth flung her arms around her, glad to see her even if she

wouldn't wish her worst enemy in this mess, hugged and was hugged hard in return. "Oh, God, you're still alive!"

"Yeah," Naomi said.

Reluctantly Ruth released her and took a good look. Naomi was now nobody's idea of a fashion plate. Her short dark hair was matted, her face was bruised, and her clothes looked as if she'd been dragged through a canebrake backward.

"Welcome—in the words of the popular broadsheet ballad—to my nightmare," Naomi said. But she was still alive. They were both still alive.

For now.

The room they were in was big—*huge*—at least a hundred feet by sixty, maybe more. The floor still gleamed dully in patches, and the light was just enough to show Ruth the shadowy pattern of marble parquetry beneath her feet. The wall against which the sword rested was lavishly ornamented, a bewilderment of niches, coffering, and crumbling plaster medallions still faintly gilded.

"I know what you're going to say. It looks like an outtake from *Phantom.* But it gets better," Naomi said.

Ruth completed her survey of the room and looked back at Naomi. Naomi's eyes were feverishly bright; her mouth was set.

"I read the book. So why don't we leave this party and go home?" And despite all her best intentions, Ruth felt hot tears prickle as past and present injustice mingled. Not fair, oh God, nothing at all fair, and if she'd been marked down to die why couldn't it have been a dozen years ago instead of now, in the dark, where being eaten alive wasn't just a sick joke but a probability?

"Good idea," Naomi said. "How?"

Ruth just stared at her.

"I've been looking around here. It's the damnedest place; looks like Miss Havisham's subway station. But the tracks don't go anywhere. They just stop. Solid rock."

Ruth took a second and more careful look, and this time she saw what her eye had missed before; the carving in the shadows there was not carving but a tiny antique railway carriage; and ahead of it were curiously narrow and delicate railroad tracks.

"I've already walked them. The tunnel goes about a hundred yards and stops. I don't think it ever went through. But there's no way out that way," Naomi said.

"We got in here somehow." She was calmer now, but now that instant panic was past, Ruth was feeling other things. Like cold, and hungry, and tired, and scared, and pretty beat up when you came right down to it.

"Yeah." Naomi looked back toward the delicate half-scale car. In the sword's glow Ruth could see her mouth set hard. "You were out a long time, Ruth; I was worried about you."

Oversleeping our specialty. But even that macabre joke couldn't raise Ruth's spirits in the face of the horror of reality. "How long?"

"About six hours. It's about seven o'clock Thursday night, if you're keeping track. Assuming my watch hasn't gone wonky after what it's been through." Naomi brandished her wristwatch, guaranteed waterproof, shockproof, and, now, *grendel*-resistant. Ruth wondered if the manufacturers would care.

"And. . . ?"

"Our host isn't back yet," Naomi added dryly. "But he-she-or-it will be."

Ruth's stomach lurched involuntarily; she looked toward the sword.

"And whoever picks that up is going to be just like him, her, or it," Naomi finished fair-mindedly.

"We don't know that," Ruth said desperately. She'd feel safe with the sword in her hands—she was sure of it.

"Ruth." The tremor of fear in Naomi's voice riveted Ruth's attention as nothing else could have. "Everything else Melior's told us has come out true, so why don't we go ahead and believe this one? Touch that sword and you'll be the new *grendel* on the block. And I don't think the other one wants to share."

I don't care! Ruth wanted to scream. Instead she drew a deep breath. "Okay. We'll leave it for Melior. If he—If he's—"

"I haven't seen him," Naomi said, and something in her voice cut Ruth's incipient crying jag off sharp. "He wasn't with the others," Naomi added flatly.

It wasn't very hard to figure out where Melior was, once Michael put his mind to it. He'd been injured in Lower Manhattan, he was in police custody, and even at his best Melior was a few sandwiches shy of a picnic by Earth-plane standards.

Where else would they take him?

It was seven o'clock Thursday night when Michael, Philip, and Jane walked into Bellevue Hospital. Carefully-phrased questions got them directed to where, by mutual unspoken consent, they all felt they ought to start: the Psychiatric Wing. There, as on other floors, there was an information desk or something that looked like one.

"May I help you?" asked a nurse, in tones that plainly translated the question into: "Oh, for Christ's sake what do you want *now?*"

"Well, you see, ma'am, we're looking for a friend of ours. We hoped he might be here."

Michael Peacock, wearing a suit jacket for the occasion, did his best to sound and look friendly, honest, and sincere, just like they taught you in Library Public Relations Courses, even though, beginning his second twenty-four hours of uninterrupted consciousness, he felt none of these things.

"Why don't you check with Information, downstairs?" the nurse said, but more kindly this time. She had never met Frank Catalpano and did not know that one of her observation patients was supposed to be held incommunicado, nor would she have cooperated with the notion if she did.

"Well, you see—" Michael began.

"No, Michael, it's okay." Philip pushed past him to stand in front of the desk and the nurse. "He's my brother, okay? Mom and Dad left him with me when they went to visit Grandma. I was sure it'd be okay." Philip said plaintively.

"He's your brother. . . ?"

"Melvil. Melvil LeStrange. But he might not have said so, especially if he got excited. He's just a little different," Philip added, putting just the right note of defensiveness into his voice. "He's got a card he usually carries, but I guess he left it behind this time." To Michael's amazement Philip dug around in a pocket and produced a battered wallet, one that Michael was pretty sure had once been his. Philip offered it to the nurse. Over Philip's shoulder Michael could see a battered and carefully-typed card containing his name and address. It even had Melior's picture, clipped from one of the Polaroids Philip had taken that first night.

"Sometimes he says his name is Rohannan Melior. I think he got it out of a comic book. Is he here? Please, could you just let me take him home?" Philip said. "He didn't do anything wrong, did he?"

The charge nurse wavered visibly.

"Just let me see him, then," Philip pleaded. "He'll be so scared," he added, as if the confession had been dragged from him with hot irons.

"Well, all right," she said, "but just for a minute."

So Philip was borne away, and Jane and Michael remained behind. Fifteen minutes later Philip was back, looking properly chastened.

"They won't let him go," he announced in the tones of a forlorn oboe. "They think he's messed up in some kind of police thing. Mom is going to kill me," Philip added, sottovoce but playing to the gallery.

"Why don't you come back tomorrow during the day and talk to the supervisor?" the charge nurse suggested.

Philip nodded and shrugged, obviously biting back tears of manly emotion. "Yeah," he said. "Yeah. You'll take care of him, won't you?"

Jane wanted to kick him. Philip was overplaying as usual. Subtlety was better, and then people could read into it anything they liked. But the nurse didn't seem to notice. "Of course we will," she said, and even patted Philip on the arm. Philip didn't try to duck away as he usually would; he just gave her a brave little smile and then turned away.

"C'mon, guys," he said.

So Michael and Jane followed him back out to the elevators. Once inside, and safe from inopportune viewing, Philip once more became his old self. He rocked up on his toes and whistled tonelessly.

"Helpful so far," Jane said. Philip smirked, still enchanted by his own cleverness.

"Look, what exactly did you do back there?" Michael demanded. Philip turned to him, bifocals flashing.

"He's up there, he's locked in, they aren't going to let him go while they're waiting for him to turn into a two-car garage. But the doors up there are all spring-locked, so I slipped him a credit card and told him we'd meet him in the parking lot."

It was half an hour before Melior joined them. He was wearing a long white coat, tattered slippers, baggy green pants, and a baseball cap that seemed to be advertising the roman numeral "ten." He carried a clipboard and looked like the White Rabbit (medical division) on his way to being terribly, horribly, late.

When he saw them, he burst into a run, stripping off the jacket as he ran. He bundled it together with the clipboard and slung both beneath a car. He kept the cap. Michael could see bandages beneath.

"Are you all right?" Michael said.

"No," Melior answered. "But I think I have the answer, and the answer finds the Sword."

"It better," Michael said grimly, "because the grendel's got Ruth and Naomi."

Their stories were exchanged on the run, heading north and west from the hospital. Ruth and Naomi, gone in an eyeblink. The grendel, real beyond controversy.

"You must not think hardly of yourself, Friend Michael. The grendel has the power to spellbind its foe if it chooses, holding him dreaming, yet awake. Thus it kept you harmless while it made its escape."

"Hypnosis," Jane said.

"Do you know the art?" Melior asked. "It will make the next task easier, can we but command a few of the grendel's arts."

*   *   *

"I did not ask the question I ought to have sought the answer to most of all," Melior told them, once they were forgathered (for safety's sake, as Melior had given the police and the hospital Michael's address) in Ruth and Naomi's apartment.

"Melior, we really don't have time for another one of your stories," Michael said with ragged patience.

"Peace, Friend Michael, this is the last of my stories and it will be brief. It was not chance that brought me here, or caused you to befriend me. The Sword was *compelled* here, by a magic which entrapped some part of the *soul* of an Ironworlder within the Sword. Falling through the worlds it sought its other part, and so came to you."

"Or to the muggers," Jane said. Melior's face twisted in pain.

"I pray not, but it could be so. I hope, rather, that it is one of you."

"Friends, are you feeling pale and listless? Write now for our free brochure describing the seven warning signs of your soul being stolen by a magic sword. Get a continuum, Elfie," Philip said.

"What is it you mean, exactly?" Michael asked.

Melior hesitated. "One among you, by accident or design, will have fallen, some time agone, into a state between sleep and death. There, helpless, with your soul caught between making and unmaking, you—"

But Melior did not get to finish this sentence. Philip sat down on the couch at the other end. He leaned back, staring at the ceiling. "Ruth," he said. "It's Ruth."

The other three stared at him. Melior's eyes were wide with horror, as if a number of things were suddenly clear.

"Ruth," he said. "My lady Ruth."

"Ruth was in a coma for eight years," Philip elaborated.

Michael looked disbelieving; Jane looked blank.

"She never told me," Jane said.

"Well, she didn't tell me, either," Philip shot back waspishly, "but it made the news in a lot of papers when she woke up. I searched her name through a database," he added.

"Fine," said Michael. "This gets us absolutely no-more-where at all."

"But now we know she is alive—oh, yes, Michael, the *grendel* will not kill such as she, who shares the nature of his treasure. Ruth is still alive, and will continue if we are in time."

"The place you want to go is the City Hall Station," Jane said.

Everyone looked at her, and Jane wished, for a faint moment, that she'd said nothing. But if she didn't, Ruth would die.

"The subway there crosses an old tunnel. The *grendel*'s got to have somewhere to *be*, doesn't it; somewhere it can sleep and not worry about getting hit by a train? Somewhere it can—put things?" Even Jane's voice wavered a little on that last phrase, knowing too well what those things were. "Look there. You remember the map," she said to Melior, "I showed you."

"Yes," Melior's voice held a faint hiss; a blood-hunger kin to the *grendel*'s. "We will seek it there. And though I will not kill it, you, Michael, will be my sword-hand."

"I can't." Michael's voice was low. Definite. Melior watched him, cat-eyes green in the darkness.

Philip's face twisted; he held a hand up as if to ward off the words, and Jane, watching him, was suddenly certain he knew what Michael was going to say.

Of course.

If he'd searched *Ruth's* name through a database, he'd searched all of them. Philip did nothing by halves.

"I killed somebody," Michael said. "I killed a kid."

Then, again, as if he needed to convince even himself, "I killed a child."

The words were ugly, heavy, clinched and waiting for their frame: their explanation and their meaning.

"I was a cop." This explanation, like the other, bereft of meaning, pregnant with emotion. "I was almost a cop."

Another pause, longer than the last.

"I was going to be a cop. My dad, my uncle—Irish, you know? Hereditary cop families, right? I knew it like I knew I was going to grow up and shave, get married and have kids. Grow up and be a cop. I did the whole thing—scholarship to John Jay, the two-year course, the Police Academy on Long Island, the works.

"So I get out, and I get a job. My first. Rookie cop. Police Academy pin-up boy. I was twenty-four. Six years ago.

"Did I ever tell you my family came from Newark? A lot you care, Mel; you wouldn't know Newark if you were standing in the middle of it. Which you wouldn't be long. Visit beautiful downtown Newark, New Jersey; a city halfway between a joke and a war zone. You talk about twenty minutes into the future. Okay. That's Newark. I've seen the future and it sucks. And my folks being from there, it meant I was a rookie cop on the Newark PD. For two weeks. In the ghetto.

"The ghetto kids, they've got a sport you might not have heard of. It's hitting the news now. They had it then. Doughnutting, they call it. What it is, a kid steals a car, goes joy-riding. Looks for a cop car to ram, maybe run down a couple officers. Fun. And they'll be back on the street again in twenty-four hours, because they're *kids*. Eight, ten, twelve."

Michael stopped, staring off into a specific place and time that was not here. His voice was even, patient, testifying for the thousandth time to an indifferent truth that was incapable of causing him either pleasure or pain.

"What they do most copshops—what they did there—is pair up a rookie with a veteran. Let some practical knowledge rub off. My partner's name was Sam DeHorst. Of course by the time I met him everyone called him Hoss. So every night for two weeks I spent eight hours in a unit with Hoss, hearing about life, cops, and Newark. The other guys called us Animal Farm—as in, Horse and Peacock. It was one of those things that was meant to be.

"And one night— And one night—" Michael took a breath and went on. "It was late. End of shift, end of tour. Quiet, clear, hot, summer. And we pull a vehicular D&D—Drunk and Disorderly, DWI—Driving While under the Influence, Reckless Endangerment, every little thing that makes life a joy. So we head off to the area where the report's from. Bad neighborhood. And all there is are these two cars piled on each other. Recent. Gasoline all over the street. So Hoss gets out to take a look.

"I should have gotten out, too. I should have. But it was late, I was tired. He told me to stay in the car. Didn't look like there was anyone around.

"I should have remembered that doughnutters travel in pairs. It came out of nowhere, and hit him, and the I did *all* the right things, make on the car, partial on the plates, "Officer Down" code. And while I'm doing that it goes right into a bunch of parked cars—having too much fun to drive, I guess.

"I can see Hoss. He's down, and he's hurting bad—broken hip, broken pelvis—but he's stable. The crash car could blow any second. So I do some more right things. I head off to the end of the block to try to get them out. By the time I get there the heap's clean. Six of them in it, probably. Swarmed out like rats out of a flooded sewer. Kids. No way I'm going to chase them. So I turn back.

"Hoss was lying in the street. He couldn't move. I could smell the gas from where I was. He was *lying* in it. In the gutter. And out of nowhere this little black kid shows up. Six—eight—with malnutrition who can tell? He was wearing a red and white striped T-shirt and tan shorts. Black high-topped sneakers. He was holding his hand out funny. And then I saw why.

"He was holding a cigarette lighter. He flicked it on. And then he threw it on my partner. Hoss went up like a torch. And I shot that baby in the chest.

"That's all. And that is why I'm not going down there with you. I won't do you a damn bit of good. That's life. That's the way it is." Michael stared off into the distance at nothing at all.

Jane risked a glance at Philip; to move meant the possibility of being noticed, but she had to know. There were high spots of color in Philip LeStrange's cheeks; he looked like a china doll that had been rouged with a lavish hand. Upstaged, and in no possible way the baddest dude in the Valley. Jane looked at Melior, but all his attention was on Michael.

"And your partner?" Melior said.

"He died after four weeks in the Burn Unit. Hero's funeral. Wife and three kids. I got a whitewash job and a psych discharge. And that's all," Michael's voice was flat, telling over the ancient maiming as if it had happened to somebody else.

"No," said Melior. "That is never all."

"Why did you have to *tell* him?" Philip cried. "Don't you see, Michael—he's going to use it, now, just the way he uses everyone to get what he wants!"

Philip gestured. The ring on his finger flashed.

"And did I not keep my side of the bargain, Child of Earth?" Melior asked. "Silver and gold."

"Shut *up,*" Philip said.

Philip, Jane noted analytically, was about as flustered as she'd ever seen him get. He glared furiously at Melior through bifocal lenses.

"I was going to leave you there. I should have. You aren't worth the grief you're handing Ruth. You aren't worth Nai taking the trouble over you. But you've got them in trouble now, so I guess you'd better get them out. I hope it kills you," Philip said viciously

"It may well," Melior said. "And as I believe so well in your hopes, Michael must come with me."

Michael stared at his feet.

"Michael, my friend," Melior said softly, "you must come with me. Who will wield the Sword, do you not? I do not think that Master Philip would prevail; the blade is not his weapon. The man who seizes it must be able to slay with it. Who will slay the *grendel,* if you do not? I ask much of you, I know, but rest assured: once you have slain the *grendel* I myself will slay you in turn."

"What?" Philip said.

Melior turned to him. "The enchantment is yet death, Philip LeStrange. Any of humankind which touch the Sword will yet become *grendel.* And since I ask Michael's help to wield the Sword, I promise him release also."

"Well, why can't *you* do it?" Philip demanded, even though he knew the answer as well as any there.

"I will try," said Melior. He spread his hands. "And perhaps I will die. I know no longer; the future I can see is dim, and perhaps only my fancy. I am no longer sure."

"What a great time for your elf superpowers to wimp out," Philip said, falling back into superiority as an only refuge.

Jane sighed. *"Leslie,"* she drawled, in bored, long-suffering tones.

Philip's head whipped around toward her. His ears turned red, and his eyes narrowed furiously.

"Michael, will you aid me?" Melior asked again, ignoring both of them. "There is little I can promise you—"

" 'But blood, toil, tears, and sweat,' " said Jane, from some oft-dredged store of quotations, " 'and gentlemen in England now a-bed/ Shall think themselves accurs'd they were not here/And hold their man-hoods cheap while any speaks.' " "And if the British Empire and its Commonwealth last for a thousand years men will still say, 'This was their finest hour.' *Henry the Fifth.* And Churchill."

"Don't you understand? *I can't do it.*" Michael said.

"If you're going to be a failure, Michael, you might as well be one underground where nobody can see you," Philip said brutally. "He won't leave you alone until you do."

Philip's face was set; for a moment he almost looked majestic. "And if nobody wants me for anything else, I'm going to see if I can shut the system down so maybe Elfie can get himself killed in peace. See you around."

The sound of the door closing was not particularly loud, but Michael still flinched.

"I blew that one, didn't I?" he asked of no one in particular. "What about you, Jane?"

Jane considered the matter. "If you give me your keys, I can get your stuff from your apartment, because the police are probably looking for you or Melior. And I've got another copy of the map I had in my room. I'll bring that, too. And I guess Naomi wouldn't mind if you make your-self dinner or something."

Michael ran a hand through his hair and looked at Melior. "I'll go with you," he said, and stopped. He made a gesture that somehow en-compassed the whole bleak quixotic situation. "Like Philip said. I might as well."

· 21 ·

The Bloody Chamber

NAOMI HADN'T WANTED her to look, but Ruth had, of course. There were flashlights in the magpie midden, and the hazard-lights could be unshipped from their moorings. There was light enough to see by, to explore every byway of their prison, even those which Naomi had already explored.

To Ruth and Naomi, accustomed to modern New York subway platforms, this strange Victorian subway platform—as if *The Wild Wild West* had chosen to set an episode in New York City, and this were some construction of the evil dwarf Miguelito Quixote Loveless—was lavishly deep; the short trackspace leading from nowhere to nowhere almost an afterthought. The engrimed, damp-rotted walls had once been gay with frescoes—allegorical depictions of the marriage of science and hedonism.

Beneath the arched cathedral space of the groined vaulting, from which hung shattered and plundered chandeliers, an alabaster fountain, dry forevermore, placed Phaeton and his fiery team in eternal and improbable juxtaposition with naiads spouting water. Even the car that had made its brief pointless journey into the darkness and back remained; moored at one end of the platform like a time-rotted but still improbably baroque gondola. Ruth started toward it.

"Don't go in there," Naomi said, but, like Bluebeard's wife, Ruth had to see.

There were bodies.

Ruth stood in the open doorway. This was the source of the sick-sweet heavy smell that she had noticed-without-noticing. Her emotions seemed cut away from intellect by an impermeable shield. On one side there was measured gratitude: that the *grendel* had been in existence only a week; that the temperature here, so far underground, was cool. On the other, there was horror, and the power of something experienced with the eyes and mind to reach out and assault.

The photographs this scene resembled did not, by their existence and by her memory of them, dull the intimate edge of it. It was no more atrocious than those sights which the generation just preceding hers had imbibed with their dinners, nor than the images brought home from a declared war to *their* parents.

But it was here, in front of her, and what Ruth's heart cried out against was not its horror, nor the pain it represented, but the *reality* of it; as if the realness of this one experience might cause all the rest of the world to match it in intensity.

The interior of the car had long since been reduced, by time and damp and mice to the bare shell of what it had once been: Victorian underground railway car. Only the iron skeletons of the seats remained. But at one end of the car, piled up against the bare rock face in careful husbandly fashion, there were bodies. There were enough bodies that there were too many to count, stacked as they were, but not so many that the situation was distilled into its own *guignol* sort of farce; less than a dozen. Several of them had been neatly beheaded, and the heads jumbled to one side. Most of the bodies had been at least partially undressed, and the ones on the top of the pile were dismembered to some extent. Blood had leaked from the bodies at the top of the pile onto all the ones beneath, and the ones at the bottom of the pile had been pressed, by the weight of their fellows, quite empty of fluids. A blackish, shiny trail led from the pile across the floor of the car, and drained, through a hole in the side, onto the railbed.

And perhaps even that could have been contemplated in quietude, except for the fact that the rich and varied underlife of the city was not absent from this part of it. There were ants, and some kind of large black beetle, and rats made tunnels through what was, after all, when all was said and done, meat.

Ruth backed away, bumped into Naomi, and screamed. She turned away, staggered half-a-dozen steps, and retched with dry mouth and empty stomach, eyes and nose running. Naomi held her up, and offered her a handkerchief when she was done.

"*No,*" Ruth said.

"No," Naomi agreed. "But there's something else you ought to know."

Ruth looked at her, exhausted, numb.

"It brought us down here and left again. It left you in that pile of junk around the sword."

Ruth thought about that.

"It left me in the car," Naomi finished.

Ruth saw for the first time that Naomi's clothes were black and clotted with something other than subway grime, and began weakly, undramatically, to cry.

It took Jane about two hours to make her various rounds and return. She carried Michael's duffel bag, stuffed full, over one shoulder, and her guitar case in her hand. When she came back into the apartment, she turned the duffel upside down, and out tumbled a strange mix of Michael and Melior's possessions: gray cape and flak jacket; high-topped boots of stamped and gilded leather and battered combat boots; scarlet tunic and black T-shirt.

Abandoning this pile, Jane turned to her guitar case. She opened it carefully, and equally carefully removed the original of the ancient survey map, illegally removed from one of the New York Library's map files in a coup worthy of Philip LeStrange. She spread it out on the table and smoothed it carefully.

Melior had been in the kitchen, eating as Michael had been unable to. Now he came out and sorted through the clothes on the floor. He picked up what was his and walked past Jane and Michael into the bedroom. Jane continued straightening what was by any standard a very large map, never meant to be folded as Jane had folded it.

"Um, Jane . . . ?" Michael said hesitantly, wondering where to begin.

"I'm not going with you," Jane said, as if finishing his sentence. "Where you're going I can't follow, and what you're going to do I can't be any part of. And besides, I'd just get in the way," she recited with sarcasm so arid Michael wasn't entirely sure he was hearing it.

"Right," he settled for.

Melior returned, dressed once more as an elf-king out of Faery. The only thing that marred the illusion was the very real-world bandage on his forehead.

Michael bundled up the clothes he'd asked Jane to get and went off in turn.

Jane sat down on the couch and began tuning her guitar. Her face was tilted to watch her hands; the pale fall of hair hid her face entirely.

"There's something you should know," she offered to Melior, "even if it's stupid."

"But you are not stupid, Mistress Jane," Melior said.

Jane regarded him, while, all unregarded, her right hand picked out, note by note, the first bars of "True Thomas."

"The way to Fair Elphame," said Jane Grayson, "is neither dark nor light, with neither sun nor moon, no wind but the roaring of the sea, and a river of blood to cross to get there. And so's the New York Subway System. You can get there by candlelight," she added, although she hadn't meant to.

"Ah," Melior inclined his head. "Fair word and fair warning, Mistress. I shall remember." He went back into the kitchen.

"I *said* it was stupid," Jane said under her breath. She pressed the fingers of her left hand down and began to weave the melody into slow mournful chords. " *'And there was neither sun nor moon/But all the roaring of the sea. . . .'* "

Michael came out, flak-jacketed and steel-toe booted, holding something in both hands as if he were afraid it would bite.

A gun.

Naomi's gun.

It was a long-barreled .38 revolver, looking like an Old West six-gun if you didn't know better. The six-inch barrel made it a good choice for target shooting, which was what Naomi used it for. Michael had helped her pick it out. When not in use, it lived in a steel box with a combination lock that Naomi kept in a drawer.

"It's loaded, but I couldn't find any spare ammo," Michael announced to no one in particular. He slipped the gun into the waistband of his jeans and pulled his shirt down over it.

Melior came out of the kitchen with a teacup into which had been poured the last of Ruth's birthday wine.

"That we three shall meet again," he said, offering it around.

"That's not the way to bet," Jane said, and drank.

It was ten o'clock Thursday night, six days from the day of Melior's arrival.

Suicidal disregard for consequence lent their actions a bitter elegance. Rohannan Melior and Michael Peacock moved directly, profligately, toward their goal. A taxi to Wall Street. A quick few blocks walk to the City Hall Station, closed still, but easy enough to force its iron gates if you simply didn't care if anyone noticed.

Down the steps. Into the station. And for Michael Peacock, into nightmare.

The gun felt *right* in his hand. *It's funny how it all comes back to you. The cop walk. The cop talk. The cop MIND.*

Michael watched as Melior leaped lightly from the edge of the platform—*covering his partner*—down into the tunnel and crouched, looking about himself. Michael followed more slowly, sitting on the edge first and then sliding over it. He held the .38 up, near his face, where it could not be knocked aside or fouled by something below eye-level. And when he saw the *grendel* again. . . .

He still didn't know if he could pull the trigger.

But the cop inside—never dead, never quite disavowed—assured him that he could pull the trigger if he had to.

It didn't say whether he could live with himself afterward. But then, he didn't have to, did he?

All he had to do was find the *grendel.*

Jane's maps were detailed but not precisely clear. The IRT line sliced through the Alfred Ely Beach Tunnel at this location, but how much of the tunnel—if any—was left after the construction, and where and how it connected with the tunnel they were in, Jane hadn't been sure.

And, in the end, they were only guessing that the *grendel* was here—and not, say, in the Second Avenue Subway, which had lain unfinished and awaiting habitation since 1975.

To *know,* apparently, they needed Ruth.

If she was still alive.

If Ruth and Naomi were still alive.

And there was just one other thing.

"There's something I've been meaning to talk to you about," Michael said, pitching the half-whisper to carry down the tunnel to Melior ahead.

Melior stopped and turned back, and Michael saw, with a certain bleak satisfaction, that Melior was *glowing,* a faint silvery aura that served to light the tunnel far better than Michael's flashlight.

"You aren't exactly as deficient in magic as you've been claiming, are you?" Michael asked, catching up to him. "I should have caught on sooner. The sword works here. And that precognition thing of yours, that works, too. And you did something to Philip."

"We had a bargain," Melior protested mildly. "With silver and gold to seal it, as one must with a Child of Earth. I did not lie to you, Friend Michael; in comparison to what I could call upon in my own place the magic I have is small, and weak, and once it is expended in this place I may not find more," Melior answered, a response that was oblique at best. "I use it now to draw the creature, if it can be drawn. You I leave to claim the Sword."

It was a sentence of death and Michael knew it, but it made him curiously happy.

"All we have to do now is find our way in," he said.

* * *

Ruth's tears did not last long; the time they had was precious. The *grendel* might come back. She hugged Naomi and said nothing, and they went on with their search.

Neither of them quite wished to try the narrow tunnel, to see if it was not as much a dead end as it looked. It was too easy to imagine being trapped in that narrow cut with nowhere to run.

They found the stairway to the surface from the days of this place's long-ago construction. The ornate brass rail and green marble steps—still bearing shreds of a carpet once red—disappeared after less than ten feet behind a pile of bricks and rubble; trash from the long-ago era of its construction.

"I wonder what this *was?*" Ruth said.

"Jane would know," Naomi answered.

"I wonder where she is?"

"I hope she's all right."

"I hope *somebody's* all right," Ruth said, with an attempt at bravery. It was hard to be brave when you were buried alive and your future looked like being eaten ditto.

Neither of them ventured nearer the sword than they had to. It glittered balefully amid its dragon hoard, promising any number of things.

"That thing gives me the creeps," Naomi said. Ruth agreed, slowly, but she didn't really agree. Some inward imp of perversity assured her that *she* could handle the sword and take no harm; that in this one thing the magic would not work as Melior had sworn it would.

They carefully explored their prison: the platform which, if this were only a book, Ruth would demand be described in all its perversely beautiful detail. The stairway to the surface (blocked). The car with its hideous contents. The sword with its trash at that end of the platform.

No escape. The car blocked half the platform. The railbed was sunk only eighteen or twenty inches below the edge of the platform; easy enough to get down to the trackbed, walk the hundred yards to the bare rock of the other end. No escape.

"There has to be a way out!" Ruth cried in a strangled voice.

"We just haven't found it yet," Naomi said, sounding calm where no calmness was possible. And so Ruth tried to be brave, in a situation where no bravery was possible.

They even, in the end, went down to the far end of the tunnel, to where the dressed stone gave way to the raw rock face, and found nothing at all. It began to seem, to Ruth, more and more possible that the *grendel* simply walked through walls, but if that were so, how did he get all these bodies here?

She had never felt so tired. All last night spent waiting up for Philip to tell them where to look; Ruth couldn't really remember how many hours it had been since she last slept, and thirst was a growing ache at the back of her throat.

Maybe they would die of thirst before the *grendel* had them for dinner.

"Maybe," Naomi said, and Ruth realized she'd spoken aloud. "There's something that looks like a canteen in that pile of junk around the Sword. I didn't grab it before because I thought it might attract the *grendel* somehow, but maybe it's worth the try."

Ruth hesitated. "I'll go," she finally said. "And don't argue with me. If—*it*—put me on that pile in the first place, it can't have any objections to my going near it. And I'm *thirsty.*"

"There might be nothing in it," Naomi warned.

"Then I'll swipe a bottle and cut my wrists," Ruth said.

"Just don't touch the sword."

The platform space seemed wider when you were crossing it waiting for a *grendel* to pounce at you. She'd made Naomi stay at the other end, back by the blocked staircase. Victorian decorator logic said that there should be one at this end, too, but there didn't seem to be. Perhaps they'd forgotten it.

The large round orange hazard light in her hand made an unwieldy lamp, but Ruth carried it doggedly. To be down here in the dark would be a thousand times worse.

She reached the trashheap. No *grendel*, and the sword still there like a brand plucked from the burning, infinitely alluring.

Ruth dragged her attention away from the sword and studied the trash. Yes, there was the canteen, and what looked like a sealed box of granola bars next to it, although you could never really trust those things to be what they seemed.

My mind is wandering, thought Ruth with an air of discovery, just as if it were an achievement. She'd better hurry.

She set the lamp carefully on the floor and was reaching for the canteen when she heard the sound. Metal on metal, and, impossibly, the subway car shifted a few feet.

And there it was; the *grendel;* spider-spread on the top of the subway car, squirming its way toward her, mad eyes gleaming. Ruth snatched the canteen—and the box—and ran.

Both were heavy in her hands, and a part of her mind must have registered that fact; why else had she not dropped them in her mad flight to simply get *away?* It was darker but not quite black without the light, and Ruth already knew the floor was clear. She ran.

Naomi grabbed Ruth as she caromed off the wall beside the stairwell. Terror modulated Ruth's shriek to a frightened whimper. It was only as Naomi grabbed her that Ruth realized the *grendel* was not behind her.

But if it had wanted to, it would have had her.

Naomi drew her up the stairwell.

"Wh— Wh— Wh—" Ruth demanded, still clutching her prizes.

"It didn't follow you. It went into the car," Naomi said. Ruth clung to her and shook.

The canteen was full. Naomi tested it cautiously, emitted a snort of disbelief and passed it to Ruth. Ruth sniffed at the opening.

"Brandy," she said.

"Brandy-and, I think," Naomi said. "Drink up." She tore the lid off the box of granola bars, trying to make as little noise as possible. The contents were both fresh and dry.

Ruth drank, and felt the bite of brandy, even though it was reassuredly diluted with a great deal of tap water.

She knew exactly how much. And she'd bought the little bottle of Courvoisier to spike it her very own self.

"This was Melior's," she told Naomi as she handed her the canteen.

"Yeah," the word came on a long exhalation of disgust. "I'm sorry, Ruth. You loved him."

"He never stood a chance," Ruth said in a small voice. Her eyes burned, but this time no tears would come. She leaned back against the smooth marble of the stairwell and wished, desperately, that she were anyplace but here.

"It explains why Philip never found anything about the bodies," Naomi said after a while.

"What?" Ruth felt groggy; exhausted beyond bearing.

"The *grendel.* It's been grabbing people all right; anyone it could find; maybe even homeless; and bringing them here—to its larder. No wonder there were never any clues." Naomi sounded more disgusted than anything else at her inability to have reasoned out this simple fact.

"So how come it left us alive?" Ruth asked unwillingly.

"Maybe it left them all alive at first," Naomi answered remorselessly. "They'd keep better that way. It'll probably leave us alone until it runs out of supplies."

"We'll be dead by then."

"And you're complaining?" Naomi asked.

They huddled together in the stairwell and tried not to think about the *grendel* and its dinner arrangements.

"Now we know where the way out is. Behind the car. Maybe. . . . When it's asleep," Ruth said hesitantly.

"I don't think it sleeps. And I don't think we could be quiet enough to not wake it up. And I don't think we could move the car enough, or climb over it, to get out."

"We have to try," said Ruth, who was trying to believe this.

"Maybe," said Naomi. She put the cap back on the canteen and tucked away the last of the granola bars. "C'mon. I know it sounds idiotic, but why don't we try to get some sleep? I'll wake up if we hear it coming."

"And there isn't any place to run anyway," Ruth said. She snuggled up next to Naomi. Naomi put an arm around Ruth's waist, and Ruth put her head on her friend's shoulder. They settled themselves as best they could against the marble wall.

And Ruth, assuring herself that she'd give it about ten minutes before telling Naomi that sleep was impossible under these conditions, fell asleep.

Dark on dark; they would have missed it entirely except that Melior's fingers, skimming lightly along the subway wall, abruptly met thin air.

Too regular to be a crack, it was as if the subway wall simply stopped and started again; an eighteen-inch gap in the concrete. It seemed impossible that the hulking *grendel* body that Michael had seen could have forced its way through such a space, but Melior's expression, eloquent of loathing, seemed to say that it could.

"Is it. . . ?" Michael said.

"A way the *grendel* uses, if not the path to its lair," Melior said in answer. He reached his arm into the crevice as far as it would go. "Bare rock," he pronounced. "Were this a castle in my own world, I would call this perhaps a ventilation shaft to the lower levels."

"That would fit with Jane's map," Michael said, hesitating. He shone his flashlight directly into the cut. Rat-eyes flared red and vanished. The walls were rough rock, the passage narrow. Getting down it would be a long process, and all they might get for their pains was stuck.

But they had to check it out. Like an alleyway door hanging open.

Like a wrecked car that might blow.

"You want to walk point or drag?" Michael Peacock asked.

When Ruth woke up, it was dark. Naomi must have turned the flashlight off to save batteries. In the darkness the distant light from the sword was deceptively intense.

And Naomi was talking.

"When I was a kid," Naomi said, "growing up in Brooklyn, and that's another story, which I guess you're not going to get to hear, no loss; everybody had relatives—uncles, aunts. I used to ask my mom, 'so where're all my relatives?' because I didn't have any, and for a Jew not to have any family, well, that's really unusual. But we had nothing. And one day when she got tired of me asking she pulled out a family tree she'd put together when she was about the age I'd been then and showed me my family. She was the youngest of eleven—I'd had six aunts and four uncles, and they'd all had families. . . .

"She had the tattoo; she'd been in one of the camps for kids. Sponsored over here in '48. Her foster parents helped her look for her real family, but. . . . Anyway. You know.

"Two hundred generations of European Jews. All gone, just as if they'd never been. It was the first time it was really real for me—just as if I were standing at the top of a ladder and somebody yanked the ladder away—and I was still standing there, only now it was *possible* to fall, because all my connections had been cut away, and there I was looking down into empty space, thinking about how I'd come this close to just not existing at all."

Ruth sat up straighter and shifted away. Naomi must be certain she was awake now, but her tone never altered.

"I don't know if you can understand that, Ruth. Understanding it is not something I would wish on anyone. But in a weird way it made me realize that I was personally responsible for continuing my own existence—for not getting erased or swept under cover as if I'd never existed. And I vowed to myself that I'd be *real,* that I'd be big and important and *noticeable.* Because I wanted to live. Because it's not enough to remember. You have to make certain that *no one* forgets."

"Naomi?" Ruth said hesitantly. She reached for Naomi's hand, but now Naomi pulled away and stood up.

"And sometimes, Ruth, the only way to live . . . is to die."

Before Ruth could react, Naomi was on her feet, skipping down the half-flight of stairs as if they were brightly lit. Ruth, groggy and now personally terrified, followed her, but she was too late. In the silence the scuffing of Naomi's feet on the marble sounded like large hisses, and in the faint radiance of the larger room Ruth saw her, a darker shadow, dashing the length of the platform to where the sword stood upright in its nest of glittering trash.

And Ruth, who had never really forgotten it, remembered that Naomi's martial art was kendo. The *sword.*

There was an earsplitting roar from inside the remains of the subway car. The *grendel* stormed out, rearing up in a terrifying bearish gesture that made the sweat of terminal fear well up in Ruth's skin. Her mouth was so dry it hurt; when she opened her mouth, no sound came.

But Naomi reached the sword. Reached it, gripped it, and pulled it free in a clangor of rolling five cent deposit cans, holding it as if it were a *katana* and facing the *grendel*.

No, please, thought Ruth in sick terror, because the intellectual sophistry of accepting inevitable death is a far cry from watching it happen in front of you. *Not Naomi. No.*

The *grendel* reached out to take its Sword back, to slay this impertinent trespasser, but all there was to grab was blade—blade which cut, and stung, and flickered out of its grasp to cut again. Naomi backed frantically, trying to stay out of reach, making useless parries at the grasping taloned hands. Parries which did not kill.

But at last the *grendel* did what every lesson swore it would, and rushed her so heedlessly that Naomi had time to step aside; presented its unprotected ribs when there was time and all the world to strike, to shape the blow that struck and sank deep, deeper, and the monster hurt at last; turning, raging, swatting at the beloved object which had become its tormentor.

Then it was possible. Then the *grendel* was weak; gushing thick black fluid from its gaping side, sliced about the arms and chest, and, finally, sinking to its knees, misshapen arms dragging limp upon the ground as Naomi struck, and hard, at the scaled folds of flesh between head and shoulder. Struck once, and again, and then again, until that hideous head hung suspended only by a flap of skin.

Dead.

Then Naomi stood, exhausted and triumphant, bleeding and gore-spattered, resting the tip of the sword on the ground.

Ruth ran toward her.

"Get back!" Naomi whirled around to face her, holding the sword en garde as if it were weightless. Drops of liquid flew from the spinning blade. Her voice was high, her eyes wide and mad.

"You can't have it!" Naomi shrieked.

Ruth stopped dead.

Naomi retreated a few more steps, but even so Ruth could see the gleam of tears in her eyes. "So this is how it is," Naomi said, her voice softly wondering. "You can tell Melior he was right about everything, Ruth. It works just like he said—and it's fast. Oh, God, it's so fast. Don't let anybody else—" she broke off.

"Naomi?" Ruth said. "Don't do—"

"What you know damn well is the only thing I can do, now?" Naomi's voice was ragged; her breathing faster now than even exertion had made it. "Get out. Go on. There's a way out around the car. Use it."

"Come with me," Ruth said. "Naomi—"

"God dammit, Ruth." The words were evenly spaced, inflectionless, read off like the ingredients of a recipe. "Melior was right. The sword *wants*—" She broke off. Ruth could see sweat trickling down Naomi's face, her teeth bared in a grimace of effort. "Anyway. This is no time to—to be as Ruth and Naomi, Ruth." Naomi managed a ragged laugh. "Get out of here. Go on."

It should have been me! Ruth shook her head, wordless with the pain, but Naomi retreated into the shadows with the sword, leaving Ruth access to the way out.

If she could take it.

The *grendel's*—the *FIRST grendel's*—body was already liquefying, melting like a Popsicle dropped on a hot summer's sidewalk. The stench was unbearable. In the silence of this man-made cave, the only sounds were Naomi's ragged panting and the drip-drip-drip of fluid over the side of the platform.

Ruth looked back. She could not see Naomi, except as a deeper darkness surrounding the Sword. She jumped down onto the tracks.

There was less than a foot of space between the body of the carriage and the tunnel wall. Ruth pressed her back against the wall and slid along it, into the darkness, eyes closed so she would not have to see what was inside. There was a bare two foot expanse between the nose of the gondola and the wall.

At first Ruth was sure the wall was solid, but then her groping hands reached an opening, a window onto nothing, rough-hewn into the solid rock. *Ventilation tunnel,* the certainty from her recent reading came.

But whether it reached the surface, or whether Ruth could follow where the *grendel* had been able to lead, she did not know.

And she would not leave Naomi.

The conviction—as stupid as it was comforting—steadied her nerves and stopped her hands shaking. She was not going to leave her friend.

And besides, the sword would be sharp.

"I have a little neck—" Anne Boleyn's reputed words mocked Ruth's nobility. It wasn't easy to die.

But she wasn't leaving Naomi alone.

She had already made up her mind and turned back when she heard Naomi's indrawn gasp of pain, amplified by an architectural trick of acoustics. She groped her way back around the end of the car, then along its length, and at last was in view of the platform with its scattershot harlequin lighting.

She could see Naomi now. Naomi knelt on the damp-splotched marble next to the fountain that stood beneath the rotunda. The sword's hilt was balanced on the carved lip of the fountain, the blade pressing awkwardly against Naomi's lap.

And even in that dimness Ruth could see the bright red welling; the running of the fast blood.

Ruth climbed up onto the platform again.

"Get the *fuck* out of here!" Naomi snarled. "Do you want to be next?"

Ruth started toward her. Naomi warded her off with glistening red hands. "It hurts," she whimpered. "It slipped. It *hurts,* Ruth."

And it wouldn't kill her, Ruth thought with sickening clarity. The sword's spell was too clever for that. It would keep her alive, somehow, and incapable of breaking free before the sword finished the work of binding her will to its.

Or to something.

"I'm going to get you the canteen." Ruth said.

Melior had gone first, and even taken Michael's flashlight to light the tunnel. Both men moved crabwise, crouching, muscles of head and neck and shoulders screaming protest. If the *grendel* came upon them from either direction, they were dead. Left alone, Michael might have turned back—not from cowardice, precisely, but from a growing feeling of futility and time wasted—but Melior forged on; if not tireless, at least determined.

Slowly the passage changed its shape, from a slit eighteen inches wide in which a man might almost stand upright to a square box-shape, angling perceptibly downward, through which they must creep upon their stomachs. Now Melior put out the light and passed it back to Michael; there was simply no point. Even the rats had deserted them, and all the world dwindled to the excruciating, abrading procession through the dark.

At last Michael ran, face-first, into Melior's boot soles. He shoved. Melior kicked back, an irritated semaphore of caution. After a pause, he slid swiftly forward, the intermittent rasp of his swordbelt on the rock escalated to a continuous singing rasp. Then he was gone.

"Come, Michael." Melior's voice, low, from what must be the tunnel's end. The silvery radiance, absent in the tunnel, grew about him again, and in the light Michael could see the opening, square-cut like a picture frame, showcasing Melior.

There was a scream.

Ruth.

Michael dragged himself forward.

*   *   *

She had pushed the canteen toward Naomi—pity, if nothing else, kept Ruth from coming too close. Naomi drained the canteen, and then worked the Sword away from the wound in her side.

That done, she lay with her forehead pressed against the cool marble, cradling the Sword of Maiden's Tears as if it were a child.

Ruth sat, as close as Naomi would allow her, and waited with her. There was nothing else to do.

"You know what my middle name is?" Naomi said after they had sat there a very long time. Ruth jumped, but her voice was steady as she answered.

"No. What?"

"Francesca. Naomi Francesca Nasmyth. I guess I got off lucky; Mom married some Wasp yuppie from Connecticut named Caldwell Kettering Chesterfield Nasmyth the Third. Duration: seven years, product: me; and then we went back to being Jews. What about you?"

"Ten generations of Ohio Methodists," Ruth replied. Her secret— the truth she had always owed Naomi—swelled in her throat, but to tell it now in the face of this disaster would seem like plea-bargaining for sympathy; a consumer-comparison of dooms. "Nothing special. I was an only child."

"So was I. You should have seen what he sent for my *bat mitzvah*. A Barbie and three trunks of clothes."

She must mean her father, Ruth guessed. Naomi's voice was slurred, now, sleepy. Perhaps she would bleed to death after all. Maybe they'd get lucky.

And maybe they wouldn't. The pool that Naomi's blood had made on the marble was beginning to dry. It had gotten no fuller. The bleeding had stopped.

"You can tell Paul. . . ." There was a long silence, until Ruth thought Naomi had forgotten she'd spoken. "Tell him I figured out the answer," Naomi said.

"I will," Ruth said. She wasn't sure Naomi heard her. The silence stretched again.

Then Ruth heard the sliding, dragging sound; scales against rock; and all her battered nerves could imagine was that the *grendel*, before it died, had somehow managed to reproduce.

There was a flare of white light.

Ruth screamed.

She saw the dark winged figure lunging for her and screamed again, scrabbling backward on palms and heels, but then Melior—Melior shockingly returned from death—had grabbed her, pulling her to her feet and holding her close.

Ruth struggled against him. "Naomi—" she cried, trying to pull free.

Melior turned and looked. He saw everything in a rush. Naomi, on her knees but trying to rise, face twisted in an unconscious grimace half of pain, half of hate as she regarded him. In her hand, glittering as she plied it as her makeshift crutch, was the Sword.

The Sword.

"Ah," said Melior, all on a breath. He held Ruth even more tightly, retreating into the darkness that was not dark to him. The cold silver light on his body flickered and died.

"Michael," he called softly. "Michael, I have Ruth and she is well, but come warily."

Michael came around the end of the subway car. He had his flashlight in one hand and, Ruth saw with some surprise, a gun in the other. He flicked the light around the platform, highlighting first Ruth, then Naomi.

And the sword.

"Oh, *Christ*—" Michael breathed.

"Hi, Michael." Perhaps the worst thing of all was that Naomi's voice was still recognizably hers; weak, but holding to its casual tone by a gallant exercise of will.

Michael stopped. *Dangerous,* the cop instincts assured him. *But she's dying!* another part of his mind protested.

"Hi, yourself," he said back. He stopped where he was. The important thing now was to find out who could be gotten out, and how, without anyone else being hurt. "Anything going on down here that you want to talk about?"

"I killed the *grendel.* I— But the sword slipped," Naomi said, leaving Michael to piece the truth together. *Then I tried to kill myself, but the sword slipped.* "Would you guys take Ruth and get the hell out of here, please, okay?"

"No." Melior's voice was low and regretful. Michael twitched but didn't turn toward him.

"Never take your eyes off the perp for a second, Cockie."

Hoss had said that.

"She will not die, Michael. The Sword has her," Melior said.

"What if you take it away? What if you take it back to Elfland?" Michael's voice was even; concealing desperation with an effort.

"It will not save her," Melior's voice held infinite regret. "Give me your weapon, Michael."

* * *

"No." Ruth's voice was small as the realization sunk in. "No you can't. Melior, it's *Naomi.*"

"Michael." Melior's voice was patient.

"Where'd you get a gun, Michael?" Naomi's voice held friendly curiosity, nothing more.

"I helped you pick it out, remember?" Michael said, then: "There has to be another way," to Melior.

"There is none," Melior said. "She is *grendel.* I am sorry, Naomi, my friend."

"Will you guys stop talking about it and do it?" Naomi said wearily. "Please. *Hurry.*"

"Oh, please," whispered Ruth, meaning just the opposite. Melior turned her against his chest and she buried her face in his tunic.

"The gun, Michael," he said.

"You can't do it."

For a moment Ruth wondered who'd spoken, then realized the ragged voice must be Michael's.

Michael drew a sobbing breath.

"You've never fired a piece before. It takes practice. I've only got six rounds. You'd *miss!*"

His voice rose to an anguished shout, and over the echoes of his last words came the crashing sound of gunfire.

"You'd miss," Michael repeated. There was a sound, small and far, of something thrown striking rock far along the tunnel.

Ruth tried to turn and look, but Melior would not let her. And when he let her go, it was only so that Michael could take her, gripping her arms as if he did not know his strength, dragging her away toward the shaft in the rock.

Melior stood until they had gone, until the sound of Michael's voice as he forced Ruth into the shaft had faded. Then he reached for the Sword, still lady-bright despite being slicked along half its length with blood and ichor.

Only the Sword of Maiden's Tears could slay the *grendel* it had made. Michael's weapon could stop it for a time, nothing more.

But at least the one who had been the warrior-maid Naomi, who, for a brief time Melior had called "friend," would not know what he did now.

He took the Sword, and did what must be done. And when he had finished he wiped it clean, and slid it into its place in his swordbelt.

Then Melior turned, and began to follow the other two. Back toward the light.

· 22 ·

And Back Again

RUTH DIDN'T HAVE any truly clear memory of the time between entering the ventilation shaft and the time she'd seen open sky; a clear blue trapezoid at the top of the subway steps.

There had been no trouble reaching it, and no one to see them, since, oddly enough, the entire Lower Manhattan system seemed to have lost power.

And somehow Thursday morning had become Friday noon without Ruth's noticing—the sky was bright, the buildings pristine, the air clear and fresh and *open* as she walked through the concrete canyons of Wall Street. Reality was mocking in its normalcy. *Do what you like,* Lower Manhattan seemed to say, *it doesn't matter to me. In fact, nothing you can do will make any difference at all.*

Exhausted, battered, the three of them had caught a taxi back to Ruth's apartment. The driver hadn't wanted to take them, especially when he saw the sword, but Melior wasn't the only one who never wanted to see the subway again. Michael had convinced him.

And then there was the silence of the long ride uptown, with Ruth feeling Naomi's absence like an abscessed tooth; renewed pain with each rediscovery. She'd reached out, cautiously, for Michael's hand, and held it. He gripped her fingers as tightly as if he were trying to crush them, and she could feel him shaking.

None of them had very much to say.

Jane was waiting for them in the apartment. She'd been watching from the window and saw the taxi stop, seven floors below. She'd been holding the door open for them when they crested the last of the stairs, and had gone to put the water on for tea without saying a word.

She hadn't asked any questions. But later, after showers and blistering hot tea with brandy and too much sugar, Michael had reluctantly realized that Philip must be called, for mercy's sake, to tell him they were safe.

That most of them were safe.

"What do you MEAN she's dead? You must have made a mistake! You should have brought her back! We could have fixed it. You didn't have to leave her there!"

Philip stood in the middle of the living room, face red and white with incredulous anger, having broken all land speed records getting there from Amsterdam Avenue.

Michael turned away and walked off.

Philip stared after him, still furious and now hurt as well. He looked around for someone to blame and saw Melior, sitting quietly in a corner. The light flashed off Philip's glasses as he turned. And Melior looked up and saw him.

Ruth, grieving and exhausted as she was, was brought to painful alertness by the lightning-flash of unleashed emotion. But Melior, as he spoke, was gentle.

"Naomi was dead, Friend Philip. All that remained was *grendel*. There was no other way."

And no one, Ruth vowed, was ever going to know what that way had been. Not from her.

Philip's eyes were very wide, and for a moment Ruth held her breath, although what could Philip possibly do that would raise a ripple after everything else they'd been through?

"Mistress Naomi is dead, Friend Philip," Melior repeated with firm gentleness. "She gave her life in exchange for Ruth's and all who dwell in this realm, if that is any comfort. I and all my Line share your sorrow."

Philip still regarded him, unspeaking, and it came to Ruth, in a slow horrified dawning of realization, what the reason had really been that Philip hung around so much. The real reason that he listened to Naomi when he didn't listen to any of the rest of them. Naomi. *Naomi.*

Philip took a deep breath. "Well, sure," he said in a bright spurious voice. "That makes it all right. Since Nai turned into a *grendel,* I guess you had to do it. Considering her hobby was cooking, she'd probably have opened a restaurant or something. *To Serve Man.* Yeah, Elfie, I guess you didn't have any choices."

Philip didn't even bother to slam the door when he left. It had hung open until Jane came out of the kitchen and closed it.

That had been Friday. And Saturday, following a notion of Melior's that seemed to be perilously close to wishful thinking, they—even Philip—had come down to the Brooklyn Subway Yards to see Melior off home.

And one of them was going with him.

"Why here?" Philip wanted to know. He hunched his shoulders against the chill, wearing a black leather jacket Ruth couldn't remember having seen him in before.

"If the subterranean way is Faery, then the approach to the subterranean way is the approach to the Morning Lands. And the Morning Lands are where we wish to go," Melior explained, patiently, for what might have been the first time. In fact, it was closer to the ten millionth time, and Philip hadn't liked the answer yet.

The moon was the traditional ghostly galleon, ducking behind cloud-wisps and painting the sky chill midnight blue. Jane and Michael, Ruth and Melior and Philip—*and never Naomi, never again*—stood outside the chain-link fence guarding the Brooklyn Subway Yards. Through the fence they could see acre upon acre of subway cars; some resting, some waiting for repair, some obviously beyond repair.

That was where they were going.

Jane and Melior, Michael and Philip and Ruth, all went down to the railway yards. To dance by the light of the moon, the moon, to dance by the light of the moon.

Have you danced with the devil in the pale moonlight? What was that from? Batman? No, something older.

The devil in the pale moonlight . . . Ruth looked at Melior beside her and thought of Coleridge: *For he on honey-dew had fed/And drunk the milk of Paradise.*

"I still wish you wouldn't do this," Michael said.

"I know." Ruth brushed her hair back; a nervous gesture. "I'm sorry, Michael."

He'd spent all morning—once she'd revealed that when Melior went home to Chandrakar she, Ruth Marlowe, intended to go with him—trying to talk her out of it. He'd called it running away. *"Naomi was my friend, too,"* Michael had said.

True. And it might be running away from people who, in their own perverse dysfunctional way, loved her, but Ruth didn't think so.

And if it was, she was doing it anyway. She had her biggest purse, and her toothbrush; four cans of Diet Pepsi, a dozen Hershey Bars, and a paperback copy of *Gone With the Wind.* All the things you'd take if you were leaving home forever.

And over her favorite cashmere sweater and the Liberty print skirt she never wore because it was "too good," there was Naomi's Kinsale cloak, taken for a thousand reasons.

"When we are home, Ruth, my father's artificers will unbind the spell from the Sword, and you will be whole once more."

Melior, trying to be comforting, and all his words did was evoke more strangeness. Her soul. The silver cord that—so Melior said—had pulled the Sword of Maiden's Tears into the World of Iron: her soul, loosed from her grip while she lay in her eight-year coma. She thought she could believe in everything else before she believed in that.

She could even believe that Melior loved her.

He was dressed again as she had seen him first, and wore the clothes that soon would not stand out in their strangeness, but would be the everyday garb of everyone. Melior was going home to Elfland, and Ruth was going with him.

"How close do you have to get?" Michael asked. Who would be practical, who would be organized, now that Naomi was gone? Would it be Michael?

Ruth would never know.

"Upon the iron road itself, I think, Friend Michael. We must go within these gates." Melior gestured, offhandedly, at the high chain-link gates, held together with chains and multiple padlocks, designed to keep trespassers out.

"What the hey; what's one more breaking and entering among friends?" Philip said.

Why, feeling as he seemed to about Melior, Philip was willing to be here at all was a Philip-mystery that Ruth would never solve. Melior's signet ring still gleamed on Philip's hand.

"You'll never know," Jane pointed out.

The paper bag she was holding crinkled slightly as she held it. None of them knew what was in it.

"Well, come on, then," Michael said heavily. "Who's got the wire cutters? Phil?"

The padlocks were beyond Michael's skeleton-key skills; in the end they went over the fence. The wire cutters had been only to remove a section of the razor-wire spooled along the top, and even in its absence— and with Michael's help—it was a difficult climb. Ruth was already battered from being dragged—*twice*—through the *grendel's* tunnel less than two days ago. When she fell and skinned her knee, it infuriated her almost beyond speech.

Well, hell, it's been a rough week.

"Here?" said Michael.

"As good a place as any to begin," Melior agreed.

"And get this over with before somebody sees us," Philip muttered.

Melior turned and strode—there was no other accurate word for it— a dozen paces away. He stood between the iron rails—silver only where the rust had been scraped away—and looked expectantly back at Ruth.

Ruth looked at her friends.

"Here," Jane said. She thrust her paper bag into Ruth's hands. It was heavy. As the top gaped open Ruth caught the honeyed smell of beeswax.

"Candles," Jane said. "For the spell. There's a lighter in there, too." Her round pale face gleamed in the moonlight, and it struck Ruth that of all the rest of them she'd miss Jane most. That Jane had wanted to be her friend, as much as Jane wished for anything she wasn't likely to get; Ruth's best friend, and not just one of a gang that happened to be all in the same place at the same time.

Jane looked at her, knowing what she knew, perhaps, or simply assuming that she knew it out of a lifetime's practice at informed assumptions. And not caring, because no amount of love and knowledge and caring and effort was going to make any difference now that the terms of Jane's reality had been set and the mind had been formed.

Knowledge was powerlessness.

"Thanks," Ruth said, and then, awkwardly, because this was not the sort of gesture there had ever been between them, she pulled Jane against her and hugged her tight. "Take care of yourself," she whispered, wishing there was someone, somewhere, who would make it their business to take care of Jane.

"Come, Ruth, we must away while the moon rides high."

Melior's cape billowed slightly behind him; his scarlet tunic was wine-violet in the cold blue light. He held his hand out to her.

"Ill met by moonlight, proud Titania." The tag was irresistible, but not apt; Ruth was no elf-queen, only cold and feeling irritable and foolish, just as she had when it had all begun. She trudged over to where he stood, hoping she would not sink High Romance entirely below the level of farce by tripping on the wooden cross-ties. She put one hand in his and held out the bag in the other.

"Candles," Ruth said.

"Ah."

Melior held his cape wide to shield the Bic lighter from the wind while Ruth struggled to light Jane's present, juggling two candles too thick to hold in the one hand she had to spare for them while trying to operate the lighter.

In the end it was Philip who rescued her, jerking the candles out of her hands and holding them like Frankensteinian electrodes while Ruth lit them.

"You're being a jerk, Ruthie," Philip said, low enough that it was meant for her ears alone.

"Shut up," Ruth answered wearily. She dropped the lighter into her pocket.

"Conservation of mass," Philip answered obliquely. He thrust the lit candles at her, and Ruth had to grab them hurriedly or drop them and have it all to do over again.

Then Philip turned his back on her and walked back to join the others. And though the night was not cold, Ruth felt cold, as if she were making some mistake she hadn't already taken into consideration and accounted for. Nerves, nothing more. *And who has a better right to them?* Ruth demanded of no one at all.

Hand in hand and each carrying a flickering beeswax candle, Ruth and Melior started down the tracks, toward the tunnel at the end of them.

There should have been more sound. Wind, carrying the far-off rhythm of subway trains on elevated tracks. Car alarms, emergency sirens; the sounds of the City, even in Brooklyn.

There was nothing. Only the prickling over her skin that Ruth associated with thunderstorms, and terror, and the last few minutes before the worst possible headaches. Melior's hand burned like cold fire over hers.

After a few moments of walking Ruth tried to look around and found she couldn't turn her head. Her muscles were suddenly painfully stiff and her field of vision had narrowed as abruptly as if she wore blinders.

Magic! And even the sudden realization that she, Ruth Marlowe, was smack in the middle of Real Magic was not enough to outweigh the fear.

Walking. Was she still walking? She couldn't remember how long this had been going on. She could not feel the weight of the candle she must still hold in her right hand. She was freezing cold, and the sweat was running off her skin like shower water.

Frightened, Ruth tried to open her mouth. Lips and tongue and palate were stuck together, immobile as if with the dust of the grave.

And Melior's hand burned, cold enough to sear flesh.

With a great effort Ruth jerked her head to the side and *saw* Melior a little ahead, walking with her hand in his down the tracks toward the tunnel ahead; blurred and shining; trailing luminous afterimages. He turned his head toward her and smiled; she saw the hot phosphor white of his teeth and the burning red of his eyes. His lips moved, though she couldn't hear what he said.

Demon lover, Ruth thought, and as swiftly another thought supplanted it. Tam Lin, and the lover claimed no matter what monstrous disguise he was enchanted into. She closed her left hand tighter over his.

Everything was fogged with halos; crisscrossing and multilayered in colors until she could hardly make out the subway cars that must be their basis. Everything was blindingly bright and much too dark to see all at the same time, and the rails of the tracks were a glittering hot-forged silver arrowing irresistibly toward a frozen nova terminus.

Now the ground—which had been perfectly flat the last time she had been able to see it clearly—was slanting upward beneath her feet. Now the footing was less certain than it had been before; still not treacherous, but a little slidey underfoot, and the gravel she kicked loose tended to roll—

—where?—

—downhill. Toward the World of Iron, which Melior was trying to climb out of. Hadn't he said he'd fallen, that the Sword of Maiden's Tears had fallen, here?

And now he was trying to climb out. Back to the Lands Beyond the Morning. Home.

Ruth gritted her teeth and walked on.

Soon the road she and Melior followed—the Iron Road—was steeper and the air was winter-chill. Ruth was glad of Naomi's cloak; the bare skin of her hands and face burned, chapped raw by some maleficent Frost King's breath. The frigid air was thin and painful in her laboring lungs: the clouds of her expelled breath added to the glittering ice-burning illusion which surrounded both of them.

But beneath it all, like cake under icing, she could see the Real World—the subway yards, the tracks and the tunnel. They weren't even halfway there.

Although she had never really been able to tell they were moving, Ruth was now aware they weren't moving as fast. Now Melior's grasp was nearly as much to pull her along as it was for comfort; without it, Ruth didn't think she would have been able to take another step. Her head spun giddily, and each step was a lead-weighted effort to defy gravity. Her mouth tasted of rust, metal, and salt, and her eyes stung with sweat.

Another step. Another. Ruth's arm ached as if her whole weight was suspended from it; as if Melior was drawing her up out of a well infinitely deep.

And if she felt this way, what must it be like for Melior, who had not only to carry himself out of the World of Iron, but her, too?

Ruth felt his muscles shudder as he fought to accomplish one more dragging step. Now progress was slowed to a series of halting baby steps, each bought at the cost of several seconds of agonizing labor.

Could he do it at all?

He'd said his magic was weak. He'd said that his only hope to return home was to ally his magic with that of the Sword of Maiden's Tears, and Ruth knew to her cost that the Sword's magic was cruelly strong.

But was it strong enough to take not only Melior back to his rightful place, but carry someone with him who didn't belong there at all?

Thin fires lanced up Ruth's arm to her neck; bruised muscles, pulled tendons. Melior would not give up. She knew that. He would not leave her behind. He would go on trying.

Could he do it?

What if he couldn't?

Did she have a right to let him risk his entire future? And not only his, but his family's, everyone who depended on him to come home with the Sword?

It was his decision to make.

And sometimes you had to decide things for yourself.

Ruth set her feet and hauled back hard against his grip. She felt him check and stagger, almost sliding backward, and that alone told her all she needed to know. Carrying her weight as well as his own, Melior wasn't going to make it home.

And he wouldn't leave her.

Ruth shouted at him, and could not even hear the sound of her own words against the clamoring silence. In the corner of her vision, the candle in her right hand glowed inferno bright.

"Can I get there by candlelight. . . ?"

Ruth concentrated. Hard. And finally succeeded.

She dropped the candle.

And suddenly there was a roaring void on her right side, chill blackness, savage and razor-edged, and here inside was her sensible cowardly self shrieking that there were bad things, worse by far than she had yet imagined, that could happen to her in these forsaken spaces if she got careless.

But now Melior's hand was not quite so solid on hers. And this time, when she pulled, her fingers slipped free.

"Ruth—!" Sound returned; she heard Melior's voice; terror and fear, longing and heartbreak, all mixed into one anguished howl but it was far too late to change her mind. She felt him rise; soaring as if a great weight had been lifted from his shoulders. Going home.

And Ruth fell, fell for hours, fell forever, fell as the Sword had fallen, down into the World of Iron.

Philip was the first one to reach her; crouched on hands and knees Ruth was treated to an intimate panoramic view of his shoes.

"You're alive, right?" he said.

Ruth sat back and looked up at him. Her face burned, her nose was running, and her lungs felt filled with pulmonary equivalent of hot green chile salsa.

"I'm alive, right," Ruth said. She located a handkerchief and blew her nose noisily. Around her the rail-yard had returned to rust, entropy, and iron. Melior was nowhere to be seen.

"What happened?" Michael, arriving, demanded. "Ruth, are you all right?"

"Physics," said Philip inscrutably. "Sure she is. She's breathing, isn't she?"

Yes. And Melior was going home. And there was too much riding on him for him to turn back, now that the hard choice had been made.

And it had been Ruth who had made it.

"So now it's really all over."

Jane, last of all to reach her, the statement flat and uninflected and just faintly accusing.

"Don't bet on it." Philip's voice had regained its accustomed sneer. "In books, magic strikes three times."

The Cup of Morning Shadows

CONTENTS

· Prologue ·

When the Magic's Real

THE WAY TO Elfland was neither easy nor straight, nor yet easy to find, but it was a road he could travel. He had paid the price.

How many miles to Babylon?
Threescore miles and ten.
Can I get there by candlelight?
And never go home again.

He lit the first candle, and the world warped; a bright flash like a coin dropped into water. He lit the second, and there was a sizzle like ice and boiling oil.

Perfect. He left them where they were, reflecting light from their pedestals of silver and crystal, and shouldered his pack. Leather, and custom-made, and it and its contents together weighed over eighty pounds.

He was glad he'd done so much weightlifting. He was glad of everything; of all the skills he'd had to master.

And now intended to use.

He ran his hand over the hunting knife strapped at his thigh.

Cold iron breaks all magic.

Then he stooped, carefully, and picked up the first candle.

The vertigo hit like an attacking shark. Cold wind whipped up from nowhere, threatening the flame of the second candle. Quickly he grabbed that one, too. It jiggled; hot beeswax spilled out over the back of his hand. It hurt, but not enough to make him drop it.

He'd learned to live with pain.

The pain of stretching his body beyond its limits. The pain of forcing his mind beyond its boundaries. The pain of having no heart—no, not any more, his heart had been cut out with a magic knife one night and he hadn't even been there.

But he was going to be there now.

And return the favor.

He lifted both the candles; five pounds each, confectionery-grade beeswax with red linen wicks. As they were in the *lais,* the *gestes,* the old tales—

The truth.

The wall shimmered liquidly and seemed to tilt drunkenly askew in every dimension at once. And beyond it, he saw the road. The High Road. The Iron Road. The Road to Fair Elphame. He tightened his grip on the candles. He set his foot on the road.

One step, and he was already gone from the World of Iron. Two steps, and the ghost-wind had sharpened to a tidal roaring, insistent as the calling of his blood. Three steps, and the road began to slant upward, toward the Morning and the Lands Beyond the Morning.

Four steps, and the iron in his bones was an aching weight, calling him back to the Last World, the World of Iron.

Five steps, six, and the Road was the only reality; the Road, and the clamoring darkness on either side.

The Road, the fire, the pain. And the chill ache where his heart used to be.

But he was used to pain.

· 1 ·

The Game of Kings

THE ESCAS SET was quite old; so old, in fact, that the pawn pieces were carved in the likeness of elves. The great pieces were the Treasures, twelve in coral, twelve in amber—a lie, in a way. There were only twelve Treasures, unique and irreplaceable. But vulnerable. Very.

No one now living knew how the Seven Houses of the Twilight had come to possess the Twelve Treasures. They had come with the Folk of the Air into the land they had renamed Chandrakar, and forever after had been the cornerstone of the Morning Lords' power. The tales of their wielding were many, but it had been long and long since Chandrakar's borders were less than secure, or since the title "Marchlord" had been anything other than a convenient honor to bestow upon an eldest son.

Even the long war following Rainouart High King's death had not changed the essential security of Chandrakar—not a small thing in a universe where worlds and lands were made and unmade in a careless thought. That the Treasures had the power to shatter worlds was understood by all.

What was less well known was that the majority of each Treasure's unique abilities were lost beyond the power of their Keepers to regain them. Only the least of the Treasures' gifts—formidable in themselves—remained: the power of the Sword to see into its opponent's heart; the power of the Cup to brew a posset that would kill or cure. These small tricks, and the mandate to guard the Treasures carefully, lest Chandrakar itself be lost, were all that was left.

Rohannan Melior of the House of the Silver Silences sat in his father's solar in his father's castle, both of which he must learn to think of as his own, and brooded, wine cup at his elbow. One day's work was done, another would soon begin. In a few days he must leave for the Twilight Court, to be confirmed by the Lords Temporal in his succession, to make known the recovery of the Sword of Maiden's Tears, to. . . .

To tell them that Eirdois Baligant, their new High King, was trying to kill them all?

Melior set out the chess pieces. Each Treasure—and its shadow-self. Conscientiously Melior lined them up in pairs down the jade-and-silver board. The pawns he left in their case.

The Sword: Line Rohannan, and safe. The coral sword and the amber one he placed to one side. They glinted in the varicolored light of candles and fire, so unlike the cold white light that came at nightfall in the World of Iron.

The Cup: Line Floire, and . . . in doubt. Jausserande had not spoken to him of her attempts to regain the Cup, but if they had been successful, she would not still be here.

And that they had not been successful in three full moons gave Melior even greater worry.

She is too young for this burden! Melior protested. But in Chandrakar that was all that was left: children—and survivors.

Like me. Melior took a sip from his goblet and wondered how the grape harvest fared on his southern holdings. You couldn't just let a vineyard lie fallow for a handful of seasons and have anything you wanted at the other end.

He hoped, nevertheless, for a good harvest. More than half the grain would have to be reserved for seed, which would mean a shortage of beer and ale, but they should at least be able to drown their sorrows in the new vintage.

Rohannan Melior of the House of the Silver Silences; Swordwarden and Marchlord; with his mind as earthbound as any of his human serfs'. Amusing in a quiet way, but not really helpful.

And what of the other Treasures? Melior sighed. Every day brought new reminders of what the war had taken from them. In the reign of King Rainouart, everyone had known who held which Treasure—it was a source of pride. But now?

Lines destroyed; cadet branches ruling; Treasures hidden for safety and their guardians slain before passing on the secret . . . Melior wondered if the Burning Lance and the Horse of Air were anywhere in any of the Nine Worlds: Line Rivalen and Line Tantris, which had held them, were gone to the last fighter. Even the peace-bonded women and children of Rivalen had died in the Red Peace; surely at least one mother would have taken her children and fled if Tantris had still possessed the Horse.

Perhaps Baligant already held the Horse and all the rest.

Chandrakar's High King had died, and Eirdois Baligant had been chosen to succeed him, but that was not where the tragedy lay. The tragedy lay in the fact that Eirdois Baligant had been chosen by the Lords Temporal to become High King over the Seven Houses of the Twilight much too late. For Baligant, passed over as a claimant before, shunted aside in the endless intriguing for alliance and advantage, was not now willing to forgive. And despite the fact that law and custom both decreed that the High King might not go to war with any of the Great Houses, nor condemn a Son of the Morning without a trial before all his peers, Eirdois Baligant had found a way to punish those he would not forgive.

Sword and Cup, Lance and Shield, Harp, Mirror, Cauldron, Comb, Cloak, Horse, Book and Crown. The Twelve Treasures of Chandrakar, each separately entrusted to one of the noble families of Chandrakar for safekeeping. All of which must be present at the crowning of the High King—and the lineage that did not come before the High Seat upon that day with the Treasure entrusted into its care would never come before it again: all rank and seizin were forfeit, and that line forever banished from the Twilight Lands.

And Baligant, it seemed, meant that to be all of them: Line Rohannan, Line Floire; all the Treasurekeepers. Driven from the land. By law.

Carelessly Melior swept all the pieces back into the box.

The safety of the Realm Eternal hung teetering in the balance, and what occupied his time? Farming and tax-collecting. . . .

But if the crop is not gathered and the rents distributed, we shall all starve come winter, and that with no help from Baligant. If only there were some proof to show. . . .

But there *was* proof. Melior straightened in his chair.

And slumped again, passing a hand over his brow. His proof was where he couldn't possibly reach it—trapped in the World of Iron.

Ruth. *Ruth.*

· 2 ·

The Glass Ceiling

"CHRISTMAS JUST WON'T be Christmas without an alarm call from the library," Penny Canaday grumbled.

She was one of those people who appear self-contained and self-consistent: plump, nonthreatening, and brown all over: brown skin, brown hair in a restless ponytail, brown eyes. Reminiscent of a gingerbread woman, and of that intermediate age (as she said) between graduation and death. Penny was wearing a set of grass-green Osh Kosh B'Gosh overalls with a white cotton shirt and bore a faint but determined resemblance to Mr. Greenjeans.

She was also the Chief Librarian at the Ryerson Memorial Library in beautiful downtown Ippisiqua (Queen City of the Hudson) New York, at which Ruth Marlowe had been the newest librarian for the last three months.

"Try to imagine it," Ruth coaxed automatically, although the thought of the last three months—and all the three months' to follow—was almost enough to send her out into the storm and back to her own apartment. Interpersonal relationships were not her strong suit these days, but Ruth dutifully did her best. And now it was Christmas, and she'd been dragooned into spending it with Penny and Katy and Nic.

Ruth wasn't sure she wanted to be here, even as insistent as her new friends had been. There were too many different horrible Christmases in her past for her to want to add one more.

Her first Christmas after coming out of the coma, spent in the nursing home. Braces on her legs and a body that wouldn't obey her—and a mind rebelling against the knowledge that it had been eight years—all her life from eighteen to twenty-six—since the last thing she could remember. Her first Christmas after Naomi died. Spent even more alone, in a hastily-rented studio apartment in Brooklyn. She'd lost track of Michael—she didn't even know if he'd graduated—but Philip and Jane were only a phone call away, finishing up their degrees at Columbia Library School.

She hadn't called them. Naomi's death had driven the once close-knit group apart, as if they were all co-inheritors of some ghastly guilty secret that made them unable to face each other. Naomi's cheerful tolerance had been what bound them all together. Without it, there had been nothing left.

Pulling her mind back into the present, Ruth looked out the window of Penny's and Katy's neat, restored-Victorian living room at white horizontal streaks of unseasonable late afternoon wind-driven snow. No, Christmas was not an especially good time for Ruth these days, but then, face it, the other three hundred sixty-four days were no picnic either.

"C'mon, Ruth, smile," Penny urged. "Katy's cooking dinner, the library isn't open, and we're going to have a white Christmas."

Ruth shook herself out of her reverie and forced the real world into focus. There was no point in pining after things she couldn't have. After things, in fact, that she'd thrown away with her own lily-white hands. Love and honor, courage and loyalty. . . .

Love.

"And anyway, if there is an alarm, you can pretend you don't hear it," Ruth said, valiantly keeping the conversational ball in play.

"Why bother?" Penny groaned theatrically. "Nic's going to have to go, and if Nic goes I might as well go, and that leaves you and Katy here."

"With a twelve-pound goose and a plum pudding with hard sauce," Ruth said, trying hard to make it sound as if they were something she wanted. Naomi had cooked, and the memories roused in Ruth by the kitchen aromas were not kind.

"But really, Penny, if the alarm goes off, it's sure to be a false alarm, and it's only two blocks away, anyway. We can all go," Ruth said, trying to keep herself firmly anchored in the here and now. She couldn't spend the rest of her life in mourning, however justified.

"It's the principle," Penny told her loftily.

Ruth was saved from riposte by Katy Battledore, Penny's clerk and—library gossip had it—the secret master of library services in the five-county area, who paraded out of the kitchen, bearing a large platter.

"Announcing the turkey," Katy said, with pardonable pride.

"It's a goose, actually," Nic Brightlaw added apologetically. He entered behind Katy, shirtsleeves rolled up and collar buttons undone, holding twelve pounds of thoroughly-cooked goose on an Armortel platter.

Nicodemus Brightlaw, the Ryerson Library Director, was one of those librarians who, Ruth thought, existed only in the fevered imaginations of Hollywood casting directors. Nicodemus Brightlaw was at least six foot two, and had eyes of blue, hair the shade of rich insistent gold rarely achieved without reference to Lady Clairol, perfect white teeth, and muscles in places most other men only had T-shirts. By rights he should have been drop-devastatingly handsome.

Ruth had distrusted him on sight. Nicodemus Brightlaw, the Library Director from Central Casting. The man with a past and no future—or possibly that was the other way around. In any event, it was pretty obvious after the first week that it was Penny, not Nic, who was running the library. The only useful function Ruth had yet seen Nic perform was to sign her paycheck. Now, three months later, she liked him (it was hard not to at least put up with the friends of your friends) and still didn't trust him.

It was puzzling.

"It's delicious," Penny prophesied. "Dinner, then presents. Yum."

"I thought you just said that Christmas wouldn't be Christmas without—" Ruth began.

There was the sound of a beeper.

Penny swore. Nic headed for the phone.

"You had to say it," Katy said to Ruth. Katy's mop of bright yellow curls and big brown eyes—and five foot two frame—always gave Ruth a shock when combined with the voice of Lauren Bacall and the diction of a cigar-smoking carnival barker. She looked like the star of the Shirley Temple remake of *The Exorcist*.

"You had to go and say it. If you hadn't said it—"

The secret of Katy's survival into adulthood was that she was also a world-class cook who felt unable, so she said, to cook for less than six people at a time. Since she lived alone with Penny in a restored Victorian on the edge of the Historic District, this meant the two of them ate a lot of leftovers. It was Katy's avowed hatred of leftovers (she said) that had first caused her to badger Ruth until Ruth accepted a dinner invitation. After that, it had simply been taken for granted that Ruth's place was at Penny's and Katy's house, for as many meals as Katy could wangle excuses to cook.

Nic came back from the phone. "It's the library," he said with a sigh. "It's just a false alarm, but. . . ." He shrugged. "You guys start without me; I'll be right back."

"Yeah, sure," jeered Katy. "C'mon and help me carry this damn bird back into the kitchen, and why they couldn't have called ten minutes ago and saved us all the trouble I'm sure I don't know."

The weather was settling down to snow in a sullen determined manner as the three librarians (and one clerk) walked down (mostly deserted) Market Street in the direction of the library. At this time of year, even four o'clock in the afternoon was twilight time. The front of the library was nearly the same color as the sky.

"Looks okay to me," Ruth said.

"Fine, let's go home," said Katy.

"It won't take that long to reset it," Nic said pacifically.

"Come on," said Penny.

Nic pushed open the inner door of the library and flipped on the first bank of lights. Ruth and the others followed. The familiar scent of wet boots, chalk, and sweetly-decaying books filled her nose. Library smell.

The Ryerson was a library of "a certain age"—about a hundred years old, Ruth had once guessed, looking at the ornate plaster medallions of the cupola—and dated from the first great flush of the American love affair with public works and high culture. Buildings like the Ryerson were the legacy of Rockefeller, Carnegie, Mellon, Vanderbilt: conscienceless robber barons who had lived like princes and acknowledged no law but themselves—and despite this had left their country an enduring heritage of public sector Arts. Many lesser plutocrats had imitated them: almost every city in America could boast a turn-of-the-century culture temple like the Ryerson.

And it hasn't gotten a good square endowment since, thought Ruth automatically, looking at the missing patches of plaster and the rusty watermarks that stained the plaster that *was* there. When the Ryerson was built, the area beneath the rotunda had probably been meant to be gracious and spacious; an architectural overture to the literary treasures within. Now it was jammed with desks, files, on-line catalog terminals, and tipsy racks of paperbacks. Study carrels vied with a massive oak card catalog for floor space on Ruth's left, and the charge desk at her right was almost completely concealed behind book racks, CD cabinets, and importunate signs listing the variety of late fines for assorted media.

Not much, but I call it home. At least I do now, Ruth said to herself, even while an inner voice told her that she lied. Home now was where Rohannan Melior of the House of the Silver Silences was, but Chandrakar was worlds and lifetimes away.

*   *   *

Ruth hadn't set out to befriend a lost elvish prince—but then, she hadn't meant to turn thirty either, and the two things had happened more or less simultaneously. She'd been living in New York City, going to Columbia Library School, all set to graduate and unleash one more over-qualified hyperlexic on the world, when she'd tripped over Melior.

Literally.

He'd been mugged.

Welcome to New York, now go home, Ruth had thought. She'd also thought he was a lost-stolen-or-strayed medievalist, but one look at his pointed ears—and pointed teeth—had cured her of that hopeful notion. But by then it was also too late to step back into the safe normal world: she'd already offered to help him, and that impulsive offer of aid to a wounded stranger had become an adventure that Ruth, all things considered, would rather not have had.

Ruth, Naomi, Philip, Michael, and Jane. Five unlikely friends, student librarians drawn together by a mutual sense of not fitting in. And before they had completed Melior's quest, and retrieved the beautiful and deadly Sword of Maiden's Tears, one of them was dead.

There were days when Ruth felt that it would have been better for everyone if she had died in Naomi's place. Or, at least, better for her.

Because she had fallen in love with Rohannan Melior, and he with her. And when the Sword was safe, he had wanted her to walk the Iron Road with him, back to his elvish land. And Ruth had agreed to go, settled her affairs, said good-bye to her friends.

And then had been forced to choose. Melior's magic, taxed by the battle to regain the Sword, was too weak to open the Iron Road enough for Ruth to pass. And Ruth faced a simple and terrible choice: between keeping Melior with her, in the World of Iron so deadly to his kind, or tricking him into returning to his land alone, knowing that when the Iron Road closed behind him, it would separate them beyond all power of elvish magic to reunite them.

"Come on," Penny said. "Let's round up the usual suspects."

"Because the sooner we do," Katy said sepulchrally, "the sooner we can get back to the goose."

Her comrades' voices jarred Ruth back to the present once more. They fanned out, not bothering to turn on most of the lights. As she walked deeper into the library, Ruth could hear Nic in his office, flipping switches to clear and then reset the alarm system.

Sixty thousand dollars. Twenty-four hours notice of battle, murder, and sudden death. Not to mention notice of changes of humidity, tres-passing mice, trucks rumbling by in the street outside, and any of a number of other interesting ephemera, necessitating midnight visits from Nic, or, failing Nic, Penny, at least once a month.

Given the approximately fifty false alarms in the three years of the system's installation, it was hardly surprising that Nic Brightlaw maintained such a cavalier attitude toward it.

Ruth went down the stairs toward the Children's Room. False alarm or no, a good check over in bad weather wasn't a bad idea. If a window had come open—or been forced—or if, God forbid, the ancient roof should start leaking, it was better to catch it now rather than after a hundred thousand dollars' worth of books had been ruined.

She took a quick tour of the Children's Room: the bricked-up fireplace with the painting of the *Half Moon* floating at anchor; the half-height bookcases with row after row of beloved classics—Eager, Nesbitt, Norton (Mary and Andre both). All windows closed, no suspicious drips. All right and tight.

Then, as if compelled by the sort of literary device found in bad fiction, Ruth's attention slid unwillingly toward the door to the Second File.

She really ought to check the Second File.

She should.

There were windows down there, too.

Ruth hesitated. She'd been in the Second File. Once.

A long time ago—say, a year and a half or so—Ruth had been a normal student librarian. She hadn't had any fear of dark enclosed places or what might live there.

That was then.

Oh, don't be a walking cliché! Ruth told herself furiously. *You know what's down there: spiders, snakes, and rats. Nothing to be afraid of.*

She walked out of the Children's Room, through the Meeting Room (in one door and out the other), and down the hall that led to the Second File.

Nothing to be afraid of. After all, you've already faced the worst Life has to offer, right?

Too true. And capitulated utterly. There was a certain dour comfort in that, come to think of it.

The Second File was—more or less, and rather less than more—in the basement, down the hall that ran behind the Children's Room. Up three stairs, open the iron door. There you were, down in the basement.

Welcome to the M.C. Escher Memorial Library . . . Ruth thought in wry self-mockery. She propped the iron door open with a brick. With an expert flick of her wrist she twisted the timer on the light switch to its ultimate max and then stepped inside.

Ruth tasted acid and copper as the smallness and darkness pressed in on her like wet rancid velvet. But there was no Sword, no *grendel,* no slain friend. There was only the solitary dark, and the memory of the cold equations that had led to the murder of her best friend.

Naomi's dead. You're alive. Act like it, Ruth told herself brutally. She took another step inside, keeping a wary eye on the door.

The basement—idealistically called the Second File, though not even Penny had been able to tell Ruth where the First File was—was illuminated in its entirety by one forty-watt bulb suspended in the middle of the space, giving the entire basement the indefinable air of a Ridley Scott movie. Piled tangles of ancient fixtures made inkblot shapes in the wan winter light from the high, narrow, and filth-opaqued windows at the back of the room. Ruth looked around, ducking her head to avoid being brained by a couple of low-flying pipes.

The basement of the Ryerson Memorial Library was, like the library, in Ippisiqua, New York, and (again, like the library) of an 1890s vintage. In the case of the basement, this meant that it was dug, unfinished, into the rocky bank of the Hudson River. It was cold, damp, and dirty, infested with bats, squirrels, and God knew what else.

For all of these reasons, the Library Gods had chosen to store their bound copies of old magazines and newspapers down here; hundred-year-old copies of the *Hudson Eagle* going to mold and dust alongside seventy years of *National Geographic,* proceedings of the State Legislature, random government documents, antique maps, and other exciting ephemera.

They said we had to have them. They didn't say they had to be accessible. Or usable, Ruth thought, staring at the shelves of magazines stored against what had been the back basement wall of the original library building; half-smoothed rock evened in places with plugs of brick and (now crumbling) mortar.

The ceiling was low here; the beams of the first floor supports just scant inches above her head. In the farthest corner, where ceiling and wall made a mad rush at each other and met in a non-Euclidean tangle, several volumes of *Life* magazine lay stacked in the middle of the floor, gathering more damp (if possible) than they would elsewhere. Ruth, a librarian to the roots of her soul, went over and picked them up. Yes, here was the space on the bottom shelf they'd come from, but what moron had pulled them out and left them on the *floor?*

Ruth reached to put the books back and stopped. The light shifted, and suddenly there was sunlight spilling into the room where she stood. Hot summer sunlight in the dead of winter, from a direction that ought to be solid rock.

Suddenly Ruth's heart was hammering and her mouth was dry. And memory, unbidden, rose up to remind her why.

In memory it was always raining, although Ruth knew that May evening had been clear. Clear and cool, and the present dissolved and left her in what Ruth thought of as the last real moment of her life.

Hand in hand and each carrying a flickering beeswax candle, Ruth and her elphen prince, Rohannan Melior from the Morning Lands, stood in a rail yard in Brooklyn, spinning the magic that would take Melior home—and take her with him. Melior started down the tracks, toward the tunnel at the end of them, and his hand burned like cold fire over hers. Melior, who had fallen out of his world into her own, and now was climbing back.

Soon the Iron Road was steeper and the air was winter-chill. Ruth's head spun giddily, and each step was a lead-weighted effort to defy gravity. Her mouth tasted of rust, metal, and salt, and her eyes stung with sweat. The way was hard for one. Impossible for two?

Melior would not leave her. Did she have the courage to leave him? Or would she, through inertia and moral cowardice, condemn the man she loved to a slow death in the World of Iron?

No. Ruth knew she wasn't a heroine, but she had enough courage for this.

She dropped the candle that bound her fate to his.

And suddenly there was a roaring void, chill blackness, and the sensation, more terrifying by far, of her fingers slipping from Melior's grasp. . . .

And so Melior was gone, and Ruth was left behind, and the knowledge that Melior would come back for her if he could was balanced by the cold truth that he could never reach the World of Iron again. And she, she had thrown away her one chance to reach Chandrakar.

But now here was a second chance. Maybe. There wouldn't be a third. Ruth knew it in her bones.

With trembling hands she tore at the hardbound volumes of *Life 1920–1950.* Hot summer sun played across her hands, light from a land where it was always summer.

The half-remembered sensation of Magic tingled along her bones. Yes. Here it was. Yes.

"Ruth!" Nic's voice, raised behind her in a horrified bellow.

A second chance. Never a third. Ruth dropped to her belly and began to wriggle through the opening.

Darkness and sunlight, and the tang of the salt sea. A roaring, and a chill burning, and as vertigo tilted down to up and Ruth felt herself slide forward in the grip of no earthly gravity, cowardly sweet reason reasserted itself and yammered that there were far, far worse things than anomie.

But it was far too late for a thirty-one-year-old librarian whose soul had been stolen to guard a magic sword out of Elphame. Ruth felt the grasp of fingers on her ankle slide free as she tumbled inexorably into magic.

· 3 ·

In Your Heart
No Love Is True

FLOIRE JAUSSERANDE OF the House of the Silver Silences, Warrior
and Treasurekeeper, had been born and bred for war, and in the seventeen years of the warrior's lifetime which was all she had to measure time
by, Jausserande had learned more than the casual observer might think
about the rhythms and textures of waiting.

She knew good waiting from bad waiting, the unbearable from the
merely boring, and, most subtle of all, the necessary from the entirely
useless.

This waiting felt like useless waiting.

In the New Peace, Jausserande had no duties for her Line but to
recover the Cup of Morning Shadows, hidden in the Vale of Stars.
Dawnheart was the nearest castle to the Vale, and so she was here: had
been since Floire Glorete had passed the Cupbearing to her, the oldest in
Line Floire willing to live untouched that she might touch the Cup.

She had been here to see Rohannan Lanval die and his death barge
launched upon the river. She had been here to see Rohannan Melior
return from the World of Iron a month later, bearing the Treasure he had
been sent to recover and a mare's nest of allegations against their new-
found High King: allegations he would not repeat to anyone with more
political power than a middle daughter of a subordinate Line of a House
now in eclipse. Would not repeat, and could not prove.

Jausserande leaned her chin on her arms and gazed out over the battlements of the castle. The wind blew her shoulder-length silver hair against its confining golden fillet.

Jausserande was tall and fair-haired, as all of Melior's House were, and her eyes were the hot jewel-violet of twilight over the Vale of Stars. Despite her youth she was a blooded warrior, a captain of cavalry. Jausserande's Ravens had led many a charge in Chandrakar's civil wars, where loyalties shifted like shadows in candlelight. Born in war, she had never known what it was to spend a summer other than in arming for war.

Until now.

Harvest Home began in just two weeks; one of the reasons Jausserande had chosen this windy perch was to evade the hordes of guests and visitors that filled Dawnheart nigh to bursting. Every reaped field for half a league was filled with pavilions, tents, and lodging carts, and even at this height the uneven music of the carpenters hammering together the booths for the Harvest Fair on the meadow below reached her ears. In a fortnight the Home would begin—just as the Twilight Court would convene at Citadel—but this year the games and gauds of neither Court nor Home would mask the maneuvering for advantage and alliance that was prelude to a winter's war.

This year they had peace.

And they would have peace, Jausserande realized with a frustrated uneasiness, even if everything Melior said about Eirdois Baligant of the House of the Vermilion Shadows was true and he could prove it at the Twilight Court.

Jausserande shook her head sharply, refusing to follow that train of thought to any conclusion. She would leave the cloud-castle building to her strange cousin, and thank all the vague lucks and soldiers' gods that the House of the Silver Silences did not look to Line Rohannan, but to the Regordane of Line Regordane. And Regordane would choose the next head of Line Rohannan, if Melior held to his mad fancies that the High King chosen by the barons after a century of war was a murderous lunatic who wished to see the land laid waste.

But her cousin's sanity was not Jausserande's immediate problem. The Earl of Silver, the Regordane of Line Regordane, had bid her make sure of her Treasure before Twilight Court convened. For the last three months she had been frustrated in every attempt she had made to reach the Vale of Stars and work the small spell that would deliver the Cup into her hands, and now her time was running out.

Tomorrow would be her last chance.

And that was all very well, and no more than she had expected from a short life spent learning that luck could not be trusted and fortune was a myth, save for the fact that, like all the heaven-born, Floire Jausserande had her rightful inheritance of the elphensight that allowed her to look a little way into the most probable of all the possible futures.

Not for her was her cousin's greater gift, that could show more futures than one, nor yet an Adept's pitiless Sight, that showed all the possible futures sharp and clear and allowed the sorcerer some chance to choose which of these futures would become the only reality. Jausserande could see only a little way, before the fog of "might be" closed in and left everything as mazy as it would be to one of the humans who followed the plow on Line Floire's demesne.

But the little way that she could see did not contain anywhere within itself the recovery of Line Floire's Treasure, nor, indeed, anything other than a peculiar tangled suspicion of battle, murder, and sudden death.

Which was ridiculous. They were at peace. The rulers of the Seven Houses of the Twilight—Silver, Vermilion, Saffron, Azure, Crystal, Indigo, and Emerald—and their vassal lords—Rohannan, Floire, Rivalen, Gauvain, Amarmonde, Eirdois, Calogrenant, and the dozen-something others—had sworn. They had all chosen Eirdois Baligant of the House of the Vermilion Shadows for the High King, and bound themselves with fearful oaths to support him and no other.

The thin shouts of the laboring mud-born on the field below drifted up to her. Happy mud-born, to have no cares beyond the next full meal and a warm place to sleep, both provided by their elphen overlords. For a moment Jausserande almost wished she were human: finite, limited, untroubled by such dreams or visions as made even Jausserande's waking hours restless.

The Morning Lords had sworn peace. And as that had been only a few seasons ago, and Baligant was not yet even crowned, it was a bit soon to be looking for treachery, in Jausserande's opinion.

Thus, there could not be war from within.

And Chandrakar was fortunate in its location among the Morning Lands: it lay between no two things of any strategic importance whatever, nor held any Gate that led so. Any invader of Chandrakar would do so for what lay within it, not through it. And at the moment, Chandrakar was much too poor to tempt even the most whimsical empire builder.

Thus, there would not be war from without.

But there was going to be trouble from somewhere. And all Jausserande could do was wait. Knowing that waiting was the wrong thing to do, and knowing there was nothing else she could do.

But if waiting perturbed Jausserande's mind, she was nearly unique in her ability to do nothing but wait. This was the height of the harvest; the grapes, the barley, the wheat, and the apples—all the produce of the

Rohannan lands needed to be harvested, the herds thinned, preparation for winter made.

And when the preparation was done, the Home would begin: the fair that had been the prelude for war since Jausserande's earliest memories, but which this year would bring peace instead. Delegates to the Twilight Court, Advocates to the High Court . . . and no war.

Why, then, did her memories of the future hold the clash of steel?

Jausserande shrugged and turned away. The battlements had brought her no peace, and so her frustrated ramblings brought her at last to a room that, no matter how overcrowded the castle became, would remain unencroached upon.

The door swung inward before she had a chance to knock.

"A small magic, but still impressive, do you not think, Jauss?" said the voice within. Jausserande shrugged and stepped through the door.

Dawnheart was a castle built for war, without any large windows in its outer walls, and so the windows in this curtain-wall tower were narrow unglassed slits barely a handspan wide. The sun's rays struck through them for only a few brief minutes each day; for all the rest the sun fell at a slanting angle upon all the three-foot thickness of good white granite that formed Dawnheart's outer walls, spreading its light a little way along the stone and leaving the room itself in darkness.

The room's occupant did not mind.

It was always night here, in the small room to which the Lady Vuissane had withdrawn after her last battle; Rohannan Vuissane of the House of the Silver Silences, Adept and Scout of her brother's infantry.

Like most of the elphenkind born during the wars, Jausserande had little training in the Great Art; enough to avoid ruining a spell, or becoming trapped in one, but that was all. Vuissane had been Adept of the Low Magic, with only the simplest tricks of fire and wind available to her from the High. The Low Magic was, so Vuissane had said, so nearly indistinguishable from common sense that it had been no burden to her to let it merge with her huntscraft and that with the ability to walk softly in another's footsteps to make her the most valuable of her brother's spies. Vuissane had been able to walk into an enemy camp and spy out its disposition down to the last barrel of ale on the sumpter's wagons, and slip away as silently as she had come.

But then, once the Lady Vuissane had been able to walk.

"Come in—and sit down—and stop jittering—and tell me what is going on in the world."

The door behind Jausserande closed with a thud. Jausserande stepped forward into the room.

There were coal fires burning at each end of the small room, and the light they shed was further augmented by the illumination from two bronze candle trees, each as tall as a standing man. One stood at each end of the high carved bed that, save for a chair, two stools, and a low table covered in books, was the only furniture in the room.

Lady Vuissane lay upon the bed, propped upright upon a mound of brightly-colored pillows. Her useless legs were stretched beneath a dyed fur coverlet, carefully bolstered with pillows to keep them straight.

"Well, here's a surprise," Vuissane said. "Three months in Dawnheart and this your second visit. What marvels may attend upon this rare visitation, eh, Equitan?"

The immense human in Rohannan livery stood impassively in the corner, saying nothing. Castle gossip said that he was as much jailer as servant; certainly Vuissane had tried many times to end her life when she saw what she had become.

To lose the use of one's limbs was, alas, not unique in Chandrakar, in all the years of war. Even elphen magic could do little to palliate the pains of those who suffered maimings and worse. Only the far frontiers of the High Magic, where such regeneration could be purchased at the cost of lives, and the twisted labyrinth of the Wild Magic, where the price was even higher, offered repair, and there were many who wouldn't—or couldn't—pay the price demanded to be whole once more.

But for the Adepts of High and Low Magic, there was not even that chimerical hope of renewal. Their years of study and sacrifice barred them by custom and oath from ever accepting another's magical help, and their training held that the powers they wielded were focused through the lens of the body—

And a broken body meant powers broken forever, beyond all hope of mending.

Vuissane shared her brother's pale silver hair and cat-green eyes. Younger than he, she was still some years older than Jausserande, and where Melior's face showed the stamp of a wary kindness and acceptance of the folly of elphen-kind, Vuissane's fox-bright eyes and pain-grimmed mouth seemed to say that the worst her people could do was only what she expected.

"Wine for the guest," Vuissane said, and Equitan went to fill his mistress' command. "Sit," she said, and Jausserande moved uneasily toward the stool indicated.

The close heat of the room made Jausserande profoundly uncomfortable and if it disquieted her, how much more must it grate upon Vuissane, who had been as free of wood and forest as any wild thing.

Before the House of the Saffron Evenings' one unwise experiment with cannon had ended all her freedom.

"Well?" Vuissane said.

"Everything's going all wrong!" Jausserande burst out. She drew breath to say more, but at that moment Equitan returned and Vuissane held up her hand for silence.

"Go outside and close the door," Vuissane told him. "As you can see," she said, making a bitter face, "I shall be well guarded in your absence. And *you* may serve us," she added to Jausserande, as Equitan set down the tray.

Jausserande poured wine into both cups, wondering why she had come. There was little enough Vuissane could do for anyone, and her company was not exactly cheering.

"But speak to me of the greater world," Vuissane said, taking ruthless control of the conversation. "How is my brother?"

"He swears he still pines for the Ironworlder—Heruthane?—and that the High King lusts to kill us all."

"Ruth, not Heruthane. And Baligant need not kill, when all he need do is follow the law."

"That the Line which cannot produce its Treasure at the Kingmaking is tainted and banished? That would—" Jausserande's brow furrowed with thought.

"Destroy twelve Lines, among them the ruling Lines of six of the Seven Houses of the Twilight: Regordane is the only ruling Line which does not ward a Treasure. And for that matter, who has the others now?"

Jausserande had no idea; so many Treasurekeepers had died in the war. She concentrated on the immediate fact that Vuissane seemed to take Melior's nonsensical theory seriously.

"It's nonsense," Jausserand said bluntly. "Baligant's the High King— what would he gain?"

"Maybe he's bored. But undoubtedly you're right, Floire Jausserande. Baligant Baneful makes no designs. His honor is pure. And you have already reclaimed the Cup from the Vale of Stars."

Jausserande flung herself to her feet with a hiss, her hand upon her dagger.

"No?" Vuissane's smile was bittersweet. Jausserande sat down again, slowly. It would not do to let Vuissane bait her.

"I do not have the Cup," Jausserande admitted reluctantly, although it was no secret. "But that is nothing to do with the High King! The roads are filled with bandits, and every wood and coppice holds some bully who would rather pillage honest men than do honest work!"

"It must be hard, when one has been a captain of hundreds, to meekly bow your head to some unblooded clerk not even of your own race," Vuissane said.

It took Jausserande a moment to realize that she was not being agreed with.

"If they dispute their rightful overlords, then they are criminals and should be punished as such! If they prefer a kingdom where humans rule, they're certainly welcome to look for one—if they can find the Gates, or use them," she added, sneering.

"Oh, do be reasonable, Jauss. Humans have no magic—how do you expect them to go Gatewalking?"

"If they have no magic, then they should do as they are told and like it," Jausserande said stubbornly.

Vuissane sighed.

"Very well. Humans are all that you say they are, and it is their malice, not Baligant's, that has kept you from the Cup. And doubtless you, now being prepared, will achieve it on the morrow."

Jausserande hung her head, and Vuissane regretted, if only a little, her biting tongue. It was true that Jausserande's sublime faith in her present virtue and future victory could wear down a sword blade's edge, but Jausserande was Cupbearer, and that was more important than her infuriating arrogance.

Besides, if she lived long enough, she would learn that Life betrayed everyone in the end. That would be revenge enough, if Vuissane wanted any.

"I don't know," Jausserande said in a low voice. "I cannot See."

"You see well enough to find tomorrow's sunset," Vuissane pointed out, kindly enough for one whose own elphensight had been broken to meaninglessness.

"Nothing I like," Jausserande said, and managed a wry smile. "Nothing that makes any sense."

There was a scuffle at the door, and both women's heads turned toward it.

"My lady is therein, churl, and do you not afford me entrance I shall prove your discourtesy upon your body!" The young voice was raised with cockerel outrage; furious with entitlement.

Jausserande coughed. Vuissane held her countenance still with an effort.

"Let him in, Equitan. I should so hate to replace you." Vuissane snapped her fingers and the door flew inward, revealing Equitan and his assailant.

Gauvain Guiraut of the House of the Crystal Wind was Jausserande's squire. He was young enough to have been too young for the battlefield, but like all the children in Chandrakar, Guiraut had been born into a land at war.

He took three long steps into the room and flung himself at Jausserande's feet. His dagger—for Guiraut was not yet a knight, and thus could not bear a sword—grated lightly upon the tiles of the floor.

"My lady!" he announced, and Jausserande ruffled his pale hair.

"Guiraut."

The boy darted a wary glance at the Lady Vuissane, whom everyone from the chief cook to the stable boys *knew* to be an Adept of undimmed and malevolent power.

"My lady," he said again. "All is prepared for our journey tomorrow. A party of the Guard will ride with us to the edge of the Vale Road and wait there until our return."

"You—" Jausserande said, and stopped. There was no reasonable reason she could give to forbid Guiraut to go, and he had done nothing to deserve so visible and humiliating a mark of her displeasure. "You've done well," she said at last.

"There is a tisane I can brew to mend that other matter for you," Vuissane said. "But it will leave you with a dreadful headache. And if you ride tomorrow. . . ."

"I will have it," Jausserande said shortly, almost as if she still ordered her Ravens into battle. "I thank you."

Vuissane looked from Jausserande to Guiraut. "I wish you fortune on the morrow," she said, in tones that dismissed Jausserande from her presence. "You will come again," she added, and it was impossible to tell if it was request or prophecy.

· 4 ·

Between the Darkness
and the Light

SICK. THE CAR. *Jimmy*— Aching fragmented memories blurred and danced, masking pain. Ruth. Her name was Ruth, and—

And what was she doing here? There was no car. That had been fourteen years ago. Ruth opened her eyes, and felt a sliding disorientation in her stomach as her preconceptions rearranged themselves.

This was none of the places she had expected to wake up in.

Half an inch from the end of her nose, an iridescent beetle climbed a stalk of green glowing grass. The hot green scent was strong in Ruth's nostrils, and sunlight made rainbows in her eyelashes. She moved her tongue experimentally. There was earth in her mouth.

Not earth. Ruth, ever scrupulous, made the last connection as memory fell into place. Not earth. Not *Earth*. Elphame.

She tried to move, and couldn't. Laggardly sensory information, checking in from the jumbled array of her body, announced that her legs were pinned under a crushing weight.

Ruth kicked. And struggled free, panting, from beneath the prone body of Nicodemus Brightlaw. She got to her knees, then to her feet, and stood there, trembling.

For a moment the sight of him blotted out everything else. She was baffled; she was indignant; she was jealous at the thought of having to share her adventure; she was glad to have someone familiar with her.

She wondered what the hell he was doing here. By a number of the cardinal rules of magic, he shouldn't have been able to follow her through at all.

Never mind that now.

Ruth brushed her long light-brown hair back out of her face. She'd lost one of her thick winter gloves going through the Second File to Elfland and this wasn't really the weather for them anyway. She pulled off the other glove and, lacking pockets, dropped it on what Ruth, a stickler for accuracy, felt one must really call the greensward.

Next, she undid the clasps at the neck of the dull green wool Inverness cloak she wore. The cloak joined the scarf and glove on the ground. The summer sun, no matter how untimely, was glorious.

Belatedly, Ruth realized she ought to see if Nic was all right, but just as the thought came to her, he rolled over onto his back.

He must have left his trench coat and gloves in his office back in the library; he was dressed as always in a conservative wool fade-to-black suit and forgettable silk tie. The tie was askew; the white oxford-cloth shirt was streakily gray with Second File dust.

He did not groan and mutter his way into wakefulness. His eyes came open, their stare as sudden and fixed as an awakening vampire's. There was a moment of nerve-stretching stillness. Then the muscles of his face came into play, assuming an expression, Ruth suddenly knew, that was both false and practiced.

There was a moment while she watched him evaluate the impossible: the noonday sun, the faery glade. Ruth, watching him watch the world, heard birdsong somewhere behind her and the murmurous plash of a running stream. Her skin prickled stickily beneath the baby-blue vintage cashmere twin set and wool Black Watch plaid kilt she wore. Her heart fluttered with emotions too complex to be named.

"Ah." Nic seemed to be trying out his voice. He arched his back and caught sight of Ruth, and got to his feet as it was occurring to Ruth that it might actually have been better to ditch her companion and take her chances on her own.

"Ruth," said Nic Brightlaw, and paused.

As if she were observing an actor preparing to go onstage, Ruth watched Nic armor himself in amiable vagueness, and the sight unnerved her far more than naked threat might.

He smiled. "Ah, any idea where we are?"

"I don't know if you're going to believe this," Ruth began in careful tones.

There was a large-animal-sized crashing through the wood.

"Damn," Nic said conversationally. Without seeming to hurry he crossed the clearing toward Ruth, scooped up her scarf and cloak from the ground, and grabbed Ruth herself with his free arm. Her squeak of surprised protest was cut short when he thrust her cloak at her; blinded by winter-weight wool she followed where he dragged her.

"Down. Don't move," Nic said softly in her ear. Ruth sank to hands and knees in the second-growth scrub that ringed the clearing, willing for the moment to do what he said. But there was no command that could keep her from looking.

She saw something large and white moving through the wood at the other side. Saw it turn, in her speculation, from bear, to deer, to—

Magic.

The unicorn was a little larger than a white-tailed deer; horse-shaped (as much as anything) with a mane that stood on end like a white silk Mohawk and a tufted lionish tail that it lashed as if it were a cat about to be bathed. Its hooves were pink and cloven.

And its horn, set with taxonomic irregularity in the center of its forehead, was spiral pearl and white gold, opal-shot.

Ruth made a sound in the back of her throat. Nic's hand pressed down hard between her shoulder blades.

The unicorn stopped in the middle of the clearing, head up, pink nostrils flaring. Its head swung from side to side, questing.

It found Ruth's glove, lying on the ground where she'd dropped it. Ruth heard Nic draw breath in a frustrated hiss.

The unicorn nuzzled the glove, pawed at it, and finally picked it up in its teeth and shook it, giving itself a momentary ludicrous resemblance to a terrier.

It dropped the glove and bugled plaintively.

It's looking for me. Ruth knew this with the certainty of a suspension of disbelief that had strained to its limits and then snapped. *It's looking for me.*

She started to get up. Nic shoved her down.

Ruth struggled. The unicorn cried out once more, then bounded away.

"*Let* me go!" Ruth demanded in a furious undertone. Nic released her, and she struggled to her feet, but the unicorn was gone. "Don't you *ever* grab me like that again!"

"That was a unicorn," Nic said in a flat voice.

Ruth stared in the direction it had gone, longing superseding all other emotions. "*The silken-swift . . .*" she quoted from some long-ago fantasy. "*The gloriously fair . . .*"

"Ruth, we have to talk," Nic Brightlaw said, in a voice that was not quite steady.

Ruth wadded the cloak she carried into a more practical bundle and tied it up with the scarf. Ignoring Nic, she walked back out into the clearing. The croquet-course smoothness of the grass was scarred by the unicorn's hooves, and Ruth, who should have been numb with shock, found herself thinking clearly for the first time since she could remember.

Forget the question of how she and Nic had gotten here; those answers could be found later. Meanwhile, they were here. What exactly had Melior told her about his world? Ruth furrowed her brow, racking memory.

Melior's land, Chandrakar, had just achieved a shaky peace after a generation of civil war. Chandrakar was one of the Morning Lands, which Ruth vaguely construed to be something on the order of a collection of little Graustarkian kingdoms. All were connected by the Iron Road which led to the World of Iron or, as its inhabitants called it, Earth.

She knew she wasn't on Earth right now, but that didn't necessarily mean, Ruth realized, that she was in Chandrakar—Melior's conversations had implied that there were a number of mail stops between his world and hers.

So where was she? And how did she get to where Melior was, without falling back to Earth?

How, in fact, did she get anywhere at all from here? Especially since the people she met here were likely to be both strange and overexcitable, as well as living in universal ignorance of the fact that she, Ruth Marlowe, was the heroine of the story.

Added to which, she didn't know what enemies Melior had made lately, let alone how to recognize them if she met them.

Ruth gazed around the clearing, excitement cooling slowly toward puzzlement, when there were more sounds from the woods. She turned hopefully in the direction the unicorn had gone.

It was back.

But it wasn't alone.

"Get back," Nic said, at a volume meant only for her to hear. Ruth edged behind him, trying to watch two fronts at once. On her left hand, the unicorn sprang and skittered at the edge of the glade, its dark blue gaze fixed unwaveringly on Ruth, but unwilling to approach any closer.

There were five men. Three on foot, two on horses, dressed in a mock-medieval style straight out of Maxfield Parrish. The ones on foot carried nets and spears. Ruth was painfully aware of her bare knees and sensible shoes.

"A maid!" one of the riders exclaimed, jerking a thumb at the unicorn in clarification. His companion laughed.

"Come here, pretty maidey, we won't hurt thee," the one who had spoken coaxed uconvincingly.

Ruth looked at the unicorn. It flung its head up and down in an agony of indecision, frantic to flee but obviously not quite able to bring itself to.

"Come, maidey; a gold ring for a few moments' work."

Ruth took a step toward the unicorn. It crouched on its haunches, poised to run as soon as Ruth had reached it.

She sensed as much as saw the riders shift their weight; to run her down; to run *it* down.

"Gentlemen," Nic began.

"Get her now; talk later." The second rider spoke.

"Run!" Ruth shrieked at the unicorn, and threw her bundled cloak at it with all her might.

The unicorn reared and fled. Ruth turned and ran at right angles to its path, into the brush where—please, God—a horse couldn't follow.

But she was leaving Nic behind. Terror and self-interest screamed at her to keep running; unwillingly Ruth stopped and looked back.

She saw a flash of metal. Nic had one of the spears in his hand and one of the footmen was on the ground. As she watched, the spear began to spin in Nic's hand—like an airplane propeller but faster, and glinting with that deadly gleam of metal.

Quarterstaff, Ruth realized in wonder. *He's using the spear as a quarterstaff.*

The others realized it, too. They spread out, trying to surround him. Ruth watched, knowing she was their next target once Nic was down, dry sickness in her throat as she realized this was not a dream, not a hoax, not a special effect. The blood and broken bones would be real.

There was a scream, following a movement that Ruth, watching closely, still hadn't been alert enough to see. One of the footmen staggered back, clutching his arm. There was a second blow, a baseball-sharp crack of wood on bone. The wounded man went down.

The second footman closed, jabbing with his spear in a fashion even Ruth recognized as amateurish. The horsemen spread and circled, but one of the cardinal tenets of war is that a man on horseback is at a disadvantage against the close work of a man on foot.

Ruth saw the flash of teeth and realized that Nic was smiling. Then— again she did not see the actual moment of the move—he was in beneath the spearman's guard. She saw the flicker of the falling spear, and then Nic was lying on the ground, one leg raised, and the ex-spearman was flying ludicrously and theatrically through the air. Nic bounded to his feet again.

One of the horsemen rode forward, leaning sideways out of the saddle. Nic moved, not fast enough, and went down. They were both on him now, blocking his attempt to rise with their horses' bodies.

And Ruth, in despair, knowing this could not end other than badly, was running through the brush toward Nic.

"Stop it— Stop— Leave him alone!"

She'd had to take her eyes off them to run; as she burst out into clear sunlight she could see that Nic was on the ground, lying still and twisted; and that one of the horsemen was afoot, and stood with a naked sword in his hand.

"Leave him alone!" Ruth screamed with all the volume she could muster. Her voice stuck and cracked, and her throat felt raw. Nic was lying very still, eyes closed.

"I'll do what you want," Ruth said in a small voice.

"No point to it now," one of the riders said. "The *losel* beast's probably halfway to the borders."

The other rider studied Ruth. His eyes were mismatched; pied; one blue, the other a brown so pale it was almost amber. His skin was a coarse, leathery, outdoor brown, deep-furrowed about the mouth. And he was regarding her, Ruth realized with a sick chill, the way she was used to regarding a package of pork chops at the supermarket: was this worth the trouble?

He turned his head to speak to his companion, confident she wouldn't run. And where, exactly, could she go, anyway?

Ruth knelt by Nic's side, not knowing what else to do. He wasn't dead, and the relief of knowing that was so great she nearly wept. But he was hurt—how badly Ruth couldn't tell, but the skin was broken and the blood was a shocking scarlet against Nic's blond hair. Gingerly she touched the side of his head. She got blood all over her hand and achieved no other particular result. Ruth gulped back nausea.

Head wounds bleed a lot. It doesn't mean anything, Ruth told herself desperately. *He could still be fine.*

"We've two men dead and nowt to show for it."

A conversation she ought to have been paying more attention to broke into Ruth's consciousness at last.

"Take the gel. Have the beast at least; there's a round *thaler* on the nail head."

The local dialect seemed to be Monty Python Northumbrian, Ruth noticed with shocky indignation. And it looked like they'd kill the unicorn after all. All her brave mad gesture of defiance had done was get Nic hurt, maybe even killed. Ruth blinked back tears and looked back down again.

Nic's eyes were open. His gaze held hers. And slowly, making sure she saw, he moved his hand down toward his belt.

She didn't know how she could have missed it before. What had to be the handle—the butt—of a gun nestled, small and brown and deadly, in a flat leather holster tucked inside Nic's waistband. The jacket had covered it.

What kind of library director packs a piece? Ruth silently demanded of the universe. But she reached for the gun.

"Come on now, maidey; fair is fair. We'll even give you a *pfennig* or two of the horn price to holpen you on your way—aye, and feed you, too. Come now, maidey, don't be shy. Leave the *jarl* for wolf-bait; that's fair, too."

Ruth, staring up at the horseman, felt the gun butt hard under her hand. She curled her fingers around it and the gun slid into her hand as if it belonged there. She pulled; it resisted for a moment then came free of the holster. Nic nodded ever so slightly.

Ruth stood up and backed away.

"I want you both to go away now. I said I'd help you, but you hurt my friend and you were going to leave him here to die. I've changed my mind. Go away."

As speeches of heroic defiance went, it wasn't much. Pied-eyes laughed and growled something to his companion that Ruth felt fortunate not to be able to hear. He flicked his reins at his horse and moved forward at a walk, obviously intending to make a game of running her down.

I am tired of being moved here and there and treated like a china doll as if what I want doesn't matter! Sudden alchemical fury—witch-fire struck alight by lucifer matches—rinsed through Ruth's veins like a drug. She brought the gun up threateningly in hands that shook, even though she hardly knew where she pointed it.

The gunshot was loud and flat; deafening, and apparently all the gun's own idea. She nearly dropped the little pistol in surprise.

But surprised as Ruth was, she was not nearly as surprised as the hunters' horses. They didn't stop to rear and whinny; they simply sought the straightest path away from the noise and took it, running flat-out and heads down. Within moments they were lost to sight, then to sound. She was lucky, Ruth supposed, that their riders had stayed on and not remained behind to make trouble.

Later she would discover that what she had fired was a double action Colt "Bulldog"; a .38-caliber revolver that would cock and fire just for pulling the trigger. Now she only wanted to find some place to ditch the noisy dangerous thing.

"Ruth, do me a favor . . . point that thing somewhere else."

Ruth looked back at Nic, and realized she was pointing the gun right at him. Nauseated reaction replaced the hot bright anger of a moment before. Carefully she placed the gun on the ground and stepped back from it.

"Good girl. Now come over here, and let's see how hard they hit me." His voice sounded frayed around the edges, but not nearly as frightened or angry as he had a right to be. Correction: as a *normal* person had a right to be.

Her sweater was ruined, Ruth thought with gloomy relish a few minutes later, but at least Nic was sitting up now. Beads of perspiration stood out all over his face, and his mouth was very set, but he was halfway to his feet and had assured her he was fine.

"I've been hit that hard before," he said wryly, "but usually with a chair. Never mind now. One question, Ruth, and I'd like a straight answer: do you know where we are?"

She met his eyes. Their gazes crossed like a romantic cliché with nothing of sex in it; only knowing. Knowing that Nicodemus Brightlaw, boy library director, was something from which all human contradiction had been carefully edited away, leaving behind something powerful and focused . . . and perhaps not quite human any more.

She wondered what he saw when he looked at her.

"No," said Ruth. "I don't know where we are. Would it help at all if I said I think I know how we got here, and where we ought to be, but not how to get there?"

"You forgot to say that it's a very long story," Nic added. He smiled as if it hurt, which it very likely did.

"Well, it is that," Ruth admitted.

"Fine. You can tell me while I recuperate. C'mon. I think I heard water over that way. Help me up. You can catch me when I fall over."

"Sure," Ruth said, relieved, all things considered, to be let off so easily.

"And, Ruth? Get the gun. We're going to need it."

Ruth went back to where she had laid it down and gingerly picked up the gun. She slid it carefully into the pocket of her skirt, hoping it wouldn't go off and shoot her in the foot. Or worse.

Then she went to see if the man that Nic had thrown was all right.

Part of her knew already what she was going to see. Hadn't Pied-eyes said Nic had killed two of their own? But part of her hoped it wasn't true.

It was. The man who lay on the emerald greensward stared sightlessly into the sun, mouth agape. His neck was broken. Ruth turned away.

Nic had killed him. Nic had killed both of them. And it didn't matter whether they were in Elfland or Ippisiqua, it was still murder.

She turned back to where Nic sat. He was looking at her.

"Yes, they're dead," he said, as if she'd spoken. "I intended to kill them, I used deadly force, and they died. Once I'd seen the unicorn, I didn't think they'd recognize the threat of a gun. Shaving the odds until they ran was the only other choice." His voice was neutral, as if he were discussing the weather.

"You could at least be sorry about it," Ruth said weakly.

"I'm not sorry about it," Nic said flatly. "I didn't care whether they killed the unicorn or not, but when you scared it away, they were set to ride both of us down. That isn't the behavior of the rule of law."

"So you killed them." Ruth hadn't intended for it to sound so much like an accusation.

"I defended the . . . personal integrity . . . of both of us," Nic answered mildly. "If you didn't like it, don't use me as a playing piece next time." He shrugged.

Where anger and outrage—some honest human feelings—should have been, Ruth only felt sick blankness; the northless spinning of a moral compass. She hadn't wanted to be hurt. Nic had saved her. To do that he'd had to kill two men.

Was the fair market value of her safety too high?

"Who . . . *are* you, actually?" Ruth said at last.

Nic smiled without joy. "The one who survived," he said. He began the painful process of getting to his feet, and Ruth, without further inward consultation, rushed to help him.

· 5 ·

Bad Blood and Risky Business

"I am sorry, Baron Rohannan." The speaker's voice was regretful.

"Are you certain?" He could not keep himself from asking, though Melior knew that Gislaine No-House—once, long ago, Rivalen Gislaine of Line Rivalen, of the House of the Saffron Evenings—would have made sure.

Rohannan Melior looked without seeing about the solar of Dawnheart. There had been peace in the land for long enough that the windows' bronze-bound wooden shutters had been replaced with airy winged glass shapes that filled the room above the Great Hall with autumn daylight—the room where rents and tithes were gathered and fee service was ordained, where one could have a private word or spy upon one's nobles with equal facility. His father's place—his, now that Rohannan Lanval was dead. And he had not even been here to lay the last-fruits upon his father's barge for its unaccompanied journey to the sea. . . .

Gislaine sighed, bringing Melior back to the here and now. "I am as certain as may be, my lord. Through all the wide Border, from Counterpane to Amalur—there is no passage to the World of Iron." He picked up the jeweled wine cup before him and stared into it as if hoping to find another truth there.

Involuntarily Melior looked to where the Treasuresword hung upon the wall of his solar. The enormous jeweled counterweight of the pommel glowed with more than the pale autumn sunlight that touched the stones of Dawnheart with gold. Ruth Marlowe's soul, wizard-bound into the Sword of Maiden's Tears, kept it balanced only precariously in Melior's world. At any moment the sword might slip free and back to its other self; to Ruth Marlowe in the World of Iron.

If only things were that easy. If only that were true.

The Sword of Maiden's Tears had fallen from Chandrakar into the World of Iron; fell because it was bound to the human soul of an Ironworlder: Ruth Marlowe. Her soul stretched between her body and the Sword; a bond unbreakable till her death. A wizard-forged bond.

A bond whose history could be resurrected, made visible for all to see. A bond whose forging might even implicate Baligant, or one of his favorites.

There were only two problems—or three, or half a dozen—with putting this plan into action.

"I do not know what else to try," Gislaine admitted. "As you know, my business lies along that border; my traffick in those things the Last World makes that the Morning Lands do not. Passage across the Border is an easy thing, do you merely know the trick of it."

"Until now?" Melior asked. Gislaine nodded sadly.

The moment Melior had reached Dawnheart's walls, he had sent a proxy back down the Iron Road, charged with a message that he prayed Ruth would believe and heed; a proxy mounted on a milk-white stallion, leading a blood-bay mare, and loaded down with encouraging gifts and suitable clothes for Melior's Lady, Ruth of the World of Iron.

He returned within a fortnight, to tell the story Gislaine was telling now; the story Melior had heard from Adepts of the High and the Low Magic; the most powerful whose service Melior could command. The way to the World of Iron was closed.

Gislaine had been his last hope—a hope that one whose trade lay along the Border could succeed where Melior's own vassals could not.

"If there is nothing more," Gislaine said delicately, rising to his feet. It was only a boyhood friendship, no longer acknowledged, that had brought him to Melior's aid at all, for Gislaine had lost more in the war than most.

And now he wished to be gone from Chandrakar again, and Melior could not find it in his heart to keep him.

Melior stood as well. "I thank you for all you have done, friend Gislaine—"

"Even though there was no issue?" Gislaine's voice was quietly mocking. "Well, and that is the way of the world in these dark times. Keep well, Baron Rohannan."

He turned and strode from the solar, a tall and slender figure dressed in a forester's dark leathers, both older and younger than his years. Melior stared into the fire, barely hearing the door close. It had all been for nothing. Two interminable months since he had walked the Iron Road—away from Ruth—and come home to find his father dead, himself the head of his Line, and the situation more tangled than it had been when he left.

Two months. And how many months and years in the World of Iron, where time sped giddily and lovers were mortal? How long until Time wore Ruth away at last and his only link to his lady would be her soul burning brightly in the Sword of Maiden's Tears?

How could the Iron Road be closed; the World of Iron barred to them? It was madness. He had to believe what Gislaine and all the others had told him, and it was still idiocy. You could not close the way to the World of Iron. It lay at the bottom of the Nine Worlds; it was the place where all the roads of all the Morning Lands led to. A trap for the unwary, a snare for the careless, a dark eidolon that drew all light and life and magic into it, ever greedy. Sorcerers and morthworkers had been trying to seal the doors into it, for safety's sake, for years. Lifetimes.

And now that someone actually wished to go there, the way to the World of Iron was sealed.

Ruth would have seen the humor in that. Ruth, who more than his love, his heartsease, was the puzzle piece he could show to the Twilight Court that would prove the Treasures had been tampered with.

As always, his thoughts circled back around to that central problem— of proving what was now mere belief: that Eirdois Baligant, their High King-Elect, meant to compass the destruction of all the Seven Houses of the Twilight. The lady Ruth was his proof, trapped in the World of Iron, out of reach.

Or—Melior steeled himself to admit the worst—dead.

He put his head in his hands.

I cannot prove Lord Baligant's fell intentions without her. I can write to the others and tell them my fears, not that it will matter. They know the date of the Kingmaking as well as I; no doubt they hurry even now to find—or retrieve—their Treasures. We have all grown untrusting through the years. . . .

Untrusting or not, he must try to tell his truth. But there was no point in asking the others to come to hear him unless he could produce his lady Ruth in proof of his accusations.

Ruth, lost beyond the power of elphen magic to retrieve—but not beyond the power of magic.

He needed a wizard.

A very powerful wizard.

Melior roused himself. There was one last hope. It was nearly as dangerous as Baligant himself, but it was the only thing left for Melior to try. He pulled inkstand and vellum toward himself and began to write.

· 6 ·

Cold Steel and Loaded Pistols

THE BROOK WAS right out of a storybook, or one of those slices of English countryside now found only in dreams. It was about three feet wide and not more than a foot deep where they were, and mossy grassy verges overhung it. Its course was starred with large round boulders green with algae, but the water was clean and fast-running over a bed of colored stones.

The sight of the clear purling water made Ruth suddenly aware of how thirsty she was. She helped Nic sit down against the bole of a large tree on the clover and knelt beside him, then looked around for something to serve as a cup.

There wasn't anything, unless she used her shoe. And questions of delicacy aside, it wouldn't be any good to walk in afterward. She knelt beside the stream and scooped up several handfuls of the water, drinking and washing her face. The water tasted wonderful, and even the specter of cholera, typhus, and dysentery didn't slow her down much. If they even had them here.

Oh, God, she knew nothing at all about this mystic fun house that she and the mysterious Nic Brightlaw were trapped in. Was she really any closer to Melior? And did it actually matter? Maybe he'd written her off and settled down with a nice elf Valley Girl.

"Help me get my jacket off," Nic said, breaking into her thoughts.

"It's ruined anyway. You're going to have to make a bandage out of my shirt, or I'll be leaving a blood trail a blind man could follow."

"If he was you," Ruth muttered, moving forward to help.

"Or someone who—ow! Let that be a lesson to you, Miss Marlowe, never ask strangers to share their toys; they won't play nicely."

Ruth eased the jacket off Nic's brawny shoulders. It was heavy, but appeared to contain only the normal mundane male impedimenta of wallet, checkbook, notepad, pens. . . . His glasses were there, thin glass lenses cracked across. All useless here, as Melior's possessions had been in the World of Iron.

Their positions were reversed now—at least Ruth hoped so. Melior was safe and in his own place, and she was somewhere outlandish, hoping for the kindness of a passing stranger.

Only the last strangers they'd seen hadn't been very nice.

Nic dragged the useless tie from around his neck and dropped it on Ruth's knee.

"Here," he said. "You might want to tie somebody up with it."

"Wrong movie." Ruth carefully rolled the tie into a ball and set it aside. Nic leaned back against the tree with his eyes closed, unbuttoning his shirt. Blood had dripped down his neck and face and soaked the collar and neck of the shirt. He looked like a bad special effect in a splatter-movie.

"It comes and goes," he said without opening his eyes. "I only hope the next outtakes from *Lord of the Rings* we meet are more inclined to be reasonable."

"It was my fault," Ruth said miserably. "If I hadn't—"

"To hell with 'if.' 'If' will kill you," Nic enunciated, very distinctly. Ruth shut up.

"Now, if you can just help me get this off, you can soak it in the stream and see what we can do to make me less a sight to frighten children with."

Ruth plunged the shirt into the river as if she were drowning delinquent borrowers. Blood made theatrical swirls in the rippling current, leaving behind only pale pink stains in the oxford-cloth button-down shirt from Earth.

She came back to Nic holding the sopping mass in two hands. The undershirt he wore did little to conceal the long bruises from the attacker's weapons that barred his shoulders, angry red welts darkening slowly to purple. She knelt carefully beside him and began dabbing blood off his face and neck with her makeshift sponge.

"Arrgh," Nic said on a rueful sigh. "I should know better than to do things like this at my age." He took the shirt away from her and pressed it gently against the back of his head, closing his eyes. Ruth glanced away. The summer sun filtered in long gold bars through the leaf canopy. The brook's song was a rhythmic noise in the background, and hesitant birdsong began again around them. As her eyes sharpened, Ruth could see flowers everywhere; tiny ones in the moss-covered bank; bolder ones peering out in hot summer hues from the gorse. As she stared, a butterfly in violent purple bumbled through the air and vanished in the leaf canopy.

All of it might be as mundane as a *National Geographic* special or as strange as *The Twilight Zone.* Ruth didn't have enough experience with even normal Earth-type flora and fauna to know.

Except, of course, for the odd unicorn or so.

And what if this was as far into the Morning Lands as she was ever going to get—stuck playing Girl Medievalist in some place that both wasn't home and didn't have Melior?

And not only her. There was Nic to consider.

"Do you think you're going to be all right?" Ruth asked, forcing her voice to steadiness.

"Um, well, no, actually," Nic said apologetically. His eyes were closed, and his voice was slightly muffled by the mass of wet cloth. "I'm going to have one hell of a headache. Could you soak this again?"

Ruth went back to the stream—only a step and a half, really, Nic's feet were almost in it—and soaked the shirt again, as requested. So this was Elfland. And here she was, Ruth Marlowe, stuck here, like a mirror, for reflection.

Reflecting on how she, no matter where she was, was caught betwixt and between. Not alive, not really, and no chance of a life until she gave up hope of Melior. Unless—until—she did, there was not only a glass ceiling between her and the rest of the world, but glass walls and a glass floor as well. Glass coffin, in which this new improved Snow White slept on, with her awakening only a dream.

What am I going to do? What am I going to do? The idiot plaint circled round and round in her mind. Here in this strange place, cut off from everything familiar, she had no idea what she ought to think or feel, and one course of action began to seem just as reasonable as another. *God, you're morbid,* Ruth chided herself. The bleak thoughts lifted themselves to flight, and, like vultures, circled only to return. *Later,* Ruth told them firmly.

She turned, wet shirt in her hands. And froze when she saw the knife.

It was only a little knife. About as long as her thumb, all in all, with a cheerful red plastic case with a white cross on it. A penknife. Nic brandished it.

"Unless, of course, you'd like to tear my shirt into strips with your teeth?" he said politely.

It was with a certain effort that Ruth refrained from simply tipping the sopping shirt into his lap. She took the knife, and discovered that a wet, well made cotton shirt resists retailoring with an inch-and-a-half blade.

Eventually she whacked enough of it apart to make a pad for the back of his head, and used the despised silk red tie to bind it on with. The finished result was rather festive and piratical.

"Better," Nic said when she was finished. Moving carefully, he maneuvered himself to the edge of the stream, washed his face, and drank. Then he sat up again and held out his hand.

"The gun."

Wordlessly Ruth dug it out of her skirt pocket and handed it to him. He inspected it closely and slid it back into its concealed holster, then leaned back against the tree.

"Conventional wisdom says that, lost in enemy country, we should make tracks for our extraction point or at least find shelter for the night. But before we do that, I'd kind of like to hear your life story, Miss Marlowe," Nic said with elaborate casualness.

"Me?" said Ruth, staring at him with wide blue eyes.

"Let me put it this way: I'd just gotten the alarm reset when it started going crazy all over again, so I cut the power and went looking for what caused it. When I got to the Second File, I found you staring down the throat of a genuine Spielberg special effect and not looking very upset about it. The next thing I know, we're here in an MGM remake of *Robin Hood,* and you don't seem too surprised by that either.

"So I think I'm entitled to an explanation—at least before you start defending any more unicorns."

Ruth winced. But if he were as right as common sense indicated, why was it so annoying? She took a deep breath and tried to feel cooperative.

"Okay. In twenty words or less the story goes like this: about two years ago in New York, I rescued an elf who'd gotten lost on Earth. They call it the World of Iron," she added, reluctant to come to the point. "He was looking for a lost sword. My friends and I helped him find it."

This was the stupidest story she'd ever heard, Ruth realized, and she'd been there.

"And?" Nic prompted.

Ruth closed her lips on the rest. He'd laugh, and then she'd have to kill him, and she didn't have the energy for it just now. "So then he found the Sword and went home. Or at least went away. End of story."

"Except that there seems to be a mouse hole to Elfland in the basement of the Ryerson Memorial Library," Nic pointed out.

And Penny and Katy must still be there looking for them, Ruth realized. What a dreadful Christmas present. She ought to be horrified or something, but thinking about them only made Ruth tired. Two more people whose lives she'd ruined, just by being alive. She closed her eyes.

Her eyes flew open again a moment later as Nic flicked water at her.

"Don't spend so much of your time on vain regrets, Miss Marlowe; nobody ever appreciates it. You haven't told me half the story, but it'll do for now," Nic said. "But you don't think this is the world your traveling elf-errant came from?"

"I don't know," Ruth said, conscious only of a vast, dragging weariness. "He said there were a lot of, um, lands on the High Road to Chandrakar." *And you're remarkably unsurprised to be here, too, Nicodemus Brightlaw, to coin an observation. I'd say you aren't what you appear to be either, but I'm not quite certain what you* do *appear to be.*

A twig cracked, sharply, somewhere nearby. Nic sprang to his feet, reeled, swore, and grabbed at the tree. When Ruth started to get up, he waved a minatory hand at her.

"Stay there," he said through gritted teeth. "I'm going to use you for bait." Still holding one-handed to the tree for support, he slipped around it, hidden.

Ruth sank back into a sitting position. There was a sound of something moving through the brush.

I could really, really, get to dislike that man, Ruth thought, holding very still. Was it the hunters coming back? Nic had killed the two footmen and she'd run the horses off. Maybe Pied-eyes wanted revenge.

There was a glint of sunlight on metal as Nic drew the little gun.

Now Ruth could hear the direction of the sounds clearly. She swore she would not look as they came closer, but at the last moment nerve and resolve both broke, and she turned.

The unicorn stepped through the stream and laid its head in her lap.

· 7 ·

Fancies and Goodnights

FLOIRE JAUSSERANDE OF the House of the Silver Silences, Cup-bearer and once Captain of Jausserande's Ravens, sat in the small elegant tower room that custom and courtesy appointed to the lady-cousin of the Master of Dawnheart whenever she should choose to visit there. She wore a loose short tunic over wide ankle-gathered trousers tucked into soft short velvet boots, every item shades of the same violet as her eyes. The tunic and trews were hand-painted in eye-teasing variations—light to dark and light again—as if all the world were purple and she a Scout who needed to hide in it.

She wished.

Though she could see the sun was setting through the room's wide windows, and fire and candles alike stood waiting, she did not call for light. Before her on the table were a battered tin cup and a squat bottle of violet glass with Vuissane's seal pressed into the wax at the stopper. The bottle held the draught that Jausserande had asked the Lady Vuissane for; the draught that sharpened the kenning of the world-*leys*. Equitan had brought it just a few moments before.

Jausserande fidgeted in her chair, sick of her own company but unwilling to seek the company of others. Once again, unwillingly, like telling over an old scar, she picked up the cup on the table before her.

It was a footed cup, of rough workmanship, such as was turned out in the marketplace by the dozen for the use of serfs and soldiers. Crudely formed of disks and triangles of rough-soldered tin, it was already pewter-black with tarnish and age. Jausserande turned it in her hands. The mock-Cup, the *tainaiste*-Cup, worthless except for the simple spell laid on it: to show the presence of the true Cup and, being thrust into shadow, bringing the true Cup visible.

But it couldn't do it from here. It could only do it in the Vale of Stars, the place where the Cup of Morning Shadows was hidden, and only on the second day of the full moon, at moonrise. Conditions finicking enough to satisfy any Adept, set around the Cup like wards to assure that it was not taken lightly from its resting place in the Vale of Stars.

A place less than a day's ride from here, that Jausserande had not reached in three moons full of days. Almost as if someone prevented her.

Jausserande shook her head angrily, banishing fancy. Oh, for her lance and bow—for a good warhorse beneath her and her Ravens around her! They had never been beaten, never left one of their own in enemy hands, and the tales of their prowess had made fine songs for the fireside at the day's end.

But no one wanted to sing those songs now. And the Ravens were gone; dispersed to home and fireside, to marriage. Miralh even had a child, and another on the way, and no time for retelling old glories with her former captain.

And in the end, they hadn't even won the war. They'd just . . . stopped. And now she was supposed to bend the knee to Baligant No-House when he set his clerkly arse in the High Seat, with that white ferret Hermonicet beside him, gloating over the way she'd been dangled like a gobbet of meat over a kennel of starving dogs and then flung to the noisiest.

It was beyond Jausserande's understanding. She tilted the *tainaiste*-Cup in her hands, so that the last rays of sunset ran round its rim like wine. All she had to do was reach the Vale of Stars with it by tomorrow's sunset, and it would call the other Cup forth. And Line Floire, Cupbearers, would have that which it must bring to the Kingmaking—or be banished, down to the smallest babe, beyond the borders of Chandrakar.

Jausserande returned the cup to the table with a snort. Melior swore that Baligant No-House was trying to gather all the Treasures to himself and then declare their erstwhile guardians attainted. She'd like to think he was. Seven, eight, ten Lines—half the Houses of Twilight—try to strip them of everything they held and drive them out of the land and there'd be a fight.

There'd be war.

Whereas, as seemed more likely, if Baligant Baneful's plot existed only in her cousin's mind, the others would present their Treasures on the day of the Kingmaking, and only Line Floire would come empty-handed.

And only Line Floire would be driven away.

Everything depended on her.

In the war Jausserande had been a warrior, not a planner of high strategy. And though she might—by right of birth and of what she held—claim a seat at the councils of her House, Jausserande had no interest in endless weary talk of marriages and dowries, taxes and *teines,* of who to send as Advocate to the High Court and who to send as Speaker to the Twilight Court. And while her sister, who had been Cupbearer before her and was now head of Line Floire, would willingly advise her, even in wartime Glorete had been too prudent for Jausserande's taste.

It was Jausserande's task alone. She would get the Cup of Morning Shadows tomorrow moonrise. She must. She would not fail Line Floire.

There was a knock on the door.

"Go away!" Jausserande exclaimed.

The door opened. Guiraut appeared, bearing a tray large enough to hold a whole roast deer without crowding. Steam and savory odors rose from it.

"Your dinner, my lady."

"I'm not hungry," Jausserande said sullenly. Guiraut, conveniently deaf, set the tray on the table before her. He looked around and noticed the darkened condition of the room. He snapped his fingers.

Nothing happened.

He muttered an oath copied from the chief groom, and violet blood rose to the tips of his pointed ears. Jausserande stared out the window, keeping her face expressionless with an effort. Guiraut wanted to impress her, and she would not mock him.

After three more tries, Guiraut snapped hearth and candles ablaze.

"You've been practicing," Jausserande said, making sure the approval was plain in her tone. Guiraut had more aptitude for the Art Magical than she did, but aptitude was nothing without practice.

He blushed again, this time with pleasure. "I have laid out your armor for the morrow, my lady. You must eat, and then away to bed," he said with as much severity as his youth would allow.

Jausserande looked at the food with faint repulsion. The sense of doom she had felt all day was back now, stronger but still as nebulous. Would Vuissane's potion buy her any clarity? Or would it simply befuddle her mind with a garden of bright images?

"I will eat if you will join me," she said finally, gesturing at the stool that stood beside the leaping fire. As Guiraut turned away to pull it forward, Jausserande picked up the violet flask and broke the seal. The liquid inside bore the cloying scent of too many flowers. She poured it into the *tainaiste*-Cup, and added wine to fill the cup to the brim.

"To success," Jausserande said, when Guiraut had filled his own cup with watered wine. And though he echoed the toast, he could not begin to know how passionately she meant it.

The predawn air was breathtakingly chill. She could almost imagine she was setting out on a daybreak scouting raid; the lightest armor, the fastest horse, and the barest sky glow differentiating the castle roofs from the sky. Almost, Jausserande could forget the Cup, the Line, and the wretched unheroic Peace.

"Art ready, Guiraut?" she cried, joy at their freedom ringing through her voice. The mouse-gray mare Sparrow danced with muffled hooves on the dew-wet courtyard cobbles.

"Ready," Guiraut answered. But it was not Guiraut at all, but her cousin Melior—to be named, by later generations, Melior the Mad—who swung into the saddle of his big gray cob, his deep-hooded traveling cloak making him hard to see in the morning twilight. The Sword of Maiden's Tears, slung over Melior's shoulder in a traveling baldric, gathered all the light in the courtyard to itself.

That was when Jausserande knew that this was a dream. She glanced around, searching for signs and portents, and saw that instead of Dawnheart's silver stone, the living red granite of Citadel surrounded them. Citadel, where the High King was made and the Twilight Court met.

Was this her future?

The mare danced; hot-blooded and impatient to run. Jausserande set that question aside. She spurred Sparrow on; the mare leaped forward like a doe before the hunters, and in moments she had left Citadel and Melior behind.

The countryside was familiar, though nothing that belonged near Citadel. Ahead the white clay road ran twisting through the valley, until the valley became a canyon and the pass too narrow for even a single armored warhorse. Beyond that pass was the Vale of Stars, and in the Vale was the Cup of Morning Shadows.

So intent was she, even in the dream, on what *ought* to be that it was not until Sparrow slipped and barely recovered herself that Jausserande took a good look at her dreamscape.

The road beneath her mare's hooves was not white, but red. Mud-red. Blood-red.

"Hold it right there, Miss."

The voice came just as Jausserande was reining in. Sparrow stopped. Ahead, Jausserande could see the pass into the Vale of Stars, and just outside it, barring her way, was a man on a horse.

The horse was the dazzling frost-on-snow color that shouted magic—

a legendary, wizard-conjured beast. The rider was not like anything Jausserande had ever seen before. He was dressed in outlandish dull-colored armor pied black and green. After a long moment she realized with a shock that he was human.

"Out of my way, earthling," Jausserande snapped.

"I don't think so," the human observed politely. His hair was the yellow of the gold that humans prized so highly and his eyes were a bright jeweled blue.

"Insolence! We'll see what taste you have for insolence after being run at my horse's stirrup for a mile or two!" Jausserande loosened her sword in its sheath and reached for her mace.

"With all due respect, Miss," the human said, with just enough emphasis on the "due" to make Jausserande grit her teeth, "aren't you forgetting that you've come for the Cup?"

At this new insolence Jausserande ground her heels into Sparrow's flanks and the mare bounded forward. Jausserande crouched low on her neck, the battle cry of the Ravens on her lips.

But as hard as Sparrow strained, and Jausserande with her, they came no closer to the false knight or the pass into the Vale of Stars.

"You're what's standing in the way of your getting the Cup, not me. And if you can't get past me, you'll never get it," the human said in tones of scholarly reproof.

The words echoed, reverberated, took on form and solidity, and caged her with bars of burning fire. Then her horse was gone, the road was gone, her dream was gone and the knight with it, and Jausserande was alone in her bed, staring out at false dawn and listening to the sentry cry the hours.

As Vuissane had promised, her head hurt abominably. And she was no closer to seeing a true future than she had been the night before.

· 8 ·

Into the Woods

THE UNICORN REFUSED to leave. It didn't like Nic though it tolerated him, but it positively doted upon Ruth. Its improbable coat was as thick and soft as a cat's fur and its long-lashed eyes were bright lapis blue. It was the size of a small deer, or a very large dog—its shoulder came as high as her ribs—and it would not go away for any money.

"Tears, threats, pleas, entreaties, vain, all vain," muttered Ruth. The unicorn nudged at her elbow hopefully. "Oh, what do you *want?*" Ruth wailed, ruffling the downy neck. All she knew about unicorns was that people hunted them.

"A maiden?" Nic suggested.

An hour's rest on the stream bank had done him a lot of good; his color was better, and the gash on his scalp had finally stopped bleeding. It was cool enough under the shade of the trees that he'd put his suit jacket back on. Worn over the wet, bloodstained T-shirt, with his head garlanded in a necktie and the remains of his shirt, it gave him a particularly raffish look. *Miami Vice* for the Hyborean Age.

"Very funny," said Ruth crossly. She was hot, tired, hungry, and lost in the woods without a yellow brick road in sight. She looked at her watch. 7:30—at least it was back home in Ippisiqua. *My, what an interesting Christmas* this *is turning out to be.*

"Well, what do unicorns usually want?" Nic went on patiently. "You're the one with all the *Twilight Zone* experience."

The unicorn nudged her again.

"My experience does not include unicorns," Ruth said brusquely.

Her eyes prickled and her mouth went wry. She took a breath and held it, fighting back tears. She'd come here of her own free will; sniveling about it now was stupid. But at this precise moment she couldn't really remember *why* she'd wanted to come here so badly.

And badly was certainly the way she'd come.

Ruth took a deep breath. "Unicorns. Their horns are supposed to be proof against poison, they represent purity, they symbolize Scotland in the royal arms of Britain. . . ." She stopped. None of that seemed to be of any particular use at the moment.

"Go on," Nic said encouragingly.

He's humoring me, Ruth realized in sudden indignation. *Well, I suppose he dislikes screaming hysterics as much as the next man.* She tried a smile, carefully. "I'm afraid that's your lot. Nothing I ever read mentioned *live* unicorns."

"Well," said Nic, leaning back against the tree trunk. "It looks like we're stuck with Fluffy here for a while. The next question is: Where are we going to go?"

"Go?" Ruth echoed blankly.

"Unless you want to stay here and learn to fish," Nic pointed out. "And so far we've seen unicorns and unicorn hunters, which doesn't rule out lions and tigers and bears, oh my—or a dragon."

Ruth contemplated the thought of a dragon and wished she could feel more hopeful anticipation at the prospect. She wished, in fact, that she could feel anything, instead of assembling her emotions by guess and by gosh and by deduction.

Maybe if she got her soul back. Yeah, right.

"You're right," Ruth said. "But I'm afraid I'm not much help. What do *you* think we should do?"

What Nic thought they should do was nothing Ruth had any stomach for, though it made perfect sense. When the three of them (Nic leaning on Ruth, the unicorn following) made it back to the clearing, their approach startled a cloud of rooks that flew up from the bodies, cawing derision.

Ruth saw what the birds had left behind and turned away, gagging.

"Wait here," Nic said firmly. "And don't look."

She would have argued, but she hadn't the stomach for it; the animal depredations of the helpless dead were etched upon her mind's eye with remorseless clarity. Nic relinquished her support and shuffled off. Ruth knelt in the grass, one arm around the unicorn.

Is this all I'm good for—to be the hapless, helpless, fainting heroine? To let Nic protect me—and get hurt because of me? That isn't fair. He didn't ask to come here. He didn't know what he was getting into (well, neither did I, but I thought I did). And this isn't even dangerous. It's just icky.

She opened her eyes. Nic was on his knees beside the nearest body, pulling at the clothes. Ruth got to her feet and walked over to him.

"I guess you could use some help with that, right?" she said in a steady voice.

Above the trees, the false-lying sun of Elfland was sliding toward the West. Ruth, no expert, placed the local time at anywhere between two and four. She knelt beside the stream, sluicing armloads of rough woolen cloth through the icy water, frightening the fish and hoping the wool wouldn't shrink too much. The dead footmen's clothing was a far cry from the expensive and exquisite traveling garb that Melior had worn when Ruth had first seen him. Baggy undyed homespun trousers were meant to be tucked into coarse knitted socks, while a wrapped breech-clout and a sleeveless slit-necked singlet protected the cloth of trousers and the green-dyed T-tunic of heavy fulled cloth from the sweat and dirt of the skin.

Heavy leather belts with horn or wooden buckles and sheepskin spats cross-gartered over stiff boiled-leather shoes completed these less than haute-couture outfits. Ruth wasn't looking forward to wearing this stuff, but Nic felt if the two of them wore the local clothes they'd be safer.

Just who is this guy, anyway?

Ruth shoved her nagging worries about her traveling companion to one side and tried to think of something useful. The unicorn (still with her) had thrown her mental balance off badly. Who'd written the rules for this place, anyway: J. R. R. Tolkien or the Brothers Grimm? Ruth breathed a brief bibliophile's prayer that it wasn't Angela Carter, but there were no guarantees.

That was the difference between Elfland and Real Life. There were no guarantees either way, but in Real Life you pretended there were. Elfland stripped away that pleasant fiction.

Ruth added yet another length of cloth to the sopping pile. Done.

She emerged into the bright late-afternoon summer sunlight, blinking owlishly. While she'd been gone, Nic had dragged the dead bodies off into the woods. Now he sat, back braced against a rock that had been padded with Ruth's discarded Inverness cloak, sorting through the contents of the dead men's belts.

Ruth chose a patch of sunlight and began to spread the clothes out to dry. The trews and undertunics might make it, but the heavy green knee-length tunics definitely wouldn't dry in the few hours of sunlight left.

And that raised the interesting question of where—and how—she and Nic were going to spend the night. She'd done some camping, true, but previous experiences had involved such comforts as a tent and a battery-powered microwave. She walked over to Nic and sat down beside him.

"So," Ruth said, by way of a conversational opening.

"So," Nic said. His plunder was spread out in little patterns beside him.

Two crude general purpose daggers, bone-hilted and slightly rusty, were laid carefully upon their sheaths. At first Ruth thought the blades were copper, but the metal had a brassier sheen. Bronze. No cold iron in Elfland. She turned to the rest of the loot. Two belt-pouches, of differing sizes and design. One drinking horn, rimmed and tipped in leather, with a loop and a bronze ring to hang it from a belt. An empty waterskin.

And, laid out carefully on Ruth's muffler, the contents of the belt-pouches. A pair of dice, crudely hand-carved. A tin spoon. A box the size of Ruth's palm, purpose unknown. A handful of copper or bronze coins, small change in any universe.

And among all these items, flagrantly, the one that did not fit.

Fine silver is as different from sterling as gold is from brass. Soft, perishable, white as moonlight, too soft for use in jewelry without the adulteration of baser metal that turns it from fine silver to sterling, few moderns have ever seen it.

The ring was fine silver, thick and wide-banded, set with a gemstone the size of an apricot pit glittering transparent and opaline in all the hot plangent spectrum of the dragon's eye.

"Don't touch that!" Ruth cried, her voice raw with fear, as Nic, following the direction of her gaze, reached to pick it up.

He stopped.

"Don't touch it," Ruth said hoarsely. "That's . . . I think it's magic." Sunlight and fire; its gemstone the chatoyant witch-fire rainbow of the jewels in the Sword of Maiden's Tears.

The sword that had killed Naomi.

"Magic." Nic's voice was neutral, neither accepting nor denying. "It's a valuable ring. What was our friend doing with it?"

Magic . . . Ruth reached for the ring indecisively. What spell, what horror, was this stone designed to release?

"Ruth? Have you seen something like it before?"

Ruth withdrew her hand. "In a sword," she managed to say. "Melior's sword. It . . . killed somebody."

Nic picked up one of the daggers and slipped its point through the ring. He lifted the ring off the muffler. The band was open behind the stone, allowing the light to pass through. The sun shining through it made a small hot point of whiteness on the muffler beneath and threw the curious carvings on the band into sharp black-and-white relief.

Ruth Marlowe was a realist, a rationalist, born into a clockwork universe that kept all its magic safely between the covers of YA fiction. Her adventures with Melior had been strange, but not enough to shake her faith in cause and effect, a world defined by objectivism.

The ring seemed to shimmer against the knife blade, saying it was a mere artifact, saying its artifactury was a lie. Malignant because unnatural, supernatural, *magic*.

"And you think this is more of the same?" Nic asked, as even-voiced as if inquiring about the possibility of rain.

"I don't know." Before she could censor herself, Ruth plucked the ring from the knife blade and held it in her hand. A cold uncanniness seemed to radiate from it into her bones, but it appeared that the message—or the spell—that it held was not strong enough to affect her.

"Magic," Ruth repeated uncertainly. She closed her fingers over it. Hard and chunky in her palm, it burned as cold against her flesh as it ought to have been hot. After a moment she dropped it to the scarf again. "Yeuch." She rubbed her palm against her skirt.

Nic picked up the ring and stared at it suspiciously, but it didn't seem to trouble him even as much as it had Ruth. His mouth set in a dogged line. "Not a piece of junk," he pronounced. "And nothing like anything else that bozo had. Why did he have it? Loot? Payment?"

"A plot device?" Ruth suggested. She'd long since discarded the bloodstained cardigan portion of her twin set, but even the short-sleeved cashmere shell was too hot for the weather. And blood-spotted as well, dammit; blood was hell to get out of woolens. "I don't know, Nic, maybe they come in gumball machines here."

"Somehow I think we'll find out," Nic prophesied. "All roads lead to Amber. Or to Oz," he added.

• 9 •

High Noon in Elphame

THE VALE OF Stars and its surrounding woods were supposed to be among the most beautiful placcs in all Chandrakar, but all its new denizens knew or cared about was that the area was easily defensible. There was only one path a horse could follow; the narrow riverine track that led between the steep hills covered in birch and pine. The road ran straight and smooth, and the trees on either side grew dark and thick.

A perfect site for an ambush.

As it had been.

The other rider had turned and fled at the first sign of trouble. The riderless horse of their victim had bolted ahead; they would find it later. Scholars in a hard school, they held their places until the birds had resumed their untroubled calling before moving out to claim their prey.

Fox reached the body first. His knife flashed, bright and quick, cutting the arrow loose from the throat and letting the dead elf's blood ooze onto the track. The edges of the wound blackened and smoked; Fox's blade was iron.

"Defiled for at least a month; let those cat-eyed weasels think about that," he said with satisfaction.

Fox got to his feet and began cleaning his knife. The others, as frightened of cold iron as any elphenborn, closed in and began stripping the body of everything useful. Fox turned his knife so its blade flashed in the sun. *Iron, cold iron, the master of them all:* a thing not easily come by in Chandrakar, where iron blistered the flesh of its privileged, silver-blooded princes.

And confounded their magic.

"Fox, what if they come for us? An open killing—that's different than a little thieving," Raven said.

And God knew, it had taken him long enough to give them the stomach for it. Fox turned toward the man who had spoken. And Raven was the best of them; wasn't that a joke? A handful of apologetic cowards to topple an empire.

"Of course it's different, Raven," he explained with a reasonable amount of patience. "It's better. When that pointy-eared bimbo gets back and puts out the word that—*quelle horreur*—*elf blood* has been spilled in the Vale of Stars, they might not even come back next month. If they don't come back, they don't get their Cup."

Raven's brow bent with the effort of following Fox's train of thought. Fox sighed inwardly. He'd thought it would be so easy, once. Before he'd seen what he had to work with—the outlaws of Chandrakar.

There were disaffected men—outlaws—living in every forest of Chandrakar; yes, and starving there, too, since their elphen overlords had the magic to hunt them down with no more aid than a lock of hair or a drop of blood any time their depredations became seriously annoying. The elphenborn spent magic with the profligacy of those expending an infinitely renewable resource. Everywhere but here, in the Vale of Stars.

Here, humans were safe to come and go and hunt and eat their fill as they pleased. All it had taken was the courage—and the brains—to come here. And that Fox had given them.

"And if the highborn don't reclaim their Treasures, there won't be a Kingmaking. There'll be another war," Raven said dutifully, in the fashion of one telling back a hard-learned lesson.

Raven towered over his companion by a good two hands' worth, and with flowing black hair and curling beard—and branded cheek—Raven looked far more likely to lead a band of human outlaws than Fox. But then, Raven had been a blacksmith, once upon a time.

And Fox had not.

"Another war. And this time, humans won't fight it for them, dying for some damned abstraction. Baligant will banish most of them and we'll take care of the rest. More humans than elves equals no elves. Simple." Fox smiled up at his companion. He would be short in any company; slender and pale and quite as dangerous as a type of blade that did not exist in this or any nearby world.

Tempered steel. Tempered in flame.

"All we have to do is hold this road a year and a day," another man— Yarrow—said.

"That's right." Fox's smile was as sweet as it was infrequent. "Hold this road, keep them out of the Vale of Stars."

And drag Line Rohannan down with Line Floire, lose Baligant two of the most powerful Treasures . . . it would be Chaos come again. *"Disorganized chaos is the worst kind,"* echoed a sudden memory voice. Absent friends, dead loves.

"C'mon," Fox said, a few moments later. He took a last look at the body, at the dull violet bloodstain in the white clay roadbed that would keep any "highborn" who saw it from setting foot on such unlucky ground, let alone using magic to find the killers.

There were some things about magic that Fox liked just fine.

· 10 ·

A New Way to Pay
Old Debts

MELIOR HEARD THE footsteps a scant instant before their cause entered the room.

"I give you good greeting, Cousin—and bring you the Cup of Morning Shadows!" the Lady Jausserande cried. Her spurred and booted steps rang harshly on the inlaid stone floor of Melior's solar. And then she threw it.

Melior did not duck; the missile was not meant for him. It landed with a dull unmusical thud on the carpets at the center of the room and rolled in a forlorn half-circle.

Melior turned away from the standing desk beside the tall narrow window. The late afternoon sunlight struck through the high windows and scattered prismed reflections across the floor and tapestries as Melior walked across the carpet. He bent down and picked up what Jausserande had thrown.

"This," Melior said neutrally, "is the Cup of Morning Shadows."

It was not, of course; merely the shadow of a shadow which—if pushed into the Otherworld in the right time and place—would bring the Cup of Morning Shadows into the world of Chandrakar once more.

As it should now have done.

Jausserande shrugged her saddlepouches to the floor with a thump more eloquent than mere words and began to unbuckle her gorget.

Melior watched as his cousin shrugged her gray-dappled travel cloak to the floor. In peacetime, in a land at peace, she wore no plate, only a sleek white doeskin tunic beneath a shirt of fine-linked silver mail. The mail gleamed silvery in the light as she worked the heavy armored collet free and dropped it, too, on the floor before she spoke.

"No . . . just a little something I picked up in the Bazaar for the douce amusement it would give Baligant High Prince when I present it instead of the Cup."

Her words were honeyed-sweet, and her tone the sweet singsong of murderous fury held barely in check. She picked up the decanter from the side table, saw the cups sitting innocently beside it, and lost what was left of her temper.

This time Melior did duck. The wine-filled flagon barely cleared his head, and with marksmanlike accuracy sailed out through the open window. There was an instant's silence, then a distant sound of shattering.

"If you misliked the vintage, Cousin, you had only to say," Melior observed mildly. A low growl was the only response.

Melior turned away, bearing the *tainaiste*-Cup back to the high desk by the window. He looked out and down, to where the decanter was a glittering crimson smear on the courtyard flags. The servants clustering around it looked up, saw him looking, and scattered. Melior continued gazing idly about his demesne, giving Jausserande time to recover herself. His eyes flickered to where the Sword of Maiden's Tears hung upon the wall.

"Oh, yes. Very well for you." Jausserande crossed the room, stray bits of half-unbuckled armor jingling, and took the cup from him. She slid the battered tinny thing inside a fold of her surcoat. She could not meet Melior's gaze, and began to pluck at her gauntlets.

"Well for you," she repeated. "Line Rohannan will appear at the Kingmaking, and all will be well—for Line Rohannan."

"And how long do you think Line Rohannan will stand alone?" Melior asked.

"If Bastard Baligant is what you say, challenge him and make an end to it." One heavy elbow-length gauntlet of gold-stamped scarlet leather fell to the floor, then the other. *Hard work for her squire,* Melior thought to himself, following Jausserande's back trail to collect and restore all her possessions. But Guiraut worshiped her; he'd think the duty no hardship.

"Where is Guiraut?" he asked without thinking.

"Feeding the rooks on the Vale Road," Jausserande said harshly. "He took an arrow through the throat. Meant for me, I think, but in the end it doesn't really matter, does it?"

"How—?"

"There are outlaws living in the Vale, Cousin. And I did not imagine they could be so bold." Jausserande's proud head bowed. She had hoped to award Guiraut his knightly spurs at Midsummer. "We'll try again, Line Floire and I. Next moon, and the moon after that. Until the Kingmaking."

When Line Floire—without the Cup—would be attainted, and the Cup, present or absent, would fall to the High King's hand to bestow upon a more worthy Treasurekeeper. Somehow, Melior doubted that Baligant would be generous.

"I share your sorrow, Cousin," Melior said formally. "And I have made up my mind that I can delay no longer in dealing with that matter of which we spoke. I shall be leaving on a journey tomorrow dawn. You are, of course, welcome to guest at Dawnheart for as long as it takes you to achieve the Cup."

"I shall achieve the heads of those mud-mannikins first," Jausserande said in low tones. "Of your charity, Cousin, a detachment of the castle guard to sweep the forests and the roads. Your outlaws and beggars have become far too bold of late."

"Granted," Melior said, "but only as far as lies between Dawnheart and the Vale. Little though you may credit it, Cousin, they are *my* outlaws and beggars, and I hold myself rather fond of them."

Jausserande made a face of eloquent disgust. "What of Harvest Home? What of Twilight Court?"

"I imagine my tenants can celebrate the Harvest without me. As for the Court, it hardly seems necessary in this time of peace to meet one's enemies beneath the branch of truce and plan the coming slaughter, does it? I have considered how I may best serve the Realm, and there is only one truth I see: I must bring the lady Ruth of the World of Iron to my side."

The calm matter-of-factness of Melior's madness swept Jausserande's grief momentarily aside. To think that Melior set so much store by some mud-born leman that he would—

Do what?

"And how, Cousin, will you bring Ruth from the World of Iron, when you have said that all that way is closed?"

"I shall seek out a wizard."

"A *wizard?*" If anything in Chandrakar could have the power to rouse Jausserande from the contemplation of her own problems, it was such a declaration. Adepts in the Art Magical were one thing: elphen scholars as loyal and trustworthy as any fighting man, masters of the High and Low Magics both Right and Left, who walked in sunlight, order, and law. Wizards were something else entirely: masters of the Wild Magic who bowed to no law save their own desires. A wizard might belong to any of the Five Races, though it was rare indeed for one of the Sons of the Morning to follow the Wild Magic's path.

"You're going to seek out a *wizard?*" Perhaps she had misheard him.

"Not merely any wizard, but one with whom I have had dealings of old. I know his price; it is high, but I think now that I have no choice but to meet it. I think he will accept my promise as sure coin."

"Bargaining with a wizard!" Jausserande burst out, "For a— A—"

"For the proof that Baligant has tampered with the Treasures," Melior said before Jausserande could say otherwise.

But his cousin was as stubborn as he. "And would this '*proof*' be so desirable, my lord Rohannan, were it not the earthling that you have sworn to be your heartsease? A pretty package, Cousin, when duty is so neatly yoked with expediency."

"And what course would you suggest, Cupbearer?" Melior's tone was distantly formal.

Leave it alone. Baligant's scheme is the air-dream of one on fire for a mortal maid. Jausserande bit her lip, unwilling to speak so plainly. She already knew it would do no good. Melior wanted the mortal for his heart's-bride, even if it was idiocy.

Marry a mud-daughter?

"I would not presume to advise Line Rohannan, my lord," Jausserande said, equally formally. "I wish you a safe and pleasant journey."

Now, if only the wizard would do as he asked, and open the Iron Road so that Ruth could come here. Melior's sturdy dappled gelding, a mount chosen for its steadiness and endurance, stood quietly in the chill of the early morning courtyard as its master made his last minute preparations.

Melior dwelt for a pleasant instant upon the thought of his lady Ruth here in his own world. But more than that, Ruth's arrival would undo the trap that bound the Sword of Maiden's Tears, and reunite Ruth with her pilgrim soul. And in that unbinding and reunion allow Melior to prove how that binding had first been done, proving Baligant's treachery to all who were willing to see.

Melior frowned. For the first time since he had hit upon this certain proof, he was close enough to gaining it to think about what having it might mean. Eirdois Baligant of the House of Vermilion Shadows, High Prince and High King to be, had been the only claimant of the High Seat all the Morning Lords could agree upon; the only one all could bear to gift with, not only the Kingship, but the white body of Hermonicet the Fair. Remove him, and war began again.

Fail to remove him, and see the Seven Houses of Twilight destroyed.

It was not a decision that Melior had a right to make alone, and so he had held his peace even after he knew the truth. But now there was proof to present to the Twilight Court, to set the yoke of this vendetta squarely upon the shoulders of them all.

It was not a vendetta, Melior assured himself. Not yet, at least. He gave one last tug to the girth, not wanting to leave that homely task to his groom.

Melior set his foot in the stirrup and vaulted into his saddle. The groom at the gelding's head released its bridle, and another waiting servant unbolted the postern gate. Melior shrugged the folds of his travel cloak more warmly about himself.

First Ruth, he promised himself, *then all the rest.*

Melior headed his gelding up into the hills, away from the plowed fields and terraced vineyards of his demesne. He did not have far to go— in Chandrakar, at least. The wizard that he sought was not here, though the way to his tower was not hard to find—once you had the key.

Reflexively Melior touched the object hung on the cord about his neck: a little knife barely a hand's width in length, with a hilt of clear amber and a blade of black glass.

A key, if you knew how to use it.

At midday Melior stopped to eat and to give the gelding a rest. He would not reach the place he sought before sunset, and there was no point in reaching it before sunset in any event: this Gate was a complicated one, opening to time, location, and proper tools.

As was the Gate the Cup of Morning Shadows lay beyond.

Would he, Melior wondered, have done any better than Jausserande, were the Cup his quest? She was young, and touchy about her autonomy; newly come to her Wardenship. Floire Glorete had never sought the Cup through all the long years of war, knowing it to be safe in the Vale of Stars. Line Floire had held the Cup since time out of mind; it had been Floire Bertraine who put it there when Rainouart the Beautiful had died, and charged no Cupbearer to come near it until the war was over. Glorete had served her entire tenure without having held her Treasure in her hands.

And now that Jausserande went to claim it, there were brigands in her way, brigands who had slain Guiraut—mostly likely by sheer accident—and now undoubtedly cowered half-mad with terror at their ill fortune. Assuming they were, in fact, honest villains, and not more of Baligant's mischief. Since the peace had been declared and the great armies of each side disbanded, such feral lostlings had become an all-too-common problem for the Morning Lords. Landless, masterless men— human men, whose sires and grandsires and great-grandsires had been raised to war—what was there for them, without place or occupation, but to roam the roads, taking what they could?

Melior shook his head sadly. No matter the reason, he could not permit it. And if the ambush on the road to the Vale of Stars was something more than honest brigandage, he could not permit that either. Baligant would not play his games in Melior's demesne.

Why? It was the question Melior always returned to in the end, the question that eternally baffled him. Baligant already had everything, and still he fought on.

Why?

Melior was not of the generation that had striven so bloodily for those twin prizes: the High Kingship and the white body of Hermonicet the Fair. The earls and barons who had battled for such riches were his uncles and cousins: even Rohannan Lanval had possessed ambitions in that direction, although it was more accurate to say that Melior's father had had firm notions of who should *not* be High King.

Yet he had lived to see Baligant chosen, and said nothing.

Melior frowned, staring unseeing at the half-eaten apple in his hand. Rohannan Lanval had said nothing, but perhaps his reasons had more to do with the reasons for Melior's silence now than with blind cowardice. Perhaps Melior's father had also held his suspicions yet had no way to prove them, and found himself forced to choose between an unjust peace and a just war.

There was no way now to know.

It was, as Melior had intended, just sunset when he arrived at the place of the Gate. The long day's ride had brought him to a place where the grass and trees were replaced by dust and rock—too companionable to be called desolation—and the eye was drawn to the horizon by the first promise of the great mountains to the north. There was nothing on this side of the wizard's Gate to make the location particularly memorable; only four boulders of a mottled dark granite arranged in an irregular circle in a place where the trail widened to obscurity.

Melior dismounted, keeping a firm hold on the gelding's reins. This Gate was one through which a mounted man might pass, and he had no intention of doing any more walking than he had to. He looped the reins about his arm and took the glass and amber knife in his right hand. The gelding nudged at his shoulder curiously as he pulled off his left gauntlet and pushed up the sleeve of his tunic.

Melior glanced around, taking his bearings. The long sunset shadows of the boulders reached out to him, straggling and elongated with the same tricky sunset light that turned the knife's golden amber hilt red.

At the last moment before darkness Melior used the little knife to make a long cut in his left arm.

The wine-violet elphen blood welled up and began to run. Melior caught the first drops on the knife blade, and at once time seemed to stop, and Melior was wrapped in the chill uncanniness of the High Magic.

He made certain the blade was well coated before shrugging his sleeve back into place. Then he sketched a door in the unchanging twilight: high enough for a rider, broad enough for a horse.

Within the area he had marked, Reality fell away as if he had cut a hole in a painted canvas backdrop. The space beyond was jarringly unlike the world he stood in—the sky the wrong blue, the soil the wrong brown. Melior unlooped the reins from his arm and remounted, pressing the cut on his forearm closed before tucking the little knife away against future need. And the gelding stepped, with only a little hesitancy, through the Gate.

At once everything changed. A thin chill wind plucked at his hair, and Melior pulled the deep hood of his cloak forward to shield himself. It was brighter here than in the day he had just left, but the sky was a deep indigo, crossed by impossible auroras, and Melior had never seen either sun or moon here.

Melior glanced over his shoulder as his mount—steady, dependable, not given to nerves—picked its way along the downward-sloping trail.

Behind him was a cyclopean jumble of white granite cast down from the cliffs above, among which two slabs had been raised as Brobdingnagian gateposts. Beyond them the wide road seemed to roll onward forever, though Melior knew that he had but to ride on for a few leagues to find himself upon it, approaching the Gate again from the direction he had come.

The land around him was mountainous and barren, a place where nothing grew. It ought to have reminded him of the World of Iron, but if it did it was only because of the differences. For the World of Iron was . . . iron, while this was a world whose very bones were made of magic; the small kingdom of an Adept of the Wild Magic, to be entered at one's peril.

Was Ruth worth it? Or Baligant's defeat? Could anyone, could any-*thing* be worth coming here?

"Yes," said Melior aloud.

The tension lifted: a soap bubble vanishing. There was the scent of laughter upon the wind. Melior rounded a bend in the trail and saw his goal.

Ahead the road stopped abruptly at the base of a sheer cliff. White as everything was in this world; bone-white and all the colors of shadows. But the cliff was not in shadow. Whatever source this world's light had, the light itself shone full-face upon the cliff.

About halfway up the cliff face there was an opening in the stone; a smooth and regular arch filled with sooty and indigo shadows.

"I am waiting," Melior observed into the emptiness.

"Don't get your bones in an uproar, Child of Air," a voice answered from the air around him. "I'm coming."

But no entity appeared. Instead, the blowing wind stopped and the light shifted, and in that still silence Melior saw the ghostly outline of a phantom staircase, curving upward to the stone doorway.

Melior shrugged within himself, and dismounted. He flung the loop of the horse's reins over the finial of an ornate and barely perceptible newel post and began to ascend the stairs.

Only a soap bubble iridescence betrayed the existence of those stairs; that, and the solidity of the treads beneath Melior's feet. The jagged boulders at the base of the cliff were starkly visible between his boot toes; the balustrade, hard and slick beneath his hand, held all the insubstantial character of water to his eye.

Ophidias had always had a sense of humor, Melior reminded himself. Of a sort.

As he reached the top of the staircase, the wind returned full force. His cloak unfurled with a snap that nearly strangled him, dragging him backward, into the empty air. He pulled it around him, and that, too, was a mistake; the wind found every entrance, filling the fabric as if it were a ship's sail and hauling at him with invisible hands.

Clutching the balustrade with one hand, Melior clawed at the throat latch of the cloak until he had worried it loose. The wind took the cloak with almost sentient glee, snatching it from his shoulders and bearing it off with a long whistling howl.

"You owe me a new cloak," Melior said, taking advantage of the respite to struggle inside.

It was warmer out of the wind, though not by much. The chamber he had entered was long and straight, the walls curving upward and inward until their meeting, if any, was lost in shadow. There was no light. The only illumination came from the tatterdemalion sky behind and the fire-like glow ahead.

Melior walked toward the light and entered a chamber of gold.

The walls, floor, and ceiling were made of gold; gold polished mirror-bright, gold wrought in a thousand styles of ornament. The floor of the room was heaped with treasure; treasure spilling carelessly from casks as valuable as their contents; the plundered excellence of a thousand worlds. But the light did not come from the walls, nor from the treasure.

The light came from the room's occupant.

"It took you long enough to think of me," the wizard said.

The wizard Ophidias was not elphen. There were Five Races in the Morning Lands which had the Art of Magic, and of these, Ophidias belonged to the oldest: the People of Fire, who shared with their namesake element the native power to change . . . and to be transformed.

"I thought of your price longer," Melior responded.

The firedrake half-spread his vast wings. His throat and stomach were the pure hot gold of embers; his sides and back the same color but slightly silvered, as if with a fine coating of ash. A pleasant warmth—at least at this distance—radiated off his skin in waves.

"You wrong me, Child of Air," Ophidias commented.

"Then, of course, you'll do what I ask without cost?" Melior responded.

"No," Ophidias said simply. "But you've had a long cold journey—and without a cloak, too. You might as well have some wine and tell me what you want."

One opal-webbed wing spread and gestured to a jade table balanced precariously upon the golden hoard. Atop it was a blue glass beaker webbed in jeweled silver, and a carven pearl cup that could ransom a hundred queens.

Melior unstopped the one and poured its contents into the other. He drank, suspiciously at first, then with real pleasure.

"Did you know," said Melior with as much artlessness as he could muster at short notice, "that the Iron Road is sealed on the Borders?"

"Ridiculous," said the firedrake. He changed position on his treasure and stretched luxuriously. Gold coins shifted and spilled beneath his weight; a cup rolled free with a clinking sound.

"Nearly as ridiculous as this mummer's play of yours. I have seen more convincing deceits on *television*," Melior said, drawing on a term from his recent excursion to the World of Iron.

"Ah, well, if you don't like it . . ." Ophidias waved one polydactyl foreclaw and everything—save the wine table and its contents—vanished.

Including the light.

Considered as a dragon, Ophidias was not especially large; perhaps as large, if you compressed the serpentine neck and the barbed whiplike tail and the vast veined wings, as one of the drafthorses that tilled Melior's acres in Chandrakar.

But a dragon Ophidias was not, any more than Rohannan Melior was human. And considered as a wizard, Ophidias was formidable.

"I thought she'd like it, you see. The expected thing," Ophidias said out of the darkness.

Light reappeared, and now the room was such as might grace any of Melior's own castles. The walls were hung with dark claret velvet. The wizard lay curled on a couch constructed to his special requirements, and regarded Melior from a glowing eye set in a long narrow head of flanged and sculpted chitin.

"Better?" the wizard purred.

"Your skill is, as always, most impressive, Ophidias, but I have not come for entertainment."

"No. You've come to ask a boon. It is a great pity you're going to ask for the wrong thing, since as high as you say my price is, you'll only be able to meet it once."

Melior stood very still. Nothing that a wizard said was idle chatter, and the aid of an Adept of the Wild Magic, bound to no law, was never free. They delighted in tricking any of the Five Races who dealt with them by speaking nothing but the truth, only in a fashion so obscure that their victims never recognized the warning until far too late.

But Ophidias was his friend, and was speaking plainer than most. What Melior had come to ask for—Ruth's summoning into the Lands Beyond the Morning—was the wrong thing to ask for. Ophidias had just said so.

Thus, there must be a right thing to ask for, if Melior could only figure out what it was.

"Then perhaps we should settle on your price first, before we come to the small matter of my request," Melior said with forced ease. He wondered how long he could stall for time.

Ophidias flicked his tail. "Now, how are we to do that, Child of Air, when you haven't told me what you've come for?"

"Surely so great a wizard—" Melior began, and stopped. Surely so great a wizard could indeed peer into Melior's mind and see what he *thought* he had come for—and sell it to him, too, even though what he had come for was the wrong thing.

And asking the wizard what he ought to want would be just as expensive, Melior suspected, as getting the thing itself.

"—will give a great vintage the respect it deserves?" Melior finished smoothly, sipping the wine.

"Of course," the firedrake agreed, a draconian rumble of mirth in his voice.

Melior reflected with well-concealed irritation that riddling with wizards was nearly as low on his list of fun things to do—as his human friends might have said—as was visiting the World of Iron.

But was that, perhaps, the boon he ought to ask? To go to the World of Iron, and this time bring Ruth away with him? Melior considered that for only a moment. He had failed once and had no greater expectation of success this time, even with his own Adepts to lend him the power to walk out of that most treacherous of all worlds. And the way was now sealed besides, beyond the power of any, Adept or wizard, to unseal it. Which must mean—

"I trust that Ruth will reach Dawnheart in time to enjoy the Harvest Fair?" Melior observed politely.

Ophidias opened his jaws wide, and light poured from his throat. The velvet he lay upon emitted a faint curl of smoke. "Oh, very good, Child of Air. Of all your line, you are the least stupid. Now ask your boon."

The whiplike tail lashed again and the opal-webbed wings mantled. Melior was to be given no more time for delay.

So. Ruth was already in the Lands Beyond the Morning and, all things being equal, could be found with the arts available to Melior's own Adepts, now that he knew where to look.

So what must he ask of Ophidias? Proof of Baligant's treachery? Once he had Ruth, he would have that; with an Adept to unbind her soul from the Sword—

Melior took a deep breath and wished he did not know how plainly Ophidias could see his fear. Ask the boon and he was pledged to pay for it, whether it was something he truly needed or not. The price might be agonizingly high, and he was bargaining with Ruth's life.

"Come once into my land, at a place and time appointed by me, and there unbind Lady Ruth's soul from the Sword of Maiden's Tears, restore her soul to her entire, and make plain to all who watch the Adept who performed the binding." *And let me hang Baligant No-House from Dawnheart's highest tower. Better death in war than this ravening treachery.*

"A clever little elf," Ophidias said. He spread his wings and cupped the air, rising from his couch as the room around him vanished like sands through an hourglass.

Now the room was dark again, the wine cup, the treasure, the world—all—vanished into this formless potential creation. This was the true state of Ophidias' world: magic shaped by will.

"Now hear me, elphenborn." The wizard's voice was everywhere: the world was made of words whose power was greater than swords, and Melior saw Ophidias at their heart like a bright flame of *logos.*

"What you ask I shall accomplish, but at the price of a life. For what I do, you will bring a human bride who comes freely and of her own will to wed with me."

Melior nearly protested aloud. Humans had no magic and thus were fearful of it; and to become the bride of a wizard, an Adept of the Wild Magic and a Child of Fire besides, was a *geas* so daunting that even many an elphen heart would quail.

Freely. Willingly. Human. Where in all the Lands Beyond the Morning would Melior find Ophidias' price?

Never mind.

"This I promise to bring you before the day that my firstborn son weds," Melior said, tempering his promise as much as he dared.

Slowly light returned, until Melior stood once more in the chamber of golden mirrors that he had first entered. Ophidias stared at him, reptilian muzzle inches away from Melior's face. Melior felt his skin tighten with the heat that radiated from the firedrake's body.

"And so you shall, elf-child—because if you don't, your son's bride will become mine, and everything you hold mine as well," Ophidias told him. "In this I have no choice, Rohannan Melior, so mark me well."

"How shall I summon you?" Melior said, ignoring the wizard's closeness—and as far as he might, the doom he had bought for Line Rohannan.

The fire-glowing head on the sinuous neck was withdrawn. Ophidias blinked once, causing a momentary flicker in the room's light.

"A ring is traditional. Cast it into fire, and I will come." A wing spread, pointed.

A ring lay upon what appeared to be a cloth of finest scale mail. It was a domed band of red gold, and set into it was a smooth-surfaced gem that was the bright clear flame color of the firedrake's eyes.

Melior picked it up. It was almost painfully warm, but he slipped it on his finger anyway. It slid on loosely, then seemed to strop itself against his skin like a contented kitten, settling to a perfect fit.

"Since you seem to have lost your cloak, take this as well. Give it to my bride, when you find her."

Ophidias was enjoying himself hugely, but Melior could not bring himself to object. He turned his back and picked up the armored cloth the ring had rested on.

Ophidias' skin was smooth, but this was not. Melior could not imagine what animal the skin had been taken from, that the perfect pearlfire golden scales should all be the same size, delicate as gilded fingernails. The cloak was not hooded, though heavy enough and more for outdoors. It had a high stiff collar ornamented with more gems of the sort in the firedrake's ring. Melior shrugged it over his shoulders and found that, like mail, the weight was not as great worn as when carried. It was lined and edged with fur softer than *vair* and as red as human blood, and it brushed the backs of his boot heels. Whoever Ophidias' future bride might be, she had better be both tall and strong.

"And now, O great wizard, have I your leave to go?" Melior said. Dealing with wizards was a tricky business, and although he seemed to have survived it, his temper had not.

"Oh, go by all means, Child of Air. Do come again, it is always delightful to see you." Ophidias lay back, fanning himself with lazy wings.

Melior swept the cloak around himself and left the chamber.

· 11 ·

Adventures in the
Greenwood

AS RUTH HAD predicted, the heavy green tunics were nowhere near dry when lengthening shadows forced her to admit that they were certainly as dry as they were going to get.

"They'll have to do," Nic pronounced, shrugging into the larger of the two. The trews and clogs that were the rest of their gruesome salvage were hopelessly too small; he settled for the green tunic and the sheepskin leggings gartered over his suit trousers.

The unicorn regarded the transformation from library director to rogue with skepticism. It shook its head and creeled, an odd, unruminant sound.

"I think I agree," Ruth said. She looked at her intended wardrobe of damp scratchy homespun with distaste. Still, her kilt and cashmere shell were almost an invitation to assault from uncouth passersby. For Nic's sake as much as her own she didn't want to get into any more fights. Traveling with the unicorn would draw attention enough.

"All right, all right—I'm going."

Fifteen minutes later Ruth stumped back out of the woods to which she had retreated for privacy. A damp baggy pair of brown homespun trousers were cross-gartered over sheepskins that nearly concealed her brown-and-bone saddle oxfords. A thick leather belt with a carved bone buckle cinched in the soggy wool tunic enough to help the drawstring waist hold the trousers up. She only hoped the things would finish drying quickly—she felt like the Second Murderer; a spear-carrier from any play you cared to name; unkempt and ludicrous.

She hated it.

"Now what?" Ruth said, more than a little crossly.

"Now we follow the stream and see where it takes us. We'll be sure of water, at any rate."

"Travel at night?" Ruth was dubious. Beside her, the unicorn's coat shimmered like a silver flame in the dusk. It nuzzled her hand and Ruth patted it absently.

"There's at least an hour of useful light," Nic said ruthlessly. "Enough to find a place to bivouac."

But the unicorn, it turned out, had other ideas.

Nic had made himself a staff from one of the spears and used it to lean on. If the blow to his head still bothered him, he didn't show it.

He started into the woods in the direction of the stream. Ruth took one last longing glance behind her at the brighter open spaces and followed.

The unicorn stood its ground, looking after them beseechingly. And then it—

Well, Ruth wasn't sure how to describe it, but it was loud. It yodeled like a cat in the throes of a hairball, like a beagle with its people away for the weekend, like a lovesick peacock and an entire cote of pigeons.

It shut up as soon as Ruth came back.

"I wonder what unicorn steak would taste like?" said Nic, with admirable restraint but perfect seriousness.

"Come on, Daisy," Ruth said to the unicorn. "We're going *this* way."

She put her hand on its neck and tried to lead it. After a few steps it broke away and skittered to the opposite side of the clearing, gazing at them reproachfully.

And then it began yodeling again.

Ruth tried making her muffler into a noose and dragging the unicorn on a leash. Same result.

"Leave it, then," Nic said. "I don't recall asking to travel with a unicorn anyway."

Ruth hesitated.

"It'll probably give up and follow if it's going to, Ruth."

Reluctantly, Ruth allowed herself to be persuaded. She followed Nic into the forest. The birds were twittering their birdish evensong high above, where the topmost tree branches still caught the last rays of evening light. Under the forest canopy it was nearly dark. Progress was slow, and Ruth began to doubt Nic's assertion that they would get any distance at all. Behind her the unicorn's cries grew louder and more frantic, and finally stopped. Ruth felt like the sort of monster usually found tying orphans to railroad tracks for her desertion.

There was a sudden crashing in the brush ahead. Ruth heard abrupt sibilants as Nic said something rude and heartfelt.

The unicorn stalked out of the thicket before them.

Like any wild thing, its eyes flashed in the half-light: not the silvery-green of the headlight-dazzled deer, but a deep, burning, predatory red. Its silky fur was fluffed out like an angry cat's; its neck stretched long and snakelike as it menaced them in weaving darting motions with its spiraled, dagger-sharp horn.

It was growling.

The unicorn advanced, growling and twisting its neck. Nic began to back up, very slowly. Ruth backed up a bit faster.

It took them very little time to reach the clearing once more, and there the unicorn, like a cat, pretended it had never been the spiky fiend of moments before. It stropped itself against Ruth, crooning its pleasure, and tugged coaxingly at her tunic with teeth sharper than any herbivore should reasonably possess.

Ruth took a couple of steps in the direction of the pull. The unicorn released the cloth and danced away cajolingly, looking back over its shoulder.

"I think it wants us to follow it," Ruth said needlessly.

"Do tell," Nic said. "I don't see a lot of choice—but if this thing is leading us into a trap, I *am* going to have that steak."

Ruth made a strangled sort of half-laughing noise. Shaking her head, she followed the white beacon of the unicorn's body into the woods on the other side of the clearing. And *they'd* been trying to save *it* from hunters!

Nic intended for them only to put a half mile or so between themselves and the unicorn hunters before stopping for the night. The unicorn had other ideas, and wasn't shy about enforcing them.

This left Nic and Ruth with a choice between following the unicorn blindly through the pitch-dark forest, or camping next to something that was howling like a defective smoke alarm and incidentally pointing them out to every emissary of the ungodly within earshot.

They followed. Until, some fifteen hours after seven o'clock Christmas Eve night, the unicorn vanished.

"I'm immoderately delighted," Nic Brightlaw said in an acid undertone.

"What?" Ruth said. Her hunger had subsided to a slow resentful rumble long since, but lack of food and lack of sleep and the clammy awfulness of her clothes combined with good old-fashioned shock to lend everything a giddy unreality.

"Your damned pet fire siren's gone," Nic said shortly. He took a step forward, and then another. "And so's the forest."

Ruth, leaning wearily against a tree that seemed to be revolving slowly about the Pole Star, decided she couldn't possibly have heard him clearly. "What?" she said again.

"We have reached the end of the forest. Stumps and second-growth ahead, then road, I think. And Fluffy the Wonder Caprid is nowhere in sight."

This seemed to call for more than another monosyllable. "What do we do now?" Ruth asked after a long pause.

"What I wanted to do in the first place," Nic said crossly. "Wait for morning."

· 12 ·

When the Deal Calls for a Sacrifice

THE CASTLE WAS a pale tower of shimmering stone. Once it had belonged to the husband of Hermonicet the Fair. Its name was Mourning.

From a distance the castle bore the appearance of a child's toy discarded thoughtlessly in the marshes that marked the eastern border of Chandrakar. It was the single vertical line in the flat marsh landscape, and what it guarded would be safe forever.

Eirdois Baligant sat within Mourning's walls upon a most comfortable chair of state in a private chamber to which he had brought the most expensive, if not the most tasteful, of his newly-won treasures. The High King-Elect was a little below average height, and his hair was a color that an inhabitant of the World of Iron would not have hesitated to call gunmetal. Before he had been acclaimed High King by the Twilight Court, he had not been accounted handsome, the elvish beauty that was his birthright marred by the decades of dissipation, greed, and anger that had carved his face into the permanent frozen snarl of a cheated bird of prey.

He no longer wore the armor of the soldier's life that had occupied all but his earliest youth. Eirdois Baligant was High King-Elect, and wore silk trousers and jeweled slippers, a velvet robe and furred mantle and rings for every finger. Delicacies from all the world—and worlds beyond—graced his table, and nobles who had once dismissed him as inconsequential now bent reluctant knee at his demand.

Eirdois Baligant was High King-Elect, with the lady Hermonicet the

Fair to his wife. He had everything it was possible to want within Chandrakar's borders. The Kingship, Hermonicet—and soon enough his enemies would be gone, on the very day of the Kingmaking that would set the seal on his triumph.

If only there weren't something he felt he might be forgetting.

It was not that he was not content—or rather, it was not that his discontent was disturbing to him, for Baligant knew himself better than some, and knew his appetites could only be deadened for a time, never slaked. That the High Kingship itself would not content him he knew; but he knew also that the High King has endless opportunities for fresh, inventive revenges, and Baligant was by nature vindictive.

He knew these things about himself and many more, having lived quite long enough to become well acquainted with his own measure of what other men called faults. To avarice he would also admit, and held that such admission rendered him superior to those who lusted and coveted and swore that they did not. In his own narrow fashion, Baligant was a shrewd and honest prince, and if Fate had fitted him admirably for a pawnbroker and then turned him loose upon the stage of greater events, this was not his fault.

Baligant rose from his chair and began to pace about the room, marking his path by the treasures which lay along it. Each of them had once belonged to someone else, and not one of their former owners would have had an approving word to say of Eirdois Baligant were he not the High King. Elect.

But at the moment Baligant felt very much like the laborer who, having worked long and hard, discovers that the coin he has been paid in is false. Baligant was honest enough to assign that fault to no one—he was to be High King, and it would be foolish to complain that the High King was ruler of a land spoiled by three generations of war.

And besides, he would tax it as if it flourished.

Baligant smiled. Let them complain—the alternative to obedience was war.

And Baligant had seen the war, every year of it—from the beginning, when every lord called up his *meinie* to wage what would surely be only the briefest of battles, to the end, when even the slights and cruelties and betrayals of a century of war could not keep the earls from negotiating their secret treaties of peace. Even the loss of the white body of Hermonicet the Fair could not incline them to battle once more.

And if they would not fight for her, they would not fight. He could do as he liked, until the grandchildren of this generation were grown.

And by then it would be too late for the Seven Houses of the Twilight. Far too late.

Baligant smiled.

"Lord Baligant?" The voice was hesitant, but that was as it should be.
He was in his private chamber, and no one would disturb him there
without overriding necessity.

That was power.

He turned, prepared to show a terrifying arrogance.

"My lord?"

It was his wizard. His *pet* wizard.

Her name was not Amadis, but it was what he had been given to call
her. Her hair was long and silken, and her form was slender and lithe, and
these, too, were not necessarily truth.

What was true was that Baligant didn't care. For someone who
trusted all his plans to his captive wizard, Baligant truly knew very little
about her. But he knew the two things that mattered. He knew she was an
Adept of the Wild Magic.

And he knew about the flowers.

He let her wait for his pleasure, studying her while he wondered—
not for the first time—how it would be to be more to her than her master.
But he was smart enough not to attempt it. That small thing might be the
one thing that would tip the balance of binding and obligation and free
her.

And he meant never to free her.

Amadis swayed in the doorway, and Baligant noted with pleasure the
green shadows beneath her skin; the hollowed, fever-bright eyes. She had
been too long away from the flowers.

"Yes?" he said at last. "I hope this is important."

Fury gave her strength; Baligant saw it flare in her eyes as it brought
her body rigidly upright. Her eyes were a brilliant copper a few shades
darker than her hair; Baligant wondered (again, not for the first time) if
the elphen form she wore were her own. So few Daughters of the Twilight
had any talent for the Wild Magic.

But if Amadis were truly talented, mere elphenborn would not have
been able to trap her.

"You may find it so," Amadis said briefly. "The soul-anchor I set
upon the Sword of Maiden's Tears has broken loose from the World of
Iron. The Sword has been carried out of this world through a Gate that is
not charted in my ephemeris. If both the Sword and the soul-anchor are
in motion through the Lands, they will meet. That is the Law."

"What do I care if one vermin-infested mud-daughter finds her way out of the World of Iron?" Baligant blustered, beginning to fear.

His wizard didn't answer—didn't need to answer, because Baligant already knew. In tampering with the Sword, perhaps the greatest of the Treasures, Amadis had left evidence that tampering had been done. And the heart and triumph of Baligant's plan lay in that his wizard's meddling should never be discovered by the elphen Houses that it doomed.

"Kill her," Baligant said simply.

The wizard did not answer. The hot bright anger that had animated her had ebbed. She put out a long pale hand to steady herself, the gesture echoing the unfolding of a dragonwing.

"But perhaps you'll want a stirrup cup to speed you on your journey?" Baligant smiled, unease dissolved in cruelty. This was his private chamber. The flowers were here.

He went to his desk and opened a jar. The moment he did, sunlight and high summer seemed to radiate from it, warming the chill autumn day. He plunged his hand into the jar, pulling out a fistful of dried flower heads.

"Is this what you want?"

He held them out. The wizard drifted closer, an unwilling serpent drawn to his piping. She stared at the crushed flowers with hungry despair.

"Not to your taste?" He held his hand over the jar, preparing to drop the flowers back in, and was rewarded by the sound of a whimpering gasp from the wizard.

"If you'd control your temper better, Amadis, you'd get more of what you want." He smiled, feeling the heat of the wizard's hatred wash over him like the wave of a summer sea. She wanted his death. But she didn't want it quite badly enough.

"On the other hand, you did tell me about the Sword," he said, relenting.

Baligant picked up a small dagger from the table. He cut the hand that held the flowers once, very carefully, and watched as his blood welled up and began to soak the crumpled petals.

Let no man say I have not shed blood for Chandrakar.

"Is this what you want?"

He held his hand out to her. The dried flowers were saturated and sticky with his blood, their pale ivory petals stained a swollen blood-red.

The wizard Amadis snatched the flowers from his hand and crammed them into her mouth, gulping and choking on them. A thin trail of bloody saliva flowed down her chin and dripped onto her long white gown. She held both hands over her mouth, hiding behind them, licking them clean.

She turned away.

"Amadis? Kill the Ironworlder before she reaches the Sword," Baligant said genially. He wiped his bloody hand upon his tunic, staining the costly delicate fabric.

· 13 ·

Traveling in an Antique Land

THE WORLD WAS called Counterpane.

Ruth sat on the bench outside the country inn, quaint as a Brothers Grimm woodcut, and let the pale morning sun bake the midnight chill out of her bones. Counterpane. Her store of local information was increased by one hundred ludicrous percent. It was—she sought through a jumbled trove of J-book memories—straight out of *A Child's Garden of Verses.* Something that started "I used to go to bed by day . . ."

Which did not, at the moment, seem like a bad idea.

She and Nic had slept the few hours until dawn huddled against each other for warmth like the proverbial Babes in the Wood. They were awakened by the sound of cart wheels rumbling along the road, and in the early daylight the two of them crouched in the underbrush at the side of a road and watched as a barrel-filled, wooden-wheeled cart drawn by four oxen rolled magisterially past. A drover dressed much as Ruth and Nic were walked at their heads.

Almost as soon as it had rolled out of sight, another party came down the road, this time on horseback.

The two in the lead were riding gray horses the improbable color of polished steel. In contrast to the earth-toned world Ruth had seen so far, the knights—somehow they looked to Ruth like knights—were in technicolor: their horses' reins were tasseled with bright multicolored flags that matched the colors in their long fringed saddleclothes, and their riders were bright and brave in sweeping feathered hats, long colored boots, striped hose, and brilliant silken tabards over white shirts trimmed in lace. Behind them, on a horse of a different gray and far less fine, rode a bareheaded young man with a plain dark vest over his laceless shirt, leading a white mule piled high with wrapped bundles, including two long canvas-wrapped ones that Ruth thought looked like skis but considering everything were probably lances.

"They look like what the SCA would do if it had money," she muttered half aloud. Nic nudged her warningly.

One of the knights reined in and stared in their direction. His companion, finding himself riding on alone, looked back and said something that Ruth was too far away to hear. After a moment more, both knights rode on.

But the squire, too, paused to stare. And without a floppy hat and trailing feathers to get in the way, Ruth could see that his ears rose to delicate points and his slit-pupiled eyes were cat-green.

Nic gently but firmly put a hand over Ruth's mouth.

The party of elphen knights rode on.

When it was entirely quiet once more, he let her go.

"Vulcans," Nic said.

"Elves," said Ruth.

"Whatever."

After that they had cautiously taken to the road themselves—once Nic had unwound the bandage around his head and scrubbed away as much blood as he could with the heavy morning dew. Half his blond hair was stained a rusty brown, but he looked much more conventional without the bandage than with it.

Once they began, Ruth discovered how many aches and pains you could have after walking all night and sleeping in a ditch. Her only consolation was that since she never wore makeup, leftover mascara was not now making dark rings under her eyes.

"Ah-ah," Nic said, after about an hour's walking. Ruth looked up. He pointed, and Ruth's gaze followed the direction of the pointing finger.

If there were buildings in Elphame at all, Ruth imagined they must be tall, airy Gothic cathedral structures entirely constructed from gleaming white marble with tasteful accents of granite and maybe rock crystal, with silk pennons flapping in the breeze and every single copper-sheathed turret roof foiled in gold.

Of course, it that were true, this wasn't Elphame.

"The Last Homely House," Nic said.

"Get real," Ruth said weakly. But the building did bear a weird and irritating resemblance to a Professor Tolkien set piece.

The building was set back a few hundred yards from the edge of the road on the right side, with a wide beaten-dirt courtyard before it. The building itself was made of wood planks weathered to gray, with a flat turf-covered roof that angled sharply backward, giving it an outline not inconsistent with that of certain Dairy Queens in Tulsa, Oklahoma. There were no windows at all in the front wall, just a white-washed door beneath a carven lintel. There was a bench on either side of the door, each rough-hewn from a single plank. Both were empty.

"Give me all your money," Nic said.

Ruth obediently dug into the belt-pouch that had come with her new outfit, rummaging until she retrieved the handful of chump change bequeathed her by its previous owner. She held it out to Nic.

He turned over a couple of the coins as dubiously as if he'd never seen them before, and slid the whole into his belt-pouch. He looked at Ruth and shrugged.

"Let's go buy some information."

They crossed the road and the inn yard, and stopped a few paces away from the door.

"You stay here," Nic said, pointing to the bench. Ruth—much against her inclinations—began to protest. Nic put a hand on her shoulder, shoving until she sat.

"Look," he said. "I can't watch you and them at the same time, Miss Marlowe. If this turns out to be more unicorn hunters, you're the one with the allies and connections here in Wonderland. So if I don't come out . . ."

"What?" Ruth asked, because he'd stopped.

"Run like hell," Nic said, and grinned.

Ruth sat down, and within a few minutes found herself fighting not to fall asleep.

A few minutes later Nic came out again. His hair was wet and slicked back, all traces of blood removed, and he carried a battered leather mug and a slab of coarse dark bread that had a slab of soft white cheese balanced on top of it. He handed them to Ruth.

"Welcome to the canton of Counterpane," Nic said, "which is one of the Borderlands—I hope I have the emphasis right—that the Iron Road runs through. This is the Merry Grigot, and its main business is serving traders. Business has been bad this spring—no caravans—and the innkeeper isn't sure why. What he does know is that some lord from one of 'the inward lands' has been crossing borders in a rather highhanded fashion, throwing his weight around."

"My, haven't you been busy," Ruth said peevishly. She took a hesitant drink from the quart-sized leather mug. It smelled like apples and had a vinegary, bubbly taste with a burning afterkick. Hard cider. She followed it with a bite of bread and cheese.

"Basic recon. Apparently they're used to all kinds of strangers through there, so neither of us should attract much attention. The name Counterpane mean anything to you?"

"A counterpane is a bedspread, if that's what you mean," Ruth offered. "Melior said he came from Chandrakar. He didn't exactly run through *Baedeker's Guide to the Perplexed.*"

"Cheer up, Miss Marlowe. Apparently you *can* get there from here," Nic said, before going back inside.

Ruth sat and drank her cider, wishing for a number of things that started with a shower and clean clothes and ended with her toothbrush. And now, because it had suddenly become possible, and because it didn't look as if she and Nic were going to get thoroughly killed any time in the near future, she thought about what she was going to say to Melior the next time they met.

She loved him, and she was pretty sure her feelings hadn't changed. But while feelings didn't change, situations did.

He hadn't come back for her, though it had taken her a long time to give up hope. Had Rohannan Melior accepted that he would never see her again, settled down with a nice second-best elf-princess, and gotten a steady day job, whatever his sort of day job might be?

Or had he not come back for her because he was dead? He'd said he had enemies. One of the traps they'd set for him had dumped him onto 116th Street in little old New York. The next might have been fatal.

These thoughts were not new, but always before Ruth had been able to bury them deep beneath the impossibility of ever finding out the end of the story. But now she was here in the Morning Lands, and it seemed very likely that she'd find out.

And which of the three possibilities—married, dead, or ready to take up where they left off—distressed her most, Ruth was not prepared, at this time, to say.

She wondered if a real person—with a whole soul—could have made an easier choice.

She finished her bread and cheese and cider, and set the leather mug beside her on the sun-warmed bench. After a while a boy appeared from around the back of the inn, collected it, and skittered off again. He returned a short while later leading a saddled horse, and a traveler in a dark cloak came out the front door, mounted, and rode away. No one gave Ruth any more notice than if she had been a part of the wall.

Eventually she did fall asleep.

A hand on her shoulder woke her. Ruth started awake with a gasp to find Nic Brightlaw gazing mildly down at her. The sun was higher in the sky; nearly noon.

He placed a cloth-wrapped bundle on her lap.

"Your lunch, Miss Marlowe. C'mon, let's move."

Ruth opened the bundle. More bread, more cheese, a couple of apples and a slab of over-roasted meat.

It looked delicious. She extracted the meat and shoved the rest into a vest pocket for later.

"Yeah, right. Where?" She stood up, biting into the meat.

Nic started for the road. He gave her time to catch up before he answered.

"Oh . . . you might call it the Unfair Faire Affair."

· 14 ·

The Fox and the Hounds

POETS MIGHT HAVE called it the greenwood, and maybe a hundred years after the event a highly-colored romanticized version of events would make its way into the popular songs. And then again, maybe not.

Fox was bored.

He lay at full length among the birches that covered the ridge and looked down on the pass into the Vale of Stars. The noonday silence was broken only by the chirr of cicadas, and the deep blue unpolluted sky was occupied only by a pair of soaring hawks.

Several hundred yards behind him and down the ridge was their village; half a dozen rude structures made of green birch saplings bent into semicircles and then covered over with peeled bark and animal hides. Warm enough, even in winter, with half a dozen fellow sleepers, but Fox was fastidious by nature and craved more solitude than this rusticity was likely to give him.

Nominally he was on watch. And should anything in fact appear on the road that led to the Vale of Stars, the willow whistle he wore on a cord around his neck would gather his men around him soon enough.

Absently Fox scratched himself inside the leather jerkin where the summer sweat made a tingling itch along his ribs. Leather might be fine to pick up girls in, but it wasn't as comfortable as a cotton shirt. Even homespun would be better.

But outlaws couldn't get cloth at all, even the coarse homespun that the cottage weavers made. And as for cotton and linen, silk and velvet, they were woven on giant water-driven looms in the market towns of the north for the sole consumption of the elf-lords and their favorites.

Fox sighed for what he couldn't have, and returned his mind to his current problem. He'd been slow enough learning the lesson that all good generals knew—that the bone and sinew of an army is people. Fox hadn't had much use for people—before. To be perfectly frank, he'd always thought most of them were extremely stupid, and in this belief he had not been disappointed by later experience. His merrie outlaw band, Fox estimated, was about as thick as two short planks. And that was on a *good* day.

But never mind. He needed them. And he had a much better idea now than he'd once had of how to make people do what he wanted them to.

Up to a point.

A waiting game was the strongest tactical position, and all very well for fellows like Wellington and Alexander who commanded a paid army that actually wanted to be there. Fox had a collection of followers who were with him only because they couldn't be somewhere else. They'd been taxed out of existence, driven from their homes, and generally disenfranchised—and far from having instilled in them by these vicissitudes a steely spine and a martial nature, all they really wanted was to be left alone.

But even if he were willing to let them sit in the shrubbery and rot, he didn't have that luxury. Without a goal, his semblance of leadership evaporated, and without leadership, the Merries would just wander off and get caught—or be sitting ducks when their numbers became too large for their former masters to ignore.

And that time—despite all Fox had done to delay it—was coming soon. His fame was spreading. Every month brought a scattering of new recruits. If his outlaws could not manage to fight when they were attacked, he had called them together only to see them slaughtered.

And though that thought would not have bothered him before, it bothered him now.

They had to be able to fight—and more than that, they had to be willing. He needed some cheap and easy victories to weld them into a unit. And it wouldn't hurt, not at all, if this cloud-castle victory allowed them a change of fare from venison, rabbit, and dandelion greens.

Besides, he thought the point-ears were getting it a bit too much their own way. He was keeping the blonde elf-bimbo away from the Cup, true, but what if he could do better than that?

What if he could *get* the Cup?

*   *   *

"Okay, is everybody clear on what's going on here?" Fox squatted on his haunches over the improvised sand table and pointed at the diagram with a peeled twig.

"Dawnheart's here. The village is over here. The market sets up in this flat place between the village and the castle, but the Harvest Fair won't be there—it's too big. It's going to set up over *here*, on the water meadow just beyond the castle."

He'd made up his mind to raid the Harvest Fair because his skittish band of rebels needed a cheap and easy victory, and what could be easier than pillaging a bunch of unwarlike merchants? Besides, Fox had found out that there was something called the Harvest Truce, which meant that nobody on the Fair's grounds would be armed.

Except Fox. And his band of merrie men, of course.

"What if they open the dyke?" Raven asked.

"The river's too low to flood the meadow this time of year. Even if we're close to the castle, we're out of bowshot—and even if they could get siege engines up onto the catwalks, they won't be able to fire into the middle of the Fair without fragging a couple hundred civilians. Which I don't think they'll do."

"What about magic?" another man asked. He was branded on both cheeks—poaching, a first offense.

This was something Fox had worried about himself, being largely ignorant of the workings of magic. But most of his outlaws had seen service on a battlefield where magic was in use, and he had listened carefully to their talk.

"They aren't expecting trouble. Magic takes time. As long as we're fast, we're safe—and once we're back to the Vale of Stars they can't even track us."

The others laughed at this, and Fox felt their tension ease, to be replaced by confidence. And once they saw that a strike at their former overlords brought no reprisals, they'd be bolder.

And so would every other human in Chandrakar.

Yippee, thought Fox dourly. *We're finally going to do something.*

"Okay, guys. We'll move out as soon as the moon is up. We hit the Fair tomorrow at dawn. And remember—the goal is a horse for every man."

The gathering around the sand table broke up. Fox took a last look at his careful map, running one more time over escape routes and pitfalls, before scrubbing the sand smooth again. By this time tomorrow he'd either have proof that he was as good as he thought he was, or he'd be dead.

Of course, maybe he'd be both. There was always that possibility.

Fox sighed. None of this was going quite the way he'd planned, back when he'd begun. He'd wanted some basic surgical first-strike revenge against elvenkind in general and Rohannan Melior of the House of the Silver Silences in particular.

So you build the tools to build the tools to build the weapon to wage the war. And if it takes long enough, you can even forget what you're fighting for. Isn't that fun?

· 15 ·

The Road Goes Ever Onward

HE WAS LOST.

Ridiculous.

Nonetheless.

Rohannan Melior—Marchlord, Swordwarden, Treasurekeeper, Baron Rohannan of the House of the Silver Silences—reined his gelding to a halt yet again.

Lost. Lost, and the Sword of Maiden's Tears with him. Lost somewhere. Lost Some*when.*

To pass through any of the Gates was to play with time. At its simplest, Time ran faster the closer one came to the World of Iron, and slower the farther away one got, until one reached the Timeless Lands where Time did not exist at all. Pass through a Gate and gain—or lose—a day, a week, a month—or more. And when dealing with the Wild Magic, be grateful it wasn't still more.

But he had thought to lose those days to threshold-*teind,* and not to a wizard's prank that seemed neatly designed to make him take the long way home.

And he had been so sure that Ophidias stood his friend.

Melior had left the wizard's lair wrapped warmly in his borrowed troth-cloak, the bargain-ring on his finger. He had ridden through the ice-pale world with its lying sky and back through the hills to the bleached bone Gate. He had seen the Gate, and clucked encouragingly to his mount, and ridden through the arch at a jog-trot.

And come here. Wherever it was. It was not Chandrakar in autumn, nor any of her neighboring Lands. Nor yet did it seem to be any of the Borderlands—Cockaigne, Broceliande, Amalur, Counterpane—that lay along the Iron Road to Earth. Gislaine had said that road was closed anyway; there was nothing for him there.

Yet if Ophidias had not lied—and no wizard, whose magical Self was created entirely through the Word, *could* lie—then Ruth had crossed that border before it closed, and wandered now in the Morning Lands.

Perhaps she was here?

Melior gazed about the wholly unfamiliar countryside, nameless and unknown despite his magical attempts to find one of the *leys;* the power-lines that would lead him to a Gate or to the Iron Road itself. A fair land, a pleasant land—but not the one he wanted, unless it held his lady.

Melior frowned. Ruth was no longer in the World of Iron. Ruth was here. Here, lost, alone, and—if he knew his Ruth—highly indignant about it all.

And so easy to kill, did anyone know who and what she was. And if she died, far more than Melior's heart would die with her. The chance to publish Baligant Baneful's treachery would die as well, and that must not be.

A man who made slow decisions would not have lived to grow older in wartime. Almost as the thought came to him, Melior had drawn the Sword of Maiden's Tears and held it before him. The bare blade shone blue in the daylight as Melior balanced it cautiously upon his gloved palms.

Perhaps he was foolish in thinking that the Sword could help him now. He was no magician, nor, it seemed, was he adept in dealing with wizards.

But for good or ill, the Sword was linked to Ruth Marlowe through her stolen soul. And Ruth was freed from the World of Iron, and walked a world as filled with magic as the Ironworld was filled with electricity.

The pommel-piece of the Sword glinted, a giant drop of frozen fire. Melior breathed a Word across it, his breath misting the polished steel on its blade. He felt the *dweomer* gather power as it left his lips, and slowly the Sword swung its ponderous weight gracefully upon his hands, until the pommel-stone pointed distinctly in a direction it had not pointed before.

Melior marked it, then flung the Sword up and caught it by the hilt in a theatrical gesture that would have much surprised his lady-cousin, who thought him dull and peacebound. And then he clapped his heels to the sides of his surprised mount, and took off across the meadow, once more upon a quest.

· 16 ·

The Unfair Faire Affair

"IF YOU DON'T mind a little vulgar curiosity," Ruth said, "just what *is* the Goblin Market? Other than a poem by Christina Rossetti, of course."

It was late afternoon on the High Road. Ruth's feet hurt, but not to the exclusion of rational thought. Their superfluous garments were bundled in Ruth's cloak and Nic had lashed it across his shoulders like a pack. Life was good. In fact, nothing had tried to kill either of them since, oh, this time yesterday.

After leaving the inn, they had walked in what seemed to Ruth to be a more-or-less easterly direction. They'd left the road three more times to make way for parties of travelers, but no one had stopped them or tried to question them.

"The Goblin Market, according to mine host," Nic replied, "is something supposed to be so well known in these parts that you'll appreciate that I couldn't ask too many questions about it. The caravans travel with special scouts whose specific job is to guide them away from it. From what I gathered, it's some sort of navigational hazard that dumps you off course and slides you across Borders."

"Which would make it pretty ideal," Ruth said slowly.

Nic smiled without humor. "If crossing Borders is what you're after, the Goblin Market sounds like the place to go. The only question I have is how to find it. By the way, we're being followed."

Nic spoke so casually that by the time the words sank in Ruth didn't react at all—which had probably been his intention, damn him anyway. Just let them get somewhere safe and she was going to have a number of tough questions for Nicodemus Brightlaw, Boy Library Director.

Of course, she had no idea how she could make him answer them.

"Followed," Ruth said, in admirably even tones.

"In the woods, off to the left."

His voice was pitched lower now, so that only Ruth could hear.

This time she did look, as casually as she knew how, and saw nothing but what she had seen all along: the beige, slightly-rutted dirt of the road, the grassy verge with its sharp drop-off into the reed-filled ditch, the expanse of grass on the other side, now mixed with bushes and skinny trees that became bigger trees with no bushes until the forest proper began. All the trees were in the full leaf of summer; you could hide two armies and a three-ring circus in that woods in perfect concealment.

I don't see anything, Ruth thought of saying, and rejected the remark as idiotic. "What are you going to do about it?" she said instead.

"That looks like a nice place to have lunch," Nic said irrelevantly. He gestured at the road ahead, where the grassy verge widened into a semi-circle bordered by the forest. Wagon ruts and burned circles on the grass showed where other travelers had taken advantage of this Otherworld rest stop.

"Yeah, sure," Ruth said under her breath. But dutifully she followed Nic off to the side of the road.

He untied the improvised pack from around his shoulders and spread it out on the ground for a blanket. "Miss Marlowe," he said, and Ruth bobbed him a mock-curtsy and sat down.

She dug out the remains of the lunch Nic had bought her at the inn and bit into an apple. The taste was sweet and tart, mouthwateringly strong, and Ruth suddenly remembered something else about the poem "The Goblin Market": the warning it contained against eating Other-worldly fruits.

But it doesn't matter. I'm not going back to Ippisiqua no matter what happens. She took another bite of the apple and bent to unlace her shoes.

"If you take those off, you'll never get them back on," Nic observed. He squatted on his haunches, watching her. Ready to move in any direction. "Your feet will swell."

"I don't care," Ruth said, trying not to sound sulky about it. He was only annoying because he was right, of course.

She unlaced the furry cross-gaiters and pulled off her bone-and-brown saddle oxfords, and then, for good measure, the blue cashmere argyle kneesocks that went with them. Her skin was winter-white, unseasonable. She took another bite of her apple.

"Have it your way. I'm going for a walk."

Nic's voice was bland. As always, Ruth watched him amble away toward the edge of the wood, the picture of unconcern, and wondered what it would be like to hear real emotion in his voice. She wriggled her toes defiantly in the grass, savoring the coolness, and finished her apple. She flung the core in his general direction, careful not to come remotely close. Emotion scared Ruth. It always had.

Not always.

As if it had only been waiting for this break in her concentration, her mind directed Ruth's attention back to that eternal sore spot: the years Ruth had spent . . . asleep. The nothingness after the accident that had stolen eight years of her life.

She did not remember how it had happened. That had been left for others to tell her, and none of them could tell her how she had felt, what she had thought.

1981. Ruth had been seventeen. She—and Jimmy, and Allen, and Kathleen—had been going to the Senior Prom. Jimmy had his father's convertible. There was dinner before, at an expensive restaurant, then the Prom itself, and afterward about twenty of them had been going back to Kathleen's house to party till dawn.

Or so Ruth had been told afterward. She didn't remember the month before the Prom; her graduation; or even why she'd bought the dress she had. She had a picture of it; a Polaroid her folks had taken when Jimmy came to pick her up. Yards of pink tulle, in every shade from baby's breath to flamingo. Fourteen years later she still wore her hair the same way; long, parted in the middle.

The need to know the truth ground against the unshakable reality that she would never know the truth. Those memories were gone, destroyed by the same thing that had pushed her into the coma.

Because somehow, somewhere, between the Prom and the party, there was a car accident, and nobody ever knew why for sure. There was no other car, no sign of anything except that Jimmy Ramirez had put the pedal to the metal and rammed a tree at something over sixty miles per hour.

Everyone else was killed. Ruth had been thrown clear, to dream the next eight years of her life—all her young adulthood—away.

The newspapers Ruth read ten years later said Jimmy must have been drinking. When she'd come out of her coma, her father had said the same thing. At the time, confused about so many things, she accepted what she was told. Ruth's memories of Jimmy were vague, like old photographs seen through carnival glass, but one thing she eventually remembered with certainty was that he couldn't have been drinking. Jimmy Ramirez' older brother had been an alcoholic. Jimmy didn't smoke, didn't pop, didn't drink anything stronger than Coca Cola.

And this was a hell of a time to dredge up ancient history.

Except that it wasn't ancient history, according to Melior. According to Melior, Ruth's soul had been stolen while she lay in that hospital bed, stolen and used to tie the Sword of Maiden's Tears to the World of Iron, so that it would fall into that last of all possible worlds, unrecoverable.

Only Melior *had* recovered it, and without enough magic to repair the damage, had taken the Sword—and, Ruth supposed, her soul—away with him again.

What could she say to him when—if—she saw him again? What could she say?

Ruth lay back, staring up at the wispy cloud trails in the sky. It was just for a moment. She should keep a lookout for Nic, and for whatever was following them. If anything.

Ruth slept.

"C'mon, Jimmy—we're going to be late!"

"Party can't start till you get there, Kath!" Jimmy shot back, laughing. He made a great show of searching for the car keys through all his pockets—the cummerbund and bow tie of his rented tux in his other hand—and then when he found them, tossed them up in the air and made a production out of scrambling to catch them. Ruth snickered.

Ruth Marlowe was sure that Jimmy Ramirez was the handsomest man she'd ever seen, and even though they knew perfectly well they didn't love each other, they both enjoyed the looks they drew as a couple. After tonight their paths would diverge: Ruth to college, Jimmy to work in his father's gas station. But tonight that didn't matter.

Jimmy finally opened the car—it didn't matter, really, since it was his dad's almost-a-classic-car convertible and the top was down, but Kathleen's dress fit like one of her mom's old panty-girdles from her armpits to her knees and she couldn't exactly climb over the side of the car. Allen handed Kath in and she slid across the seat and then Jimmy walked around the car and opened the door for Ruth.

She tossed her head, flirting with him, both of them knowing it was all for show. He'd brought her a corsage of white roses to go with her dress and Mom had pinned it into her center-parted hair. Her ombréd-tulle dress swirled around her calves, and her satin pumps were dyed to match the darkest shade of pink in it. They had glittering rhinestone buckles on them that matched her earrings, and Ruth could not imagine a future occasion on which she would be so perfectly dressed. She got into the car. Jimmy closed the door.

There was a shortcut to Kath's place—a back road, not very well lit, not exactly two lanes wide, although everyone pretended it was. It was one in the

morning, and real unlikely that anyone else would be on it. Ruth held her
hair in place with her lace shawl and shivered deliciously in the whipping
midnight slipstream.
    There was a flash of light in the road ahead.
    "Shit," Jimmy muttered, thinking of cops, of tickets, of his dad's refusal
to ever let him borrow the car again. But the lights weren't flashing red-and-
blue. It was a coppery fiery light, and Ruth, straining her eyes, suddenly
saw—

    "Nuh—*oh!*" Ruth struggled awake, pulled by terror and a feathery,
whiskery touch on her cheek. She opened her eyes, and the meaning of
the dream dissolved into spangled fragments, leaving only the fear behind.
    Her unicorn was looking down at her, blue eyes wide and pink nos-
trils flaring. Around its neck it wore a garland of flowers, each bloom the
bright intense improbable color of one of the Crayolas in the Deluxe 64
Color assortment. The scent pouring off them suggested that someone
had machine-gunned the perfume counter at Bloomingdale's. It nuzzled
her again.
    "Yag," said Ruth, and forgot her dream entirely. She struggled to a
sitting position. The unicorn backed up politely and sat down, looking
rather like a large friendly dog that happened to have hooves and a single
horn growing out of its forehead.
    "Where have *you* been?" Ruth asked it. She stood up, wincing as she
put weight on her bare feet. Nic had been right, of course; her feet were
swollen. If she'd known she was coming to Elfland, she would have worn
hiking boots.
    The unicorn got to its feet and shook itself all over. It trotted a little
ways away and looked back over its shoulder hopefully.
    "Oh, no. Not this time." Ruth looked around. Where was Nic?
"Hello?" she said tentatively.
    The unicorn trotted back to her and nudged her arm. Urgently.
    Oh, the hell with it. "Nic!" Ruth shouted at the top of her lungs. The
unicorn added its trilling bugle to her shout and then looked at her
expectantly. Ruth shook a minatory finger in its face.
    "We are not going anywhere without Nic. We started out with Nic,
and we are finishing up with Nic, whether you like him or not. And, really,
you ought to be a little grateful."
    The unicorn was unimpressed.
    "And where did you get those flowers anyway? A secret admirer?"
Ruth reached out to touch the flowers. The unicorn skittered back just
out of reach.

Ruth looked around, turning her whole body to do so. Where was Nic? If what had been following them was the unicorn, then he wouldn't have been able to catch it, but he would have come back. And if it hadn't been the unicorn that was following them, had Nic met up with what was?

And what happened then?

"Damn," Ruth said inadequately. And everything had been going so well just five minutes ago.

With quick angry motions she bundled the cloak and its contents back together as she'd seen Nic do and yanked on her socks. Getting her shoes back on took more determination, but Ruth was mad enough now not to care how much it hurt.

Or, to be honest, scared enough. But mad was better. She'd rather be angry than scared, any day.

"*Nic!*" She looked around hopefully, but he didn't appear. It was, to coin a cliché, later than she'd thought. The sun would be setting in a few hours, heralding the start of another wonderful night spent sleeping on the ground in her clothes with no blankets. "Nic! Nico*de*mus!"

She'd give him one last chance to show up before she really lost her temper.

But he didn't, and secretly she'd known he wouldn't. Nic Brightlaw thought she had survival skills one notch above those of free-range linoleum. He would not leave her alone for this long if he'd had a choice.

Unless, of course, he's simply abandoned you.

"Cute, Ruth. Real cute. C'mon, Fluffy. Let's go hunting."

· 17 ·

Midnight Is a Place

THE TOWER WAS in no place, at no time. And that was precisely the way its lady liked things. To age meant to change, even for the Sons of the Morning and the Daughters of the Twilight.

And the lady liked herself just the way she was.

Here in her tower, time passed just as she wished it to. Quickly, slowly, backward . . . or not at all. Here she dreamed and made her plans, and wielded the small subtle weapons that bent the great and powerful to her will.

A small thing, in the midst of war, to single out Baligant No-House and put into his mind the thought to hide the Treasures. Easier still, to direct him to the Adept who could aid him in this—the Adept whose weakness she had discovered.

And no trouble at all to conceal from Baligant the fatal idiotic flaw in his ambitious plan—that even though their absence would allow him to attaint and destroy the seven unruly Houses of Twilight, without the Treasures, Baligant could not be made High King of the land, much less hold its borders. No trouble, because Baligant was . . . dazzled.

The lady regarded her image in a mirror and allowed it to reflect a faint expression of contempt. A fool, a greedy and jealous mediocrity who might never have been noticed all the days of his elvish immortality, save for the war that had cast him upon his betters' regard just as if he were some deep-sea refuse tossed ashore by a storm.

Weak and flawed, but those very qualities were what made Baligant No-House such an able tool of destruction.

Her tool. And when this working was done, nothing would be left—

not High King, not Morning Lords, not the very boundaries of Chandrakar itself.

Hermonicet—called the Fair—regarded her image in the mirror. And smiled.

· 18 ·

The Broken Swordsman

NIC MOVED INTO the forest, letting it close around him like the sea, touching him all over. And, like the sea, a disturbance in any part of it would be transmitted to him here.

He did not think about Ruth. He did not worry about the impossibility of their arrival here by way of a haunted bookshelf in a library basement, or about her half-told tale of sorcery and power politics. Nic Brightlaw had learned in a very hard school to focus his mind in a deep and narrow track, avoiding speculation about things he could not affect.

Just now, his mind was focused on achieving the Objective: ID-ing the stalker who followed them.

He wished, momentarily, for the toys that belonged to another world and another life: grenades, rifle, LAW. Then he put them from his mind. He had a knife.

At first he headed away from the direction of the presence. He intended to circle around, and if he drew the Unfriendly away from Ruth and toward him, so much the better.

He stopped, sheltered by a stand of trees. He stood until the birdsong resumed, and knew by its resumption that his quarry was either equally motionless or absent entirely. He continued his sweep. Neutralization would be second best. Live capture and interrogation would be better. Who were they, who did they report to, why were they following him and Ruth, what did they want—

Ahead the forest thinned. Second-growth vegetation, legacy of a recent fire. A clearing. The sort of place he'd wanted to look for so that he and Ruth could camp for the night. He saw a flicker of color and movement in the clearing ahead. He moved closer, and stopped.

A horse. A roan mare.

In the afternoon sunlight her coat blazed like polished copper. She swung her beautiful sculpted head toward him and flicked her ears back and forth. The sun turned her eyes as red as her coat, and her mane and tail fell in a long silky curve, fine as a woman's hair.

Nic's lips curved in a sardonic smile. He had a certain amount of experience with horses. Enough to tell him that the presence of this one was suspicious.

"The *phooka*," he announced in loud, conversational tones, "is an Irish fairy able to take three forms: dog, human, and horse."

And to tell him that there was no more point in playing hide and seek. He couldn't break a horse's neck. And a horse couldn't talk.

Scratch Objectives One and Two.

On the other hand, the knife in his hand was iron.

"Iron, Cold Iron, the Master of them All." I hope.

"I'm not a *phooka*," the woman said. She was red-gold and ivory, and she was absolutely naked. Her ivory body shone like every dream of goodness and honor he'd ever had.

"All hail, O mighty Queen of Heaven—isn't that how it goes?" Nic said. If she'd expected her magic to unnerve him, she was doomed to disappointment. *Du ma nhieu, Charlie.* Goodness and honor were dreams. And dreams were lies.

She shook out her hair and it fell over her shoulders, highlighting her nakedness instead of concealing it.

She was alone. If she weren't, she and her partner would have tried a flanking maneuver against him and Ruth on the Road long since. The only question was, were they after him or after Ruth?

The smart money was on Ruth. She had a history with the local politicos.

"And then I am to tell you that name does not belong to me." She smiled. The effect was heartbreakingly beautiful, meant to keep his eyes riveted to her face.

Nic looked past her, moving his gaze without moving his head. Beyond her, at the edge of the clearing, he saw the unicorn. Its head was down, neck extended, the very picture of a dog trying to pull its head out of a too-tight collar. There was a black strap digging into the flesh just behind its head. The other end of the strap was looped around a tree. The creature struggled in desperate silence.

Nic looked back at the Queen of Air and Darkness. He focused all his attention on her, banishing the unicorn from his mind. He took a step sideways, as if trying to get a better view of her.

"What do you want with me?" he asked, because it was the next obvious stupid civilian question.

There was an infinitesimal pause, a ball-lightning crackle of electrical potential on his skin. *She's checking something.* He took the opportunity to shift position slightly.

"You are a great warrior, Nicodemus, unjustly betrayed by your leaders. There are those among the worlds who have noted that betrayal, and would give you the means to set it right."

"You can't know what you're talking about," Nic said pleasantly.

"But I do," the Lady said. "Time is mine to command. I can give you a sword to shatter worlds, and return you to your own place at any time you wish."

She waved her hand, and hanging in the air was the image of a sword. A Prince Valiant, King Arthur, Conan the Barbarian wet dream of a sword, with a blade as long as his thigh and an edge sharper than a razor.

"Yeah, I can just see me walking into Firebase Delta carrying that."

"It is invincible," the Lady purred, and whether she was lying or not, he believed her. It would chop through the barrel of an AK-47 like it was balsa, and go through a man like he was made out of Jell-O.

She waved her hand again, and a doorway appeared beside the sword. Rank, fleshy, yellow-green vegetation filled the opening, and the light was the shadowy bluish light that was all that filtered through the jungle canopy.

It was the place that had become home, because it had burned away the memory of any other place. He smelled cinnamon and burnt rubber, the rank brackishness of canal water and the glass-house humidity of the jungle.

"Take it," the Lady said. "Go." She gestured toward the doorway. Offering him life. Offering him the real world.

One step forward, one to the side. "I like it here," Nic lied.

She snapped her fingers, and sword-image and doorway both vanished. She turned toward him, just as he wanted. If you moved slowly enough, most people would turn to face you without really noticing.

"Then stay. I'll sponsor you." She held out her hand. "I can promise you adventure beyond imagining, and—" she dropped her eyes demurely, "—other things."

Her hand was white and soft, the nails gleaming seashell pink. And the glamourie she was exuding would have melted the tires on an eighteen-wheel semi tractor trailer.

But not Nic Brightlaw, who believed in neither Beauty or Truth in any possible combination.

"The trip down Memory Lane was really special, but if there wasn't something you wanted, we wouldn't be talking." He took another step. The unicorn's tree was almost within reach.

The woman stretched, raising her arms and pushing the copper-gold mass of her hair off her neck. Nic felt power and intention reach out for him—and miss, as if he had almost intercepted a message meant for another.

Interesting.

"You didn't come here willingly. It was an accident, in fact. Come with me, and I will make it right."

Almost there. Time to set off the fireworks.

"And Ruth?" Nic said.

"Ruth has her own destiny to follow," the Lady said glibly. She smiled, and her teeth were long and white and sharp. "Come to me, Nicodemus Brightlaw. I have waited for you for so long." She held her arms out to him, welcoming him.

He knew who she was now. She was Death, and he'd strung her about as far as he was going to be able to.

He threw himself sideways, toward the tree. The penknife in his hand sliced down at the strap circling the trunk. He'd expected a struggle, but when the blade touched it there was a recoil sharp as an explosion, and the little knife flew out of his hand. The strap parted with a teeth-setting scream, and the unicorn plunged free.

He rolled to his back just in time to meet the leopard's rush. She hit him like a football player going for the winning tackle and her open jaws stank of blood and roses. He kicked her off him and knew he couldn't do it twice. He scrabbled to his feet, back against the tree.

She crouched, sleek and beautiful, her copper coat spotted with improbable vermilion florets. Her ears were flat and her jaws were open, and her beautiful eyes flared as red as dashboard warning lights.

The jaws could grind his bones to powder. The foreclaws could lay him open like a fistful of razors. But the hind claws would kill him fastest, disemboweling him with unstoppable force.

But whatever she was, she had wanted the unicorn trapped, and he'd freed it. Maybe that gave Ruth a chance.

"Nice kitty," said Nic. He bared his teeth in an expression that had very little to do with a smile. He knew someone who'd killed a leopard bare-handed. He'd died, but then so had the leopard.

And she deserved something for waking up the memories he'd buried so carefully.

The leopardess sprang again. Nic flung himself away from the tree, and she slammed against the trunk with bruising force. He saw what he wanted, half-buried in the mulch of the forest floor, and dove for it. The cat came up in a blinding flurry of fur and fangs, and a small dispassionate timekeeper in the back of Nic's brain told him he had only a few more seconds before she tried something more effective.

But now he had a rock in each hand. And when she launched herself at him again, he brought both hands up, trying to make them meet in the middle of the big cat's skull. His fists struck with a hollow wooden sound, and bounced away again.

She flung herself away from him in mid-leap, defying all the laws of physics. Nic scrabbled backward, adrenaline obliterating weakness. His feet skidded and slipped on the leaf mold of the forest floor and he saw, for only a moment, the image of the copper-fire witch-queen, her face bloody and bruised.

You will die a thousand deaths! screamed the voice inside his skull.

She flung her arms skyward as if summoning heavenly vengeance, but instead her body rippled, pulled like taffy. A wave of furnace heat tightened his skin. The dragon-thing spread her wings, blotting out the sun.

Maleficent. Jesus, I always hated that movie.

She reared back to strike, all beauty and inevitable grace. First him— because he'd made her mad. Then Ruth.

Only he didn't give a damn whether she turned into a dragon or a two-car garage. She wasn't getting Ruth.

The gun was small. A pocket pistol. The noise it made would scare horses, not dragons. But the load was steel-jacketed hollowpoints.

Steel. *Iron.*

She swung a head the size of a Japanese sedan at him, mouth wide with rows and rows of teeth. The scent of blood and roses was enough to make him gag. He thrust his arm down her throat and pulled the trigger.

The jaws closed. Oblivion for Nic Brightlaw came with the speed of a collision.

· 19 ·

Shop Till You Drop

THE GOBLIN MARKET was one of the most dangerous places in all the lands, and in the end, it was inevitable that every Gatewalker should find himself there at least once. If dealing with a wizard took all one's skill, surviving the Goblin Market without loss took all one's skill—plus luck.

The rules of commerce there were simple: you could only sell what you wanted to keep, and purchase what you already owned.

Melior, on horseback, sat on the crest of a hill and looked down into the Market. Painted tents and ribbon-decorated stalls spread out across the floor of the valley. Gypsy wagons occupied the edges of the pitch, and also on the perimeter were the horse-copers' lines, filled with horses worth—well, what you paid for them. Literally.

Every road out of this valley led to a different Land. No road led to the same destination twice. Even experienced travelers, when caught in the Goblin Market's turbulence, let its power fling them where it would, and made their way home from that more stable Land with gratitude for the ability to do so.

Power and opportunity. Or, in other words, danger. The Goblin Market.

The Goblin Market never closed, but its character changed sharply with nightfall. It was safer, by far, to chance the Market during the day.

Melior looked at the sun, balanced a bare hour's worth of daylight above the mountains. Go down the path to the Market an hour from now, and there was every chance he'd lose the Sword again. And Ruth was not worth that, no matter what his heart told him. That cold equation had been solved before, and nothing yet had changed. He would die to save Ruth. But he would not give up the Sword.

But it was only a chance he would lose the Sword, not a certainty. And Ruth *was* there. If he waited for her to pass through the Market and enter a less hazardous Land, he might lose her forever.

There were no certainties.

Melior clucked to his tired gelding and urged him down the path to the Market. In its sheath upon his back, the Sword of Maiden's Tears flamed palely.

"What—to coin a phrase—fresh hell is this?" Ruth demanded of the unicorn. It had been willing enough to follow her into the forest in search of Nic, but inevitably she'd gotten lost. The unicorn had brought her to a trail, and the trail had brought her here.

If the inn this morning had been vintage Hildebrandt, the scene before her now was pure Howard Pyle.

There were wooden stalls, some with bright-colored cloth awnings. The counters were piled high with all sorts of things—hats, it looked like over there, and those were gloves. . . .

"Whoa," Ruth said. "It's the Hollow Hills brand of Nieman Marcus."

And it was filled with people, more people than Ruth had seen in one place since she'd fallen through the bookcase. Some behind counters, more—far more—strolling the lanes between the stalls in garb from every possible historical period and fantasy kingdom.

Here was a lady wearing a gown that Ruth could reasonably assign to fourteenth century France—save for the fact that the gown was made from layer on layer of sea-green gauze, and the lady's headdress was a cone-shaped *hennin* of spectacular height, swathed in more sea-green veiling.

There she saw a man whose silky black hair hung nearly to his waist. He did not look toward her, but shouldered his way through the crowd, wearing full plate armor of breathtaking rococo splendor that looked as if it had been emitted from a cake decorator, chrome-plated, and then Turtle-Waxed. A tiny woman with hair the bright improbable blue of Egyptian faience darted up to him from between two stalls. He bent his head toward her, listening, and they went off together.

Ruth hesitated, then stumbled forward as the unicorn nudged her—hard—in the back of her knees. Ruth swung toward it and it bounced sideways, out of reach, shaking its head at her in silent laughter. It tossed its head, and the wreath it had worn lay in the road at her feet.

Then it turned and trotted off, back the way they'd come. In a few moments the white flash of its body was lost to sight.

"Abandoned," Ruth said out loud.

She took a step in the direction it had gone, and stopped. It obviously didn't mean to be followed, this time. The bushes closed behind it, and the path she'd followed to come here looked narrow and unappealing.

Ruth blinked hard against tears. She'd miss the silly thing. She supposed it was gone for good this time. She stooped and picked up the flowers it had dropped. Something to remember it by, at least.

She'd expected it to be rigid, like a horse collar or a wreath, but instead the flower garland was as flexible as a lei. She draped it around her neck. The perfume radiated from it like a more benignant form of a particularly virulent Air-Wick.

Ruth turned back to the fair. Was this Nic's Goblin Market? Probably.

And because it was as likely that Nic was there as anywhere, she walked toward it. Ruth Marlowe had faced hordes of sixth-graders with an assignment due tomorrow and five minutes until the library closed. A Goblin Market full of elves, fairies, and little men shouldn't faze her in the least.

The race is not to the swift, nor the contest to the strong, but that's the way to bet. James Thurber.

There was no formal entrance to the Market, only two posts about eighteen feet tall and slender and straight as teenaged telephone poles, striped black and white in a cognitively-dissonant symbolic blend with railway-crossing barriers. Ruth passed between them and into the colorful, noisy, busy babble of the Goblin Market.

The setting sun gave the place the fluorescent jewel-brightness of a medieval Book of Hours. And, as in a Book of Hours, there were small cylindrical tents of bright-colored felt flying pennants of gorgeous, rippling, many-colored silk, banners on poles, and liveried lackeys of every stripe. There were piemen in motley hawking their wares, pushcarts draped with brightly-colored banners, strolling minnesingers; the New York City bustle that Elfland had so far lacked.

It took all Ruth's attention just to navigate through the press of crosstime patrons without trampling or being trampled. Fortunately she didn't have to worry about getting her pocket picked. She didn't have anything worth stealing.

"What d'ye lack?"

Ruth swung around again, menacing oblivious fairgoers with the bundle she carried over one shoulder. While she'd been staring, one of the wandering *handelsmenchen* had waylaid her.

He was wearing red and gold striped hose and purple velvet boots

with tiny golden bells sewn around the dagged cuffs. His shirt had billowing white sleeves, and over it he wore a quilted vest of deep green leather.

Ruth regarded this vision with fascination. His hair was red and his
wide eyes were a green-hazel, and when he saw that he had Ruth's attention, he smiled more broadly. His wares were piled on a tray he carried
hung from a strap that went around the back of his neck.

"What d'ye lack?"

"Everything," Ruth sighed with weary comprehensiveness. "Have
you seen—"

"Old loves, lost causes, true dreams, new hope—tell me what you
lack; for I've the key to every lock and the word to every riddle."

"I'm looking for my friend," Ruth persisted. "He's tall—" but there
were any number of tall men in the Goblin Market "—and he was hit on
the head. Have you seen him?"

"Friends, ah, lost loves are the sweetest. The Market has what you
lack if I do not—but before you go on, won't you buy a faireing from
me?"

"I haven't got any money," Ruth said apologetically.

"Barter me, then—the knife at your belt, useless thing, for any piece
on my tray. No, better yet—any two." He smiled coaxingly.

Ruth considered, staring at the tray. There was no reason not to,
after all—and though she was probably going to be cheated of the real
value of the dagger, she didn't have any use for it anyway. She took a
closer look at the items on the peddler's tray.

There was a red glass heart on a chain of pearls, a gossamer scarf in
grays and blues, a mirror the size of a half-dollar with a silver frame
shaped like a snake swallowing its tail. There was a set of what first
looked like bondage gear for hamsters but which Ruth eventually identified as a hood and jesses for a hawk. Glass bracelets, gilded nutmegs,
embroidered ribbons . . . an entire jumble of possibilities.

"Choose what you lack," the peddler urged.

Ruth pulled the dagger from her belt and handed it—still in its scabbard—to the peddler. He inspected it briefly and slipped it into his vest.
Around them large competent-looking men in more sober dress carried
baskets of torches, stopping at intervals to set one in a socket on pole or
stallside and light it. The warm scent of burning resins tickled Ruth's
nostrils.

"Any thing—any two things—that you see," the peddler urged.

She plunged her hand into his tray almost at random. Beneath the
jumbled surface of ribbons and silks, her fingers hit something hard. She
pulled it out.

Scissors. Well, that's useful. Maybe I can cut my hair. Or my throat.

The scissors looked as perfectly ordinary as any Ruth had in her sewing basket back in lost New York: about four inches long. The eyes were gilded, and textured with some sort of design that Ruth couldn't make out in the twilight. The blades gleamed needle-sharp; embroidery scissors.

Tangled through the scissors' eyes as if it belonged there was a long red ribbon with a tiny gold bell at each end. Gold embroidery on the ribbon glittered in the torchlight.

"I'll take these," Ruth said. "And if you see my friend—"

But the man with the tray was already bowing his way out of her presence, searching for new customers. Ruth found an unoccupied pouch in which to stow her purchases, and walked on into the Market.

She had not had time to see much of it in daylight, but it seemed to Ruth that the character of the Market changed perceptibly in torchlight. All the middle ground in shapes and colors vanished, and all that was left were the brightest brights and the darkest darks.

And it was no longer possible to fool herself that Nic was here. She was the one who was here, in the place that people paid good money to stay away from, so Nic had said. She'd lost him—and the unicorn—and herself—and she felt not so much threatened as maddeningly ineffectual.

"Ruth!" A voice called her name.

They would say, when it was time to compose his epitaph, that Rohannan Melior was a fool. So be it. He was a fool. The sun's light had fled the Goblin Market and he was still here.

A wise man would not try to ride his horse through the twisting maze of alleys and fairways that made up the Market, and so Melior had left his in the place provided, bribing the attendant suitably to assure that he came back not only to a horse, but to the same horse he'd left.

He carried the Sword of Maiden's Tears upon his hip; an awkward position for a sword of that length, but it enabled him to use it as his compass in his search for Ruth.

And either its magic had failed entirely, or Ruth was dead, or she was here.

What a comforting selection of possibilities to choose from.

But the flame that was Ruth's soul burned clear and bright in the pommel of the Sword, and while there was a chance of finding her, Melior knew he would not leave, fool though that marked him.

He paced through the Market, oblivious to its temptations. Scraps of music and conversation swept past him like clouds scattered by a storm wind, and Melior ignored them all. Natives and visitors alike spared him a respectful distance, for the sword that Melior carried held one-twelfth the magic of an entire Land, and such power commanded respect even here.

He was so focused on finding Ruth before the Market did her harm that the sound had been in the air for several seconds before he noticed it. The sound of wings. *Large* wings.

He looked up. The bowl of night was filling slowly, pale stars visible only at midheaven in a sky only just darker than an October day's. The flying thing could be seen against that background quite clearly, the last rays of day striking greenish-copper light from its hide. Its wings were a dark insectile blur about its torso.

Warwasp. Not a natural creature. A form assumed by wizards and Adepts Major for the damage it could do. Created for war. Faster than a dragon, more poisonous than a manticore, able to burn with the lethality of a salamander. Melior had seen a warwasp destroy an entire unit of cavalry once.

Around him others who had seen it too were spreading the news; in moments this collection of unrelated people would be a mob. Or a riot.

He looked down, choosing his retreat. And then he saw her.

"Ruth!"

He recognized her even through the motley rags Fate had dressed her in. For some impossible reason she was wearing a Gate-garland—the ornament that assured you exited through the same Gate you had entered by—around her shoulders.

She swung toward the sound of her name and stared straight at him. Above him, he heard the thin song of the monster's flight change pitch as the warwasp prepared to dive.

She wasn't ready, was Ruth's first thought. She'd turned at the sound of her name, thinking Nic had somehow found her after all, and seen him. Rohannan Melior of the House of the Silver Silences. And she found she was nearly as afraid of him as in love with him.

He was wearing a cloak the metallic orange-gold color of enameled monarch butterfly wings. It glittered in the torchlight, and in his hand he held the Sword.

The Sword of Maiden's Tears.

The Sword that had killed Naomi.

As she stood, indecisive, the press of people that had seemed pliable and permeable suddenly took on solidity and direction; a solid mass of people, pushing her away from Melior. She struggled against them, trying to go the other way, and then at last she heard the sound that everyone else had heard before her Ironworlder ears had.

A dive bomber? Don't be—

Ruth looked up.

A nightmare, vexed to madness by a thousand Japanese monster movies: a wasp the size of a subway car, glowing dull red as if stoked by hell's own furnace. Its giant bubble-eyes gleamed wetly with unclean phosphorescence, and when Ruth looked up she knew with a sick certainty transcending logic that it was looking at *her*.

Melior drew his sword; a white-hot neon blur that bleached his surroundings to a ghost of daylight brightness. And the determined self-interested exodus around Ruth became a full-scale rout.

She struggled to keep her feet, knowing that if she fell she would be trampled. Reaching Melior, finding him, was abruptly less urgent than surviving to find him again.

Melior took a step toward Ruth, knowing that he could never reach her through this mob; that by the time he might search for her again she could be half a hundred Lands away. Then he drew the Sword of Maiden's Tears and pushed Ruth from his mind.

The Goblin Market was sacrosanct: to use sorcery near it—or *in* it— was a violation of custom and treaty so vast that Melior could not begin to imagine the retribution that would be exacted. And the warwasp was a creature of Chandrakar and those Lands near it. Paranoid intuition indicated that the creature was here for him.

Or for Ruth.

To save Ruth; to deflect the Heartlands' retribution from Chandrakar, Melior had to kill the warwasp. Here. Now. Quickly.

The Sword flared nova-bright in his hands, heterodyning magic from the creature above him. He saw the nightmare yanked from its intended path by the compelling magnet of the Sword's power, and took the last moment before it reached him to feel fear that for the first time the Sword's hidden weapon was his to wield.

Each of the Twelve Treasures was more than it seemed. The Sword of Maiden's Tears was unstoppable, unshatterable—but more than that: the Sword of Maiden's Tears gave its wielder the opportunity to know the mind of his opponent.

As Melior would know the mind of the warwasp.

He unclasped the hindering cloak and flung it away.

Then the warwasp was within reach.

Against beasts, spears and bow. Against men, the sword. Against a true dragon, the only defense was prayer. And the warwasp was none of these.

It hovered above him, as large as three cart horses and their wagon. He slashed upward, and it dodged out of reach, nimble in an element

Melior couldn't enter. Heat radiated off it like a furnace. The body was scaled; six grasping legs ended in claws, and mandibles glistened like black glass. It descended on him and this time Melior retreated, hampered by close quarters and the inability to bring the Sword to bear. The mandibles clicked, inches from his face.

But he had seen something. Behind the head, high in the chest between the two forelimbs, was a tiny fleck of blue-white light, as if there were something inside the warwasp, burning.

That was its vulnerable part.

Melior backed between two market stalls, hoping the warwasp would follow. The intuition granted him by the Sword assured him that it wouldn't. The monster snatched itself into the sky again on its black gauze blur of wings.

It wanted Ruth, not him, and now Melior knew it. But the wizard whose creation this warwasp was couldn't search for Ruth, not while the Sword of Maiden's Tears flared magic like a balefire, eclipsing all lesser lights. The warwasp would attack the Sword until the Sword was destroyed, or until it gave up and left without its prey.

So he was risking the Sword after all.

He looked around, trying to find his enemy. The space he was in was a narrow alley between two rows of stalls. The top was covered with canvas. He saw a clear space ahead, and started to move toward it.

The canvas above him bulged inward. The stall timbers edging it began to groan and splinter. The canvas smoked, catching fire, and black mandibles sliced through it, seeking him.

Melior cut upward, and the canvas split with a high buzzing shriek, dropping the hindquarters of the warwasp into the alleyway with him. The barb in its tail dripped greenish vitriol that smoked and stank.

The Sword bit into the creature's thorax. Only a glancing blow, but enough to make the warwasp disengage. Only this time, when the monster tried to rise into the air, it was tangled in the burning canvas. It thrashed like a dying horse, spraying poison from its trapped hindquarters.

Melior ran. Behind him the walls of the market stalls began to burn.

He heard the crashing as the warwasp floundered free, and a distant, bookish part of his mind wondered what indemnities the Heartlands would ask against Chadrakar for the bringing of its war into the Goblin Market. He wondered what coin his pillaged kingdom could find to pay in, after a century of war.

But what he wondered most was if he could find a clear area ahead so that he could seduce the warwasp into another attack.

Buying time, so that Ruth and the other innocents here could flee.

And Ruth would be lost to him again.

Ahead, the alley opened out into another thoroughfare. There were still people here, cowering or merely watching. He saw a blue-eyed lion the size of a pony regarding him unblinkingly.

Melior turned back the way he'd come, and saw the warwasp rise into the air again. Bright gold blood dripped thickly from its torso, setting fires wherever it dropped, and the werewizard itself glowed like a stoked kiln.

The night was full dark now, illuminated only by torches, random fires, and the light that flamed from both combatants. The monster sighted the radiant Sword and flew toward it.

Its heat sucked the breath from his lungs and pulled his skin taut. Melior raised the Sword for the downward cut—through the shoulder, into the spine—that experience and training swore was the surest kill. The bright blade flung itself forward.

And the lower part of the warwasp whipped forward like a second attacker, and a chitinous barb the size of a boarspear slashed at Melior.

Its venom had been expended in the first encounter; the droplets remaining were only enough to burn, not kill. The barb struck his thigh and stuck, then tore free to drag a smoking furrow up his body before Melior flung himself out of reach.

The Sword passed cleanly through untenanted air as the warwasp reared back. A miss. And the swift instants in which Melior might have won the fight through surprise and misdirection were gone, and all that was left was a war of attrition. A war that Melior Treasurekeeper, elphenborn or not, would inevitably lose.

And though the roads through all Lands crossed here, by the time another warrior came to his aid it would be too late.

He would be dead.

And Baligant would have the Sword.

The wound in his side burned, poisoned and seeping. Melior's vision blurred. His body shook with waves of hot and cold, and not even the incandescent insectile proximity of his foe could warm him. It seemed there had been poison enough remaining, after all.

The warwasp hung in the air before him, just out of reach, savoring the moment. It was a tactical advantage Melior had been taught to look for—that those creatures who loved slaughter often stopped to admire their work. It would not be enough to save him, but if he could cripple it, another might finish the task.

This, too, Melior had been taught.

He slashed down. The Sword hit the barb in the warwasp's tail with the sound of an ax hitting wood. And the barb broke and the Sword did not.

But the Sword was so heavy. . . .

Up again, with the weapon that now felt as awkward as a bar of farrier's bronze clutched clumsily in his hands. Stroke to the midline; open the belly.

He missed.

And while his clouded senses were still registering the fact, the warwasp closed on him. He brought the Sword up barely in time to save himself, all the while knowing it was only a temporary respite.

Through a hot poisoned fog Melior felt himself falling backward, felt the dulled impact as he struck the street. He saw his hand clasped around the hilt of the Sword, and the warwasp's maw upon it. His fingers lay just outside the flexing mandibles; safe. But the blade was being pushed back toward Melior's own throat, and his other arm was trapped beneath him.

And through the Sword he felt his opponent's intentions. No ambiguity there, only madness, blood, and flowers. And the furnace heat, beginning to sear.

"Father!"

The shout cut through Melior's concentration, forcing him to look. A brown-haired girl, her face a subtle blending of Ruth's features and his own, stood in the street behind the warwasp.

His daughter.

And in her hands she held a sword that was twin to his own—that *was* his own, duplicated by Time refolded like a silk ribbon to touch itself. It was not the warwasp's poison alone that had sickened him; the air was glutted with the magic that had let this be; a stifling rarified atmosphere that choked the breath in Melior's lungs and made his vision dim.

Not what will be, but what may *be.*

The Sword in his hands vibrated like some mad Ironworld machine, threatening to tear itself apart through proximity to . . . itself.

The warwasp turned, sensing, impossibly, the magic that bespelled it, redoubled. It lifted off him to confront this new threat, and Melior freed his trapped arm and snatched the Sword from its jaws; felt his hands, burned and cut to the bone, slide upon the sharp dimpled substance of the hilt.

Then the warwasp jerked and reared up, screaming silently as it was attacked from behind. Melior felt the blow that had struck it vibrate through its body and into his, and at last he had the clear target he had been trying for.

With the last of his endurance, Melior thrust the Sword of Maiden's Tears, point first, into the glowing patch in the warwasp's throat.

He felt the Sword turn icy and sullen in his hand as it transfixed the node of molten iron burning in the warwasp's breast. Reflexively he jerked it sideways, clearing the blade with a snap-wristed jerk, and fell to the street, sick and dizzy.

The warwasp flung itself into the night sky, body rippling as it threw off the form that had served it so ill. Melior didn't need his Sword to tell that it was abandoning the attack.

And it hadn't killed him.

But the riptide of Wild Magic might.

He scrambled to his knees and looked through the veils of shifting smoke to his daughter. The daughter who had not yet been born, who might never be born, despite her appearance here today. Who had saved his life, at the cost of a greater magic than Melior thought there was to buy.

She smiled at him, pushing her hair up off her forehead in an achingly familiar gesture. He could see the street beyond through her body.

". . . Father . . ." her voice was faint, as the Time River that had never been meant to merge here separated itself again before the worlds tore themselves apart.

"Your name! Child, your name!" Melior shouted, willing her to hear him. Suddenly it was important to know, to properly honor this spirit-daughter.

He saw her lips move in answer as she faded. No sound reached him, but he didn't need to hear to know.

"Naomi. . . ."

· 20 ·

For the Love and for the Glory

A PLAN. I need a plan.

Ruth Marlowe was no ordinary interdimensional traveler. Possibly unique among the visitants of the Goblin Market, she had survived rush hour in the New York Subway. In the crowd that swept her away from Melior she kept both her feet and her head, looking for an alley to dodge down.

She worked herself to the edge of the press of bodies and pulled free, the force of the maneuver sending her sprawling into a display of baskets. As she fell, the scissors jabbed her sharply; Ruth swore and tucked them somewhere safer, rolling into concealment. No one saw her here, no one was idiotish enough to stop and "rescue" her. Ruth tried to catch her breath and think sensibly. Melior was back there. And it would be vapor-brained to the ultimate max to do anything but get back to him as soon as possible.

There was a blinding flash of light and Ruth cringed instinctively deeper into the baskets. She thought about that *thing* that Melior was currently fighting and shuddered, a mutinous panic building in her. It belonged in a monster movie, not in Elfland.

She didn't like adventures. She didn't like surprises. And most particularly she didn't like monsters, whether they flew, shambled, or swam. She closed her eyes tightly, stricken paralytically by the certainty that twelve-foot wasp knew who she was, knew she was here, and was coming for her.

And someone showed up to rescue her after all.

"—shut up. Your pardon, demoiselle, can we be of assistance?" A man's voice, light and amiable.

"We. I like that." A woman.

Ruth opened her eyes and looked up. Two of the people she'd seen before—the man in the wedding-cake armor and the woman with the blue hair—were standing in front of the stall. The man was looking at her. His companion was looking at him.

He looked like a sword and sorcery pinup designed by a particularly vindictive armorer. His hair was black, his eyes were blue, and his strong sculpted face had a faintly Oriental cast to it. His hair was longer than Ruth's own and straight, caught back in a jeweled ring and falling free over his shoulder. His armor was intricately jointed and elaborately chromed. He had an earring, equally bright, in his left ear, and the open, friendly expression of an All-American Hero from a thirties pulp magazine.

His companion barely came up to his elbow. Her hair was shoulder-length, a bright false cerulean blue that clashed weirdly with her old-ivory skin and slanting amber eyes. She was wearing a fussy, elaborate costume that incorporated every form of dagging, slashing, trapunto, bead, button, and ribbon ornamentation of Western Europe from the fourteenth to the seventeenth centuries, inclusive, but far from making her look ridiculous, it simply increased her resemblance to some fabulously expensive jeweled clockwork doll. Her boots had curled toes and her cape resembled a fuschia suede artichoke that someone had edged heavily with gold bullion fringe. Her gloves had lace trim.

Ruth took a deep breath and tried not to surrender to an hysterical urge to laugh.

"Might you perhaps have a particularly large can of Raid?" she asked carefully.

The man smiled, an especially dazzling smile on an entirely human face. "No," he said, "but I'll happily stand you a cup of wine. No obligation."

His companion made a noise like an enraged cat sneezing.

There was another flash of light. Ruth flinched. The man's expression sobered slightly, then lightened.

"Oh, don't worry about that—just some local elf-lord bringing his war to Market. One of them'll kill the other, and everything'll be fine. I'm Perigord, by the way, and this is Azure Bowl." He held out his hand and Ruth took it. He helped her to her feet.

"You don't understand. That's *my* elf-lord, and—"

"I knew it!" Azure Bowl shrieked. "Peri, you inbred son of a peripatetic sphinx, I *knew* she was trouble!"

"And I suppose I should have just stepped over her and gone on?" Perigord shot back. He looked over his shoulder, and Ruth followed the direction of his gaze. Fires. He turned back to her.

"If the elf-lord's your friend, then I hope he wins. But he's going to have to win without me." Perigord shrugged.

"No money in it—and too much trouble," Azure Bowl snapped, but unease radiated from her.

With an effort alien to her nature Ruth shut her mouth on her next remark, which was that if the giant bug killed Melior, it would be coming after *her* next. Why should she tell these people that? She didn't know them.

And they might decide that it *wasn't* too much trouble to simply hand her over to the wasp-thing in the name of peace and quiet.

"The offer of a drink still stands," the man—Perigord—said, and Azure Bowl threw up her hands in the universal gesture of one who has nothing to do with events. She regarded Ruth with a measuring eye.

"Maybe you should buy her some clothes instead, Peri," she purred.

Pure irritation wiped every other thought from Ruth's mind for an instant, and she took a quick self-inventory: borrowed clothes, the wrong size to begin with, that she'd worn for two days; her hair full of brambles; her possessions much the worse for wear. And her cloak—Naomi's cloak—was gone.

"It's been a long day," Ruth said tightly, and didn't add: *"Just who's calling who a fashion victim? I've seen better dressed Macy's Thanksgiving Day Parade floats."*

"Don't mind my charming companion," Perigord said, with a haste suggesting this was a speech he had to make frequently. "She used to be a librarian and she's never gotten over it."

"Better a librarian than a prince," Azure Bowl rejoined. Perigord took Ruth's arm and led her in the direction in which the crowd had been running.

Librarian? Ruth wondered.

It was perhaps fortunate that visitors to the Goblin Market were a uniquely sophisticated clientele. Most of them were only interested in getting out of the way of the immediate danger. Though half the Market seemed to be burning, the customers grouped around the wine seller's stall were completely nonchalant.

Perigord handed Ruth a battered tin goblet full of wine. She started to raise it to her lips, trying to phrase some graceful way of thanking him for such disinterested kindness, when suddenly the ground . . . shimmered.

"Magic!" shrilled Azure Bowl. Perigord clutched her in his arms, which would have surprised Ruth if she'd had any inquisitiveness to spare.

The world had taken on a form only seen in nightmare, where there was vision without light, sensation without perception. Everything seemed both distorted and horribly clear; vertiginous, hot, cold, greasy, and dryly gritty. Ruth felt as if the air had turned to rubber cement, gelid and chill. In her sight the objects around her pulled like taffy and flickered like a riffle of playing cards.

The Market was there. It wasn't.

It was a forest.

A city inhabited by huge insects.

A featureless plain.

The Market.

And Ruth felt the shock wave strike her, as personal and intended as if someone had found the loose trailing ends of her nerves and yanked on them. It was terrifying enough to numb her entirely, and without a backward look for her new friends she ran toward where she had last seen Melior, though the ground beneath her rippled and bucked like a fun house attraction.

I have to get out of here, was Melior's first clear thought, and then: *The cloak. Not mine. Ophidias' gift to his bride. I cannot leave it.*

But where was it? And was it, for that matter, still there?

He got unsteadily to his feet and looked around. The Market was burning. The smoke hung in a low pall, reflecting back the light of the fires. Several of the stalls were smashed, their inventories strewn about the street. In a few moments their owners would return, and Melior hoped to be gone by then. Or, at least, to blend into the crowd.

Small chance of that, battered as he was, and with the Sword he carried. Melior grinned mockingly at that, and winced, and staggered as the world did another slow revolve. Now distinct from the disorientation of High Magic, the warwasp's poison burned in Melior's veins. He looked down at tunic and trousers shredded and soaked with blood.

He could still die here.

With flayed and shaking hands he sheathed the Sword of Maiden's Tears. He drew breath to voice the Word that would show him Ruth's location, and realized that to expend even so little magic would use all his remaining strength.

The cloak. Then his horse. If either was still there.
Now. He had come out of that alleyway. . . .

The alley was smoldering and venom-fouled, but Melior didn't dare
choose an alternate path, lest he lose his way entirely. He was rewarded
by the sight of Ophidias' cloak just where he'd left it, and risked losing his
balance completely to bend and retrieve it.

New strength seemed to seep into his bones as its scaled golden folds
settled about his body. There was a wine seller's stall across the way, and
Melior stopped to retrieve an unbroken flask from the wreckage, carefully putting a silver penny in its place. Another wave of dizziness roiled
through him and he clutched at a wooden pole for support. Still gripping
the pole, he broke the wax seal on the bottle and drank. Brandywine,
spiced and potent.

False strength surged through him with the liquor's heat—enough,
perhaps, to get him to his horse, but far from enough to allow him to pass
through a Gate of his own choosing, or to find Ruth. That much, at least,
the warwasp had succeeded in accomplishing.

He had hated Eirdois Baligant before. But now Melior swore that he
would kill him, no matter what else happened, no matter what the consequence to Line Rohannan. For forcing Melior to abandon Ruth here,
Eirdois Baligant would die.

Childish runesinger nonsense, Melior scolded himself. A battle was
not a campaign. And Ruth was not lost, nor was he.

He hoped.

But Baligant would still die.

Grimly, Melior set himself to reach the horse lines.

"No!" Ruth screamed it in pure terrified fury. She skidded to a stop,
the leaf-and-pine-needle-strewn track treacherous beneath her saddle oxfords. She spun around, glaring behind her, already knowing what she'd
see.

Or wouldn't see.

The Goblin Market was gone. And here, where simple physics and
the logic of Ruth Marlowe's top speed, even terrified, both assured her
should be approximately where Melior was fighting the Return of the
Creature From Beneath the Id, wasn't.

It was as if she'd run *through* the Market, unheeding, but even so she
should see it behind her.

I HATE magic! Ruth stamped her foot, and rejected every swearword
she'd learned in a lifetime of obscure reading as simply . . . inadequate.
The Market—and Melior—were gone.

It was night, and Ruth stood just inside a forest, on a long straight track that, looking back, she could see led out into a gently-sloping meadow lit a bright unreal blue-silver by the full moon. In the distance were more trees, and beyond that a different darkness that could be mountains or clouds or both.

No Goblin Market.

Ruth walked out into the middle of the meadow, finding that moonlight was everything its detractors had ever said it was: tricky and lying and full of illusion. Though the light seemed nearly bright enough to read by, objects seen by moonlight seemed to possess a sort of insubstantial vagueness that made it difficult to navigate, even if she did stay on the path.

And she couldn't see the Goblin Market from here either.

By the time she reached the middle of the meadow Ruth realized she was still clutching the wine cup. It had long since been emptied by her headlong flight, and whether it had been Prince Perigord's or belonged to the Market wineshop, Ruth saw precious little hope of returning it.

She thought of throwing it away, but a lifetime of reading Andrew Lang's fairy-tale collections stopped her. Whatever else it was, the cup wasn't *hers*.

And besides, that would be littering. She stuffed the cup into her tunic and hoped she wouldn't lose it, too. She'd lost Nic, she'd lost the unicorn—*Oh, I've lost Britain and I've lost Gaul and I've lost Rome, but most of all*—she'd even lost Melior, although she hadn't really had him, and although she now knew that he'd gotten home to Chandrakar alive, she didn't know if he was alive *now* and had a number of reasons to think he wasn't, so she really didn't think she was ahead on points. . . .

And she was lost, with no idea of which way to go, a pretty good idea that there were people and *things* around that didn't like Ruth Marlowe very much at all, and no basis for choosing a direction.

That, at least, was solved for her with the first cold drops of rain, falling miraculously out of a sky still moonlit and star spangled, but even as Ruth stared upward indignantly the question of whether the dark shapes on the horizon had been clouds or mountains was answered as the clouds slid across the sky like scenery being changed between acts, blotting out the moon and bringing rain in earnest—wet, soaking, cold, pneumonia-producing rain.

Ruth ran for the nearest possible shelter: the forest she'd just left.

The rain became a full-fledged downpour, complete, suddenly, with thunder and lightning and noisy whipping wind. And while the forest canopy was a roof of sorts, it was a very leaky one, and the gusting air was damp and chill.

The thought of holing up in a hollow tree with a woodland assort-ment of spiders, woodlice, and rabid squirrels actually began to take on a certain charm as Ruth stood, shivering, in the dark. After standing there long enough to realize exactly how miserably uncomfortable and out of alternatives she was—about two and a half minutes—Ruth began groping along the path that led deeper into the forest, guided by intermittent spasms of lightning, seeking some place drier and out of the wind.

Navigating by lightning was exhausting enough that Ruth stopped at the first halfway suitable spot. She sat down among the gnarly sheltering roots of the enormous tree and set her back firmly against its trunk, and vowed to sit there forever, or at least until a kindly old fairy godfather came along with a pair of red shoes.

And what would I wish for and where would I go? Ruth wondered. Then she thought about Melior, and put her head on her knees, and wept.

She thought she'd probably dozed, because when she roused the storm had spent itself, and the only sound was a faint but constant drip-ping as the rainwater spilled from leaf to leaf in search of the forest floor. She was so cold that everything hurt; her fingers felt as if they'd been boiled, and if she wasn't as wet as she would have been out in the meadow, she was at least much wetter than she liked.

And there was a light.

Ruth stared at it for a while, numb-brained and fuzzy, and tried not to think that it was what it so very much looked like: a porch light, or one of those retro coach lanterns people hung on their gates or over their garages.

But it didn't move, and it didn't vanish, and eventually Ruth got wincingly to her feet and tottered off in the direction of the friendly yellow light.

He was, Melior realized, in what his cousin Jausserande would have called real trouble (to distinguish it, Melior had always supposed, from the numberless samples of unreal trouble she was constantly exposed to).

The Goblin Market was deserted. And that could not be the case, nor ought it be that the Market's rulers would hesitate to make their feelings known to him, and that at once. Yet he saw no one and heard nothing, only the crackle of the fires that burned in half a hundred locations.

Even the gypsy wagons were dark and silent when he reached them. Melior shook his head, wishing he could be more regretful of the unpleas-antness his future undoubtedly held. He clutched at the side of one of the gypsy carts, using it to hold him upright as he made his way past it and to the horse lines.

Ah. So that explains it, Melior thought with light-headed clarity. At least it would save him the sorry task of informing Line Rohannan of this latest disaster. He tried to remember who was next in the succession at the moment, and failed. Was it Rollant? Acevelt?

All the horses were gone—the horses for sale and trade, the pack animals with their watchful trader masters, the light, long-legged couriers and the savage, heavy-boned warhorses. Even the donkeys, mules, and oxen. All of the animals were gone.

Save one.

It advanced upon him with a slow, measured gait—but this horse was not one which had to run—or that any in the Morning Lands wished to hurry.

It was pale gray, this horse, its mane and tail a darker gray than its coat. Its long hooves were unshod, yet Melior could hear each step that fell upon the soft turf clearly. Around its eyes, and at its muzzle, its coat was soot-dark, and out of that darkness, its long-lashed eyes flared red.

Melior knew this horse. He had seen it on innumerable battlefields. Some called it beautiful, and some hideous, but it had never been his to ride.

Until now.

It walked toward him without hurry, and when it reached him, it stopped.

"Now?" Melior said. "But I have suffered deeper wounds than this—"

And why, he thought with regret and indignation, should he still suffer all the hurts of the body, when the presence of this new mount showed that Rohannan Melior was beyond them?

The horse nudged him with its nose, soft and implacable. Melior stretched his hand out toward its mane.

No! If he must choose to mount this horse, then it followed that he could still choose otherwise. He recoiled from the pale horse and stumbled away, toward the forest.

Behind him, he heard the footsteps of Death follow patiently after.

Ruth stumbled creakingly toward the light at the aching pace of an arthritic snail. If the storm had not passed, she could not have managed, but the blue bars of moonlight filtering down through the leaves gave just enough light to move by.

As she got closer, the one light became two, and once she was closer still, Ruth saw that the light came from two lanterns hung one at each side of a set of wooden gates.

The forest path branched there; one path leading on into the forest, one leading toward the gate. Two carved posts, each with an iron hook to hold a lantern. Between them the gates—about five feet high; low enough to peer over without too much difficulty. Gates of what must be a purely ornamental nature, because anyone who chose to leave the path and step into the bramble of the forest for a step or two could simply walk around the gates: there was no fence.

Ruth did not leave the path. She tottered up to the gates and looked over them. As she pressed close, she felt the soggy wreath she still wore around her neck squish against the wood, pressing water into her clothes. She pulled back and hung it over one of the gateposts, then gripped the top of the gate with blue and aching fingers and peered over.

On the other side of the gates the path was graveled, wide and silver in the moonlight. The forest receded from the sides of the path until it was gone altogether; the path itself ambled on for a little distance until it reached the house.

In the pale moonlight what Ruth saw was a house that could very well have come out of her own world. It was a Tudor manor house, with a half-timbered, lime-washed second story, and high narrow windows set with diamond-shaped panes of glass. The flagstone path spread out to a courtyard that ran the length of the front of the house. Beyond the house Ruth could see a low stone wall and the regular planting of trees that meant an orchard. There was a lantern burning over the front door, but all the windows were dark.

Ruth hesitated, wanting to run to the safety and normalcy the house proclaimed, but knowing that here, in Melior's world, things were . . . different. The householders might welcome her with open arms. Or chain her in the basement. Or serve her for dinner. And there were no cops to call, and she didn't think the American Library Association would take much of an interest either.

She might be much better off just staying with the forest, and starvation, pneumonia, lions, tigers, and bears.

In the end it was the homely ordinariness of what she saw that persuaded her to risk it. Surely people who lived in a house that looked like that would at least be . . . civilized.

Jennet Jourdemayne Memorial Society, here we come.

Ruth ran her hand down the front of the gate, looking for a latch, and one wing of it slid inward under her hand.

Ruth was cold and wet and hungry and tired and not in the mood for extended debate. She stepped through the gate, stopped to close and latch it carefully—*but if the latch is on this side, and it was closed, how come it came open?*—and hurried on down the path.

It was, if anything, colder out in the open than in the forest, and the air had the crystal-bright stillness of long after midnight. Ruth walked as quietly as she could, but her progress was marked by the sharp crunching of saddle oxfords on gravel.

Then she stood at the house's front door and tried to gather up enough nerve to knock. At least, if you were meeting someone under normal circumstances, you had a hint of what you should say, and some idea, however unfounded, of what sort of person they were. Not here.

And it was late, and she was a stranger knocking on a country house door. And bringing trouble with her. Ruth had to admit that here even if she hadn't admitted it to her new acquaintances at the Goblin Market. Trouble was following her.

She stood in front of the door for a long moment in silent frustration, then finally grabbed the dangling chain of the bell that hung beside the door, and pulled.

There was no sound. *I HATE magic.* Instead, the door slowly swung open.

It was warm inside, and light. Ruth hesitated only a moment before walking in.

"Hello?"

Profoundly disinterested silence answered her.

Ruth stood in a front hall facing a staircase. The hall was dimly lit by candles in glass bowls in sconces on the wall. The floor beneath her muddy shoes was polished wood, and Ruth conscientiously backtracked to wipe her feet clean on the rag rug just outside the door.

"Hello?" she said again, a little louder this time. There was no sound from deeper in the house. She glanced around the hallway nervously, wondering what she was looking for and how she'd know if she saw it, anyway.

No one and nothing. An empty house.

The wall on her right was half-timbered; golden wood below, white-washed plaster above. The staircase took up the left wall, its newel post fancifully carved with leaves and acorns. There were sliding parlor doors—closed now—in the wall to her right, and straight ahead a half-open door led to a parlor with a fireplace. Ruth could see the shadows the firelight cast upon the wall, and went toward that source of light and warmth as if drawn by a magnet.

This room was empty, too, but Ruth didn't care. She huddled in the arch of the fireplace, hands nearly in the flames, and winced in silent discomfort as the blazing fire baked the bone-deep damp from her body.

A few minutes later, the worst of the chill gone, Ruth gave the room a careful inspection.

Not a modern house after all. Something more in the Colonial Williamsburg line, from the high-backed settles on each side of the fire to the high, narrow windows swathed in velvet curtains worthy of Scarlett O'Hara's dressmaking abilities. There was a narrow, brocade-covered couch, two deep padded chairs, and, to one side of the room, a table swathed in white linen upon which two candelabra burned.

Ruth left the fireside and advanced upon the table, an unsettled feeling of triumphant dread in her throat. She knew what she was going to find.

On the table was a glass goblet, a pewter bowl, a silver spoon, and a folded square of white linen. There was also a green glass carafe filled with red wine, a loaf of bread on a wooden dish, a wedge of cheese on a patterned china plate with a silver knife beside it, a wooden bowl of apples, and a blue and white china tureen with a silver ladle beside it. Ruth lifted the lid of the tureen. It was warm under her fingers, and the tureen contained steaming hot stew.

I know where this is.

Abruptly Ruth wondered if she would have seen a rose garden if she'd walked all the way around the house. Was there a garden here, in which the roses bloomed even in winter, and was one of them a blue rose, fairest of the fair?

I know where this is.

The Beast's castle, to which the weary traveler came in the dead of night and found food and drink, clothes and shelter—and no master. The house was familiar in the way dreams and childhood are familiar. No wonder she had recognized it.

Ruth considered her options. Suppose this was the Beast's castle—or house—just as advertised? If it was, she should be perfectly safe, providing she stayed out of the garden and didn't steal the spoons.

But what if it wasn't? What if—

Oh, God, she was so tired. And there was one thing left to do. To make the proof that she needed, because Ruth had no faith left in her to give to anything.

She picked up one of the candlesticks from the table and left the room. She slid open the doors to the parlor—cold fireplace, more Jacobean furniture—then climbed the stairs.

On the second floor she found two bedrooms, a dressing room, and a study with shelves of books and a writing desk. She did not stop to look further, because all of them were empty of inhabitants.

The last room she entered—a back bedroom—was not dark like the others.

She opened the door into light. Burning candles on the table, well-made fire in the grate. The room contained a large four-poster bed with carved walnut posts and garnet velvet bed curtains fringed with bullion, a dressing table, and a clothespress. There was a patterned carpet on the floor, and a fireplace with a roaring fire built up in it, and in front of the fire, sheltered by canvas-covered crewelwork screens from the draft, there was a copper hip bath full of steaming water.

Beside the hip bath stood a narrow can shaped like a cone with the point sliced off, also filled with water. There was a stack of fawn-colored towels with a square cake of orange soap and a wide-toothed comb lying upon it. There was a puffy yellow bath sponge, and, best of all, on a bench near the fire was a long soft heavy gown very nearly the color of the firelight with a pair of fur-lined soft boots beside it.

That does it. Ruth surrendered to her fate with a sigh. She could pass up any number of roses, and she could even, with an effort, pass up dinner, but she could not bear another moment of being filthy and unwashed and grubbing around wearing a dead man's clothes.

She kicked off her oxfords and began to undress.

Some minutes later, a pink, wet, and naked Ruth sat in the bath and gouged the last of the burrs and elflocks out of her hair with the sandalwood comb. She was warm—really warm—for the first time since she'd fallen through the bookcase in the Ryerson basement, and clean besides. And now she was going to wash her hair.

If she hadn't been stupefied with exhaustion, stress, and unaccustomed exercise she might have thought twice about participating in this setup for a Masterpiece Theater remake of *Psycho*. But Ruth was numb past hysteria, and so she bent her head between her knees to wet her hair, and then lathered it thoroughly with the soft orange soap.

Afterward there remained the problem of getting it really rinsed, but with the aid of the second can of water Ruth managed to get her long brown hair "clean enough for government work," as she thought of it. Then she rubbed off another layer of unwanted skin with the hot rough towels and picked up the robe.

It was a simple T-tunic, generic to the point of parody; the garment all moderns thought everyone in "The Middle Ages" wore and none of them actually did. The tunic had a close round neck with a short slit in front to let the head through, fell to just below the calf, had slightly-flared three-quarter-length sleeves and otherwise fit like a unisex sack of potatoes. The fabric had a close smooth hand and was the color of pale apricot flame; a color that Ruth was quite certain could not be achieved in Nature before the introduction of coal-tar (aniline) dyes in 1857. It was thick and rather stiff, the way wool blankets or drapery fabric are stiff, and reminded Ruth vaguely of one of those one-piece acrylic fleece sleepers for infants.

It was also clean and soft and she hadn't had to peel it off a corpse. Ruth put it on. The slippers were soft suede fur-lined ankle boots, obviously meant to be worn indoors, and Ruth put those on, too. Then, compulsively and apologetically tidy, she shook out and folded the clothes she had come in, and spread the towels she had used over the fire screens to dry. Then she sat in front of the fire and combed her hair until it fell in a soft, loose light brown curtain. *Clean.*

Ruth braided her hair in a fat tail over one shoulder, and was standing there, holding it, and wishing in frustration for her long-lost purse or even one good rubber band, when she remembered the hair ribbon she'd bought at the Market. That sent her on a (one-handed) search through her possessions until she unearthed it.

She found more than that, though.

Ruth stood, absentmindedly tying off her braid with the red silk ribbon with the tiny golden bells and looking at the object now lying on top of her discarded clothes. She'd forgotten all about the ring.

Ruth's worldly goods as of this moment, exclusive of clothes, consisted of a battered tin cup stolen (probably) from a Goblin Market wineshop, a pair of golden embroidery scissors, Nic's wristwatch (how had she gotten that?), and a ring, a silver ring with a golden stone that glittered uncleanly of magic. The ring the dead man had been carrying, back in the meadow where she met the unicorn.

Nic had said it was out of place where it was, and Ruth could only agree. She also knew that it made her profoundly uneasy. She was tempted to throw it into the fire, but the firm resolve not to trespass against her unseen host's graciousness stopped her.

With some reluctance, she unearthed the one remaining belt-pouch in her possession and shoved ring, scissors, and goblet into it. She hesitated for a moment more, looking about for something to hold it on with, then went over to the bed and unhooked one of the golden ropes that held back the curtains. It had a heavy fringed tassel at each end, and easily went round her waist with a good deal to spare. She slipped the strings of the pouch over one of the fringed tasseled ends and tied the makeshift belt tight over the housegown. She didn't want any of the pouch's contents, but she didn't think it was fair to leave them lying around loose for someone else to trip over.

She snuffed all of the candles in the bedroom except the one she'd brought with her from downstairs, and went back down. Her soft booted feet made no sound on the oak-planked floors of the empty house.

In the parlor the stew was still steaming hot, just as it had been an hour before. The candles were no lower, nor were the logs on the fire any more consumed. It was as if, in this room, time had stopped while Ruth was elsewhere.

The thought made her uneasy, but not profoundly so. Not after however long it had been since Christmas Eve.

She tried to remember exactly how long it had been, how many days she had been here, but the only thing that came to mind were scraps of misplaced poetry about a sleep and a forgetting.

She wished she *could* forget. Or remember. Or something.

The stew was very good, and the wine had spices in it. Ruth finished both. Sometime tomorrow she'd have to try to find the kitchen. But somehow it didn't seem like a very good idea just now, so Ruth finished her stew and her wine and then, like a good actor patiently following his assigned if rather bewildering role, Ruth took her candle and went back upstairs to bed.

Here, however, things were not just as she had left them. The hip bath and towels were gone, the screens were folded and stacked against the wall, and there was an enormous marmalade cat sitting on the pile of Ruth's neatly-folded clothes.

He must weigh twenty pounds! was Ruth's first marveling thought. As if it had heard her, the cat turned its head and regarded her, unwinking butter-yellow eyes fixed on her with a feline look of disdain.

"Hello, moggie," Ruth said. "I'm Ruth Marlowe, the traditional benighted traveler who comes to the house in the woods and doesn't ask awkward questions about where the owners are."

The cat closed its eyes and began to purr, kneading the fabric beneath it with its paws.

"I'm going to bed," Ruth added, feeling only a little silly to be having this one-sided conversation. "You're perfectly welcome to join me. In the morning, all things being equal, I expect to be on my way. Even if I don't know where I'm going. Or how to get there. Or—" Ruth yawned, hugely. "G'night, moggie."

The bed was already turned back, revealing an expanse of white linen sheet trimmed in French point lace. Ruth sat down on the side of the bed and kicked off the house boots, curling her toes at the cold before sliding them beneath the covers. There was a hot brick wrapped in flannel at the foot of the bed; Ruth wrapped her toes around it and sighed. All the comforts of civilization.

Civilization. And in the word the edges of some larger concept than could be embodied in flush toilets and tax collectors; something about expectation and reason and the rule of law.

She unknotted the curtain tieback from her waist and pulled the leather pouch off of it. She put the tieback on the table beside the bed and the pouch (with reluctance) on the pillow next to her. She snuffed the candle, but the room remained rosily lit by the fire on the hearth. She lay down and pulled the covers up to her neck.

There was a thump on the bed as the marmalade cat joined her. It walked the length of the bed, toward the pillows, and stopped as it encountered the pouch. It regarded it for a moment, sniffed at it, and sneezed. Then it began pawing at it, making the universal "cat covering up something" motions on the pillowcase.

"Oh, for heaven's sake," muttered Ruth. She snatched at the pouch and moved it to the night table. The cat settled into the pillow with a deep-voiced purr.

Time slipped from his ordering like a willful serpent, and if anyone knew when and where he was, it was not Rohannan Melior of the House of the Silver Silences.

Head of Line Rohannan. Was that event far in his past, or still yet to be?

At least the Sword was with him. It had been Melior's task and obsession for a human lifetime, and its absence would have left him more than restless.

He stood in his father's solar in Castle Dawnheart. A wild witch-storm battered the walls; cover for Arneis' and Gratien's move of troops along the border of the Vale of Stars, so Rohannan's scouts had said. As soon as the storm died, Rohannan Lanval and his son would be after them with two troops of horse and Jausserande's Ravens—if she got back here in time—and hope to pin them at the edge of the Vale until Rohannan infantry and Adepts could come to support them. At any cost, Arneis and Gratien must not be allowed to come to Medraut's aid with fresh troops.

"Melior." His father's voice recalled him to himself. He turned from the window. Rohannan Lanval was staring at him intently.

"Father?"

"You know that our Covenant forbids us to use that which we guard against one another—"

Melior frowned. Of course he knew it. They all knew it. With every hero-tale and elementary lesson in simple magic came the lore and warnings surrounding the Twelve Treasures. They must be kept. They must be presented at the Kingmaking. They must not be set against the other Treasures,

*for the Twelve Treasures were only vulnerable to themselves, and the destruc-
tion of any of them was the death of all the Seven Houses of Twilight.*

"—yet I would have used it tomorrow."

Melior stared at his father in shock and felt disjointed time slide around
him like chill oil.

"The Sword of Maiden's Tears is gone, my son. Find it. Find it. Find—"

Where was he? In the middle of some retreat, but the Sword of
Maiden's Tears was with him, and Melior had never carried it in war.

The rain fell in distinct echoing *pock!* noises through the canopy of
trees, and Melior was soaked; his silver hair sleeked dripping to his skull
by the rain that slid down his skin and beneath the collar of the ornate
cloak he wore to soak the clothes beneath. His boots, too narrow and
high-heeled for this activity, squished soddenly with each step. There was
nearly enough water to wash away the blood, until he felt life flow out of
him with the trickling rain.

It seemed, however, important to go on.

Chills and fever racked him alternately, and Melior knew his senses
could no longer be trusted. He was giddy with blood loss; unbearably
thirsty. He had stopped once, to inspect the wound and bandage it as best
he might, with strips dagger-cut from his undertunic, and then he had
seen that the edges of the long slashing wound were iridescent and slimy,
glowing with the residue of poisoned magic that would finish him, with
time.

He paused, leaning against a tree, and a chilling douche of water
from above caused the time-ocean to recede momentarily and beach him
in the Now.

He was Melior Rohannan. His father was dead and he was alive, and
lost somewhere in the Heartlands with the Sword of Maiden's Tears.

He looked over his shoulder and saw the gray mare. Her mane and
tail fluttered in the breeze as if no rain reached her, and she walked in a
shaft of moonlight reserved for her alone.

He would not ride.

Melior turned and stumbled on. And once more the world slid away,
until he was only a soldier in an endless war, slogging through the rain
without knowing why.

"C'mon, Jimmy—we're going to be late!"

Ruth tossed restlessly in the strange bed. Sleep had hit her like an
auctioneer's hammer coming down on a quick sale, but it hadn't brought
oblivion. Lost in the Lands Beyond the Morning, Ruth dreamed.

There was a shortcut to Kath's place—a back road, not very well lit. It was one in the morning. Ruth sat beside Jimmy Ramirez as he slewed the Oldsmobile around the curve.

There was a flash of light in the road ahead; a coppery fiery light, and Ruth, straining her eyes, suddenly saw—

It was in the middle of the road, and she saw—

She saw—

It was gold, copper and gold, and she saw—

"Oh, please, no," Ruth said in a tiny voice. She was awake, sitting bolt upright, staring into the embers of the fire. The marmalade cat was curled in her lap.

And this time she remembered her dream. For some unreasonable reason, here in Elfland the memories the doctors had told her were gone forever, destroyed by accident and trauma, were hers again, at least in dreams.

She would remember the moment of the accident soon. She knew it. And she couldn't bear it.

Ruth took several deep breaths and tried to stop her hands from shaking. Horrible as the nightmare was, it wasn't what had awakened her. Something else had.

What?

There was no point in trying to go back to sleep, and for Ruth the question of whether she would like to sit in the dark and brood or do it by candlelight was easily answered. She gently set the cat aside and groped around the edge of the bed until she found her boots. Then she put them on, slid out of the bed, and took her bedside candle to light at the hearth.

Naomi always said the SCA'd come in useful some day. For the first time in a long while, thoughts of her dead friend didn't bring pain. Ruth held the lit candle aloft, feeling absurdly like a remake of the Statue of Liberty, and watched it chase shadows back to their hiding places in the corners of the room.

Then she went back downstairs.

The marmalade cat followed her, complaining volubly: it was too hot, it was too cold, what was she doing up at this time of night?

Ruth didn't know. She was still tired from the long walk that day and all that had followed it; exhaustion thrilled in her bones like a stubborn vibration. But the hope of sleep was gone.

The parlor that was her first entry to the house was dark; there were banked coals on the hearth, but everything else was tidied away, waiting for morning. Even the remains of Ruth's dinner were gone, and the white linen cloth of the table as chaste and unsullied as ever.

Simple tricks and nonsense, Ruth thought wearily, pleased through it all at her lack of reaction. Why, magic was becoming just as ordinary as ordinary to her.

There was a coruscating flash. Multicolored light forced itself through the chinks in the curtain in a neon Armageddon, as if someone had just detonated Times Square outside her window. Ruth yelped and flinched backward, to tangle herself inevitably with gown and cat and go sprawling.

The candle and its silver candlestick sailed in a wide arc toward the hearth, where the candle struck, broke, went out, and began slowly to melt in the greater heat of the fire.

The fall hurt, even though *she* was not hurt. The cat was all solicitude, stropping and purring and favoring Ruth's chin with a few random licks.

"Moron," Ruth muttered, pushing it away.

There were no further explosions, and after a moment to collect the shreds of her courage, Ruth limped over to the window, and pulled back the drape.

The moon was a ghostly galleon that illuminated the scene in monochrome clarity. Beyond the windows, a terrace; beyond the terrace, a garden. Nothing to frighten. Nothing to call her up out of bad dreams.

No source for the Filmore East Revisited light show, come to that.

The cat jumped up on the sill and thrust its furry face against her shoulder. Ruth stroked it absently. *Poor thing. It must be lonely. I wonder if—*

She jerked as if someone had shouted her name, and stood baffled the next moment, the cat in her arms. Nothing. No sound.

Something is going on, Ruth thought with grim certainty. But what?

If she were one of the peculiar natives of this place, Ruth had no doubt, she could simply whip out some highly enchanted mathom from her strait-waistcoat and thole the whole situation to the ultimate max. Hefting her handy crystal ball or notebook computer, she—

She was in a terrible mess because she didn't know the local rules, and it was about to get worse.

"Help me get out of this, Jonesey; there's a good moggie," Ruth whispered to her furry companion.

There it was again. The sensation that someone was shouting for her—someone in terrible danger. Only she didn't hear anything.

Any number of Ruth's acquaintances back in college would have been happy to suddenly manifest psychic powers at a juncture like this and be perfectly certain they knew what was going on, but Ruth was not so made. She liked her facts manifest and incontrovertible. Or at least visible.

She didn't hear anything, and she couldn't force herself to pretend that she did. And that stubbornness, Ruth realized with a sinking feeling, might very well be the death of her.

Or of someone else.

He was lucid enough, in his periods of lucidity, to know that they were infrequent and becoming rarer. He might as well have mounted the nightmare back at the Goblin Market and saved himself all of this. It wasn't as if there was anywhere for him to go, or anyone who could help him. Chandrakar was worlds away, and Melior had no allies here. He didn't even know where he was. Some forest. Broceliande. Avingnon. The Forest of the Night. The Wherewood. Somewhere.

His feet slipped on the muddy forest path, and Melior staggered, working desperately to keep his feet. Fall and he would never get up again.

He shook his head to clear it, and the pain washed his senses clear for a moment. And he realized that here, in this rain-damp autumn forest, he smelled flowers.

Flowers. A moment later, looking for them, he saw them; a garland of many-colored blossoms hanging on a post. A Gate-garland. Ruth had been wearing a Gate-garland in the Market.

A small eternity later he reached it; hewn wood, a gate, and on one gatepost a garland—

Melior lost his balance and fell against the wood, crushing his wounds against the planks and smearing the wood with his blood. He groaned, sliding to his knees. Only his grasp on the Sword kept him from falling on his face.

The horse was closer now. And he had no more flight left in him. He reached behind himself, and pounded weakly upon the gates. No matter whose dominion lay beyond them, entrance to it was better than death.

The gates didn't open.

Reason, sweet or otherwise, was a poor substitute for faith or intuition. Either of those could have told her what to do, but Ruth lacked them utterly, and all that Reason could do was grant her answers that were some sum total of information she already had.

GiGo. Garbage In, Garbage Out. Ruth paced the parlor in frustration. In here she was warm, safe, fed, and protected. Out there it was the middle of the night. It was cold. It could rain. The house might vanish the moment she was over the doorsill. There was nothing out there, no reason to go out there, nothing out there that she wanted, come to that.

But at last Ruth realized that the choice boiled down to this: be stupid or go mad. And with this paradigm defined, she picked up a fresh candle and headed for the front door.

Instantly the cat was underfoot, explaining loquaciously to Ruth that there were needs, urgent needs, feline needs that must be addressed upon the instant. Needs in favor of which Ruth's petty priorities must be set aside. Surely she could not abandon a cat, a small and lonely cat, in a large empty house in the woods, could she?

Yes.

"I'm sorry, moggie, I really am—and it's undoubtedly the wrong thing to do, and I can tell my own self I told me so, but I haven't got any choice, you know," Ruth told it. With gentle firmness she scooped it out of the way and opened the front door.

The night was still out there, black and chill. And it came to Ruth, with the blatant irresistibility of the Improving Homily at the end of some nineteenth-century Moral Tale, that she was turning her back upon Safety and Normalcy to forge off into Chaos and Uncertainty.

"Crap," muttered Ruth under her breath. She pulled the door carefully shut. She was going up to the gate, and then she was coming back— if she could. And then she was going to find the wine cellar and get royally drunk.

She was heartily kicking herself for even this much of an indulgence in hysteria by the time she got to the gate. The candle had blown out before she'd gotten two steps, she was just as cold as she'd expected, and the soft slippers had introduced her to every sharp flint pebble in the path.

But she ran the last few yards to the gate—almost, Ruth thought self-mockingly, as if she knew what she was going to find.

She peered over the top of the gates and then wrestled them open, dragging one wing inward. It grated on the flagstones, creaking in protest. She hadn't recalled it making so much noise the last time.

Melior lay upon the threshold, looking like a high Victorian knight back from a seven-year party at Elf Hill. His skin was pale and rain-soaked, and his lips were blue.

He didn't seem to be breathing.

"Melior? Mel?" Ruth's voice was an overwrought croak. *Oh, Jesus*—

There was the sound of a hoof striking against stone.

Ruth looked up and saw the pale horse, and abandoned Reason and Logic in a rush. The horse was Death, and if it reached Melior, he would die. It stepped forward slowly, neck stretched toward Ruth questioningly.

"Get away from him." Even at the time Ruth had difficulty believing it was her own voice. Fury and adrenaline banished cold, pain, and common sense. "Get away from him, you bitch."

Its head snapped up—almost as if she'd insulted it, Ruth thought, stifling a suicidal impulse to laugh. She paid no more attention to the nightmare; there was nothing she could really do to stop it, except, perhaps, get Melior through the gates. She grappled awkwardly with the dead weight of him, trying first for a grip under his arms and flinching back when her hands came away wet with blood.

The horse took another step. Ruth gritted her teeth and plunged her hands into the blood-soaked cloth, grabbing and dragging and pulling Melior's body in through the gate and down the gentle incline of the flagstoned path that led back to the house.

The moment she was through them the gates shut with a snap, as if spring-loaded. Ruth heard the clatter of the mare galloping off and drew a breath that sobbed with the force of her relief. Then she looked at Melior.

"Oh, God," said Ruth. "What a mess."

· 21 ·

The Fall Is All That Matters

AND SO, IN the end, the Lady Floire Jausserande of the Silver Silences was back once more where she had begun: upon the walls of Castle Dawnheart without the pleasant serenities of grace that had lapped her as little as a week before. Guiraut was dead, and the castle's lord, Rohannan Melior, was gone, and that he had not returned home again argued persuasively that he had found his wizard—the one who would bring him his human concubine at whatever price Melior was willing to pay.

Human.

The upwash of fury was as perilous and irresistible as the flames of a spring balefire. Jausserande yielded to it even as she recognized the danger. Coolness, unemotionalism, were the hallmarks of a good commander. Detachment was what saved your life in battle.

But there had been no battle, and still Guiraut was dead. Struck to stillness between one breath and the next, all his might-have-beens forever unriddled. Dead. There would be no knighthood, no Adepthood for Guiraut now. He had ridden out with his lady on a bright fall morning and human brigands had squandered his blood in the dust of the Vale of Stars.

And she, his lady, had stayed not to defend or avenge him, but, burdened with the *tainaiste*-Cup that could not be lost lest the Cup of Morning Shadows be lost with it, had run.

If she had possessed the true Cup, she could have saved Guiraut. The

Cup could cure. A formless murder coiled itself around Jausserande's heart, dark and subtle. The Cup could also kill.

The thought horrified her even while the fury whipped fire to ice and settled around her in seductively numbing armor. The outlaws who had killed Guiraut would die. Her Rohannan cousin was not here to stop her. She would hang their bodies in chains from the castle walls.

"First catch your coney," Jausserande whispered.

It could be done. She was Cupbearer and Treasurekeeper, even without the Treasure in her hands. When she gave orders, there were few in the land that would say her nay. What she willed would come to pass.

And was it so wrong, to sweep the land free of human wolves that preyed upon their betters and upon Melior's contented human sheep?

Yes, a last scrap of sanity protested.

But Guiraut had trusted her, and they had killed him—now, in the New Peace, when through all the long years of war Jausserande had not lost anyone she loved. But now she had, and the pain was unbearable. The only refuge left to her was in revenge.

The outlaws in the Vale would die. She would take them by whatever means she must, and see every one of them dead.

Jausserande took a deep breath, and felt cool clarity settle over her like a cloak once the decision was made. A pretty problem, this. How to proceed?

The villains were within the Vale of Stars. Magic did not work in that sacred precinct; violence was forbidden there. It did not matter that humankind broke that law. Elphenkind, bound by magic, could not.

Very well. She must drive them *out* of the Vale.

What drove out vermin?

"Fire," Jausserande said softly, and began to sing, quietly, under her breath.

His brain was on fire. Nic Brightlaw groped painfully back to consciousness, afraid of what he would find if he allowed himself to reach it.

But against all expectation, the fire behind his eyes was not a foretaste of crisped and suppurating limbs, shards of candied white bone spangling the earth, silvery loops of intestine uncased and garlanding the jungle trail—

He opened his eyes, horror within banishing horror without. And found himself alive, intact—not whole, but not the ruined meat-puppet of unimaginative memory.

He lay on his back in a woods. His clothes were shredded. Blood made a sticky mask of his face, and the scalp wound had opened again.

He rolled over; every muscle protested and the crusted gouges in his arm began to bleed again.

He'd fought a dragon and lived. Nic gritted his teeth and sat up. Unfortunately, so had the dragon—since, looking around himself, Nic could see nothing, anywhere, that even slightly resembled a dead dragon.

And that meant that it was alive and after Ruth.

He tried to tell himself that it wasn't his problem. He tried to tell himself that Ruth didn't look for him to protect her. He tried to tell himself that it was far too late; that Ruth was already dead anyway; that once upon a long time ago there had been people who'd looked to him for rescue, for loyalty, and that all of them were dead.

Swearing, he dragged himself to his feet. Bone bruises were a dull ache, mixed with the bright heat of torn muscles and the sick damaged sense of open wounds. The head injury, gotten a day or maybe three before, throbbed chillily with this fresh mistreatment. He tried to close the hand the dragon had savaged, and watched the fingers clamp painfully into a half-numb unresponsive claw as the blood dripped brightly down. Torn muscles, damaged nerves. Impairment.

There was no point to this. It didn't matter how long he'd been unconscious. Five minutes or an hour, the dragon already had Ruth. There was no point. This wasn't his problem. This wasn't his fight. His war was over more than fifteen years before.

Ruth hadn't even wanted him here.

Nic drew a breath and found the strength to laugh. Don Quixote of the poisoned lance; he knew what he was going to do. There was no point in trying to bargain his way out of it. He was going to find Ruth if he could, save her if he could. And if he couldn't, he was going to kill her killer.

Or die trying.

Starting now.

"Courage, Miss Marlowe," Nic murmured. "One rather shopworn white knight, on his way."

The wood bordering the Vale of Stars was a ghostly monochrome in the dawn light. Fox's outlaws moved silently through their camp, gathering up their weapons: bows, staves, here and there a salvaged lance or sword.

This morning of all mornings there were no fires to warm them. Better cold comfort than the risk of attracting unwanted attention here while they were most vulnerable.

And later?

Fox looked around at his men, wondering which of them would be dead by noon. He saw them watching his expression for some sign and smiled, as approvingly as if he thought they'd all live forever. Their tension relaxed, and Fox continued moving among them, making the last minute plans that would take them all to the Harvest Home by routes that would let them merge with the travelers, unremarked-upon.

One last time he coached Raven and Yarrow, his lieutenants, on what they must do and where they must go.

"Once you've got the horses, don't wait for me. You got that? Don't wait for anybody outside your group. Keep them together, keep track of them—and get out when you've got what you came for."

Yarrow was a tall sandy man missing both ears; a bit quicker than Raven to see the ways of the world, but too easily discouraged.

"And what if you don't come back?" Yarrow said.

Fox sighed inwardly. In the old days, he'd never needed to look at people and measure their capacities as if they held a list of ingredients for his recipe. Now things were different.

"If I don't come back, Yarrow, you and Raven will have to make up your minds what to do." Hopeless, when centuries of slavery had buried the human capacity for self-determination beyond Fox's ability to retrieve it.

"But I'll be back. You can bet on that." And if he didn't come back, he'd be dead, and would hardly be in any position to concern himself with broken promises.

Raven smiled brilliantly. "And if you don't come back, we'll rescue you."

Two chances of that. Slim and none. "Sure," Fox said.

He didn't like the way he felt; this treacherous sense of obligation and responsibility. But he didn't like most things in his life since the moment he'd first set eyes on Rohannan Melior, and for this thing, too, Melior was responsible.

"Come on, guys. Let's move out. Nobody wants to live forever," Fox the Outlaw said.

Jausserande had hoped, superstitiously, that Melior would return for the Harvest Home. She'd sat awake all night in his solar, watching the road that led up to the castle as intently as if it held her last hope of salvation. Watching, and not seeing him. Beyond the walls, in the Water Meadow, the circling sparks of torches told of midnight arrivals and late construction on the booths and dancing floors of the Harvest Home. Tomorrow, outliers from every corner of Melior's fee-lands would come to the Home, bearing samples of the harvest, the *teind* they paid to Line Rohannan. And Melior would not be here to receive it.

Nor, Jausserande realized with tardy dread, was Melior here to go to the Twilight Court to be confirmed by the Seven Houses as The Rohannan of Line Rohannan. It was custom that named him head of his Line as his father's inheritance, not law.

And the Peace had only ended the war, it had not healed the divisions among the Seven Houses of the Twilight. There would be those who would argue against Melior's accession for spite or advantage. Melior *must* be at the Twilight Court to speak for himself, else he would lose the guardianship of Line Rohannan to another.

He had known all that, and stil he had gone to seek the wizard and be taken out of Time. For what?

Not for the mud-born, daughter of Earth. He had come back once without Heruthane—Ruth—and had not gone after her again. No, he had sent messengers, and mere common sense argued that now, when the stakes were so much higher and the penalty for absence so much more great, Melior would send messengers again, with gifts if needful, to the wizard whose assistance he desired to court.

Jausserande swung herself to her feet. Seven paces to the window, where the High Road gleamed white in the moonlight. Nine paces from that to the wall where Melior's Treasure, the Sword of Maiden's Tears, hung when its master was in residence. The empty pegs were black punctuation to the pale stone. Jausserande slapped the wall in pure frustration; the sound was muffled and flat.

He had gone for something more important to him than Ruth.

Jausserande stood in the middle of Melior's solar, the pale dawn light crowding around her like the enemy host. She must see Lady Vuissane at once. Perhaps she—

"So there you are."

Jausserande whirled to face this new threat. It was the human knight out of her dream, still dressed in his bizarre black-and-green armor, but even as she registered that, she understood that he was not here at all. An aftereffect of Vuissane's potion, or some baffling weight of futurity pressing its shadows into the real world.

"Who are you?" Jausserande said tightly.

"I'm nobody: who are you?" He smiled; teeth dazzling white against skin burned brown by the sun in human fashion. His eyes were cold as winter glass.

"Why are you here?" Jausserande persisted.

"You're supposed to be the ones so familiar with the unseen world, lady. I'm here because you keep calling me. You need me. Without me, you can't get the Cup."

Lies and illusion, Jausserande told herself firmly. *"I* need? And what do you need?"

"A windmill," the phantom answered maddeningly. "I need some tilting practice. A windmill will do."

Jausserande felt the anger take her, making her voice and movements abrupt and precise. So the *inconnu* wanted windmills, did he? When she found him in the flesh, she would chain him in a mill until he was sick of it. Sick to death. She took a step toward him, saw his smile widen with maddening mockery—

And then it was full day, the light of two hours past sunrise streaming in through the windows, and Dawnheart's steward stood where the apparition had been, holding a tray laden with morning bread and beer.

"A good day for fairing, Lady Jausserande," Arnaut suggested.

Jausserande blinked, the thoughts and visions of the night sliding and jumbling around each other until they were battered to fragments. She forced a smile, though she felt more like screaming.

"A good day, indeed," she answered, and every instinct told her that she lied.

She spoke with Arnaut a few moments more; small politenesses, forgotten as they were spoken. He was barely gone when she, too, left the chamber.

In her tower room, Jausserande dressed to go a-fairing. Perhaps her answers were there. At any rate, going to the fair would take her away from Dawnheart, with all its reminders of unkept promises. But the clothes she selected from her clothespress were not the garments of a young lady of fortune bent upon dalliance.

The doeskin trousers were soft and gray, molding to her skin like supple armor. She selected, and rejected, several pairs of boots before settling upon a high-cuffed pair in dark shagreen leather, broad-toed and low heeled and hobnailed for far journeying. The undertunic she chose was soft cream linen; nothing white to draw the eye; and over it a tunic of wool sheared black from the ram, a darker gray than her trousers. She pulled the laces at the neck tight and then let the ends dangle upon her chest.

The belt was the only touch of luxury to her outfit, buttery black leather studded with chased and enameled silver plates depicting ancient victories, its silver rings ready to hold a purse and dagger. Jausserande took neither: Lady Jausserande of Line Floire, Cupbearer and Treasurekeeper, would need neither to show coin nor defend herself at the Harvest Home. She picked up her cap from the windowsill and set it on her head. Soft dark leather, low and flat, and at one corner brooched with a red-eyed silver raven.

The badge of Rohannan's Ravens. Who had never left one of their own to the enemy—dead or alive. Who had never been defeated in battle. She had kept this one piece after all the rest of her battle livery was gone. As she turned to go, she caught sight of herself in the mirror.

Where am I going and what do I seek? Jausserande asked her mirror. The image seemed almost about to speak, but Jausserande did not know what to say.

And if she could step through that mirror into the time before the New Peace, would she?

Jausserande turned and hurried from the room.

The Harvest Home was all that anyone could ask of it. Memories of childhood walked with Jausserande here, and she bought that imagined child fried cakes spangled in sugar and hair ribbons stamped with silver foil stars. But even the horse lines could not hold her attention for long; the animals were sleek and powerful, but Jausserande had no cavalry troop to buy for.

It was then that she saw him.

There were humans everywhere at the Fair. That was understandable; the Home was one of the few places where the Sons of the Morning and their human vassals mingled freely. Humans came to sell. Elphenkind came to buy. This was as it had been all the autumns of Jausserande's life.

This year was different.

This human was different.

He was tall and gaunt, dressed in worn clothes and a hooded tunic. When he glanced in her direction, Jausserande saw pale sandy hair and pale eyes; an expression that made her think of a yellow dog kicked once too often. And when he turned away, a madcap flirt of autumn wind blew his cowl back and revealed the pale hair lying smooth and unimpeded along the sides of his head. He scrambled to pull the hood forward again, concealing his shame.

Both ears docked, Jausserande noted automatically. *Thieving.*

And as she began to wonder what fool had let such a man leave his master's lands to travel to the Fair, she saw the others.

They were not together, not taking overmuch notice of one another, but each one had the same air of subtle wrongness as Crop-Ears did.

Petty prigs, Jausserande thought, but even as she tried to convince herself, Jausserande's steps were taking her back toward Dawnheart and the guard barracks. Despite all law, custom, and the Harvest Truce, one of the outlaw bands that plagued Chandrakar in such numbers since the war had come to Rohannan's Harvest Home.

* * *

Dawnheart's main gate was closed, its master being absent and its steward a prudent man. Jausserande went in by the narrow postern gate.

Outer court. Inner court. The doors to the Great Hall were barred, and rather than summon someone to open them, she took a shortcut; up the outside stair to the second-floor gallery open to the air. The wall had a wooden walk behind it for archers to shoot from. Jausserande ran along the top.

Dawnheart had five towers set into its eighteen-foot-thick outer wall. In this time of peace, several of them were connected to the buildings of the inner castle by high-slung suspension bridges of ropes and planks, swaying and delicate. Jausserande found the one she sought and plunged down it without hesitation, her hobnailed boots catching and chattering on the smooth planks. The door at the far end was open to the warmth of early autumn. Jausserande lunged inside.

Nothing and no one. Nearly everyone was at the Fair, another reason to keep Dawnheart shut up so tight, that it could be guarded lightly, releasing its soldiers to their pleasures. But Richart, Captain of the Guard, should be here. She scanned the room, saw the down-flung quill spattering its ink across a curling sheet of vellum. Richart had left in a hurry.

She could not waste the time to find him. In the middle of the suspension bridge she looked out toward the Fair, and through the lazy curling of blue smoke she saw the flash and flicker of pikes and helmets. Richart did not need to be warned. Richart was at the Fair already.

The Harvest Truce was broken.

Melior was right! was her first outraged thought. But right about what, she could not say; all that Melior feared was Baligant No-House, and if the High Prince was bent on murder, he was hardly fool enough to tip his hand at a simple Harvest Home on Rohannan lands.

Across the bridge and down the wall. Back along the gallery, and this time her path took her along the hall and through the solar, the quickest shortcut to her tower room and weapons.

In the middle of the room she stopped, as abruptly as if the air before her had become stone.

Someone had been here.

She turned in a circle, looking around. The books on her cousin's desk had been moved. There were papers strewn around that she did not remember seeing. The bread and ale left for her this morning by Arnaut and left, by her, untouched, were half-eaten.

"Looking for me?" a voice said lazily.

Jausserande turned, scrabbling at her belt for the dagger she was not wearing.

The speaker stepped from behind a pillar. It was a man, blond as in her vision, but not that man at all. That one was an immovable barrier. This man was a stiletto, to break all locks.

"Or just looking around?" he went on. His hair was as long as any elf's, caught back with a leather thong to fall in a silky whip down his back, and he was dressed in the same shabby leathers as the outlaws she'd seen at the Fair. In his left hand he held a stout staff several inches taller than he was.

On his right hand was Melior's ring.

It flared with magic in the dim light of the room. This was how this outlaw had bypassed all the castle defenses; the magical traps and wards that should have alerted the guards and kept him out. Melior's signet. The signet of Baron Rohannan.

Was this why Melior had not returned?

"You are a dead man," Jausserande told him. But incredibly, he did not seem afraid.

"Watch me shake. You're Jausserande, right?" He took a step toward her, and Jausserande's sight was drawn toward the flicker in his right hand. A knife with a gray blade, darker than silver and somehow harder. Iron. *Iron.*

"Lord Arnaut!" Jausserande raised her voice in imperious summons, and the intruder smiled.

"He's a little busy right now. Somebody seems to have set a fire in the granary."

"A fitting place for rats—and mice. Run along, little mouse, and perhaps you can still escape," Jausserande said scornfully, but it was a bluff, and he seemed to know it.

"Maybe you can answer something that's been keeping me up nights. How come you didn't go back after your buddy on the Vale Road?" He took another step.

Jausserande had retreated from the iron that would burn her before the sense of his words penetrated. The Vale Road.

He was the one who had killed Guiraut.

Red murder filled Jausserande's vision, driving out tactical thought and making it hard to breathe. Her eyes flicked left and right, searching the room for a weapon.

"And while you're answering questions, Tinkerbelle, where's Mel and his patented glow-in-the-dark Magic Sword? I'm taking up a collection."

Jausserande turned and ran, for as many steps as it took her to reach the hearth and the display of hunting weapons mounted above it. She yanked down the first that came to her hand. A boar-spear.

"Oh, very good, Tinkerbelle," the intruder sneered.

She grounded the butt of the spear and menaced him with the fire-hardened point. "Tell me your name, before you die."

"Call me Fox. But I'm not going to die." The smile on Fox's face widened, and became a burning, predatory thing. "And neither are you. Which is too bad—at least you're going to think so."

And then he lunged forward, knocking the point of the spear aside with his staff and lashing at her with the deadly iron blade. Jausserande leaped backward, barely far enough. The blade touched the sleeve of her tunic and the fabric began to spark and flare as the small magics in the weave guttered and died. She shifted her grip backward on her chosen weapon, trying to find the balance point that would let her lift and swing it. She backpedaled, lifting the spear barely in time to ward off a blow from Fox's staff.

"Historically," Fox remarked, "oppressed groups have not been allowed access to state-of-the-art military technology—in your case, Tink, swords and spears. Big deal."

The staff struck the heavier spear and bounced off, spinning in Fox's hands to strike again. Jausserande was barely fast enough to convert a blow meant to cripple to one that was only glancing. But even that glancing blow was enough to send bolts of tingling numbness down her arm.

"And also historically," Fox went on genially, his predator's smile wider now. "The oppressed people have managed to develop a pretty effective martial technology out of leftovers. Prepare to lose big time, elf bitch."

He struck, but Jausserande was not there. The spear clattered to the floor as she dropped it, and she sprang backward, gaining the refuge of a tabletop.

"I have not lost yet," Jausserande said, hefting a candlestick. "And you talk too much, Fox."

"Yeah, probably," Fox said. And threw the knife.

He aimed for none of the possible targets where a throw meant to disable could miss, and kill. The point of the iron hunting knife he carried sank into the meat of Jausserande's leg a little above the knee, sliding home as if it entered water, not flesh.

It felt to Jausserande as if every nerve in her body had been dipped in acid. She smelled the stink of her burning flesh in the moment before the pain hit, and as she drew breath to speak, the shock of raw agony slammed an iron vise around her lungs and throat, staggering her heart in its rhythm and blotting out every sensation except the pain. She did not feel herself fall from the table to the floor, nor hear the hard wooden sound of her solid impact. And when Fox turned her over and yanked the knife out of her leg, the blessed cessation of pain brought dreamless oblivion, and she did not hear the bitter sound of Fox's cursing.

· 22 ·

The Manor of Roses

IT WAS WET, it was raining, she was kneeling in the mud over the bloody, dying body of a man who was not only her hopeful lover but a dead weight she could not possibly drag to true safety.

Ruth Marlowe had had better days.

"Melior," Ruth whispered under her breath. "Oh, God damn it to hell."

Rohannan Melior did not respond. He lay on his back in the road, wearing a gaudy fantastic scaled cloak the hot urgent color of monarch butterfly wings and holding the Sword of Maiden's Tears as if it were a walking stick. His face was pale as a beeswax casting; as still as if he slept.

And this would be a moment of high Victorian tragedy, except for the fact that Ruth's knees hurt from the gravel and her fingers ached with cold. The rain plastered her hair to her scalp and made it hang down her cheeks and back like dripping snake-locks, and there were urgent things to be done and no form of aid forthcoming anywhere.

But she could not simply let her lover die due to lack of imagination. The house held warmth and safety and a promise of life. If they could reach it.

If it would let them in.

Ruth rose stiffly to her feet and looked back the way she had come. The house was dark, and after a moment she realized she could not see the expected lights through the windows: the lights that had been burning when she left. Ruth set her jaw stubbornly. She would *make* the house let her in.

She turned back to Melior. The icy soaking rain still pocked noisily on the cobbled path around them. The edge of the forest still loomed just beyond the gate. The lantern at the gate still burned; light enough to show Ruth her lover. One hand was still clutched tightly around the hilt of the Sword of Maiden's Tears. The other flexed feebly against the ground.

"Melior?" Ruth said quaveringly.

His eyes opened when she spoke. He saw her and smiled, an effortful redrawing of the lines of pain in his face.

"Don't try to talk," Ruth said hurriedly. "There's a house, I—"

He was already trying to get up, eyes closed against the pain. Ruth saw what he was doing and put her hands under his arms and pulled back and up, trying to get him on his feet.

He was taller than she was and heavy; the strain sent needles of warning pain down the long muscles in her back. But if she dropped him now, she would hurt him worse; Ruth clung to that thought just as Melior clung to her, grimly dragging them both upright. The point of the Sword grated along the cobbles as he dragged it, point first, to serve as a prop for his weight.

His clothes were soaked with blood and rain; the sodden front of his tunic was pressed against her, soaking the robe she wore and beginning to drip. She felt no warmth from his body; cold, sodden, and chill, he was a faery knight dragged from a watery grave, a burning brand bare in his hand. The strain of holding him upright was a tight fiery ache in her neck and shoulders, and ran quicksilver wires of strain down her back and leg muscles.

You're babbling, Marlowe. Get the lead out.

"Melior." She spoke his name loudly, willing him to attend. "Put the Sword away. Put it away, okay?"

She didn't know if he heard, but she knew that the touch of the Sword of Maiden's Tears would do worse than kill a human. She didn't need lamplight to see it; it glowed with a faint rotten phosphorescence—witch-fire and marsh gas; poison.

But he wouldn't leave it behind, and she didn't dare drag him toward the house while he clutched it naked in his hand.

"Melior!"

He heard her at last; with awkward, laborious grace he lifted the blade and slid it into its sheath. Deprived of its support he leaned even more heavily on Ruth; she felt her knees begin to buckle as he clutched at her again.

She felt her muscles begin to tremble as she forced her legs straight. She had to get him to shelter or he'd die. To do that, all she had to do was walk there. With him.

She took one hand from beneath his arm and tried to unlock his hand enough to turn him. Finally he released his bruising death grip on her shoulder, only to transfer it to her hand, so that for one moment they stood poised like demented dancers in the rain. Slowly Ruth turned, moving with agonizing care, so that they stood side by side. Melior seemed to understand what she was doing; he let go of her and slid his arm across her shoulders, transferring his weight to that new support. With his other hand he clutched her arm. The fingers dug in cruelly, bringing first pain, then numbness, then, finally, a chill, bone-deep ache.

I can't move. The realization almost made Ruth laugh out loud, and only the fact that she would fall if she did stopped her. It was all she could do to stand supporting Melior's weight. Walking was impossible.

"Walking isn't impossible, Ruth. It's just going to be hard to learn."

A woman in white. The first of many days of mindbending frustration and pain. But she'd learned. Ruth Marlowe had learned to walk once before. She could walk now.

First one step. She unbalanced them so that she could move. Heard Melior groan as his weight shifted. Slid her foot forward quickly. Caught her weight on that hip-knee-leg, and felt the muscles quiver and burn with strain.

A step.

Then another step. Legs heavy and aching and unresponsive, it was just like learning to walk again, wasn't it?

If she tore a muscle, if she hurt herself too badly, if she fell, it would be all over and Melior would be here, helpless, with no one to see if he lived or died.

A step. Then another step. Her feet pressed against the ground with more than twice her normal weight, and every sharp stone in her path was a possible assassin. But now the door was only a few yards away.

Locked and dark.

Unheeded tears ran down her face, mixing with rain and sweat. And Ruth, beginning to plea bargain with Fate in a rote litany of empty extravagant promises, stopped short with the chill certainty that here, in this place, words had meaning. What promises she made, she would be held to.

"Oh, please let us in," Ruth said very softly to the dark and shuttered house. Her words came in breathy staccato gasps of air drawn into lungs aching and strained with effort. "I don't have a kingdom and I won't marry some stranger and I won't work for a wizard for seven years." *I'm losing my mind.* "But there must be something you want. I promise to help—as much as I can and if it doesn't hurt anybody else. That's enough, isn't it? Please, please, oh, please—"

She was almost to the doorstep, and knew, with a soul-dead certainty, that she could not take the step that would lift Melior over the threshold. The door swung inward. Faint and low on the wall inside Ruth could see the shifting glow of a chamberstick. In the open doorway the marmalade cat stood, looking up at Ruth accusingly.

Ruth opened her mouth to say something more, but all she could do was gasp for air with a ratcheting bellows sound. She had carried Melior perhaps a hundred yards, if that.

The door opened wider, and Ruth, determined to the point of madness, found the strength to drag herself up the one low step, and Melior after, and then pivot, swinging him around her and into the sure support of the door frame.

He slammed into it harder than she'd meant, and cried out as if the impact hurt him terribly. And then his knees buckled and he began to sink to the rain-wet threshold, and Ruth, all passion spent, slid down with him, unwilling to let go. Together they lay in the doorway, spent and shaking.

She must shut the door. The thought occurred to Ruth in a vague detached fashion. Melior's head was pressed firmly into the hollow between her neck and shoulder, and she was rain-chilled on one side and only slightly less cold on the other. The stiff immense sodden weight of Melior's cloak hung about them like a tent; Ruth smelled wet fur and leather and cinnamon, and even the trembling quivering aches of her shaking body were remote and forgettable. How pleasant to simply stay here until someone else solved all her problems for her.

There was a pat-pat-pat of a velvet paw against her face, and an outraged miaowing, as of a cat forced to stand in a cold and drafty hall when a warm fire was available.

Reluctantly Ruth opened her eyes and stared into the yellow eyes of the marmalade cat.

"I'm coming, I'm coming," she muttered hoarsely.

She crawled out from under Melior. Freed of her support, he slid the rest of the way down the doorjamb to sprawl on the stoop like an unstrung puppet. Ruth surveyed him for a moment and then grabbed him by the tunic and dragged him forward until his entire body was inside the house.

The latch was a carved wooden peg; she latched the door and slid the bolt home.

Now that Ruth was indoors again and safe, all the nagging annoyance of being cold and wet and dirty returned with full insistent force. Angrily she pushed the thoughts away and turned back to Melior.

In the shadows of the hall it was difficult to see how badly Melior was hurt, but she could smell his blood. She took the chamberstick and lit the hall lamps; in the pale candlelight, Ruth saw the outline of bones stark beneath his skin, the pale eyelashes wet and spiky and gilded with flame.

The cat wove back and forth around Ruth's feet, looking up at her with feline opacity and singing a constant chantpleure of its needs and injuries.

"Oh, do be quiet, there's a good moggie," Ruth pleaded, and knelt beside Melior.

His eyes had opened, and his gaze was fixed, not on her, but upon the marmalade cat.

"I cry your pardon, Lord," Melior said, his voice thin and effortful. "I would not have come here had I known. But Ruth is my lady," he added, almost apologetically.

"Melior," Ruth said. He reached up and took her hand with fingers that were cold and trembling, then he closed his eyes again as if he had exhausted all his strength.

Ruth bit back a yelp of tearful laughter. His hand went slack in hers, and she laid it down gently. Her chest ached, and there was a lump in her throat that made it difficult to breathe. If this was love, she'd take a good book instead, thank you very much.

Because if Melior died, she couldn't bear it. And she didn't think there was anything she could do to prevent it. The realization made her hands shake even harder, and the tightness in her throat expanded in a burning, strangling ache.

"Mir-*RAO!*" The cat of the house was tired of being ignored. It sat on the newel post and wailed. Ruth jumped, and stared up at it guiltily before seeing what lay beyond it.

The parlor door was open.

Not the Parlor where Ruth had eaten her dinner, but the small one in the front hall that she had examined and dismissed; an odd unlikely room, useful mostly for spying upon the dooryard. Ruth got up and peered inside.

There was a roaring fire in the small fireplace. The heat tightened Ruth's skin and made her numb hands ache with returning life. There was a pallet of canvas-covered straw laid out beside the fire, and a pile of blankets beside, and on a nearby stool draped with a white cloth there were bandage rolls, lint, and cord, knives and probes and forceps. There was a squat green bottle of brandy and a wide copper basin of water.

"Thank you," Ruth whispered, tears prickling her eyes. She turned back to Melior. Warmth, and life, and everything else he lacked, only a few steps away. *"What d'ye lack?"* echoed the ghostly remembered voice of the redheaded vendor at the Goblin Market. If Melior died, Ruth would lack everything. Forever.

But she could help him live.

All she had to do was get him into the room.

"Only a little more," Ruth promised. She undid the beautiful jeweled clasps that held the golden cloak close about his throat and dragged him free of it, toward the safety and haven of the small front room. There was a rasping sound as the scabbarded Sword was pulled across the floor, but she did not stop until Melior lay upon the blankets in front of the fire.

In the bright hot light she could clearly see Melior's injuries at last; the slashes that crossed his leg and torso; the torn leathers and the ruined flesh beneath. Bile rose in her throat and she swallowed hard. But the bleeding seemed to have stopped, or slowed down at least, and if she could only get him warm and dry—

First she had to get the Sword away from him.

In a world not this, Ruth, whose hobby was costuming, had once had the opportunity of a long and detailed acquaintance with Melior's clothes. The straps and buckles were not unfamiliar to her now, and soon she had uncased him of belt and baldric. She unbuckled the high horseman's boots with their tassels and gilded spurs and pulled them off, and then eased the leather straps of the sword harness from beneath him until he no longer lay upon them.

To move them any further she would have to touch the Sword.

"No, no, no . . ." Ruth whimpered. It wasn't fair; she was willing to do anything else.

Anything but that.

Once there had been five friends: Ruth and Michael and Philip and Naomi and Jane. And they'd rescued an elf named Rohannan Melior, who told them his magic sword—the Sword of Maiden's Tears—would do worse than kill any human who touched it. The Sword would turn that human into a *grendel*, a mindless cannibal who lived only to kill, who could only be killed by the Sword. And Naomi had taken up the Sword. . . .

She stood in a tunnel far below the city, bleeding and gore-spattered, resting the tip of the Sword of Maiden's Tears upon the platform floor, the body of the slain grendel *liquifying at her feet.*

The last grendel.

Ruth ran toward her.

"Get back!" Naomi whirled around to face her, holding the sword en garde as if it were weightless. Drops of liquid flew from the spinning blade. Her voice was high, her eyes wide and mad.

"You can't have it!" Naomi shrieked.

Ruth stopped dead.
"Naomi!" Ruth said. "Don't do—"
"What you know damn well is the only thing I can do, now?" Naomi's
voice was ragged; her breathing faster now than even exertion had made it.
"God dammit, Ruth." The words were evenly spaced, inflectionless. "Melior
was right. The sword wants—" She broke off. Ruth could see sweat trickling
down Naomi's face, her teeth bared in a grimace of effort. "Get out of here.
Go on."

Naomi had taken up the Sword. And died for it.

There was a poker by the fireplace. Ruth shoved at the Sword with it
until it was safely on the other side of the room. She threw Melior's boots
after the Sword and then crouched beside him, clutching the poker.

But she didn't have time for this now. She turned back to Melior. His
eyes were open again; she smoothed his hair back from his forehead with
a hand that trembled only a little.

"Everything's going to be fine," Ruth said.

"And so it is," said Melior, his voice a bare whisper, "I have rescued
you, my lady Ruth. There is nothing to fear." The corner of his mouth
quirked upward in a wry smile. "It is cold here," he added, in a tone of
faint apology.

Cold? In front of a fire that baked Ruth's skin like custard and filled
the room with the wet scent of stewed wool? Ruth lunged for the pile of
blankets that lay beside the pallet and flung several of them over him. She
remembered the brandy and uncorked it. There was no cup, but then she
remembered the cup in the bag on her belt and pulled it out, filling it and
holding Melior up to it to drink.

He drained it as if it were water. "Again," he said, and Ruth refilled
it. "Better," he said, when it was empty again. She laid him down and
sighed deeply, still holding her hand.

"There is so much to tell you," Melior said. Then his eyes closed, and
he was unconscious again.

Ruth studied him with desperate attention.

His skin was pale, but it had always been pale. His hair was drying
now in the furnace heat of the fire; Ruth smoothed his hair back; his skin
was chill and clammy.

Was he healing? Dying? And if he was dying, what could she do?
Ruth remembered the pale nightmare in the forest outside and shuddered. The nightmare would not have Melior.

If she could help it.

The only thing she could think of to do was to get his wet clothes off
and bandage his bleeding wounds. And then—

What? Blood transfusion? Amputation? Antibiotics she didn't have?

She couldn't imagine the extent of his injuries and had less idea of how to treat them. But she had to do something.

"You're going to be all right," Ruth said, wishing it were true. Then she set to work.

There didn't seem to be any place here for false modesty, but even so it was difficult in a purely practical sense, working with her hands beneath the sheltering blankets to remove tunic, mail shirt, jerkin, and undertunic—all sodden—without hurting him further. Melior stirred and muttered as she shifted him, and Ruth recognized at last that this was not healthy sleep, but feverish delirium.

Why? He was wounded, not sick. And it was only a few hours since she'd seen him at the Market—there hadn't been time for infection to spread.

She worked the soaked woolen tunic up under his arms at last and tossed it into a corner. The mail shirt beneath was a fine-woven silvery thing, but crumbling and discolored in places, as though—

Ruth dropped the blankets back over Melior and grabbed the tunic. It dripped as she shook it out and held it up. The gapes she'd thought were cuts were *burns*—something had eaten through it.

A horrible realization spread through Ruth's mind. She turned back to Melior. Where the silvery mail had been splashed, it was flaking and black, and she brushed metal ashes aside to expose rotting leather beneath.

She dithered for a moment before she used the knife to cut the leather thongs that bound the mail shirt closed and worked it off Melior's body. He stirred and muttered, but whatever he said wasn't in English. A ring with an orange-red stone gleamed on his left hand, brilliant and out of place. Magic. She left it alone.

The leather jerkin beneath the mail had been white once; now it was soaked, rotting away where the monster's poison had spilled on it. It was a tighter fit than the tunic and harder to remove; Ruth worked carefully to keep the rotted places in it from touching either Melior's skin or her own. Beneath it, the linen undertunic was yellowed and burnt, and even the skin underneath was faintly reddened. Ruth pulled the blankets down to Melior's waist to sponge him clean of the last possible traces of poison before swaddling him in blankets again. He shivered beneath them as though neither the blankets nor the fire were there.

"Oh, God," Ruth muttered under her breath. "Oh, God, oh, God—"

But the worst injuries were below the waist, where the armor did not cover him. The doeskin of his breeches was glued to his skin by the blood of reopened wounds, and she had to sponge, and cut, and sponge again, before she could peel them off.

But once she had, she could see the injuries Melior was dying of.
Whatever had wounded him had struck up from below. It had dug a
deep gouge above his left knee before ripping free to slice a shallower
trench across the front of the thigh and then, at last, to score a dark welt
across the top of his right hipbone where the mail did not protect him.
The splashes that corroded his mail followed the same trajectory, as if
Rohannan Melior had been attacked by some mad mix of bayonet and
acid-gun.

No. It was no use pretending she did not know what had made these
wounds. Memory of the monster she had glimpsed at the Goblin Market
made her shudder. It had looked like a giant wasp.

And a wasp's stings were poison.

Panicked hopelessness sluiced through her veins like ice water. If he
was poisoned, he was going to die.

No. There was a chance. People survived wasp stings and even snake-
bites without medical intervention. If she could just keep him warm and
safe . . .

The water in the basin was too bloody now to be of any use and her
neck and back were a screaming knot of tension, demanding release.
Ruth covered the exposed gashes with a square of bandage, then stood
up. She could not think of anything else to do; it should be safe to leave
him for a while. She stretched her cramped muscles gratefully.

She looked down at the basin. She needed somewhere to dump and
refill it. She stood, and picked up the basin of bloody water and went out
into the hallway again.

The cat was still sitting on the banister.

"Any suggestions?" Ruth asked it. Melior had spoken to it as if to an
equal, but Ruth was too tired to manage more than simple politeness.
That must have been sufficient, because the cat trotted off down the hall
in a purposeful way, tail up and glancing back at her. Ruth followed,
carrying the basin gingerly.

So this is the kitchen, Ruth said to herself a few moments later.

It looked like most English kitchens before 1750; a low room with
small windows high in the walls; a hearth big enough to hold a whole
roast ox and encumbered with a number of hooks and swivels that Ruth
realized were bronze, not iron; a table or two in the middle of the floor
and a whole catalog of hulking, unidentifiable furniture along the walls.

She located the back door and emptied the contents of the basin out
it in a great watery crimson arc. The bloody water spattered on the stones
of the walkway, and it was a shock to see, in addition to a well-tended
kitchen garden, that the rain had stopped and the sky was lightening.
Dawn.

The cat strolled in and out of the open doorway, looking up at her as if anxious she should approve the place. Ruth looked over her shoulder into the kitchen, worrying her lip in indecision. She didn't want to take anything from the house that wasn't freely given, but she needed water, water in quantity, and preferably hot. Finally she shut the bottom half of the door and went in search.

One of the cupboards Ruth opened held food. A half-cut wheel of yellow cheese, a bowl of white butter, a loaf and a cut loaf of bread, and a crock of milk.

Habit alone made her think of eating. Common sense and a lifetime of reading fairy tales was stronger. But the cat was winding around her ankles, prrt-ing and miouwrling just as if it were any kitchen cat, any cat that had never been fed in this or any other lifetime, and so she went and got a dish from one of the other cupboards and filled it from the crock. She set it down on the floor and the cat immediately deserted her, lapping at the milk and purring loudly.

Ruth continued her search. If she could just find one of those jerricans that had appeared at her bath, it would be practically perfect for what she wanted.

She located one eventually, and ten minutes of excruciating exercise with the pump enabled her to fill it. Every single one of her strained, abused, and exhausted muscles objected to their treatment, and once she'd filled the can, it was nearly too heavy for her to carry. But she managed to bring both it and the empty basin back to the room where Melior lay.

He'd thrown off the blankets. Ruth set down the can and basin hastily and hurried over to him. He thrashed back and forth, defending himself against some absent enemy, his eyes wide and unseeing. Blood soaked the cotton pad and spilled down his leg, soaking the pallet beneath him, a richer red than human blood. Ruth put her hands on his shoulders, trying to push him back down to the bed.

She hissed in pain as his fingers clamped on her arm, finding old bruises with unerring accuracy. She'd forgotten how strong Melior was. He struggled against her, and even leaning all her weight against him, she could not get him to lie still.

"Stop it!" Ruth cried in frustration. She would gladly have shaken him, if she could only get free to do it. At last she simply lay across his chest, trapping his body wit her own. He struggled against her for a few moments more, then subsided.

Ruth rose awkwardly off him and replaced the blankets, sopping up the oozing blood as best she could. It didn't seem possible that one person could contain that much blood, but on the other hand, look how much tea a teacup could be found to have contained once you spilled it. . . .

The sun was rising now, and the little room was filling with daylight. Ruth looked down at what she was wearing; the robe that had been so pretty when she put it on the night before; it was draggled with mud and blood, and still damp from the rain. She exhaled and closed her eyes, a weariness great enough to bring tears to her eyes dragging at her very bones. She felt like a swimmer, pushed beyond her strength, in that last moment before the ocean closed over her head forever. A small traitorous part of her mind assured her that no blame could come to her if Melior died, and then she could stay here forever, *free.* . . .

No.

She turned back to the doorway and picked up the can and basin. She found the hook in the fireplace that instinct had told her must be there, and hung the can on it to warm the water. While she waited, she retrieved the brandy bottle and the tin cup from the Market. She poured it half-full of brandy and raised it toward her lips, glancing down into it as she did.

The cup was filled with cool blue streamers of glowing light, coiling into the depths of the brandy, swirling down and down, as if she stared into a tiny holographic maelstrom.

Ruth was tired and her reactions were slow, or else she would simply have dropped the cup. But as it was, she only quivered slightly, staring into the liquid. The fire seemed to drift out of the walls of the cup. It spiraled into the dark red brandy, turning it a rich, luscious, impossible purple. It might be a trick of the light, but now, dazed, half dizzy with the need for sleep, Ruth thought she recognized the faint unnaturalness of magic.

The cup was magic.

Whatever this was, it did not bring the instant lightning revulsion that the magic ring she had taken from the outlaw did. Good magic, then, if there was such a thing.

But what did it *do?* Other than make brandy change colors and glow in the dark? Hesitantly she dipped a finger into the brandy and licked it dry. She felt no different, tasted no strangeness.

Recklessly, Ruth belted back a healthy mouthful of the brandy. Then she blinked once, very slowly, in astonishment.

It was like drinking sleep. Sleep, rest, health . . . she felt like she'd had two Excedrin and a nice cup of hot cocoa.

Ruth looked at the cup and looked at Melior. There was no possible way she could get him to drink now. She took a tag-end of clean bandage and moistened it in the brandy, and wiped at the burned and poisoned skin on Melior's thigh.

Was it her imagination, or was the redness less red, the puffiness decreased?

Alcohol was a good antiseptic, anyway.

She filled the cup from the bottle again, and watched as cerulean witch-fire drifted out into the brandy. When it seemed to be about as magical as it was going to get, she went back to her task, drizzling brandy from the cup to the cloth and swabbing Melior's skin until she'd wiped all around the gashes in his leg.

But the wound itself still had to be cleaned.

And if she poured alcohol into an open wound, it'd hurt like hell, magic or not.

But would water have the same effect?

The water in the jerrican was pleasantly hot now. Ruth drank the last mouthful of brandy and dipped the cup into the water. The blue streamers of light were fainter now, or possibly only harder to see against clear water in full daylight. But after a few moments the liquid was perceptibly bluer.

Maybe the cup was running out of charge, or something. She'd have to be careful. Not waste it.

Carefully she poured the water over Melior's leg.

He jerked once as the water touched him, but almost as if he'd started in his sleep. Ruth's stomach clenched as she realized the water was literally filling the wound, the way rainwater would fill a rut in the road. An iridescent scum rose to the top of the water and Ruth swallowed hard, trying not to gag.

She poured another cup of water into the wounds on Melior's leg. It spilled over, carrying the scum-residue with it. Ruth mopped and swabbed, noting with resigned despair the growing pile of soggy, bloody, *messy* cloth. She blotted the gashes dry and then poured water over them a third time. This time the water ran nearly clear.

The bleeding had stopped.

She did not question her good fortune, but used the last of the dry pads and the bandage rolls, brisk efficient wrappings and tyings learned in what seemed another lifetime. She lifted Melior's leg carefully, propping it up against her knee so she could wrap the bandage all around his thigh, crisp and clean and sane and white. Then she covered him in blankets until he lay like a little hill before the embering fire.

There was nothing more to do. And Ruth, unable to push her mind past the moment, lay down beside him on the bare wood floor.

And slept.

* * *

"C'mon, Jimmy—we're going to be late!"

Ruth tossed and turned, realizing too late that sleep had been a bad idea. The dream that had followed her into the Morning Lands had seized her again and not let go.

And now they were on the back road to Kathleen's place, on their way to the accident that had stolen eight years of Ruth's life, and she could not wake. Jimmy Ramirez was driving, and Kathleen and Allen sat in the back, and in a few moments all three of them would be dead.

Desperately Ruth attempted to wrench her inner vision away from the sight of what must be. There were flashing lights around the corner of the road ahead, and at the moment Jimmy thought they were cop-car flashers, but the lights weren't red-and-blue. It was a coppery fiery light, glowing as balefully as the stone in the brigand's ring, and Jimmy, slowing, slewed the Oldsmobile around the corner and Ruth saw—

And Jimmy screamed—

The car jumped forward as he floored the accelerator—

"No!" Ruth jerked herself free at last. She lay on the floor, staring unseeingly at the legs of unfamiliar furniture, while her heart battered the inside of her chest like a demonic washing machine on eternal spin cycle.

A hand touched her shoulder. Ruth screamed and flung herself away, scrabbling at the floorboards like a maddened armadillo.

She looked back. Melior was staring at her with an expression of bewildered concern.

"Oh. It's you," Ruth said lamely.

"Yes," Melior said.

He was, if not completely recovered, at least *going* to recover. He was propped up on one elbow among the blankets in front of the ashes of the fire, one hand was still raised in the gesture of touching her.

He did not ask who it was she thought might have been in the room with her.

Ruth scrabbled to her feet and sat down on the settle. Heroines of fiction might have seized the moment to throw themselves into their lovers' arms, but she just didn't feel like it right now, she told herself crossly.

"You came back to me," Melior said marvelingly.

And it was true, she knew it was true; she remembered, vividly, Christmas Eve in Ippisiqua, and wanting him, and knowing there would never be any peace or happiness in the world again. And finding the door that had led her here.

Ruth began to cry. All that, and now that she had him, she couldn't think of a single thing to say.

She was so absorbed in blotting out the world that she did not hear him move. Only the faint unstartling susurrus of wool as he sat down beside her on the wooden bench and gathered her into his arms. He smelled of brandy and wood smoke and damp linen, and Ruth clung to him both as if she would keep him safe forever and punish him for unspecified wrongs.

"Your leg," she said, a long damp time later.

"Does not pain me so much as some wounds might. And as the dead feel no pain, I should be grateful for the discomfort," he responded.

Ruth looked at him with suspicious embarrassment. He had one of the blankets draped around himself. One fold of it covered her bandaging job. She scrubbed at her eyes with the back of one hand. He was well enough to have gotten over here, at any rate.

"How long has it been in the World of Iron?" Melior asked.

"About two years," Ruth said. "Well, a year and seven months. It was Christmas, when—" She stopped.

When she had fallen through a hole in the world with Nic Brightlaw right behind her.

"Nic! Ohmigod, I— How could I just have forgotten about him? We've got to find him. He's my boss, the library director at Ryerson; he fell through the bookcase with me and then the unicorn got me lost, and he's *out* there—"

Melior shook her gently. "The round tale, from the beginning. And— not following my example—omitting no details whose omission could prove inconvenient or fatal later."

Ruth stared around the room. Late afternoon sunlight streamed through the narrow windows, and the place looked as messy, rumpled, and disorganized as Ruth felt. There were piles of bloody rags everywhere, the scraps of Melior's clothes, and, abandoned in one corner, his riding boots and the Sword of Maiden's Tears.

"But perhaps not at once," Melior amended. "Lend me your aid, and we will see if my strength extends to leaving this room, and what generosity this house's master may be moved to. The magic that runs here is not to be accomplished in the sight of eyes," Melior added, as if annotating some guidebook for her benefit.

"There's a cheese in the kitchen," Ruth offered. Melior shook his head, saying nothing, and after a moment Ruth got to her feet and helped him stand. Then Melior pulled her toward where the Sword of Maiden's Tears lay on the floor.

Ruth dug in her heels, pulling them both to a stop.

"I must bring it with me," Melior said quietly. "It will not hurt you."

"It—kills people," Ruth said, from a throat drawn suddenly tight. *Naomi . . .*

"That is the nature of swords," Melior answered implacably. "But it lacks the particular power you fear while it is in my possession."

"You mean you can turn it off," Ruth said flatly. Melior sighed.

"While I am its guardian—while it is *mine*—it will not trap human-kind into *grendel*form, nor will humans covet it. The sword is harmless now, Ruth, and I must keep it with me. It is my duty." Plainly this was not a subject for discussion.

And Ruth knew that Melior would not lie to her, nor lead her into any danger. But it was still hard to help him over to where the Sword lay, to pick it up by a loop of swordbelt and hand it to him. He looped the strap over one shoulder. The silver-chased scabbard dragged on the floor. Ruth turned to go, Melior's arm around her shoulders. Then she remembered the other thing that it would not do to abandon.

"My cup!" she said. "Oh, well, it isn't really mine, but—" She stopped babbling with an effort, and guided Melior to the door frame where he could stand supported while she scurried back over to the hearth.

Ruth found the cup without difficulty and stuffed it into the pouch with her other (wanted and unwanted) possessions, and returned to Melior. Together they went out into the hall.

The back parlor where Ruth had eaten her dinner the night before was sun-drenched and welcoming. Through the long leaded windows she could see a flagstoned walk and a low wall, and beyond the wall an entire orchard of apple trees, bare-limbed in the fashion of early spring. Beyond the orchard was another low wall, and then a long meadow, punctuated with stands of blue and yellow flowers. Hyacinth. Daffodil. At the foot of the meadow, Ruth was certain, there was a stream, and beyond the farther bank of the stream a forest—

There was bread and wine laid out on the sideboard, and Ruth consoled herself with the knowledge that a skimpy breakfast was better than none. Melior sat on the sofa with the Sword propped up beside him while Ruth cut bread and poured wine.

"Tell me how you came to this place, Ruth," Melior said. Ruth turned back to him, forgetting about the forest.

"It was raining—" Ruth began, and with the help of Melior's patient questioning was able to tell him most of what had happened since she fell through the enchanted bookcase. Nic, the unicorn, the inn they'd found— and what had happened after.

"He said there was someone following us. He went off into the woods to look. I thought it might be the unicorn, and it *did* show up again, but Nic didn't. And it wanted me to go with it, and, well, I already knew what happened if you didn't. So I did, and I didn't find Nic, but I got to the Goblin Market—"

"And were lucky to escape unscathed," Melior said sternly. He didn't ask how she'd managed to bring him back from the dead—perhaps he didn't know how badly he'd been hurt. Or maybe she was the one who was wrong about the extent of his injuries.

"Unscathed," Ruth echoed unsteadily. "That *thing*—"

"The warwasp sought to kill you," Melior said bluntly, "and was dazzled by the bolder magic of the Sword. It is a creature of Chandrakar; I think Baligant wishes your death before you can be used against him."

"Me?" said Ruth. "Used against him? What am I going to do—miscatalog his books?"

Melior looked into her eyes, and Ruth realized with a small thrill of unease that he was deciding how much he should tell her.

"I want the truth," Ruth said flatly. "All of it."

"There is a court," Melior said after a pause, "which settles matters among the Houses of the Twilight—matters that are not the concern of the High King. I believe that Eirdois Baligant, the High Prince, works to harm us, and it is at the Twilight Court that I must tell the tale to the Earls and their vassal lords. But what is a tale without proof, in a time where I stand to be confirmed in my father's holdings, or have my rights set aside for another?"

"I don't know," Ruth said, feeling like a straight man. "What *is* a tale without proof?"

"Useless. But I *have* proof. You are my proof, Ruth Marlowe." He looked into her eyes and smiled, with the faint hint of self-mockery that told her he knew she wasn't going to like this, whatever it was.

"I think you'd better explain that," Ruth said, with sinking heart.

So Melior did.

It was in the World of Iron that Melior had discovered that Ruth Marlowe's soul was tangled somehow into the magics that had wrought the Sword of Maiden's Tears. Now Melior went on to explain that some wizard Ruth had never met was going to make a public spectacle of putting her soul back together and getting it out of the Sword while everyone at the Twilight Court watched. It would, he hoped, prove that Baligant was behind the plot to destroy the Treasures.

It sounded if not actively painful, at least luridly public and humiliating.

"And what if I don't choose to cooperate in this?" Ruth said tightly.

There was a very long pause.

"Do not ask me that, Ruth," Melior said tonelessly.

Before she was quite knew it herself, Ruth was on her feet and out of the room, running down the hall just as if she had someplace to go. Running away before she said something she'd regret to the man who, last night, she was sure she'd die without.

And who now intended to use her as a pawn in some elphen chess game, no matter how she felt about it.

"Prr-RRING?" said the cat, from halfway up the stairs.

Ruth picked it up. The marmalade cat was a warm ecstatic weight in her arms, indicating by every means known to catkind that Ruth was surely the wisest of mortals to be devoting her time to *him*.

She walked the rest of the way up the stairs, cat in her arms, then down the hall to "her" room.

Once again there was a tub before the fire and clothes laid out, and this time there was the mouthwatering smell of hot venison pie and a. bowl of candied chestnuts laid out on the table before the bow window. The cat leaped down from her arms and began making sure the accommodations were up to standard. Ruth stood and inhaled.

This time hunger overcame cleanliness. The cat jumped up onto the bed and settled itself to watch her eat, and Ruth, standing so as not to get guck on any of the furniture, wolfed the pie in large inelegant swallows, washing it down with mugsful of the hard cider provided.

It was better fare than that laid out below, she reflected.

"Don't like Melior much, eh?" she said to the cat around a mouthful of pie. The cat purred.

"Don't blame you," Ruth said generously. "Don't like him myself at the moment." She filled her cup with the last of the cider, drained it, and sighed.

"But I love him, I think. And he's *responsible*—to the Court of Twilight, whatever that is. To prove the truth to them about that other guy. Baligant."

The cat stopped purring, and regarded Ruth with gold oracular eyes.

Ruth pulled off the robe, folded it fastidiously, and climbed into the bath. "You see," she said to the cat, picking up the soap, "if he doesn't get back with the Sword, or if Baligant manages to get all the Treasures and screw everything up, that means Naomi died for nothing, doesn't it?"

The cat watched her.

"Or maybe I'm just crazy, talking to a cat. But I don't think so. I wish—"

Ruth thought of the garden and the orchard and the meadow beyond. About the clean clothes and hot dinners; comfort, order, and civilization. About calm comfort, untroubled by love or politics. *I wish I could stay here.*

"But I can't," Ruth said aloud, and bent to wash her muddy, bloody hair.

As if it had already known her intention, the clothes laid out for her to put on were traveling clothes, even though the shadows stretched toward evening. Ruth tried to remember whether any of the rash and hasty half-promises she'd made yesterday included a promise to only spend one night here.

But whether or not she'd promised, whatever she'd promised, the house seemed disinclined to welcome Melior. And that seemed to mean they would have to leave tonight.

It did not occur to her to stay without him. She had no idea if she could really be happy with him, but the idea of not finding out was unthinkable.

And so, Ruth thought primly, she'd better get dressed.

There were knitted woolen stockings that gartered above the swell of the calf with bright braided ribbons, brown boots lined in sheepskin with stout formidable soles, an airy linen smock made opulent with tucks and pleating and delicate white embroidery over which Ruth, professional costumer, tied with ease one wool and two cotton petticoats followed by a sleeveless chemise of silk, which was in its turn surmounted by a soft, thick, serviceable and dependable double full circle skirted T-tunic in dark green wool.

The neck of her dress laced closed with a scarlet ribbon, and at the wrists and above the neckline the immaculate white embroidery of her smock could be seen. The neck, placket, and wrists of the dress, and a band eight inches above the hem, were brave with bright multicolored silk embroidery in designs that were vaguely Celtic, in the way the clothes she wore were vaguely historical.

But the twelfth century T-tunic did not go with the fourteenth century petticoats, and the sleeveless silk chemise was from no historical period.

Still, it was warm.

There were gloves, too, long gauntlets of supple green leather whose cuff-embroidery matched that of her dress. And a snood, of green velvet ribbons and lined in darker silk, that Ruth gratefully seized upon as an answer to the eternal question of what she should do with her hair.

There was a belt of green-dyed braided leather that she fitted about her waist, threading it through the drawstrings of the pouch she carried and returning the tasseled cord to the bed curtains. The free end of the long belt wove back and forth through D rings; Ruth folded the excess over and through, making it dangle properly.

The last item there was Naomi's Kinsale cloak.

Ruth was sure she'd lost it at the Goblin Market. She thought the matter over carefully and became positive. She'd been carrying it at the Market. She'd dropped it sometime there, as she certainly hadn't had it in the forest.

And now it was back.

Welcome to Elfland. The Lost and Found Department . . .

She picked it up and slung it over one arm. The cloak was heavy and it dragged, but she clung to it like a last lifeline to home. How many times did she have to leave safety and comfort and at least the semblance of normalcy, just to follow Melior? There ought to be a limit to what she was asked to give up, somehow, somewhere. . . .

You've buttered your bread, Ruth Marlowe, now lie on it.

She turned to the cat and held her hand out toward it tentatively. It allowed its ears to be ruffled and its jaw to be rubbed.

"Do take care of yourself, moggie. And I remember my promise."

But this time, talking to the cat, she felt silly instead of wise. She shrugged the cloak into a more comfortable position over her arm and went out the door.

It was no particular surprise to see Melior standing at the foot of the stair waiting for her, fully dressed. The Sword was slung over his back again, and he leaned upon a black walking stick as long as he was. His clothes were a match for hers, down to color, cut, material, and embroidery, save that he wore his own boots and the orange scaled cape.

And it was too soon for him to be up and around; he'd been dying the night before. She could tell he was hurt; his mouth was set firmly and his gloved hand clenched tightly on the stave.

"Looks like we're both ready to go," Ruth said, trying for the bright neutral tone that had served her many an hour at the Reference Desk.

"Yes. The Border should be easy enough to cross from here; we might even find the Road again. But I confess my plans take me no farther than the nearest inn."

"Why—" Ruth began, but a gesture from Melior stopped her. She came the rest of the way down the stairs and followed him down the hall.

The front door stood open. And standing on the threshold, knowing she would never see this place again, Ruth felt a wild clutch of homesickness drag at her heart. This place was not home, she had been here barely a night, but somehow it was the distillation of all of Ruth's best times and places, and leaving it would be like abandoning all her happy memories.

"Come, Ruth." Melior's voice was abrupt with tension. Out of sheer inertia, she crossed the threshold and set foot on the path outside. Melior's measured pace was easy to match, even in her bulky unfamiliar skirts.

She would not look back. She held firmly to that resolve. She would not look back for a last sight of a place she could never go home to again.

The sun was setting, and despite the fact that it had been autumn here last night the sky was the pale crystal-white of clear spring sunsets. Dusk and the season made everything sharp and rainwashed and vivid, and tiny details leaped out at her, from the green of the moss overgrowing a rock to the even distinctness of the cobbles edging the walk. Bare bushes and early grass became trees within yards of the walk, and here and there Ruth could see clusters of spring flowers closed against the oncoming night. Melior's footsteps were loud beside her.

They came to the outer gate, the one that divided the house's grounds from the forest, a double recurve of weather-grayed wood. There were clusters of flowers at the foot of each post, and the garland she had hung the night before was still draped over the gate. The lamps were already lit, their candles feeble against the bright twilight.

She could still go back.

Even now, the house would take her back, and there would be long walks in the twilight, through the orchard and the meadow to the river beyond.

Melior put his hand on the gate, and it swung away from him as if it did not like to be touched.

Four steps would take her onto the forest path. And the gate would close forever.

It did not matter what she might have with Melior. What she was giving up here was real, and good, and precious, and she would miss it all the days of her life.

Ruth wavered. And Melior yanked her arm so that she stumbled forward, through the gate. She gasped as she heard it swing shut behind her with gunshot finality.

Melior looked down at her. "Some day I will explain, if you still wish to hear. You have been done great honor, Ruth Marlowe, in that place."

Ruth shook her head, blinking back tears, and wiped her eyes on the sleeve of her tunic. Melior held out his free arm and she put herself inside it, resting her hand on his hip and leaning her face against his tunic.

This was what she'd chosen. For better, for worse, with malice aforethought. This. Melior.

Then he shifted his weight, hissing a little to himself as he leaned his weight upon the stave, and the two of them began to walk down the forest path through the darkening wood.

· 23 ·

Between the Knife Edge
and the Skin

THERE WAS A long time of pain and sickness, of wandering alone crying out for any of her own to find her, to answer her. She was hot and cold by turns, and fought the hands that held her back when all she wanted was to run.

At last, exhausted, Jausserande fell into dreamless sleep. Some uncounted time later she drifted toward consciousness, only to be lulled back into dreams by the familiar sounds of an armed encampment.

"—don't know why you brought her."

From somewhere outside the place where she lay, Jausserande heard voices, but it was too much trouble to wake to them.

"Everybody else got to bring home a souvenir. I didn't get time to shop."

Jausserande heard the words without caring. She felt weak; lazy. Every muscle in her body ached with past strain.

"The men won't like it."

"Then the *men* can go find somebody else to play with, Yarrow. I'm the Daddy; either they do what I tell them, or I'm taking my toys and going home."

How strange. She must have taken a head-hit in the last raid. That would explain everything. How Miralh would laugh.

Jausserande drifted back into sleep.

* * *

"Wake up, Tinkerbelle," a voice said, very close.

Jausserande jolted awake, fully conscious this time. Fatigue resolved itself into separate aches. Her head. Her leg.

The Harvest Home. *Fox.*

Fox was standing over her, holding a bowl. Jausserande lunged for him, reaching for his throat—

And was yanked back by the collar around her neck. Its leash was tethered securely to something that would not yield; her hands were prisoned behind her, in a carven yoke such as she had seen prisoners wear in wartime, half her life ago. She fought her bonds, gritting her teeth at the nausea and weakness that rode over her in waves.

"Quit thrashing. If Raven couldn't break that—and he tried—you can't. I thought you *aristocrats* were supposed to have a few brains," Fox sneered.

Jausserande stared up at him, violet eyes wide with shock as the full horror of her situation sank in. She was in the hands of the enemy. She looked around.

Jausserande lay on a crude pallet in a primitive hut. Her boots and her belt were gone; she lay on the pile of skins in her linen undertunic and drawers, with a large bandage wrapped high on one thigh. Through the squares of bark that formed the hut's outer covering, she could see chinks of daylight shining, and could hear the sounds that had mocked her with their familiarity. The sounds of an armed camp, yes—but the camp of the outlaws.

Fox stood over her—wearing, she noted with almost ludicrous indignation, her gray wool tunic over the same crude leathers she had seen him wearing at Dawnheart. His skin had darkened with exposure to the sun, as humans' skin was wont to do, and the hairs on his forearms were almost elf-silver by contrast.

And Melior's signet ring was on his finger.

Fox gazed passionlessly down at her, as if she were a litter of pigs he was deciding best how to cull. Then he squatted, setting the tray down on the floor of the hut within easy reach.

"Going to behave, Tink? You try to kick me, and I'll knock you silly."

Jausserande swallowed, through a throat gone suddenly dry. This was not clean war, where prisoners were ransomed. Fox and his losels had nothing to lose. He might do anything.

And there was nothing she could do to stop him.

It was a new sensation, and a year ago she would have fought no matter the odds, as blindly as an unbroken colt. But she was Cupbearer now, and the honor Jausserande had taken up so lightly held her more brutally than Fox's shackles could. She had responsibilities that stretched far beyond her own desires. She was Cupbearer; and while the Cup of Morning Shadows was safe still . . .

The key to the Cup was not.

"Lie back," Fox said, and reached for her leg.

Despite her best intentions, Jausserande flung herself away from him. Her arms were twisted awkwardly behind her by the shackle, and the leather collar at her throat chafed. The bad leg buckled agonizingly under her when she tried to use it and Jausserande bared her teeth at Fox in hopeless defiance.

Fox sat back on his heels.

"What? Afraid of me, a—what was the quaint native term again?—'mud-born'? Afraid of *something* at least, Tink? Finally? Fear, you know, is the beginning of wisdom. Mao Tse-tung said that, I think. You won't ever have heard of him."

Jausserande watched him, spellbound as the lark before the cobra.

"But maybe you've heard of gangrene? Stupid bitch," Fox added in an afterthought. "All of you damn elves think you're so irresistible. You just come waltzing in and expect everybody to be struck stupid by your ineffable beauty—and then you start putting the boot in. Well, the boot stops here, Tink. No more elves. No more magic. No more Twelve goddamned Treasures."

She had thought the situation was as bad as it could be, and had been wrong. It had just gotten worse.

The human was mad.

"What are you going to do?" Jausserande demanded, her voice harsh and low. "And what have you done with The Rohannan?"

"Who?" Fox's surprise was genuine enough.

Now it was Jausserande's turn to be nonplussed. Had he killed Melior and looted the body without even knowing his victim's name? She stared at Fox's hand.

He saw the direction of her stare and smiled, the sweet smile of a saint seeing Paradise. It transformed his face to something neither human nor elphen, and Jausserande did not care for it.

"Oh, the ring. He gave it to me, Tink, and that was his first mistake, and too bad for him not his last. But you asked what I was going to do, so in good villain style I might as well tell you. I'm going into the Vale and getting the Cup of Morning Shadows. Then I'm holding you and the Cup for ransom until I see if Melior is going to come and get you back. If he does, I'm going to shoot him in the back and see what a hammer and anvil'll do to his Sword."

The Sword of Maiden's Tears. Line Rohannan's Treasure—destroyed?

"You can't do that!" Jausserande gasped.

"Wanna bet?" Fox reached into a pouch dangling from his belt and pulled something out. Jausserande desperately tried to shut her eyes, but couldn't bear not to see.

Her cup. The *tainaiste*-Cup, that would find the true one. In Fox's hands. The attack on the Fair had been a feint all along. The outlaw did not seek plunder, but to strike at the heart of Chandrakar itself. At the Twelve Treasures.

But who could be so crazed?

No one. Unless her cousin, whom she had thought mad, was not. And the human, though mad, was not crazed.

"Tell your master the High Prince he will never succeed in his depravity—not while any of the Treasurekeepers retains his charge!" Jausserande raged.

The surge of fury left her weak. Jausserande closed her eyes, and through the tide of weakness felt Fox's fingers at the bandage on her leg, unknotting and unwinding. Almost, she did not care.

"You'll live," he said, when the wound was bared to his inspection. "Jesus, a five-year-old with a slingshot and a box of paper clips could take over this place in twenty minutes. Assuming he could get anybody to get off their ass and rebel. How do you ever expect to develop any decent technology without iron?"

His words meant nothing to her, and his scornful manner whipsawed Jausserande between fury and a hard, hopeless fear. There would be no rescue for her here, and even the small magic she could command was beyond her in this weakened state. She tried to shut out the day, the place, the sight of the *tainaiste*-Cup in human hands, Baligant's madness, to put all the Treasures so at peril.

The feel of a wet cloth on her skin shocked her to alertness again. Fox was bathing her wound. She stared; it was a short ugly violet gash, swollen and raised but obviously healing cleanly. Such a small injury, to cause such agony.

Jausserande's eyes teared unwillingly at the memory. She had ridden all day once with a bone-deep sword cut to the leg, but the sword had been bronze, and nothing, *nothing* to the pain of iron.

"I'm going to leave the bandage off so it can get some air. After all, you aren't going anywhere, are you?" Fox said.

Jausserande didn't answer. She turned her head away, dismissing him.

"And now, Tink, it's dinnertime. There's just one thing I'd like to share with you before I read you the list of tonight's specials. Look at me, elf bitch."

His voice had lost its light note of self-mockery.

Unwillingly Jausserande met his eyes. They were blue; pale blue and opaque, like expensive glass. His face was expressionless, his tone emotionless as he spoke.

"If you give me trouble, I won't feed you. If I don't feed you, nobody will. They're afraid of you. That probably sounds like a good deal to you, but it means my men won't come anywhere near you—unless, of course, Yarrow cuts your throat. He's that kind, you know; inclined to panic. And he gives up too easily—but on the other hand, you're tied up. Not much of a challenge.

"But since I know Yarrow's that kind of guy, I've got Raven keeping an eye on him. Raven wouldn't touch you with a ten-foot pole. He's kind of an idealist, you might say.

"So if I don't feed you, I don't think the rest of them are going to give it a real high priority. Think about that. You'll die of thirst in about four days, assuming you're anything like a human, and you know, somewhere along about your third day without water you'll be willing to do practically *anything* to get a drink."

The smile that followed that bland recitation of horror was all the more terrifying for its easy brilliance.

"So why don't you be a good Tinkerbelle, and cooperate, and we can all keep our illusions a while longer. Okay?"

He knelt beside her, watching and waiting, and all Jausserande could think of was that if she died here, the Cup of Morning Shadows would be lost to Line Floire forever. And Line Floire would in turn be lost.

And Baligant would win.

If fury could have cut her bonds, Jausserande would have been free. If desperation were a weapon, Fox would be dead. But they were not.

He was waiting for her to answer, Jausserande realized. And when he was tired of waiting, he would leave. He would not come back. And she would begin to die.

The need of her Treasure broke her own need before it.

"I accept your terms," Jausserande whispered.

If her capitulation pleased him, Fox didn't show it. There was none of the gloating or bragging Jausserande expected from a human who had captured one of the Morning Lords. Instead, he simply moved forward and helped her back into a sitting position. Her leg gave twinges of pain as she shifted, but she thought it would soon be strong enough to bear her weight.

And then she could get free. Get the *tainaiste*-Cup. Kill Fox.

Jausserande leaned against the post she was shackled to; a tree trunk, lopped and left rooted in the earth. Fox brought a waterskin and held the nozzle to her mouth; Floire Jausserande, Cupbearer and Treasurekeeper, gulped thin warm flat beer until the waterskin was withdrawn.

"For what it's worth," Fox said, turning back to her with a bowl containing boiled grain, "my plans don't include killing you. But you can kiss your Cup good-bye."

Never, Jausserande thought fiercely, but there was puzzlement in the thought. Didn't Fox know that the loss of the Cup meant death for every man, woman, and child of Line Floire? How could Fox think to promise her life and withhold the Cup?

"Whatever you have been offered to do this, Line Floire will match it, for my freedom and the return of the Cup. And more—Gate passage for you and all you choose to a land where humans rule," Jausserande said. Surely Baligant could be offering nothing more. "Think, before you cleave to your bargain with the High Prince. A lord who has betrayed one will betray all."

Fox stopped with the spoon halfway to her mouth. "Very pretty, and very noble. And you'd probably even keep your word, which is a nice gesture considering what we mean to each other. Too bad you got me wrong, Tink. I don't give a damn about the home rule situation in Elfland. I'm a freelancer."

Jausserande opened her mouth to protest. Fox filled it with a spoon of porridge.

Days passed. Jausserande brooded as her injury slowly healed, wondering how she could kill the outlaws' leader. In her captivity she saw no one other than Fox, though she heard his men on every side. He slept in the hut beside her, and in the darkness Jausserande would lie awake, listening to his breathing and watching the progress of the waxing moon through a chink in the roof of the hut. He had the *tainaiste*-Cup. She could not kill him until she knew where it was.

During daylight hours Jausserande had the hut to herself, Fox usually being absent on his mysterious business of rabble-rousing and thievery. She listened carefully to the careless talk that went on outside, and after a few days had collected a good idea of the extent of his following. The knowledge made her no happier.

Fox was the touchstone for every spark of foolish human disaffection in all her cousin's wide lands, it seemed, and had gathered about himself not only the brutal losels that one might expect to find accompanying a forest outlaw, but also men of a dangerously high quality.

Jausserande suspected that there might be women in Fox's band as well, and that was the gravest news yet. It meant that this band of Fox's was no summer rebellion, with disaffected serfs returning to their hearths and masters as soon as the first snow fell. If the women supported Fox, then he might find welcome and support in any village in Chandrakar.

Ungrateful, stupid creatures, to turn so on their overlords just as peace had come to Chandrakar at last. It was their great-grandsires who had first gone to war; surely they themselves should be grateful to put an end to it.

As she had been? Jausserande was honest enough to ask herself that question. If she could imagine no life beyond war, how much less imaginative might these short-lived humans be?

It mattered not. Their duty was to obey their overlords. There was no excuse for their rebellion. When Melior returned, he would not be allowed to be as soft with them as formerly. Line Floire would sue for Jausserande's blood-price, and Melior must pay it. Fox and all his band would die: gelded, hanged, and then beheaded to deck the Traitors' Gate of Dawnheart.

If Melior returned.

And even if Floire took its vengeance, what would happen to the Cup?

In the late afternoon after the night she had watched the full moon pace the sky Fox came to her. It was early for the evening meal Jausserande had come to expect from him, though he carried a wooden tray with food on it.

But instead of feeding her, today he untied her hands.

Freed, it was absurdly easy to untie the braided leather leash from the tree; Jausserande stood, holding to the post for support. Her muscles trembled with the unaccustomed exercise.

"Why?" Jausserande said, stretching to ease the stiffness of long stillness. She could kill him even bare-handed, she was nearly certain, but if she knew that, Fox must know it as well. She rubbed her wrists and eased her shoulders, not looking at him.

"Eat your dinner, Tink; we're going walkies. And although it's hardly necessary to mention it, I will: the Cup is hidden somewhere that only I know about."

Jausserande sat again and reached for the tray. There was bread and ale, proof, though she hardly needed it, that Fox had sympathizers in the local villages. She did her best to ignore him as she fed herself. His trick was only what she had expected. It was only what she herself would have done, had one of the other Treasurekeepers fallen into her hands during the war.

But today Fox was edgy, keyed up and minded to talk.

"The way I figure it, if you kill me, no Cup. If you escape, you can't dally to search every rock, rabbit hole, and tree. The only way you can think of to maybe get it back is to string me along. In other words, cooperate."

"What makes you think it means so much to me?" Jausserande said crossly.

Fox laughed, a short sharp bark such as his namesake might have uttered. "If it means as much to you as the Sword does to Melior, you'll do whatever it takes for a chance to get it back."

Jausserande nodded, slowly, acknowledging what was no more than the simple truth—and wondering, not for the first time, why the outlaw Fox seemed to claim such intimacy with her cousin. She reached for the wooden mug on the tray and then stopped, speaking almost without thinking.

"Fox, what do you truly want? Destroy the Treasures and you destroy us all, elf and human alike—you cannot want that."

"I want," said Fox, with the soft passion of a man at the edge of endurance, "to be able to sleep again at night. So I'll destroy Chandrakar? Fine by me. It's a damn shame Chandrakar didn't think a little harder about what it destroyed. But it didn't—so Chandrakar—and its Treasures—and its elves—have me."

Another of Fox's brilliant smiles, which Jausserande was coming to distrust as the indicator of Fox's truly nasty temper.

"Like the man says. I'm not your judge, I'm your judgment. Get dressed, Tink; we're going for a ride."

He'd brought her most of her own clothes, with a heavy sheepskin vest to take the place of her lost tunic. He even brought her cap with the Ravens' badge, and Jausserande could not say whether such consideration pleased or discomfited her.

Since knowledge was the only weapon she had, she considered the matter carefully. Fox did not treat her with the respect a worthy enemy deserved. He was not cruel out of fear of her strength. He treated her with the distant kindness she used toward her human servants, as if he were so high above her that there was no way she could drag him down.

Realizing this, her eyes kindled, and she glared at Fox, settling the cap on her head. He regarded her with mocking acknowledgment.

"It's show time, Tink. C'mon."

"My name—"

"Is really, *really* unimportant to me, Tink. C'mon." He turned his back and ducked out through the hut's low doorway.

After a moment, Jausserande followed.

Her first view of the camp showed it much as she had imagined it would be. Shelters made of bent but still-rooted saplings roofed over with hides and squares of bark, small fire pits were scattered here and there, carcasses and food bundles hung from tree branches—all the signs of a long-kept base camp, yet so portable and ephemeral that an hour's hard work could erase it almost as if it had never been. She counted perhaps thirty men, and knew there must be at least half again as many that she did not see.

Fox led her to the edge of the camp, where, within a concealing lattice of branches, six horses stood, saddled and ready—fruits of Fox's raid on the Harvest Home.

Fox looked at her, a slanted sidewise knowing glance.

"See anything you like?" Fox asked her, still in that blithe untrustworthy mood.

Wait for your chance, Jausserande told herself. She spared a sweeping glance for Fox, the stolen horses, the outlaws standing around.

"Nothing."

Fox laughed.

He rode well, an uncommon skill in the mud-born. The horse Jausserande rode was the worst of them, easily caught by any of the others should she incite it to bolt, and haltered to Fox's saddle besides. Four of his men rode with them, and Jausserande had seen the flash of sword and dagger as they mounted. Fox led them with easy certainty onto the road that led into the Vale itself.

Jausserande watched Fox's back and the long tail of pale hair, and wondered who he was and what she should believe about him. Even if Melior's theory was true, she did not think that this one looked to Baligant Baneful.

But if he did not, *why* did Fox want the Treasures? They were of no use to the mud-born. Humans had no magic—*they* could not wield the powers of the Twelve Treasures. And, though the Cup of Morning Shadows was not so guarded, no human could even *touch* Rohannan's Treasure, the Sword of Maiden's Tears.

Yet if she could believe him, the Sword was more Fox's goal than the Cup, though he wanted the Cup as well.

Why?

For the first time Jausserande wished she had paid more attention to her lessons in the Art Magical—or, even better, had an Adept Major to consult. Because Fox said that his intention was to *destroy* both Cup and Sword, and Jausserande had no idea what would happen if he succeeded. Chandrakar would be doomed, that was common knowledge, but doomed *how?*

As her horse's hooves struck the white clay road, Jausserande felt a familiar warning tingle of sensation. This was the road into the Vale of Stars, where elphen magic could not be used, lest it twist itself and turn upon the wielder. Even the enchantment upon the Cup was a simple thing, a mere mechanism, related to the works of the Art Magical as a child's hobbyhorse was to a war destrier and thus safe from the power of the Vale.

Did that very simplicity mean that Fox would be able to use its magic as well?

The terrain rose around the mounted party in the gathering dusk, until they rode down a gleaming bone-white road between the steep dark walls of a great defile, and at last passed through into the Vale of Stars.

Beyond the walls of the pass the road dipped sharply, arrowing down into a tiny perfect valley. Though the sky was already dark, and the crowding hills shut out the sunset light, the Vale shone with its own illumination. There was a faint glow to the mist that hung over the vivid green meadow, and even in this season the trees were filled with pale flowers that gave off their own light.

All was perfect; Jausserande could hear the purl of a quick-running stream, see the flicker of grass stems bent beneath an evening breeze. To this place, unique in Chandrakar, the war had not come.

Until now.

Fox chivied his mount down the narrow track. Jausserande was pulled unwillingly with him, wondering if it was best to vault from her saddle and run before Fox could attempt to compel her help.

She didn't get the chance.

"Tie her," Fox snapped over his shoulder, and before the horses had stopped, Raven yanked Jausserande from her saddle. She fought him, but his strength was as great as Fox had foretold, and he was able to hold her as another of Fox's men jerked her hands back and bound them behind her.

Not enough to restrain her, save for the noose that went about her neck. Run and she would hang herself.

"There. All comfy now?" Fox asked, dismounting. The man behind her tossed Fox the free end of the halter. He caught it and looped it about his wrist.

"I will see you hanged from Dawnheart's walls with your own entrails," Jausserande grated.

"Why is it that people complain when others do things as well as they would themselves? Your problem, Tink, is that you get really bent out of shape when you start to suspect you aren't going to win."

Around them Fox's men were dismounting and picketing the horses, but Fox and Jausserande might have been alone. Her fury was a palpable weight, pressing against her skin until only gritted teeth kept her from panting for relief from it. For a moment she forgot even the Cup.

Fox turned away and strode off, pulling the rawhide leash taut between them. A sharp shove between the shoulder blades sent Jausserande stumbling after him, muscles trembling at her narrow escape—though from what, she wasn't sure.

He does not know where he must stand. The realization broke through to her consciousness like a rock that she could cling to. How could he know, when even she had only Floire Glorete's handed-down directions to a place Glorete had never seen?

What had Glorete said? Jausserande frowned, summoning memory under unpromising conditions. *On the second day of the full moon*—that was now—*at moonrise, the presence of the shadow-Cup within the Vale of Stars would show the presence of the true Cup and, being thrust into shadow, bring the true Cup visible.*

Moonrise would be very soon. And when it came, the *tainaiste*-Cup would cause an image of the true one to appear for a few moments somewhere within the Vale of Stars. Glorete had told her to hold the shadow Cup within the image of the other one, but even Glorete hadn't been able to tell her what would happen then.

Could Fox do that much? Would he even see it? Would he ask her aid—and kill her when she did not give it?

For the first time Jausserande forced herself to think about what would happen if the Cup of Morning Shadows were lost here—not as a vague possibility, but as a real likelihood.

Chandrakar would still be safe, since the Cup would still be within the land. And perhaps Line Floire would send someone to the Vale to search when Jausserande was known to be dead. And perhaps that one would find it.

And if they did not?

On the day of the Kingmaking, with Eirdois Baligant in the High Seat, Floire would be called upon three times to present its Treasure. And when it had been called for the third time, and failed . . .

Line Floire would be no more. Before the sun had set, every man, woman, and child of the Line would have been driven beyond the bounds of Chandrakar, banished and attainted with no more possession than the clothes they wore. Landless wanderers, thrown upon the mercy of Lands that had none.

It could happen.

Fox stopped near the middle of the tiny valley. If not for the luminescence filling this place, he would not have been able to see; overhead, the sky was dark indigo velvet powdered with bright autumn stars. From the corner of her eye she could see two of Fox's men in the distance, standing with lighted lanterns beside the horses. The lanterns' warm light clashed oddly with the cool illumination that emanated from the grass and trees.

She glanced behind her. There was Raven, the black-haired giant who—so Fox said—feared her. When he saw her look toward him, he looked away, obviously ill at ease, and it occurred to Jausserande that if she could manage to be alone for any length of time with Raven, she could probably bend him to her will.

Beside him was the man who had bound her hands. Remarkable among Fox's band, he was not marked or branded for thievery or trespass, but his eyes would mark him in any company: one blue and one brown, they gave his face an oddly unfinished look. He regarded her with a knowing disrespect that irritated Jausserande even as it worried her. Such irreverence toward their overlords was not natural to the mud-born.

"Well, Tink, here we are. Just you, and me—and this."

Fox reached to his belt and pulled out the shadow-Cup. Melior's signet ring flashed on Fox's hand as he raised it.

"You had it all along!" Try as she might, Jausserande could not keep the note of betrayal out of her voice.

Fox smiled and spoke—for him—with compassion.

"But you couldn't know that. And with stakes so high, you couldn't risk it."

"How can you know that—and still do what you do!"

"I'm just one surprise after another, Tinkerbelle," Fox said, turning away.

Raven came forward, making a wide detour around Jausserande. Fox handed him the end of her leash, and Raven looped it around his wrist.

"Don't drop that."

"Fox, shouldn't we—" Raven began.

"Once we've got the Treasure, Raven, things'll be different," Fox said.

"They'll be worse!" Jausserande cut in swiftly. "Let me go now and—"

"If I have to shut you up, Tink, you won't like it," Fox said mildly, and the man still standing behind Jausserande chuckled.

Jausserande shut up.

Fox gestured, and Raven moved aside until the rope about Jausserande's throat was pulled uncomfortably taut. Now Fox lifted the simple pewter cup higher. The light from the meadow played along his jaw and the underside of his raised arm, but the darkness of his hand nearly blended into the dull pewter surface of the cup.

"Such a large area to search. And such a short time to do it in.

Moonrise, isn't it?" Fox turned back to her, and his bared teeth were predatory.

Jausserande raised her chin and stood silent.

"And somewhere—some *particular* where—here in the beautiful Vale of Stars we swap *this* one—" Fox tossed the Cup into the air and caught it, "—for *that* one. I wonder where?"

But he didn't wonder, Jausserande suspected in growing horror. If he did not know—or think he knew—how to retrieve the Cup of Morning Shadows, Fox could not be so gaily confident.

Surreptitiously she tested her bonds. Her hands had the numb tingle of having been tied too tight for too long, but as she pulled, she felt the leather cords creak and stretch.

She could get free.

She worked at the bindings on her wrists as Fox wandered, seemingly in random circles but actually covering a good amount of territory, as full night fell and moonrise drew nearer.

The pied-eyed man moved far enough away that Jausserande could watch as he unslung a crossbow from his back and held it ready, but she was still close enough to see that some of the bolts were tipped with a bright grayish metal.

Iron.

Raven's hold on her leash never slackened, but Jausserande had taken care to turn away from him and make no abrupt struggling movements. The leather bonds on her wrists continued to stretch. It began to seem that she had deluded herself during the days she had spent in the outlaws' camp. The most important thing was not to get the Cup of Morning Shadows.

It was to keep the Cup away from Fox.

"Ah-hah." Fox spoke softly, but Jausserande was so keyed up that the sound made her jump. The movement made the cords slide loosely on her wrists.

The moon hovered on the edge of the ridge, dispelling the luminescence from the Vale by its greater light. In the distance there was a spark of gold.

"Bring her along."

The source of the stream she had heard was a spring, round and perfect as the Cup itself, that bubbled up out of the earth at the crown of a small rise. Above it hung the faint balefire flicker of the Cup of Morning Shadows. The *true* Cup.

Jausserande stared, her heart hammering in anticipatory terror. In a moment he—

"Hold on tight," Fox said, but not to her.

Raven's hands settled on her shoulders in a crushing grip. Fox grabbed her arm and yanked. Her hand slid easily out of the loosened cords.

"Naughty," Fox said, but not as if he cared. And wrapped her fingers around the *tainaiste*-Cup.

She knew what he meant to do in the instant before he did it, but there was nothing she could do to stop him. She felt the hot callused roughness of Fox's hand over hers as he held her hand closed on the Cup, and Raven's grip on her shoulders was bruisingly tight.

And Fox used all his strength to force her hand, filled with the shadow-Cup, into the gleaming ghost-image of the real one. It would be her touch that retrieved it, not his.

Jausserande struggled until every muscle burned and her heartbeat was a hammering concussion in her temples. Her breath was a rasping repetition and there was the taste of blood in her mouth. Nothing had any effect.

And, at last, the Cup in her hands and Fox's passed through its golden mirror image.

The icy suction that Jausserande associated with High Magic pulled at the marrow of her bones, and through the Cup's gleaming illusion she could see the *tainaiste*-Cup catch fire, dull metal gilding.

And vanishing.

She felt it melt away in her hand, and for a moment she was as stunned as Fox. Raven released her and backed away, and she heard the words of a mud-born prayer against magic.

Magic.

Shadow and image both gone—and no Cup. But then she realized that Raven and her need to protect the Cup no longer held her, and the only hands on her were Fox's.

He was powerful for a human, but no match for elphen strength. Jausserande tore free and whirled away, only to slam into Raven's massive bulk. She knew he was stronger than she, but his fear of hurting her placed him at a disadvantage. In a moment she would be free of him, too.

"No, Hathorne—you'll hit Raven!" Meaningless words that she did not bother to listen to. Now Raven's grasp was loose on her wrists, and then she was running, a jagging path to baffle the crossbowman. The evening grass was cool on her legs as she ran for the trees and safety.

She did not hear the whistling arc of the slingstone that struck her unconscious.

· 24 ·

Queen's Play

IN THE SPACE of one short night she had been maid and mare, leopardess and dragon, warwasp. . . .

And defeated.

Amadis could still not believe—could not *understand*—the moment when her carefully made plans had dissolved like sugar in hot wine. Though the mortal man she had left for dead had wounded her, the Wild Magic had rippled through her like pure power incarnate, obedient to her command, and even the death-metal embedded in her throat was only a minor handicap. It had been simple to follow the soul-anchor to the Goblin Market; one snap of her mandibles and the soul she had spun out like flax would be free to inhabit the Sword of Maiden's Tears for the rest of its eternal existence, and the *proof* that Baligant's rebellious nobles might bring against him would be lost, lost, lost—

Only that was not what had happened. The Swordwarden had been there, the magic of the Treasure that he bore blinding to her supernatural senses. She had lost her prey, but the Swordwarden's death would serve almost as well, and so she—

Had been defeated by him. By Rohannan Melior, and the Sword of Maiden's Tears, and a magic greater than her own. If she had not fled, she would have died there.

Which might, Amadis considered, have been better than what faced her now—to go and tell Baligant High Prince, her master, that she had failed. That Ruth Marlowe, who had been the trap to bring the Sword of Maiden's Tears into the World of Iron, was still alive, and must inevitably encounter—and be used by—the Sword and its bearer.

No. Amadis considered the matter carefully. To die was worse than having to make such a confession, it was true. But it was far better to be able to report success than to confess to failure. She had possessed the strength and wit to return secretly; Baligant would not know to demand her presence yet. But the little time before the need that measured the seasons of her life was once more acute was short, and when that time was gone, she must go to Baligant High Prince in hope of slaking it again.

Without success to offer him, Baligant would deny her. And though he would not deny her unto death, the long agonizing humiliation that stretched before her as the payment for failure was something it was worth any exertion to avoid.

So when Baligant asked of the outcome of her hunt, she must have a better answer for him then than failure. In the chamber set aside for the wizard's use in the tower by the sea, Amadis made her preparations.

In this chamber the floor was inlaid with lines of silver; the gross geometries of the true world and its Gates. All lines led to the center of the room, where a low black cube of glass supported an enormous alabaster bowl, also webbed with silver. These were the trappings of the High Magic, which any Adept Major might presume to master.

In Amadis' hands, these objects became something more.

She set the wards, which would confine the powers she raised within the cube of space defined by the walls of this chamber. She set another such binding on the white bowl, that it would retain its shape regardless of the energies poured into it.

Then Amadis gestured, and cold green fire gushed from her hands into the bowl. Her form and the form of all the room's contents became mutable, the shapes they displayed merely a consensus shaped by her will and by the Word. The bowl flared sun-bright all along its silver inlays, and the fire that filled it, refined by its own weight, became darker and quieter until at last the bowl was glutted with an emerald liquid dark as blood.

In this speculum, Amadis began to search.

She did not see the forest house where Ruth had sheltered, for sight of that was barred to such as she. And from the Market, paths multiplied in such bewildering profusion that it could take a very long time to search all the Lands they led to.

Amadis took the time, though she could not draw upon the Word for as much energy as she spent. That was her peculiar misfortune. But her need was great enough to spend herself so.

She had not only space to search, but Time, which shifted its rate at every border, spinning faster and faster until one reached the World of Iron and Time became a blur, snuffing out the brief lives of that world's mortal inhabitants in an instant.

And at last, because she must, she found the moment and the Gate wherewhen the Swordwarden and his heart twin, Child of Earth, crossed the border into Chandrakar.

There. She marked it: *there.*

The viridian phlogiston sank away into the walls of the bowl and vanished. The light left her hands, her body, the walls of the chamber, returning them all to this world: creatures of matter, with fixed and immutable shapes. The riptide of Wild Magic ebbed and ebbed and ebbed, until for a moment Amadis wondered if she had cast the spell that every wizard fears—the unrepaid outwelling of power that takes all with it, even the life force of the wizard and his Covenant with the Word.

But it wasn't. Not this time. Still in flesh, Amadis slid to the chill stone floor and lay there with her cheek pressed against the icy glass of the altar cube. And the hunger for the drug that was weakness, that was *power,* burned demandingly within her.

An hour passed, then two, before she recovered the strength to stand. She swayed slightly as she got to her feet, still graceful as a willow in the wind. Now to finish the task that Baligant had set her, and kill Ruth Marlowe.

She raised her arms, willing the transformation, but even as she did the impulse flickered and died.

Not enough.

She put her hand to her throat and touched the faint white scar where the lump of iron had lain. Gone now, but death-metal destroyed magic as rain quenched fire.

She must have time. But a hammering upon her door told Amadis that time was something she did not have.

"I trust you come to tell me that the Ironworld daughter is dead?" Baligant said.

"I *came* to tell you nothing," Amadis reminded him.

In contrast to Baligant High Prince's elaborate jeweled and embroidered robes, the gown Amadis wore was of unornamented silk with a surface so bright it seemed almost to be made of the copper its color mimicked. Her hair gleamed in coils against it, its surface only slightly less hard.

"Don't toy with me, wizard. I can be spiteful and exceptionally unjust."

Baligant sat at his ease in his favorite room, the one that was crowded with treasure extorted from those whom Baligant suspected of being better than he. Amadis stood, as she had stood since Baligant's lackey had summoned her to him.

"I merely remark that you demanded a report. I did not come to bring you news."

"Did you or did you not slay the Ironworlder bound to the Sword of Maiden's Tears?" Baligant snarled.

"Slain or not, Line Rohannan would retain the Sword," Amadis remarked, as innocently as if it were an observation on the weather.

Baligant, like all clever men, could sometimes be dazzled by his own cleverness. There might be something in that which she could use, as Baligant used her. Amadis waited, dispassionately hoping, and dreamed of revenge.

"Line Rohannan would retain the Sword," came Baligant's inflectionless acknowledgment. His scrutiny came to rest on her, a slow weight. "Am I to understand, my . . . wizard, that you have *refrained* from slaying the earthling in order to bring me a greater triumph instead?"

"It is known that The Rohannan has obtained the Sword but has not yet brought it to the Twilight Court. Nor is he confirmed as the Lineholder. Now he is out of the world. No man knows where. His own cousin will swear that he went in search of the Ironworlder, and every servant in his castle knows that he has thought of nothing else."

"And should he disappear, and the Sword with him . . ."

"Then his name would be remembered as that of a fool. And another from Rohannan would go to seek the Treasure Rohannan Melior had lost."

Baligant smiled. "Fail me twice, creature, and I will make you beg for death."

He would, and she would. But she would not die, nor would he cease to make use of her.

Baligant held out a filled and bloody hand.

And for a moment there was bliss; freedom from pain.

Power.

· 25 ·

Dress in Black and Lose
Your Heart Beyond
Recall

ONCE HE'D RECOVERED a little from the thrashing the dragon had given him, Nic circled the glade he'd awakened in until he found the unicorn's tiny split-hoofed prints.

He'd followed the tracks hopefully, but they led, not to Ruth, but to a stream he didn't remember crossing. He stopped, and drank, and salved his injuries as much as he could with the icy river water.

His head hurt. Also his arm, his back, and the rest of his recent injuries. The Hyborean Age was no place for a forty-year-old library director, no matter what he might have been once.

And if that much were true, then by extension this was no place for a thirtysomething librarian, no matter what she was now.

At least, not alone.

An hour later, unhappily satisfied of the unattainability of Ruth Marlowe or the main road, Nic sat down on a fallen stump to think.

About unicorns. Unicorns wearing handmade, man-made garlands. Unicorns right out of a medieval tapestry, unicorns that Miss Marlowe, who at least had some small familiarity with this place, had not recognized as familiar when she had seen them. Unicorns that appeared and vanished with suspect facility, and had a vested interest in herding him and Miss Marlowe straight down the middle of the High Road that led to Fair Elphame—to coin a ballad.

In the cold clear light of hindsight, it looked very much like Fluffy the Wonder Caprid had been a player, and, presented as he had been with such painfully real evidence of the existence of at least two sides, Nic wondered which side it had been on. The opposite side—or *an* opposite side—from the Dragon Lady, almost certainly. But that didn't mean it was on Miss Marlowe's side, whatever being on Miss Marlowe's side might constitute at any given moment.

Nic smiled ruefully. You could take the boy out of the country, as the saying went, but the boy would never stop expecting smoke and mirrors. He'd gotten too attuned to hidden meanings in his youth to stop looking for them now. The only thing he could be even sixty-five percent certain of was that the possession or destruction of Miss Ruth Marlowe was important to at least some of the sides.

Nic took a deep breath and held it, and blew it out, looking down at the split and ruined remains of his expensive leather wing tips. Suitable shoes for a life it didn't seem he was ever going back to.

It would be nice to know what was going on, not that *not* knowing what was going on had ever been much of a handicap in the past. You just kept going on until you made enough trouble that the other guy took his toys and went home, a tactic Nicodemus Brightlaw had found particularly useful at meetings of the Ryerson Library Board of Directors.

On the other hand, it didn't seem to be of much utility when he was looking for somewhere to spend the night. And Ruth Marlowe, come to that.

Nic got to his feet, took his bearings from the sun, chose a direction at random, and began to walk.

Melior had been perfectly serious about advancing no farther than the nearest inn, Ruth discovered. It had been a matter of only a half-hour's walk along the forest road until they saw the lights in the distance.

Why did it seem that she had come so far?

If not for the dense forest surrounding it, Ruth would have taken this place for the inn she and Nic had found their first day here. The same sloping roof, the same Brothers Grimm wood carving.

Maybe it was a chain, like Howard Johnson's. *Come to the Otherwhere Hilton, where you can check out any time you like, but . . . Oh, quit whining, Ruth Marlowe. You've got what you said you wanted. You're here.*

And somebody's trying to kill you.

"Come, Ruth," Melior said.

* * *

Melior entered the inn's common room as if he'd just bought the place on a long lease. The landlord scurried toward him as if he'd been included in the price.

"Dinner," Melior said succinctly. "A room. In the morning I will require two horses, one for my lady."

"Yes, my lord. At once, my lord."

And how are you going to pay for all this? Ruth wondered. Two locals—if there could be locals in a place like this—took their dice and tankards and vacated a table near the fire. Melior led Ruth toward it.

The inn was one room, so large that the black-beamed ceiling seemed very low. In one corner, enormous kegs were racked on their sides, bunged and ready for tapping.

So that's what a hogshead looks like. I've always wondered.

A board on trestles provided a bar of sorts, as well as a place to stack empty clay jugs, pewter goblets, and leather quart-jacks. The fireplace was large enough to store grand pianos in, and in addition to a roaring fire contained a covered clay pot as well as a whole roast sheep hanging on a spit swung out of the way of the flames. The opposite wall of the room was filled with an enormous oven, cold now.

The table was round, its thick oak planks polished satiny by years of handling. The chairs were three-legged stools with a cricket bat-shaped backrest.

It was all very odd.

Melior lifted Ruth's cloak off her shoulders and threw it across one of the chairs, then piled his own dragon-mail mantle atop it. He leaned the ebony walking stave against the wall. Then he sat down, and Ruth saw that one reason for the odd chairs was that their arrangement allowed a man with a sword slung across his back to sit down without removing it.

They must get a lot of wandering paladins here.

Melior arranged himself with his back to the fire, wincing as he eased his weight off the wounded leg. He pulled off his long gauntlets as the landlord hurried anxiously over with two pewter cups and a clay jug. Ruth ducked out of his way, pulling at her own gloves, sitting down next to Melior as the landlord set down the cups and began to pour.

"Have you no better vintage?" Melior demanded ungraciously.

The landlord stopped in his tracks and retreated, rattling out a string of unintelligible promises. Melior rubbed his forehead wearily, face drawn.

"Rohannan is—*was*—known for its vintage," Melior said, as if that were an explanation.

"You didn't have to snap at him," Ruth said.

"His kind understands nothing else."

Ruth bit her lip to keep from snapping something unforgivable back at Melior. She was seeing a new side of his personality now that he was in his own world, one that she didn't think she liked. Not even arrogance: a matter-of-fact assumption of privilege that grated badly upon Ruth's republican ideals. *This* was her own true love? This . . . *monarchist?*

"If you say so," Ruth said tightly.

Melior glanced quickly toward her, his eyes flashing golden-green in the firelight. "Yes. I say so."

The landlord returned, this time with a large, dusty, dark green bottle with a protruding cork covered in red wax. He cut through the wax and drew the cork, and a scent like summer flowers in honey filled the room. Melior smiled. The landlord looked relieved.

"And there is game pie, my lord, and new bread, and apples in honey for the lady. And a bath, should either of you desire—at your word I will have the tub brought up—"

Melior raised his hand and the man stopped speaking.

"Bring what I have asked of you, and that will be sufficient," Melior said briefly.

The landlord retreated once more.

Melior inspected the cups critically, and then filled them both, pushing one toward Ruth. He drank, and leaned back carefully.

"I hope you know some way of paying for all this," Ruth said sourly, not touching her own cup. The conversation seemed to be sliding irrevocably into one of those nasty snippy little fights she hated—and could see, here and now, no way to keep from having.

Melior glanced at her through lowered lashes and smiled faintly, and in that moment Ruth saw the man she'd fallen in love with such a very long time ago. Her mouth quirked upward in answer.

"Ah, Ruth, did you think I bought and could not pay? It is true that we do not *spin plastic* in the Morning Lands as you do in the World of Iron, but be sure that the innkeeper will receive his—certain to be outrageous—due." Melior refilled his cup and drank again. "Magic is the coin between the realms, and he shall have what sorcery he asks on the morrow."

"You didn't have to be so rude to him," Ruth said, retreating to her original complaint.

"And is the friendship of Rohannan Melior such a desirable commodity, that you would offer it to every passing stranger?" Melior looked even more amused. "We are hunted—it is not hard to imagine by whom."

"B-Baligant," Ruth got out, remembering the name at last. She took a deep swig of the contents of her cup and choked, her nose and mouth filled with sugar and heat and the scent of summer fields.

Melior hissed slightly, a warning to Ruth to hold her tongue. The landlord reappeared, this time leading a girl dressed as if there were a Bavarian comic opera rehearsing next door. "Buxom wench" was about the only way to describe her, politically incorrect though it might be, with the tight red leather of the woman's gold-laced bodice thrusting her chest up and out in that uncomfortable-looking Playboy Bunny fashion.

The serving girl set a tray stacked with food down in front of Melior, and smiled in a fashion Ruth tried very hard to mistake for something else, and lingered in front of him to place the dishes on the table. In the firelight, Ruth saw that what she had first thought was glitter and then bad skin was actually *scales.*

She blinked, and tried not to stare. A tavern wench with scales?

I don't think we're in Kansas any more, Toto.

"If there is anything else," the landlord said hopefully.

Well, thought Ruth, *yes. For dessert we can always manage to get this place leveled by something out of a science fiction double feature.*

"The horses in the morning," Melior reminded him.

The landlord bowed and smiled and rubbed his hands together in a way that made Ruth wonder how expensive—or overpriced—those horses were going to be. Then Melior turned his attention to the food and so did she.

There were, as promised, game pie and new bread and apples in honey. Ruth, who had eaten well not that long ago, picked at a portion of apples. They tasted as if they had been boiled in honey, impossibly sweet. She pushed them away and concentrated on the wine, while Melior finished both servings of the pie, a heel of the loaf, and the rest of the apples.

"Ah," he said at last, leaning carefully back in his seat. The gem on the pommel of the Sword of Maiden's Tears glowed with opal rainbows in the firelight. Ruth regarded it mistrustfully.

"And now to bed, Lady Ruth. And tomorrow, home—or at least the Road," Melior amended truthfully.

Another of the inn servants followed them, to bring the cloaks and the half-finished wine, and to carry the candle and light them up the stair. Melior mounted the steps with apparent ease, and only Ruth knew how his hand tightened on hers. His injuries were far from healed; God knew what he was going to do with a horse tomorrow. God knew what *she* would do, come to that—Ruth had never ridden a horse in her life.

The room could be nothing but the inn's best, but despite that it was small, with a tilting ceiling and closed wooden shutters where glass windows ought to be. But there was a fire burning in the corner, and at least the place smelled clean.

And it contained a very large bed.

There was a thump as Melior dropped the bar into position across the door, and another as the head of his walking stick struck the white plaster wall beside it. Then the creak and pull of leather, as he unbuckled the harness that held the Sword in place.

Ruth sat down on the bed. And down, and down, and down, through featherbeds piled one on the other, because here at the Elphame Hilton the mysteries of the innerspring mattress had not been revealed unto them.

Melior regarded his lady, who was staring resolutely off into space, and wondered if he would have to manage his boots by himself. It was true that he could have gotten one of the lackeys to do it—if he had wanted to publish the fact of his injuries to all the wide world. It had seemed more desirable to have a barred door between him and them instead, but now he wasn't so sure.

Melior told over his memories of Ruth's world, and decided he would have to get his own clothes off. And then—

Return to Chandrakar as fast as they could, and hope and pray that the Twilight Court still sat. Summon Ophidias, unbind Ruth from the Sword, lay the evidence of Baligant's tampering before the convened Lords Temporal—

And, oh, yes, arrange to be confirmed in his lands and honors at the same time. Find some way to meet Ophidias' price. Discover what doom the Heartlands would call down on Chandrakar for the attack at the Goblin Market. Collect the taxes. Collect the harvest. Discover whether Jausserande had yet been successful in retrieving her Treasure. Sweep the forests for outlaws, and decide what to do with them when he caught them. Perhaps Richart would have some idea—many of them would be ex-soldiers, after all. Perhaps they could go to the guard, where a roof and a meal and a warm cloak would do much to discourage thievery.

Keep the sword. Keep his life. And, somehow, in all of this, incline his lady's heart once more to him. She had been willing to leave her own world for him once.

But that had been long ago, as mortals reckoned time. And if it were true that she no longer loved him, each day would be less bright than it might have been.

"Ruth?" Melior said.

*   *   *

She turned at the sound of his voice, and felt the corners of her mouth twist downward. But underneath the automatic pain was the unnerving certainty that her responses weren't *real;* that somehow she was only faking what a real person would feel.

Because she wasn't real. In the truest sense of the phrase, Ruth Marlowe was not "all there."

Against her will she looked toward the Sword of Maiden's Tears. That was where her soul was—the thing that would let her be real. Melior said he would return it to her. Until then, all she could do was pretend.

She got to her feet and went over to him.

"Need help?" Ruth said.

Melior smiled up at her and reached for her hand. His fingers were warm over hers, and she wished—

"I need to find Nic," Ruth blurted out suddenly.

Melior frowned and tightened his grip on her, as if he were afraid she would suddenly pull away.

"If he is here, it is wizard work, or do you think that the Iron Road is open to any who choose to stroll it for a day's pleasaunce?"

"I think I don't know where he is. I think he's in trouble and needs help. I hope you'll help me find him," Ruth finished in a strangled tone.

Melior lifted her hand and lightly brushed it with his lips. Ruth wanted to hug him to her; wanted to push him away. She stood perfectly still.

"I shall do all that I may to find your friend, once we are home," Melior said.

"But—"

"My lady, do you think we ourselves are safe?" Melior said gently. "We are in danger as great as the power of the wizard who hunts us. In my own place—" The last word was a drawn-out sigh, and Melior's head drooped a little.

"We'll be safer," Ruth finished for him. *Poor Melior; no wonder he's been so bitchy. If I knew what was going on, I'd be scared to death, too.*

As it is, I'm merely terrified.

"Yes," Melior said. He released Ruth's hand and looked down at his boots, and Ruth's imagination painted vivid holographs of the ragged tears and gouges that the warwasp had left in his flesh.

"Let me do that for you, okay?" Ruth said.

Though in the course of her association with the Society for Creative Anachronism Ruth Marlowe had been given occasion to assist both fops and fighters with that one item of garb which, when properly worn, it is almost impossible to remove unaided, it did not mean she was particularly expert at it. The first boot came off easily enough. The second, for all her determination, resisted until Ruth was tugging with all her might, whereupon it slipped free and sent her sprawling.

Still, it was probably easier on Melior than trying to remove them himself.

She looked up at him from her inelegant seat on the floor and grinned hopefully. And Melior, who had been trying hard not to laugh at her, gave up.

"So elegant a chatelaine," he teased, holding out his hand and smiling at her.

"I never claimed—" began Ruth.

"To be anything but my lady. My—dearest—lady. My heartsease."

He pulled her forward until Ruth knelt between his knees, her face turned up to regard him. And then he brought his lips down on hers; so slowly, so carefully, that she was mad with impatience by the time contact was made. It was as if the touch completed some circuit of power, filling meek Ruth Marlowe with a borrowed wildness. She reached up to put her arms around his neck, but instead of pulling him downward, the gesture raised both of them to their feet.

And finally, for a while, everything was all right.

She awoke near dawn, lying nestled in featherbeds with Melior's arm across her. At one point during the night he had opened the shutters, and from where she lay Ruth could see the faint proto-lightness of the sky. Mist overlay everything, so that only the sharp black-green tops of the pines protruded.

Dawn had always had the power to lift Ruth's spirits. To see dawn was to have survived the night, and there had been times when surviving was the only triumph Ruth had been able to claim.

Not any more. Now there was Melior. And if she was too old to believe that love could solve all her problems, at least she could believe that now she had an ally against them. That no matter what tricks of temper and imagination might intervene, there was no longer an invisible wall dividing the two of them. They were together, and all their future problems could come from that.

Ruth smiled to herself and nestled deeper into the bed.

All the mist had burned away and true morning had come when Melior escorted Ruth from the inn. The stave had been left behind; this morning Melior walked without it, and the effort it cost him was visible for no one to see.

An ostler led two horses into the yard for their inspection. Both were saddled and bridled. The dark gray one had saddlebags behind the saddle.

"Ah," said Melior, in rueful tones.

The large gray horse—as differentiated, in Ruth's nonequinephilic mind, from the small white horse—tugged at its lead rein when it saw Melior. He walked over to it, and it lowered its head to nuzzle him roughly, until he staggered. He grabbed at its headstall.

"This," Melior announced, "is Cobant."

Ruth looked blank.

"The horse I began with," Melior elaborated. "And lost."

"They sold him back to you?" Ruth said.

Melior shrugged, as though being sold one's own horse was no more than a wandering elf-lord could expect. "Assist my lady to mount," he said to the ostler.

After last night Ruth knew that Melior's injured leg would not bear the strain of her added weight, but she still wished he were the one who would be helping her onto the beast's back. She regarded her destination with wariness.

The white horse was really a pale gray, with dapples like rain spots across its shoulders and rump. It regarded her as if it had been expecting bad news and she was it. On its back was a carved wooden saddle with a high padded back and prowlike front, much as if someone had miniaturized an old-fashioned sleigh and then converted it to a saddle. The wooden stirrups were shielded by wide leather skirts, half flapping in the breeze like unhinged automobile cowling.

A second groom came forward with a mounting block, and there was nothing for Ruth to do but step up to it as if she'd been doing this all her life.

Two steps up, then a foot through the stirrup, then a hop and wriggle and Ruth was in the saddle, smoothing her wide skirts carefully back into place while her pleasant seat sidled mistrustfully beneath her.

The ground looked very far away.

The painted leather reins lay on the horse's neck, and Ruth, for something to do, picked them up. As if that were a signal, both ostlers stepped away, and the horse took a step forward. Ruth clutched at the curled saddle-prow before her and dropped the reins. The horse stopped.

Then Melior, without benefit of mounting block, swung himself aboard Cobant. He collected the reins and the horse moved as if it were merely an extension of Melior's will.

He tossed a handful of something that sparkled to the ostlers and moved his horse next to Ruth's.

"Ruth," said Melior in tones of sudden suspicion, "you *have* seen a horse before?"

"Sort of," Ruth said truthfully. Why hadn't he asked earlier?

Melior shook his head and smiled. Reaching across, he took the reins from her clutching fingers and unknotted them. He threaded one through a projection on the front of her saddle and wound the other through his gloved hand. He turned Cobant away. Ruth's horse followed on the lead.

"You ride like a basket of dead fish," Melior told her half an hour later.

"Thank you," Ruth replied sweetly. "How many baskets of dead fish have you seen go riding?"

It had to be admitted, though, that at the moment she *felt* rather like a basket of dead fish: walk, trot, and canter alike were bone-jarring, and she always seemed to be going down just as the saddle was coming up.

"Enough to know that you greatly resemble them. It might be easier," Melior said, "did I take you up in front of me."

Ruth glanced sideways. Melior's saddle, though nothing out of a John Wayne Western (the sum total of Ruth's previous exposure to horses and riding), was still flat enough fore and aft that what he suggested looked possible.

"I don't want to hurt you," Ruth said.

"Cobant can carry us both this while. And I am anxious to strike the Iron Road and return home as soon as I may," Melior said. "By your leave, my lady."

"And find Nic," Ruth said, just to remind both of them, though in truth it was rather difficult to stay worried about Nicodemus Brightlaw after the things she'd seen him do. By now he was probably king someplace, just like Conan the Barbarian.

"And find your companion," Melior agreed.

The transfer was more easily accomplished than Ruth would have thought, and soon she was seated sideways across Melior's thighs, one arm around his waist.

Cobant broke into a trot, but this time, cushioned by Melior's body, the motion was fluid and peaceful. The road branched and branched again, and each time Melior took the wider of the branches. Her horse followed along behind.

There were any number of things she should ask about—the unicorn, the warwasp—but Ruth kept silent on all of them, as if to name events would be to acknowledge that they had happened. And she didn't want them to have happened. It was as if the time in the forest house had

drawn an eraser across all that came before it, and now the only thing
Ruth wanted was Melior and peace and quiet.

Then they came to a third crossroads, and Ruth, glancing up toward
Melior, surprised him sketching a glyph in the air. The lines he had drawn
sparkled for a moment and then faded: faery-fire.

"You said you didn't have any magic," Ruth said, as if he'd been
deceiving her.

"*Small* magic only—and less than that in the World of Iron," Melior
corrected. "But enough to find our way. Now we will stop, and rest, and
perhaps strike the Road by evening."

They picnicked beneath a tree at the edge of the road—or, rather,
Ruth picnicked, the horses grazed, and Melior ate and drank something
beside the tree, the Sword of Maiden's Tears handy to his hand, and kept
watch.

It was a disturbing reminder of how far from home she was. It was
true that there was street crime at home, but Ruth would never have gone
into the worst neighborhoods of home, let alone stopped to have lunch in
a place as dangerous as Melior seemed to think this one was.

"We must give the horses ease, if we are to use them later," Melior
said, catching the tone of her thought.

"Where are we?" Ruth asked.

"In the Morning Lands, near the Iron Road. Once we reach it, Chandrakar is not far, and Dawnheart a day's ride, if that, from the Gate."

"Which tells me precisely nothing," Ruth informed him helpfully.

Melior smiled. "Were you an Adept, my lady, I would refer you to
your ephemeris, but as you are not, I know not how to lesson you. This is
not the Last World, where everything is fixed and in its appointed place
forever. These are the Morning Lands. Things . . . change."

"Except you," Ruth said.

"As to that, my lady Ruth, perhaps some day even such as I may learn
wisdom, though not if wisdom means I must renounce you. Come, if you
are sated, and we will try if we might make your ride a little smoother."

When they finally reached the Road, it was late afternoon. The trail
had been rising steadily since they'd stopped for lunch, and the air had
taken on an alpine sharpness. Oak had given way to poplar and birch,
then to pine, and Ruth was stiff and sore with the effort of keeping back
straight, knees in, heels down, and wrists cocked. It was possible, she had
discovered with pleasure, to not come down quite as hard—or as far—on
the white horse's saddle as she had that morning, and the ground did not
look quite so far away now that she was more certain of staying in the

saddle. Despite—or because of—this, she was looking forward to to-night's inn with active interest.

"There," Melior said, and pointed.

Ahead the trail merged with a wider track. There was a tightness, an anticipation in the air, as if some enormous engine were running. The air above the wider track shimmered as if with heat, and the surface of the road changed and rippled in the wavering air—now claylike, now hot white radiance, now opaline gravel.

Magic.

"No!" Ruth cried. She hauled up and back on her horse's reins, and the beast obediently stopped. A cold chill of revulsion struck through her, and what had seemed so harmless when Melior used it to find their way, so reasonable when he proposed it in the morning light, was suddenly horrible.

Go on *that?* Ride along it, touch it, let it touch *her?*

"No," Ruth said, with what she hoped was more calmness. "Not on that."

Melior had reined in also, and sat regarding her with blank puzzlement.

"You can *see* it?" he said after a moment.

Ruth nodded miserably.

"A terrifying sight, is it not?" Melior asked.

"Don't humor me!"

"But it *is* a terrifying sight, Ruth—for any of the Five Races, let alone for a—"she saw him stop, and decide to go on, "—for a human, a Child of Earth, who has little experience of magic."

"I've had enough," Ruth said tightly, glaring mistrustfully at the sword Melior carried. *Enough to know that magic kills.*

He caught the direction of her glance. "But that explains it," Melior said. "You are bound to the Sword, and it lends you some of its magic." He looked back toward the Road. "I swear you will take no hurt from the Road, Ruth. Magic is not always baneful."

Ruth shook her head. How could she explain that it didn't matter whether it was harmless or just as lethal as it looked?

"But it is the Road, Ruth. There is no other way," Melior said help-lessly.

"There has to be," Ruth said, with the irrational desperation of the phobic. "I can't go on that."

Even at this distance she could feel the presence of the Road; a heatless proximity pressing on her skin. It felt as Ruth imagined exposure to lethal radiation must feel—insidiously toxic, destructive beyond death.

"None as certain, as simple, nor as fast," Melior answered honestly, "and we are in desperate haste." He sidled his horse over to hers and put out his hand. Ruth flinched away from his touch, but he only covered her gloved hands with his. "If I hooded you, or cast a darkening about the Sword so you did not see the Road, would that serve?"

Ruth felt her eyes begin to tear from sheer stupid terror, and fury at her own helplessness made her voice hard. "But it would still be there, wouldn't it?"

"You see the Road as the Children of Air may see it—in all places, and none; the silver cord that binds the Morning Lands together."

Which meant "yes," she guessed. And there was no other way. But—oh, God—to set foot on that road felt like betraying Naomi; making common cause with the magic that had killed her friend.

And what would it do to *her?* To Ruth Marlowe—not fish, not flesh, not good red herring? Gazetted Sleeping Beauty, certified elphen pawn—would it fling her back into the World of Iron and lock the door behind her?

Did she want to stay so much?

She opened her mouth to try to force the words of acceptance out, but as she did, Melior turned violently in his saddle, listening intently to something she could not hear.

Then he drew the Sword of Maiden's Tears.

It flashed like an airplane wing against the sky, and hummed with the thin sweet croon of high-voltage power lines. Melior's face was grim enough that for an instant, watching him, Ruth forgot all her reasonable terror of being trapped between the Iron Road and the Sword in the fear of whatever made him look so frightening.

"They've found us," Melior said. He patted Cobant's neck absently, as if judging what reserves of strength the horse had left to give him.

"We must reach the Gate before they do—that is our only safety."

Ruth strained her ears, her eyes, her mortal senses, but the link to the Sword that had given her elphensight enough to see the Road gave her nothing more.

"Forgive me, Ruth," Melior said—and swung.

The flat of the blade hit her horse square across the haunches, and the horse, already infected by Ruth's fear, squealed and lunged across the little distance that separated it from the Road. Ruth, flailing desperately to stay in the saddle, felt the pressure of the Road crescendo; felt a heatless, lightless sizzle envelop her—then she was *on* the Road, and Cobant was crowding her horse to turn it along it. The mare bounced and shied; Ruth clutched at the saddle, afraid of being pitched beneath those fatal hooves.

The horse's plunging, kicking trot at last became first a canter, then a gallop, then a flat run. The hammer, hammer, hammer of the horses' hooves merged into a steady machinelike thunder, and now Ruth could hear sound behind them like the distant clamor of a mob—but loud enough to be heard over the jangle of bridle and thud of hoof. Ruth's new-learned horsemanship deserted her completely; she bounced help- lessly in the saddle and focused all her will on not falling off.

That was all she could do. Her safety was entirely at the mercy of the muscles and will of a frightened animal running out of control.

Just as the car had been out of control.

The intrusion of the dream-memory into her waking fright was jar- ring. For a moment it blotted out the real world with its presence—

A back road, not very well lit. One in the morning, Prom Night. There was a flash of light in the road ahead, a coppery fiery light, and Ruth, straining her eyes, suddenly saw—

The creature that blotted out the sun merged seamlessly with the terror-image of Ruth's nightmare. It was dark against the sun dazzle, and despite its wide leathery wings Ruth thought of spiders and blind squirm- ing eyeless things churned up out of the earth.

She barely had time to register its presence before it banked and dove for them. It passed low over her head, close enough for her to smell sulfur, blood, and the cloying scent of roses. Ruth crouched like a jockey, and the animal beneath her seemed to elongate, stretching its neck for- ward as if shrinking away from the monster above.

Suddenly there was a sound, a flash; lightning, thunder, nuclear war. She saw Melior's horse Cobant pass her, riderless and running flat out. Where was Melior? She wound the reins around her hands and pulled back as hard as she could.

Nothing happened.

· 26 ·

So You Want to Be a Hero

IN THE END, as it turned out, the unicorn was of some use after all.

In his circular sweep—looking for a road, looking for clues—Nic came upon the unicorn's track again, impossible to mistake. The print was slotted like a deer's hoof, but shorter and rounder, and in one place, where the tracks passed too close to a thornbush, there was a tuft of familiar white down caught among the twigs.

" 'Where are you come from, Baby Dear/Out of the everywhere into the here?' " Nic quoted softly to himself. He followed the tracks, pushing the pain of his injuries as far into the background of his consciousness as he could. As it always had, a job to do settled Nic Brightlaw's mind wonderfully, letting him banish everything but the need to do it well.

It was the light that gave him his first warning that things were worse than he thought.

Ever since Christmas Eve, when he'd fallen through the enchanted bookshelf with Ruth Marlowe, the sun had behaved itself. It had risen, crossed the sky, and set in a reasonable fashion.

Not any more.

Nic stopped, and straigtened out of his half-instinctive crouch, wincing as bruised muscles and torn flesh protested. He was in a spring forest with a heavy canopy, garden perfect: everything in new leaf and no sign anywhere of last autumn's leaves. The light was the rich mellow gold of late afternoon.

Just as it had been when he'd woken up—several hours ago.

Nic looked up. The leaves gave the view the aspect of a green and starry heaven—an ever-shifting, nearly solid viridian canopy through which light penetrated in white glittering chinks.

He turned around slowly, abruptly conscious of how unsteady he was on his feet; how dizzy, how likely to fall. There was no place where the sky, seen through the leaves, was brighter than any other. The light had not changed, or shifted, or dimmed, in hours. He braced himself one-handed against a tree trunk and continued looking for the source of the sunlight.

There was none. There was no sun.

Unreality washed over him in a slow wave of contused nausea. No matter what else had been strange, the physical world had always played by the rules. Now, it seemed, there weren't going to be any rules. Now, in the roots of his neglected soul, Nic Brightlaw believed he was in Faery. Where there was neither sun nor moon, only inhuman malice.

Perhaps he ought to have been frightened. But he felt, instead, a vast stubborn rage pushing at the edges of his self-control. He was here to do a job and *They*—whoever They were—were withholding information. Changing the rules.

It was an unexpected and not entirely pleasant thing to feel anger when the ability to feel anything at all had been dead for so long. To give it a focus—because anger, like lightning, needed a focus if it was not to destroy everything—Nic concentrated his anger on the unicorn. This was all Fluffy's fault.

He was going to find it. And once he got his hands on it—

A twig snapped.

Nic froze. He looked around carefully. Only his eyes moved.

There was a flash of white.

Fluffy the Wonder Caprid was back in town.

If this isn't the oldest trick in the book, it's certainly a main heading in the index, Nic thought with a flash of grim amusement. He knew how silently the unicorn could move. The noise it had made had been deliberate. Apparently he wasn't following fast enough.

But apparently, too, he was supposed to follow without knowing he was being led, and that spelled "trap" to Mrs. Brightlaw's little boy.

The nice thing about traps, Nic had always found, was that the people setting them were rarely paying much attention to anything else.

Nic blundered—gracelessly and with as much dramatic effect as he could muster—in the direction of the silvery flash. He caught a brief glimpse of Fluffy—*sans* flowers, but otherwise much the same as the last time he'd seen it—for one brief shining second before the unicorn plunged away.

Nic stopped. He was supposed to follow, of course. Instead, he headed off at right angles to the direction of the unicorn's flight. If it was smarter than a man, this trick wouldn't work. It might not work anyway, of course, but at least it would give him something to do.

When he was far enough away from where he'd seen the unicorn, he turned and walked parallel to its line, moving as silently as he could in his condition, looking for the right tree.

After a few minutes he found it: a massive, dense-foliaged oak, with a thick overhanging branch suitable for Errol Flynn to stand on while making speeches. Nic had other plans for it.

His first attempt to climb it made him abruptly aware that his right hand was entirely useless to him. He fell back, and found he'd reopened the deep gouges in his right arm. New blood seeped through the tight windings of Nic's makeshift bandage. The pain was exquisitely demanding, even overshadowing the pounding in his head. A fine countertrap he was setting here, lying on the ground waiting to be caught.

Hissing through clenched teeth, Nic rolled to his feet and hooked the useless hand through his belt before trying again, one-handed this time.

He made it onto the branch, but the pounding trembling weakness in every limb, the flashing light behind his eyes, told him how close to the edge of failure he really was. Catching the unicorn was his best and only shot.

It should come back for him. The unicorn was supposed to lead him . . . somewhere. Once it realized he wasn't following, it ought to turn back and try to draw him out again. When it didn't spot him on its back trail, it should circle to find him. Eventually, it would show up here. Nic stretched himself full-length along the branch and waited, hidden from watchers below by the dense overhang of leaves. One of the advantages of being the aggressor was not having to wait until the other guy did something.

Time was hard to judge without the sun to mark it by, and his watch had vanished long ago, probably in the fight with the dragon. In this woods there was only Now, and Now seemed to last forever. As he waited, Nic began more and more to think that this was not a place where human beings could safely remain. This was the dark side of Faery, deadly as poison, and Nic hoped, with the desire of one who dreams of a life free from complications, that he would not meet the rightful masters of these woods.

The unicorn came back.

Head up, pink nostrils flaring, tufted tail twitching like an inquisitive cat's, the creature minced into the clearing below Nic as if it were slumming royalty.

Nic slid off the branch and dropped on it.

It was only when he was in midair, unable to change his mind, that he spared a fleeting thought for the unicorn's exceedingly sharp horn. But its mind was on flight rather than attack. Fortunately.

Its legs buckled beneath his weight, and Nic twisted to grab it before it recovered. He was barely in time. The unicorn fought, all furious coiled muscles. It reminded Nic of wrestling alligators, the skills for which, once learned, were always with you, just like riding a bicycle. He clutched the unicorn to him, back to belly on the forest floor, his good hand clenched about the base of its horn, his other arm around its barrel just behind the furiously windmilling forelegs. It thrashed and squalled, but helplessly.

So he thought.

He was hoping it would run out of strength before he did, when suddenly the hairs on his forearm and the back of his neck prickled with some unsettling electrical charge. *Incoming artillery!* his idiot instinct yammered, and Nic threw himself sideways, still clutching Fluffy, to escape something that couldn't possibly be there.

And fell into a pit that couldn't be there either.

The fall was darkness and numbness—long enough for him to frame a coherent thought about failure and betrayal and dying alone. This time he landed on the bottom, and the pain that lanced through his skull made him close his eyes against the brightness. Then light returned, and he clutched tighter at the unicorn.

"Let go of that, son. I'm a thought fond of it, in my fashion."

Nic opened his eyes. He saw the biggest orange lizard he had ever seen. And it had wings. The fact that it could talk, too, was almost an anticlimax.

Nic carefully let go of the unicorn. It didn't move, and for a moment he thought it was dead. Then it shook itself and rolled over, gaining its feet and staggering away from him—toward the dragon—shaking its head.

The unicorn collapsed beneath the shadow of one enormous wing, looking rumpled and tired, and closed its eyes with a sigh. Nic was absurdly reminded of Christian iconography, the lion lying down with the lamb. But Fluffy was no lamb, and this was no lion.

"That's a sight friendlier," the dragon said amiably.

Its hide had the satiny-rough sheen of sharkskin and the bright ruddy color of California poppies, Monarch butterfly wings, and fancy goldfish. Its eyes were burning pupilless gold, set in a long triangular head belonging to no known taxonomy—bird and beast and insect all blended together into something out of heraldry set at the end of a serpentine length of plate-crested neck.

It was lying on the grass, but even so, it could look Nic in the eye—and even so, it was much smaller than the last dragon he'd seen. Maybe that was why he didn't feel immediately threatened. Endangered, perhaps, but not threatened.

"I'm a friendly kind of a guy," Nic said mendaciously, glancing around unobtrusively. He was in open country, as manicured as a golf course, and the sun was a blessedly determinate point in the sky.

It took him a couple of tries to stand up, during which he kept his gaze warily on the dragon. He wondered if it could actually fly, or merely glided once it had launched itself from a height.

"Oh, I manage to get around," the dragon said.

"I'm glad," Nic said.

So it was telepathic, although it seemed to talk. On the other hand, it did not have the lips or tongue or palate to form those familiar English words he heard so clearly—just gleaming rows of teeth indicating a highly carnivorous lifestyle.

Outclassed. Game, set, and match to magic. Every muscle hurt, he was bleeding steadily, and the next fight he was in he'd lose.

Unless he could put it off long enough. A year or so seemed about right.

"I'm looking for a friend of mine," Nic began. "I wonder if you might have seen her?" *I wonder if you might have killed her, Puff, and if I can believe a damned thing you say, anyway.*

"Trust is a virtue," the dragon observed.

"Virtue is found only in Heaven," Nic responded.

"Does your friend have a name?"

"Ruth Marlowe. Do you?"

"Have a name?" the dragon asked, spreading its wings until the sun shone on Nic through a golden dragonsilk canopy. "Oh, many. But for the moment, you can call me Ophidias. It's a name much known in these parts," it added.

What, not Gandalf the Grey? "Okay, Ophidias, have you seen Ruth Marlowe?" Nic asked patiently. Although why he should assume that every talking dragon he met was a wizard—

"Not a dragon. Please. Dragons are such obsessive creatures; you wouldn't enjoy meeting one, believe me. I'd prefer you thought of me as a firedrake—or salamander, if you have a classical education."

Firedrake. Salamander. Creatures of fire. Creatures of Faery.

"Ruth Marlowe?" Nic asked yet again.

"My you are persistent. No, I haven't seen Ruth Marlowe yet. But I will." The dragon—firedrake—preened itself in the sun. The light struck golden rainbows from the chitin of its muzzle and crest and turned the unicorn's silvery coat saffron yellow.

So she was still alive. Nic felt a pang of relief.

"The question now is, what shall I do with you?" Ophidias pursued.

Here it comes. Nic tensed. He could see trees, behind him and to the right. Could he reach them before the creature reached him?

"No. The question, *firedrake,* is why *that*—" he pointed toward the unicorn, "—has shown up every other minute since Miss Marlowe and I arrived. And where it was leading me just now—and why. And while we're on the subject, you owe me big time for rescuing it a while back before Cruella DeVille turned it into unicorn *en brochette.*"

"Ah." The firedrake mantled its wings. "You want to buy."

"Maybe," said Nic. "But you still owe me."

Ophidias graciously inclined its head, agreeing.

"Where was the unicorn taking me?" Nic asked.

"To an inn where you would be fed, clothed, tended, and housed."

Nic started to ask why, and stopped himself. "Why" was something he could worry about later. There were more important things to ask.

"Where is Ruth Marlowe?"

"In Chandrakar, in mortal peril," the firedrake answered promptly, and waited.

Three questions were the traditional payment in fairy tales, and if Ophidias was a traditionalist, Nic had better not waste the third one.

"Can you take me to Ruth Marlowe?" he said carefully.

"Well," said Ophidias, after a long pause, "no. I can open the Gate for you, of course. But you're in no shape to go charging after her right now. Have some wine."

The firedrake spread its wing, and the unicorn was gone. Where it had lain, Nic saw a small table with a decanter and a single glass on it. Nic looked from the cup to the firedrake.

"Am I supposed to trust you?" Nic asked mockingly.

"Do you actually have a choice, Child of Earth? I could spin you a tale about being a great wizard unable to interfere directly in the affairs of the Morning Lands. I could go on about chess games of the gods, and grand illusions, and young Adepts reaching for powers they don't understand, and the mistakes of ancient enemies giving me the chance to thwart their plans, but the brass-nailed bottom line is, you either trust me for the hell of it and drink the wine, or hit the road just the way you are, Jack—if you can—but don't forget to look over your shoulder."

Nic walked to the table, poured the cup full, and drank it off without stopping to breathe. The sweet, raisiny taste almost gagged him, and standing this close to Ophidias was like standing in front of a roaring fire.

"That's no way to treat a fine vintage," Ophidias objected mildly, but Nic wasn't listening.

The wine slid honey-hot down his throat and set up a comfortable burning in his empty stomach. And as the warmth spread, his headache cleared; the aches of used and abused muscles dulled into the background and then faded altogether.

He flexed the hand that had been in the dragon's mouth. The fingers moved, feeling returning to them in a tingling rush. Already guessing at what he would find, Nic peeled back the bloody makeshift bandage to look beneath.

The gouges were feverish, deep pink, and welted, but the fang marks were closed. There was no bleeding. As he stared at his arm, the color of the scars continued to fade.

"I trust you consider yourself repaid?" Ophidias asked.

"Yes." *If it lasts.* "Thank you."

"What a very suspicious young man you are. Now. Did you wish to bargain for passage to Chandrakar?"

Past overlay present with unwelcome suddenness. Sunlight. A crumbling sidewalk cafe in a city where the humidity molded your clothes to your skin even before you'd finished dressing. Across from him sat a smiling dark-skinned man, who smiled and smiled and offered his services in just such mild tones as Ophidias did.

Black market is black market, no matter where.

"Naturally I'm interested in listening to whatever proposal you care to make, but you'll appreciate that my resources are a bit limited at the moment," Nic said, falling into the old ways. He looked down at the cup in his hands, rolling it between his palms, then set it down on the table and took a step backward.

Nothing hurt.

"Well, son, I'm afraid your resources may turn out to be a bit of a problem. In fact, I don't think I'd be overstating the case to say that you really haven't got much to dicker with at all—except your life," Ophidias said in the bland tones of a Tennessee moonshiner.

If Ophidias had wanted his life, the firedrake could already have taken it with one snap of those long fanged jaws.

Don't listen to what they say. Listen to what they mean.

"So you'll put me in Chandrakar in exchange for my life," Nic said. "That doesn't do me a lot of good—unless you'd consider leaving me part of my life to use myself after I get there?" Nic said, equally blandly.

"You're good, boy." The firedrake flicked its tail and settled itself more comfortably, for all the world like an old hound dog in front of the woodstove. "How much time do you think the rest of your time is worth—once we deduct the cost of the travel?"

How the hell should I know, old man? Nic kept his face smooth. What was important here was the Mission Objective. Reality was for those who couldn't handle a good fantasy.

And Logic was the greatest fantasy of all.

"We haven't been talking about time until now. We've been talking about life. What will you give me for the part I've already lived?" Nic said logically.

Now Ophidias reared up on its hind legs, spread wings blotting out the sun. Nic didn't flinch.

"A *paladin*," the firedrake said, and now there was respectful amusement in its voice. "What do you offer?"

Nic considered carefully. What wouldn't he give, to lose the years and the knowledge he most needed to keep? But Mission Objective was paramount. What would he be, if those were gone?

"Leaving me physically as I am now, and with all the abilities I presently retain," Nic began carefully, "I offer you my life from birth until June 17, 1971—eighteen years—and from January 1, 1976 to December 24th of this year. That's a good length of time."

"Give me the five years you're keeping, and you can have the transport, plus a horse and weapons," the wizard countered quickly.

It was tempting. *But what is ability without memory?* Nic thought. He'd phrased the offer so that—as far as he knew—if it was accepted he'd jump straight from the end of his last tour to Christmas Eve, at least as far as his memory was concerned. He didn't know what that would do to him. But if he didn't keep his tours, he was just another civilian. He needed what he'd learned.

The horse and weapons would have been nice, though.

"No," Nic said. "The offer stands. How much is it worth?"

Ophidias seemed to smile, though the shape of its face could not possibly change. "Not enough. But don't worry, boy, you've got more. What about the life you haven't used yet?"

"What if I trip on a rock tomorrow and die?" Nic gibed.

"What if you do?" returned the wizard equitably. "Don't worry about me, boy; I know the value of what I'm dickering for."

And I don't. Terrific.

Mission Objective.

"For transport, horse, and weapons—my choice—the life I've offered, plus what I have left, minus one year—"

"Seven days," the firedrake interrupted, with a flick of its tail.

"Six months," Nic countered.

"One month." Lash-lash, went the long whip of tail.

There was a pause.

"Okay. Minus one month of it," Nic agreed. "But including transport to hospitable terrain within, oh, five miles of Miss Marlowe and allowing me free access to her, that should be fair enough. And the time starts after I've reached Chandrakar and runs till it runs out. Without interruption."

The firedrake half-closed his eyes, thinking. Nic tried not to wonder how badly he'd been rooked, bartering his past and future for one month's grace. Still, if he couldn't reunite Miss Marlowe with her boyfriend in thirty days, he just wasn't trying.

Ophidias made up its mind.

"Remind me not to play poker with you, boy. Okay. For transport, horse, and weapons. The horse is my choice, and no discussion. The weapons are your choice from a selection I supply. A fair selection, my promise for that; no good ever comes of cheating a paladin anyway, even if I was of a mind to. You have one month from the time you reach Chandrakar. Then I collect. Deal?"

A choice from weapons the dragon supplies. Not a great offer, but probably the best I'll get.

"Firedrake," Ophidias corrected.

Nic took a deep breath.

It's like dying! a part of his mind screamed, and another part answered: *Don't be stupid. You died a long time ago.*

"Deal," said Nic Brightlaw, and held out his hand. Ophidias brought its wing forward so that the clawed tip—just—brushed Nic's palm.

There was a lightless flash, a chilling sensation of no-space, no-time. *Medic! Get a medic! I'm hit!* his mind screamed.

Then he was real again.

His mind staggered and groped; the cognitive analog of a man with both legs blown off trying to stand; the attempt to rely on systems no longer there, that habit insisted hysterically *must* be there.

Cautiously, with real fear, he tested what was left. Was it enough? He knew he'd sold the years of his life between twenty-four and forty in order to survive in never-never land. Was there something there he needed to keep to survive?

But he remembered that he'd survived them. That was enough. It had to be.

And his childhood, his parents, the town where he was born—gone. His first car, his first girl, the things that had brought him to the recruiting sergeant in 1971. Gone.

He didn't need them. Nic took a deep breath—wondering suddenly, with new and frightening ignorance, why the parents he must have possessed had chosen to name their son "Nicodemus."

Ruth Marlowe. The Mission Objective.

A brown-haired, blue-eyed girl with the bitter depthless eyes of a survivor. How long had he known her? Had they been lovers? Had she told him what had made her the way she was?

He'd have to ask her, wouldn't he, when he saw her again?

Find Ruth Marlowe. Someone was trying to kill her, and Ophidias had said she was in deadly peril. Stop the killers. And never mind "why." "Why" would kill you. "How" was what mattered.

Mission Objective.

"A horse, weapons, and a Gate," Nic said.

The wizard gestured, with one wide silk-sail wing, and Nic looked at what had not been there a moment before.

There was a horse that gleamed as if someone had spray-painted and varnished it. Its coat was as white as the unicorn's had been, as the fur of a very white cat, so white that its pink skin shone like pearls along its muzzle and around its dark watchful eyes. Its hooves were as pink as Nic's own fingernails, and there was a narrow white gleam of metal between the hoof and the ground; silver horseshoes. It wore a halter of pale blue velvet and a narrow rope ran from the halter to a brass ring bolted to a whitewashed post.

The post stood in front of a circular tent that looked like a miniature circus tent. It, too, was white and pale blue, and there was something faintly familiar about it. Not a real memory, or even a memory-of-a-memory . . .

Ivanhoe. A movie. He'd seen it on base one night.

Nic glanced once more at the firedrake, and walked toward the tent. The horse stretched its head out to him as he walked past, and Nic paused to stroke its muzzle and neck. The hide beneath his hand was glass-slick with grooming, hot with the sun, and its mane glittered with sunstruck iridescence; not like a horse's mane, but like a woman's hair. He ran his fingers through it.

Congratulations, Sergeant Brightlaw, you have just won a magic horse of your very own.

He gave the horse a last friendly slap on the withers and walked into the tent.

The thin fabric of the tent walls didn't keep the sun out. It was nearly as bright inside as out; a circle, perhaps twelve feet in diameter.

There was no floor. The tent's contents were laid carefully on the grass.

There was a saddle and bridle, he noted with relief. Either they counted as weapons, or the wizard was being generous. Then he looked further, and revised his opinions.

No guns, no rifles. No grenades, bazookas, no C-4, and certainly none of the more elaborate black budget dirty tricks that Nic was used to.

Seems like just yesterday, doesn't it? Nic told himself with gallows humor. He looked further. The wizard had promised him a selection to choose from, and so the contents of the pavilion were not simply what an Ivanhoe-knight would carry to tourney. Nic began to search, and to sort.

There was a huge triangular shield, painted to look like the Ace of Spades. Black and white, and a pretty redhead in black silk stockings and not much else superimposed on the center pip. It weighed nearly twenty pounds. He set it aside.

There was a sword in a scabbard of heavy, pale-blue leather, stamped in silver leaf with more spade Aces. Three and a half feet from point to pommel, with a blade three inches wide and sharp as his morning razor all the way up.

But he didn't know how to use a sword. He set it beside the shield.

There was a mace. Short. Light, after hefting the sword, but you still wouldn't want to stop it with your teeth. A possibility. He started a second pile.

Knives. Everything from a belt-knife Bowie point-heavy enough to use as a machete to delicate throwing knives that were each barely three inches long. Eight of them studded an arm's-length bracer that concealed one more surprise: the four silver knobs at wrist and elbow of the bracer could be pulled free, leaving you with a narrow, rigid, six inch long steel pin with a wicked point. Eight knives, eight pins.

A coil of rope, thin as climbing line and as strong.

A slingshot. A wicked cage of blackened bronze, held in the hand and braced against the forearm. The cup was leather, but the strap was strong elastic. The bag of shot with it weighed easily a pound and a half, small round lethal lead bullets.

Climbing hooks that could be used in the hands like claws, or attached to a rope and swung.

Caltrops. Spiky shapes that thrust at least two points skyward no matter how they fell. A horse that stepped on one was crippled. They'd survived past the days of cavalry, however: a car that drove over them was crippled as well.

A quarterstaff. Four feet long and lead-weighted. Nic slid his hand over the smooth wood and smiled.

A thinner coil of cord. It might support his weight. It might not. But what it *would* do, without uncertainty, was strangle a man. Or make a mighty fine trip wire.

A bow and its arrows joined the sword and shield. So did a crossbow. The crossbow had been the equivalent of the Saturday Night Special in its day: you needed very little training to become accurate, and it punched through armor as if it were swiss cheese.

But Nic didn't know how to use one, it had a limited number of bolts, and anything he might kill with it he could probably kill with the sling.

Spears and lance. Same objection as to the sword. Ax. Too big to throw. Looked easy enough to use. Might not be.

After some hesitation, Nic started a third pile.

The full suit of plate armor, complete with bucket helmet topped with dyed ostrich plumes, went the way of the sword without a moment's hesitation.

Good boots joined the mace, quarterstaff, and rope.

He hesitated for a long moment over the mail shirt.

Retro kevlar. It would stop a knife, probably stop a spear or sword. It felt like heavy velvet.

Then he hefted it again and heard the faint rustling jingle as it slid over itself and the links shifted. He'd never sneak up on anyone wearing that. It joined the sword.

He was drawn first by the leather shirt's false familiarity. It was not the "Come And Kill Me" blue of the sword's harness. The shirt was stippled in broad swatches of green, black, and darker browns. Breaking up the silhouette.

It had a round neck, and rawhide lacing all along the shoulders and outer seam. The sleeves looked as if they'd reach the elbow or a little below—these were the magical gifts of a wizard, and Nic didn't even have to question whether everything was in his size—and had a small notch at the cuff about an inch wide, edged with eyelets and strung with a rawhide cord. Pull it on and lace it tight, and it would fit like Superman's costume. Nic picked it up, puzzled.

It was heavy, so heavy he dropped it once. Then he flipped it inside out and saw that the dappled doe-leather shirt was entirely lined in thin pale chamois. He saw the careful marks of stitching, where thin pieces of metal had been sandwiched between two layers of chamois, assembled piece by piece into a silent armored jigsaw, until to wear the shirt was to be invisibly sheathed in metal.

Whoever thought this one up, I love you. You've got my kind of twisted mind.

He added the shirt to the pile of things he would keep.

There was another wrist-brace, similar to the first except that it had no concealed pins or sheathed blades. It was heavy enough that Nic was willing to bet it concealed another shaped metal plate. He took it.

There was a sack of coins, which any parfait gentill knyghte would have scorned. But money was also a weapon. Money was cooperation. Nic took the money.

He took a firebox: flint and steel, and a space for tinder.

He took a mirror, a polished square of metal the size of his hand.

He took a three-foot length of leather braided with horsehair with a heavy ball weight on each end. Bolo.

He took a small wooden box with a sliding top that was filled with black grease and green grease. He tried them first, suspiciously, on the back of his hand and then with his tongue. They tasted vile, but he knew what they were, then. Camouflage.

He took the pants that went with the tunic. They were wool, not leather, and they didn't have metal plates sewn in, but they were lined with thick fleece, and there were shaped pieces of stiffer leather covering kidneys and groin. More protection than none.

There was a cape with a hood, longer than he was tall. It was thin dark wool, shining with grease, and had wooden loop-and-toggle buttons halfway down the inside. Flap-covered slits let you poke your hands out when the cloak was buttoned.

Rain poncho.

He took a foolish-looking helmet that looked as if someone had mated a football helmet and the old *Wehrmacht* coal-scuttle helm. The cage on a pivot that gave it its resemblance to a football helmet could be hooked in place like a visor and protect eyes and nose, or swing down as far as the helmet would permit and protect the lower jaw. There was also a chin strap.

What is this? Wardrobe left over from Santa Claus Conquers the Martians?

And suddenly the voices from a time that ought to have been buried safely by almost two decades of living were painfully bright and close, and Nicodemus Brightlaw was gone. What was left was Sergeant Brightlaw of the United States Army Special Forces. "Saint" Nic.

Sniper, infiltrator, specialist in covert penetration and field intelligence. Field intelligence was walking through your lines and theirs, walking far enough that you'd have something to bring back. Papers. Prisoners. Intelligence. The truth.

Find the truth and the truth will set you free. Jesus on horseback.

Nic shuddered.

Let it go, Saint. They're all dead, and you are, too, and what Puff the

Magic Dragon out there is counting on is that you're going to come apart right here and he scoops it all for free.

He added the helmet to the things he would take. He added a belt that incorporated a shoulder strap to distribute the weight that would hang from it, and pouches to hang from the belt because there wasn't a backpack and if you trusted the other man to carry what you needed the other man might just wind up raspberry roadkill and your stuff with him.

Then everything in the tent seemed to be sorted into those three piles. By now the illumination in the tent was less, and the tent's contents were harder to see. He didn't worry. Time started when he went through the Gate. And he had a month. In a month, Ruth Marlowe would be either safe or dead.

Nic took a last look at the ax and the mace and reluctantly added both to the pile with the armor and the sword. Too heavy. Everything he chose, he—and the horse—would have to carry.

He stripped off the clothes he'd taken from the man he'd killed in the clearing when he and Ruth had first arrived, and the last of the clothes left over from a life he no longer remembered, on a Christmas Eve that now never was. He remembered that day from its beginning; getting out of bed, getting dressed.

But the memories were slippery and senseless, hard to hold on to, because the day before that, his mind assured him, he'd been at in-country waiting for the Sikorsky that was going to medevac him back to the rear echelon country club, home, and Mother.

Away from the nightmare.

He looked at his body. There were scars where there had been fresh wounds day before yesterday. Old scars. Years old. And he was old. An old man of forty; impossible age to contemplate from twenty-two.

If you'd thought this was going to be easy, Saint old son, you wouldn't have done it.

He dressed in the firedrake's gifts, lacing and buckling everything carefully: heavy, calf-length boots that would protect the foot running or riding. Pants, gray-green wool lined intermittently with leather. The shirt was hard to lace down by himself but he managed. It was much less heavy worn than carried, and hugged his outline like a tight T-shirt.

He had a sudden desperate wish for a cigarette, even though he'd given up the habit the first week of his first tour. Charlie didn't smoke. Charlie could smell you if you did. End of incentive program.

Next came the bracers. Nic strapped the knife-studded one onto his right arm. He could throw left-handed, and he'd rather block with his left arm for a while anyway, magic healing drink or no. Nic fumbled the buckles awkwardly closed with his left hand.

The other bracer was easier. He strapped the heavy leather cuff that concealed the metal plate onto his left arm. It should foil any number of attacks. The edge of the bracers came to the cuff of the shirt, just as if someone had known he would select these items to wear from all that had been offered.

Someone had.

He swung his arms, stretching, trying to learn how the weight and constriction would hinder him.

Not too bad. He bent over and picked up the belt, noting how his center of gravity seemed to have shifted. Have to watch that. He straightened, buckling the belt around his hips, its tongue-and-toggle fastening eerily reminiscent of his web-nylon utility belt.

Bowie knife. Dagger. Sling and shot. Money.

But even that much weight made him waddle like a pregnant duck. Sapping his energy. Tiring him.

And God knew what the horse that had to carry all this and him besides would think.

He looked at the mace, the caltrops, the water bottle, the other knives. The claws. The bolo. The two coils of rope. The quarterstave. The cloak.

Triage time, dogbrain. Nic unloaded the pouches.

He kept the bracers; they were replacing a shield, as well as containing a number of samples of Sentry Surprise. He kept the big knife, and would at least until he could decide whether he'd need it to move through the jungle.

Forest. It's a forest here, not jungle. He kept the belt with its two deep pouches; he had to have a way to carry things. And it was something he could get rid of later. Ditto the poncho. Ditto the quarterstaff. Ditto the water bottle, because it was a forest-not-a-jungle, and there were fewer places to get water in a forest. He kept the claws.

He dropped the box of camo cream into a pouch. The memory of how much disadvantage a blond-haired white boy was at while trying to sneak anywhere in a jungle was still fresh.

He hefted the bag of lead bullets, then poured out half, dropped them in the pouch, and threw the bag into the first pile. He slid the slingshot into the pouch with the ammo. The right angle of the wrist brace protruded slightly, but it didn't look like it would fall out.

The caltrops joined the shot bag on the discard pile. Fun was fun, but there were other ways to sabotage a line of retreat.

He picked up the bag of money, easily as heavy as the bag of lead bullets. Trick question time. Did he need money or didn't he?

He poured the contents of the bag into his hand. Copper, silver, gold, and some coins of a greasy gray metal that looked like polished pewter and hefted like lead. He picked those out and discarded them.

Copper for the working man, silver for the maid . . . Something . . . Something . . . Gold for the ruler who sits in the hall/But Iron, Cold Iron, is the master of them all.

Scraps of Kipling danced through his head. Poet of Empire. Advocate of a rousing good brawl. But Kipling had believed there should be honor on both sides in war.

There wasn't. And cold iron wasn't what Nic wished for, it was hot lead.

In the end, he took less than half the money provided. Gold was for bribes, because Nic was betting that human nature wasn't that different here and a gold coin was a dazzling sight that could make anyone lose his head. Some copper, some silver, to pay for his own needs—assuming there was anyone to buy from. He put the money in the other pouch.

It clinked. Nic sighed. He retrieved the money pouch, poured the coin he was keeping into it, wrapped it tight, and stuffed it back in the pouch.

Blessed silence.

He picked up the tinderbox, and found that the slippage of the light was such that he had difficulty picking it out against the grass. Into the pouch with the money.

He picked up the coil of rope and the coil of line and slung them over his left shoulder, then picked up the cloak and stave, testing the arrangement.

Better. He'd worn heavier packs and carried more equipment, but he didn't have a pack and he hadn't seen a single example of lightweight, rotproof, ripstop nylon superfabric since he'd gotten here.

He used the stave to hook the helmet up off the floor and let it slide down the length of the quarterstaff into his hand. He tucked the quarterstaff awkwardly under his arm and put on the helmet. He pulled the strap tight through its D ring closure and left the protector down, shielding jaw and throat with its leather-wrapped metal cage.

Thus burdened, he turned back to the saddle and bridle.

Here too, he discovered, a choice was offered.

There was the saddle that went with the plate armor. It looked like a rococo rocking chair and Nic grunted with the weight when he tried to lift it. The bridle that went with it had wide ribbonlike reins with tassels, and the bit was a complex arrangement of several hinged bars.

He reached for the memories that would tell him what this apparatus would be doing in a horse's mouth, and ran, once more, into the impervious blankness of lost time.

And Nic realized with a sense of grim amusement that his knowledge of horses and the ability to ride was a skill picked up in his vanished childhood.

Score one for you, lizard-breath.

But he'd bargained for a horse, and he had a horse, and he needed a saddle for the damned thing, that much he knew.

There was a stirrupless pad—two sheepskins sewn together, fleece out—with a braided circingle and D ring close. It went with a braided-leather line consisting of one rein ending in a loop that would slip over the lower jaw, and no bit at all. Maybe he'd been that good a rider, once. Not now.

The last available choice still looked like nothing Nic had ever seen, though it was his by default. It was the same streaky black and green—though what good camouflage would do him mounted on a horse that white was a mystery—and looked rather as if someone had incorporated a racing saddle into a throw rug; a rectangular shape of heavy felt that would hang nearly to the horse's knees on each side. On the horse side there were two leather straps and a sheepskin pad. On the rider side there was a covered wooden shape of teardrop-verging-on-oval that rose only very slightly at the back.

Short pieces of rope that Nic identified, after a moment, as cargo tie-downs fringed the saddle seat like tentacles. Two at the front, where Nic mourned the complete absence of a saddle horn, four at the back. The stirrups were nothing but long leather straps that hung down to the edge of the saddle skirt. The strap ended in a long blunt fishhook shape, and you made a place for your foot by sliding the hook end through your choice of holes in the strap. The shorter the stirrups, the wider the loop. Nic hooked them through the bottommost hole.

The only unrejected bridle had a straight bar for the horse's mouth with a ring the size of a bracelet at each end. There was a rope with one end woven unbrokenly over the ring; twelve feet of rope. There was also a strap attached to the ring, with the now familiar double D rings braided into it about a third of the way back from the free end. Between the D rings at one end and the bit dangling unanchored from the other, there was another strap. This had a flat loop at each end and slid freely up and down the strap until stopped by the hardware.

It took Nic some moments of puzzling until he decided that the bit went in the mouth, the long strap went up the horse's cheek, around the back of the head, through the free loop on the dangling strap (which would go under the horse's chin, Nic decided from hazy recollections of John Wayne movies) and down to the ring on the other side. The rope was obviously meant to function as a rein, but the only way Nic could see to make that work was to run it through the free loop on the other side and either tie it there or hold the loose end in his hand.

Fortunately saddle and bridle didn't weigh very much. Nic added them to his burden and walked out of the tent.

The horse was still there. But Ophidias was gone, and it occurred to Nic with the persuasive force of intuition that there was no Gate in his future to measure time from; he was already in Chandrakar.

Perhaps he'd been in Chandrakar all along. Perhaps only since he'd sealed the bargain.

Why hadn't he asked where he was, when he was asking questions?

Would it really have mattered, in the end?

"Great going, Puff. But where do I go to pay up?" Nic asked aloud.

Don't worry, paladin. I'll find you.

The voice in his mind had the fierce unreachable irritation of an itch beneath bandages. Nic shook his head violently to be rid of it. He turned back to the horse.

The tent behind it was gone.

Smoke and mirrors. "You sure you don't have relatives in Washington, big fella?" Nic said aloud.

This time there was no answer. Nic set his detachable possessions aside and advanced upon the horse.

There followed a brief interval where he cursed the firedrake and himself indiscriminately for his sudden lack of information that, as it turned out, he probably needed far more than he needed the memory of how to open a can of Army-issue beer with his utility knife.

He put the bridle on the horse. To do that he had to remove the velvet halter, and he had enough presence of mind to put a loop of the halter rope around the horse's neck, make a slip knot, and tie the horse to the post on a very short leash. Next stop, the bridle.

He got it assembled in place, but before he got it buckled the horse shook its head violently. The bridle went flying. Nic went and picked it up. He looked back. The damned thing was laughing at him. He was sure of it.

On the second try he got the bridle on and buckled. The horse shook its head again, and then delicately tongued the bit into Nic's hand. The bridle fell off.

Then he was ready to try again and the horse wasn't. It tilted its nose in the air, holding its head out of his reach. He had no way to bring its head down, and belatedly considered he should have put the rope-loop higher. But he outwaited it, grabbed it by the forelock, and held on grimly while he shoved the bit at the horse's lips one more time. The hand holding the forelock held the strap, while the bit slewed sideways and Nic groped for the throat-strap. Get the strap. Thread tab A into slot B. Then yank the strap through the bit-ring until the D ring hardware touched it. Thread the strap through. Tuck the hanging end between the layers of doubled strap. Wrap the single rein around the horse's neck and pass the free end through the empty bridle-ring. Tie it. Remove the rope. Recoil it.

The horse regarded him placidly, as if it had never moved in its life and didn't mean to start now.

Nic picked up the saddle.

The first miss was his fault; he got the saddle on its back and realized only then that the straps to tie it on were bundled beneath it.

Take it off and try again.

On the next attempt he let go of the saddle once it was on the horse's back. It shrugged—Nic would swear it shrugged—and the saddle slid off. The horse casually lifted one foot and set it firmly on the saddle skirts.

After some negotiation, Nic was able to lift the foot and kick the saddle out of the way.

Third try. He kept one hand on the saddle and crouched forward, looking for the straps. He'd never properly considered how wide a horse was when you were trying to get your hands on something hanging down on the other side of one. It began to sidle away from him, edging around the post like a sweep second hand.

But in the end that maneuver hoisted it on its equine petard. After a couple of circuits it had wrapped the slack in its rein completely around the post. The front end of the animal had to stand still. Nic kept the back end from moving by finally getting his hand on the loose end of the back strap and pulling it toward him. He buckled it, drawing it as tight as he dared. The front strap was easier, now that he didn't have to hold the saddle in place.

Once the saddle was in place, Nic unwound the horse from the pole and decided he'd try boarding it. It looked easier on television. It had probably been easier for him, once. He grabbed a double handful of mane the color of moonlight and put his toe into the stirrup loop. He stepped down into the stirrup, swinging his other leg up—

The saddle slid unhurriedly in the direction of his weight. Nic fell, carried off balance by the unfamiliar weight of armor and weaponry. He sprawled on his back in the grass, looking up at the horse's undercarriage, and at the saddle slung beneath its body. He felt a moist caress on his cheek. The horse nuzzled him, dark eyes wide with innocent inquiry.

"That does it. Just hold that thought, Shadowfax; in another moment you're going to be singing soprano."

He got to his feet and grabbed the horse's reins in one hand while he shoved the saddle upright with the other. Then—as he should have done at first—he began hauling on the girths alternately, tightening them until the leather creaked and there was a faint but perceptible indentation in his mount's satiny white belly.

Nic backed away, panting with exertion. The horse looked at him innocently. It did not seem to be particularly uncomfortable with the saddle's tightness.

"All right. Good. Fine. I'm glad we had this chance to get to know each other," Nic muttered to himself. He put his foot in the stirrup again, and this time swung his leg across the saddle without trouble.

He looked around. From horseback the landscape flattened out. He could see farther, move faster, and—if he only had the technology and training—smite enemies in their hundreds with sword and mace, lance and shield.

The mounted horseman. The cutting edge of military technology for two thousand years. The cavalry that had smashed empires.

"Heigh-ho, Silver," Nic said without enthusiasm. The horse shook its mane, pulling on the reins.

He swung down again. He picked up his goods and chattels, and used the trailing lengths of rope behind the saddle for their proper function; to tie his cape and other possessions firmly into place. After some hesitation he lashed the quarterstaff on top of the pile, seeing no other way to carry it. It stuck out ludicrously on both sides. Wide load.

This time, when he mounted, he held the reins bunched in one hand and the mane in the other. His legs hung awkwardly, even in the stirrups that kept his knees bent—as if this were a Harley, not a horse—and he had no idea what to do with the reins, other than not drop them. But after some joggling and swearing he got the animal moving, and even pointed in the right direction.

Once he'd untied the horse from it, the hitching post had disappeared as soon as Nic took his eyes off it, but he ignored that. If he'd done all that he'd done in order to be able to find and protect Ruth Marlowe, then finding and protecting Ruth Marlowe was what was important—not magic tricks.

And after a few minutes a-horseback, he realized that the dragon had kept its part of the bargain. All the abilities Nic had possessed at forty were all still there, including the instinctive operator's manual for Horse (One), Single Operator Equine Transport Unit Mark One (Magic). If he didn't think about what he was doing and why he should do it, he was fine.

Now all he had to do was find Ruth Marlowe, and see what rescuing her required.

In one month.

Starting from now.

· 27 ·

Cold Steel and Chance Encounters

IT WAS DAWN in the Vale of Stars, and Fox the Outlaw Brigand was a man with a problem. The problem was his hostage.

He didn't particularly mind the loss of the Cup. Fox hadn't been after the Cup in the first place. Having it vanish was almost as good, for Fox's purposes, as having it himself. But since he didn't have it and couldn't either bestow or withhold it, he also had no particular control over his hostage. Even if he kept her tied hand and foot (as she was now), something would happen. With the cup gone, Tinkerbelle was a loose cannon; an elf bitch with nothing to lose.

Fox could almost sympathize.

His spies at Dawnheart had told him yesterday that The Rohannan—whom Fox had known as Mel the Elf—was still away. No one knew when he might return. Since what Fox really wanted was Melior and the Sword of Maiden's Tears, his hostage was no good to him if Melior was not around to be lured within reach. The logical thing to do was to get rid of her and try again later.

Logical, sensible, and safe.

Of course, there arose a question as to method.

It was not that Fox was a stranger to killing. He had killed—or helped to kill—five people already in his career: three humans, the elf on the Vale Road, and one hominid neither human nor elvish—though Fox was not prepared to say, even to himself, what it *had* been. He remembered every face, though he didn't know all of their names.

He made no excuses for himself. He knew he could kill again if it was necessary.

But was it necessary to kill Tink? *That,* as Hamlet said, was the question.

Hathorne rode ahead, his horse picking its way carefully up the trail that led to the pass into the Vale. Fox followed, leading the horse that carried the hostage. Behind them came Raven, then Ash and Otter. All present and accounted for.

Fox thought the matter of Tink through carefully and decided he did not have to kill her, providing he was prepared to take a few risks.

If he dumped her at Foretton, the village at the edge of the forest—across the valley from Dawnheart but well within sight of it—they'd fall all over themselves to return her to the castle. It was reasonably safe. She didn't know where the camp was, exactly, and it was time to move it anyway.

And now that Fox'd seen inside the Vale, he thought that its one pass could be properly defended by very few men. They could set up a free human village here, safe from elvish magic. He owed them that much, considering he didn't intend to devote his life to them.

It had seemed so impossible for him to succeed that he'd never thought past the moment when Melior was dead and the Sword destroyed. Now it seemed at least possible, and Fox, ever the clever general, tried to push his mind past that moment.

The few experiments he'd been able to conduct had indicated that he could not leave Chandrakar by the same sort of magic he'd used to bring himself here. Possibly he *could* walk the Iron Road again—but without magic, he couldn't *find* it. Without the magic to find the Iron Road, he was trapped in Chandrakar.

And in Chandrakar, Fox was a hunted—and, he prided himself, famous—outlaw. Even if he left Domain Rohannan and Canton Silver itself, Melior (aka The Rohannan), the Earl of Silver, and any number of other high-nosed elves would undoubtedly make sure that none of the other six Cantons would harbor him; at least, not for long. At least, not unless Fox could be of more use to them than Silver Silences' displeasure was harm.

Fox really, *really,* hated the idea of being of use to any elf. To anybody, for that matter; he had always been remarkably evenhanded in his disdain for other sentient life.

Live fast, die young, and leave a pretty corpse, he thought philosophically. *Maybe I CAN start a full-scale peasants' revolt.*

It was something to think about.

An hour's riding brought the outlaw party to the place where they would leave the Vale Road for the sheltering woods that edged it.

"Here's where we kiss and part, gang. I'm sure you'll all agree that Tink here has been a great little hostage, but the clock on the wall says—"

Raven, Ash, and Otter stared at Fox like a field of grazing sheep. He sighed, and took a deep breath, and tried again, resisting the temptation to count out the words on his fingers.

"We don't need the elf any more. I'm going to take her back to Foretton and let her go."

"Not kill her?" asked Raven with guilty relief.

"Not kill her," Fox said. "I'll meet you back at camp. Tell Yarrow to get ready to move. Everything positively must go. This once in a lifetime, never to be repeated—"

"I'll take her," Hathorne said, interrupting.

Fox studied the man as if his own life depended on it—which it might. He knew little more of Hathorne than his name and his claim of being wolfshead—outside the protection of the law—but that was true of a number of the members of Fox's merry band of murderers, poachers, and thieves. He knew that Hathorne had done enough peacebreaking since he'd joined them to swing for it if Hathorne were caught, and he knew that Hathorne was as quick to speak against Chandrakar's elphen overlords as Fox was himself. That much being said. . . .

"No, I feel like a little jaunt," Fox said, smiling his sweetest smile.

"I really think—" Hathorne began.

"No, you don't," Fox assured him kindly. *And I do.* Any local boy who hated elves that much could hardly be trusted alone with one.

Fox swung down from his horse. "Raven, help me shift her. You can use the extra horse back at camp."

Between them, Fox and Raven shifted the unconscious Jausserande to Fox's horse. She would have roused hours ago from Fox's sling-stone blow, save for the sleeping draught he'd given her.

Sleeping draught, hell; nothing beats a Seconal dissolved in half a cup of wine for sweet dreams and no regrets. Boy, is she going to have a headache when she wakes up.

He swung himself back into the saddle behind his hostage, conscious of Hathorne watching him. The man's mismatched eyes were brilliant in his weather-browned face. Fox wondered what he wanted with Tink—other than the obvious. Maybe he was overreacting. Maybe Hathorne was just thinking of going into the kidnapping and extortion business for himself.

"See you guys later," Fox said, kicking his mount into a canter. Hathorne watched him out of sight.

Something, Fox thought, was going to have to be done about Hathorne.

The first thing that returned to Jausserande was the pain, a dull, sick, jarred-loose throbbing in her head that meant she'd hit it very hard. Or had it hit *for* her.

There was a taste in her mouth as if she'd been eating river mud, and she focused on that. She would not think of the night just past, or the red murder waiting to be loosed in her one final time would find that its time was now.

If she didn't throw up first. She breathed deeply and steadily, forcing back pain and nausea and taking stock of her surroundings. She was somewhere in the open air, lying facedown across the withers of a horse. Its rider's body pressed her against the saddle. She smelled leather, horse, and grass, wood smoke and cut hay—

They must be near a village.

The horse slowed.

"This is your wake-up call, Tink," a hated and familiar voice said. "I'll spare you the conventional villain speeches, except to note that I'm sparing your life—which is more than you'd do for me."

The horse stopped. Its rider put his hands on her, lifting her away from the saddle. Jausserande struggled, and found that she was tied hand and foot. Fox heaved her off the horse as if she were a sack of meal and flung her to the ground. She landed hard and awkwardly in a pile of leaves, and by the time she had struggled onto her side and gotten her breath back, Fox's mount was a retreating flicker of motion seen through the trees.

Pure outrage gave her the strength to drag the buckskin strips from her wrists, oblivious to the pain. In a moment more, her ankles were free as well. Jausserande lunged to her feet, shaking with the need to kill something.

But there was nothing here to kill.

She kicked savagely at the leaves and looked around. Dawnheart was a white shape on a distant hill, brilliant in the late afternoon sunlight, and the sloping valley between it and the forest edge was a brown and gold patchwork of autumn meadows and harvested fields. Foretton. She remembered its name; it was the last village she'd passed with Guiraut before reaching the road that led to the Vale Road—

The road she would never need to ride down again.

The magnitude of her failure left Jausserande momentarily breathless. Where could she begin to repair the loss suffered by Line Floire? She strained her eyes to look across the valley, but could not see the scarlet-and-silver pennant flying from Dawnheart's tower that would tell her that her cousin had come safely home. But even if Melior were still absent, any of Rohannan's serfs would give her any aid she desired. If she could build a fire, she could even signal the castle directly—Richart's sentries still walked the wall, and after what had happened at the Harvest Home, the captain of Dawnheart's Guard probably had patrols out sweeping these woods as well. Help was as close at hand as the village below her.

But Jausserande didn't want help. She wanted Fox's throat between her hands. She shoved her hair out of her eyes, streaking her pale skin with dirt. She wanted Fox in her hands, at her mercy, with a passion greater than any she'd ever imagined—a passion greater than her need to possess the Cup of Morning Shadows.

Before anything else, Jausserande wanted Fox.

And she was going to have him.

Jausserande turned her back on the castle and began to follow the horse's track into the wood.

Blurred events taking only seconds seemed to stretch and slow with the deadly inevitability of a dream.

Ahead, Cobant pulled farther and farther away, and Ruth's own horse seemed determined to close the distance. A shadow occluded the sun as the monster passed overhead once more. Ruth looked up, blinded by her own whipping hair, and could not be sure what she saw.

The knowledge that Melior was lost and the realization that her horse was bolting came to Ruth Marlowe at the same moment.

"Stop!" Ruth screamed, dragging at the useless reins. There was no response. Foam dripped from the animal's mouth and rose up from the sleek hide as if the white horse were a rug being shampooed. If the horse stumbled—if she fell off—Ruth Marlowe would be as dead as any car wreck could make her.

There was a sound behind her like baying. Something hunting. Something hunting *her*.

Ruth clung to the saddle, to the reins, trying not to think about how vulnerable she was on horseback. The pounding gallop began to be an active hurt; each hoof impact upon the road sending a stabbing pain through Ruth's knees and spine and head. She couldn't feel her legs, couldn't feel her hands; tears streamed down her face from the whipping of wind and hair and mane, and the world was reduced to blurred and meaningless light.

She even wished she were more afraid: fear seemed to have sharpened every thought and feeling to the point of pain; imagination raced even faster than her mount, painting vivid pictures of every possible way she could be hurt. Safety was over the border—but Melior had said it took magic to reach it, and Melior was lost.

The howling rose to a cheated crescendo behind her, and then, at last, panic might have come, save that pain came before it: pulling, tearing, sick fire in the marrow of her bones, twisting and burning and ripping until nothing, nothing, nothing was left. Ruth screamed in agonized protest through a jarred disjointed jolting that ended with falling and landing and left behind it only the memory of pain vivid enough to make her bones throb.

Silence.

The quiet was the first thing she heard. Quiet, and stillness—no baying hunters, no thundering hooves, only an odd rhythmic sound Ruth couldn't identify. She gasped blindly for air and got a mouthful of earth. Choking and gagging, she struggled to her knees. There was no Road and no pursuer anywhere in sight. She scanned the sky with anxious terror. There was no dragon either.

Ruth's horse lay on its side a few yards away. Her hind legs were outstretched and her forelegs tucked near her belly, as if she'd been shot while in full flight, but her side heaved like a working bellows and Ruth could now identify the sound as the high whistle of her gasping breaths. The mare's coat was covered with foam, almost steel-colored with wet, and foam and drool streamed from her nose and mouth. And down low, toward the hoof, one leg was twisted, and shards of white bone showed like slivered almonds through the blood.

"Oh, God. Oh, Jesus. Oh, God." Ruth tried to stand, and fell, and crawled on hands and knees toward the horse.

"Well met, maidey," a voice said behind her.

"Please, can you—" Ruth began, turning.

The words died in her throat. It was the odd-eyed man, the one who'd tried to kill the unicorn and Nic when she'd first arrived in Elphame. He was alone, on horseback, and looking at her.

"Best to be saying your good-byes now, maidey," the man said as he dismounted. He took a step toward her, one hand down by his side.

He was holding a knife.

He reached her and hauled her to her feet, and Ruth, scrabbling for balance, felt the lancing pain of a twisted ankle as she tried to stand. The pied-eyed man hefted her easily, pulling her back against him and raising the knife.

"Hathorne!"

The name rang out, sharp and imperious. The man jerked, as if part of him wanted to respond.

But he didn't. He raised the knife.

"Let her go," the voice said again, so familiar that Ruth was sure constant terror had unhinged her mind. "Let her go *now,* Hathorne. If I shoot, I'll hurt her. But I'll kill you."

There was a moment where Ruth, nauseated with terror, felt Hathorne weigh the usefulness of her death against his own. Then he released her with an ungracious shove. Ruth fell forward and scrambled onto her back in an unladylike sprawl. Her ankle was a nexus of white fire.

She looked up.

"Hiya, Ruthie. Long time no see." The man known to his followers as Fox smiled.

Ruth stared. She saw a blond man in a gray tunic, his long hair pulled straight away from his face to fall in a silky tail that hung forward over one shoulder. He held a crossbow balanced on his hip. His pale eyes were startlingly blue against the sunburnt brown of his skin, his forearms were sculpted with muscle, and he stood with the unconscious arrogance of the athlete.

"Philip!" Ruth squealed, but Philip—if it *was* Philip—wasn't looking at her.

"This is Ruthie, Hathorne. She's by way of being an old friend of mine. I'd like to know what you thought you were doing."

"I wasn't going to hurt the maidey," Hathorne said unconvincingly.

"You weren't going to rape her either—not in that position," Philip/Fox said, completely uninterested in excuses. "What I want to know is why I had to tell you twice to let her go."

"Philip?" Ruth said, in a whisper meant only for herself. Could this be Philip LeStrange—this cold-eyed master of men? When Naomi had been alive and the five of them had been together, Philip Leslie Le-Strange had been weedy, blond, short, twenty-two, and the product of respectable parents who were sure that his health was too delicate for anything more than a quiet career as a librarian. He'd worn bifocals and backpacks and the only weapon he'd been familiar with was words.

But she hadn't seen Philip in over two years. Things seemed to have changed.

"I meant no harm, Fox," Hathorne said again. "Didna thole the maidey was thy kith."

His Monty Python dialect was growing thicker by the minute. Ruth clamped her teeth shut over the urgent information that Hathorne had already tried to kill her once before. This wasn't the time to mention that. Not when she wasn't sure whose side Philip was on. Hathorne had called him Fox, which was just the sort of name Philip would choose for himself if he were picking an alias, but what did the fact that he was using it *mean?*

"Yeah, well, don't let it happen again. If you want a woman, go to the town and buy one. You know the rules: no messing with wives or sisters or girlfriends. It's stupid. The *elves* are our enemy, Hathorne—not humans."

There was another long pause. Hathorne bowed his head in acceptance.

"You okay?" Philip said to her.

Try as she might, Ruth could not reconcile what she saw with what she remembered. How could Philip have made himself so at home beyond the Morning in only two years?

And how had he gotten here?

"I—" Ruth began, and coughed. "My horse—" She gestured.

"Wait there," Philip said.

She watched as Philip—*Fox*—turned away and led Hathorne back toward her horse. She watched them talk, Philip gesturing. His head barely came to Hathorne's shoulder.

Well, he was still short, at least.

She saw Hathorne crouch by the horse's side, and look up at Philip. Their voices didn't carry. Philip made a chopping motion with his hand, explicit in any language. Hathorne knelt on the horse's neck to cut its throat, and Ruth, shuddering, looked away. She closed her eyes. Her fault. Her fault *again.*

"There wasn't anything we could do. Broken leg." The words came from above. Ruth looked up at Philip. No, at *Fox.* "Too bad. We can always use horses. Do you want the saddle?"

"The saddle?" Ruth said blankly.

"Yeah, Ruthie, the saddle. The part that goes around the middle of the horse; you sit on it?" he said condescendingly.

"Leave me alone," Ruth said wearily.

"I ought to," Philip said, still in that nasty sneering voice, "but you're too damn much trouble to leave wandering around loose."

Ruth stared at him in dawning disbelief.

"Get your ass in gear. This is not optional. In case you hadn't noticed, it's getting dark. And there's all kinds of things that come out after dark."

Ruth put her head on her knees again and closed her eyes. "Somebody wants to kill me, Philip. They're chasing me. There was a dragon, and we were on the Road—the Iron Road, you know?—I think it's got Melior."

"Where's the Sword?"

The question—simple, intelligent, cutting through everything else—made Ruth feel insensibly better. No matter what else might be true, this was Philip. Her friend, as much as he was anyone's, and the thing that Philip had always been best at was cutting to the chase.

"I don't know. We were together." She tried to remember whether the Sword of Maiden's Tears had been in its scabbard or in Melior's hand when the dragon had attacked and couldn't. "I think it's with him."

"Well, that's just fine," Philip said, so warmly that Ruth stared at him in faint surprise. "We can work with that. Now come on, Ruthie—we gotta go."

"I hurt my ankle," Ruth said, knowing it sounded childish. She fought down the tightness in her throat. She'd die before she'd cry in front of Philip. Fox. Whatever.

"Don't worry, I've got the best MASH unit in all Elfland. Now come on. Put your arm around my neck. No, don't look over there; Hathorne's butchering your horse. Shut *up*, Ruthie, there's no sense in wasting meat. Close your mouth. Which ankle is it? No, keep your eyes on my *face*. Look at me, Ruthie, upsie-daisy. And don't worry; this is going to hurt."

Philip was right. He put her arm around his shoulder and his hands on her waist and lifted. Pain like lightning shot through her back and legs and she yelped.

"If you think that's fun, wait till we get to the part where you get on the horse. Here we go. Lean on me, Ruthie, I'm not going to drop you." Philip kept up the easy encouraging patter as she hobbled toward where his horse was tied. His arm circled her waist like an iron bar, easily supporting her weight. Her arm pressed down on the hard, well-built muscle of his neck and shoulders. Scrawny, unhealthy Philip was muscled like a kick boxer.

She was gasping with effort by the time they stopped. Philip wasn't even breathing hard. She looked up at the horse. It was bigger than hers had been; the saddle an impossible height from the ground.

"I'll boost you up across it. Swing your leg over, but don't put your feet in the stirrups. I'll get up behind you."

"Philip, I don't think I—"

"One-two-three—" Philip said, ignoring her. He put both hands on her waist and lifted her straight up over his head. It hurt, and when she grabbed at the saddle edge and used it to pull herself forward that hurt, too—just as he'd promised, a part of her mind reminded her.

But falling would hurt worse, so she scrabbled, yanking at her skirts and cloak, until she had one leg on each side of the saddle and was sitting more or less upright.

Philip vaulted lightly up behind her. "There we are," he said, as if to a backward child. "Now just sit here and let me do all the work." He reached around her to collect the reins.

Ruth was forced back against him as he settled in the saddle and shifted his weight forward. He reined the horse around and set it through the trees at a walk. He rode as if he'd been born on horseback, and Ruth tried to remember if Philip had ever mentioned horses when she'd known him before.

It had been spring on the Road, but it was autumn here, wherever here was. The trees had dropped most of their leaves, and what remained on the trees were as gaudy-bright as the contents of a box of breakfast cereal: raspberry red, lemon yellow, orange orange. The sun was at the right late-afternoon angle to slant through the leaves in translucent golden bars, yet, despite all the gold, Ruth was glad she had the cloak to pull around her.

"Philip—"

"Call me Fox." There was no hint of apology or embarrassment in his tone. "It's the kind of name they use here, for one thing."

"Where are we?" Ruth asked. "Fox." It wasn't that hard to say. What was hard was to think of him as Philip.

There was a pause of surprise behind her. "Chandrakar. I thought you knew. Dawnheart's just the other side of the valley; about ten miles."

"Dawnheart?" Ruth asked. "Your camp?"

There was a short bark of laughter; for a moment Fox sounded distinctly like his namesake.

"I wish! No. Castle Rohannan, you could call it. Mel lives there when he's home."

"Oh, God." Ruth leaned forward with sheer despair. Fox put an arm around her waist and pulled her back against him. "What am I going to do?" she whispered, not intending him to hear.

"Well, you could start by telling me what's going on. Start with how you got here and go on till you get to the end. We've got about an hour before we reach camp; I don't want to push the horse when it's carrying double."

"You've changed," Ruth said.

Another laugh, with nothing of humor in it. "I've changed, Michael's changed, everybody's changed."

"I haven't," Ruth said bitterly. Maybe only people with souls could change.

"No," said Fox noncommittally. "But you will."

Ruth began her explanation with Christmas Eve at the Ryerson and immediately received another shock.

"You got a job there? So did I. Intern the summer you graduated. They still talk about me?"

"Why?" said Ruth.

"Because I vanished without a trace—assuming they noticed. There's a Gate to Elfland down in the Second File."

For the old Philip, this would have been unusually talkative, but Ruth didn't pay any attention.

"I know," said Ruth, "I fell through it."

Fox snickered, and sounded exactly like his old self for a moment. "Of course you did. The Sword is on this side. The Sword fell to Earth to be near you, once upon a time. Then you fell to Elfland to be near it. Quod Eras Demonstratum, or, in the vernacular, thus always to tyrants."

"Not all the way. And not alone."

Ruth explained about finding the Gate and falling through into a place called Counterpane. About Nic Brightlaw, who had accidentally come with her, who'd saved her life and then disappeared.

"You brought my boss to Elfland?" Fox said in disbelief, and Ruth realized with a jolt that of course he would have known Nic if he'd worked at the Ryerson. The thought was disturbing in a way Ruth couldn't quite place.

"Wow. Old Mr. Brightlaw in Elfland. But go on, Ruthie. Jesus, you never did know how to tell a story."

"Well then it's just as well I wasn't going to be a J-librarian, wasn't it," Ruth snapped, nettled. She explained briefly about the unicorn, about reaching the Goblin Market, being attacked. Finding Melior, losing him, finding him again. And, now, losing him once more.

"And there's something else you ought to know, Fox. That friend of yours with the charming manners? He showed up almost as soon as Nic and I did. He said he was hunting a unicorn, and at the time I believed him. But now I don't think so."

"Hmm." Fox's breath tickled her neck. "So Hathorne's been walking the Road, has he? Have to be; aren't any unicorns in Chandrakar to hunt, and you saw one at the same time. Hathorne's been a naughty boy; I wonder who his patron is, and what his patron wants?"

"I don't know what you're talking about," Ruth said.

"It doesn't matter anyway," Fox said. "All that matters is finding

Melior and the Sword. Oh, yes. At last. Thank you, Ruthie," he said prayerfully.

"I'm sure he'll help you, too," Ruth said, although she wasn't exactly clear on what kind of help Philip/Fox needed. "But how do we find him— where do we start?" Ruth said. "Oh, God, he's dead—I know he's dead." Tears would have been appropriate, but tears wouldn't come somehow, and her protests of Melior's death tasted like lies. She shook her head. Fox poked her in the ribs.

"If he's dead, he's still going to be dead when we find him. If it's a stupid elf vendetta, they probably want to talk him to death. And anyway, I know who's got him."

"Who?" demanded Ruth, trying to turn around in her seat to look at him. Fox prevented this.

"Jesus, Ruthie, use your head. Who hates Melior, who wants the Sword of Maiden's Tears, who screwed up your life in the first place? Eirdois Baligant of the House of the Vermilion Shadows, known to his friends, loved ones, and other intimates as Baligant Baneful. *He's* got Melior.

"And maybe even Nic Brightlaw, Boy Librarian."

· 28 ·

Love in a Faithless Country

HE DID NOT wish to wake, because the situation, in addition to being hopeless, was also perfectly clear.

Baligant had won. Line Rohannan was doomed.

Melior drifted just below the surface of waking, letting the eddies of sleep carry him where they would. Vertigo became the saddle of a horse, with Ruth's horse just ahead, and miles of undefended open Road to cover before reaching a Gate to any land, let alone to Chandrakar.

Then he was looking down on the running horses, as the cruel claws of the wizard-dragon gripped his arms. Saw Cobant running free as Ruth's inferior mount struggled valiantly to keep up. Saw the pack behind—not wizards, but wizard-called: hellhounds, creatures of magic who could run the Road and pull down any prey.

And then the pain, as the wizard used pure brute power to make a Gate where a Gate *might* be, but was not.

And then darkness.

Melior drifted deeper, seeking oblivion, and his vision took on the jangled logic, not of memory, but of dreams. He saw the *grendel* once again, but this time it was Philip LeStrange who held the Sword of Maiden's Tears to slay it. And who did not become *grendel* in his turn, but kept outward human seeming and changed within—into a creature far less human and more deadly than any *grendel*.

He saw the Cup of Morning Shadows, blazing bright gold and filled with power. But it was not Jausserande who held it, but Ruth—Ruth who cried as she held it, consumed by flame, for only that which was untouched might touch the Cup, and Ruth was his, his, his, his heart twin, his lady bright.

He saw Jausserande, her face in agony as she lost that which meant more to her than the Cup, and the pain was everywhere, burning, pushing him up out of dreams.

"It was time you awakened, Baron Rohannan." A woman's voice.

Melior roused to consciousness, and the burning came with him; a brand in the shape of a flower, angry garnet against his ribs. The woman holding the iron that had marked him stood watching, her sharp white teeth denting her full underlip.

She was as fair, perhaps, as the white Hermonicet—Hermonicet the Fair, whom Melior had never seen, and for whose sea-cool kisses the seven elphen Houses had gone to war. But this woman was fair as the sun, not the moon—as beautiful and deadly as sun fire; all the shades of gold and copper and blood. Hair the color of firelight rippled over her shoulders, eyes the hot color of burning coals gazed into his.

Mad eyes.

He tried to move and found he could not, hung in chains like any felon in his own dungeons. There was rough stone against his bare back, and his feet were bare also; his toes barely skimmed the floor. The pain in his shoulders of his unsupported weight was a burning pressure that would only grow worse with each passing hour.

The lady set the iron aside into the brazier to heat once more. Though her outward seeming marked her as one of his own race, the Children of Air, Melior knew she was not.

"I awake," Melior said, watching her. "What would you have of me?"

The lady sighed, as though his question wearied her unutterably. "Peace," she said.

Melior would have said more, but she turned away, circling the room, her fingertips running along the wall as if she were any bored child seeking to amuse itself. Her hair, unbound like a maiden's at her betrothal, hung in a rippling metallic curtain nearly to the floor.

Melior could smell the sea, and—if he turned his head—at a price paid in sickness and pain he could see a narrow window-slit set in the curving wall. There was another opposite it, and though the thickness of the wall denied Melior sight of the outside, he could see pale daylight against the stone.

Aboveground. Near the sea. He thought he knew where he was. Castle Mourning, the seat Baligant had chosen to occupy until his

Kingmaking in order to be near his bride. The Eastern Marches, then, and all Chandrakar away from Domain Rohannan of Canton Silver in the West.

But why?

"Yes-s-s-s" said the red-gold lady of Mourning, completing her circuit of the barren tower room and returning to Melior's side. "It is *good* that you are awake."

She picked up the iron, cherry red once more. She chose her site with care, and pressed the glowing metal home.

There was a soft groan from her chained victim.

"You to the Sword, the Sword to she. Then I have you all three, and my master's favor. What could be more desirable?" asked the mad lady of the sea-tower.

Five miles, more or less, was the bargain he had struck with Puff the Magic Firedrake, as he recalled. Five miles separated Nic Brightlaw from Ruth Marlowe at the moment he mounted the horse.

But in which direction?

There was a white castle on a distant hill, pat and perfect as something out of a *Boy's Own Paper*. He'd ride up to it as a last resort; in Nic's newly-abridged experience, wealth and corruption went hand in hand. Meanwhile, he rode through a world where everything was new, impacting on his senses with a vividness found only in the memories of childhood. These were the lands a child's eyes saw, unblinded by years of grinding dailyness.

As his eyes were now unblinded.

The road was well kept, the foliage cut decently back, white stone markers set at the verge, carved deeply with letters in some alphabet that Nic couldn't read. The air was autumn-crisp, and through the gaps in the hedge he could see harvested fields, orchards stripped of their summer bounty, vine stocks pruned and tied back in anticipation of winter. Tidy, prosperous, peaceful.

At least now. Because as he rode, Nic could see other things, too. A hillside that glittered as if it were covered in ice, although it wasn't ice—it was vitrified stone; glass called up out of earth and stone by some firestorm worse than a thousand lightning strikes. A swath of woodland burnt to charcoal. The place where a village had been once, and now only foundations remained.

Now that he knew what he was looking for, he could see the subtle irregularities in the plantings that terraced the valley hills—plantings lately begun, plantings that attempted to follow the outlines of those abandoned years before and which could not match them exactly, because the memories of the original husbandmen were bone and ash on the battlefield this once had been.

War. Miss Marlowe had said there'd been a war here. And it was Nic's experience that wars were never over.

After he'd been riding for an hour on a road that climbed slowly as it ascended the hillside, Nic came to a village. It looked much like the villages that were still fresh in his edited memory: a sprawl of huts made of sticks and grass (some, here, of stone), a well in the dirt square that served as the center of town. The wells he remembered had pumps, of a sort, while this one had a crank and bucket, but there was more sameness than difference.

He tugged on the rein and his mount obediently stopped. Nic sat, and looked at the well, and wondered how to get water out of the well and into his horse.

"Can we aid thee, lord?"

Nic instantly pegged the speaker as the village headman, a round brown individual wiping his hands on a leather apron as he approached, looking understandably nervous. To Nic's relief he was speaking English—at least, it *sounded* like English, which was all Mrs. Brightlaw's favorite son asked of life.

"Water for my horse. Beer. And some information."

The man looked relieved, nodding. Nic dismounted, pulling off his helmet, and the man's expression became confused, wary. After a moment Nic understood why. *It's the ears. Mine are the wrong shape. Elves are the bosses here. Pointed ears.*

"Do you come from the castle?" the man said carefully.

Saying "yes" could be checked too easily. And Miss Marlowe hadn't told him nearly enough to be able to pass here.

"Americal Division," Nic said, just as if it would make any sense to his listener. Never mind that the Americal had been disbanded in 1971, long before Nic's tour. "I'm on a long-range recon; humint penetration and survey. I'm afraid I got separated from my unit, so I'm looking to resupply and hook back up. You can check that with Captain, um, Ryerson, if you like."

It was nonsense, but it had the right sound. The headman relaxed again. "No, that's fine." A child who had been watching from the shadow of one of the houses came forward. "You can leave your horse with Wing, he'll take care of him, good master . . ." the headman hesitated, fishing for a name.

"Saint," Nic said. "Call me Saint."

* * *

From the tavern—a shed with three walls, a roof, some crude benches, and a roof that wouldn't leak so long as the weather was dry— Nic could watch as the boy Wing filled the trough for the horse one bucket at a time. A piece of silver to the headman brought grain for the horse and food and beer for Nic. The beer was warm and sickly-sweet. He drank it without complaint.

The other men of the village—close at hand, now that harvest was over—collected slowly beneath the tavern roof. Nic produced more silver, and paid a round for all.

And got, as he hoped, information.

There were brigands in the woods; a cunning band, led by someone called Fox. There'd been a raid on the Harvest Home, and the castle had been set afire. Arnaut the steward had sent to the Earl of Silver—Baron Regordane as he'd been, whose father had fought so bravely in the War— as their lord, the Baron Rohannan, was from home and the poor lord's sister not able to command by way of the injuries she'd taken. And his cousin the Treasurekeeper, who might have done aught, was gone this fortnight and feared murdered and slain by the same villians—

That you are sheltering, supplying, and spying for, Nic finished silently. He'd heard this song too many times in the past to mistake the tune. He wondered how many of the men here drinking with him raided with Fox—who would have to be his next stop, that much was clear.

"Your bandits are your problem, not mine," Nic said. "I'm not here for them. I'm looking for a girl." His description was simple: brown hair, blue eyes, a stranger. He didn't mention the unicorn. He wondered if this Fox had a useful taste for gold.

No one had seen a blue-eyed girl stranger. They were quite forth-coming on that point—and honest, too, since Nic had framed the question in such a way that the answer could exclude any mention of nonlocal men.

Then it was time to go. This time the whole town stood around to watch him: the men and boys in a body in front of the alehouse, the women and younger children from the doorways of their houses. Nic mounted his horse and turned its head toward the road that led into the forest. He thought a moment, hesitated, and then said the words that would set him on an inevitable collision course with the outlaw leader.

"There's a gold piece for whoever brings me the girl I'm looking for," Nic said.

Clucking to his mount, Saint Nic rode out of the village.

It had been early afternoon when Fox had dropped her on the hill above Foretton. Jausserande found and lost his trail a dozen times in the

hours that followed—she and her Ravens had been cavalry, not scouts—
but she continued without dismay. Every time she thought she'd lost it
unrecoverably, some luck, some instinct, found it for her again, as if she
and Fox were destined to meet once more.

Here he'd stopped a long time, to judge from the disturbance in the
leaf-mold. And when he moved, it had been fast—she saw the deep
gouges left in the damp leaf mass by the horse's unshod hooves. She
looked in the direction he had gone, peering with sight far superior to her
quarry's into the deep blue evening shadows that filled the woods as if
they were a bowl.

That was when she saw the body.

It was all white ribs and blood, the roosting place of feasting crows.
Such larger scavengers as remained in Chandrakar after a century of war
had also been at the body—pigs and dogs, perhaps; it was too early in the
season for wolves.

A horse.

Fox's?

She advanced on the carcass carefully, conscious that other predators
might be doing the same. The crows launched themselves into sluggish
complaining flight—alerting the whole forest that someone was here.

The horse was not Fox's. What hide and hair remained were gray,
and Fox had been riding a bay. The gray had been skinned and dressed
out, and after another moment she saw why: the shattered fetlock.

But whose horse was it? What other riders used these woods?

Jausserande circled the clearing. Here was sign that two horses had
been here, there a clear point that told her Fox's was one of them, and
the scraped branch where he'd tied it. She saw a glimmer of out-of-season
color among the leaves and retrieved a green velvet snood. Jausserande
ran it through her fingers and sniffed at it. There were strands of light
brown hair caught among the velvet ribbons and the cloth held a flowery
perfume.

Human. Some human girl lost in these woods, set upon by Fox's
bandits and stolen away. It was almost a plausible story, save that the
splendid hairnet argued that she was the daughter of some rich farmer or
some hedge lord's petted mistress. Where, then, had been her escort?

Suddenly there was the sound of someone on horseback coming
nearer.

Jausserande looked about for some place to hide.

By the time he'd left the village, Nic had figured out the other joker
in the wizard Ophidias' deck. The lizard-wizard had promised that Nic
would be no more than five miles from Ruth Marlowe at the moment he

entered Chandrakar. But—as Nic had already figured out for himself— there was no guarantee that Miss Marlowe would stay put. Which meant that one direction was nearly as good as another—and there was always the bandit chief. It was Nic's experience that if you could only get in good with the hill bandits in any region, your job was half done for you.

Up ahead he heard the caw and flurry of crows. He pulled his horse to a stop, listening, then went forward at a slow walk. Ambush at worst, confrontation at best. Unavoidable, at least if he wanted to do something more than wander around in circles.

He entered the clearing where the butchered body lay. Deer, he thought at first, then, accurately gauging its size, horse. Dressed out as neatly as any deer ever poached—

And not a scavenger in sight. How odd.

"Come out, come out, wherever you are," Nic Brightlaw said, raising his voice slightly. And though he had expected it, even he was surprised when the woman dropped out of the tree.

It was the human warrior from her vision.

To be truthful, Jausserande had recognized the horse first—not the animal itself, but what it *was*. Creature of magic, and therefore being ridden by no human enemy.

Then she saw that she'd been wrong—its rider *was* human. He had ridden out of her dreams.

"What do you here in Rohannan's woods?" Jausserande demanded boldly.

The rider shifted comfortably in his saddle and looked at her, his eyes a clear and untroubled blue. She recognized nothing of his clothing and equipment, and he displayed no badge to say what lord claimed him.

"I might ask you the same question," the rider said. "Your horse seems to have met with a mishap."

His voice reminded Jausserande uncomfortably of Fox. This voice, too, held no proper note of subservience.

"I am Floire Jausserande, and hold freedom of the wood by my cousin's gift. The horse belonged to another. Come now, churl, and explain yourself or face my just punishment."

The stranger blinked midly, as if surprised, and said, as if to himself, "If this is Chandrakar, I don't think Miss Marlowe is going to like it here." He turned his attention back to her. "I am . . . Saint, and I go where I damn well please. As it happens, I'm looking for a man called Fox. You wouldn't have seen him, by any chance?"

Jausserande's hand dropped to her belt, to the sword she did not currently possess.

"Ah," the stranger said in satisfied tones, "you *do* know him."

"I'm going to geld him, then skin him alive, then hang him in chains from the castle walls," Jausserande said flatly.

"First, catch your rabbit," the stranger said mildly. "For my part, I only want a short conversation with him about a friend of mine. You wouldn't have seen her, would you? Her name's Ruth Marlowe."

Ruth Marlowe. The Ironworld mud-daughter that Melior had formed such an unsuitable passion for. What connection did this stranger have with Ruth Marlowe?

And what connection, for that matter, with *her?*

"Well if you haven't, you haven't. A very good evening to you, Miss." He turned his horse to go.

"Ceiynt! Wait!" Jausserande cried.

He stopped, and looked over his shoulder at her. In the lengthening shadows his face and hands were dim blurs, his horse a white beacon in the darkness.

"How will you find Fox?" Jausserande said.

"I don't expect to," Ceiynt said. "I expect he'll come looking for me."

"He'll kill you," Jausserande said quickly, "and even if he had Heruthane, she belongs to my cousin, not to you."

Ceiynt turned his horse about, until he faced her once more. Jausserande felt the flicker of warning danger, but at least she had his attention.

"It was my understanding that Miss Marlowe belonged to herself. And since a number of rude strangers are apparently out to kill her, I'll trouble you for a declaration of intent. Lie if you like. I will mention that I don't think I can miss at this range."

She saw the paleness of his raised hand in the gloom, and, gripped between his fingers, the thin dull-colored feathershape of death-metal.

It was too much. Jausserande sat down, not entirely of her own will, on the ground. "Strike then, upstart maggot! No doubt Fox will reward you for it. I don't care."

"Tell me about Fox. Tell me about why you recognize Miss Marlowe's name. Take your time." Ceiynt's voice was gently insistent.

"I have told you, mud-man. She is my cousin's—and she is *not* here, because if she were, he would seek her here, and he does not." Silence. "My cousin is the Rohannan," Jausserande said, impatient with Ceiynt's silence. "He has told me of his venture into the World of Iron, and of Heru—*Ruth.* And you also come from the World of Iron—do you come seeking her to take her back?" Jausserande finished, struck by a hopeful thought.

"Seeking her, at least." There was the rustle of motion as he sheathed the death-metal weapon once more. "And what are you doing out here all alone in the woods, Little Red Riding Hood?"

"Killing Fox." The words were muffled; Jausserande leaned her cheek against her knee and wished the mad mud-born would leave her in peace. That he would not, she already knew; this close to him her undependable elphensight burned bright and certain, lighting a few hours of the future. "And now you will say that you will ride on, and will not, and will offer me a share of your fire for my aid in leading you to this Fox— who has done that for which the Earl of Silver would hang him, did not Rohannan or Floire reach him first."

There was a pause.

"I suppose in that case, I'd better build the fire," Ceiynt said. "Do tie this thing up—or whatever you do with them," he added, tossing her the reins of his horse.

It was full dark when Ruth and Fox reached the outlaws' camp.

They'd stopped once so she could wrap Naomi's cloak around both of them. Fox's arms were around her, his hands on the reins, and it began to seem to Ruth that she had spent her entire life seated on one saddlebow or another. She heard the signal whistles as they passed beneath the trees, and Fox's soft snort of satisfaction. A moment later they reached the camp itself.

It was familiar as things imagined out of books are familiar—the scattered small fires, each with its tripod-hung kettle; the men in rough furs and leathers, with club or quarterstaff kept near to hand. Fox tossed the reins down into waiting hands and slid off the horse.

Ruth stared.

"Welcome to fucking Sherwood, Ruthie—now get off the horse," Fox said sweetly.

She'd forgotten the twisted ankle. Fox hadn't. He took her whole weight as she staggered and swayed, hissing in pain.

"Raven! You've got a customer! And where's Hathorne?" Fox called.

No one, it seemed, had seen Hathorne, but in answer to Fox's cry, Raven appeared.

He was the largest man Ruth had ever seen; well over six feet tall and with shoulders as wide as if he juggled cart horses every morning before breakfast. His hands were the size of gallon milk jugs, and curling black hair seemed to cover him everywhere. He wore a deerskin tabard with the hair still on, sleeveless, laced loosely at the sides. His brown eyes were mild.

"Raven used to be a blacksmith," Fox said, then, to Raven, "This is—"

"Don't you *dare* call me Ruthie!" Ruth hissed swiftly.

"Ruth. This is Ruth. Ruth is a friend of mine. She got hurt," Fox said blandly.

"And the highborn?" Raven asked. His voice rumbled, deep and slow.

"The highborn is *fine,* Raven. I let her go at Foretton. She's probably up to her neck in a hot bath right now. What's for dinner?"

"Philip, what are you up to?" Ruth demanded in an undertone.

"It doesn't exactly matter, from your point of view, does it, Ruthie-Ruth? Come on, let's go to my office."

"Philip—" Ruth began. Fox's grip tightened, hard enough to steal the air from her lungs. No, not Philip. Not any more.

Between them, Fox and Raven got her to one of the little huts that ringed the clearing.

"I'm not going in there," Ruth said, looking at the tiny enclosed space.

"Raven," Fox said. She felt his muscles flex as he made a gesture she couldn't see.

She thought they were going to force her, and prepared to fight, but Raven simply went and began to cut the cords that fastened the green hides over the hut's wooden frame until it was no more than a shelter half, open to the night.

"Better?" Fox asked, in noncommittal tones.

Ruth felt tears of weakness prickle behind her eyes. "Yes," she said in strangled tones.

The hut-as-was was a little larger than a pup tent. Through the hole in its wall Ruth could see an uneven earth floor, scrubbed smooth, that supported two piles of skins and pine boughs. At the head of one of the makeshift beds was a tree trunk, lopped short, with a carved groove circling its trunk about six inches from the top. Fox helped her through the side of the hut and eased her down onto one of the beds.

She sat there, feeling every muscle reminding her of its recent ill-treatment, and watched as Fox lit a candle and set it inside a mirrored lantern-box that sat upon a plain wooden box. That was all that was here.

"I used the last of the Seconal on Tink. Is there any of the wine left?" Fox said to Raven. The blacksmith nodded and backed out through the low entrance. Fox rocked back on his haunches and looked at Ruth. The candlelight cast his face into harsh lines.

"Pray that ankle isn't broken, because if it is, we can't set it very well. For what it's worth, I don't think it's that bad, but first we have to get your boots off and see—*that's* going to take two strong men and a boy," Fox smiled with all the poisoned sweetness Ruth remembered.

"Why?" she said, tiredly puzzled.

"Because it's going to *hurt*, Ruth. There's no morphine here, no penicillin. Not even an asprin. There's just *magic*, and mere humans don't get the use of much of that." Fox's voice was vicious, and Ruth recoiled from the bitterness in it.

"But I don't understand—why don't you just ask Melior to help?" Ruth said, bewildered.

The words hung in the air, and suddenly Ruth was conscious that she'd said something very wrong.

"Ah, here's the steward with the wine list," Fox said. "Sorry the service doesn't run to cups—" he went on, taking the leather bag from Raven.

"I brought my own," Ruth said with sudden remembrance, hoping she hadn't squashed it flat. She upended the beltpouch, producing Nic's watch, the magic ring, the gold scissors she'd bought at the fair, a length of red ribbon, and the battered tin cup.

Fox took the cup and filled it with wine.

"Chug it down—when you've had that and another one, we'll see if we can get your boots off."

"But I'll be drunk!" Ruth protested, "and—"

Fox put a finger on her lips, effectively silencing her; Philip had never touched anyone, or liked being touched himself. She gaped at him.

"—and you're worried about you're virtue," Fox said, picking up the thread of dialogue and twisting it effortlessly away from its original meaning. "Cheer up. I prefer sheep." He wrapped her fingers around the goblet and raised it to her lips. "Drink."

Ruth drained the cup—the wine had no particular flavor other than alcoholic harshness—and then, at Fox's bullying, another.

Rich warmth spread through her, as though her veins were filling with hot honey. Without any particular self-will she lay back on the pallet and gazed at the ceiling from a place where her body was only a distant inconvenience.

There was some tugging and prodding, nothing to do with her. The night air was cool on her bare feet and she curled her toes.

"Ruthie? You still alive?"

Scraps of talk swirled through her head like smoke.

"Christ, she's out like a light. Was that the wine with the hemp seeds in it?"

But she wasn't asleep. She was just floating.

"Is that it? Doesn't look too bad. Do we have any green hide to wrap it in? She can soak it off at the other end."

But what was the other end? *Journeys end in lovers' meeting,* but hers had ended in lovers parting.

She had to find Melior.

She felt some one winding something around her ankle. It tickled.

"There's elves hunting her, Raven. But I don't want anything to happen to her. Not yet."

Raven's response was an unintelligible mumble.

I was a child and you were a child, in a kingdom by the sea . . .

"Yeah. Out like a light."

No.

Yes.

Fox snuffed the candle and climbed out the side of the hut ahead of Raven. It was a good thing he'd dumped Tinkerbelle this morning—he didn't think she and Ruth would get along.

And besides, Ruthie made a much better hostage.

Fox was clever, and, when setting out on a hopeless crusade, knew better than to scatter his shot. His goal had always been small and simple: to smash the Sword of Maiden's Tears while Rohannan Melior watched helplessly. No more than that, and, being a realist, Fox had accepted that what he actually accomplished might be less: to destroy or hide the Sword in Melior's absence, for example.

Or to kill Melior while the Sword went safely to other hands, although killing Melior was really his last choice. The dead didn't suffer nearly as much as Fox felt Melior deserved to suffer.

He had not considered the effect of his plans on Ruth before. Ruth, after all, was *there,* at the far end of the Iron Road, while Fox and Melior were *here,* beyond the Morning, and whatever happened, Ruth would never know.

Well, now she would.

Fox had been in Chandrakar a period of time he privately termed Long Enough—at least two winters, and he'd been somewhere else before that for a while—to know things about the place that their good buddy Mel apparently hadn't thought important enough to mention to Ruth. Like the fact that Chandrakar—seven Cantons, twenty-seven Domains, the Twilight Court and the Lords Temporal, the High Court and the High Prince, and the Holy College with its High and Low Adepts—was a hierarchical ladder that made Dark Age Europe look like an upwardly mobile love-in, and humans weren't even on the bottommost rung.

Mud-born. Or, if you were being kinder, Children of Earth—the only one of the Five Races that couldn't use magic.

Which wouldn't be so bad, if the elves' use of magic hadn't stopped medicine, engineering, and the rest of science dead in its tracks. Why invent the telephone when you had telepathy and teleportation? Why study pharmacy and surgery if you could set bones and take away pain with a touch? Why build better roads if you could fly—or print books when you would live long past the day when the book had rotted to dust?

If you were an elf. If you had magic. If you didn't care about what humans could do, providing only they did what you wanted and kept your vineyards and dye-yards running, worked your looms and mills, tilled your fields and bred your servants.

And remember, always, the inevitable expansionism of a race that lived forever—and still bred nearly as fast as humans. And so was now, despite the war, despite everything, not only displacing humans from society, but from the very world. Someday, perhaps, there would be low-born elves who would toil as serfs in Chandrakar's fields, but by then all the human serfs would be extinct.

Two years, Ruthie'd said it'd been since she'd seen Melior last. Fox didn't know how much longer it had been for him.

It felt like forever.

But he looked cheerful as he wandered through the camp in search of a bowl of stew—or, more likely, cold meat, what with the camp being moved. He was looking in a desultory way for Hathorne, even though he didn't really expect to see him. If Hathorne was after Ruth with elvish backing, Fox wanted to know what Hathorne's backers really wanted.

But as he made his circuit, something else drove thoughts of elphen politics completely from Fox's mind.

"Yarrow, how come nobody's packing and all the horses are here? We need to send riders to Foretton and Black Bridge and get a bird to fly to Avernet. We're moving, remember? Bring the wives and kiddies."

Fox squatted beside the cookfire with its gently-steaming copper cauldron that should long since have been emptied and readied to move.

It was late—i.e., about two hours after sunset, and while sentries and a few others were still awake, most of the outlaws would be either asleep or preparing to be. A society without artificial light rose and slept with the sun.

"But you said that wasn't till next week, Fox."

"I sent Raven, Ash, and Otter back to tell you guys to move *now*," Fox said, working hard to keep his voice low and even.

Yarrow's brow cleared. "But then Hathorne said he'd talked to you later, and you'd changed your mind."

Fox took a deep breath. What a moron he'd been not to check *immediately* that his orders were being carried out. It was true that the camp had looked much the same when he'd ridden in, but all he'd really seen had been things they'd been going to abandon here anyway.

And if Hathorne had countermanded the order to move—

"When did he tell you that, Yarrow?" Fox kept his voice low and even. His control over his band was slight, usually consisting more of getting them to do what they were going to do anyway more efficiently than of overt innovation. Push or hurry them, and he risked losing any control over them at all.

"He rode after you and the highborn, just in case you needed help . . . an hour after Raven and the others got here, say."

Which, made it something Hathorne had done before he'd found Ruth—but a betrayal regardless.

"Yarrow," Fox said gently, "Hathorne *lied* to you. He's betrayed us. We've got to move the camp *now.*"

Yarrow had lost both ears for theft in one of Canton Silver's northern cities and didn't want any more elvish justice. He sprang to his feet, ready to bolt. Fox grabbed his arm and yanked him to a stop.

"Quietly. Together. Like we did it at the Fair." Fox stared into Yarrow's eyes. "Rouse the camp. Do it quietly. Everything's going to be fine." When he saw that Yarrow was going to behave, at least for a few minutes, Fox let him go.

Rouse the camp. And send the men *where?* The Vale was still the best choice, even though Hathorne knew about it, because magic would not work there.

Or so Fox had been told. But he recollected that he'd also been told that humans couldn't work magic—and he'd worked magic to get here. So had Ruth, from everything she'd told him. So, for that matter, had Hathorne, every time he walked the Road.

Fox hesitated, thinking fast. What he knew about the Vale might not be true, but even so, the elves believed in the Vale's legend. And there were some members of his band who could not simply blend back into the towns and villages of Domain Rohannan. They had to go somewhere. It would have to be the Vale.

The quiet camp began to resemble a kicked ant's nest as Fox's outlaws were roused and alerted. Fox had little time to think of Ruth. She was safe enough where she was. His men might steal her boots if they thought of it, but they wouldn't hurt her.

"Raven! Get me three horses—fresh ones. Stay with me."

He could send Raven off later. For now he needed his support here. There were beggars to outfit, plans to pass on—all the while knowing the plans would not be followed—food and spoils to share out so that every man would have an equal chance of surviving. He sent them on their way in twos and threes, knowing that any man traveling at night was suspicious, knowing that half of them couldn't read the sky to find their way, knowing that instead of this unplanned exordium they should have been settling into a safe place to winter.

Knowing that many of them would panic at the first sight of a pointed ear, and babble enough to get themselves hanged.

At his direction they tore down the skin huts and covered the fire pits. Maybe Hathorne would be confused if the place looked different enough. Fox didn't think so. *He* wouldn't be.

Damn Hathorne. And damn the inevitable for happening, right on schedule.

It was long after midnight. The last few of his band were sitting, talking, waiting for their turn to go. Waiting because too large a party of humans traveling together would rouse even more suspicion in their elvish masters. Fox stood, watching them, not really daring to sit for fear he'd nod off. Last night he had been in the Vale of Stars, and he hadn't gotten any sleep then either.

Never mind. There'd be plenty of time to sleep when he was dead.

He went over to where Raven, a tree-tall shadow in the dark, stood with the horses Fox had reserved for himself, Raven, and Ruth.

"You could take one of them and go. If anybody stops you, tell him you're taking it to the smithy. It could work," Fox said.

And if Raven could get out of Canton Silver where he might be recognized, even the poacher's brands on his cheeks might not matter too much.

"And shall I leave my Dowsel and the hills where I was born? And you, Fox—what would you do without me?" Raven said, after a moment to think it over.

Dowsel had been Raven's wife. She was buried in an unmarked grave somewhere along the Dawnheart Road, and Fox knew from experience that when her name was invoked it was useless to argue.

Raven wouldn't go, and Fox felt a faint flutter of relief, even though the reality of it was that it meant he would probably watch Raven die. But Fox was weary to death of stories he didn't know the ending of. This ending, grim as it advertised itself to be, he would see.

And maybe God would let him broker a miracle. So he said:

"You always were the brains of the outfit, Raven. I guess you'd better stay."

"And the little earthling girl?" Raven went on, meaning Ruth.

"Earth girls are easy, so the saying goes," Fox said, his mind elsewhere. If Hathorne wanted Ruth, and was working for Baligant Baneful

(Fox did not entirely rule out the possibility of another employer), then he probably had a way to track her by magic. If he didn't have magic, he'd come first to the camp and then to the Vale of Stars.

He would probably not go to Dawnheart.

"Come on, Raven. I've got an idea."

The man most recently called Hathorne—and who had answered to many other names in his life—roasted horse meat over a fire as he waited for true night to fall. This particular item in the bag of wizard's tricks he'd been given to play with did not work in sunlight.

His camp was among rocks, sheltered from the wind, and to casual eyes—if there were any—he appeared to be no more than a harmless traveler on innocent business. As he waited, he thought about Fox.

Hathorne had always suspected that Fox had come, if not from the Iron Lands, then at least from the Borders where cross-traffic was known to be common. It was only the worst sort of luck that Fox should come from the same world as Hathorne's quarry did. Hathorne's orders were explicit and simple: get the girl and kill her without witnesses. Bad luck, for now Hathorne must report to his master that he had neither got nor killed the girl. Best to rely on the old lag, that, seeing how complicated the game had grown, he had done nothing rather than do that which his employer would dislike. It might serve, and it might not, but what was nearly certain was that he had lost as much of Fox's trust as he had ever had, and with it, the possibility of using the outlaws whom Fox had gathered.

On the other hand, he could tell his master that Line Floire's Treasure, the Cup of Morning Shadows, was itself truly lost; that he himself had seen Floire try to retrieve it and fail.

He could tell his master that.

At last the darkness was complete, and Hathorne took the ring out of his pouch. He did not put it on, but took a clay bowl out of his saddlebag and filled it with water. Then, hesitating for a moment as if he were about to do that which he did not wish to do, he dropped the ring into the water.

The ripples it made entering the water did not die out, but increased, shadowed and tipped in light, until the whole surface of the water in the bowl was a blinding chiaroscuro of motion. Hathorne did not look away— he had learned better.

"Who calls?" The voice was honeyed-sweet, sexless and inhuman, and as always the sound of it was like an ice dagger in Hathorne's guts. No face formed itself in the bowl whose surface was now a liquid sheet of hot silver; but its baneful glow dazzled the eyes, inviting them to embrace illusion.

"It is Hathorne," he said from a dry throat, adding nothing as he had been given no honorific to add, though fear and deference were explicit in his every tone.

"My Hathorne. Have you brought me the news of where the Ironworlder girl's grave lies?"

And now it was agony to speak, agony to stare into that fiery bowl—but the alternative would be far worse.

"She was where you said she would be—but you did not tell me that she was Fox's trull of old. He had taken her back with him alive to his camp, on the day after he failed to achieve the Cup of Morning Shadows."

There. All said in one breath, and neatly, too, so that the silver hellgrammite he served could not blame him for telling the one thing first and withholding the next.

There was a long, nerve-racking silence, broken only by the sighing of the wind through the trees and the hiss and pop of the tiny fire. Hathorne's eyes watered, and tears streamed down his cheeks, but he kept his eyes fixed on the bowl.

And now the blazing silver cleared, to show him the outlaw camp—not deserted, Hathorne had made sure of that, but in a flurry of activity through which that white witchbreed Fox stalked like a man demented.

The scene changed. He saw the Ironworlder girl he had hunted so long and so fruitlessly lying in dimness in one of the huts.

And then he saw a figure on a white horse—magic white, white as a unicorn—with a rider whose face was in shadow. Beside him was the elphen maid that Fox had captured, whose throat it would have felt so good to slit, and then fire, fire, fire rose up to cover all.

"Kill the Ironworld girl before they meet, or forfeit your own life," the sweet metal voice told him. *"Kill her now."*

The bowl went dark, and in the blessed silence there began a stabbing pain behind Hathorne's eyes.

"There's magic about," Jausserande said, sitting bolt upright. In the fireless darkness, her face was a pale blur.

She was wrapped in Ceiynt's cloak, and had burrowed down for sleep into a pile of leaves so that only her pale hair showed. Now she was sitting up, staring out into the night as if an explanation would be forthcoming from leaves and branches.

The man Jausserande called Ceiynt felt it, too, although he wouldn't have called it magic. What Nic Brightlaw would have called it was "trouble"—the feeling of "something's about to fubar" that presaged a sniper or mortar attack. The feeling of being in a suddenly discovered minefield.

He got slowly to his feet, crouching, cursing the absence of his M1 and the AR15 he'd swapped it for. Jausserande was standing blithely upright, staring into the dark.

"That way," she whispered, and Nic took off in that direction, moving silently through the dark.

He saw the flare of the campfire from a hundred yards away though it was built small and sheltered among the rocks. One man, one horse. The man was sitting cross-legged before the fire, staring into a bowl as if there were no hooligans in all the wide world. Light shone out of the bowl as if from an arclight, and in the blue-rinsed illumination Nic could see that his hair was curly, reddish, worn long.

He was talking.

No, that wasn't right. He was listening.

"Kill the Ironworld girl before they meet, or forfeit your own life. Kill her now." The voice made the high mechanical moan of a wet crystal goblet when you run your finger around the rim. Nic's hackles stood on end, and every instinct urged him to blot out both voice and auditor.

But he held his hand.

The bowl went dark and slid from the man's crossed ankles. It tipped and spilled, and water flowed into the fire, making it hiss and gutter.

Nic charged.

To capture a man without hurting him in any way that matters is a task more difficult than merely killing him. And when the 23-year-old mind attempted to command the body two decades older, it was inevitable some miscalculation must occur.

Nic's lunge fell short, striking the man about the knees instead of the shoulders. He felt the clench of seasoned muscle under his hands, and then the other attacked with a silent desperation that marked him as guilty in Nic's mind. Guilty as charged.

Neither dared to let go. They rolled across the fire, putting it out completely. In the midnight darkness they fought by touch.

Here was a rock, to gouge into the stiff complaining muscles of the back. There, an exposed tree root to batter the enemy head against. The other sought for every advantage, used every dirty trick that Nic had ever learned a counter for, and if they were evenly matched, how could he manage to hold the enemy without killing him?

There was the dull sound of rock against skull, and the desperate struggling man in his arms went limp.

"I thought I told you to stay where you were," Nic said.

"You did," Jausserande responded coolly.

Nic pushed the body off and she grabbed it.

"I hope you haven't killed him. He was talking to someone, and I'd like to talk to him," Nic said.

The darkness was absolute—no, not quite, because he could see Jausserande—no, more than see her. She was glowing.

As he stared, the white radiance increased until Nic's shadow straggled across the ground. Jausserande cast no shadow, being the source of the light—an incongruous glory, given her tattered and mudstained appearance.

"Magic," Jausserande said, though whether it was a dismissal or an explanation wasn't quite clear. She rolled the body onto its back. "Ah. His name is Hathorne. He knows where Fox's camp is." She worked quickly and efficiently, searching Hathorne's body, stripping him of cloak and vest and shirt.

Nic stared down at the man. He'd seen him before. This was the man who'd tried to kill him just as he and Miss Marlowe had arrived—and in this world, coincidence was no coincidence.

Apparently his elphen ally knew him, too. Nic felt no particular need to burden her with the additional information, however. Not when the Mission Objective was the only thing that mattered.

"And he'll lead us there?" he asked.

"He will when I've finished with him," Jausserande answered with quiet certainty. She pulled Hathorne's boots off and tossed them aside. Shadows flitted and danced in the silvery elvish light, but Nic ignored that, watching what she was doing with such innocent efficiency.

Victor Charlie did that with his prisoners. Barefoot Americans were at a disadvantage in the jungle—soft-footed, easy to recapture. Easy to track.

He could smell the war that had been here. He could see it in every move the elf-girl made, moving sleek and efficient through the forest as if she were a part of it. He was worlds and decades away from home, and nothing was any different.

"I need something to tie him with," Jausserande said peremptorily, raising one silver-glowing hand.

Nic looked at the pile of discarded clothing and held out his knife. Her reaction to that surprised him: she shied back, rather as if he'd offered her a grenade with the pin out.

"You do it," she said tersely.

Now this was interesting. Nic shrugged, and began reducing Hathorne's leather shirt to strips.

Jausserande prowled around the campsite. She found Hathorne's horse where he had tethered it for the night, and beside it, its saddle and pack. The pack had little enough in it: some skin-wrapped chunks of meat, salt, and a tinderbox—

And—victory. Jausserande's fingers closed over a thin wallet of silk, its surface rough with silver-embroidered designs. She slid it inside her tunic for later study and went back to where the fire had been.

Its place was now no more than a flat and muddy sprawl. The shards of a broken bowl were embedded in the mud, and Jausserande's study of them was rewarded by her discovery of the ring. She pried it out of the ground and picked it up.

A wide band of fine silver, the metal preferred by Adepts and wizards for its ability to hold the imprint of magic nearly as well as crystal. Around the band, inside and out, unreadable writing flamed into existence and guttered out as she turned it, radiating outward from a reddish stone the size of her thumbnail.

The power imprinted on the object made Jausserande's fingers tingle, and she frowned. Wizard work at the very least, but who were the Adepts of the Wild Magic to interest themselves in the affairs of Chandrakar? And, more than that, why use as cat's-paws humans and *losel* outlaws like Hathorne?

Fox had not lied when he told her he did not serve Baligant Baneful, so it seemed. But had he *known* what the real truth was?

It really didn't matter, since she intended to kill him anyway. But it would be nice to know.

Jausserande slipped the ring into the wallet with the other things. She went back to the horse and saddled it.

"Satisfied?" Nic asked. Jausserande inspected the work and nodded briefly.

"Bring him along." She was leading a saddled horse—Hathorne's—and, having delivered this last order, rode off, glinting like a distant star.

Leaving him, on foot, to carry the prisoner.

Nic looked down at his prisoner and shrugged. It was true that the lady was rude and condescending, but one had to expect that from one's allies. He bent and picked up the unconscious man and followed the glowing figure. Too bad Charlie hadn't glowed in the dark—they could all have been home by Christmas.

Expectation and reality met and quarreled in the unfamiliar strain on overtaxed muscles as he started down the slope with his burden. Was this what being old was like?

That wasn't important. What *was* important was that Hathorne's talking flashlight had told him to "kill the Ironworld girl."

And the only Ironworld girl Nic knew of in these parts was Ruth Marlowe.

· 29 ·

Hymn to Breaking Strain

HIS FIRST PERCEPTION was of heat, followed by the smell of wood smoke and the sound of a fire. Hathorne rejoined the world, knowing that something had gone wrong.

A pointed stick jabbed him in the stomach. He tried, reflexively, to bring his hands around to cover himself, but they were bound behind his back.

"Welcome to the world, Chucko." The voice was unfamiliar, but when he opened his eyes, the face was not. This was the man who had accompanied the Ironworld bitch through the Gate—the one Hathorne had been given no orders about.

Pity. He'd thought the *losel* wight was dead.

"You have the advantage of me," Hathorne said, wheedlingly.

"For a change," the man said.

"Stop coddling him, Ceiynt." The elf bitch—in the flesh this time, and not in a vision. He wished he'd killed her when he'd had the chance. Correction: he wished he'd worked harder to *make* the chance, and damn Fox's soft heart.

Something had gone very wrong indeed.

Strong hands hauled him upright. Violet eyes whose slitted pupils shone with the cat-green of elphenkind glared into his. She held him upright by one fist twisted in his hair, and smiled, and leaned very close, so that he could see the curved wolf-teeth in her smile.

"Ah, Hathorne—have you no brave words now?" Her voice was rough velvet, quivering with anticipation. Hathorne began to sweat. It was well known that the Morning Lords placed no value on *human* life.

The pointed stick jabbed at his naked and unprotected belly once more. "I would hear your voice," Jausserande said.

"My lady—" he began, and gasped as the stick jabbed and slid aside, scraping a deep welt along his ribs.

"So humble, now that *I* hold the leash! I do not ask you, Hathorne, but tell: you will lead us to Fox's camp."

"Yes. I'll do that. I'll do just as you say, Lady—" the words came out tumbled and too fast, but Hathorne didn't care.

"I have a couple of questions, if you don't mind," Ceiynt said. He yawned, and his boredom in the face of all this made Hathorne even more uneasy.

The elf bitch's eyes flashed as she turned to look at Ceiynt. "What matters? He will do as he is told."

"You're a trusting soul," Ceiynt said. "How do you know he'll lead you to Fox instead of just around in circles?"

"Fox's camp can't be more than two hours from here. If he takes longer than that, I'll cut off his thumbs," the elf bitch answered with sweet reasonability. The firelight flashed on Hathorne's own good knife— bronze-bladed and horn-hilted and very sharp—in her hands.

"Um." Ceiynt appeared to consider this. "What if he told you it was just a little farther, or that he was lost, or if he fell and pretended he'd twisted his ankle and couldn't walk?"

"I'll cut off one thumb," she said promptly. "And give him a chance to save the other."

"Suppose his job was to delay you until his reinforcements arrived?" Ceinyt said again.

The elf bitch sighed. "Ceinyt, what is your *point?*"

The blond man smiled, holding all of Hathorne's fascinated and horrified attention. He'd fallen into the hands of ghouls.

"I just want to ask him some questions," Ceiynt said reasonably.

Jausserande pulled out a whetstone and began to hone Hathorne's blade. "Ask him, then. It will pass the time until dawn."

The sound of metal on stone was loud in the shadows.

In the merry greenwood the night inched over the summit of midnight and began to slide down the other side. Everyone else was gone. Fox, wrapped in Naomi's cloak, half-dozed while Raven kept watch. The attack (if one was coming) would come at dawn. Therefore they would leave just before dawn.

And see what was following them, and if they could finesse or outrun it. A thousand possibilities, but, like Holmes, Fox preferred not to theorize in advance of his data.

He wished Ruth weren't here. Poor Ruth, sleeping ice princess, but sleeping was better because at least then you didn't feel. And when Melior had come along and opened little Ruthie's glass coffin, she'd had no waking defenses.

Everything that magic touched it hurt. And whether Ruth had ever gotten over Melior or not, if she'd stayed in the Real World at least she wouldn't have been hurt again. But here she was, hip-deep in Elfland, leading with her chin.

Fox dozed. And inside the hut, Ruth slept heavily.

"C'mon, Jimmy—we're going to be late!"

The dream, the memories began again, unspooling toward its predestined end.

Ruth fought them—the car, the dead children, the midnight slipstream carrying her forward to an unsolicited epiphany.

There was a flash of light in the road ahead.

"Shit," Jimmy muttered, thinking of cops, of tickets, of his dad's refusal to ever let him borrow the car again. But the lights weren't flashing red-and-blue. It was a coppery fiery light, and Ruth, straining her eyes, suddenly saw—

A nightmare in the road ahead; an undigested vision out of the Saturday Monster Matinee. Ruth had a confused image of mocking red eyes, of needle-sharp fangs in a gaping maw, of poison, ruin, and pain. She saw the monster spread its burning wings as the Oldsmobile rounded the corner; heard Jimmy scream as it reached out for him. . .

Felt Jimmy floor the accelerator, desperate to find escape for them all.

Heard the mocking laughter inside her head as the creature vanished.

Saw the tree—

—and, with the desperate strength of terror, broke free.

It was a mistake.

Blind. She was blind. Chill in the roaring void, more naked than an absence of clothes could make her. Hovering unsupported in a lightless abyss where pure information, disenchanted as computer code, printed pictures in her mind.

Will this work? A dark voice, brown, stinking of ambition. *I must be certain, wizard.*

See this? It is an Ironworld soul, still bedded in its mortal host. And I shall weave it to the Sword of Maiden's Tears and set the Sword—so. If he but touches the Sword, it will fall through all the worlds.

This voice flared and guttered, flame-bright like burning roses, thick with decay. *It will fall. I have the soul here.*

The soul.

Her soul.

Her.

Ruth struggled to wake, struggled to run away, to hide from the newborn memory of lying helpless on the grass, flung free of the wreckage, awake and aware while a wizard out of Elphame tore out her soul.

But all she did was wrench herself into yet another vision.

"What do you want?"

Here there was light and sound, color and form and line. A room, visible, but with the shifting insubstantiality of a dream.

"What do you want of me?"

But it was no dream. She knew the man within it.

His legs had long since lost the power to bear him up. He hung from a beam in the center of the room by his shackled wrists, every muscle in chest and torso pulled taut.

"What do you want?"

His skin was mottled with the marks of whip and rod and knife, each pattern of horror left somehow unfinished, as if this torture were only the evil pastime of some easily-distracted child.

"I want nothing." In Ruth's dream she could not see the speaker, yet the voice called up a clear image of red-gold horror. *"My master wants the death of the Ironworld wench, and so he will have it. He would have the Sword lost to Line Rohannan, and so he will have that, too. All for my master, all, all, all—"* the mad little voice sang, swooping and skirling as if its owner danced.

"And what for yourself?" Ruth heard Melior ask, in a voice weary with pain. *"Is there nothing you want for yourself?"*

"All, all, all—" sang the voice. *"All, all, all—"*

"What do you want?" Melior cried.

Ruth awoke, struggling with monsters.

"Jesus, Ruthie—lay off, willya?"

Philip—no, *Fox*—the voice oddly unfamiliar in the dark. He held her pressed tight against him until she realized where she was.

And where Melior was.

It was like the knowledge that someone stands behind you; the burning intuition that makes the hackles rise even when you stand in a room you thought was empty.

"Fox! I—" she gagged on the New Age idiocy of the words but got them out nonetheless. "I had a vision. I know where Melior is."

She could see Fox outlined against the sky in the predawn light. The air was chilly, and when he let go of her and she kicked off the blankets she was colder yet, but she didn't hurt as much as she expected to.

"Okay," said Fox.

"No! I mean I can *find* him. We've got to find him—" Her throat closed with the Technicolor immediacy of her dream.

Melior was being hurt. And things that were only entertaining in lurid fiction or nothing to do with you in the dryly inaccurate report of a newspaper mattered desperately when they were happening to someone you loved.

Not a dream, not a hoax, not an imaginary tale—

"They're hurting him," Ruth finished flatly.

There was a pause, in which something that ought to have happened, didn't.

"So you can find him," Fox said, halfway between comment and question. He backed away on knees and toes and then stood.

"Yes. I think so. I mean—"

"Fine." Fox was not interested in equivocations. "C'mon. Get dressed. It's time to go."

Ruth got to her feet, having forgotten about the ankle. Fox hadn't, and moved forward to support her, but there was no need.

She was fine.

Fallen leaves crackled beneath her bare feet. Experimentally she put more weight on the injured ankle.

Nothing. No pain. Fox stared at her.

"Okay. It wasn't as bad as we thought. So get your boots on and c'mon—unless you want to wait for Domain Rohannan's police to raid this joint—and trust me, Ruthie, they are *not* going to read you your rights and then let you call your lawyer."

"Raid? Fox, what's going on?"

"*Put* your boots on," Fox snapped, completely out of patience. He stepped through the hole in the side of the hut and stalked off.

Ruth sat down and groped about for her boots and stockings. She wasn't pleased with the thought that Fox had had his hand halfway up her leg last night—or with much of anything else she could think of at the moment. She ran her fingers through her hair and dislodged a number of leaves and brambles. Maybe Fox had a comb.

She unwrapped the sticky rawhide bandages from her ankle and brushed away as much of the residue as she could, then pulled on stockings and boots. The day was already perceptibly lighter by the time she was done—was it only yesterday that she had watched the dawn, safe and

warm with Melior in the bed at the inn, and thought that everything
would be fine now?

Oh, God.

Ruth followed Fox out into the camp and saw him standing beside
some horses with another man—Raven, that was his name. The giant.

"Here." Fox threw Naomi's cloak to Ruth and went back to the
shelter. He came back carrying the lantern and the box, with the skin
blankets draped around his shoulders. Ruth swung the Kinsale cloak
around herself, feeling the weight settle on her shoulders with a tug.

"Need a leg up?" Fox said.

"Where are we going? For that matter, what's going on?"

Fox sighed, and leaned his head against his horse's flank. "Ruth, I
will answer any question you have—after we're moving. Now get on the
damned horse." His voice was hard and adult, and he looked desperately
tired.

Ruth got on the horse.

It was nearly true dawn by the time they were underway, Fox in the
lead and Raven at the rear. Fortunately for Ruth, today's horse had few
ideas, and all of them involved following the horse ahead of it.

"I don't see anyone," Raven said hopefully.

"Maybe I was wrong," Fox said wearily. "But if we're all alive next
month, we can get together and sing about it."

"Fox?" Ruth said cautiously.

Fox half-turned in his saddle to look at her. "Poor Ruth," he said
mockingly. "They should have said that no one'd be seated after the
intermission."

"Just a synopsis, that's all I ask." The invisible Melior-compass in her
head pulled Ruth east, toward the rising sun. They were riding at right
angles to it. "And—we're going after Melior, aren't we?"

"Yes." Fox added nothing to that. "Which way is he?" he asked, and,
when Ruth pointed, said, "thought so. We'll head that way eventually, but
right now it's down to Foretton for breakfast, supplies, and gossip. Then
we circle around to reach one of the main roads."

It sounded plausible, and that, from the man she had once known as
Philip, was enough to make her suspicious. "The synopsis?" Ruth
prompted.

"Well, in this unlicensed remake of Francis Ford Coppola's *Robin
Hood: Men in Traction,* the Merries had just discovered a spy in their
camp and are trying to get out of the way before whoever they were sold
out to arrives to collect his new purchase."

Ruth considered this. She was cold and preparing to be hungry, hunted by wizards and tormented by a vision of Melior in agony, but she wasn't brain-dead.

Item: Philip was in Elfland. More particularly, Philip was *here,* in Chandrakar.

Item: Philip, now known as Fox, was the self-confessed leader of a band of outlaws.

"Oh," said Ruth inadequately. Something didn't add up. Ruth tried another question, with an increasing sense of the surreal. "Who's after you—us?"

"I wish I knew. Someone's backing Hathorne with serious magic, and I'd like to think he was just after you—"

"Thanks so much," Ruth snapped.

"—except for the fact that it's *my* group he infiltrated, *my* group he's been supporting with general rural lawlessness, and *my* men he's set up to get killed."

"But he was waiting for me when I got here. How could he do that if he was with you?" Ruth asked.

"Time's different here. A function of geography. If you take the right route, you can get somewhere before you've left. And then, there's always teleportation," Fox said blandly.

"You're kidding," Ruth said.

"Straining at gnats again, Ruthie?" Philip LeStrange had always possessed the power of being infuriating to the max, and he hadn't lost it just because he'd changed his name to Zorro (the Fox).

Ruth refused to dignify his comment with a reply, and as a result, they rode along in silence for nearly an hour while Ruth brooded. Because there were too many holes in Fox's story, too many stops and starts with convenient lacunae in between.

During the silence the sun came up and they struck a trail, a munificent throughway fully four inches wide and mostly covered in leaves. The icy autumn air gradually warmed, and everything was shades of gold, from the smoky barred sunlight to the drifts of leaves through which the horses plodded. Enough leaves still remained on the trees to color and soften the light, and break every vista up into a dappled Impressionist landscape.

Nothing gold can stay. Robert Frost said that.

Did she really need to know the answers Fox could give her? Why not? This was, after all, *Philip,* the annoying little cyberpunk eight years her junior. Without computers, what could he possibly be doing that would cause much trouble?

Don't answer that, Ruth told herself. The man who'd faced down

Hathorne in the greenwood, who'd carried her back to his outlaw camp, was not the guy she'd gone to Library School with.

Too many unanswered questions.

If Philip had been here in Chandrakar, why hadn't he gone to Melior?

If he'd found a way to get here, why hadn't he taken her with him?

"Fox, what were you in the greenwood rebelling against?" Ruth finally asked.

Fox sighed and rubbed the back of his neck.

"The elves, Ruth. We're at war with the elves."

The questions Saint Nic had for Hathorne were many and varied, and kept coming back to the same one: who wanted Ruth Marlowe dead?

Along the way he learned that Miss Marlowe was, indeed, with Fox, that Fox was her kin from the World of Iron, that Fox wished to be High King in Chandrakar, and that Hathorne, for love of the true High King or anything else they pleased, would take them to Fox on the instant as soon as the sky was light enough to see the way.

"Lying mud-sucker," Jausserande commented, without interest. The knife had long since been honed to sharpness and she was whittling a long piece of fell-timber into a spear, holding the point over the fire at intervals to harden it.

"Well, yes, probably," Nic admitted. He hadn't even had to get particularly rough with Hathorne to get his answers so far; whatever else they were familiar with, the natives of these parts had no particular experience with the relentless disinterest of a field interrogation. Keep asking them the same questions over and over and they came all to pieces.

Of course, the fact that his partner—bloodthirsty little savage that she was—frequently offered suggestions as to body parts that Hathorne could afford to lose (without impairing his utility in the least) did not hurt matters, especially since neither Nic nor Hathorne had the least doubt that she'd do it.

"Then why do you keep talking to him, if you know he's lying?" Jausserande asked.

"To see what he says *this* time. And what would you do with him?— bearing in mind that we need him in more or less one piece to lead us to Fox."

Jausserande stopped what she was doing. A mound of pale wood shavings lay among the leaves at her feet. The weapon in her hand was some three feet long, one end sharpened to a wicked sturdy point. The whole body of it was scraped smooth, and midway down the shaft was ringed and checked to make a textured handgrip.

"Thumbs," said Jausserande, with whom this amputation was apparently an article of faith. "He'll sing then."

"He's singing now," Nic pointed out. "And if you take his thumbs off, what inducement has he got to help you?"

"If he cooperates, I kill him or let him go. If he doesn't, I take him back to the Castle to be racked to death. It isn't nice," Jausserande added, apparently moved by an impulse to accuracy in reporting. "But it works."

Hathorne had gone greenish-pale, his skin as wet as if he were drowning.

"Or broken on the wheel," Jausserande went on, "although you don't really break them *on* the wheel," she emended scrupulously, "you break their joints and their long bones—you can rack them first, that makes it easier—and then you hang them on the wheel to die. It does make them scream, I'll say that much; you wouldn't think they'd still have the energy for it, but they do. Dying can take days, especially if there's rain."

"Thank you for sharing," Nic said, modernist irony dredged up out of the memoryless void.

"Of course, I couldn't do something like that if he had a patron," Jausserande went on, apparently addressing her knife.

Nic held in a smile with an effort. *Little girl, I love you—you've hooked him, now play him.*

Jausserande looked up at Nic, her violet eyes wide and innocent. "Well, it's *rude,* you know," she said, as if he'd spoken. "Killing other people's mud-born. And we're at peace now"—a long sigh—"and the Rohannan doesn't want to start another border squabble. And neither do Floire or Regordane; no one in The House of the Silver Silences does, as a matter of fact. But I don't think any of the Silver lines is his patron. If he has a patron."

Nic glanced back at Hathorne. "Who sent you to kill Ruth Marlowe?" he asked gently.

Hathorne didn't answer. This time, Nic could see, it was an effort.

"Tell us who your patron is. We can't hurt you then."

Hathorne wanted to answer, Nic could see—wanted it desperately, in fact. But there was something that frightened him more than that little elf hellion did.

"His patron might be from outside Chandrakar," Jausserande offered. "That's probably it," she said, with the satisfaction of one discovering the answer to a puzzle.

The knife, apparently, was dull. Jausserande got out the whetstone again. "Among the Seven Houses of the Twilight, Rohannan would succor him—how not, if he rescued the lady Ruth? And Regordane gives ear to the Swordwarden. No harm to it—what's one thief more or less among the mudborn—so House Silver itself would stand his patron—if he aided Line Rohannan now."

Scrape, scrape, scrape went the knife on the stone. It was irritating enough to Nic, and he didn't have being broken on the wheel to look forward to.

"You heard the lady," Nic said—softly, insinuatingly. "Who sent you? Who wants Ruth Marlowe dead?"

It had been a good try; they'd played it just right, and they'd very nearly had him. But, looking at Hathorne's face, Nic could see it wasn't going to work.

"Or," said Jausserande, "we might just notify his patron now and save all the fuss."

She reached into her tunic and pulled out a ring, twirling it between her fingers. Snapshot identification came clear in Nic's mind. A ring like the one Miss Marlowe had found on one of the men he'd killed—one of Hathorne's partners.

The effect on the prisoner was even more dramatic.

"No!" Hathorne's howl was desperate. He lunged for Jausserande. Nic grabbed him. He struggled wildly, heedless of his bound hands. Trying to get the ring.

"No— Don't do it— You'll kill us all, Lady!"

Jausserande looked at Hathorne with eyes as flat and bleak as winter ice.

"I don't care."

It was easy enough then. Hathorne would do anything to avoid having his patron summoned; even tell all he knew. It was just disappointing, after all that buildup, that he knew so little.

He was a Borderer, from the Borderland called Cockaigne, but he'd left there long ago. Wizard-touched and lucky, he had the knack for slipping through some of the greater Gates (Jausserande seemed to find this part of the story unremarkable, and Nic didn't care), and eventually he'd come to the attention of his current patron.

Whose name, face, home, and race, Hathorne did not know. He had never met his patron, never seen or spoken to his patron save by magic. Couriers delivered his gold, and such other items as he might be supposed to require. He had an amulet that let him see the Iron Road, and once upon it he relied upon his patron's power to pass him through such Gates as Hathorne needed to pass. The ring, dropped into any vessel of water during the hours of true night, would summon his patron's attention. If his patron wished to summon him, the ring would grow hot.

He had been told to insinuate himself into Fox's outlaw band, and he had not found it too difficult. There had been other tasks, now and then, some that took him out of Chandrakar.

Then, one night, he had been shown Ruth Marlowe's face in the bowl and told that here was one he must kill. He had taken to the Road immediately and passed through, and when he had entered the inn to which he had been directed, he had found companions in the same service. There he learned that their task was to hunt the unicorn through the nearby wood—and slay it and the woman they found with it.

"Only no one said as you'd be there with the maidey," Hathorne said plaintively.

"It was an impulsive decision," Nic said.

After losing the girl and her unicorn and searching for them in vain, Hathorne had come back to Chandrakar and stayed with Fox until he'd been summoned again to meet Ruth Marlowe at Road's End. He didn't know why Ruth Marlowe was supposed to die, nor who wished her dead, and meanwhile he had been playing a double game of his own, passing information to Lord Richart at Dawnheart about the outlaws' movements in hope of winning gold and a free pardon.

"And passage out of this luckless land—aye, to the World of Iron itself, even, if that's far enough!" Hathorne snarled in disgust.

"Do as you are told and Line Rohannan will see you taken care of," Jausserande said. "Now. It's light enough. Take us to Fox."

Nic and Jausserande rode, with Hathorne on foot before them. His hands were free, but it was not as trusting an arrangement as it might appear, for Hathorne had one end of a coil of rope tied around his neck and Nic held the other end.

Whenever Hathorne moved too slowly or appeared to mistake his way, Jausserande would prod him with the end of her improvised lance.

They found the camp by midmorning.

"Gone!" Jausserande was cheated fury itself.

"Where?" Nic demanded, but Hathorne, exhausted, had sunk to his knees and did not answer. *"Miss Marlowe!"* Nic shouted, but no one replied.

"She'll be with him. Fox likes hostages," Jausserande said. She vaulted down from her horse and quartered the camp at a fast trot, reeling off her finds as she did so.

"Fires hours cold—huts here that they've taken down—half a dozen huts—horse lines here—they're not coming back before Spring, that much's clear—" she ducked inside the only structure still standing and with a small cry of satisfaction came out with a deerskin and a pair of green leather gloves.

"She was here!" Jausserande crowed.

They'd known that, of course, but it was nice to have proof.

"So where is she? Where are they?" Nic said. Just his luck, to get a line on the bandit king and arrive too late.

"Where?" Jausserande demanded, glaring down at Hathorne.

"Perhaps—they were going back to the Vale—" Hathorne began.

"No," Nic said suddenly. "I know where Fox is going. Where I'd go. And I know how to get there."

Jausserande glanced quickly up at him, then used the end of her lance to lift the loop from around Hathorne's neck and toss it to Nic.

"Then we ride," she said.

Nic kicked the magic horse into a jog trot—back toward Foretton, and what all good outlaw leaders, bandit kings, and rebel terrorists craved. Information.

Jausserande turned her horse to follow.

"Wait! Lady— Lady Jausserande, you said—" Hathorne gasped.

"Aye." She reached into her tunic and pulled out something, concealed in a fist. "Then go to Dawnheart, and tell Guard-Captain Lord Richart that you are to be housed on my word until I return."

She opened her hand, and Hathorne's ring fell from it into the leaves. "Or call your patron." Jausserande wheeled her horse again and took off after Nic.

Fox's raids on the road were based in Foretton and the other local villages; their return to camp with their spoils was a matter of two days on foot. On horseback the journey took a little over five hours. They started at dawn and reached the hill overlooking Foretton a little before noon.

But instead of riding down into the village as Ruth expected, Fox dismounted and pulled Ruth down from her horse. Raven led all three animals into the deepest cover the autumn forest provided.

Fox looked at Ruth's clothes and sighed. "You show up too much. Wrap up. And stay back."

Ruth glanced down at her dark green dress, brilliant against the dun leaves, and pulled the gray cloak around it as much as she could. She thought of the first cloak she'd seen Melior in, back in the World of Iron: its spotted, mottled gray-green coloring would have been perfect camouflage here.

She looked at Fox dressed in ragged grays and browns and a deerskin tabard still covered with its previous owner's gray winter coat. He pulled a corner of the blanket up to cover his pale hair, and knelt in the leaves near the edge of the drop and seemed to stop moving completely. Raven came back and sat down, back against a tree, waiting with that same patient immobility.

Ruth found an appropriate rock and sat on it. From this vantage point Ruth could see across the valley, and on the southern hill the terraces, planted with fruit trees, that led up to the distant white castle. Dawnheart. Melior's home.

"What's going on *now?*" she asked several minutes later, keeping her voice low and hoping she sounded patient. Melior's presence was a maddening tug eastward, and they didn't seem to be heading that way any time soon.

"We're watching to see who's in town." Fox spoke without moving.

"We could always go down and ask," Ruth pointed out scathingly, although if Fox were a hunted outlaw—and wasn't *that* the culmination of a lifelong dream?—that was the last thing he could do.

"Sure. Only in these current middle ages, Ricky over at the castle's going to know we don't belong in the village. They don't issue travel visas—mostly because most people can't read or write—but the point-ears sure as hell want to know what you're doing when you're off your land."

"You don't make the place sound very nice," Ruth said, after a while.

"It isn't very nice. Humans are *serfs* here, Ruth. Peasants, bound to the land. And every single one of them belongs to one elf-lord or another."

"But Melior said—" *He said he wanted to marry me.*

There was a long pause, then Fox spoke again, sounding reluctant. "Mel might have been tenderhearted, or stupid, or optimistic, or buttering us up because he needed us. He might even have thought he was telling the truth."

"But he wasn't," Ruth said flatly.

"No," Fox said simply. "Feudalism isn't pretty, but it gets downright ugly when you add in racism."

"Melior said there was intermarriage," Ruth protested.

"Maybe. I don't know. I only know what I've seen."

And what is that? Ruth wondered. *"Feudalism isn't pretty,"* Fox said, and he was right. Hangings, beheadings, brandings, maimings, murderous taxes, and no law, no justice, no protection for the lower classes, whose only hope lay in not being noticed. Justice for the rich. Obligations for the poor.

If Fox was telling her the truth. And if he was . . .

Where did Melior fit into this? Where did *she* fit?

And . . .

"Fox," Ruth said carefully, "what would you say if I asked you what you wanted with Melior?"

The silence stretched.

"In about an hour we should know whether Ricky the Rodent—that's Guard-Captain Lord Richart to you—has eyes in the village," Fox said, his voice perfectly even. "We can go down then."

Nic's and Jausserande's goals were actually in reasonable agreement: he wanted to see Ruth Marlowe safe from her enemies, Jausserande wanted someone named Fox dead.

Nic could not recall Miss Marlowe mentioning someone named Fox. And as for the matter of murder, his own hands weren't so clean that he could sit in judgment on someone else's hobbies. And so they circled around and came up into Foretton by the main road a little after midday.

"Company," Fox said, looking down into the village. "Jesus, what did he do, *bleach* that horse?"

"It's a magic horse," Raven rumbled, craning forward to look. "Shod in silver. They come purpose-sent, and go in their own time."

"I don't like this," Fox said.

"No more do I. Fox—"

"Shhh-h."

Ruth stood up and peered, but she couldn't see the village from where she stood.

Abruptly Fox scuttled backward and stood up.

"Raven, get the horses—that's Tinkerbelle down there, and it looks like she's got some high-ticket help. Come on, Ruthie. Hoka-hey."

Hoka-hey. It's a good day to die. It took Ruth several minutes to trace the quotation to its source: Sitting Bull. The Trail of Tears.

Did Fox expect to die here? Had Melior brought her all this way only so *she* could die here? She tried to remember what he'd said about her *surviving* the plans he and his wizard had for her, and couldn't.

And the memory of that other wizard, that other magic, froze her like the memory of a rape. She would *not*—

They did not go down to the village, but circled around it, heading east at last, paralleling the road along the heavily-forested top of the hill.

Roads are where they are for reasons. The road on the hill leading to the valley below was the easiest path; here above it their way was blocked by boulders, rock slides, fallen trees, and deep-cut dry creekbeds. Fox and Raven were leading their horses, but Fox had insisted that she stay mounted, and Ruth was just as glad not to have to try to climb over this stuff in a long cloak and heavy full skirts. After an hour of that, they stopped to rest.

"If they catch us, Ruthie, don't fight and don't run. Just tell them you belong to Melior. Say it early and often. They should back off."

"But Melior's—" Ruth said.

"Captured. But it won't make a difference to them where he is if you belong to him. Try to get away, though. For immortals, they've got short memories," Fox said. He was talking as if he expected to be caught, and it scared her.

"Tell them you belong to him, too, then. Fox—Philip—he was our friend—"

"He wasn't my friend. And it wouldn't work anyway."

"Philip, you can't blame him for Naomi's death. I know you loved her—"

Fox glanced up sharply at Ruth; she had the disturbing feeling that she'd finally gotten his attention. "It isn't like that," Fox said, with the flat patience of one whose emotions are long dead. "People fall in love and one of them dies; there isn't any point in making a federal case out of it." He took a deep breath.

"But this is different. Melior used all of us: you, me, Michael, Jane— to get the Sword back. Because the end justified the means, in his eyes. Do you understand?"

"No," said Ruth tightly. The horse shifted under her.

"The end does not justify the means, Ruth. The means *are* the end. The way you travel determines your destination, and sometimes you can't get there from here."

"So you think Melior was wrong."

Fox sighed. "No. I think he was neither right nor wrong. But if I . . . disapprove . . . of the means, the only appropriate response is to punish the end."

"You mean, destroy the Sword?" Ruth asked, baffled but knowing it was vital to figure out what Fox was telling her.

"If you like. Think of it as free-market economics: an item has no intrinsic value. An item's value is set by a free market. Right here, right now, magic is more valuable than human life. But if I devalue magic, that changes."

"But if you destroy the Sword—"

"Yeah, yeah, yeah—I've heard all the arguments, too. Baligant would kick all the elfie-welfs out on their collective ass. Chandrakar would, um, let me see if I have this right, 'cease to be.' " Fox snorted eloquently.

"As for point one, if they just cooperated with each other for ten minutes, they could all refuse to leave the party, and what exactly could

Baligant do about it? Intrinsic value, Ruthie—a thing has only the value
people place on it. And as for point two, get to the part where I care."

Fox stopped talking and looked away. He seemed to be finished.
Ruth stared at him.

"You're nuts! You— Thousands of people would die!"

Fox smiled at her, very slowly. "Are you sure, Ruthie? Are you really
sure?" He turned and walked off, leading her horse with him.

"They haven't been here," Nic said.

Jausserande looked around the village. The headman was desperate
in his desire to satisfy, but unable to produce what wasn't here.

"You said they'd be here," Jausserande said.

"I said they'd come here. But if they saw us coming—"

Both of them stared upward, to the hillside above the village. A
perfect vantage point—and very near the place where Fox had left her the
day before.

Jausserande wheeled her horse and spurred it along the forest path.
After a moment Nic followed. His horse easily overtook hers, and only a
few minutes took them to the hillside overlooking the village.

"They were here," Jausserande said grimly, and even Nic could see
the scrapes and mars of horses' hooves in the leaves.

"But where did they go?"

"Come on," Jausserande said cryptically. "We'll make faster time on
the road."

"Fuck it," Fox said, some backbreaking time later. "There's the road.
If they're behind us and we can reach Black Bridge, maybe we can lie low
long enough to lose them."

She really hated being scared without knowing what was going on,
Ruth thought crossly. Fox and Raven were trying to get away with desperate haste, that much was clear. But she could see no one following them.

"Heads up, Ruth. Elevator going down."

Fox tossed her the rein and started down an incline, that rapidly
became, as far as Ruth could see, a sheer drop. Her horse lurched and
slid, jerking Ruth from side to side in the saddle and making muscles that
were trembling and weak from hours in the saddle ache ferociously.
When they reached the road, she was shaking.

"You did that on purpose!" she said accusingly.

Fox didn't answer. He got on his horse.

"I'm not going with you!" Ruth said wildly.

"Go on, Raven. I'll talk to her. We'll catch up," Fox said, in that soft,
reasonable, *lying* voice.

Raven favored both of them with a troubled look eloquent of his doubts, but turned his horse down the road and set it to trot.

Fox walked his horse back to Ruth's.

"You *hate* Melior. You blame him for Naomi," Ruth said. "I'm not going to help you find him just so you—"

"Fine," Fox said. "Then who's going to help *you* find him?"

Ruth stared at him. Fox shook his head, as if marveling at her stupidity.

"Mel is back and Baligant's got him. You and I know that. And you might be able to get Tink to believe you—if she didn't cut your throat first. But no one else. Baligant's their *king*. Nobody's going to pay attention to *mud-born.*"

"I've only got your word for that, you know," Ruth told him shakily. Strong emotion scared her. It always had. And Fox's passion burned like acid.

"Fine. Go to Dawnheart. Shout it from the rafters." Fox smiled unprettily. "See what kind of help you get."

"Whatever you've got in mind for him, *Philip,* isn't help."

Fox took a deep breath. It occurred to Ruth, belatedly, that if she was afraid of Fox on Melior's behalf, perhaps she ought also to be afraid for herself.

"Political Science 101. It doesn't matter what my wishes for England are. With me, you have a better chance of reaching Melior than without me. Along the way I could change my mind and be nice to him. You could kill me when you have no more use for me. You can abandon me *later.* Or you could be your own sweet normal stupid self," Fox finished nastily.

"I got this far by myself," Ruth lied stiffly.

"Fine. If you change your mind, leave word at the Gallows Oak in Black Bridge." Fox wheeled his horse and galloped after Raven.

Ruth sat there, listening to the hoofbeats of Fox's horse fade into the distance and finally die away completely. Overhead the afternoon sky was a deep October blue, and high in it she could see the faint shape of a circling hawk. There was a scent of wood smoke in the air, and, in the distance, the faint tolling of a bell.

But other than that, silence. Silence, and solitude, and in the absence of frenzied escape attempts, the call of Melior's pain burned bright and insistent—and, unfortunately for Ruth's pride, from the same direction Fox had gone.

Maybe Fox had been right. Maybe it didn't matter what his motives were, as long as he was useful.

The cold-bloodedness of the calculation pulled her up short. That the end justified the means was a trap and a lie.

But she didn't know what else to do. Nic was gone. She'd driven Philip away and, if she could trust a single thing he said, she could expect no help from any of Melior's friends.

She looked back over her shoulder to where Dawnheart was a white shape on the hill.

Item: she needed help to rescue Melior. Going by herself was almost the same as not going. The people who held him prisoner wanted her dead. They'd be delighted to have her show up, wouldn't they?

Item: she should be able to get help at the castle. All else aside, it was Melior's castle, and his retainers should be loyal to him—shouldn't they? *Were* they?

Going to Dawnheart was the only sensible thing to do. She wouldn't have taken Philip's advice in New York. She wasn't going to take Fox's advice in Chandrakar.

With reluctant resolution, Ruth kicked and shoved at her horse until she'd turned it toward the castle, and then kicked it some more until it began to walk.

What Fox had not expected was Raven's response to the news that Ruth had elected to leave them. Raven reined his horse to a stop and stared at Fox with a level accusing gaze.

"She has no more sense than a babe unborn. You should have brought her, Fox."

"Yeah, well, how?" At least they wouldn't hurt her, if she had the sense to open her mouth. Everyone in Canton Silver knew that Melior'd been trying to get his mortal maid out of the World of Iron ever since he'd gotten back.

"Tell the mortal maid you meant her lord no harm," Raven said reasonably.

"*Raven!* I'm trying to *kill* him. How could I tell her that?" Fox said in exasperation.

"Lie," Raven said simply. He sat his horse unmoving and gazed at Fox.

Fox ran his hand through his hair and looked back in the direction of Jausserande and her wizard, who might be less than an hour behind. He ran his hand through his hair and clung grimly to his temper.

"Let me get this straight. You want me to go back there, backtrack, catch up with her, and tell her I've *changed my mind?*"

"I will do it," Raven said with hurt dignity. "And happen she will come with me, and we will meet you at the Harp in Black Bridge."

" '*Happen*' she won't believe you," Fox said. "Look. You go to Black Bridge—"

"Thou'rt a poor tale-spinner, Fox. We shall both go, and I shall say I lessoned you to prudence."

His two choices, it seemed, were letting Raven ride back alone toward Tink—who would recognize him instantly as a member of Fox's band—or go with him. To talk sense into Ruth. *Ruth.*

He should have coldcocked her. He should have brought her along bound and gagged. He shouldn't have rescued her in the first place.

Raven was right. He should have lied.

But he hadn't wanted to lie to Ruth.

One more social taboo about to be broken.

"Come on. Maybe we can find her before she falls off her horse and breaks her neck," Fox said.

"How much traffic is there along this road?" Nic asked. They were moving at a trot, to spare Jausserande's unmagical horse—and, privately, Nic doubted his ability to stay on if Shadowfax II elected to gallop.

"Some," Jausserande said. She'd told him there was a market town called Black Bridge about two leagues down the road. If Fox was on the run, he'd head for someplace with more people, where strangers would be less noticeable. Besides, Black Bridge had a garrison, and Jausserande could enlist them. "Not as much as in the spring," she added. "No caravans—and the great lords are at Court until the moon rides full again."

The moon had been just past full the night before, as Nic recalled. So the great lords were at Court for the next month.

And a month was all he had anyway.

"So—" he began.

"Hist!" Jausserande hissed, hauling her horse to a stop. Nic reined in and listened, but it was several minutes before he heard it.

Hoofbeats.

Ruth was getting the hang of it now. Horses were just like cars, except instead of shifting and stepping down on the gas, you kicked them in the stomach until they were going as fast as you wanted them to.

At least in theory. At any rate, she'd gotten it going faster than a walk, and the staccato bu-da-dum rhythm its hoofbeats made gave her the illusion of doing something.

And it got her away from Fox.

She had just gotten used to the relief of feeling she was doing all she could do to move matters forward when she came around the bend in the road and saw the riders. One of them was on a horse so white—

The white horse Fox had been talking about.

The people he'd been running from.

She hauled back on the reins, and, to her surprise and relief, her horse actually stopped. It took a few steps backward, shaking its head, but when she loosened the reins, it remained blessedly still.

The man on the white horse stayed where he was.

The silver-haired boy on the brown horse walked his mount forward. When he was halfway to her, Ruth realized that "he" was a she, and she was an elf. Ruth moistened her lips nervously and wished she didn't look as if she'd slept in her clothes. Well, now she could test her theories against Fox's.

"Name yourself, human woman," the elf-maid said. Where Melior's eyes had been cat-green, hers were a shade of violet found only in expensive underwear. Beneath the scrapes and dirt and the tattered clothing she was exquisite. Her silver hair gleamed like polished metal in the sun, for all it was pulled back into a rough horsetail and hadn't seen comb or brush for far too long. But that didn't matter, apparently. There were no bad hair days if you were an elf.

"I— I'm going to Dawnheart," Ruth said.

"Aye, very likely," sneered the elf. "And your escort lost along the way."

"I didn't have one. Look, do you know a man named Melior—"

It was as far as she got before the elf grabbed her by the front of her tunic and dragged her off her horse.

"Tell me what you know of my cousin!"

"*Let me GO!*"

Fox and Raven heard the scream from the bad side of a blind corner. When they rounded the corner they saw—in no particular order—the white horse and its rider, Jausserande, and Ruth, stuck unrescuably in the middle.

Fox swore.

Jausserande looked up and saw him. He could see the color of her eyes plainly, even at several yards' distance. She dropped Ruth, who sat down in the road. Fox kicked his horse into a turn and headed back up the road at a hammer gallop. He could hear Raven behind him.

And behind that, a ululating howl of delight.

"Let me go!" Ruth demanded, and, abruptly, the stranger did. Ruth sprawled backward in the road, only dimly registering the sound of several horses leaving.

"Fox!" She started to her feet.

"Miss Marlowe?" a voice above her head said.

She stared up. Stared for an instant at yet another large hostile stranger in weird clothes before she saw—

"Nic!" She clutched at his arm. "Nic! Oh, God, it's you—I'm so glad you're here! I thought you were dead—we've got to stop her—she's after Fox."

He smiled faintly. "The lady's name is Jausserande, and I don't think that anyone interfering between her and Mr. Fox is going to have much luck," Nic said. "I think she means to hang him and cut off his thumbs— I'm not particularly clear on the order, but—"

Miss Marlowe stared at him as if he was crazy. Nic reminded himself firmly that this was a *civilian;* she hadn't been there.

"Oh, God. He was right. He was telling the truth. Nic, you've got to help me help him get away! He's my *friend!*" Ruth said with agitated inaccuracy.

This presented an unfortunate conflict of interest, if true. "Come on, then." Her horse had wandered a few yards away and was unconcernedly browsing. He ran to it and led it back, tossing her up without asking if she needed the help.

"Follow me," he said, and turned his horse in the direction Jausserande had gone.

And a pillar of fire rose up out of the center of the wood.

Fox couldn't believe his luck—all bad. Ruth was caught and Tinkerbelle was on their tail. Tink had Hathorne's horse, from the markings, and that meant Fox's horse might be able to outrun it.

But Raven's horse, with its greater burden, couldn't.

Ambush time.

He turned off the road into the wood, knowing that Raven would follow. Spotted a likely looking tree, kicked free of his stirrups, and did a flying dismount into a pile of leaves. Rolled to his feet, barely escaping being trampled by Raven, and scrambled for the tree. A second later Tink appeared, too hot in pursuit to think clearly.

Fox jumped.

And the world exploded into flame.

Fire. The first spell, the simplest spell. She had little power and less interest in the Art Magical, but for days Jausserande had lived in fire, fire waiting to burn.

She nearly had them; moments more and she could throw the giant from his horse. And then something hit her, and the Word was ripped from her very bones, following the outlaws as she could not. Fire. She heard a horse scream.

And then she was down, but the spell had distracted her attacker long enough for her to gain the advantage.

Fox.

She twisted, bringing Fox's body under hers, and struck hard at his face with the butt of Hathorne's dagger. He fell back, scrambling out of reach. In a moment he would be gone. She gazed wildly around herself and then thrust to her feet, running away from him.

Toward the fire.

What burned now had been dead already; a lightning-blasted oak, tinder dry. It had gone up like an oil-soaked torch at her Word. The giant's horse had shied, and the giant was no rider. He lay sprawled among the leaves like a stunned ox.

Jausserande vaulted him and set her knife to his throat.

"Don't!" Fox shouted.

Nic's horse stood fast, its ears swiveled away from the sound of burning. Ruth's tried to shy; she hauled back on her reins like grim death until it danced in a circle. The pillar of fire was visible through the autumn trees, lethal and unnatural.

"What?" Ruth said, staring anxiously from the forest to the sky and back. But there was nothing to see but the fire.

"I don't know. Come on—we'll go around. *And find out who called in an air strike later.*

"Why not?" Jausserande asked. One hand was fastened in the unconscious outlaw's black hair. The other held the blade, razor-sharp, at his throat. The pressure of his pulse fluttering against the blade had already made it break the skin, and a thin gaudy line of red trickled along its edge. "You're outlaws. Your lives are forfeit," she said, as if Fox needed reminding.

"What about a trial?" Fox said. Jausserande snorted.

"You'd rather have me than him," Fox pointed out. She couldn't see him any more, only hear his voice. The heat at her back made her skin itch, but she hardly noticed. Her gamble had paid off—Fox was trying to bargain for his companion's life.

"I have both of you now," Jausserande pointed out.

"Kill him and I run for it," Fox said promptly. "Want to bet I catch one of the horses before you do? And I'll be back—but before that, the story of what a jerk you are will be *samizdat* from here to the border."

Jausserande didn't know what "samizdat" was and didn't care.

"Ceiynt will grind your bones to powder. The ears first, I think, to wake him." She lifted the knife. The mud-born in her arms began to stir.

Fox appeared.

He was crouched on an overhanging branch about ten yards away, and half his face was masked in blood from where she had struck him. In his hand was the iron knife.

Jausserande flinched; she couldn't help herself. Fox saw it and grinned.

"Checkmate," he said.

Raven groaned. "Fox?"

He opened his eyes and froze. From where he was Fox saw all the color drain out of Raven's face. Jausserande smiled down at him, tender as a new mother.

"Yes, mud-born. You are going to die. But not here. I don't need to kill you here. You'll come back to Dawnheart; they'll rack you sweetly on *my* word, no matter where my cousin bides. And you, Fox, I'll run to earth another day."

She got to her feet and pulled Raven to his knees. He stared at Fox in miserable terror and Fox knew there was no fight in him. Raven would go like a lamb to the slaughter, just because Jausserande was *highborn.*

"Let him go," Fox said flatly. "Let him go and I'll surrender. You won't have to wait."

"Fox—no! They lie, the highborn; their promises are like smoke," Raven cried. Jausserande snarled and jerked his head back.

"Well, I've taught you that much," Fox said. "Think fast, Tink; if you kill him, there goes your shield—and I kill you."

"I will not pardon him," Jausserande said through gritted teeth. She held the point of the dagger to the side of his throat; one shove and Raven was a dead man.

"Pardon, hell. Just let him go and he can take his chances. You can hunt *him* down another day. Right, Raven?" Fox said bracingly.

"Fox, I—"

"All this damn time and you haven't learned to follow orders yet? *Run away,* Raven. It's a chance, at least."

"Drop the knife," Jausserande said, growing impatient.

"Let him go and I will," Fox said.

"All right. Surrender and he goes free this day. My word on it."

It was weakness. He was throwing away his last chance—for nothing. All he'd gain Raven was a head start, and it wouldn't be enough. And if he couldn't escape before Tink got him back inside Dawnheart, he'd bought a one-way ticket to hell.

He'd known how it would end. But after everything he couldn't bear
to watch Raven die.

Fox's knife dropped from his hand, into the leaves below. The sound
was muffled by the crackle of flames in the burning tree. *One more social
taboo broken.* He jumped down after it, and stood, staring at Raven.

"Kneel," Jausserande said.

Fox dropped to his knees.

She stood up and away from Raven, releasing him, and took a step
toward Fox.

"Find a horse and go, Raven," Fox said. Raven got slowly to his feet.
"Go *on,* goddammit."

Raven stared at Fox for one last frozen moment then turned away.
He could have attacked Jausserande, but Fox knew he would never think
of it.

"On your face," Jausserande said, and Fox lay down. She walked over
to him, yanking a length of leather out of her tunic, and knelt on his back
to tie his hands.

There was a sound of hoofbeats—a pair of riders. Fox jerked convul-
sively where he lay.

"No," Jausserande said, "he goes free. If they bring him to me, I will
free him." She stroked Fox's hair. "Your life for his this day."

The smoke and fire from the burning tree was probably visible for
miles, and its sparks would almost inevitably start other fires soon.

"Would it do any good at all to tell you to stay here?" Nic asked.

"I don't think so," Ruth admitted.

He dismounted, his eyes on the figure silhouetted by the blaze. He
tied his horse to a tree and took the quarterstaff from its packs. He tied
Ruth's horse to another tree, and helped her down.

"At least let me go first," Nic said. Ruth nodded. He moved off,
quarterstaff in hand. Ruth followed.

Jausserande got to her feet when she saw them, and pulled Fox up
with her. He looked like a splatterpunk special effect, half his face covered with blood and dirt.

"Welcome to the party," Fox said. "Hi, Ruthie. Welcome to Introduc-
tory Social Science. Who's your wizard friend?" For a man in so much
trouble, Fox sounded remarkably cheerful.

"He isn't a wizard—he's Nic Brightlaw from Earth!" Ruth said.

There was a pause as the two men stared at each other.

"Philip," Nic finally said, sounding more puzzled than anything else.

"Hi, Mister Brightlaw," Fox said with fulsome smarm, sounding for

an instant remarkably like Wally Cleaver. The act collapsed. "Good.
Great. Fine. *He* can help you find Melior."

"Let him go," Ruth said to Jausserande. "I mean it."

Jausserande looked at her and laughed. "So you are my cousin's
Ironworld heart twin, Ruth? I wish him joy of you."

"Melior's in trouble," Ruth said quickly. "We were coming here, and
he was captured—by Baligant and a dragon. Him *and* the Sword. You
have to help. And let Fox *go.*"

Jausserande sighed, as if the news had aged her. "I will bear that
news to Dawnheart, and evil news it is, but the fate of The Rohannan is
Line Rohannan's business, and this rebel brat is mine, so—" Jausserande
raised her dagger.

"He's got the Cup," Fox said swiftly.

Jausserande stopped, lowering the dagger, torn between hope and
the certainty that anyone in Fox's position would lie. Ruth started forward and Nic stopped her with a hand on her arm.

"Think about it, Tink," Fox said quickly. "I don't have the Cup. You
don't have the Cup. It wasn't in the Vale of Stars in the *first* place,
remember? When Mel was on Earth, he told Ruth and me that Baligant's
master plan was to get his hands on all twelve Treasures. Now, sweet-
cakes, where do *you* think the Cup is?"

Jausserande turned and backhanded Fox—hard—across the face.

He struggled to keep his balance, but couldn't with his hands bound.
He fell back and sideways, unable to break his fall. When he was down
she kicked him. Her boot landed solidly in his ribs and Ruth heard his
gasp of pain from across the clearing.

"No!" Ruth tried again to fling herself at Jausserande; Nic held her
arm tightly while she jerked and struggled. "Let him go let *me* go—
leave him alone—*what kind of animal are you?"*

"Satisfied now, Tink?" said Fox breathlessly from the ground.

Jausserande stood over him, only a little less breathless than he. "So
Baligant has the Cup—your word on it. I thank you for this advice and
will act on it once I have hanged you."

"Nic, what's the *matter* with you—it's Philip—make her let him *go!"*

Jausserande turned toward Ruth, the knife heavy in her hand and a
feral triumph in her eyes. Ruth backed up against Nic, feeling the hardness of metal against her back even through all her layers of petticoats.

"I wouldn't," Nic said mildly to Jausserande. "After all, we know *her*
patron."

"She's his proof," Fox said. He'd managed to get to his knees and
shook his head to clear it. Blood sprayed from his gashed mouth and

spattered the leaves; he spat. Jausserande jerked back around and glared at him.

"Mel needs her. She's his proof," Fox repeated. He got carefully to his feet, never taking his eyes from Jausserande's face. "When they were together, he told her, and she told me. There's a spell that ties Ruth to Melior's sword, the Treasuresword; the Sword of Maiden's Tears. He's found a way to undo it and prove who cast it. Ask her."

"He must go before the Court of the Twilight," Jausserande said slowly, reasoning it out. "And until then I will seal his Ironworlder in Dawnheart to keep her safe. And I will kill you," she added.

"Fine," said Fox, leaning against a tree as if he hadn't a care in the world. Where Jausserande had struck him, his face was purple-red and swollen, and the split lip blurred his speech—but only a little. "Enjoy yourself. Of course, Mel, the Sword, your precious day-glo Dixie Cup—and ten other exciting Treasures—are all lost. Somewhere. I don't suppose you're planning to look for any of them? And have I mentioned that Ruth can lead you to Melior? She can."

"Don't. Fox—don't," Ruth begged.

There was a pause, and when Jausserande spoke again, it was in a voice false and rich with mockery. "Oh, Fox. Dear little Fox. Are you actually pledging to aid me to find my cousin in exchange for your life?" She laughed, as if he'd told a joke she found particularly amusing.

"No." Fox made an aborted motion, as if he'd wipe his bleeding lip and had been prevented by his bonds. "I want to find Melior myself. Ruth can do it—she's still tied to the Sword, in case you'd managed to forget that. And she isn't any safer in the Magic Castle than she is with us—there's a wizard trying to kill her. If you find the Sword, you'll find the Cup. Or that's the way to bet."

Jausserande hesitated, her face a study in betrayed bewilderment. She raised the knife again, her face set, and it was plain to all three of the others that Jausserande intended to reject all this talk of plot and counterplot for something she could understand.

"You took it from me. I'll kill *you."*

"Look," Nic's voice was quiet, as nonthreatening as he could make it. He knew her kind now; her war wasn't over. Didn't Philip realize that? Or was he as crazy as she was? His memories of Philip LeStrange were blurred and unreliable; memories of memories from a Christmas Eve that seemed to have receded into legend.

"Getting Melior and the stuff back is the main thing. You can always kill Fox later. Where's he going to go? And we might need cannon fodder some time," Nic said reasonably.

"Cannon?" Jausserande said blankly.

"No cannon," said Fox, and now his pain and weariness showed in his voice. "No cannon, no gunpowder, no *iron.* Catapult and crossbow. And, of course, *magic."*

Jausserande dropped the knife to the ground and stalked away toward the burning tree. Nic let go of Ruth and she ran to Philip/Fox.

"Oh, *God*—" Ruth said. She blinked; tears spilled down her face.

"Untie my hands," Fox said. He half-turned, leaning against the tree for support, and offered her his bound hands. They were already bluish, the dark leather biting into the flesh.

"I— I can't. It's—"

"My knife's on the ground somewhere here. It's steel. Find it."

Ruth scrabbled on hands and knees around Fox's feet until she came up with the blade. She sawed through the leather until it was raveled enough to break.

Fox sighed and worked his shoulders, then looked down at his swollen hands. "Keep the knife. It's iron—well, steel. It burns them—elves. Badly. I think I'm going to sit down now," he added, and did, leaning back against the tree.

Ruth scrubbed at her stinging eyes. "Was it true?" she asked.

" 'What is truth?'—to quote Pontius Pilate." Fox rested his arms on his drawn-up knees, working his hands.

"Where's Raven?" Ruth asked guiltily. She looked all around, but didn't see him.

"He's got a head start. I wish he had the brains to use it, but he doesn't. He's dead meat, Ruthie; we all are." Fox leaned his head back against the tree trunk and closed his eyes.

"How could—" Ruth stopped. There were just too many questions. She looked behind her. Jausserande was standing staring into the burning tree. Nic was standing near her, talking.

"You were right, Fox. I'm sorry," she said. "Maybe Melior— I'll *make* him change things."

Fox laughed, then swore at how much it hurt. "Jesus, Ruthie, he's got the High King trying to kill him and you want him to take up civil rights, too?"

I want him back. Alive, Ruth thought. "Maybe," she said aloud. "Fox, what do we do now?"

"It depends on them. I take back what I said earlier, Ruthie. It's never a good day to die."

· Epilogue ·

The Court of Illusion

IN THE CASTLE called Mourning, at the edge of the world, Eirdois Baligant, who was beginning to realize that he had surrendered more than he knew for the privilege of being named High King of Chandrakar and husband of Hermonicet the Fair, waited upon the pleasure of his wizard to attend him.

That was not how it should be.

Nothing was as it should be.

A human lifetime ago he had begun his conspiracy. The Seven Houses were at war, and so the matter was a simple one: steal the Twelve Treasures of Chandrakar, the entities which held within themselves the power which maintained Chandrakar's existence in the Morning Lands, and by their absence gain both ultimate power for himself and destruction for his enemies—for whomsoever did not present the Treasure that was his Line's to guard at the Kingmaking, he and all his Line would be banished beyond the bounds of Chandrakar and stripped of all they owned.

Why wasn't it working out that way?

Baligant paced. Simple equations, as rational and reasonable as the columns and figures that had occupied him as a clerk in Rainouart's Instrumentality of Taxation: The Sword of Maiden's Tears, Line Rohannan's Treasure, had been spell-trapped by Baligant's wizard to fall into the World of Iron when its Treasurekeeper touched it—thus its Treasurekeeper would be lured to his death and the Sword remain lost to Line Rohannan. The Cup, the Lance, the Harp, the Crown—Twelve Treasures lost, stolen, or strayed, leaving Baligant the victor.

Only Rohannan Melior had not died. He had retrieved the Sword, he had come back to Chandrakar, and he had brought with him *proof* that Baligant's wizard was the one who had tampered with his Treasure.

Baligant's wizard.

He would like very much to blame her—he *did* blame her, in fact—for the calamity he saw looming before him; but unfortunately he was also clearsighted enough to see that it was *he* who was in trouble no matter who was responsible.

What would he do? What could he do? Proof was proof, no matter what; his complicity would be undeniable.

Surely they would deny him the High Kingship then.

Or . . .

. . . would . . .

. . . they . . . ?

Where was his wizard?

"I am here, my prince," Amadis said.

She was, as always, beautiful—in the way that swords' edges and fire and high places are beautiful—a taunting, deadly, and inhuman limmerence that obsessed even while it threatened. Her hair was a fall of copper fire, her eyes were garnet sparks, and she wore the shadow of elphen beauty like a fatal cloak.

He had sent her to kill Ruth Marlowe, for Ruth Marlowe of the World of Iron was Melior's proof that the Sword had been tampered with, and, when she had failed, had sent her forth again. She should be desperate now for what only he could provide.

"You are tardy enough in coming," Baligant growled.

"Perhaps," said Amadis insolently. Baligant glanced sharply toward her.

"And, having taken so much time, you naturally have progress to report," he went on with heavy irony.

Amadis smiled, small and secret, and said nothing.

Baligant gazed around his treasure room, buying time to put down his growing unease.

Amadis was his wizard, mistress of the Wild Magic, and, like all such Adepts, paid a high price for her power in those things she might and might not do. Such prices were kept secret by their disbursers, but Baligant knew hers, and that knowledge was part of his power. What had shaped the spell that held her, and molded her to his will, and made its necessary flaw the bone-deep addiction to the ice roses unique to Chandrakar's heights.

And not the flower alone, but the flower mixed with the blood of Chandrakar's High King. Without them both she would expire in agony.

In which case, why wasn't she dead?

Like the clerk he had once been, Baligant was meticulous in details. His blood alone could keep her alive, and he did not wish her to grow too independent. He kept her closely; she should have been begging his favor long since to replace the power she had expended in doing his will. Even if she had done nothing, she ought to have reached the limit of her endurance by now.

He turned his back and walked to the window. The Eastern Marches stretched flat and silver to meet a polished pewter sky, and in the distance he could see the tower wherein his bride dwelt until their wedding day. The wind off the marches was cold. Winter was coming. Soon the Twilight Court would rise and the Lords Temporal return to their kingdoms, and the Morning Court would sit and the Prince-Elect tend to his taxes and his pleasures.

If there were to be any pleasures this year. And next autumn . . .

He gazed at the jar that held the dried roses, their petals still supernaturally pale.

"Would you hear what I have done?" Amadis asked.

Baligant turned. *I would hear more than that.* "No doubt you will tell me what you see fit to relate," he said dourly.

Amadis folded her hands upon her flat belly. "I have made a trap, and set out my bait, and the Ironworld girl Ruth Marlowe is even now drawn to my lure. I have made certain that she and Rohannan Melior will not meet, nor that he may wield the Sword against you. And she will die."

So Ruth Marlowe was being drawn to Amadis' lure, was she? The girl was human; she could not make a Gate-crossing unaided; Ruth Marlowe must be alreay in Chandrakar if Amadis trusted her to walk into her trap. And Amadis had also said that the Sword and the Ironworlder would be drawn together—so where was the Sword, that Amadis was so certain they would not meet?

"I told you to kill her," Baligant reminded her. *So why do you not tell me that she is dead?*

"And so I shall kill her," Amadis said with some impatience.

"Do you wish to displease me?" Baligant began—and stopped at the sight of the indifference in his wizard's eyes. "I think you are not being entirely forthcoming with me," Baligant observed mildly.

"What must I say?" Amadis said. "I have captured Rohannan Melior, and he, his Sword, and what pitiful magics he possessed are in my chamber room even now. He is the lure, and soon Ruth Marlowe will come that I may kill her," Amadis said with innocent satisfaction.

There was a pause.

"You . . . did . . . *what . . . ?*" Baligant said hoarsely.

No. He must have heard her incorrectly. Not even a wizard of the Wild Magic could be so unworldly and inhuman as to arrange such a way of fulfilling the orders he had given her. He had told her to kill Ruth Marlowe. That was all he had told her.

"It is what you asked of me," the wizard said.

And he had. Oh, he had—now Baligant saw the disaster he had made for himself—he had told her to kill Ruth Marlowe by any means. Any means at all.

He had *not* told her *not* to kidnap The Rohannan, head of Line Rohannan and Swordwarden, and imprison him in Baligant's own tower. He had not told her *not* to steal the Sword of Maiden's Tears—which was now known to be in Melior's possession—and hide it here in Castle Mourning.

He had not, in short, desired her to refrain from a number of actions she, being thus unrestricted, had straightaway committed.

And if they saw— And if they found—

"I will see you dead," Baligant gritted.

"No," said Amadis, as calmly as if venturing an observation on the weather. "I have what I need."

Baligant's hand ached with the need to strike her, but on the day that he touched her with anger or lust his control over her would end, and he did not know what her vengeance might be on that day. He clasped his hands together and ground them closed until the gems on his hands squeaked and squealed with the pressure.

"Go from my sight," he said hoarsely. "And stay within the place appointed you until I summon you again. Work no wiles; abstain from the Art—do *nothing,* do you hear me?"

"I hear and obey, my lord," Amadis said. She bowed very low, but as if it amused her, not as if she meant it. Then she turned, and left, and only the solid sound of the bronze door sliding home again marked her exit.

She looked remarkably healthy.

Baligant sat down upon his carved and cushioned throne. About The Rohannan's presence here in Mourning something would have to be done, perhaps involving a slender dirk and a body left to fatten the pigs, but he would let that wait until he was certain what the best course might be. In that matter, in the matter of the Sword, he had time.

And what of the wizard?

"I have what I need," Amadis had said. But if he had shed no king's blood to slake her hunger—who had?

The Cloak of Night and Daggers

DEDICATION

For Neal Christiansen (got
it right this time, guy!) and the *real* Escher
Hilton in Rye Town, New York. . . .

. . . for Dr. Thomas M. Stallone, who makes
sure my characters take the right pill at the
right time <g>. . . .

. . . and for the guys on Genie SFRT 1: Zette,
Nic, Andi, and the rest of the gang—here's
looking at you, kids.

ABOUT THE AUTHOR

Best-selling fantasy author Margot Leigh Reasoner is five feet four inches tall, mumble-mumble years old, and lives in a semirestored Victorian house in Shelbyville, Indiana, with her harlequin standard poodle, Longshot, and her orange cat, Crusher. Her hair is brown, her eyes are green, and she is the head (and only) librarian of the Shelbyville Association Library. Besides writing, her other hobbies include coming up with reasons not to get her hair cut, destruction-testing new diets, and cataloging the many alternative uses for books found by patrons of the Shelbyville library.

"The House of the Silver Silences is one of the Seven Great Houses of the Twilight. As we rule over the Men of our land, so does a High King rule over us, and that he shall have died is the cause of tragedy both in my world and your own.

"Yet it is not the death of the one who is known now in death as Rainouart the Beautiful, High King of Elphame, which is the tragedy, though the Sons of the Morning and the Daughters of the Evening Star do not die in the time and season of Men. The tragedy came once the funeral games were ended, and Rainouart's funeral boat was set upon the bosom of the wave. . . ."

—From *The Chronicle of House Silver,*
Rohannan Melior, Baron Rohannan

CONTENTS

· 1 ·

Too Real for Fantasy

THE CASTLE WAS a pale tower of shimmering stone, set in the Eastern Marches. Once it had belonged to the husband of Hermonicet the Fair; now it was the seat Baligant had chosen to occupy until his Kingmaking in order to be near his bride. All Chandrakar separated it from Castle Dawnheart in Domain Rohannan of Canton Silver in the West. The tower's name was Mourning, and it had been built over a century ago by the Marchlord who was once husband to Hermonicet the Fair.

From a distance the castle bore the appearance of a child's toy discarded thoughtlessly in the vast flatness of the fen country that marked the eastern border of Chandrakar. It was the single vertical line in the flat marsh landscape, and what it guarded would be safe forever.

The Wizard Adamis stood outside the closed doors of Baligant High Prince's chamber. After a moment she drew a crystal from her robes and stared into it intently as if what she saw could help her now, although the scene she conjured was long past.

"WILL THIS WORK?" *The voice was Baligant's—not yet High Prince in those days, nor High King-Elect, but already ambitious, certain that victory would come to him in the end.* "I MUST BE CERTAIN, WIZARD."

SEE THIS? *she had replied to him then, gleeful in her skill.* "IT IS AN IRONWORLD SOUL, STILL BEDDED IN ITS MORTAL HOST. AND I SHALL WEAVE IT TO THE SWORD OF MAIDEN'S TEARS AND SET THE SWORD—SO. IF HE BUT TOUCHES THE SWORD IT WILL FALL THROUGH ALL THE WORLDS." *Her voice had flared and guttered, flame-bright like burning roses, thick with decay.* "IT WILL FALL. I HAVE THE SOUL HERE."

The soul.
Her soul.
HER.

Ruth struggled to wake up, struggled to run away, to hide from . . . something. Something looking for her. Though the nightmare brought her only half awake, discomfort did the rest.

Ruth Marlowe was thirty-two, blue-eyed and brown-haired and stubborn. She hadn't intended to rescue Rohannan Melior of the House of the Silver Silences—but then, she hadn't meant to turn thirty either, and two years ago the two things had happened more or less simultaneously. *Welcome to New York, now go home,* Ruth had thought as soon as she'd seen him. But by then it was too late to step back into the safe normal world she'd been born into; she'd already offered to help him, and that impulsive offer of aid to a wounded stranger had become an adventure that Ruth, all things considered, would rather not have had.

It had cost lives and friendships, and when it was over, Ruth couldn't even hate Melior for the part he'd played in the death of her friend Naomi—because Ruth had fallen in love with Melior, as he with her. But the only magic he could conjure to take him back to the world where he belonged was not strong enough to take her with him, and they had been separated—in Ruth's mind, forever. She had tried to get on with her life, but she couldn't even mourn him properly—how could you mourn someone who was still alive, somewhere, some*when?*

Then Ruth had stumbled onto magic of her own, in the basement of the Ryerson Memorial Library in Ippisiqua, New York—a Wild Gate that opened the border between Ruth's own World of Iron and the Lands Beyond the Morning. Ruth was wizard-bonded to the Sword of Maiden's Tears—one of the Twelve Treasures that contained all the magic of Melior's own land and kept the Seven Houses of the Twilight strong and secure against their enemies—and that magical link had opened the Wild Gate and pulled her through.

It had also, of course, pulled her boss, Library Director Nicodemus Brightlaw, through after her. If Ruth had learned one thing in her sojourn here, it was that magic was not only perilous but also not particularly dependable. She'd been separated from Nic the day after they'd fallen through the gate; in looking for him she'd found Melior instead—in a house beyond the Goblin Market—only to lose him again almost immediately.

Madness takes its toll: Please have exact change, Ruth thought flippantly. And if stupid jokes were a universal constant, then so were treachery and political backbiting. The power of the conspiracy that had first cast Melior's Sword into the World of Iron was even more formidable here on its home turf, the Lands Beyond the Morning. That conspiracy had stalked Ruth from the moment she'd fallen through the Gate, and, once she had reached Melior, her foe had targeted him as well, capturing him and separating them with frightening ease. Now Melior was being held captive . . . somewhere, and only the wizard-forged link that bound them together offered Ruth any clue to his location.

There was no one else to rescue him if she didn't. By the time she got anyone here in Chandrakar to believe that he'd been captured, he might well be dead. And she would never in a thousand years succeed in convincing any of the Morning Lords of what Melior had come to believe— that the architect of the plot against Ruth, Melior, and the Twelve Treasures was the one man in all of Chandrakar who had the most to gain from their safety, Eirdois Baligant of the House of the Vermilion Shadows, High Prince and soon to be High King of all Chandrakar. After a century of war that had ended with the Lords of the Twilight all agreeing to make Baligant High King, they would not oppose him without much more reason than the unsupported word of a mere human who hadn't even been born there.

If she was going to rescue Melior, she would have to do it with the help of people that she could convince—or who didn't care whether she was telling the truth or not.

She had three. And considered as a heroic rescue, this one didn't seem to have a very auspicious beginning.

Ruth was lying on the stone floor of the burned-out shell of a house in Canton Silver, in Chandrakar, somewhere between Foretton and Black Bridge, wrapped in her cloak and the heavy skirts and petticoats of her traveling dress. Black Bridge was where the garrison was; Foretton was the nearest town to Castle Dawnheart, where Melior lived.

What an amazing fund of useless information you've become, Ruth told herself mockingly. Sleep was impossible now. Ruth sat up stiffly, pulling her cloak tightly around her. Everything ached, and she was cold. It was autumn here, even though it had been Christmas Eve in Ippisiqua when she'd fallen through the bookcase and summer in the first of the Lands Beyond the Morning she'd reached. In Chandrakar the winds blew cold, and the trees had dropped most of their leaves. They lay in drifts on the ground: She'd been sleeping on a pile of them until another of the usual nightmares had wakened her.

"Can't sleep?" Fox's voice was slurred. It was a wonder he could talk at all, Ruth considered, what with the beating he'd taken earlier today— yesterday, now—from Jausserande.

There was a small fire just inside the doorway of the ruined building, not enough to give much heat but enough to show Ruth the livid purple bruises on Fox's face. His mouth was swollen, and dried blood from his split lip made crusty black slashes and smears along his jaw. Even looking at it hurt. Melior's cousin, like Melior, was a Treasurekeeper, and Jausserande held Fox personally responsible for the loss of her Treasure, the Cup of Morning Shadows.

"Oh, *look* at you," Ruth mourned. Fox turned his head away, disgusted.

When Naomi had been alive and the five of them had been together, Fox had been Philip Leslie LeStrange, and Philip had been weedy, blond, short, twenty-two, and the product of respectable parents who were sure that his health was too delicate for anything more than a quiet, respectable career as a librarian. He'd worn bifocals and backpacks, and the only weapon he'd been familiar with was words.

But until yesterday, when she'd stumbled into his outlaw camp in the forest near Castle Dawnheart, Ruth hadn't seen Philip in over two years.

Things had changed.

Now Philip was no student librarian in a red James Dean jacket, but a hard-faced blond man dressed in ragged grays and browns and a deerskin tabard still covered with its previous owner's gray winter coat. At the moment one of his pale eyes was swollen shut, but the other was startlingly blue against the sunburned brown of his skin. His long hair was pulled straight away from his face to fall in a silky tail down his back, and his wiry body was sculpted with muscle.

Ruth hadn't actually been looking for Fox. Meanwhile, Nic had been looking for Ruth, and Jausserande had been searching first for the Cup of Morning Shadows and then for the outlaw Fox. Jausserande had enlisted Nic—here called Ceiynt—as an unlikely ally in her search. Fox had been trying not to be found and (more or less incidentally) to keep Ruth safe from her pursuers. Ruth had wanted to rescue Melior.

The paths of the four of them had crossed in a woodland glade. Fox had fled when he'd seen Jausserande. Ruth and Nic had followed, but they arrived a few minutes too late. Fox had already traded his companion's freedom for his own, and Ruth had discovered that everything Fox had told her about the social position of elves in Chandrakar was true.

If Fox had not managed to convince Jausserande that the High King-Elect Eirdois Baligant of the House of the Vermilion Shadows had the Cup of Morning Shadows—as well as Melior and the Sword of Maiden's Tears—Jausserande would probably have killed Fox right there—or, worse, taken him back to Dawnheart to be racked to death. Fox was an outlaw here, a criminal under Chandrakar law, and Melior wasn't around to protect him.

Even if, Ruth realized soberly, Melior wanted to.

But for the moment Jausserande—the Lady Floire Jausserande of the House of Silver Silences—was willing to aid them, and that was important, because in this land elves ruled, and the three humans could do very little—including follow Melior—without elphen backing. Maybe the four of them—Ruth, Nic Brightlaw, Melior's vicious cousin Jausserande, and the outlaw now known as Fox—could actually rescue Melior.

Although, considering everything, Ruth thought that what was going to happen was that they were all going to die.

Ruth moved over to where Fox lay and helped him to sit up. He wasn't tied up—in theory the four of them were equals now, allies—but a fall from a horse followed by several enthusiastic kicks to the ribs made movement excruciatingly painful.

"How are you feeling?" she asked.

"What about Mel?" Fox asked, changing the subject.

"The same," Ruth said shortly. Like a chorus of Greek ghosts, the sensations returned: not a memory, because somewhere far to the east it was happening *now*.

Ruth shuddered.

Above ground. Near the sea. The woman who stood over Ruth's lover was fair as the sun, not the moon—as beautiful and deadly as sunfire; she displayed all the shades of gold and copper and blood. Hair the color of firelight rippled over her shoulders, eyes the hot color of burning coals gazed into his.

"WHAT DO YOU WANT OF ME?"

He hung from a beam in the center of the room by his shackled wrists, every muscle in chest and torso pulled taut.

"WHAT DO YOU WANT?"

His skin was mottled with the marks of whip and rod and knife, each pattern of horror left somehow unfinished, as if this torture were only the evil pastime of some easily distracted child.

"I WANT NOTHING. MY MASTER WANTS THE DEATH OF THE IRON-WORLD WENCH, AND SO HE WILL HAVE IT. HE WOULD HAVE THE SWORD LOST TO LINE ROHANNAN, AND SO HE WILL HAVE THAT, TOO. ALL FOR MY MASTER, ALL, ALL, ALL—" *the mad little voice sang, swooping and skirling as if its owner danced.*

"AND WHAT FOR YOURSELF?" *Ruth heard Melior ask, in a voice weary with pain.* "IS THERE NOTHING YOU WANT FOR YOURSELF?"

"ALL, ALL, ALL—" *sang the voice.* "ALL, ALL, ALL—"

* * *

"Ruthie?" Fox said, jarring Ruth out of her reverie.

"I told you not to call me that!" Ruth snapped, her voice a whipcrack of pure frustrated fury. But even the anger seemed unreal somehow, faint and assumed for the occasion. Underneath the automatic pain was the unnerving certainty that her responses weren't *real,* that somehow she was only faking what a real person would feel. Because her soul was absent—trapped in the Sword of Maiden's Tears.

"Is everything all right in there?" Nic asked.

He walked into the cellar—after a century of war, Chandrakar was plentifully supplied with ruined buildings—and for a moment, as he passed by the fire, Ruth could see him clearly: wearing an odd assortment of gear that suggested both King Arthur's Court and Southeast Asia. Nicodemus Brightlaw was at least six-foot-two, with eyes of blue, hair the shade of rich insistent gold rarely achieved without resorting to Lady Clairol, and perfect white teeth. By rights he should have been drop-devastatingly handsome.

But there was something not quite . . . right about Nic Brightlaw, boy Library Director. Ruth had thought he was strange from the moment she'd met him back in Ippisiqua, and since he'd reappeared here in Chandrakar, she'd thought he was even stranger. It was almost as if he no longer recognized her, although they'd come through the Gate in the library's Second File together and he still called her "Miss Marlowe" in that oddly formal way of his.

One more mystery she didn't have time to solve. Not while Melior was being used as a cat's-paw to draw her to her death. And there was nothing that she could think of but to go.

"We were just fighting," Ruth said sheepishly, ashamed to have called Nic in off watch. Baligant and his agents aside, the roads of peacetime Chandrakar were not without peril.

Nic shrugged.

"How are you feeling?" he said to Fox.

"Just peachy," Fox answered. He tried for an irritating sneer, but couldn't quite manage it through his bruises.

"Are you going to be able to ride tomorrow?" Nic said.

"I'm going to have to, aren't I?" Fox said evenly. "Where's Tink?" He called Jausserande "Tinkerbelle," with a bravado that made Ruth wince every time he did it.

"You shouldn't bait Jausserande," Nic said mildly.

Fox shrugged and grimaced when it hurt. "I don't exactly have a lot to lose, do I?"

"She's outside," Nic said, answering the previous question. "I don't think she likes you very much, Fox, and I'll just remind you that the lady is our local liaison. If she decides not to cooperate in our little crusade, all she needs to do is walk into the garrison at Black Bridge tomorrow and hand the two of you over to the authorities."

"She won't hurt Ruth," Fox said quickly.

"She's unlikely to take her on a rescue mission after her elf-friend, either, and if you're thinking that an official force would have a better chance of extracting him from wherever and whoever has him, well, inconvenient loose ends have a way of just disappearing when the person they're inconvenient to is the next king," Nic said.

Fox regarded Nic with mockery in his pale blue eyes. Ruth knew better than anyone here what Fox's hopes for Melior were.

Fox wanted him dead.

Ruth, Naomi, Philip, Michael, and Jane. Five unlikely friends, student librarians drawn together by a mutual sense of not fitting in. And before they had completed Melior's quest all those months ago and retrieved the beautiful and deadly Sword of Maiden's Tears, Naomi was dead. There were days when Ruth felt that it would have been better for everyone if Ruth had been the one to die instead.

She suspected Fox would agree. He'd loved Naomi, and when Naomi had died, Fox had blamed Melior for it.

"Melior used all of us: you, me, Michael, Jane—to get the Sword back. Because the end justified the means, in his eyes. The end does not justify the means, Ruth. The means are the end, and if I . . . disapprove . . . of the means, the only appropriate response is to punish the end."

Melior. The Sword.

His goal, so Fox had told Ruth, had always been small and simple: to smash the Sword of Maiden's Tears while Rohannan Melior watched helplessly. Being a realist, Fox had accepted that what he actually accomplished might be less: to destroy or hide the Sword in Melior's absence, for example, or to kill Melior while the Sword went safely to other hands, although killing Melior was really his last choice.

The dead didn't suffer nearly as much as Fox seemed to feel Melior deserved to suffer.

"So what are we going to do?" Ruth asked Nic quickly, to banish those bleak thoughts.

"If we survive Black Bridge," Nic said, "and everybody behaves himself,"—this was addressed specifically to Fox—"we can pick up remounts and supplies at the garrison, and then . . . we follow you, Miss Marlowe, and see what happens."

What a wonderful plan. Ruth didn't say it aloud. It might work. For a while. If Jausserande didn't decide Fox was lying. If no one killed them on the road. If there was some way to rescue Melior from the tower by the sea. If they could get there before his captors killed him.

    If.

• 2 •

My Heroes Have Always
Been Space Aliens

HELICON WAS THE largest science fiction convention still located within a day's trip of New York. It was held the week before Christmas, traditionally a dead weekend for conventions, but there were usually enough people, lured by an excuse for going somewhere other than home for the holidays, to keep HeliCon in the black. In the decade when America celebrated its Bicentennial and the first *Star Wars* movie came out, HeliCon had still been held within New York City itself, and the tales of its destruction of upmarket Manhattan hotels had been the stuff of legend.

These days George Lucas was filming prequels, people weren't sure what a bicentennial was, and HeliCon was held in the wilds of, alternately, New Jersey and upstate New York. The New York hotel was the Hotel Escher, which was located in Manningtree, an area of Westchester County that had hit economic rock bottom when IBM left. Five hundred SF fans could do what they liked: they could not equal the damage done by the recession. And so this year, once again, December saw the Hotel Escher filled almost to capacity with the few, the proud, the cream of New York area SF fan-and-prodom and its associated life-forms.

"Check-in sucks," Holly Kendal observed succinctly, standing behind a bulwark of duffel bags in the middle of the Escher's shabby, overcrowded lobby. She and Carol (who'd flown in from Idaho yesterday, obsessively overpunctual as always) had driven out to the airport to pick up Margot—whose flight was supposed to arrive at noon and was late, as if it knew it carried Margot Leigh Reasoner and had a tradition to uphold—and then headed straight for Manningtree in Holly's car, an antique Honda station wagon named Rosinante. Unfortunately, at least a hundred other people had all had the same idea. They'd all converged on the Escher lobby in time for the 2:00 check-in carrying more mismatched luggage than had been seen at the wrap party for *Voyage of the Damned.*

"It wouldn't suck if you weren't bringing enough gear for two men and a boy. The hotel does have beds, you know," Margot replied, eyeing Holly's tent and sleeping bag.

"I'm going to an event next weekend," Holly—known in the Society for Creative Anachronism as Lady Fiametta of the Danelaw—responded weakly, with a glance at four extra-large cargo duffels. Margot snorted elegantly.

As a professional writer—or, as Margot put it, a *Professional Female Fantasy Writer* (her current series, *The Quest for the Phoenix Throne,* the detailed adventures of the feckless Prince Perigord and his companion, the runaway librarian Azure Bowl, had reached Volume 5, a cliff-hanger ending involving the Goblin Market and a talking sphinx)—Margot Reasoner felt called upon to deck her Junoesque contours in a manner reminiscent (as she occasionally said herself) of some unearthly combination of Miss Piggy and a Wagnerian soprano.

Thus the cape, Holly thought with a combination of resignation and envy. It was silk velvet, Holly knew with costumer-trained instincts, a deep violet-tinged indigo with a glittering star field pattern worked somehow into the weave. It was lined in bright primrose satin, and, draped over Margot's robust frame, made her, well, difficult to overlook. She'd worn it on the plane, which meant she was wearing it in the lobby. This being HeliCon, it drew only a few envious looks.

"Maybe if you guys, um, left the luggage with me?" Carol suggested hopefully.

Carol Goodchild was shorter than either Holly or Margot and a great deal more self-effacing. Carol had white-blonde hair and gray eyes and despite these advantages managed to look like an apologetic sheepdog most of the time. She also had much less luggage. Carol lived in Twisted River, Idaho (population 1,465 if you really stretched things), and was the sole suzerain of the Twisted River Association Library. Two years ago she'd worked at the Brooklyn Public Library. Of course, two years ago Carol had been married, too.

It had taken a combination of threats, pleas, and downright bribery (Margot had promised the Twisted River Library a large donation of books from her publisher) to get Carol to HeliCon, and only the reminder that Carol would be just a few hours drive from Ippisiqua and could therefore include a visit to her friend Ruth to see how she was settling in to her new job had finally been enough to swing it.

"Yeah, right, okay, sure, whatever," Holly said, in answer to the luggage question. She began heaving duffel bags in the direction of Carol's feet with a reckless disregard for anyone who might be in the way.

"Jeez, lady, what's *in* these things?" the bellman said, at the same time Holly said:

"Oh, never mind, let me handle those—" and Margot said: "Room 555; the neighbor of the Beast."

Carol pretended a great interest in the opposite wall.

With the ease of long practice, Holly swung one of the bags up off the luggage cart—it clanked alarmingly—and carried it into the suite, waddling only a little. By the time the bellman had finished schlepping Margot's nine pieces of lipstick-red hard-sided Samsonite into the main room, Holly had gotten her duffels stacked in a corner. He regarded them dubiously as he finished moving Carol's two battered no-brands into the room. Margot gave him a twenty. Carol closed the door behind him in relief.

"Really, you *guys,*" she said.

"England expects," Margot said cryptically, opening the door that led to the bedroom.

Holly flopped down on the couch in the main room. She was glad Margot had insisted on a suite—they weren't much more expensive than a triple, and for Margot it was tax deductible. And with the amount of luggage each of them had . . .

"There is no room," Margot announced, returning to the main room, "in the closets."

"Oh, I don't have to—" Carol began. Both of the others turned on her.

"There are times when I think you're too self-effacing for your own good," Holly said to her friend.

"Assertiveness is a virtue," Margot added. "I owe everything I am today to being unreasonable."

"If you don't think passivity is a virtue, you've never listened to the members of the Twisted River Library board trying to decide whether they really ought to do anything at all," Carol said dryly. "If it'd been left to them to vote the money for civilization, we'd all still be living in trees."

"And *loving* it," Margot shot back, à la Maxwell Smart. "But seriously, folks—"

"You need the space in the closets for your masquerade stuff," Carol pointed out.

"This is true," Margot said reasonably.

"What are you doing this year?" Holly asked, genuinely curious. Margot's entries nearly always got at least a Judge's Mention.

"Ballgown from *The City With No Name*," Margot said promptly. "You know, Ellen Kushner?"

Holly frowned. She knew the book, of course, but . . .

"And since the ballgowns're never mentioned and never described, who's to say that whatever I do isn't accurate?" Margot finished triumphantly. Carol snorted and took her suitcase into the bedroom to see if Margot had left any empty drawers.

Holly was the first one to finish unpacking. Margot was emptying her suitcases as methodically as if she were moving in for life, and Carol was sitting on one of the beds watching raptly, but Holly's own preferred method was simply to *find* the bag that held her con clothes and leave them in it.

"Hey, guys?" she called through the door. "I'm going to go down and find out about registration, okay?"

"Bring back Pepsi!" Margot called. Holly waved—though neither of the others could possibly see her—and let herself out of the suite.

Holly Kendal was five-foot-ten, with brown eyes and russet hair which, when braided, fell to her waist. She was an RN with a psych specialization, and for the last several years she'd worked as an EMT in New York City, which meant that the muscles she'd earned spending weekends swinging a sword in the Society for Creative Anachronism came in very handy on occasion. Holly liked the SCA. Even with Kingdom politics, it was about as far from reality as you could get.

The only thing farther was HeliCon.

It helped that they held it in the Hotel Escher, which had been renovated some time in the 1960s by an architect who'd apparently received his early training designing tesseracts. The hotel had seven floors. They were not, however, stacked one on top of the other. To get to the seventh floor, you took the elevator up to five and walked across. At the far end of the seventh floor was a staircase that went down one flight—whereupon you were in the ballroom, which was on the first floor.

Robert Heinlein would have loved it.

Since Holly had been attending conventions here for a number of years, she navigated the selection of half-staircases and two-floor elevator rides needed to get her from the suite floor (five) to the function rooms (seven) from which she could reach registration (one) on personal auto-pilot, her mind on next weekend's "White Mare: Frigidare" camping event in the Shire of ValCoeur. She was just entering the Transdimensional Corridor when she saw the stranger moving slowly down the empty corridor, one hand on the wall.

Holly's mind pegged him easily and instantly as a "not part of the con," even though the Escher was rapidly filling with conventioneers and it would not be entirely outside the realm of possibility for one of them to be wandering the halls in a bathrobe and jammies. It was partly the way he moved, as if he weren't entirely sure that the prosaic corridor around him was real, and partly that he looked miserable, as if there were no more fun anywhere in the universe. As she got closer, Holly revised her opinion further. Not just a misplaced mundane. Not at all.

The stranger was downright skinny; hollow cheeked and gothic as a Russian vampire, and his wrist, where the sleeve of the dark blue ter-rycloth robe had fallen back from it, was slender and frail-seeming, the veins and tendons clearly visible beneath the skin. He was about an inch shorter than she was—that put him around five-eight or -nine, short for a man—with a spiky mop of hair the color of new butter that was long in spots and short in spots and looked as if someone had tried to trim it with a three-hole punch. His skin had the fishbelly pallor that Holly, a nurse, automatically associated with great age or a prolonged hospital stay: whiter than white, nearly translucent, with an almost violet undertone to it. Like some faster-than-an-intern computer, Holly's streetwise brain sorted through all the possibilities and came up with one that seemed all too likely.

Escaped from an institution.

By now she was even with him—close enough to see that one eye was green and the other was hazel. In the dim light of the corridor, they seemed to shine like a cat's. He didn't seem very old at all: some interme-diate "adult" age from twenty to forty, old enough to be out on his own, certainly, but . . . Her eyes flicked to his left wrist and saw what she expected to see: the plastic patient ID that every admitted patient in every hospital wore.

"Can I help you?" Holly said in her best professional nurse's voice. She wanted a closer look at that bracelet: It would tell her his name and where he was from. He turned toward the sound of her voice, slowly enough to tell Holly as plainly as if he'd said it aloud that he was heavily medicated. It was a moment before his eyes focused on her.

"No," he said, enunciating with great clarity, as if speaking to the foreign-born. "I don't think so."

Holly suppressed an unprofessional sound of amusement. Well, she'd *asked* . . .

Just then a gaggle of con-goers appeared at the ballroom end of the stairs, all talking at once. They were wearing HeliCon badges and flourishing the rest of their program packets, obviously looking for something along the Transdimensional Corridor—probably the dealer's room.

The effect on the stranger was startling. He threw himself backward into a doorway, his eyes flickering from side to side as he searched for some escape route. It was several seconds before he located the sound of the noise, but once he did, he relaxed almost at once.

The conventioneers passed between Holly and the stranger without sparing the man in the bathrobe a single glance. They turned the corner and vanished from sight, and before the stranger could focus on her again, Holly stepped across the hall and seized his wrist. She held the ID band up to the meager light in the hall. The stranger did not resist. She could feel his pulse fluttering, hummingbird-fast, beneath her fingers.

"It's okay," Holly said, in automatically soothing tones. "Nobody's going to hurt you."

The end of the sentence was slightly strangled as she got a good look at the bracelet. *A bar code. Who the heck bar-codes their patients?* For one stunned moment Holly entertained the notion that this was some new weird form of hall-costume, and in a moment the stranger would announce he was a patient from, say, Vulcan General Hospital, but Holly couldn't force herself to believe in her own theory. As an EMT in New York, second-guessing people was a survival skill, and Holly'd become very good at it. This guy wasn't faking anything.

"Yes, they are," the stranger said seriously. Holly was baffled until she played back her own last words in her mind.

—Nobody's going to hurt you.

—Yes, they are.

Without thinking, Holly pushed up the sleeve of his robe. When she saw the skin at the inside of his elbow, she sucked air in through her teeth in a hiss.

The skin around the needle tracks was purplish and mottled— bruised as well as inflamed, Holly was willing to bet, although the color was strangely wrong for that. These were the marks of weeks—maybe months—of injections, unskillfully given or perhaps given for so long that the skin was starting to break down regardless of the care that had been taken.

"Who's going to hurt you?" Holly asked. The corridor was too dark to see very well in, but her sense of something wrong was growing all the time. The man in the robe seemed too lucid to be a mental patient, and the only other reasons she could think of for those tracks—rehabilitating junkie, AIDS victim, terminal cancer—didn't fit the rest of what she saw. Holly tried to think of all the hospices, secondary-care facilities, and hospitals in the area that were close enough for a sick, frail man to walk from to the hotel Escher on an afternoon in late December.

"I don't know." The voice was weary, defeated. "Let me go." He swayed against the door, turning his head away and putting his free hand up to cover his face. His hair—long on this side—fell forward, and Holly got a better look at what she'd only glimpsed and half-imagined before.

He had pointed ears.

Holly stared and felt her preconceptions realign with an audible thunk. It couldn't be a stunt—nobody she knew would carry a gag to such ridiculous lengths—but real people didn't have pointed ears. They just didn't.

She had a nagging feeling of something she'd forgotten, but she brushed it aside. Whoever this guy was, he was hurt and lost, and no matter what else was true, that made him her business.

"Why don't we come over here into this nice room and sit down?" Holly suggested brightly. She led him through the first open door she saw.

The first item on the program was at six; at a quarter of four the function room was deserted, with rows of pink chairs facing a white-swathed expanse of table. Holly led the man she already thought of as her patient—a real busman's holiday, this, she acknowledged wryly—to the nearest chair and then went over to the table to fetch him ice water from one of the waiting pitchers. On the way back with the pitcher and an empty glass she detoured to shove the door to the hall shut. With a little luck, nobody would open it again for a while.

"You have to let me go," the stranger said when she returned to his side and poured the water. But he took the plastic glass from her and drank gratefully.

Holly stared at his ears. She couldn't imagine how she could have missed them before, even in the dim light of the hallway. Real genuine *Star Trek* pointed ears, without any sign of spirit gum or scar tissue anywhere. Real? *Oh don't be silly, Holly Amanda Kendal,* Holly chided herself.

He—she was going to have to think of something to call him soon—held out the empty cup for a refill, and Holly poured, trying to think. She almost wished he were bleeding—at least she knew what to do for that.

"Is there somebody chasing you?" Holly asked. He smiled slightly and didn't answer. She frowned, trying to think clearly, intuitively—and fast.

He'd said somebody wanted to hurt him, but he could be confused, delusional, or just plain wrong. She knew he was drugged; Holly only wished she knew what he'd been shot up with, and how much, and when. She refilled the plastic cup again, and he drained it once more. Thirst could mean any of the downers, all of which caused "cotton-mouth." The pitcher was almost empty. Anyone could come in to this room and discover them at any time.

"Do you think I could look at your eyes?" she asked cautiously. She waited, but he didn't answer, gazing off into space with his mismatched eyes. " 'Stoned again,' " Holly muttered irreverently, and gently put her hand on his face to tilt his head back into the light.

He didn't squint or flinch away from the brightness. He didn't have to. When the lights from the ceiling shone fully into his harlequin eyes, the pupils contracted to vertical slits. And Holly made a slow inhalation of dismay and remembered where she'd seen someone like this before.

"Hi, my name is Holly Kendal, and I'm your EMT for the morning."

The unit was already rolling. They'd found this guy down on the tracks on the "E" line, and, with the city's subways all but closed down by the Subway Slasher, Holly was relieved to discover that their client's injuries didn't seem to be much worse than a whack upside the head, even if he was now bound for Bellevue under police escort. She brushed his hair back, very carefully, to see if she could tell what was bleeding and what wasn't and what she needed to do at the site.

The client had pointed ears.

She glanced automatically at his eyes. They were the bright leaf-green of expensive contact lenses, and the pupils had contracted in the light until they were little more than vertical slits.

The client wasn't human.

But this was New York, and Rule Number One, even for Emergency Medical Technicians, was "mind your own business." She hesitated, chewing at her lower lip.

"How are you feeling?" Holly asked carefully. "Do you speak English?"

"Dizzy," the man on the gurney said, closing his eyes. . . .

A few minutes later he'd fainted—at least, he'd closed his eyes and didn't say anything else during the trip—and when the unit got to Bellevue, Holly'd gotten him into Emergency and dropped off the paperwork and that was that. They'd gotten a call for another run almost immediately, and for a while she'd forgotten completely about the entire incident, eventually adding it to her "weird but meaningless" mental files along with so much of life in New York City. She'd never found out what happened to their client.

He might even still be at Bellevue, even though that had been more than two years ago, because this guy was not him. Same *species* maybe. . . .

Get a life, *Holly!* For a moment she wondered if something had gone drastically wrong with her meds—but no, she'd been on the same protocol for years, and it was working just fine. And right now it didn't matter if he was Starman or the Creature from the Black Lagoon—what was she going to *do* with him? She couldn't just walk away.

"My name's Holly Kendal. I'm a nurse." Silence. "I'd like to help you. Do you belong in the hotel?" Silence again. "What's your *name?*" Holly asked mournfully.

The wanderer regarded her with the same vague, sweet, apologetic smile. "Name?" Holly persisted.

"Ma . . . Mak—" he stammered, and looked worried, as if this were a secret he wasn't supposed to tell.

"It's all right; it's okay," Holly soothed. Automatically, Holly smoothed the hair back out of his eyes, wanting to calm him. She couldn't imagine any place that wouldn't at least give its patients a decent haircut, she mused irrelevantly.

Her fingers recognized the injury before her mind did; Holly was already recoiling with nausea before her eyes had time to focus on the dime-sized shiny pink burn on the side of his head. There was one just like it on his other temple.

Electrode burns. And a snapshot out of memory: the reek of Lysol and urine, and Eddie-the-orderly's whining, self-justifying voice—

"Aw, c'mon, Hol, it's not like they can really feel it. A few thousand volts through the old bean and they're just meat—see?" And then he'd taken the cigarette and . . .

She'd nearly lost her RN's license over that one, and she *had* broken Eddie's jaw. Everyone had been very gentle with her afterward and murmured condescendingly about how brave she was to even try to lead a normal life with her condition, but hatred of patient abuse wasn't an entry in DSM-IV. She hadn't hit Eddie because she was one of the Pendulum People. And now she didn't work Psych any more, anywhere, because no matter what you did, it wasn't always your shift and you couldn't stop what happened on other people's shifts.

She took a deep breath. *Hold your center, Holly-girl.* She looked at the marks again and frowned. Electroshock shouldn't leave marks like that, though Holly was certain those were contact burns on his temples. And almost nobody used it any more, but those burns were still pink—recent.

She felt the decision in her bones even before she made it consciously—an unyielding new fact of her life, as absolute as gravity.

"C'mon," said Holly, putting an arm around Mac's bony shoulders and hauling him to his feet. "Walkies."

"Run away," Mac said.

"Margot? Carol? I'm back. There's somebody with me," Holly added quickly, just in case either of them was naked.

Carol came into the living room, wearing jeans and a sky-blue sweater with a white unicorn knitted into it—her own work. She stopped when she saw the man with Holly.

"Holly . . . ?" Carol questioned ominously.

"I found him wandering the halls," Holly said quickly, as though that were enough explanation. "I think his name's Mac—something like that, anyway." She led him over to the couch and lowered him onto it. Mac sank into the cushions gratefully and lay back; he'd gotten progressively less steady on his feet over the last several minutes until Holly had almost ended up carrying him the rest of the way back to the room.

"Hi," Carol said to Mac uncertainly. He closed his eyes.

"He speaks English, but he's pretty doped up right now, I think," Holly said. "And he's got pointed ears."

"He's got what?" Margot had walked out of the bedroom on the last sentence, still wearing the maroon business suit and killer heels she'd flown East in. She looked like some kind of high-toned corporate raider rather than a female fantasy writer. When she spoke, her voice was curiously flat.

"Pointed ears," Carol repeated helpfully.

"And you brought him *here?*" Margot asked.

There wasn't time to pursue that curious statement. "I don't know where he goes," Holly said, looking back and forth between her friends and Mac. "He's got an ID bracelet, but it's bar-coded, and he's all doped up, and . . . other stuff," she finished on a note of fastidious distaste. Carol had been a New York City cop's wife, and Margot was pretty tough, but there were just some things Holly didn't want to say out loud if she didn't have to. Things like the bitter truth of what happened to helpless patients in warehouse facilities when there was no one to care or to stop it.

"Hello-o-o . . ." Carol waved a hand back and forth in front of Mac's face. He opened his eyes and gazed at her fingers with complete blankness.

"Cut it out," Holly said sharply.

"So what," asked Margot, ignoring the byplay, "are you going to do with him?"

Holly sighed, and girded for argument.

* * *

"It's just for a couple of hours," Holly said for the fourth time in as many minutes. Mac was asleep on the couch. Holly hadn't been able to get much more information out of him before he'd caved in. He'd walked to the hotel. He was running away.

He didn't know his name, or where he'd been, or even who the current President of the United States was (come to that, there'd been an intense debate among Carol, Holly, and Margot as to whether George Bush was still in office, so that probably didn't mean much).

He had pointed ears, one green and one hazel eye, and slit pupils like a cat's. And his burns and bruises were a strange color, as though his blood weren't quite red.

"When the drugs wear off I'll find out where he belongs, and—" *and send him back there,* Holly tried to finish. But could she really send him back to a place where he'd been so badly mistreated—no matter *what* he was?

Maybe she'd get lucky. Maybe he'd just been transferred to this new place from whatever snake pit he'd been in last.

And what about those eyes and ears, Holly-girl? Where's the local extended care facility for elves these days?

"What about dinner?" Carol inquired, in the bright determined way of one warding off what promised to be a brutal argument. "I'm hungry. And Margot and I still have to register."

"Yeah," Holly said, gratefully seizing on the distraction. "Aren't you on programming, Marg?"

"Crimenentlies!" Margot groaned, with a guilty glance at her watch. She hesitated, looking at the sleeping elf.

"Look," said Holly briskly. "Why don't you guys go register and see if Margot's supposed to be anyplace? Then you could take my car and go get a pizza, or something, and bring it back here. . . ."

"That's just what we'll do," chirped Carol determinedly, as though she were about to offer to rent a barn to put on the big show. "C'mon Margot, let's go. Don't forget your coat—better take the jacket instead of your cape; it's started snowing—" She sounded as if she were channeling the Doughty Girl Companion in one of those Girl Sleuth Series' from the forties, and she didn't stop talking once until she and Margot were out the door.

Once they were gone, Holly stared at the hall door in puzzlement. Carol had just broken the indoor land-speed weirdness record—but then again, Margot had been acting pretty strange, too, and Carol had known Margot longer than Holly had.

I wonder what set her off? Holly wondered. *Of course, it is the first time*

I've brought a strange man to the room, and Mac looks like he's stranger than most. She looked toward the window; it was after four by now, and the December light outside was a kind of battleship gray. It was also, as advertised, snowing. HeliCon was usually lucky with its weather; the snow arrived after the convention started, and if you were still snowed in by Monday, who cared?

Holly turned back to Mac. He was sleeping the sleep of the completely exhausted; there were dark shadows under his eyes, and if not for the slow, shallow breaths he took, it would have been easy to think he was dead, not unconscious. Holly frowned, looking at his feet. They were chafed and scraped; if Mac had ever had slippers, he'd lost them a while back. He hadn't been limping, so he seemed to have escaped serious injury in his barefoot walk, but there was a long wicked scrape along his anklebone. Still frowning, Holly went into the bathroom and wet a Kleenex, then came out and dabbed at the scrape.

Mac stirred but didn't wake. The scrape cleaned up nicely, just the sort of scratch you'd get from a bramble or some roadside trash; she hoped his tetanus shots were up to date.

A few slow beads of blood collected in the scrape once she'd cleaned it and Holly blotted them up, too, and then stared at the tissue in her hand, a cold coil of rock-bottom realization uncoiling in her stomach.

They could do amazing things with contact lenses these days.

Plastic surgery could account for the ears.

But no power on earth could make a normal human being bleed *purple.*

Francis Marion Catalpano—the few people who were on a first name basis with him called him Frank—did not want to be here. He hadn't wanted to go to a number of places he'd been sent in the past two years, though, and he'd gone to them, too.

A science fiction convention, though, was definitely the worst.

The people were loud. And *friendly.* And interested in you, themselves, each other, and the arts of rhetoric and personal adornment, in approximately that order. Denise—Frank's former wife, a liberal-arts space cadet with a Vassar education—would have loved them all, Frank was sure. And there were a lot of them *to* love at the Hotel Escher, a lot of (presumably) liberal-arts space cadets with no particular concept of personal space. The people at HeliCon offended his fastidious nature. Frank Catalpano was a master of subtlety, of inconspicuousness and blending in.

And how in God's name did you blend in to a convention full of exhibitionists?

He supposed they all had day jobs somewhere. Frank's day job—and nights, and weekends, and holidays—was with a mostly unknown agency with the curious distinction of being the only private-sector service provider in a field usually reserved for governments, friendly and un-. Information Management Systems (information was power, and managing information was controlling reality) leased its services to the United States Government, which paid very well indeed for an exclusive lien on IMS's time. This was not to say that Frank's employers did not have other clients, only that they did not do for these other clients what they did for the United States Government.

At least in theory.

And, being an exclusive private-sector subcontractor to the biggest employer there was, it was easy for Frank's bosses to move mammal-fast around the ankles of the Federal dinosaurs, so that when it was necessary to react in a . . . timely . . . fashion, Frank's people could react.

For example, it was only six hours since Gauvain Makindeor of the House of the Crystal Wind had escaped from some place Frank didn't feel the need to know about, and Frank's people had already tracked him as far as Manningtree. That put the matter squarely on Frank's plate, as Frank had actually seen one of these Seven Houses guys close up and personal, and well enough to ID another one like him. And if there were any helpful civilians around his target this time—the way there had been the last time—Frank intended to make sure they were in no condition to mess up his routine handoff this time. He intended, in fact, to turn loose ends into dead ends.

It would be incorrect to say that Frank Catalpano didn't know right from wrong. In fact, Frank had a highly developed sensitivity to right and wrong and could always tell them apart. What he was doing was wrong. He was, however, on the side of the angels, if you defined the side of the angels as the side of the law.

Laws, it must be noted, can be rewritten, from time to time, for expediency's sake.

Watching the lobby for any sign of Makindeor, Frank brooded on the one that'd gotten away two years ago, one Rohannan Melior, probably of the House of the Silver Silences. In one brisk half-hour clip when Frank's back was turned, Melior had slipped out of what was supposed to be a secure holding room in a New York City hospital and vanished before he could be turned over to Frank's masters.

Frank had backtracked Melior, of course. The trail had run smack into a gaggle of kids: Jane Grayson, Philip LeStrange, Michael Peacock, Ruth Marlowe. Frank suspected they were the ones who'd gotten his prisoner out of Bellevue. They'd all claimed innocence, but there was something clandestine there. There'd been a fifth member of their little group, Marlowe's roommate, Naomi Nasmyth, who nobody could find and none of them wanted to talk about.

None of the four had wanted to talk about anything much, actually, even though Frank'd had all the New York City Police Department ID necessary to encourage proper cooperation from the innocent. IMS had kept a distant watching eye on them over the next couple of years, though, and Frank kept in touch. Except for Peacock, they had gravitated upstate to a city in Patroon County, New York, and LeStrange seemed to have vanished off the face of the Earth.

It might be time to pull the girls in for a little chat, once he'd handed Gauvain Makindeor back over to his minders. A little *permanent* sort of chat.

· 3 ·

Magic by the Book

HOLLY FUSSED AROUND the suite, pulling together stuff for Mac to wear instead of those blatant hospital clothes. One of her sweatshirts and a pair of sweatpants would probably fit him, and she could probably pick up a pair of Jockeys in the hotel giftoid shop. Shoes would be a problem, but if she switched to the leather boots that went with her armor, Mac could wear her Reeboks. He'd need shoes for the trip back to wherever he'd come from, wherever that was. *It couldn't be a good place if it let him get out,* a small inner voice insisted.

The next time she found an excuse to pass by the couch, his eyes were open.

"Hello," said Holly carefully. "How are you feeling?"

Those harlequin eyes—green and hazel—searched the room wildly for a moment before focusing on Holly. Then Mac lunged to his feet.

"Hey—take it easy—nobody's going to hurt you."

The motion had carried him only halfway up; when Holly grabbed him to steady him, even that gentle resistance pushed him backward. He sat down on the couch, looking like a frightened egret.

"I'm the one who rescued you, remember?" Holly said coaxingly.

After a moment comprehension came into his eyes, and she was rewarded with one of his sweet vague smiles.

"Ah," he said. "Foolish of you."

It was so far from what Holly had expected to hear that she was startled into laughter.

"That isn't very gracious," she pointed out.

"They pursue me, my hunters," Mac said quietly. He looked around the room.

"Well, nobody saw you come in here—and this is HeliCon, anyway; believe me, you'll fit right in. There're probably zillions of people out there in the halls right now with pointed ears."

"Other—?" Mac began quickly, and stopped. "I do not remember," he said plaintively. He covered his face with his hands. "I can't remember. Don't ask me."

"It's okay," Holly said, though privately she thought it wasn't okay and was getting less okay by the moment. She'd seen psych patients of every possible diagnosis, and none of them had ever presented quite like Mac. She didn't think that even a full-blown Ted Bundy sociopath could sell her quite this convincing a bill of goods.

And there was the fact that he was an elf to consider.

"Can you tell me your name?" Holly suggested.

"No," Mac said gloomily. He raised his head and looked at her, then shook his head. "I am not from here."

"I figured that out," Holly said, but she didn't know what to say next. Asking him where he *was* from went against every professional instinct. "You started to say something like 'Mac' before," she finally temporized. "It might come back to you. We'll just call you Mac for now, okay? Just until we find out who you are."

"Mac." He didn't sound as if he liked the taste of that very much. "Mac, then, Holly Kendal. A not-name for a man who does not even exist seems well enough. I do not know how it is that I came here, or who I am. I cannot even name my House," Mac went on despondently. "If I have fallen to the World of Iron, why do my jailers ask me to read the *Book of Airts*? Answer that, if you can."

"What's the *Book of Airts*?" Holly asked automatically. Mac shot her a look of narrow-eyed suspicion.

"Okay, let's move on," Holly said hastily. *Paranoid delusional structure?* "You don't know your name, you don't know where you are, and you don't know where you've been. Why don't we clean you up while we discuss what we're going to do with—what you want to do now, okay?"

Holly moved Mac into the bathroom, where she sat him on the edge of the tub and proceeded to even out his hair with the help of a set of bandage scissors from her first-aid kit.

She wanted to leave it long enough to cover his ears—by some instinct she didn't question, Holly thought that concealing Mac's ears was a good idea—but she also wanted him to look a little less like a post-Punk Borrible. By the time she'd finished trimming, he looked a little bit like Sting and a little bit like the King of the Goblins but more adult, somehow. The ears were quite conspicuously visible. On the other hand, now he looked as if he meant to have that haircut—and anyway, she had a gimme cap he could wear.

"Would you like a bath?" Holly asked next, folding the wisps of cut hair into the towel she'd draped around his shoulders. In her professional capacity, she was no stranger to the male body, and there were a lot of reasons that she wanted to get a good look at his, scrapes, scratches, and needle tracks all included.

"Yes," Mac said. Holly turned to the tub and opened both taps up full. Conversation was impossible over the roar of the water, but when she glanced at Mac, she found him watching her, a wary intelligence in his eyes.

She was starting to get used to the idea that he really wasn't a human being. She'd called him an elf when she'd first seen him, but it was actually more likely, all things considered, that he was really a space alien. She remembered an old story written by a friend of Margot's called "Is Your Coworker a Space Alien?" So, was he? That theory made as much sense as any other explanation.

And whoever he was—elf, alien, none-of-the-above—what was he doing *here?* He'd escaped; he was being chased. Sure, she'd gotten that far, but escaped from where? Being chased by whom? And for that matter, came to Earth how?

Drugged, shocked, malnourished, amnesiac—if Mac had already been treated this way by the "proper authorities," Holly wasn't sure she wanted to turn him back over to them.

What to do, what to do. . . .

She couldn't take him home with her to her Brooklyn apartment. Her roommates already thought the SCA was weird; they'd never put up with an alien elf.

She could take him on to the White Mare: Frigidare camping event, at least. That would put off the final decision for another week.

But no. Holly shook her head. Taking him to White Mare: Frigidare would mean keeping him here in the hotel all weekend and then taking him with her to spend Tuesday night with Rook, stopping on the way to drop Carol off with Carol's friend Ruth in Ippisiqua.

That wouldn't work.

The tub was full. Holly twisted the taps off and automatically tested the temperature of the water. Not too hot, not too cold, and fortunately most hotels these days—including the Escher—came equipped with safety rails inside the tub enclosure.

"Do you need any help?" she asked.

"No," Mac said. But he didn't ask her to leave, either. He was still unsteady on his feet, and Holly hovered in the doorway, hoping he wouldn't fall.

He pulled off the tatty blue terrycloth bathrobe and tossed it to the floor. Beneath it he was wearing a worn cotton smock and drawstring pants in a washed-out pale green; standard institutional ODs. Stenciled across the front and back of the smock were the letters "HMPS."

For Holly Kendal, it was like getting a look at his driver's license. *Half Moon Psychiatric Center.* Half Moon, New York, was just north of Ippisiqua in Patroon County. It was one of the largest residential-care facilities in midstate. HMPS. That was where he must have come from.

Holly didn't say anything.

Holding onto the towel bar, Mac pulled off the tunic and dropped it to the floor, facing away from her. Holly could see that the skin of his back was the same unearthly white as his face, hands, and feet, with the off-colored wine-violet patches of pressure sores where no patient would get them—unless he'd been kept strapped down for hour after hour, day after day.

The unhappy knot of tension in Holly's stomach grew. Gross misconduct on Half Moon's part, barely excusable if the patient was extremely violent. But Mac wasn't. And if he were a career-institutionalized uncontrolled bipolar on his way into a deep depressive phase, his presentation would not be this . . . conventional.

He might be a few sandwiches shy of a picnic. He was not Thorazine-electroshock-and-round-the-clock-Foley-restraints crazy; she'd bet her license on it.

Mac worried at the drawstring of the trousers that had been helpfully knotted shut by some nursing aide somewhere and finally simply snapped the cord between his hands. It was a small display of strength, but it impressed Holly nevertheless. The trousers joined the shirt. There were pressure sores on his hips, too—not bad, yet, but enough to indicate he'd been kept under heavy restraint not long ago.

Why?

A moment later she stopped wondering about that at all. When Mac turned sideways to step into the water, Holly saw the battle scars.

At first Holly couldn't imagine what they might be. The only scars she was used to seeing were surgical ones, placed on the body through injury or design and neatly and regularly closed thereafter. These marks looked as though somebody had been taking a swing at Mac with . . .

. . . a sword. *They looked like sword cuts.*

Palest purple, the long-healed scars pulled and twisted the skin like a thin coating of paraffin, above the knee, along the ribs. Battle scars.

Without thinking, she took the few steps needed to cross the room and get a closer look. *Car accident? They can't be what they look like—*

Mac turned back and saw her. His face was only inches away, his eyes on a level with her own. Green and hazel, the colors of leaf and forest . . .

"Need help getting into the tub?" Holly asked calmly. She held out her arm and Mac took it, wincing slightly as he lowered himself into the water.

"Why would somebody want you to read a book, Mac?" Holly asked a while later.

Her new patient was freshly scrubbed, sitting on the couch and dressed festively in Holly's dark green sweatpants and a bright red sweatshirt with a white bull's-eye silkscreened onto the back beneath the words "Security." A *Star Trek* cap was perched on the back of his head, giving him a slightly surreal appearance. Holly hoped that—in combination with the clothes—the ears would be taken for makeup.

"To see what it says," he said, after a moment's pause.

"Well, can't they read it themselves?" Holly asked reasonably. "Or get somebody more cooperative to do it."

"No," Mac said quickly. "Only—" There was a pause. "I can't remember."

"Part of that might be the drugs," Holly said. "High dosages of some of them can cause temporary disorientation and amnesia. It should wear off; give it a couple of days."

"And if it doesn't?" Mac asked, with real anguish. "And if I can't remember . . . anything?" he finished lamely.

He isn't telling me the whole truth, Holly thought to herself, but she could think of no reason offhand that he should. Trust was a fragile thing; it took more than a few hours to build. "We'll find out where you belong," she said firmly. "I'll take you there."

"You?"

Mac was plainly skeptical, which roused Holly's competitive instincts.

"I've got two weeks off," Holly pointed out. "I can't think of anywhere we couldn't get to by then." *Elfland, Poughkeepsie, Mars. . . .* "Look, Margot and Carol ought to be back with dinner soon, and for right now I've got some chips if they aren't squished—you want Coke or something?"

"Things go better with Coke," Mac said with a faint wistful smile. "The *tell-y-vision* says so."

* * *

Holly walked down the hall to the fifth floor soda and ice machines, jingling the change in her jeans pocket. One or two people—nobody she knew well, but obviously belonging to the convention and therefore her brothers and sisters in fandom—passed her in the hallway, some with luggage, some already with badges, which reminded Holly that she still had to register.

She wasn't sure it was one of her better ideas to leave Mac alone in her room, but it was only for a minute or so, and there wasn't much he could do. Even if he were larcenously inclined, she didn't think he could *lift* her armor, much less steal it, and Carol and Margot had their purses with them.

She'd brought the ice bucket with her and was juggling four cans of soda under her arm while trying to fill it when something made her look up. She flinched back, heart hammering, as automatically as the rabbit cowers from the shadow of the hawk. It happened and was over in a flash, so that only when Holly replayed it over and over in memory, taking it apart to understand it, did she really begin to understand her fear.

The silence was first: the peculiar strained, unnatural silence that comes when everyone else already sees a danger you haven't spotted yet. Holly looked up and saw the gray man.

It was not that he was gray; it was more that grayness radiated from him like a tangible force, a bleak leaching of color from everything he touched. He had mouse-brown hair, cut corporate-short, and no-color eyes that gave an impression of paleness. He wore a gray suit, neither cheap nor expensive, and had the indefinable look of middle managers everywhere.

But there was just something about him: that half-beat when he hesitated, walking down the hall, and Holly froze under the stress of his regard like a jacklighted doe. Then he was gone, and Holly was left to the gradual process of becoming afraid.

And of remembering where she'd seen him before.

It had been at Bellevue, two years ago. He'd been there, asking her ambulance crew if they'd seen their subway patient again after they'd dropped him off. He hadn't explained why he was asking, and none of them had really felt like questioning him.

It was the same man. Holly was sure of it.

And he was here, and so was another "elf."

She was shaking by the time she could coax herself to move out of the cover of the machines and back into the hallway.

"Maybe he's gone," Margot said hopefully. She was balancing three large garbage pizzas on top of each other. "What time is it?"

"Six. Ish," Carol said. "How come you don't like this guy so much, Marg? He's just another one of Holly's humanitarian projects."

"I've got the Mill 'n' Swill at nine, so that should be enough time for dinner and a change," Margot said, ignoring Carol's conversational gambit to change the subject obliquely to the con event more properly known as the "Meet The Pros" party. "Hey, look at that."

Margot didn't have to point for Carol to know what she meant. It was like a "What's Wrong with This Picture?" illustration: men in the lobby, men in suits, men with ties, men wearing sunglasses in Westchester in the middle of December.

Men, in short, who didn't belong within light-years of a HeliCon. Men in Black, strange invaders from another fashion sense.

"Is the President in town?" Margot said to Carol, sotto voce.

"Maybe there's an *X-Files* programming track," Carol suggested, but her voice was worried.

They counted three of the MIBs by the time they reached the elevators, and that was three too many for a small Westchester hotel at seven p.m.

"Anybody know what's going on?" Margot queried of the assembled fans in the elevator. Some of them had noticed the MIBs, some hadn't. None of them had an explanation.

"And there haven't even been any fire alarms yet," said a tall man in a Polar-Tec jacket with "Darkover Ski Team: Ski The Hellers" appliqued on the back.

Carol shrugged. Margot juggled pizzas. They reached their floor and got out.

It was hard to worry when you didn't have any of the facts, Holly reflected. She'd gotten back to the room, found the chips (not too mashed), and poured sodas for herself and Mac, and then turned on the TV. Mac seemed quite willing to be occupied by an endless loop of trailers showing the delights of all the in-room movies they could be watching at this very moment for a mere $8 per, charged to your room. Holly fidgeted, pacing back and forth until she finally noticed what she was doing.

Who was that man? Why was he here? Who was this elf, and why was *he* here? And what, if anything, was Holly Kendal, RN, EMT, supposed to do about it?

She didn't know.

Finally Holly gave up pretending to be calm. If she was going to fidget, she'd fidget constructively. She rummaged through her duffels until she located her cleaning kit, then turned to the case that held her sword. It was a long narrow case, the kind that looked as if it might hold a really skinny Stratocaster or a dwarf bassoon. Holly flipped open the locks, and there she was, Holly's lady-bright, lying on her bed of red rayon plush looking like sunrise and moonrise and starlight all fused together.

Her name was Lady Fantasy III; she was one of the last swords Stephen Mallison had ever made—thirty-six inches from guard to tip; drop-forged carbon steel with a rutilated quartz counterweight in the pommel, horsehair-wrapped double-handed haft, and a three-inch wide blade that Holly kept sharp enough to shave with. Thirteen pounds of unstoppable war engine, lethal and irresistible.

The terror of watermelons from Oestgard to Atenveldt, Holly thought to herself. She'd carried Lady Fantasy III in choreographed renfaire demos, but she'd never used her for real. Lady Fantasy was a lethal weapon. Holly lifted the blade out of her case and flourished the sword carefully. Lady Fantasy glittered in the evening light.

Mac looked up—and stopped. His mouth hung open, as if he were trying to say something and had forgotten every word.

Belatedly, unbelievingly, Holly's mind made the connection between the scars she'd seen on Mac's body and the weapon in her hand. Sword wounds. They didn't just look like sword scars; they *were* sword scars. Sometime, somewhere, Mac had been in a battle fought with swords— real ones.

There was a scrabbling at the door, a rattle-bash-thump-click of key-card in lock and bodies softly colliding with unyielding technology. Holly stared at Mac for the frozen moment before Margot and Carol tumbled through the door on a wave of pizza-scent, both talking.

"—isn't any kind of you know *mundane* convention here at the hotel and besides it's the wrong—"

"—don't look like any editors I've ever seen and in the second place Team Avon and the Tor-eadors aren't—"

Both of them stopped at about the same time.

"Oh," Margot said in a flat voice, looking at Mac. She set the pizzas down on the table and walked off to the bedroom.

"Um . . . hi," Holly said weakly. Feeling vaguely embarrassed to be caught playing, she went to put Lady Fantasy back in the case. She could oil and sharpen the sword later.

Carol looked from Margot's disappearing back to Holly and then at Mac. She set down her sack of groceries next to the pizzas and took off her jacket.

"How are you feeling now?" Carol asked him politely. There were still scattered snowflakes melting in her long fair hair, a legacy of the snowy evening outside.

"Better," Mac said. "I do not think I can long remain here, Child of Earth," he added seriously.

Carol looked at Holly for assistance with the conversation. Holly shrugged. Mac was right, but the situation seemed to be getting more tangled by the moment without any input from her.

"There's some strange guys downstairs," Carol said casually, opening the pizza box and surveying the contents.

"What kind of strange guys?" The memory of the gray man came back to Holly in a rush, frightening her all over again and making her voice come out in a strangled croak.

"Guys in suits," Carol said, before she looked up. "Holly, what's wrong? You're white as a cliché."

"I'm . . . not really sure," Holly said slowly. She swallowed hard, willing herself to be calm and collected. "Let me get back to you on that."

Carol turned to the grocery bag and began unpacking paper plates and paper towels and two six-packs of cold soda. "Margot? Are you going to eat pizza?" she called over her shoulder.

There was a pause before Margot came back out of the bedroom, having changed her blazer and blouse for a leopard-print velour top marginally more suitable for eating pizza in. She shot Holly a vaguely challenging look.

"So," said Margot, sitting down in a chair across from the couch. "He's still here. You guys have much of a chat?"

"Well," Holly said, "Mac's still a little disoriented, but I think I know where his clothes came from, at least."

Margot turned to Mac, still with that same atypical aggressive look.

"I don't know how I got here," he said humbly. "But I am not . . . delusional." There was a faint hesitation over the last word, as if he'd heard it somewhere and was quoting it without entirely understanding its meaning.

"Nobody said you were," Margot said with cool indifference. She reached for a slice of pizza and scooped it onto a waiting plate, then reached for a can of Diet Pepsi. "How'd you get here, do you know?" she added with elaborate casualness.

She bit into the pizza, reminding Holly that no matter how weird everybody was acting, she'd missed lunch and was starving. She got plates and served herself and Mac two slices each, relieved to see that he was able to manage for himself.

"I am not certain," Mac answered hesitantly. "I remember being in the library—"

What library? Holly wondered.

"—and then I was in the World of Iron; here. And Children of Earth were asking me about the Book."

Over Mac's head Holly could see Carol, who was doing an elaborate pantomime (around a mouthful of pizza) that Holly was having no trouble decoding: *What about the ears, Hol? Is this guy for real?* What *book?*

"The *Book of Airts*," Holly amplified.

"What's an airt?" Carol wondered.

"A direction," Margot (who, being a fantasy writer, was presumed to know these things) said harshly. "Like north, south, east, west." She hesitated, as if she were going to say more, but subsided.

"And whoever they were," Holly said to Mac, "they weren't treating you very well, were they?"

"They were torturing me," Mac explained, as simply as to an idiot. "Because they wished me to read the Book for them, and I would not."

Carol—who had been swallowing—began to cough, and there was a brief flurry while the others made sure she could still breathe.

"Torture!" she exclaimed, looking at Holly.

Holly hesitated. Mac could be a real genuine elf and still be delusional—or mistaken. "Could be," she said hesitantly, thinking of the marks she'd seen on his body. "And there's something funny going on here."

"Just one thing?" Margot drawled derisively.

"There's this guy," Holly said.

The four of them finished two of the pizzas and part of the third while Holly explained about the other man with the pointed ears that she'd taken to Bellevue two years before, and about the gray man who'd taken such an interest in him then and there, and now was here.

"And he's . . . I don't know. *Creepy* somehow—and this is just such an unlikely place for somebody like that to be, anyway. I mean, an SF convention? And a little regional one at that."

"Everybody's got to be some place," Margot pointed out.

"Do you suppose all the guys in the sunglasses are with him?" Carol asked. " 'Creepy' is right, as in, 'I'm from the government, I'm here to help you.' " She looked unhappy.

"The U. S. Government is persecuting elves?" Margot asked. "Sounds like an *X-File* to me, Scully."

When she put it that way, it did sound silly.

"Well, why not?" Holly asked, nettled. "Art has to convince, life just is, and so are those MIBs in mirror shades. Mac, honey, don't you remember *anything?*"

"I remember Chandrakar," Mac said seriously. "I was . . .." He pressed his hands against his forehead, as if it hurt. "I was librarian to the

High King. I remember how it rained the day we laid Rainouart the Beautiful upon the wave, as if the sky itself were weeping. . . ." His voice trailed off; there was a long pause, and then Mac sighed heavily. "But I remember nothing useful. Why should I be here in the World of Iron at all? I should be home preparing for the Kingmaking."

It was a beautiful story, and Holly could see that Carol believed it, but unfortunately Holly had heard any number of delusional paranoiacs spin equally plausible tales that Holly knew were false. *Elf* and *crazy,* she reminded herself. Or lying.

"Well, if you came from Chandrakar," said Margot rudely, "why don't you just go back there?"

"Margot!" snapped Holly, automatically. The resentful undertone of hostility in Margot's voice wasn't an undertone now. Point against Mac: Margot didn't like him, and Margot's radar for character was pretty close to infallible.

"Oh, will you both stop *fighting?*" Carol wailed.

Everyone looked at her.

"What are you going to do, Holly?" Carol added in a quieter voice.

It was as if Holly had only been waiting to be asked the question. "Well," she began, reasonably, "we—Mac—can't stay here."

Margot snorted derisively.

"For one thing," Holly continued, talking louder to cover the sound, "we don't know that all these guys in suits are connected with Mac, but I'm starting to think that they might be, and I'm not sure I trust them, so the sooner he's out of here, the better."

"Where are you going to go?" Carol inquired.

"Well, if you can't impose on your friends, who *can* you impose on?" Holly said with a triumphant grin. "I have a cunning plan. . . ."

By 8:30 Friday night, everybody at HeliCon knew that *somebody* was looking for *something,* and four people had a pretty good idea of what it was.

While Holly was still bandaging up Mac's feet prior to putting shoes on him—Carol had been able to contribute a pair, so Holly did not have to sacrifice her only non-garb footwear—Margot had come back from the Meet the Pros event to say that the Men in Black had descended on it, asking everyone questions that were marvelously nonspecific.

"Like, Had we seen anything out of the ordinary?—at *HeliCon!*" Margot said, with a fine disdain. "But you've got to get him out of here, Hol—and take your luggage with you. I think it's a good thing you didn't get around to registering, you know."

"Are you serious?" Holly asked. Margot was already digging through her wallet and producing a wad of cash big enough to choke at least a miniature horse. Margot always carried enough cash to bankroll a small revolution, explaining that the only way female fantasy writers could achieve respect was through bribery.

"Take this. You can pay me back later. But don't use any credit cards until this is over, okay?" Margot said.

"You *are* serious," Holly said. She got to her feet, smiling at Mac in what she hoped was a reassuring fashion, and abruptly realized that a gimme cap and red shirt weren't going to fool anyone about those ears if there was a serious search going on.

Mac regarded her with an expression of sober humor and began to pull on a pair of Holly's white gym socks.

It took Holly another hour to get out of the hotel with Mac and her luggage, and by the time she had, she was heartily glad she was going. The Friday night reveling had taken on some of the behavior of a dance band on the *Titanic;* and Holly had the faint feeling of some impending disaster that only her absence—and Mac's—could avert.

"Don't forget your meds," Carol said. Holly had already made two runs down to her car, to pack it, clear the windows, and make sure that there was no visible trouble in the parking lot; this last trip out she would make with Mac.

"Zoloft and Lithobid right here," Holly said, patting her purse. *Better living through chemistry.* "Ready, Mac?"

He was wearing Margot's J. Peterman cashmere watch cap, a down vest of Holly's, and Carol's hand-knitted *Spiderman* gloves. To Holly's jaundiced eye, he didn't look terribly convincing as fan, mundane, or human being.

"Ready," Mac said gamely. Dark circles of weariness showed beneath his eyes, and his pale skin had the translucent fragility of exhaustion.

"Don't call," Margot said urgently. "Leave a message with Sheila at DAW if you want to reach me. I'm having lunch with her Tuesday and I'll ask her if there's anything."

"Hey," Carol said worriedly. "You're really spooked, aren't you? Maybe we should just call the police?"

"And tell them what?" Holly and Margot returned in chorus.

"Well," Carol said thoughtfully, "we could ask the Sheriff's Department who's tromping with their big muddy feet all over WCSD's jurisdiction—if anyone."

"Spoken like a true Idaho taxpayer," Margot quipped.

"Maybe you might like to try that after I'm gone," Holly said, reluctant to let her friends involve themselves further. "Look. We're just getting crazy. Everything's going to be fine. I'll see you later."

"I'll go first," Margot said. She swept from the room in her evening suit like a Wagnerian soprano with attitude.

"Well . . . see you," Holly said lamely after a pause. Carol smiled wanly.

Some convention this's turned out to be, Holly thought gloomily. She took a deep breath, squared her shoulders, and took Mac's hand. She could feel his fingers tremble even through the thick red knitted wool.

" 'C'mon, men. They can't stop people who really want to be free,' " Holly muttered to herself. She opened the door.

After that much of a buildup, the corridor was anticlimactically empty. She didn't even see Margot.

Holly checked her watch as she and Mac started down the hall. A little after nine. Dealer's room closed, programming in full swing, room parties on the rise. She thought that the elevators were a little less crowded than usual, but that might simply have been a fannish love of intensive recomplication: additional stairwell use to baffle the ungodly, who kept asking who everyone was and where they were going. Holly held her breath as the elevator traversed the three floors to the lobby and the doors opened.

She didn't see anybody at all wearing a suit.

The lobby seemed as if it were a thousand yards wide. Holly's heart hammered in panic. This wasn't like showing up at the site of a car crash or brawl where everyone was depending on her to stay calm and save lives. This time Holly herself was the casualty-to-be, and she didn't like it. By the time she reached the lobby doors and freedom, she could have shouted out loud with relief, she was that wired.

It was snowing harder than it had been since her last trip out: Rosinante, her almost-an-antique Honda station wagon, was covered again with a sparkling dusting of snow, despite the fact that she'd swept it clean once already. She hadn't been able to bring herself to leave it unlocked with Lady Fantasy inside, even though that would have made things go faster this trip. With fingers stiff from clutching them inside her pocket, Holly fumbled out her car keys and opened the passenger side door. Mac got in, and Holly went around and opened the driver's side door.

Safe. She locked her door, dumped her purse on the floor at Mac's feet, and reached across to belt him in and lock his door. The sound of the engine catching had a soothing effect on Holly's nerves, and she felt

like bursting into song as she slewed the Honda out of the snowy parking lot and onto the still-clear main road. *Come on, Rosinante, do your stuff—*
"Holly?" Mac said.
"Just a minute," Holly said, looking for the entrance to the Taconic.
"Holly," Mac said, more urgently. "Holly, we have to go back."

· 4 ·

The Truce of the Bear

AFTER SPENDING THE night in the ruined shell of the house the four of them prepared to ride onward the following day—Ruth and Jausserande on their own horses, Nic on that ridiculously white, ridiculously bright horse that Fox's companion Raven had said was magic, and Fox on Raven's horse, which Jausserande had caught as it wandered riderless.

In the morning light, Fox's bruises showed livid and hurting against his brown skin. Jausserande watched him like a hungry tiger, and despite that—or because of it—Fox seemed to take an almost painful pleasure in baiting her.

"S'matter, Tink, don't you think this is going to be *fun?* A hopeless quest, a kingdom in the balance; it's just the kind of stupidity you point-ears dote on," he mocked as he mounted.

Ruth wondered idly where Philip/Fox had learned words like "dote." She supposed it was the same place he'd learned his horsemanship; even battered as he was, he sat his horse with a calm assurance that only Jausserande could match.

" 'Ware your tongue, little Fox," Jausserande had answered sullenly. "I need my cousin's heart twin to find him and the Cup. I don't need you."

"Hurt him and I won't help you," Ruth said quickly, though she knew such brave rebellion was a lie.

Jausserande turned all her attention to Ruth, and Ruth felt the impact of that burning violet gaze like a blow. Ruth wasn't helping Jausserande *now*. She was trying to reach Melior the only way she could, to somehow make whoever had captured him leave him alone. And there

was something terribly dangerous about Melior's lady-cousin Floire Jausserande of the House of the Silver Silences: dangerous because not sane,
not answerable to reason. But no matter what happened on the way, or
who she had to ally herself with, Ruth could not bear to abandon Melior.

"Hinder me, you mud-born sow, and I'll—"

"I really don't think this is productive, your ladyship." Nic's voice cut
across Jausserande's: quiet, deferential, and not to be argued with. It
stopped her—something that surprised Ruth—and Jausserande turned
toward Nic, regarding him with narrowed, suspicious eyes.

The former Ryerson Public Library Director was wearing armor that
looked like nothing Ruth had ever seen in either her intermediate-length
career in library science or several years of hanging around the edges of
the SCA. The black-and-green-painted leather tunic made him look terribly competent, and the odd studded bracers covering his forearms looked
formidably dangerous. He carried neither sword nor shield, but strapped
to his belt was a Bowie knife as long as Ruth's arm, and balanced across
his horse's rump was a metal-shod quarterstaff. Ruth had watched him
kill two men with an improvised quarterstaff only a few minutes after
they'd come through the gate to the Lands Beyond the Morning, so she
could understand why he'd brought this one, even if the way he was
carrying it did make it look stupid.

Jausserande set her mouth and waited.

"And I'm sure you wouldn't want to do anything to hurt Miss Marlowe," Nic continued, "as we're all . . . allies, you might say."

There was a silent battle of wills that made Ruth's teeth ache with the
force of it, and even Fox had the sense to keep his mouth shut while it
went on.

"As long as she cooperates and takes me to the Cup, Ceiynt, no harm
will come to her," Jausserande grudgingly promised Nic. She swung up
onto her mount. "She owes me that service by right; it was *her* confederate who lost the Cup to me."

So now Fox was *her* confederate? Ruth thought to herself. It would
be almost funny if the stakes weren't so high.

But Fox wasn't done yet. He leaned forward confidentially over his
horse's neck and addressed Jausserande.

"Don't you get it yet, elf-bitch? The Cup was never *in* the Vale of
Stars. You spent Guiraut's life for nothing, trying to get to a place that—"

Jausserande kicked her mount forward at the same time Nic did.

"Put up!" he roared, though neither Fox nor Jausserande was carrying a weapon.

Nic grabbed Fox's horse's bridle before Fox could spur his mount to bolt. It was a few moments before Nic was able to sort things out and stop Jausserande from dragging Fox off his horse.

"Now," Nic said, and Ruth could hear the gritted teeth from the other side of the clearing, "Fox, you apologize to Lady Jausserande and don't do it again."

"No," Fox said simply. He looked at Nic. "Just how are you going to make me, Mr. Brightlaw? Just what is it you're going to do that's worse than what *she's* going to do?"

"I'm closer," Nic said.

There was a moment when Ruth saw him struggle with his temper, and thought it would be a frightening thing to see if he ever lost it.

"I ought to give you to her and let her do what she wants. As far as I can see, you're a petty little murderer not worth the powder to blow you to hell."

"I'm depraved on account of I'm deprived," Fox said archly. He bowed over his horse's neck. For a man facing the likelihood of a severe beating at the least and death by torture at the worst, Fox looked remarkably serene. He looked, Ruth thought, like a man with nothing to lose.

But he didn't really have anything left to lose, did he? And all Ruth had left to lose was Melior.

"Fox," she said. "Please. You said you wanted to get to Melior. . . ."

Fox smiled, a sweet and not particularly trustworthy expression. "You're right, Ruth. I should be more considerate of other people's feelings. After all, Mel's a really lovable guy, isn't he?"

Ruth didn't answer. There wasn't any point, when she knew what Fox really thought of Melior. Fox thought that Melior was responsible for Naomi's death; that he'd held all of their human lives as expendable in his quest for the Sword of Maiden's Tears and should be made to pay for that act.

"Come on, could we?" Ruth said wearily.

After that, none of the others trusted Fox to ride unsupervised, even though the horse he rode could not possibly outrun any of the others'. Nic tied Fox's rein to one of the D-rings on his saddle and led his horse. Jausserande rode ahead, ignoring all three of them. Her silver hair glittered in the morning sun. Ruth stared at it.

Everything fit together like a not particularly pretty Rubik's Cube, Ruth mused. Nic and Fox, Jausserande and her. Ruth traveled to find Melior in the direction that the tie pulled her—east, across most of Chandrakar. To cross Chandrakar, Ruth needed Jausserande. Jausserande went because of the belief that where Ruth found the Sword and Melior, Jausserande would also find the Cup of Morning Shadows, and Jausserande was its Cupbearer. Fox came with them whether he would or no as a sort of quasi-prisoner, because Jausserande would not even consider the possibility of his going free and Fox had business of his own with Melior. But what was Nic's excuse?

Or as Jausserande called him, Ceiynt.

Ruth brooded over that question all the rest of the way to Black Bridge, incidentally disentangling the pun involved: Ceiynt—Nic—Saint Nic. A jolly old elf, so the poem said. It was too bad that her Saint Nic was neither jolly nor an elf. But they were going to have to make do with the manpower at hand.

Jausserande didn't turn anyone in to the Earl of Silver's garrison at Black Bridge. Ruth supposed she ought to feel more grateful for the circumstance than she actually did. What she felt, actually, was numb.

The town of Black Bridge was one of those jarringly bucolic elfland scenes, commonplace Beyond the Morning, composed of a ye olde quaynte country inn, a large businesslike stone building that must be the garrison, and a few other buildings of the smithy-and-stables variety. The four of them crossed a covered bridge on the way into the town, but it wasn't black as far as Ruth could see.

Jausserande stopped in front of the inn. There was a sign over the door: a golden harp on a green field. The gilding on the harp glowed in the sun.

Ruth looked longingly toward its door. She was cold and stiff with several hours of riding and hungry besides, and she doubted any of the others felt any better than she did.

"I shall acquaint the garrison with our business and send messages to the Earl of Silver and to the castellan at Dawnheart. Perhaps we can get better horses here—and we must find a healer for you, sweet Fox," Jausserande added with sugary malice.

"No," Fox said briefly, but his face was drawn and grayish beneath the tan, and he rode holding himself as if it hurt to breathe.

"Oh, but I fear you must have sustained injuries," Jausserande continued in that feline way, watching Fox as closely as if she were a cat and he a particularly appetizing mouse. "And our journey is too long to allow you to suffer so. I am not myself a handy spellwright, but I am certain we can craft your healing here. In fact, I insist on it."

"No," Fox said again. With an effort, he favored Jausserande with one of his more brilliant smiles. "I couldn't possibly put you to any trouble."

It was the magic, Ruth realized. Fox didn't want magic used on him, and Jausserande knew it and was toying with him. For once Ruth found herself in surprisingly strong sympathy with Fox. Ruth feared and distrusted magic in all its forms—and Fox knew more about it than she did.

"Leave him alone," Ruth said shortly.

"Ah, the mud-born leman speaks. And what will you have for a wedding gift when you mingle your false blood with my cousin's? Shall I resign you my blood-claim on this outlaw's life? I am not the only claimant, you know."

The trouble with talking to Jausserande, as Ruth was beginning to discover, was that her conversation hinged on rhetorical questions that you had to understand—if not answer—to make sense of the conversation. All Ruth really understood from Jausserande's speech was that she didn't like Ruth—and Ruth had already known that.

Why had she come to Chandrakar anyway? Ruth wondered wearily. It had all seemed so simple, until Fox had told her something that Melior had never mentioned—that the racial intolerance of elves for humans was vicious and deep. The magic-wielding elves were the overlords and the helpless humans their natural victims.

And nobody cared. Except possibly Fox, for whatever that was worth.

"Let me see what I can do for our friend," Nic said to Jausserande conciliatingly. "Why don't you go on and check in with the garrison? We'll wait for you here." Nic indicated the Harp Tavern. "He won't run."

"If he does, I will raise the hue and cry for him. My cousin is not here to sign the warrant, but I can have one in hand from the Regordane within a fortnight, and there is no one in this Domain who does not know it."

Fox opened his mouth to say something. Ruth skewered him with a glare of murderous intensity and he subsided, his face a mask of stoic denial.

Jausserande cantered off, looking regal and autocratic despite her dusty and mud-spattered state.

Nic dismounted from his horse and whistled. Ostlers came running—skidding to a stop when they caught sight of Nic's Ajax White Knight horse, then approaching more cautiously. One of them held the head of Ruth's mount while Nic hauled her out of the saddle. She clung to him for half a minute before stepping away, wincing at the protests of her sore muscles. It felt odd to be on foot again.

"Mr. Fox, if you please," Nic said, reaching for his horse's bridle.

"I'm coming," Fox snapped, his voice ragged with pain.

Ruth saw him grit his teeth, and kick his off-leg awkwardly free. He tried to swing his leg over the horse's back and failed, falling sideways out of the saddle rather than dismounting gracefully. Nic dropped the bridle, moving forward to catch Fox before he fell. He pulled him backward; Fox tried to get his feet under himself and stand—Ruth saw him make the effort—but it was more than even his stubbornness could manage. His face went whiter than before, and he fainted.

"Cracked rib," was Nic's laconic assessment a few minutes later. He'd commandeered the inn's private parlor, laying Fox out on the table and pulling up his tunic to expose the skin.

The diagnosis was rather lacking in dramatic flavor, considering the color of Fox's torso, Ruth thought. *Red and black and yellow and purple and green. . . .* It looked like a lot more than a cracked rib, and Ruth said so.

"She got in a couple of good kicks yesterday that I saw, and probably some more that I didn't. And these things seem to be a lot stronger than a man."

These things. Nic's casual categorization of the elves only depressed Ruth further. She was in love with one of "these things," wasn't she? At least, she was riding after him into almost certain death, because no matter how delusional her whimsy, she could not imagine herself and Fox—even with Saint Nic's help—defeating so much as a moderately well-equipped Girl Scout troop, let alone a monster like the one who'd carried Melior off. She shuddered at the memory.

"They are," Fox said hoarsely. Ruth saw his forehead bead with sweat at the effort speech cost him. "Stronger than a man. On the average. Do you mind? There are ladies present—or at least Ruth."

"Thank you so much," Ruth shot back promptly. It gave her an uncomfortable feeling to realize that here in this time and place, Fox—with all his social handicaps—had a strong claim to the title of being her oldest friend.

Because everyone else is dead, Ruth thought bleakly.

Nic helped Fox sit up, a process that left the outlaw sweating and shaky.

"I can strap them, but it isn't going to help very much," Nic told Fox. "Maybe you ought to let her—"

"Use magic? Hey presto, good as new—but just because one of the point-ears has a use for me. Work yourself to death on their lands, die in their wars, and see what you get. I'm not going to be anybody's showpiece."

Fox gripped the sides of the table and took as deep a breath as he dared, then pulled his tunic straight with the careful fastidiousness that reminded Ruth, once again, that somewhere beneath the skin of the outlaw leader Fox, student librarian Philip LeStrange remained. "In other words, no."

"Fox, be reasonable," Ruth pleaded. "You said yourself there wasn't any other kind of medicine than magic."

"Fuck reasonableness," Fox enunciated carefully. "I am not a reasonable man."

"All right." For some reason, Nic seemed to think Fox's position was a legitimate one. "Let's get some whiskey into you, then, before we start. It's just a good thing she didn't stick you with a knife; I don't know what we'd do with something like that if it went bad."

Fox laughed, short and shaky. "We'd *die,* Mr. Brightlaw. That's what mud-born are *for.*"

Nic had gone to see to the horses and to collect the supplies to treat Fox. Jausserande was still away. Ruth stood in the doorway of the parlor, looking out to the main room of the inn.

By good luck or some form of intuition, in choosing the inn Nic had picked the right place to wait. There were far more humans than elves in the outer room; a small party of humans probably wouldn't be bothered here, even without Jausserande hovering in the background to vouch for them.

It was daunting, Ruth realized, how quickly she had come to size up situations in terms of elves versus humans, pointed ears versus round—to see every elf as a potential threat solely on the basis of race. To see the world as Fox and Jausserande did.

It isn't right! Ruth wailed to herself. But it didn't matter if it was right, because it was fact—and to change it would be another long and bloody struggle for a land that seemed to want no more war no matter what the reason.

"I brought something for your laddie," a woman said, rousing Ruth from her reverie.

She was obviously a barmaid, wearing the short tunic over long tunic that had been the nearly universal Western European costume for a solid thousand years. She held a rope-wrapped jug in one hand and a cup in the other, and she nodded toward where Fox sat huddled in stoic misery on a bench at the corner of the room.

Ruth stood aside and let her pass.

At first Ruth thought Nic must have sent the woman with the whiskey he'd prescribed. The woman put the cup on the table and poured, then set the jug down and leaned close to offer it to Fox. His hand closed over hers to take it. They were such a perfect picture of a flirting couple that for a moment Ruth accepted the unspoken explanation unquestioningly—until she realized, with a cold pang of understanding, that broken ribs aside, Fox was the last person on earth who'd be flirting with *anyone.*

The woman straightened up and walked out. Ruth stood beside the door, almost holding her breath. Did they realize what she'd seen—and what she'd made of it?

The outlaw leader Fox. It wasn't until this moment that Ruth had really realized what that meant. Robin Hood—but not the Disney version. Fox was a hunted outlaw, a decidedly unglamorous murderer and thief. He also had a lot of support from the local humans. Hadn't he mentioned Black Bridge as a place to rendezvous when she'd been riding with him? Ruth tried to remember but wasn't sure.

But if he *had* mentioned Black Bridge, it was probably crawling with his people right now. Raven had escaped yesterday. He would have warned them. And what was more likely than that they intended to rescue their leader?

Ruth looked toward Fox, as conflicted as her absence of a soul would allow. She could help him escape and vanish into the peasantry. Nothing would happen to her if she did—at least, she was pretty sure it wouldn't. No sane person would want to stay—if Fox remained her prisoner, Jausserande would see him dead if she could. But if Fox got away, any help he could give Ruth in rescuing Melior would be lost.

"Philip—" Ruth said. Philip or Fox, and would either *persona* be willing to help her? Her voice emerged as an unsteady whisper.

Fox looked at her, his eyes flat and hostile, opaque with pain. The clay cup was in his hand. Ruth walked over to him.

"Don't do it," she said in a low voice. "Please. I need your help." The moment she'd spoken, Ruth felt ridiculous. All she was going on was her overactive imagination—wasn't she?

"You're probably thinking Mel will pardon me," Fox said, his voice slightly breathless with the effort of camouflaging his pain. He drank, emptying the cup—abstemious Philip, who once had never drunk anything stronger than Classic Coke—and shuddered. "Unfortunately, he can't. Line Floire and House Crystal—to name only a few—also have an interest in my welfare. It would take the Earl of Silver himself, and he won't. Trust me on this one. Tink wants to see me go down, and as far as Morning Lord justice is concerned, she'll get her wish."

"I need you," Ruth pleaded, though Fox had admitted nothing, certainly not an escape attempt.

He smiled mockingly. *"Moi?* I can't even save myself. Pour me another one, will you? If you want to see me suffer, just wait until Saint Nic tapes up my ribs. Tink'll love it."

Ruth refilled the cup. "If you do this for me," she said evenly, "I'll make Melior do whatever you want."

"Die?" Fox asked ingenuously.

Ruth winced inwardly, though she'd expected nothing less from Fox. "No. But I'll make him give up the Sword and leave Chandrakar—if you want me to." She was almost certain she could get Melior to do that—not abandon the Sword, not place it in danger, but pass it to someone else in Line Rohannan and come away with her.

"Swear to it, Ruthie? No matter what happens?" Fox's voice was utterly intent.

"Yes." The consequences of her promise loomed before her, unimaginably awful. Melior loved his homeland, and his guardianship of his line's Treasure was something he'd devoted half his life to. "I swear. I'll make him give up the Sword and leave Chandrakar if you come and help me rescue him."

"You've got it," Fox said promptly. "My company until you've got him back for your promise after you do. Silver and gold to seal it, air and earth to know it." He slipped the ring off his finger and held it out.

It was Melior's signet, given to Fox long ago in the World of Iron to trap Philip LeStrange into the bargain that had ended in Naomi's death. It gleamed on the palm of his hand: silvery setting and featureless oval hematite stone. Ruth took it reluctantly. She felt a faint electric shock when she touched it. *Silver and gold to seal it.* Melior had said those words to Philip once, worlds and years ago. And look where it had gotten them all . . .

"Miss Marlowe?" Nic's voice from behind her nearly made Ruth drop the ring, but it didn't matter now. She'd already accepted it—and Fox's bargain.

"Pull it tighter." Jausserande said. Her voice was cool and clinical. If there'd been the slightest trace of gloating in her voice, Ruth didn't think she'd have been able to stand it, but there was none.

"I'm not sure I can," Nic said mildly.

Fox sat on a stool in the middle of the room, a short piece of wood clenched between his teeth. The stick was not to keep Fox from screaming, Ruth had discovered, but to keep him from shattering his own teeth when he ground them together against the pain. Nic had several feet of light, six-inch-wide canvas bandage in his hands—he'd told Ruth the ostlers used it to bandage horse's legs—and he was winding it around Fox, cocooning him from armpits to hips.

"He won't be able to ride like that," Jausserande said.

"You might have thought of that before you kicked his ribs in," Nic said, and Ruth braced for an explosion; but Jausserande only laughed.

"But sweet Ceiynt! I had it in my mind to kill him then, and now I

want to keep him alive as long as possible," Jausserande explained reasonably. "Here. Don't let him fall; I'll do it."

Before Ruth or Nic could stop her—and by now Fox was past caring—Jausserande took the strip of canvas and hauled on it with all her
might. Ruth saw the tendons stand out in her neck as she pulled, and she
remembered what Nic and Fox had said about elves being stronger than
human beings. With deft brutal motions she took several turns around
Fox's torso, then dragged the bandage tight and tied it off.

"Does that hurt?" she asked, tapping—hard—at Fox's ribs.

"No more than it does when you don't," Fox said levelly, after spitting out the stick. Ruth could see the clear prints of his teeth in the wood,
a perfect half-moon on each side. He drew a deep breath and coughed.
"Lovely," he said.

Jausserande refilled the clay cup and handed it to him again. Fox
drank, moving only a little stiffly.

"I have remounts from the garrison and some supplies. You say the
trail leads east?"

"East," Ruth agreed. She turned Melior's signet stone-in on her hand
and closed her fist over it.

"Then we ride in an hour, before the mud-born here realize I have
Fox the brigand with me and start trouble. We can make the inn at
Avernet by night if the trail and the road continue to run together. Then
all that remains is to track these losel wights to their lair and make an end
to them." Jausserande looked pleased with herself.

"Has it occurred to you, Tink," Fox said with the careful overpreci-
sion of one who has had nearly a pint of brandy on an empty stomach,
"that if Mel was right and this whole Oliver Stone joyride has been set up
by Baligant No-Brainer, you are going to find more than a parcel of
rogues at our ultimate destination?"

Jausserande shrugged, and suddenly her face looked stark and old. "I
have left word for my heir. I must gain the Cup. If I do not, Line Floire
ends here."

True to Jausserande's word, an hour saw the four of them fed,
washed, regarbed, and prepared to take to the road once more on the
remounts (except for Nic) that the garrison had provided. The horse that
awaited Jausserande in the stable yard was a gleaming black mare who
seemed to have as much nervous energy as her mistress. In a bedchamber
of the inn, the scruffy elf-maid who had ridden into Black Bridge had
vanished; the lady Floire Jausserande was now dressed as befit her station, her embroidered tunic and cape and soft high boots leaving no one
in any doubt that here rode a prince of elphen. Jeweled rings glittered in

her ears, and a silver clasp with violet stones held back her silver hair. The black cap with the Ravens' enameled badge was set at a jaunty angle upon her head, and she now wore a sword gleaming at her belt.

Ruth had no idea how all these things had been arranged, but she suspected magic, and the thought made her nervous. Still, Ruth was glad enough to be leaving. She'd managed to gag down a bowl of stew, and her hair was brushed smooth and pinned back into the snood that Jausserande had returned to her. Her clothes had been made for travel; she supposed she was as comfortable as she could be under the circumstances. She brushed her hands down the green skirts of her dress— brushed and cleaned but still the dress given to her by the cat in the forest house—and tried not to borrow trouble. She'd be satisfied to get rid of some of the trouble that had already been delivered, if she could.

When she stepped out into the stable yard, the first thing Ruth was aware of was the size of the gathered crowd—unnaturally quiet and ostensibly all on business—and the number of guardsmen in half-armor who stood among them. Their four horses stood waiting, each with its attendant groom. Having nowhere else to go, Ruth walked forward and stopped. From her place by the horses, she could watch the others.

Jausserande followed Ruth out. The elphen woman's wine-colored eyes swept the crowd, and a small angry smile played about her mouth. She made as if to move forward, turning swiftly around when Fox came through the door.

Fox was now dressed as Jausserande's squire.

The amber wool tunic, buckskin trousers, and full red cloak were warmer and finer than the all-but-rags Fox had worn as an outlaw, and there were sturdy boots with golden spurs to go with the garb. Jausserande had been generous, if only to her self-image—but she'd had to rip Fox's old clothes to shreds and threaten to break the rest of his ribs before he'd wear them.

That shouting match had left Ruth with a headache that hadn't faded yet—as well as a new respect for Fox's command of the minor Elizabethan dramatists—but she understood the reason for the battle far too well. Here in Chandrakar, cloth came from the mage-driven looms of the north. Garments such as those Fox now wore marked the human who wore them as an elphen servant, less free than one of the serfs who worked the land. The serf, at least, might not see his elphen overlords from year's end to year's end and could at least pretend in his heart that he was free. Fox's fine livery was a constant and explicit reminder of his new servile status, and when he rode out of Black Bridge, every one of his supporters would see that he wore it.

Ruth wondered if that had been Jausserande's intention. Despite the elphen Treasureseeker's airy prediction that it would take hours for people to realize his identity, Ruth suspected that the only person in Black Bridge who didn't know that the outlaw Fox was here was the captain of the garrison, and Ruth wasn't sure about him. It seemed as if the entire complement of the guard patrolled the streets, keeping order in the face of a growing—and sullen—crowd of humans.

But true to his pledge to Ruth, Fox had done nothing that might be considered an escape attempt, even though Ruth had seen him speaking again to the serving-girl who had brought the brandy. His face was flushed from all the drink, but other than that Ruth could see very little difference between Fox cold sober and Fox after a bottle of brandy.

"The only difference is, Hamlet goes gay in the third act," Ruth quoted to herself out of packrat memory, the tag line of a notorious review of a performance of Hamlet featuring a famous Welsh drunkard.

Jausserande turned back toward the doorway as Fox emerged. She made a small tossing motion once he was through the doorway, and Ruth saw a glitter in the air.

"There you are, my fine brigand," Jausserande purred. "Lest you should be tempted to leave me."

Ruth heard the short ugly sound of Fox's curse. He took a half step backward, colliding with Nic. His hand was at his throat, clawing awkwardly at it as if something strangled him, and when he took his hand away Ruth could see a small pinpoint of light: a jewel gleaming against Fox's skin, bonded to it as if it were a part of it.

Fox looked down at his hand, where he must have touched the gem, and Ruth saw an expression of revulsion cross his features. Ruth's skin crawled in sympathy. She could not imagine how it would feel to have elphen magic welded to her skin, and Fox hated magic as much as she did, and with as much reason.

Jausserande's words had carried, easy to hear; Ruth could not hear what passed between Nic and Fox a moment later. But Fox squared his shoulders and walked out into the yard, head high.

None of the humans watching made a sound, but the air was as taut as a drawn bowstring. One word from Fox and there would be a riot.

Jausserande knew it. Ruth could see the knowledge of it in her face— that, and the puzzlement. Floire Jausserande of the House of the Silver Silences could not imagine any reason why the "mud-born" should resist their lawful overlords, and that frightened Ruth. Ignorance killed so many more people than simple malice.

Jausserande mounted, ignoring the crowd, and collected her mare. The animal danced and fussed, alive to the tension in the air.

Nic and Fox crossed the yard together. Fox's hair shone like flaxen silk in the harsh autumn sunlight, and beside him, Nicodemus Brightlaw looked like a warrior out of legend. He followed Fox to the horse chosen for him, and boosted him carefully into the saddle. Fox sat his saddle stiffly, gaudy as a whore in his new livery, his face completely blank. He stared straight ahead, his eyes fixed on nothing, the only color in his face two spots of red high on his cheekbones. Fury.

Nic turned to Ruth next, to help her onto her horse. Ruth clutched the reins and the front of the saddle together, the leather of her gloves squeaking on the leather of the pommel. She held her breath, willing this to be over without anything happening.

Nic mounted his magic-bright steed, so white it looked as if it stood beneath a separate sun.

Jausserande didn't bother to lead Fox's horse this time. She didn't need to. Whatever she'd done had hobbled him more effectively than all the bronze shackles in the Lands Beyond the Morning. With magic to hold him, Jausserande didn't need anything else. She wheeled her horse and started off. Fox followed.

"Miss Marlowe? After you," Nic said, and Ruth realized she'd been staring after them, her horse immobile beneath her. With some coaxing, the animal beneath her started into motion, and Nic's steed followed.

There were people all along the road; not lining it, which would have been too suspicious for the garrison to ignore, but near it.

The humans stood like a guard of honor, in silent homage to a fallen hero, and it did not take Jausserande long to realize that this was what they were doing. There was nothing she could do, however, but pretend she didn't recognize it for what it was.

It took the four riders a very long time to reach a place where none of Chandrakar's humans waited to watch the passing of the outlaw Fox.

· 5 ·

Full Moon and MTV

"GO BACK *WHERE?*" Holly demanded. Rosinante—fifteen years old and a *good* little car, Holly assured it fervently—rocked and skidded as she took the curve of the on-ramp a little too fast.

"Back to where I came from," Mac said. "It is a place north of here some leagues—"

"I know where it is," Holly said. *So you've decided to remember where you came from, have you? And you want to go back there?* "It's a place called Half Moon Psychiatric, about two hours upstate. I wasn't exactly going there, Mac, honey, but—"

"I think I must go there," Mac said. "There are . . . things which are mine. I think I may have brought them with me into your land. They may be there."

Or they may be gone—or never have existed at all, Holly couldn't help thinking. "Well, let's go there, then," Holly said unwillingly.

Holly supposed that Rook must have a last name somewhere. The mailbox down by the road said "Saunders," but Holly didn't pay much attention to that, knowing that Rook was an A. A. Milne fan. In the Society for Creative Anachronism, of course, he was Sir Rook of Outremere, but you couldn't exactly put that on a driver's license.

What she did know was that Rook was her friend.

Rook lived in the town of Half Moon at the northern end of Patroon County—about ten miles, as it happened, from Half Moon Psychiatric Center—on a parcel of land that bore a strong resemblance to landfill but was actually, he'd once told her grandly, a rural slum. Rook lived in a trailer that was a few amenities shy of a Certificate of Occupancy, and, in addition to being a jack-of-many-trades, he bred (as he put it) "fine Rottweilers for home and office use." There was a covered run and a shed out behind the trailer.

Holly gave a deep sigh of relief as she pulled into the long drive and saw that the lights were on in Rook's trailer. The snow had gotten steadily heavier and lengthened her driving time; it was closer to eleven at night than to ten when she arrived, and the last two miles on this back road had been a treacherous business, with snow piling up on the road and not a plow in sight. Mac, exhausted, had fallen asleep near the Westchester border, and Holly hadn't had the heart to wake him, even though she would have enjoyed the company.

The Honda proceeded grandly and silently—and without much concession to traction—over the surface of Rook's snow-packed dirt driveway and toward the waiting woodpile. Patroon County believed that plowing was for sissies.

As Holly feathered the brake, coaxing the car to a stop, half a dozen muscular black-and-tan dogs boiled out of cover in the runs behind the trailer and began to bark.

"We're here," Holly said to Mac, as he began to stir. She unbelted first him, then herself, and got out of the car.

It was colder here than it had been in Westchester. The sky was an all-devouring black, and the snow was an endless white pattern in the white beams of the security spots around the trailer. Holly shivered in her jacket and wished she'd thought to put on some of the long underwear she'd packed for the camping event next weekend.

Rook came to the doorway, a dark-skinned football-player-sized man holding a short leash with a large Rottie at the end of it in his hand.

"Rook?" Holly called.

"Lady Fee!" Rook said, sounding pleased. "Who's your friend?"

"It's a long story," Holly (aka Lady Fiametta of the Danelaw) said.

". . . so things were getting enormously bizarre at the con, and I couldn't think of anywhere else to go," Holly finished apologetically.

The hefty stoneware mug looked small and fragile cradled in Rook's fingers. Curls of steam eddied up from the depths of the cup, and Rook gazed down as if he were going to find his answers in a cup of Stop'n'Shop Special Drip Grind.

Holly was not quite certain what instinct had brought her here. In the SCA, Rook had been her squire before he'd received his A.O.A. (he'd joined later than she had, and new fighters often began as a more experienced fighter's squire), and though now a knight, he was still a member of her household. But so were a number of other people in the tristate area, and Holly hadn't gone to any of them.

The three of them were grouped around Rook's tiny kitchen table, in the front of the narrow trailer. Joletta, the Rottie bitch, was back in her box in the corner with her new litter, but she watched Holly closely, mild suspicion on her blunt, intelligent face. Whatever built-ins it had originally possessed had been ripped out long ago in order to accommodate Rook's spartan refit. Banners—including the big hand-painted one for House Churnadryne that made it to Pennsic every year—and painted shields hung on the walls, duct-taped rattan swords were stacked in corners, and pieces of armor and pieces of junk were accumulated in specious orderliness.

"Margot didn't think I ought to go home, and anyway my roommates both know I'm going to be gone for a week. They've probably already rented my room." Holly grinned.

Rook grinned back at her, his dark skin shining in the feeble electric light. "Since there's no place like this place anywhere around this place, this must be the place," Rook said. "You did right to come up here, Fee. Ain't nobody going to bother you two here." He nodded toward Mac, who regarded him in an open, innocent, friendly—if sleepy—fashion. Now that he'd removed the watch cap, his butter-yellow hair stood up like the peaks in a bowl of meringue. His pupils were narrow ovals in the dim kitchen light.

Holly released a breath she hadn't known she was holding. And Rook hadn't said a word about Mac's ears, either, though she was certain he had noticed them. But Rook was the type who saw a lot and said little. Holly knew she could trust him.

"I need to go back inside the hospital," Mac said to Rook and Holly both. "There will have been some sort of warrant, to place me there. I need to see it, to find out what else they know of me."

"Are you sure you want to do that, friend?" Rook rumbled in his deep voice. "You're talking about Half Moon, right—over there across Shakykill Creek? There's a lot of bad stuff going on in there. Weird bad stuff."

"What kind of stuff?" Holly asked. Rook wasn't prone to exaggeration.

"Choppers. There's a sound you never forget. Flying in and out, real late at night—and you tell me what use is a loony bin going to have for an air force? And, oh, just a few too many city types underfoot, you know what I mean? There's some kind of hoodoo going on up there, Fee."

"Yeah," Holly said unhappily.

"So," asked Rook, "when are we going in?"

" 'We'?" Holly echoed, startled. "Rook, all I'm looking for here is a place to crash where nobody's likely to find me. I don't—"

"Don't treat me like a mundane, Fee," Rook said. "Your buddy didn't just walk off the set of *Star Trek: The Elfquest Years*, did he? And now you want to just go waltzing into Half Moon, and I've already told you it's gone over to the Dark Side of the Force. So whatever you're planning to do, you're going to need help."

Holly looked at Rook helplessly. She'd never expected anything like this. Rook had been supposed to stay here, safe, and let her and Mac chase their troubles around in circles.

Rook smiled, watching her face. "I'm forty. You don't know what that means, do you, Fee? I'll tell you. I'm a child of the sixties, in that ghastly phrase. And, you know, I can't be the only one who thinks we sold out, gave up, got tricked into surrendering when we might have been able to win—ideals, promises, the last gasp of Camelot and all that; we were going to change the world, you know, and overthrow all the bad old tropes of the Age of Capricorn and make sure everyone got a fair shake. We were going to bring happiness back into the world. Might *for* right, don't you see?

"But somehow the years went by and it got to be too much trouble, and each of us decided we were the one the Movement wouldn't miss. So in the middle of the night we stole away, one by one, and left King Arthur to face Mordred all alone. And now we look back on the ruins of that shining city, and we want it all back, because we've lived in the world we vowed to destroy and it isn't very pretty.

"But we're locked out of Camelot now, because that chance comes only once if ever at all, and what haunts some of us is how close we came to having the only thing that ever mattered and then threw it away because it was too much trouble to fight for," Rook said softly. "So when you get a chance to do something right, you do it—not because it's right, or because you even think any more that it's going to make any difference, but to sort of pretend to yourself that you really could have done the right thing back when it would have mattered."

Holly didn't know what to say. She glanced toward Mac and found him watching Rook with his wide, strange eyes.

"If you want a fight, Sir Rook, I fear one will be easy to provide. But a victory . . ."

"Taking on a fight you can win is for wimps," Rook told him, and smiled.

An hour later Rook's battered old pickup ghosted onto the Half Moon grounds. The hospital was a turn-of-the-century building executed—and Holly used the term advisedly—in institutional red brick, a legacy from the time when society's answer to the problem of the mentally ill and "developmentally challenged" had been to hide them as far away from "normal" people as possible.

It was close to midnight, and the snow—still falling heavily—gave everything a spectral, insulated quality, as if nothing were quite real.

"Are you sure you know what to do?" Rook asked again.

"Relax," Holly answered. "I almost worked here once." And it was true that one sanitarium was much like another not only in the way it was laid out but in the way the people inside acted.

"Well, I'll take the truck down by the Shakykill and wait. I showed you the place; there's a spot where you can get under the fence there to hook up with me again."

"Right," Holly said, but most of her mind was already on the task ahead.

"Locked," Holly said in disappointment. She rattled the door latch to the staff entrance again.

Holly and Mac had left their winter coats in the car. In a battered blue cardigan over her nursing whites—Holly blessed the packrat instinct that had led her to bring *everything* to HeliCon—she looked as if she fit right in, and dressed as he was, Mac could pass as anything from a resident to a doctor.

Holly looked at the doorbell beside the door dubiously. She'd hoped it would still be open, but at 11:45-and-change, the 11 to 7 staff was already on station, and it looked as though they weren't expecting anyone to be late. If she rang, someone would be almost sure to let them in—but that might raise more questions than she could handle.

"Let me," Mac said. He put his hand on the doorknob and pulled. For a moment light seemed to shine out through the coarse knit of the Spiderman gloves, then the door opened.

"It must just have been stuck," Holly said doubtfully. Mac smiled. They walked in.

Business as usual. First Floor: Administration, Admitting, and Cafeteria. Patients: Left, Right, and Up. Basement: Laundry. And—at this hour—nobody in sight. At midnight there was only a skeleton staff anyway: no doctors and very few nurses.

"Anything look familiar yet?" Holly asked Mac in a low voice.

For a place where—so Rook said—maximum hoodoo was going on, the building was surprisingly insecure, in the sense that neither Mac nor Holly saw anyone at all on the first floor.

"Not yet," Mac said warily. If she hadn't felt that they needed to move fast, Holly would have given Mac a day or two's rest before trying this. He was frail, exhausted, and the drugs he'd been given were still working their way through his system.

But if they'd waited, Holly suspected it might have been too late.

"Is this too easy?" she asked Mac. He shrugged.

By now they'd walked through the building from the back to the front. The decor had altered markedly, from scarred linoleum and gas-chamber green walls to parquet marble and wood paneling—battered and underloved but as explicit as a sign that said *Here There Be Doctors.*

"There," Mac said, and pointed.

The brass plate on the door said *Eudora Egan-Light, M.D., Supervising Director,* and there was no way on Earth that a door with a sign like that on it was going to be unlocked.

Well, what did you expect? Holly asked herself. She looked around. She'd been hoping for a secretarial desk she could rifle; the pink-collar brigade usually kept a spare set of their boss's keys.

"Come on, Holly," Mac said.

Mac was standing in the open doorway of Egan-Light's office, beckoning her in. Holly felt the hairs rise up on the back of her neck. That door *had* to have been locked. She'd swear it. Elves were one thing—mystic powers were something else entirely, and Holly didn't think she was ready for them.

On the other hand, she hadn't tried the door herself, had she? Holly followed Mac into the office.

The room was indistinctly lit by light coming in from outside, and Holly carefully did not turn on the lights. They'd have to make do with the small flashlight in her pocket; what they were doing here was illegal by any rubber yardstick, and she'd just as soon not have to try to explain it to police, security, or a certifying board.

"Is there anything else you'd like to unlock while we're here?" Holly asked, looking around. Like every other shrink's office she'd seen, this one had a treatment couch, a comfy chair, a desk, some file cabinets, and a wall of bookshelves. What it did not have was any real look of belonging to somebody. She glanced at the wall beside the door. No diplomas or other certificates. Well, some doctors didn't display them. Holly went over to the shelves. There was a rattle as Mac opened the file cabinet. The files inside looked normal from what Holly could see of them.

A thought occurred to her suddenly.

"Mac, honey, what name were you admitted under?"

Mac looked toward her, and Holly flinched back involuntarily. His eyes shone like a cat's in the dim light—unmistakably alien.

Buck up, Holly. You knew he wasn't from around here anyway.

Mac looked apologetic. "I don't know, Holly. I don't remember. But this is the woman who questioned me with iron and fire. That I know."

"Great," Holly muttered. She came over to stare into the file drawer. As if willing to resign that part of the investigation to her, Mac moved to the desk.

"If I don't know what file to look for," Holly asked Mac, "why are we here?"

"We seek the *Book of Airts*. They wanted me to read it for their enlightenment—how, if it is not in their hands?"

"Did you ever see it?" Holly asked.

"It must be here," Mac said with weary stubbornness.

Welcome to the Home Delusion Shopping Channel, Holly thought sourly. She began paging uselessly through the files, having little else to do. Holly thought there was something not quite right about the case files she was looking through, although she couldn't put her finger on what it was. But they did contain photographs of the subjects, so Holly thought she had a good chance of finding Mac if he was in here. She pulled one out at random and began to skim it.

She wasn't sure what they were doing in the Chief Shrink's office, anyway; while it was probably too much to hope for that Mac's things were in his room, the personal effects he'd had when he'd been admitted must be stored here somewhere in the building—but what *name* were they stored under? The more tangled up she got in this mess, the less Holly believed that she was going to get straight answers any time soon.

She's prescribing enough Thorazine to stop a charging rhinoceros, and I've never even heard of some of these other things. And what's "Protocol 2 Therapy"? Holly stared at the Treatment Record. Whatever it was, Holly suspected she wouldn't like it. She put the file back and reached for another.

"Holly." Mac's voice was filled with suppressed excitement. "I've found them."

She turned away from the files. Mac stood behind Dr. Egan-Light's desk. All the drawers hung open. He was holding something small in his hands—a pair of eyeglasses. Holly came over to him and took them from his hand. The frames seemed to be made of lead, or of some soft silvery metal she'd never seen before. The lenses were rectangular, of antique glass, not even optical glass: green and bubbled and ripply with an oil-slick iridescence on the surface.

Holly stared into them, puzzled. *Maybe some kind of knickknack? They can't be for wearing.*

"They are not for looking in," Mac said, watching her. "They are for looking Out."

He put them on. The lenses flashed and shimmered, glowing like moonstones.

"What—?" Holly began.

There was an interruption in the light.

They'd left the venetian blinds at the windows open—the windows were the only source of light and Holly hadn't wanted to change anything. The security floodlights streamed through, zebra-striping the room in projected shadows.

But now the shadows had changed. Someone was walking outside, silhoutted against the lights. Holly saw a snow-obscured shadow, the long outline of a rifle barrel. If they were heading where she thought they were, they'd reach the front door in seconds.

"C'mon, Mac, we've got to get out of here."

"But, Holly, I must find—"

"Not now," Holly cut him off. "We've got to get out of here, unless you don't want to leave at all."

"Miss? Miss? Could you come back here, Miss?" The voice that called after them was courteous, nonthreatening—and terrifying. Another few seconds and they would have been bottled up in the office. Holly fled, dragging Mac behind her.

She heard a sound—a *loud* sound, nothing like what movies and television had taught her to expect—and her estimate of the importance and dangerousness of what she and Mac were doing here skyrocketed upward. The guard was shooting at them!

Another shadow on the wall made Holly veer away from the staff entrance, heart hammering. Not only were these guys better armed and with more security than Holly'd ever seen, there were more of them, and they were smart.

"Come on!" Holly gasped, veering toward the door marked "Laundry."

The two of them clattered down a flight of metal stairs. Holly could hear Mac's whistling gasps behind her, and she knew he didn't have the stamina to make this a chase, even if she had faith that they could outrun a bullet. She shoved open the door at the bottom of the stairs, breathing a fervent prayer.

It was answered. There was a light still burning in the vaulting basement and, even better, a loading chute at the far end of the room.

Like most small hospitals, Half Moon did only some of its own laundry, farming out the majority of it to a commercial linen service. The outgoing bags and incoming parcels had to load and unload somewhere. Here. In the basement. The laundry chute.

Their detour wouldn't fool the pursuers for long. Holly grabbed Mac and bullied him ahead of her, toward the shining silver tube—and safety.

"Get up that," she panted, "and open the doors on the other side."

"But, Holly—" Mac began. She didn't listen. She shoved him into the tube's gaping maw and climbed in after him.

Her shoes squeaked on the sides of tube, and her shoulders very nearly didn't fit. Mac was slenderer but not in as good condition. He ended up almost sitting on her shoulder as Holly pushed both of them higher into the tube.

"It *burns,*" Mac whimpered.

All the lights in the room outside went on. Holly froze, holding her breath and praying Mac would do the same. His words made no sense— nothing was burning. The metal walls of the chute were cool.

She heard squeaking sounds as the canvas carts full of laundry were shoved aside, hard-soled footsteps echoing across the cement floor. The air was heavy with the smells of disinfectant and bleach, and Holly wondered with a kind of detached horror whether she was going to sneeze.

There was some more banging and clattering, the audible evidence of a rough search, and over those noises Holly heard the hiss and blurt of a walkie-talkie. This was like no hospital security she'd ever heard of.

Finally the light went out, and Holly heard the door boom closed, but the paranoia educated by a thousand hours of movies held her still. What if that guy wasn't gone? What if he was standing down there in the dark, waiting for them to betray themselves.

As the seconds lengthened into minutes, Holly realized they could wait forever, wondering. They had to chance it.

"Mac?" she whispered.

"Yes," he said, sounding breathless. He shifted position, and for a moment she was supporting his entire weight.

"Can you open the hatch?" She'd been counting on that, Holly realized. She didn't really believe that the file cabinets or the desk—or for that matter, the office door and the staff entrance—had all been unlocked before they'd gotten here. What she believed was that Mac could open doors.

"It's dark in here," he complained, and a moment later it wasn't. A faint silvery light seemed to emanate from Mac's body, hovering over his skin and clothes like silvery fog. He looked down; Holly looked up.

"You can do that and you can't remember your name?" Holly asked skeptically. For some reason he didn't frighten her—but if she had to choose between being frightened of Mac or of those smooth, falsely polite voices with guns, she knew which she'd pick.

"They weren't asking me to do this. They *were* asking me my name," Mac said, a faint chiding note in his voice.

Great. Amnesia on demand.

"The hatch?" *They're going to figure out that we have to be down here sooner or later. If they take a good look around outside, they're sure to find Rook. The truck's wheels are going to show up real good in snow, and they'll know just how we came in. Oh, why didn't I think of that sooner?*

"The portal is locked," Mac reported a moment later. "And it is iron," he added chidingly.

"I know that," Holly answered, with what she personally thought was commendable patience. "Can you unlock it?"

"Not exactly," Mac's voice was puzzled. "The door is *iron*, Holly."

Whatever that meant.

"Oh, damn." Holly had never felt more like crying. They were trapped, and somehow she didn't think they were looking at a scolding here, or even a simple arrest.

"Holly?" Mac's voice interrupted her spiraling fear. "I can open this portal, but if I do what I must to clear it, there will be a lot of noise. And afterward I will have nothing left to me. I will not be able to . . . unlock anything any more."

"Ever?" Holly asked, although part of her mind could not imagine why she was choosing now to have this conversation.

"Maybe." Mac sounded despondent.

"I think you'd better do it anyway," Holly said gently. *And then all we have to do is outrun them, get to the trunk, and get away without becoming a statistic.*

"All right," Mac said. "Hold on."

There was a pause.

She thought she heard the door to the basement open again, but she wasn't sure. Mac's glow went out, and then everything blew up.

Or rather, *out.*

There was a sort of fizzy flash, a tingling, tearing push and a roar like a thunderclap, and suddenly there was a waft of cold air skirling down the tube. Holly set her shoulder into Mac's rump and pushed. Far in the distance, there was a loud bang as the metal storm doors returned to earth.

Mac sprawled full-length on the ground and Holly climbed out over him. Freedom had never felt so good, even if it was only a temporary situation.

She looked around, standing over Mac and taking her bearings. Peace, and quiet—and a field of virgin snow across which their tracks would show like arrows pointing "This Way To The Wabbit."

There was no choice.

"Come on, Mac."

Holly hauled him to his feet. She could feel his slender body trembling with exhaustion in every limb. She didn't think he was going to make it more than a few yards, but they didn't have any choice but to try.

In the end, it was the snow itself that saved them. When Mac fell, Holly simply dragged him. Her elphen companion slid over the few inches of December snowfall with all the grace of a bag of wet laundry, but she could move him.

Holly told herself that this wasn't as bad as going jogging in full armor. She told herself she was grateful to be able to run away at all, grateful for whatever mental glitch or operational oversight it was that had led to the two of them *not* being followed on snowmobiles by men toting high-powered rifles.

Their progress was pitifully slow. Halfway to sanctuary, Holly dragged Mac behind an ornamental stand of evergreen bushes and flopped to her knees, panting. She knew it was less than ten minutes since they'd climbed out of the laundry chute, but the time seemed to stretch and turn back on itself as in a nightmare.

"Why aren't they following us?" Holly asked, as soon as she had enough air to talk.

"They're afraid of me." Mac, though exhausted, still sounded very pleased with himself. "Even if they know which way we're going, they're afraid I'll do something like that again."

"But you can't," Holly said.

"Holly, I'm too far from home," Mac said plaintively—whatever that meant. "I am at their mercy now."

"Not while I'm alive," Holly said grimly. At least Mac seemed to be right about the pursuers being afraid. They were probably waiting for orders as well because, though Holly saw a lot of flashlights in the distance, nobody seemed to be coming their way. Yet.

"This is not how I'd planned to spend Friday night," Holly muttered. Melting snow soaked through her clothes, and she was feeling colder by the minute.

Off in the distance to her right lay the sprawling Victorian Gothic pile of Half Moon Psychiatric. Ahead and to her left there was nothing but endless vistas of golf-course-short snow-covered lawn sloping slowly down to the Shakykill, dotted with stands of pines and stands of birches and impossible to cross unseen. The falling blowing snow made the visibility poor, cutting it back to only a few yards. The fresh snow might even be covering their tracks, but Holly wasn't willing to bet on that.

Mac squeezed her hand and Holly forced a smile. *I hope tonight was worth it, Mac, honey, 'cause I've got a feeling it was real expensive.* If she'd had the brains Goddess gave a TNG Trekkie, she'd have planned this better in the first place. "Ready to go?" she asked.

Mac smiled sardonically and shoved himself to his hands and knees. "Ready," he said evenly.

They ran again, falling and sliding in the clinging, wet snow. The fence and the river seemed farther away than ever, and in her heart Holly began to worry that even if they reached it, Rook wouldn't be there, that he'd been captured or simply wandered off.

They stopped to breathe again, Mac clinging to Holly for support. Even through both their layers of clothes she could feel the triphammer beating of his heart and knew that the next time he fell, he wouldn't get up.

That was when she heard it. A wailing on the wind, its source too far off to see, but brutally apparent. It rose and fell like sirens but had an all too-mortal source, and Holly shuddered with atavistic fear.

Dogs. They'd set dogs on them.

"Come *on*, Mac," Holly said. She pushed him ahead of her, breaking into a shuffling run.

The howling of the dogs galvanized them both; Holly found energy she hadn't known she had left, and Mac kept to the pace she set. The farther they got from the hospital's security lights, the darker everything got, until they were running through a featureless arctic gloom. She couldn't even hear the dogs behind them any more, though she knew they were there.

She ran into the fence before she saw it, slamming into it and dislodging a shower of precariously clinging snow.

"Mac?" Holly said.

Rook had said the gap in the fence was impossible to miss, right behind the hospital, but Holly didn't see it and she didn't know how far south of the building they'd veered as they'd run. "Mac?" she said again.

"I don't . . . want to do . . . that again . . . Holly," Mac gasped, his voice faint.

Holly clung to the fence with burning, cold-numbed fingers and thought she'd give anything if only she could just rest. "Not much farther," she heard herself say. She began feeling her way along the fence.

They'd been closer to it than she'd known. The snow had drifted up to conceal it, but the weight of her feet made the snow disguising the furrow's downward slope give way, and Holly nearly slid right through.

"Yah," she said comprehensively, dragging herself back up onto firmer ground. Her Reeboks were full of snow now, and she couldn't feel her toes.

"Here?" Mac asked hoarsely.

"You first," Holly said. Mac dropped to his knees and slid through, feet first.

Holly looked around but could see nothing through the shifting veils of snow. She followed Mac.

In spring flood time, the Shakykill might easily reach its banks and beyond. In December, the stream was a thin, fast-running icy trickle down the center of its bed, trying to make up its mind to freeze. Holly slid down the bank and found herself sitting in a drift of leaves too frozen to be muddy. It was pitch dark in the riverbed, and the footing was treacherous; she groped in her pockets for her flashlight and found she'd lost it somewhere behind them.

"Mac?" whispered Holly.

There was a faint rustle off to her right. "Here," Mac whispered.

Groping through the dark, Holly found Mac and lifted him to his feet. Stupid, to try this *Mission: Impossible* stunt with a man barely better than an invalid. They were both going to pay for that now.

With grim determination, Holly got them across the trickle of creek. Her feet got thoroughly wet and throbbed with a burning cold that warned Holly she'd better get them dry and warm Real Soon Now unless she wanted to spend the rest of her days in the Society known as Fiametta Ninetoes. Then she stood facing the snow-dusted curve of frozen mud and realized that the top of the crest might as well be on the moon—she had no reserves left.

"Outremere Taxi Service," Rook said from the bank above her.

"So what exactly did we accomplish here tonight?" Rook asked.

An hour later, the three of them were sitting in an all-night diner on Route 111, about half an hour away from Half Moon. Holly was wearing a dry pair of hutboots and felt much better after a steak, a milkshake, and a large slab of apple pie. And Mac looked as though he'd reconsidered everything and decided to live.

"Show him the glasses, Mac," Holly suggested.

Mac rummaged around in his down vest and retrieved the odd glasses that he'd taken from Dr. Egan-Light's desk. With only a little reluctance, he handed them to Rook.

"And these are yours?" Rook asked.

"He says they're for looking Out," Holly offered.

Rook put them on. His dark eyes looked curiously distorted through the bubbly lenses.

There was a long pause.

"Holly?" Rook said in a strange voice. "I can see . . ." he pulled them off, "wondrous things," he finished. He offered them back to Mac.

Holly pounced on them and put them on, closing her eyes as she did so. Despite the fact that Rook had just worn them, the metal was cool and heavy against the bridge of her nose, pressing down with more weight than she really thought a pair of glasses ought to have. She looked around.

The inside of the diner was brightly lit, a standard-issue monument to chrome and formica and pseudo fifties tackiness, but that wasn't what Holly saw.

Through the glasses, Holly saw a vast darkness broken only by a faint tracery of colored lines. They seemed to warp and bend off toward some vague horizon, meaningful and meaningless all at once.

She looked down.

She'd been playing with the menu that came with their booth: desserts on one side, dinner specials on the other. Despite the fact that the diner wasn't there, she could still see it, and all the information it contained—and more—slammed into her mind all at once.

The blue-plate steak was reconstituted from meatscraps and blood-glue. It was microwaved and fried, not grilled; the grill-marks were painted on. The lettuce in the Caesar Salad was shipped from Argentina, where they were still spraying the crops with DDT; the hard-boiled eggs were sliced from a reconstituted hard-boiled-egg-loaf that had MSG and stabilizers added. The base for the salad dressing was corn syrup—

Holly jerked the glasses off. They tumbled toward the tabletop. Mac caught them and tucked them away, regarding her severely. Holly stared at him wild-eyed.

" 'Looking Out'?" she demanded. She looked down at the menu in her hand. Caesar Salad. London Broil Special.

She was just as glad she hadn't read as far as the meat loaf.

"For looking Out," Mac said. "They are to read the *Book of Airts* with—or any other book, truly, but that book most of all."

"This is getting too weird for me," Holly said. She looked toward Rook. He shrugged and looked back at Mac.

"So where did you say this book was?" Rook asked.

"I don't know," Mac said seriously. "But I will once I read this."

From another pocket in his vest, Mac extracted a slim black book with the word "ADDRESSES" stamped on the cover in gold.

· 6 ·

All Along the
Watchtowers

THE NEXT MORNING was Saturday, and the three of them gathered around Rook's kitchen table to plan their strategy.

Rook was cooking breakfast: A dozen eggs and a pound of bacon shared an enormous skillet while a pan of quickbread browned in the stove. The weather had broken; this morning the sky was a crystalline blue, and the temperature hovered near zero. The reflection of the sun off the snow was blinding; when Holly had gotten up earlier, the unsullied surface had been a smooth, unbroken expanse, without even last night's tire tracks to mark it. Holly had been obscurely comforted, even though she knew that the Men in Black must have more hi-tech ways of tracking them than simply following tire tracks to Rook's home address. And now they were planning to carry the war to the enemy again.

Rook slid bacon and eggs onto a plate, placed it in front of Holly, and then did the same for Mac. He took a cautious bite. A night's sleep had done more to restore him than Holly would have expected, but she hoped they could keep all future felonies to the low-stress kind.

"How do you like Earth food?" Rook asked.

"Better than hospital food," Mac said, and Rook laughed.

"How long were you there at Half Moon, Mac?" Holly asked. They were placing an awful lot of trust in Mac and his silly little glasses, she thought moodily—even if she had seen them work.

"Long enough," Mac said, reaching for a piece of the quickbread and drizzling honey on it. "I remember the last few months, but before that, if there was a before . . ." Mac shrugged helplessly.

"Why *you?*" Rook asked, sitting down and reaching for his fork. "Why should those guys be going after you—what have you done?"

"I don't think they have guaranteed access to . . . us," Mac said, his voice flattening as another gap in his memory appeared. "It is not what I did, Rook, but what I am—none of their blood can read the *Book of Airts.*"

"So what's this book, that they're so hot-and-bothered about reading it?" Rook asked. "You wouldn't think it, would you, the way literacy's going in this country?"

Mac looked from Holly to Rook, his face expressionless.

"My feelings," Rook announced, "are going to be really hurt if you don't trust us on this one, my friend."

Mac sighed, seeming to give in all at once. "The *Book of Airts* is the Regalia Catalog, describing each of the Twelve Treasures of Chandrakar and the protocol for the Kingmaking. With the *Book of Airts,* the Chief Archivist can discover the location of all the Treasures. Who holds them is not supposed to be a secret, but in these dark times . . ."

"What dark times, Mac?" Holly asked gently.

"Since the war," Mac answered, as if they ought to know. "Since the earls and the barons rose up to contend for the white hand of Hermonicet the Fair and for the throne."

"There are Seven Great Houses of the Twilight," Mac began, "all of which together rule Chandrakar. As we rule over the Men of our land, so does a High King rule over us.

"But Rainouart died, and once his funeral boat was set upon the bosom of the wave, it was time to say who from among the Seven Houses would be High King thereafter, for Rainouart had left behind him no heir, nor made provision for one."

"That was stupid," Holly said. Mac bowed his head in acknowledgment.

"Yet the Sons of the Morning and the Daughters of the Evening Star do not die in the time and season of Men, and it may be that Rainouart thought he had more time to make his choice. He was a quiet man, and thoughtful, and perhaps he should not have been King at all." Mac sighed and put his head in his hands. "He was my friend."

"But what about the war?" Rook asked. "And what does that have to do with this book, or what's going on over at Half Moon?"

"Rook, my friend, I do not know," Mac said. "I would have said it is none of the Last World's concern, for the succession concerns only Chandrakar, and the Morning Lands have no ties with the World of Iron. Yet those of your blood do seem to meddle in the affairs of our world."

"Acquit me," Rook drawled. Mac shrugged.

"The war, then. The High King was dead, and Chandrakar must have another. At Harvest the Twilight Court met to choose one of their number to ascend to the throne. At first it seemed that the succession might be settled with reasoned council—"

"Yeah," said Rook, bitterly. "And we'll all be home by Christmas."

Mac laughed sharply in agreement. "There was a woman, a lady among the Houses. Her name was Hermonicet, who was the most beautiful lady born to the Houses of the Twilight in the memory of elphen or the reckoning of bards. Her father had betrothed her when she was only a child to a Lord of the Marches, who lived in wild solitude at the very edge of the sea. That her father was wise and kind the Morning Lords only knew later. Then, they knew that the Marchlord, her husband, had lately died, and so the Lady Hermonicet was free to remarry how she would. And she sent to the Court to say that she would marry none but the next High King."

"That's right," Holly muttered. "It's always a woman's fault."

"Had she but announced her choice a month later," Mac said, "I would have no quarrel with her, for the new King would have been made, and the others would merely have grumbled. But she spoke, and the Lords Temporal tarried not one moment more over their deliberations, but each went forth to arm and to raise his troops and to prosecute his claim above all others. And there was such war as lasted a handful of Men's generations."

"So who won?" Holly asked, when it became apparent that Mac had reached the end of his story.

"No one. But after so long, those who survived were willing to compromise on a High King no one theretofore had thought of, whom no one likes. But we have peace."

"Typical," Rook muttered.

"But all the Treasures were lost in the war?" Holly asked, "And only this *Book of Airts* knows where they are?"

"I do not know that," Mac said. "But I know that the Children of Earth are not the custodians I would choose for the power that binds my Chandrakar into being. And so I must take back the book if I may, and destroy it if I may not."

Which explained, Holly supposed, what she was doing twelve hours later crouched in the back of a pickup truck with her sword and wearing her armor, tootling down the road to a former IBM office building located in the geometric center of nowhere.

Her armor rattled slightly as she turned her head. She might have been cold if any part of her had really been exposed to the midnight clear, but Holly Kendal was in full hand-forged fourteenth-century tournament plate, with Lady Fantasy III strapped to her hip. After the previous night's adventures, Holly had wanted to take precautions, and those were the only precautions she had.

"Why am I going there in full armor? Because it's stupid. And the cops won't stop me, and a sword isn't illegal to carry. But, Mac, honey, my armor's 90-gauge sheet steel lined in Kevlar, and Lady Fantasy III is thirteen pounds of carbon steel and every inch of her is sharp. I can cut their guns to pieces before they realize I'm trouble."

Besides, anyone who saw her would probably think he was hallucinating, which was all Holly asked out of life if she was committing her second burglary in two days.

Since IBM's pullout from the valley at the end of the eighties, thousands of square feet of office space had gone begging, and the building whose lot they pulled into was a prime example. "For Sale or Rent" signs were prominently displayed in most of the upper windows, and if not for Mac's glasses and Dr. Egan-Light's purloined address book, Holly would have thought the building was completely deserted.

The truck drifted to a stop. Mac's elphen door-unlocking powers might be gone, but Rook had spent the afternoon drilling him with a ring of skeleton keys from who knew where until Mac could be pretty sure of opening any door they were likely to find.

And get the book—assuming it's here. And then what? Holly, these are crimes you're committing here; they've got comeback. You just took Mac's side without giving it another thought—what if it's the other guys who are in the right?

But they weren't. Holly didn't care what anybody said—she'd seen the marks on Mac's body, and that was enough for her. The good guys didn't torture people.

Rook came around and let down the tailgate. Holly hopped out, fairly nimbly considering her articulated steel jammies. She skidded a little in the snow before she compensated for her higher center of gravity. Stephen Mallison had made her armor—it and Lady Fantasy together had cost her over a year's wages—and it was as flexible as a fine machine. This perfection, however, fell several degrees short of the flexibility of the human body, and it always took her a few moments to get used to wearing it again.

Mac approached from the passenger side door. He looked oddly normal, all things considered. In hopes of preparing an insanity defense beforehand, Mac was wearing SCA garb, and from his soft knee-length deerskin boots to the dark blue knee-length tunic belted in tightly and covered with an only slightly tattered purple velvet cloak clasped with a copper penannular brooch, he looked as if he'd been born wearing it.

The pair of us look as if we'd gotten lost on the way to a renfaire.

"You ought to let me do it," Rook said again.

"You don't have any armor that'll stop a bullet," Holly said reasonably. "And it was my idea—I should be the one to break the law."

"Ever heard of 'accessory before the fact'?" Rook asked sardonically. Holly shrugged as well as she could in the armor.

"Don't wait up. If you hear anything, Rook—*anything*—you get out of here. We'll take our chances. These people are dangerous."

"Fee, why won't you ever listen to your own good advice?" Rook asked the sky. He patted her on the shoulder; his class ring clanked against her armor. "See you in a few."

Holly waved. Rook got back in his truck, and Mac started toward the door. Holly followed.

The outside door of the building opened easily, and then the inside door. Holly followed Mac. She hadn't asked how reading that address book with his glasses had allowed him to find this place; to be truthful, she didn't want to hear the explanation. If so many weird things were possible, then how could anyone know what was impossible any more?

The lobby was the usual corporate horror of plastic fake-wood paneling, tired beige carpet, and plastic plants in baskets. Holly looked around, nervously clutching the pommel of her sword as if an archaic piece of steel could actually be any help in the current situation.

"Up there." Mac pointed. Holly looked around. There was a stairwell. She followed him up. The armor moved like a part of her now, its presence forgotten.

The second floor was like the first, only darker, but this time they had a flashlight with them. Mac shined it around.

"What are you looking for?" Holly whispered.

"The right door," Mac said.

Figures.

Mac found the door he wanted and began trying keys. Holly looked over his shoulder. The plate on the door identified what was behind it as WHOLE EARTH TRANSPORT SYSTEMS, LTD., which was nice and vague, for Holly's money.

This is too easy, why do I feel like this is too easy . . . ?

Mac got the door open.

The office behind the door was almost anticlimactic. Mac's flashlight beam danced over stark utilitarian walls and closed office doors, looking much like any other. Holly wasn't sure what she'd expected—CIA agents in robes and pointy hats? Wiseguys with magic wands and Uzis?—but it wasn't this.

Holly wandered over to the receptionist's desk. What did somebody who worked for someplace called Whole Earth Transport Systems do all day?

"Holly." Mac's voice was strained with excitement. She followed the sound.

What did I expect? I expected something like this, some idiot part of her mind babbled numbly.

She stood beside Mac in the doorway of a room that belonged in a Lucasberg movie, not here. The room was a small one, about fifteen feet square, and the floor was hard and shiny enough to be the black glass it so much resembled. Around the edge of the room there were seven of the largest quartz points Holly had ever seen—each about the size of a two-drawer file cabinet—arranged in a horseshoe shape; at first Holly thought the lines in the floor were reflections, but then she realized that somehow there were lines embedded deep below the surface of the floor, forming a shape not quite a star that hung suspended in the black glass.

In the center of the room, on a perfectly ordinary Levenger's cherrywood dictionary stand, stood what was almost certainly the *Book of Airts.* It was bound in a violet leather so dark as to be nearly black. There was an elaborate symbol stamped upon its face in gold, and there were metal clasps encircling the book, their twin hasps secured by tiny silver locks. If a book could be said to look smug, this one did. There was something almost trite about its appearance.

"Is that it?" Holly said in a whisper—as if there were any other possibility. Mac nodded.

"They can't get it open, can they?" she inquired next.

"No. Only the Royal Librarian or the Chief Archivist can open the Catalog."

Holly looked sideways at Mac. He wasn't her idea of a librarian, but then, *Carol* was a librarian, so you couldn't always tell.

"And you're it," she said. "So go on, get it and let's get out of here."

"I can't," Mac said. He gestured at the room. "It's *protected,* Holly, can't you see?"

"No," Holly said, looking at the room, and then: "By a bunch of rocks?"

"They serve as a reservoir for the power that has been called to ward the Book. I fear someone was killed to provide it—and should either of us try to cross that barrier, our lives will surely add to it."

"So we just leave?" Holly said.

"Well, I think you ought to just walk on in," a new voice said.

The lights went on.

Holly was certain her heart stopped beating completely; she felt it clench into a hard painful knot in her chest and refuse to move. It was the hardest thing she'd ever done to turn in the direction of the voice.

"Cute costumes, kids, but you're a few months too late for Halloween." The gun in his hand did not waver.

The man didn't look as if he were much older than his midtwenties, and even in the middle of all this, Holly felt a moment's pang of relief that it wasn't the gray man from HeliCon. The young gunman was wearing a dark suit, mirror shades, and thin black leather gloves. His black hair was slicked straight back, and he had the sort of pallor that people who spend a lot of time in front of computers get.

"Nice to see you again, Makindeor. You're not going to make any trouble for us, are you?"

Holly knew this was the moment for the heroine of the piece—her by default—to make stirring speeches and possibly even fight back, but all she could do was stare down the barrel of the gun with a sort of horrified obsessive fascination, as if it were actually something interesting.

"If you wanted the Book, all you had to do was ask. We'd have been happy to give it to you any time." The gun in his hand did not waver.

Holly was not completely sure where it was pointing—at Mac or at her—but either one was bad.

"I will not read it for you." Mac's voice was low but determined.

"Come now, Makindeor. You don't *really* want to convince us of that, do you? You wouldn't be a lot of use to us if that were true, you know. Now step over here. I've got some business to finish up with Joan of Arc here."

"You can't get away with this," Holly said. Her voice quavered, and the words were not what she'd have chosen for an epitaph, but they were all she could think of.

The gunman smiled.

And fired.

The impact knocked her backward into the room; an impact as abrupt and powerful as a car crash. Holly was flung off her feet. She fell, helpless and dazed, and hit the gap between the crystal points.

There was a flashbulb pop and a flare of stark blue light, a stench of ozone thick enough to send the heart staggering into danger rhythm and a sizzling frying sound. If being shot was like a car crash, then what followed was like being struck by lightning.

And she wasn't dead. Every cell in her body ached with unexpended adrenaline, and she was lit up like the billboard in Times Square; but she was not dead. Time seemed to slow to a crawl. The lethal magic raced over the surface of her armor, shorting itself out harmlessly. Holly saw the gunman bring his weapon into position again. This time he would aim for her face, and her visor was open. There was no Kevlar to protect her eyes.

Holly did not think about what she did next. The gunman's downward aiming motion echoed an overhand sword cut and Holly reacted without thought. Lady Fantasy cleared her scabbard with a tearing sound, as she rose to her feet.

Step. Her blade swept up, hitting his hand. The gun flashed as it fired and missed, but Holly didn't hear the sound. She was doing what she'd trained for on a thousand summer afternoons.

Disengage. Step. Step. *Cut.*

At the last instant she realized what she was doing and its cost; she screamed as Lady Fantasy sheared down, razor edge and irresistible power, into the trapezius muscles between neck and shoulder. With a rattan sword on padded steel or leather the blow would have rocked back, but now it sliced down through clothing and meat and bone, cutting deep into collarbone and spine.

Shock or training kept Holly's hands on the sword as the blood from the gunman's wound sprayed the room in arcs, fountaining one—two— three—with the spasms of the dying heart. Then he fell, with the limp irrevocable sound of death, the injury in his neck gaping open, showing white flecks of bone and the bubbling multicolored cartilage of the neck. *No. Please, no.*

Holly stared down at the body, unable to let go of her sword even now. He'd bled to death in seconds. With all her nurses' training, there was nothing she could have done. *I killed him. I murdered him.*

There was blood on her armor, blood on her face, blood spreading in a stinking puddle beneath the dead body—a smell familiar from a thousand accident scenes, a thousand dismembered fatalities, but this one was different. This one Holly had caused.

She felt nausea rising in her throat as the mechanism of shock took over. Cold and sick and dizzy, still clutching Lady Fantasy, Holly stepped away from the body, feeling a black and reckless exultation rising through her veins. Nothing could be worse than this. There was nowhere lower for her to sink.

"Holly. *Holly.*"

She turned toward the sound of Mac's voice. *Makindeor.* That was what the man with the gun had called him. She'd been close after all.

"I killed him," Holly said. There was blood on her face; she could feel it when she spoke. She raised her hand to brush it away, and jumped when her gauntlet—an intricately jointed mechanism of small plates that she'd used to think was pretty—brushed against her visor, pushing it back down. She tried to push the bail back again but couldn't manage it one-handed. *My sword. I have to clean her; she'll rust. . . .*

"Holly," Mac said again.

This time she turned around.

Mac was standing in the middle of the room, the *Book of Airts* in his hands. The quartz terminals around the room's edge were crazed and blackened; a couple of them were shattered, and Holly wondered for an instant what had happened. Then she guessed.

My armor. Like putting a penny in the fuse box. The charge had run harmlessly through the steel of her armor, leaving her unscathed, and grounding the power.

"Holly, look at this! The Cloak is *here*—in the World of Iron," Mac said.

"I *killed* him," Holly said.

Mac set the book aside and came over to her, hovering close, as though he yearned to touch her but didn't dare. "Never before?" he asked. There was a mixture of bafflement and incredulity in his voice.

"I'm a *nurse,*" Holly said, as if it were an explanation. "I don't kill people."

"Then this . . . ?" Mac said, indicating her sword and armor.

"It was for play," Holly whispered through a throat that was aching and tight. "It was all a game."

And no matter how hard she'd hit and been hit in the lists, with the marshals standing by to judge each blow's fairness, winners and losers had all been alive, able to drink and laugh together later.

"Holly." Carefully Mac walked around her until she was looking at him. "This is no game. He would have killed you and taken me back to his torture chamber. You saved my life and your own."

Holly closed her eyes. "I killed him," she repeated numbly. Nothing else could be as important as that horror.

"Holly!" Mac's face was very close to her own. "Do you know what it is to beg for freedom? To have your tormentors laugh as they inflict such agony as I have no words to describe—to be burned alive over and over by a fire that leaves no mark behind? I would gladly have slain him myself to keep from returning to that place. He came here armed—he meant to have your life. He was no innocent, Holly. He tried to kill you—look."

Mac's fingertips hovered over the breastplate of her armor. Holly looked down, lowering her chin with difficulty. If she strained, she could look down at her armored chest and see the three bright silvery smudges in a close grouping over her heart, where three soft-nosed lead dumdums had been stopped by sheet steel and Kevlar.

Any one of them could have killed her.

A coldness more profound than shock slid through Holly's veins. She'd worn her SCA armor almost as a joke, but if she hadn't, her life would have ended here tonight.

Holly took a deep breath. "Okay, Mac. I'm okay. Let's—"

There was a blurt of static; a radio's open line. Holly spun around.

"Red Rover, cross over. Over." There was a walkie-talkie lying on the rug in a spreading pool of blood; the gunman must have been carrying it. *"Red Rover, Red Rover—"*

"Two of them," Holly said dully. Whoever was on the radio was going to come looking for Red Rover pretty soon. He might already be on his way. She looked down at the sword in her hand. She couldn't go through that twice.

And then the thought came that banished every other thought like a blow to the heart: *Rook is down there.*

"Come on," Holly said sharply. Lady Fantasy was a featherweight in her hand as she strode toward the door.

Mac caught up with her seconds later, the *Book of Airts* cradled in his arms as if it were a child. Holly barely noticed him as she strode back up the hall, out through the door, and into the hall beyond. *We should have turned the office lights off,* Holly thought a moment later, but it was already too late. They were already on the first floor, almost home free, the front door and safety already in sight.

"You first," Holly said, pushing Mac toward the door.

"Why?" he asked, though he took a willing step forward.

"Because they won't shoot you," Holly said, her face beneath the helmet stretched in a wolfish death's-head grin. But there was no one in the parking lot when Mac stepped out through the door with Holly close behind him.

While they'd been inside, the night sky had clouded up again. Fresh snow fell with a faint hissing sound, like pouring sugar, the swirling flakes making the parking lot lights into white speckled cones like transporter beams. Except for the tire tracks from the pickup, the asphalt was covered with two to four inches of pristine white.

The truck itself was nowhere in sight.

"We're screwed," Holly muttered.

Mac was turning—to ask her the same unanswerable question: where was their ride?—when Holly saw his expression change. She swung around to face what he was looking toward, her steel sabatons skidding in the snow.

She saw a man who could have been the slain gunman's twin: He wore a Langley topcoat and mirror shades even in the snowy dark. There was a walkie-talkie in his gloved hand, and for one brief fatal moment all his attention was concentrated on that.

Holly raised her sword and felt a wild recklessness well up from somewhere inside her. She took a deep breath and emitted the blood-curdling howl she'd once learned from a fighter in an "Atenveldt by the Grace of God" T-shirt, moving forward as she did. It worked in Patroon County as well as it had at Second Manassas; the MIB dropped his radio and took a hesitant step away from her—then ran.

Holly stared after him, uncertainly triumphant. There was the sound of an engine behind her, the crunch of tires on snow. Holly pivoted again, raising her sword, determined to sell their lives dearly.

"Hi, guys, did you—Christ, Holly, what happened to you?" Rook said.

The three of them had driven back to Rook's trailer through elaborate back-way routes that took them halfway around the county. Rook had a police-band scanner mounted under his dashboard, but all it picked up was the normal Sheriff's Department chatter of a slow December night. Even so, they'd done the last two miles on a dirt road Holly wasn't sure was there at all, bumping along slowly with the lights out and the windows rolled down to catch any sound.

"This is too easy," Rook pronounced as they coasted slowly toward the trailer a little while later. A part of Holly could only agree; someone should have noticed what she'd done and followed them. Where were the police? Every time Holly closed her eyes, she saw the dead man and relived the horrible moment of glee that she'd felt just before she'd killed him. She couldn't bear the memory of that moment when she'd been stripped bare of all inhibitions and restraints—and what she'd done with that freedom.

The truck rolled to a stop. They were here.

"Too easy?" Holly said bitterly. "That all depends, doesn't it, on your definition of easy?" She climbed out of the truck and went up the steps of the trailer, following Rook inside.

Joletta came padding across the floor to greet them. She stopped, smelling the strange smells on Holly, and lifted her lip. Rook went over to soothe her and then snapped a short lead on the animal's collar.

"I'm going to take her out for a quick one and then get Gabriel in here. We might need some backup."

Holly crossed the room to lay her unsheathed sword on the kitchen table. The red blood had dried to a dark burgundy smear, but looking at it still made Holly's stomach hurt.

"From where I sit, it hasn't been easy at all," Holly said, lost in her own thoughts. She jerked off her gauntlets and started pulling at the straps on her helm. Mac sat on the battered couch on the other side of the room, head thrown back and eyes closed. It reminded Holly how frail his health really was.

"Rook, help me uncase," she said when he came back in. Joletta was still on her lead and now Gabriel was nosing helpfully along behind. Rook snapped his fingers and pointed, and both dogs went to lie down.

With Rook's help, Holly was soon free of the elaborate weight of armor. Blood had soaked through the shoulder seam to stain the padding and T-shirt beneath, and her chest ached where she'd been shot. She pulled the neck of her T-shirt away and saw a livid wine-colored blotch bigger than her hand just over her heart: the painful forerunner of a really spectacular bruise. She drew a deep breath. It hurt enough to make her wonder if her ribs were cracked, though she knew they probably weren't.

"My, my, my, my. What a mess," Rook said, holding up her chest plate and peering at it. "I can see we've got our work cut out for us."

"Leave it," Holly said. The exhaustion of shock made her words come out in a mumble; it seemed like too much of an effort even to move, but she had to at least clean her sword before falling facedown onto the nearest mattress.

Rook put down the chest piece and headed toward the stove.

"Holly, Rook, we needs must conceal this Treasure," Mac— *Makindeor,* Holly mentally corrected herself—said. He was holding the Book in his arms, his face grave.

"Okay, we'll do that," Rook said. He put the teakettle on one of the burners and began taking down canisters of sugar, tea, and cookies from the cabinet. "Holly, you have to eat something," he said firmly.

"Yeah," Holly said. *Hot sweet liquids, first aid for shock.* "Boil me some Coca-Cola, would you?"

Rook snorted. *"Holly,"* Mac repeated. "This is important."

Important enough to cost a man his life and get everyone I know in trouble, Holly thought to herself bleakly. *Everyone I know . . .*

"Can't you just take it home with you?" Rook asked. "You know— back to Elfland?" The kettle began to steam; he poured boiling water into mugs and glared at it impatiently, waiting for the tea to steep.

"Find a Gate?" Mac said. "Oh, yes—if I had an ephemeris that showed one or a few weeks to take the measurements to find one myself. But I do not—we must hide this *now*, before the Ironworld villains who held me in thrall come to lay hands on all of us again. I was not certain before that they knew what they had, but now that I have seen the arcane safeguards they laid upon it, I know they did. And with the possession of the Catalog, can they only unriddle it, the Children of Earth can achieve all of the Treasures, no matter where they bide."

"Burn it," Rook suggested. "Drink this, Holly." He thrust a mug of dark tea, thickly sweetened with cream and sugar, into Holly's hands. "And put on a sweater or something, okay? Your lips are turning blue."

"Go ahead and try," Mac said to Rook, talking across the other conversation. He tossed the book to Holly's former squire, an expression of bleak amusement on his weary fine-drawn features.

Rook lit the stove again and boldly held the Book over the burners. The blue propane flames played over the leather and the edges of the pages without affecting them at all.

"It is *magic*," Mac said simply. "In a sense it is also part of Chandrakar's magic; it cannot be destroyed in the World of Iron because in some sense it is not here."

"But not, heaven knows, in any sense that counts," Holly muttered.

"So we've got to hide it," Rook finished for him.

"Yes." Mac took the Book back and opened it.

Holly drank down her tea in one scalding gulp and held the mug out for more. Rook handed her a second mug and the tin of cookies. Holly cradled them awkwardly to her bosom—sore, with the ache spreading across all the muscles of her chest and shoulders and back—and went to sit down at the table. She felt the sugar in the first cup of sweet tea hit her like a jolt of adrenaline.

"So where would you hide a book, Mac?" Holly asked. A book important enough to cost a man his life and get everyone she knew in trouble. *Everyone I know* . . .

"I'm not sure," Mac began, his voice slightly distracted as he opened the *Book of Airts* and began to look through it, searching for something he didn't want to tell the others about.

"In a room full of other books, of course," Holly said, a faint note of smugness in her voice. "There's got to be a—" she broke off as a thought occurred to her, and when she resumed speaking it was in a different tone entirely.

"Mac . . . ?" Holly said, her tone worried.

Makindeor looked at her. He'd put on the odd glasses; she could see his eyes, amber and green, distorted by their uneven lenses.

"My friends—" She didn't want to ask, didn't want to know, but the vivid memory of the gun pointing at her with lethal intent told Holly Kendal that this was a question she had to have the true answer to. "They came looking for you at the convention and they're still there. Are my friends going to be in trouble?"

"At the convention," Mac echoed, as if he hadn't heard a word she'd said. "Holly, one of the Twelve Treasures of Chandrakar is at your convention—or very near it. We have to get to it before the others find it."

· 7 ·

Waltzing with Dreamers

THE FOUR OF them rode until long after dark to reach Avernet, and by the time they got there, Ruth was too tired to know whether Melior's pain drew her on or whether it was just inertia.

Almost before they were off the horses, Jausserande was calling for hot baths, and liniment, and other things for Fox's comfort. She vanished into the inn, dragging Fox after her with a remorseless efficiency. Ruth was left behind, staring at Nic, baffled and uneasy. Jausserande *hated* Fox. What new kind of malice was this solicitousness?

"I wouldn't worry, Miss Marlowe. She isn't likely to hurt him. Some of the hill warlords were like that about their prisoners; it's a matter of face, more than anything else."

"The hill warlords *where?*" Ruth asked suspiciously. Nicodemus Brightlaw had changed since he'd vanished outside the Goblin Market, and Ruth wasn't sure she liked it.

He shot her a startled look. Though Nic had a good ten years on Ruth—midforties at least—for a moment he looked very young. Young and almost frightened.

"Upcountry," he answered, briefly and obliquely. "Come along, Miss Marlowe, we'd better get inside." With inflexible courtesy, he dismounted and helped her from her horse, ushering her forward.

The inn was much like others that Ruth had seen—she was becoming quite a connoisseur of Inns Beyond the Morning—and it seemed that Jausserande had found time to give orders for her and Nic's comfort as well. The table by the fire was waiting for them, complete with a fat, round, and anxious man who could only be the landlord hovering beside it.

"Where's Fox?" Ruth asked in a tight voice, before realizing that it probably wasn't a good idea to be asking after one of the more notorious outlaws in Chandrakar in a public room. "What has she done with him?"

"The lady's squire—" The innkeeper hurried up to them, Ruth thought ungraciously, just as if they were elves. "The lady has gone to put him to bed. She has bespoken rooms, dinner, a table by the fire—" The little man gestured.

"I don't suppose there's any beer?" Nic inquired hopefully.

There *was* beer, as it turned out, but from the expression on his face Nic didn't think much of it. Nevertheless, he'd drained one tankardful and was working on a second by the time Jausserande returned. Ruth had been served wine; she stared at the untouched cup on the table in front of her as if it were a personal enemy.

Somewhere during the time they'd been waiting, Jausserande had taken the time to remove her cloak and gauntlets and wash the travel dust from her face. In the dimness of the inn room Jausserande sparkled like a killing engine fashioned of fine silver and white gold. She looked at Ruth, her expression one of distant courtesy.

"We ride at dawn tomorrow, if it suits you, mortal Ruth," she said.

The frustration, fear, and disappointment of the last several days boiled up all at once, and Ruth spoke before she thought:

"What do you care what suits me? All you've done since we've gotten here is push me around; and the way you treat Philip—Fox—I don't care what he's done, he's—"

Cat-quick, Jausserande had closed the space between them; her hand on Ruth's wrist was a crushingly painful grip.

"Hold your tongue, you mud-born fool; do you wish to advertise our business to the world?"

The bruising pressure did not relax until Ruth was seated once more, but still Jausserande did not release her grip.

"You do not care what Fox has done and mark me as the villain? Then it will not trouble you to hear all the round tale, madam—it makes a pretty hearing. I shall tell you of Fox.

"Once I had a squire, a likely lad in arms. He was the son of one of my commanders who could no longer fight; she had married into House Crystal, a cadet line whose founder had cast off his place in the succession to tend the books of the late king. The boy I speak of was named Gauvain Guiraut, and I would have made him knight next year at Midsummer.

"He was . . . young," Jausserande said. A puzzled note had crept into her voice, as if she had never understood Guiraut's youth and now never would. "He was begotten in the last years of the war, but he knew nothing of it. The war did not strike deeply into Canton Crystal; it was possible to live there and see nothing of it, especially if one were a child. And the New Peace was declared before he could bear arms, so his mother sent him to me so that I might lesson him gently in the knightly arts." She looked toward Ruth; in the dim inn room the pupils of Jausserande's elphen eyes glowed a baleful silver.

"He is dead now. A child, not yet a warrior, his body meat for the rooks and swine, slain in his place at my side as I rode seeking the Cup. Slain . . . by Fox."

Ruth had gone pale during this slow recitation, somehow anticipating the conclusion to Jausserande's tale. But she still shook her head in automatic denial. Killed? No. Not Fox. Not *Philip*. She looked beseechingly at Nic. He was listening, a statue-stillness about him.

"Guiraut took a dart meant for me—an arrow through the throat," Jausserande continued grimly, "and that is generally considered a fatal wound. But I could not stop to see, nor avenge him, nor even recover his body for proper sending forth, because I must flee to save myself—because I was Cupbearer.

"You do not understand what it means to be Cupbearer, do you, Child of Earth? Baligant rises toward his throne, and I must present the Cup of Morning Shadows at the Kingmaking or I and all my Line will be banished beyond Chandrakar's borders—the aged, cripples, the sick, sucking babes and all, cast out to die. There are many who will use that moment to avenge old injuries upon my Line, though we were all commanded by our Houses to set aside vendettas in the New Peace."

Jausserande's voice was deadly even. She had no need for dramatics when she told a story such as this one. She spoke with the weary patience of one who reports inevitable disaster.

"Am I making myself clear, Rohannan's leman? All those of my Line will die, do I not present the Cup next Harvest Fair. And knowing all that you do now, in the Vale of Stars, Fox took it from me, as he took my squire's life—for foolishness and mud-born pride, and his sense of petty grievance. Your pretty comrade owes a greater debt than he can ever repay."

There was perfect and profound silence when Jausserande had finished speaking, and Ruth felt the borrowed fire of her own emotions gutter awkwardly into darkness once more.

"You can't hurt him," Ruth said lamely.

"I can do with him as I wish," Jausserande said flatly. "I hold the Low Justice and Rohannan the High. I may do with Fox as I choose and do no other than he has purchased with his own madness—but only after he is of no other use to me. He has said that the Cup of Morning Shadows which Floire bears may be with Rohannan's Treasure, the Sword of Maiden's Tears, and you are wizard-spelled to lead us to that. Do I achieve the Sword and find that the Cup is not—"

Jausserande covered her face with her hand, and for a moment Ruth almost thought that the elphen maid was going to cry.

"—then I will see what magics I may buy to tell me where else I can search in the time left to me. And I will slay any who troubles my path," Jausserande finished.

And I made him promise to stay with me—and once Jausserande roped him in with magic, he didn't have any choice. Oh, Fox—

Jausserande pushed herself away from the table and strode to the back of the taproom, calling for wine in a harsh crow's voice.

"Dammit," Ruth said inadequately. It wasn't fair. Jausserande's idea of justice was enough to revolt any sane person, but Ruth couldn't quite bring herself to say (even if only to herself) that it was all right for Fox to have killed someone. If only the stakes weren't so high—without the presence of the Cup at Baligant's accession ceremony, several hundred people would die. Ruth looked at Nic.

"At least now you know where she's coming from," Nic said neutrally. His antique slang was another jarring note in a universe where everything seemed out of place. Ruth closed her eyes and felt even more like crying.

"We know where she's coming from, all right," Ruth said tiredly. "The basement of Gilles de Rais. But what about you? What's your story?"

"You know, I thought we'd get around to this. Are you sure you don't want to leave it alone?" Nic asked, still in those same calm, uninvolved tones.

"No," Ruth said doggedly. "I mean yes." She still felt bludgeoned by the emotional force of Jausserande's speech; she picked up her wine cup and drank its contents down, slugging back the rich, bitter stuff as though it were water. When it was empty, Ruth wiped her mouth and shuddered.

"Eat first," Nic advised. "It's a tragedy of a sort, and all tragedies are boring, even one's own." He raised a hand in a signal; one of the servants approached cautiously and was gifted with the information that the travelers wanted their dinner delivered without delay.

"Yes, good master, of course," the man said. "Instantly." The servant fled before they could ask him to do anything else.

"That means at least half an hour," Nic said. "So while we wait, you

can go see if the nice elf-lady was being forthcoming with us about our
friend Fox's accommodations."

His whereabouts were no secret. Fox was in a ground-floor room at
the back of the inn, and Ruth tracked him down easily. She opened the
door and walked inside, ducking her head to clear the low doorway. The
room was redolent of the strong scent of liniment.

Fox was lying on what was probably one of the finer available beds.
From the piles of gear lying around the room, Jausserande expected to
sleep here, too, though Ruth couldn't see where, unless she shared Fox's
bed. And that was a concept that ought, by right, to appall them both
equally.

The room was lit not by candles but by a small glass-sided lantern
that contained a glowing blue ball. Ruth picked it up and looked at it. The
tiny globe of silvery-blue light seemed just to hang reasonlessly in the
middle of the lantern.

"S'matter, Ruth, don't you believe in fairies?"

Ruth looked toward the bed again. Fox reclined beneath a blanket, if
not at his ease, then at least not in obvious pain. He wasn't wearing
Jausserande's livery now, but he was still swathed in mummy-bandages at
least as far as the edge of the coverlet.

"It's elflight," Fox explained, as if it were something Ruth ought to
know. "Cheaper and longer-lasting than candles, but it lacks ambience,
don't you think?"

"Are you all right?" Ruth asked awkwardly. "Did she hurt you?"

Fox smiled. He looked very tired, and the remains of the boy that
Ruth had known were nearly gone from his face. This man was all but a
stranger, and the chasm of memory was an unbridgeable gap.

And, looking at Fox, the concept entered Ruth's mind with a painful
longing: *I want to grow up, too.* To grow, to change, to *be*—no longer
trapped in the emotions and expectations of the eighteen-year-old girl
she had once been. To *change.*

"No more than necessary," Fox said, answering her. "I'm fine,
Ruthie-Ruth. She needs me alive and you happy. Come and sit down.
Have some wine."

"I've already had some wine," Ruth said, hearing her voice slur with
the effect of it. She came and sat down beside Fox on the bed, not even
bothering to resent the hated nickname.

On the table beside Fox's bed there was a clay jug and a battered tin
mug, obviously the local elphen equivalent of a Dixie cup.

"Sorry there's only one cup," he said. "And you'll have to pour."

"That's all right," Ruth said, "I've brought a spare." She pulled the footed pot-metal cup she'd gleaned from the Goblin Market out of her belt-pouch and filled both it and the tin mug with wine.

"Visit scenic Elfland, home of the closet alcoholic," Ruth said, drinking. Either Fox had gotten a better quality of wine than they served in the common room or her taste buds had died; it didn't taste quite as ghastly this time.

"It's better than having to deal with the local reality sober," Fox said lightly. "So what can I do for you—or is this really a tender inquiry into the treatment of political prisoners in Elfland?"

"Jausserande said—" Ruth paused to take another fortifying drink. "Jausserande said you killed somebody."

"Her squire," Fox answered without hesitation. "She told me his name, but I've forgotten it, sorry."

"Why?" Ruth said, almost wailing. "If—" *If all this is about revenge for Naomi, because you think Melior killed her, then why kill someone else? It isn't—*

"Oh, Ruthie. Disabuse yourself of the notion that all this is about fairness. It's about war," Fox said.

"It's about revenge," Ruth said.

"No," Fox said flatly. "It isn't. So Naomi's dead, young and unfair and all the rest of it: It happens all the time, and do you see everyone else heading off for Elfland to off some guy? This is for more than that. Mel wasn't the cause, Ruthie, he was the last straw. The ends do not justify the means. The means *are* the end; that's the great secret of the twentieth century—you really can't get there from here. So if I disapprove of the means, all I can do is punish the end."

"But Jausserande's squire wasn't even *there,*" Ruth said. "He had nothing to do with Melior, with Naomi, with *anything!*"

"I want your elf-boyfriend to rot in hell," Fox said flatly, as if he were finally too exhausted to deceive her, "but I'd settle for making his entire life useless. Naomi died because Melior thought that magic was more valuable than human life. But if I devalue magic, that changes."

"You can't do that by killing children," Ruth said stubbornly. "That boy you killed? His name was Guiraut. He was a child—Jausserande said he was younger than she was; and she's not that old," Ruth added, still hoping for something that sounded like remorse.

"I'm sorry he was in the wrong place, if that helps. I'm not sorry I killed him. For the record, Tink is seventeen," Fox said levelly. "Her squire was fourteen at a close guess. And if you want to discuss relative injustice in Chandrakar, I can bury you in cases. Raven's wife, for example. He was a blacksmith. That's a skilled trade here; he made enough money to buy Dowsel off her father's land so she could come and live with him in town. He even paid enough to get a real Morning Lord doctor—an Adept of the Low Magic—to come and use hoodoo when their last kid was born, which was the only reason Dowsel lived through it. They lost the baby, though; don't ever confuse an elphen healer with someone who actually knows as much basic anatomy as a first-year medical student. And for all that, Raven might as well have saved his money because a month later a pack of point-ears came around looking for a little fun and took her off with them while Raven was down at the forge. By the time Raven found her, she was already dead, and I'm sure I can leave the rest to your overactive imagination.

"So he buried her in an unmarked grave somewhere out there because after the Adept he didn't have the money to have her cremated like all good Children of Earth are when they die. And he went to the magistrate of his district and laid his complaint like a good serf. When the Morning Lords involved were found—and they were found, Ruth, the police here aren't stupid—their leader said that Dowsel'd asked to go with them, and for all the rest, too. A woman still in bed trying to put her insides back together after having just about bled to death a few weeks before. So Raven hit him. Strategy's never been his strength.

"The magistrates branded Raven on the cheek for assaulting a Morning Lord and dismissed the charges he was trying to bring and told him to go home and shut up, and by the time Raven got back to his village there was nothing left—his kids were gone and everything he had was trashed, and three guesses who by? There's a million stories in the Naked Forest, Ruthie, and they're all just like that one, so don't come bleating to me about poor innocent elfy-welfs. The point-ears deserve to suffer."

"It's funny," Ruth said in a small tight voice, getting to her feet, "but Jausserande said the same thing about you."

She didn't think she could stand much more self-actualization tonight from any of her traveling companions. From Fox's room Ruth went outside, unable to face Nic. Dinner was the last thing she wanted, especially followed by whatever horror story Nic was holding in reserve.

Ruth wandered aimlessly around the inn yard and stables until she found a place where nobody else would bother her—half a bench, its broken end propped up with stones, sandwiched in between the back of the stable and the trees beyond.

Chandrakar seemed to have a lot of trees. A gently rural feudal sort of a place. *"A greenery-yallery, Grosvenor Gallery, foot-in-the-grave young man!"* Ruth's packrat mind echoed, but *Patience* was not her strong suit.

It was only after she'd sat on the bench for half an hour in the autumn dark that she realized that Fox had never answered her question at all. He said this was war. But whose war, and why was Fox involved? *He* was the one who'd killed Jausserande's squire, not Raven. He wanted *Melior* to suffer; he'd said so, and that vendetta at least had some faint vestige of logic about it, but where did Jausserande come into it. Why take on everyone in the entire kingdom?

None of this makes any sense, Ruth thought with mournful weariness—except for the fact that once his usefulness to their quest was ended, Jausserande would surely have Fox tried for murder and executed in some grand guignol fashion. *If she even bothers to do what passes for due process here,* Ruth thought bleakly. And why should she? As someone once said: "Power delights, and absolute power is absolutely delightful." Why should Jausserande be more generous than a human in her place would be?

Ruth had nearly managed to work herself all the way into a flat black depression when Nic finally found her. He carried a bundle of cold chicken and bread wrapped in a napkin, and this echo of the first day they'd spent together Beyond the Morning made Ruth feel something like a faint discomfiting tangle of mixed grief and panic.

"Here you are," Nic said. "I started without you, I'm afraid, but I saved you some. If you'd like to eat out here, be my guest, but you really ought to come back inside; you'll freeze out here, you know. It's too cold for grand gestures."

"I don't care," Ruth said mulishly, turning away from him. "I wish Jausserande *had* killed Fox back there in the woods; everything would be so much neater. Which side am I supposed to be on now? Fox is my friend—he *was*—but he killed that boy—Jausserande's squire—he told me he did, and—" Ruth broke off, swallowing hard. She had no reason to think Nic wanted to listen to her problems, even if he'd indicated a willingness to tell her his. "And I don't know what to think," Ruth said in a low voice. "I don't know what to think about anything at all."

"People die in war," Nic Brightlaw said austerely. "Their war isn't over here yet; they just don't know it. There've been—" he stopped. Ruth looked at him.

"I would say there've probably been too many betrayals for it to be over just because somebody declares peace and gets out," Nic finished, as carefully as if he were walking around land mines.

"Let's declare victory and get out." Someone had said that somewhere a long time ago, before Ruth had been born.

"You said you'd tell me why you're here," Ruth said slowly. She didn't want to know, especially after talking to Fox, but knowledge was power, especially here, and she might need Nic's information desperately sooner than she thought. "About what happened to you? Where you got that uniform you're wearing? I'm sorry I dragged you into all this; I'm not even sure how you got here—I don't know how you're going to get home, and it isn't very safe here, really—"

She was babbling, Ruth realized, exhaustion and alcohol taking their mortal toll at last. But Nic didn't seem to notice; with a courteous hand beneath her elbow, he levered her to her feet and walked her back inside.

Ruth saw Jausserande sitting in a corner of the inn room as she and Nic walked in. The room was thinly populated with individuals who looked as if they asked nothing more than to be allowed to mind their own business; Jausserande seemed to have that effect on everyone in Chadrakar but Fox. Nic walked Ruth past all of them, into a smaller room concealed behind sliding wooden doors. He pulled them shut behind him.

The room was lit by fat candles burning in pewter dishes and heated by a small brick stove; shutters were half-pulled across a row of tiny-paned windows. There was a bench built into the wall beneath the windows, a table, a chair, and a stool: an empty and intimate room, a room meant for conspiracies and treasons.

There, Nic bullied Ruth until she'd eaten the bread and chicken. He stuck to beer—the innkeeper came in and refilled his tankard while Ruth ate—but ordered more wine to be brought for Ruth, this time cut with hot water and sweetened until it reminded Ruth of the wine coolers you could buy in any grocery store back on Earth: a sort of alcoholic soda pop. But she felt better after she'd eaten and drunk—and worse.

Worse, because no matter how hard she tried to believe in her own fantasy, Ruth could not imagine how the four of them were going to rescue Melior from any kind of durance more formidable than a two-car garage. And in trying to rescue Rohannan Melior of the House of the Silver Silences, they were—so Fox had said, so Melior had implied— going up against no less an enemy than Eirdois Baligant, the future High King of Chandrakar, and his tame wizard.

"What are you thinking?" Nic asked her. He was sitting in the chair at his ease, looking like the "Cat Who Walked By Himself," his feet stretched out toward the heat of the stove.

"I'm thinking that we're all going to die," Ruth said, surprised into honesty.

Nic laughed, a short mirthless bark, and sat up straighter in his chair. "Probably. But Lady Jausserande has a certain obligation in that regard and it's a better deal for Fox than he'd get otherwise. I don't have anything better to do, and that just leaves you, Miss Marlowe."

"What about the Ryerson Memorial Library?" Ruth asked, and was rewarded—if that was the word—by a brief return of the haunted blankness to Nic's face.

"You don't remember it any more, do you?" she accused hotly. "What's going on here—why—?"

"I made a bargain," Nic said. "It might not be a good one, but it's the one I made. There was this dragon—well, a firedrake, he said he was." Nic shrugged. "I'm twenty-four."

Ruth stared at him. Nic Brightlaw was no twentysomething-year-old; he was a good decade older than she was at the very least. She shook her head, not understanding what he was saying.

"My life: I signed up when I was eighteen for a two-year hitch; went over for my first tour in '71. The war was starting to wind down then; in Geneva they were arguing about the shape of the conference table, and I bet you were wearing braces on your teeth. I don't remember anything after 1975."

It took Ruth a moment to understand what he'd said, and it still didn't make sense. "After 1975? How can that—? How can you—?"

"I told you, I met this dragon. He bought . . . my *time,* he called it. I sold my memories, my experiences, for a horse, and weapons, and transportation to wherever you were, Miss Marlowe. After what we'd already run into, I thought you could use the help."

Ruth thought about the brigands and the warwasp and the monster that had snatched Melior from the High Road and flown off with him. It was true: She needed all the help she could get. But . . .

"For me?" Ruth asked. "You did it for me?"

"You were in trouble," Nic said. "That much had already been made abundantly clear by a rather changeable lady I ran into a little earlier. Don't look so appalled, Miss Marlowe—it wasn't that much of a sacrifice."

But it's your life. That's what you're talking about. You swapped your life for the things you'd need to come and rescue me.

Ruth looked at him, puzzled and wary. Nic looked away from her, staring into the flame of one of the candles.

"You wanted to know why," he said, the attenuated ghosts of fury stirring in his voice. "I suppose someone ought to know, and now that Lady Jausserande's told you her story and Fox has told you something of his own, I suppose you ought to have mine to make a coordinated set. As stories go, it's a pretty familiar one. It happened a long time ago, even if that's sort of . . . hard to remember now. It was a long time ago, a chess game in a far country, and all the players are dead." Nic stopped, and lifted his tankard and drank.

"Don't—" Ruth whispered, but he didn't hear her.

"Once upon a time," Nic said quietly as if to himself—and Ruth knew that the time he meant was neither long ago nor fictional—"once upon a time there was a tender young man who spent his time in the greenwood wandering here and there and taking things that didn't belong to him. Well, one day—"

Nic took a deep breath, and ran his hand over the back of his head. He turned toward Ruth. His pale eyes glittered, as if this were an amusing story. His face was drawn in sharp white lines, as if it were not.

"One day he was told to go off into the forest with a bunch of his friends to get back something that *did* belong to him. To them. To all of them. A senator's son, something. And IPW'd come across for us. We even knew where he was. So off we went, heigh-ho. Only . . . only some of us had different orders."

Nic smiled at her. It was the meaningless rictus of a man on the rack, and Ruth's heart beat faster, afraid of what she was about to hear, afraid of what summoned that expression to Nic Brightlaw's face.

"Ten of us, waltzing in to lift thirty-five GIs out of a dink hotel. It just wasn't going to happen. In fact, it hadn't ever really been the plan. Maybe there wasn't even a senator's son to begin with. I don't know."

He wasn't really there with her any more, Ruth realized. Nic Brightlaw was gone, reliving the events that had made him glad to give up his life so casually two decades later.

"We were a day away from where HumInt said we needed to be. And then the captain gathered in all his tender young men, and told them they weren't here to rescue anybody. It wasn't a rescue mission."

Ruth sensed what was coming. She held up her hand to ward it off, but Nic could not be stopped. And she owed it to him to listen, so that somebody would know. Even if nobody cared.

"We were supposed to go in and kill everyone in the compound. We were supposed to go in and kill American soldiers. Our own guys. Not rescue. Execute."

There was a long pause then, as if the narrative continued on some frequency that Ruth simply couldn't hear, as if some things were far too painful to be said aloud.

"I remonstrated with my superiors over this minor point of military protocol, of course, so with one thing and another the captain eventually pointed his weapon at me," Nic said, as if he really were taking up the narrative at some later point. He fell silent again. His hand sketched a shape in the air, drawing pictures of a scene Ruth could only dimly imagine.

"He wasn't quite ready to shoot me just then, or maybe they wanted me to think I was going to get out alive. They took my boots, which didn't cripple me the way they thought it would, and my rifle, which was dammed annoying; I'd swapped two cartons of cigarettes and a case of beer for it. And they made camp and tied me to a tree and figured they were safe."

Now Nic's eyes focused on Ruth as if he were finally really seeing her—seeing her and somehow trying to apologize for having told her what he needed so desperately to tell. But apology was a human act, and what Ruth saw when she looked into them were the eyes of someone who had been human once but whose humanity had been burned away beyond any hope of recovery.

"I'll cut to the chase," Nic said, and now even the memory of emotion was gone from his voice, and once more it was the light, easy voice of someone for whom absolutely nothing could ever matter again. "They were my buddies. I killed them. I tried to get the grunts out of the camp by myself. It worked as well as you'd expect. I stumbled back into base alone three months later with a septic leg wound full of maggots and a story to tell. I didn't tell it. The Eagle and I parted company. Years passed. And here I am."

Ruth's throat worked, but no question came out. *Why? Why here? Why this?*

"It's as good a place to wait as any," Nic said, answering the question she hadn't had the nerve to ask.

After that, the only place the evening had to go was to worse, and it did, with the aid of most of a jug full of unwatered wine. Ruth didn't really remember getting to bed at all. She thought vaguely that she must have ended up bundling in with Nic, but the following morning she was up and washed and dressed and confronted with her horse before she was entirely sure where she'd actually slept. It hadn't seemed much like sleep, anyway, with its endless nightmares of pain and cruelty. Melior's pain drew her like a remorseless compass arrow, chill and sure.

Ruth tried to remember being in love, being happy, feeling that Melior could make her happy. She tried to summon up the memory of the feeling that if she were with Melior, everything would be all right. It was hard to believe now that she'd ever been that innocent. Had she really believed that any fairy tale could have a happy ending?

I don't know if I can survive this, Ruth said to herself as she shivered into wakefulness in the inn yard. The early morning air already possessed some of winter's bite, and mist hung between the trees. Ruth's stomach slowly revolved. She supposed this must be a hangover; all she knew was that it felt like a combination of a sinus headache and the flu.

"Drink this." Nic Brightlaw pushed a leather-covered jack into her hand. Steam rose from it; Ruth sniffed cautiously and smelled what seemed to be hot boiled beer. She recoiled fastidiously.

"Um . . . no thanks."

"Hair of the dog," Nic said. "You'll feel better."

The conviction that she could not feel worse—and the faint hope that it might poison her—was what caused Ruth to take the container. She closed her eyes, held her breath, and chugged down as much of the tepid contents as she could in one go. There was a brief moment of intense nausea, after which Ruth began to feel better.

"Thanks," she said, finally trusting herself to face Nic. Ruth was under a spell, her soul stolen—that was why she felt as if there were a shield of unyielding glass between her and all of the living world. What must it be like not to have that pleasant excuse? To be someone whose emotions had all been burned away until there was nothing left but the mind's firebrick and a strange detached courtesy?

"Specialty of the house," Nic said, taking the tankard and draining the rest of it. "I understand we stop in a few hours for lunch, so you needn't feel the omission of breakfast too keenly. And here comes the rest of the tour group."

Ruth turned back to the inn's front. Melior's ring was a hard weight on her hand, its bezel turned in toward the palm. Fox came through the door, followed closely by Jausserande. Either no one here had recognized the notorious outlaw Fox, or they were better at hiding their interest than the people at Black Bridge had been.

Ruth realized with a pang of conscience that all her bargaining had been for nothing; when you came right down to it, it didn't really matter if Fox came along or not. She'd made a bad bargain—hadn't Nic said something like that last night? She'd promised Fox that if he would come with them, she would persuade Melior to leave Chandrakar.

And so Fox had set aside his one best chance of escape in favor of the thing that he valued more than life—Melior's destruction. And Ruth found herself bound to a useless promise in a contest where the sides shifted like the banks of a river at flood tide. One more person wasn't going to make any difference to their chances of getting Melior out of wherever he was. Ruth had wanted Fox along for his company, because she'd thought he was a friend.

And he wasn't. She didn't know who lived behind those pale blue eyes now, but it wasn't the Philip LeStrange she'd gone to library school with.

Fox said something and Jausserande laughed, the mirth as candid and unfeigned as a child's. As if she were not the vengeful harpy Ruth knew her to be. As if Fox had not murdered her squire on his way to declaring holy war.

Am I the only one here who's sane? Ruth wondered. It was a frightening thought, but possible. She already knew about Fox's fixation, Melior's cousin was a homicidal maniac, and Nic was aloofly friendly, but . . . strange.

Maybe this was what normalcy boiled down to. Passing for normal, not really being there. *You are now leaving Normal, Ruth* mentally intoned. *Please adjust your preconceptions.*

The others joined them, and the horses were brought around. Ruth mounted with Nic's help. Being on horseback was already starting to seem normal; she might even learn to ride before something got her killed.

Fox swung himself into the saddle with an effort, but he managed. Nic followed suit, and so did Jausserande—easily the most accomplished rider of the four.

"Whither away?" Jausserande called gaily, and suddenly Ruth realized it all came down to her. Without her internal compass, her link to Melior, the others didn't know where to go.

Of the other three, only Jausserande had any real interest in going wherever they were all going, and that was because she was on quest to recover the Cup of Morning Shadows, not because she wanted to rescue Melior. Melior, Ruth had come to realize, placed a distant second in Jausserande's interests, though she'd be happy to mourn for him—once the Cup was safe.

Except it wasn't going to be. Whatever was waiting for them at this place they were heading for was going to get them all killed and have the Cup and Sword for dessert if it could get them. But oddly enough, that wasn't Ruth's problem. She couldn't really afford to care about something so irrelevant to what she wanted. Now she finally understood what Fox had meant when he'd spoken of the ways enemies could be allies, back on the road before Jausserande had found them. Ruth needed to get to Melior. She needed these people to get her to Melior. She'd use them to get her where she was going for as long as their purposes paralleled hers. She'd use anything.

Ruth took her mental bearings, honing in on the direction from which the intangible psychic pull was strongest.

"That way," Ruth said impassively. "Over there."

· 8 ·

The Fall of the House
of Escher

THERE WAS A certain reckless excitement about being able to go into a situation that was already as bad as it could be and trying to make it worse, and Holly couldn't suppress an anticipatory thrill at the prospect. As she headed Rosinante back toward the Taconic, she tried to bring her spinning thoughts into some sort of order, but all she could really focus on was how wonderfully detached she felt from the hideous events of the night before.

It was hard to believe she'd ruined her life so completely in less than forty-eight hours, but there you were. In mundane terms, she was a murderess—a fugitive from justice—although she found it very hard to regret the man she'd killed. She only hoped that despite her paranoid imaginings, the gray man hadn't tracked down Carol and Margot. He knew her name from the other time he'd questioned her. Why hadn't she thought of that? He only had to check registration to know she was supposed to be at the convention this weekend, and almost anyone at HeliCon could tell him she was rooming with Margot and Carol!

Maybe his being there was just coincidence. Maybe he didn't work for the same people who'd tortured Mac. Maybe she could just surrender. Because even in less pragmatic terms than worrying about how to avoid being arrested and going to jail, finding whatever it was that Mac said was here at HeliCon wouldn't bring anything Holly could think of closer to a solution, though Mac assured her that having something called the Cloak of Night and Daggers would be an enormous help.

"—because the Cloak gives its wearer both invisibility and the ability to spy unseen over vast distances, providing it is used at night—" Mac assured her. "Holly, aren't you listening? Don't you see? The Cloak is Line Amarmonde's Treasure—or it was—and—"

"Yeah, right, whatever," Holly muttered under her breath. She didn't care if this Cloak and Dagger thing had an MBA and could get its own coffee—she didn't think that even having an Oscar could get all of them out of this mess if it was even half as bad as she thought it was. But she had to try—even if the only thing she could think of to try was showing up and getting killed.

She'd tried to get Rook to come back with them for safety's sake, but he'd refused, saying he had enough to do with taking care of five Rottweilers and a boxful of puppies.

"And I don't think the hotel'd be too wild about letting all of us in, somehow. Besides, Fee, you might need a safe bolt-hole, and if I'm here I can make sure this place stays one. So don't do anything stupid, and if nothing happens I'll see you at the tourney."

"Yeah, right," Holly had told him unhappily. Even though she expected to come back to Half Moon before the event, she'd packed her armor and sword to take with her again, both because she could not bear to leave them someplace she was not, and also because taking them with her would make Rook look less like an accessory after the fact—which he was, though Holly had not told him what she'd done and Rook hadn't asked.

Rotties or not, she ought to have made him come with her, Holly fretted all during the drive down, but she'd been too anxious to get back and find out what had happened to her friends to put enough effort into browbeating her former squire. Fear for Carol and Margot knotted her stomach. She'd foolishly left them behind, and the stakes had been revealed to be too high to believe they were all right.

It was late Sunday afternoon as Holly and Mac pulled into the Hotel Escher parking lot.

Frank Catalpano was not having a good weekend. For as long as he'd worked for Information Management Services, he'd been the hired gun— go in to a situation, make a lot of people unhappy, go on to the next job.

But the Sunwise Account was breaking all the rules. Frank had gotten a telephone call from Denver early Saturday morning, which made it clear that Sunwise was now Frank's baby all the way. Frank had never been particularly fond of babies. And the more he found out about this one, the less he liked it.

Frank gazed with baleful dispassion at the six men sitting in awkward assembly around his hotel room. One was the station officer from Half Moon Psychiatric Center, who hadn't yet provided a particularly convincing explanation of why they hadn't simply shot the trespassers the moment they'd seen them. One was Gilman's partner, Doyle, who looked as uncomfortable as any man could who'd let someone decapitate his partner with what Forensic Response said was one hell of a cutter. Doyle wasn't too forthcoming so far on what had happened after that, but he would be. Fortunately he'd had the sense to get Gilman's body out of there and deep-clean the site, so at least IMS wouldn't be hip-deep in local yokels and some backwoods murder investigation.

"Perhaps, Mr. Doyle, you'd like to explain again just why it was that you were unable to apprehend Gauvain Makindeor at the secondary site. You told Control that you'd seen him. And take off those damned sunglasses," Frank added without heat.

"I'm not sure it was him, sir," Doyle suggested hopefully.

Without the mirrorshade camouflage his face was naked and young; he'd only been with IMS for a little over eighteen months, and the secondary site had been supposed to be a standard Meet and Greet under the supervision of the more experienced Gilman. What had happened was certainly not Doyle's fault, but Frank didn't care.

"You're not sure it was him. A skinny guy in a cap and someone in a suit of blood-drenched armor carrying a dripping sword. After you've let them get away, you go on in and discover that the office has been tossed, Gilman's dead, and the object that our client has lent to us is gone. You're right, Doyle. It was probably a coincidence," Frank said with labored irony.

Doyle was going to take the full hit on this one. IMS had little use for field agents who couldn't cover their asses when the need arose, and Frank was not in a charitable mood. He was Account Manager in Charge, now, not here to be liked.

Not that people had liked Frank even before this.

"We will table—for the moment—the question of why it was that Mr. Doyle was too shy to approach two citizens and ask them their business and move on to why it was that these two citizens were still free to annoy Mr. Doyle after their visit to Half Moon. Mr. Baudino?" Frank looked at the station officer.

"We knew that the subject and a still-unidentified woman had clandestinely entered the building," Carmine Baudino said. "They penetrated Dr. Egan-Light's office and triggered the silent alarms. I tried a soft approach and they fled, going to ground within the building. I cordoned the site, called in off-station personnel, and began searching the first floor and basement areas."

Frank allowed himself to look impatient. All of this had been in Baudino's original report. Baudino surveyed Frank's face and made his report march.

"He must have gotten his hands on a bazooka, is all that we can figure. They escaped through the laundry chute after blowing the cover off—padlock, chain, and all—so we hung back in order to avoid provoking another response like that . . .'"

If Baudino had actually thought he was facing a bazooka, Frank would be very surprised. But he'd learned a long time ago that most of the personnel attached to Project Sunwise were scared silly of their study subjects. Baudino'd probably figured that Makindeor had been holding out on them for all those months and was going to turn him into a goddamned toad or something.

Frank sighed.

"Now let me get completely clear on this," he said patiently. "You had this Gauvain Makindeor in extreme restraint, from which he escapes. You tracked him to the Escher Hotel, where I was supposed to take custody of him, and he escapes again. He next appears back at the original custody site in the company of an unidentified woman in nursing whites who may well be the same individual who had monitored access to another of the subjects. At Half Moon, you lose Makindeor for a *third* time, and even though it is abundantly clear that he has had unconstrained access to highly sensitive material in Dr. Egan-Light's office—and may I remind you that Dr. Egan-Light is the supervising clinician for *all* of Sunwise East Coast?—you fail to adequately safeguard the secondary site.

"So Gilman is dead, the object that we have been attempting to induce the subject to operate for us is gone, and Gauvain Makindeor of Chandrakar is out there somewhere making little friends wherever he goes and telling them . . . oh, could be almost anything."

There was complete silence in the room once Frank had finished speaking. The others stared at him blankly, as if they were convinced that it was now Frank's responsibility to think up an excuse for them. But Francis Catalpano was nobody's fall guy—a fact which he intended to communicate to them in simple, easy-to-understand terms.

"IMS probably doesn't consider this acceptable case management. I know that I don't, gentlemen. Exhibitions such as these not only indicate that the lot of you require an *exhaustive* review of each of your personnel files to make sure that you're really happy with us, but they have jeopar-

dized the future of the entire account. May I remind each one of you that
the reason we control this account in the first place is so that the client
can maintain total deniability? Now, let's make a real effort here to shut
down all the peripherals on this one. Loose ends will become dead ends,
is that clear? Now Mr. Doyle and Mr. Baudino, do you think that the two
of you would care to oblige me by handling any dingleberries in the
vicinity of Half Moon?"

The Hotel Escher was jumping. Even though some of the conventioneers had already checked out and would be leaving the hotel later
today, by tonight the place would be zoological in its crowded chaos. Its
lobby was filled with people who hadn't been to bed yet or who had
gotten up only a few hours before and were gearing up for a night of
serious partying. As Mac and Holly walked in, things looked relatively
normal, and there was no sign of any Men in Black. Holly greeted some
acquaintances with barely a bobble; it hardly mattered now if people
knew she was here, did it?

Now, where were Carol and Margot likely to be at this hour? Heli-
Con would run through Monday, so the big masquerade was scheduled
for tonight instead of Saturday. Margot, Holly knew, was staying over
Monday and then heading down to the city. She had lunch with Sheila at
DAW scheduled for Tuesday, a flying pre-Christmas visit. Carol was planning to go to Ippisiqua to visit her friend Ruth, and Holly had the tourney
in Patroon County. She'd been going to drive Carol up to Ippisiqua, drop
her off at Ruth's, and then continue on to Half Moon and stay the night
at Rook's place.

Only Holly wasn't too sure it was a good idea to go back there again.
Most of all, she had to talk to Carol and Margot, and tell them . . .
something.

Holly was too keyed up to bother with the courtesy phone in the
lobby, prudent though it might have been to use it; instead, she went
straight up to five, Mac tagging behind, and used her key card on the
door. The suite's window curtains were still drawn—or drawn again—and
the room had the awful refrigerated silence of a cut-price tomb. There
was a tag on the door asking the maid not to enter.

"Carol? Marg?" Holly whipped through into the next room and was
relived to see that their luggage was still strewn around. At least she knew
they were still at the hotel.

All eight pieces of Margot's luggage lay open and half-filled on the
dresser, the tables, and the chairs. Her dress for tonight's masquerade
was laid out on the bed. No wonder she hadn't wanted the maids in here.

It was supposed to be the dress of a duchess from *Swordspoint,* and

Margot had used Elizabethan period costume as a jumping-off point. The overdress was a brilliant blue-green, and the stomacher and underskirt were both appliqued with a repeating pattern of crossed swords, executed in silver lamé and clear crystal beading. Matching hand-painted slippers nestled in a shoebox on the floor, and the rest of Margot's accessories were scattered about the coverlet.

Holly looked at her wristwatch, forcing herself to focus. It was after three, late in the day but hours before Margot would be back to dress for the masquerade. And Carol might be anywhere in the hotel.

"Is there trouble, Holly?" Mac asked, coming in. Rook had given Mac's hair a slightly better trim than Holly had, and now it showed a tendency to break into butter-blond ringlets when left alone. Rook had also managed to get him a better set of mundane clothes than the ones he'd driven there in, but in jeans, chambray shirt, and navy V-neck pull-over, with the *Book of Airts* concealed in a green nylon backpack, Mac looked like a refugee from some alternate planet where Ralph Lauren had collaborated with J.R.R. Tolkien on the set design for *Lord of the Rings,* or someone who ought to be running a news group called *alt.peter—pan@lostboys.com* somewhere out on the Web—wholesome and exotic all at once.

But he sat down on one of the beds almost immediately, trying to look as though he didn't need to. Though his powers of endurance were courageous, it was impossible for him to conceal the true state of his health from Holly. The unknown period of imprisonment and torture had exacted its toll.

"Trouble? Not as such, I guess," Holly said slowly. "They're okay, I guess. They just aren't here."

"I have to find Amarmonde's Treasure," Mac said fretfully. He stood and walked back out into the other room, unslinging the backpack he carried.

The phone rang.

There were two phones in the suite, each a half-tone off from the other, so that when they shrilled in unison the discord was enough to set even a tone-deaf person's teeth on edge. Holly stared at the one yowling and flashing beside the bed as if it were a cobra.

"Do not heed it," Mac suggested.

"Oh, thank you so much for that input," Holly snapped. "That was just what I wasn't going to do." She felt instantly sorry for her flare of temper, but Makindeor didn't seem to notice. Though it seemed much longer, the phone only rang four times before surrendering to the inevitable and going to voice mail. Holly let out a deep breath as she saw the red "Message Waiting" button begin to flash a moment later.

I wonder who it is? Oh, don't be silly, Holly, just go pick up the message and see . . . she punched her way through the necessary numbers, and a moment later the message played.

"Holly? This is Frank Catalpano. You probably don't remember me, but I interviewed you a few years back at Bellevue about one of your EMT runs. I'm in the hotel, and there's another little something you could help me out with, if you would. I'm on the floor right below you, Room 455. Could you give me a call?" The voice was bright, upbeat, spuriously cheerful. As if there were no cause for alarm and never would be. A friendly, helpful, professionally cheerful voice.

False. Lying. The voice of the gray man, who had found her at last.

Holly began to laugh breathlessly. Just when she thought things couldn't get worse, just when she thought events were going to start to leave her *alone,* something like this happened. It was just like a god-damned movie!

"Holly?" Mac put the *Book of Airts* down on the nearest table and came over to her. "Holly?"

He shook her, but she couldn't seem to stop laughing.

"Don't you see, Mac—it's funny? We're all in a real-time role-playing game, only they forgot to give us our badges—"

"Holly—don't do this—I need you—" Mac shook her again, but she couldn't stop; she felt herself sliding from the shallows of hysteria into the deeps, into some dark otherwhere in which she would drown and die and go on laughing.

There was a flash of aureate fire in front of her face, and a peppery scent in her nose. Holly sneezed, and sneezed again, and groped for a Kleenex. She blew her nose—a forlorn, furious honk—and shook her head, wiping at her eyes. The toxic wildness was gone, seeping somehow out of her blood. Mac regarded her, looking shaken and drained, holding onto the doorframe for support.

"What did you—? I mean, thanks, Mac. I guess I must be pretty scared," Holly said dutifully.

But as a matter of fact, she didn't feel scared at all. She'd never felt more alive, as if she could defeat any challenge.

"It was my pleasure," Mac said with grave courtesy. "A simple thing, not like unlocking doors. But here in the World of Iron, my magic is a finite thing. I have already used far more than I safely may. But if I can only find the Cloak . . ."

Holly put a companionable arm about his shoulders and hugged him. "I'll try not to take too much out of you, then. But that guy on the phone? He's bad trouble. I guess I'd better explain—"

So she did, quickly, about an ambulance ride two years before, and another man with pointed ears and glowing cat's eyes.

"—I never found out his name or what happened to him, but he must have gone missing somehow, because the gray man—I mean Frank Catalpano, I guess—came back around asking all of us—well, Dave and me—questions about had we seen him again. We hadn't. I wonder what happened to him?"

There was a silence as Mac sat down to consider her words intently. The short haircut Rook had given him showed the pointed ears plainly, but it was hard to think of Mac/Makindeor as alien or even elvish. Holly felt an odd sense of kinship with him, as though she knew him too well for them to play at being strangers.

"I do not know; that he was one of my own people seems undeniable. But that he should be called to come to the World of Iron argues a grave emergency—or arrant folly."

"Why?" Holly asked, half idly.

"Why should we come here? The very air is our death, and there is deathmetal all around us, though it is not quite so poisonous as it is in our own place, where we are linked to the magic of the land. But rather I would know how it is that your own people know to hunt us—and for what purpose? I confess that puzzles me more than all the rest—what use can the Children of Earth have for magic?"

"What's 'deathmetal'?" Holly asked. Why did everything that Mac said when he got going only lead to more questions?

"Iron, Holly," Mac said quietly. "Were I to take up your beautiful sword, her blade would burn me like the fire of a true dragon—and I could not bear the touch of your armor at all."

"Oh," Holly said inadequately. She tried to remember how many things in her daily life were made of iron or steel, and could only think of her stainless steel wristwatch band. Had she ever seen Mac handle any of them? She couldn't remember. And most of the fixtures on the inside of a Honda were plastic. . . .

"But that is not the issue at hand," Mac said firmly. "What matters is that now I know that my imprisonment was but part of a larger design that the World of Iron has to make war upon Chandrakar, baffling though that seems. And so I must retrieve the Treasure which is here and travel home to warn my kindred."

"Home—to Chandrakar?" Holly said.

"Yes." Mac stood up and began to pace, turning toward the Book and then away, as if something about it drew him against his will. "It is possible—with an ephemeris, which I do not have—but there must be a Gate; I can find it, given time—but do I have the time?"

"Mac, honey, you're making my damned head hurt," Holly said. "Could you just grab the *tchotchke* and argue with yourself later?"

Mac stopped and looked at her and gave her one of his infrequent smiles. "As you say, Holly. We shall gain the *'chach-key'* and use it to unlock the rest."

He picked up the Book and settled his strange glasses on his nose, paging quickly through the volume as if he knew what he was looking for. "It's here—or rather, it occupies the same space in the same ethereal plane as this place, contingent with the Last World, so that—"

"If there's no place like this place anywhere but this place this must be the place," Holly finished for him, getting restlessly to her feet and going to look out the window. The day was crystal bright, the colors sharp in the arid air of winter, but the light was already beginning to fail. "Why does he want to talk to me?"

"Who?" Mac said, nose buried in the Book.

"Frank." Holly bounced down on the couch again. "Catalpano. Why me? Unless—he knows I killed that guy?" It was the first time she'd said it out loud, and the memory was suddenly unbearably fresh. Holly was silent for several minutes, fighting back treacherous tears.

"It's no good," Mac said. "I am going to have to go looking for it. This is a large holding with many rooms—it might be in any of them."

"You haven't heard a single word I've said," Holly accused. Mac looked at her with blank innocence. *Oh, well, I guess you've got problems of your own,* Holly thought to herself. "What do we do now? If that Catalpano guy's looking for me, I want to find Carol and Margot before he does."

"Then our ways fall together," Mac said, holding out his hand to her. "You will search for your friends, and I will seek the Cloak."

"Do you know what it looks like?" Holly asked.

Mac shrugged. "It can look like anything that may be worn. That is a part of its nature—deceit."

Right. One particular cloak—or something—in a hotel full of elf-wannabes, SCAdians, rogue Comyn, and free-lance Kindred six hours before the big masquerade.

"At HeliCon," Holly said aloud, taking his hand. His clasp was warm and dry, the pressure of his slender fingers strong against her own. "Good luck," she said, to both of them.

Each time she walked into danger Holly was surprised at how abrupt the transition was. Sitting in the suite behind a locked door, everything seemed easy and possible. The moment she opened that door and stepped out into the hallway, tension closed around her like a vise, making every new decision painful and paralyzing thought. She jumped at the sound of Mac closing the door behind them—the heavy metallic sound of its click sounded too much like the sound of the slide on a pistol being pulled back.

"Okay," Holly said in a breathless undertone. "Okay." *Where do we start? Where would they be? The dealer's room? The art show? The Con suite?* "C'mon," Holly said, trying to slow her spinning thoughts enough to think. "We're going to registration."

Without a badge they wouldn't be able to get in to any of the places they needed to search. Of course, if *she* were an elfhunter for the FBI (or whatever), that was the first place she, Holly, would have staked out. They were going to have to risk it anyway.

Registration—if you weren't a program participant—was in the open area in front of the art show and the Main Ballroom. It was just about completely unoccupied after four on Sunday; Holly gave cash for two one-day memberships to a preoccupied gopher wearing a "Gophorit: HeliCon 1997" T-shirt and received in return two blank badges (it was why she hadn't picked up her prepaid membership: a small circumspection, but better than nothing), pocket programs, two glossy full-color program books, and the (verbal) information that the art auction was what was running now in the Main Ballroom. It would close at five for Tech Set-up, open at seven to the masquerade participants, and the masquerade itself would start at nine.

"Assuming the auction ends on time," Lenore said, and she and Holly both laughed, because they never did.

"Good makeup on your friend," Lenore said. "Is he entered? They're death on media costumes here, but he looks really good."

"Um, yeah," Holly said, "but it's okay because he's going as the Mirror Universe David Bowie." *Where did her mouth come up with these things?* she asked herself in vain.

"Oh, that should be great," Lenore said, just as if Holly's explanation were reasonable. "Sort of a Thin White Vulcan, huh? It'll be great."

"I hope so," Holly said, with more enthusiasm than she felt. "Nice talking to you. C'mon, Mac, let's go find some people."

The art show was closed for the auction, so the others couldn't be there; Holly and Mac slipped into the back of the auction itself for a few minutes, watching the bidding quickly rise into the stratosphere over a Tom Canty sketch. Holly looked around, trying to spot Margot, and then thought to dig out her pocket program.

"It isn't here, Holly," Mac said with faint impatience.

"Just a minute," Holly said, flipping back and forth between the schedule pages (panel titles only) and the alphabetical listings, which included the participants. Finally she established to her satisfaction that Margot'd had a reading at 9:00 a.m. (Holly winced in sympathy: nobody came to 9:00 a.m. Sunday morning programming), a signing at 12:00, and nothing else today. There was no chance of catching her at a panel unless she got lucky at second-guessing her whims.

When Holly looked up, Mac was gone.

Holly bit her lip and swore silently, playing back his last few sentences in her mind. He'd said that the Cloak of Night and Daggers wasn't here in the auction, and he had just wandered off to find it. She'd *kill* him.

But before she could kill him, she had to find him—find all three of them.

Where would *she* go, Holly asked herself, if she were a mystic elphen Cloak and its several-sandwiches-shy-of-a-picnic seeker?

Checking all of the function rooms at HeliCon (including Con Ops, the video room, and the raffle) was a daunting prospect, so Holly decided to start with the easiest thing: the dealer's room.

To call it the dealer's room was the first in a series of many misnomers. It wasn't a single room at all but two sets of linked function rooms just beyond the Transdimensional Corridor.

And to say that there was any room in it was just plain ridiculous.

Holly wedged herself through the door—a process not unlike that of a salmon swimming upstream to mate—and began looking for Carol, Margot, or Mac. The progress of her search was severely limited by the fact that she couldn't see past the press of bodies more than a few feet in any direction, and all three of her search-objects were rather short—even Margot, whose flamboyant forcefulness tricked the eye of memory into thinking of her as a tall woman.

Holly worked her way through the first compartment with a cheerful brutality but didn't see her quarry anywhere—not by the jewelry, not by the books, not by the T-shirts or the videos or the buttons. She squirmed out of the first room and prepared to cross the hall to the other side.

There was a Man in Black in the hall, talking to the gopher at the door.

Holly ducked back inside, banging into the person behind her with a gabbled apology. Who was the man in the suit looking for? Her? Margot? Mac? Carol?

Holly'd worked her way back to the center of the room and was standing enraptured by a display of fake ID cards when he poked his head in through the door. Holly kept her head down. She'd tucked her braid under her vest—hair as long as hers was a dead giveaway to her identity, even if a lot of fans had hair this long. Holly could only hope that after two days of looking and not finding, the MIB was ready to give up.

Unless they already had Margot and Carol. Unless they'd caught Mac, and that was why they were looking for her.

But as Holly watched from the corner of her eye, the searcher only looked in from the doorway and didn't come into the room. Holly held her breath until he withdrew and then for another several seconds just for luck, but he didn't come in and he didn't come back. It was just as well that he didn't, she told herself—his nice black suit would never have survived the experience.

It was another minute or two before she could force herself to move, and that only after buying a clip-on badge signed by Darth Vader himself that identified her as Imperial Security. She took an obscure comfort from it as she clipped it below her HeliCon ID. *If you can't impress them with sincerity, you can always baffle them with bullshit,* Holly reminded herself.

Or you could just hit them over the head with a big stick, preferably rattan wrapped in duct tape, which was what she was going to do to Mac if he didn't turn up real soon. Holly looked both ways cautiously before she ducked into the second room, her heart beating as fast as that of a fox fleeing before the hunters. At first it seemed as if this room might be as unproductive as the other, but then she saw a familiar blonde head at the far end of the room. It was Carol; she was here, inspecting a rack of hooded cloaks just as if there'd be some place to wear one in Twisted River, Idaho.

Holly hastened down the row—past Poison Pen Press, two other booksellers, and a jeweler famous for her work in cut-and-pieced gold. She slid in next to Carol, who was concentrating on a calf-length hooded cloak in mulberry wool that was trimmed in a white and gold brocade patterned with roses.

"Carol," Holly said, feeling curiously out of breath.

Carol Goodchild turned toward Holly, her automatic expression of pleased greeting fading as she remembered that she wasn't supposed to be pleased to see Holly—that, in fact, she wasn't supposed to be seeing Holly at all.

"Where's Mac?" Carol hissed under her breath.

"Where's Margot?" Holly hissed back. "Carol—these guys all over the hotel—they aren't cops. I don't know what they are, but they aren't cops. We—I—we're all in a lot of trouble." Trying to tell everything at once and not tell too much, Holly explained about being shot at in Half

Moon, nearly killed the following night, and having Frank Catalpano phone the room less than an hour earlier.

Carol listened seriously, her gray eyes wide. "We've got to find them—and you've got to stay out of sight, Hol. If he's phoning you up, he's *got* to know what you look like." With sudden determination, Carol turned back to the dealer. "How much for the pink one with the roses?"

"I know she'll be back in the room by six," Carol was saying a few minutes later, as she and Holly walked down the hall. Holly was wearing Carol's new purchase, with the deep hood pulled well forward, and the blank one-day HeliCon membership badge pinned to its front. Perfect anonymity. "She was having lunch with a friend of hers—you know, that romance author who's crossing over?—and I was supposed to meet her back at the room to help her lace into her corset. We could check the coffee shop, but they might have gone outside to eat, if her friend drove."

"Don't you remember who it was?" Like all resident New Yorkers, Holly kept running mental tabs on all of her friends, acquaintances, and not entirely total strangers who had cars.

"You know I don't know all of Margot's friends," Carol said. "But what about Mac—you said he was a—"

"An elf librarian," Holly finished for her. "And frankly, Carol, I'm inclined to believe him. He did things . . ." She fell silent, thinking of the things she'd seen Mac do that simply couldn't be done. Not outside of the Twilight Zone, anyway. Or Elphame. "Anyway, if he says—and he does—that there's a magic cloak running around HeliCon and that he's got to grab it and go home to Elfland, I'll help him all I can."

"Well, I will, too," Carol said loyally. "At least he isn't asking me to cheat on my taxes or something fatal like that." She shrugged and tried to smile. "But he must have done *something* wrong, Holly—or else why would all these guys be after him?"

"Oh, Carol, you are too much," Holly sighed wearily. "When did somebody ever have to do something wrong for reality to fall on them like a ton of bricks?"

By this third day of HeliCon, the waitstaff at the Hotel Escher coffee shop were used to seeing people of all shapes and sizes advance upon them seeking tables for four. The reservations clerk didn't even blink when Carol and Holly asked if they could come in and look for a friend.

But Margot wasn't there.

"Figures," Holly said, rubbing her nose. The unlined wool was making it itch, and she spared a moment to wish that Carol could have picked up some little number in Polar-Tec or something hypoallergenic. "And Mac isn't here either."

"Hist!" Carol said. She dug her fingers into Holly's arm. "Holly," she said urgently.

But Holly had already seen him—one of the MIBs, walking casually out of the coffee shop with a carton of "coffee-to-go" in each hand.

And, across the lobby on an oblivious collision course, Mac was walking straight toward him.

"Oh, *no,*" Carol breathed. In another moment the MIB would walk from the coffee shop into the lobby, and Mac was in plain sight.

"Nuclear Tag!" Holly suddenly yelped. She shoved Carol backward, swirled her cloak around her with a Lamont Cranston flourish that imperiled the early dinners of several patrons, and lunged forward with a rebel yell.

She caromed off the MIB in the doorway. He dropped his cartons of coffee. They hit the floor, and their contents fountained upward, drenching his trousers.

"Sorry—sorry—sorry—" Holly caroled, fleeing past and semaphoring apologies and laughing all at once. Her cape belled out behind her as she ran straight toward Mac, leaping up over the back of the couch in the lobby and jumping down off the seat. Everyone stared.

"Nuclear Tag!" Carol cried gamely, and ran after her. She hoped Holly knew what she was doing.

"Nuclear Tag—" Holly yelped, running straight into Mac. She flung a wing of the cape up over his head, hoping it would look like an accidental tangle to any watchers. "They're in the restaurant," she hissed in his ear. Without untangling him, she began to drag him toward the elevators.

"But Hol—" Mac began. Holly stuffed a fold of the cloak into his mouth.

"Nuclear Tag!" Carol shouted, ramming into both of them from behind. "They're going to throw us out of the convention if they catch up with us," she added in an undertone.

It wasn't until they were around the corner that Holly felt safe enough to unwrap Mac and take a deep breath.

"What the *hell* were you doing—wandering off like that? There's one of them in the restaurant, and they're all over the fucking convention! Don't you ever—ever—ever—" She took him by the shoulders and shook him, inarticulately furious.

"Holly." Carol put a hand on her arm. "It's after five. Margot should be back soon. Why don't we go up to the room to wait for her?"

"How could you be so stupid?" Holly demanded of Mac.

"But I have to find the Cloak," Mac said. "The ley lines lead in that direction—I think it's outside this building, and—"

"You were walking right into him," Holly snarled, angry beyond reason. The thought of losing Mac to his former captors filled her with a rage that made her heart hammer.

"Come *on,*" Carol said. She rummaged beneath the hem of the cloak until she found Holly's braid and yanked hard enough to snap Holly's head back.

"To the room," Carol said when Holly looked at her.

Holly sighed, the quivering tension vanishing in a breath. "Okay. Come on. You too, Mac—and let's hope they haven't got it staked out."

But it wasn't as easy as Holly had hoped to get back to their suite. Either the MIB were breeding like amoebae, or Holly and her friends were just unlucky.

Or they *were* staking out the room.

"This isn't going to work," Holly finally said. "And they're going to get suspicious if they keep seeing us veering off like this."

They were standing in front of the elevators on Four, having ducked hastily back into the elevator one more time. No matter which way the three of them tried to approach the suite, there always seemed to be someone in sunglasses and a suit in the hall, and Holly was terrified that finally it would turn out to be Frank Catalpano himself.

"Why can't they just go off and watch the program?" Carol said mournfully. "Holly, maybe it would work out if I went up to the guy on Five and distracted—Holly? Holly, are you *listening?* Mars calling Earth?"

"I think I have an idea," Holly said in an odd excited voice.

The hotel fire alarms rang almost simultaneously on floors Four, Five, and Seven. In the corridors the klaxons mingled, each howling in a slightly different key from the next, until the discord was enough to sterilize cockroaches at fifty paces.

"Do you see him?" Holly whispered to Carol, still a little breathless from running up and down the fire stairs to trigger as many alarms as she could. Her mouth was right next to Carol's ear; if it hadn't been, neither of them would have been able to hear anything over the din of the alarms and the excited conversations of a corridor full of fans.

"No." Carol shook her head.

Holly gave her a little push. *"Go."*

Wrapping her arms about herself as if to hold her luck in place, Carol scurried out of the stairwell and down the hall.

Brank—brank—brank—the fire alarms bleated on.

"*Go.*" Holly pushed Mac out next. She was bringing up the rear both because she thought of herself as more expendable and because she thought the chances were better that she could get Mac away from the bad guys than that Mac could rescue her. He ran, wrapped and bundled in the mulberry cape, just another anonymous HeliConner.

Holly counted ten, listening to the cacophony with an experienced ear. She got to her feet as some people—fans—came running up the stairs and held the doorway open for them to pass.

Now's as good a time as any, Holly thought to herself, and followed them.

She forced herself to move easily, as though this were an ordinary day. The corridor was full of people, HeliConners having come out of their rooms to wonder what was going on, or heading back to their rooms to salvage possessions just in case there really was a fire. It was this well-populated confusion that Holly had been counting on, and she blessed it as she hurried down the corridor toward Room 555.

She heard the quality of the pandemonium change as one of the distant alarms was silenced. In a few more moments it would all be over, but she didn't need much more time; the door was right ahead, and Carol was holding it open.

Holly slid through, so keyed up that she threw the deadbolts and night locks once she'd got the door shut. She leaned against it, her eyes glittering with excitement. "Two down, one to go," she said cheerfully. "How you doing, Makindeor?"

"I am well, Holly. But we won't find the Cloak here." He flung off Carol's new cape with a practiced gesture and took his strange glasses out of his pocket. He settled them on his nose, peering through them with an abstracted expression.

Sheepishly, Holly reached for the deadbolt and chain. It wouldn't do them any good to barricade themselves in while they were still expecting Margot. She glanced up. Carol was looking at her, a thoughtful, puzzled expression on her face.

There was a scrabbling at the other side of the door, followed by a rattle and a bumping as someone tried a key and ran into the security lock.

"Carol?" the muffled familiar tones of Margot Reasoner, FFW, came through the door. "Carol, you had better be *in* there—"

Holly jerked open the door and stared at her friend. Margot's eyes widened in shock.

"You!" Margot said.

Why does everyone keep saying that? Holly wondered to herself. She pulled the door open wider and gestured Margot inside.

Margot swept in—she could hardly do anything else wearing a full-length rhinestone-studded indigo velvet cloak lined in flame-colored silk charmeuse. She pulled the mantle tighter around her—giving her something of the look of a Gothic vampire princess—and squeezed past Holly into the room. Behind her, Holly locked the door up tight again, mostly out of nervous reflex.

"Boy, am I conditionally glad to see you again," Margot said. "What's going on out there? The whole place is a midnight zoo; don't they know you're only supposed to pull false alarms in the middle of the night? But I'm glad you're back, Hol. Did you ditch the—" She saw Mac and stopped dead.

"There it is," Mac said, a note of wonder in his voice. "She has it. *She* has the Cloak of Night and Daggers."

· 9 ·

Treason Is the Season

EIRDOIS BALIGANT OF the House of the Vermilion Shadows bided within Castle Mourning's walls upon a most comfortable chair of state in a private chamber to which he had brought the most expensive, if not the most tasteful, of his newly won treasures. The High King-Elect was a little below average height, and his hair was a color that an inhabitant of the World of Iron would not have hesitated to call gunmetal. He was dressed in sumptuous, jewel-sewn silks and fur-lined velvets. The shoes upon his feet were gilded with gold so fine and so thick that it could be scraped from the leather with a fingernail. And he had a problem.

It seemed an unlikely condition for one such as he to find himself facing, for Eirdois Baligant was High Prince, soon to be High King, with the Lady Hermonicet the Fair promised as his wife. He had everything it was possible to want within Chandrakar's borders and as much that could be brought from beyond as his inventive greed could contrive.

It was true that he was not content, but that the High Kingship itself would not content him he knew, and it was no surprise to him. He knew also that the High King would have endless opportunities for fresh, inventive revenges, and Baligant was by nature vindictive, with a spiteful nature honed by a hundred years of war.

He had been a young man when it began, a minor clerk from the most junior line in House Azure. Before he had been acclaimed High King by the Twilight Court, he had not been accounted handsome, and no one, from his childhood tutors to the Chief Archivist under whom he had toiled as a young man, had thought him clever.

All this had changed. Better men than he had died through the years of the war—handsomer, cleverer, nobler, and more worthy of life. Baligant had survived—and flourished. He had possessed the best of motivations to do so. The Lady Hermonicet, called the Fair, most beautiful in all the Seven Cantons which made up Chandrakar, had chosen him from all the Morning Lords who fought for her hand. Had chosen him, though she had sworn she would wed no man save he who would be High King now that Rainouart the Beautiful was dead.

Since that moment many years before, when a message from White Hermonicet had come to him, Baligant had lied and intrigued, made alliances only to betray them, worked and schemed and planned. And over the years, with the help of his Lady, he realized that the moment he had plotted to reach was not the Kingmaking yet to come. The Lords Temporal thought they knew the scope of his ambition and that the moment of his glory would be then. They thought him a malleable and grateful choice, but they did not know the extent of the malice that drove him. His ambition would not be realized at that moment when twelve elphen lineages presented the Treasures which they guarded . . . but when they did not.

At that moment, with their own law to be their fetter and their lash, he would destroy the power of the Seven Houses of the Twilight forever, and any of the Morning Lords who remained in Chandrakar thereafter would do so by his whim and at his sufferance, knowing him for their master.

Amadis was the key. Amadis, whom Hermonicet had bound to him. Amadis, Adept of the Wild Magic. A wizard.

Adepts in the Art Magical were masters of the High and Low Magics both Right and Left; they walked in sunlight, order, and law, and any of the Children of Air who chose might bend themselves to mastering the rigorous disciplines of the High or Low Magic according to their talent. Without the Adepts, the very fabric of life in Chandrakar would unravel.

But wizards were something else entirely: masters of the Wild Magic who bowed to no law save their own desires. They might be of any of the Five Races; they lived in palaces belonging to no Land, strongholds crafted from the fabric of the Morning itself through their covenants with the Word, and their personal histories were the stuff of legend. Their powers were vast, their loyalty could not be bought, and the price of their services was immense and permeated with subtle trickery.

Except for Amadis.

To gain mastery of the Wild Magic, each wizard had to accept some weakness that corresponded in its intensity to the scope of his power. As wizards were hugely powerful, their weaknesses were as bitter as death itself, and as jealously defended against. To know a wizard's secret was to forge a magical covenant that bound both the discoverer and the wizard in an unbreakable pact.

Or, at least, in a pact that was *thought* to be unbreakable.

Baligant began to pace. It did not matter to him that the movement exposed his agitation for any to see—there were no watchers here; in this one place Baligant could lay aside the masks of state . . .

And wonder how Amadis had managed to betray him.

He wondered again, as he had many times, how it was that the wizard Amadis had bargained her way into such a fatal weakness in the first place—that the dried petals of the ice-rose, which grew in so many of the Morning Lands, mingled with the blood of the rightful King of the Land in which they were gathered, was the wellspring of Amadis' power. Baligant knew, though knowing little of magic, that her covenant with the Word was not as secure as that of other wizards, that the power that she expended in her sorcery was not returned to her by the Word, and that she must weave lesser magics to harvest the power she needed to survive. Magics like those of blood and roses, fire and ice.

But in the end, those puzzles mattered less to Baligant than that knowing her weakness was what bound Amadis to his will.

It was she who had sought out the Treasures at his orders while the land was still at war, she who had catch-trapped them, rehidden them, stolen them, and flung them from the Land according to her own good pleasure—save for the Mirror, which Line Eirdois held for all to see. And those Treasures that Amadis could not find to hide were surely lost beyond the power of any to retrieve them, which suited Baligant's plans just as well.

What did *not* suit his plans was that his wizard—his tool, the chief architect of his plot—seemed to have found some way around her need for his blood. And if she did not need him to survive, he could not command her.

Although even when he had been sure of his ability to command her, Baligant thought bitterly, things had not often worked out precisely as he had intended them to.

He lifted a thin-walled vase carved from cloudy emerald from a delicate mosaic-topped table crafted in a far-off land and gazed sullenly into its viridian depths, remembering.

The Sword of Maiden's Tears was Line Rohannan's Treasure, one of the most powerful of the Twelve, rendering the Swordwarden nearly invincible in battle. And so Baligant had known that it was necessary to destroy not only the Sword but its Guardian as well, and with his wizard he had crafted an ingenious trap.

The Sword itself they had hidden in one of the Borderlands, difficult enough to find that its Rohannan seeker would not be suspicious. But what they had not meant him to know until it was too late was that the Sword of Maiden's Tears was bespelled, balanced so that the moment it was disturbed in its hiding place, it would fall through the worlds to the Last World, taking its Guardian with it. Amadis had tied the Sword to an Ironworlder soul, making them indivisible, causing them to seek one another wherever they lay.

That trap, Baligant had to admit, had worked. Rohannan Melior had achieved the Sword and had fallen through to the Last World, where Baligant had confidently expected him to quickly die of its deathmetal poisons.

It was then that things had begun to go wrong. Melior had come back to Chandrakar—*with* the Sword—and, worse, had sworn to any who would hear that he would have none but the Ironworld mortal Ruth Marlowe to be his bride. And Ruth Marlowe, Baligant had quickly discovered, was the earthling mortal to whom Amadis had tied the Sword. But still disaster could be averted, so long as Ruth Marlowe remained in the World of Iron. Mired in the swiftly spinning passage of the Ironworld years, the mud-daughter would surely be dead almost immediately as Chandrakar reckoned time.

Then Ruth Marlowe unthinkably found her way into the Morning Lands, and Baligant had no more leisure for mercy. He had dispatched Amadis to kill her before she reached the Sword.

But his wizard had inexplicably failed him, and Ruth Marlowe had reached Chandrakar itself. Disaster unqualified came when Baligant discovered that instead of abducting Ruth Marlowe, Amadis had seized Rohannan Melior and the Sword of Maiden's Tears, bringing them *here*, to this very keep. Amadis planned to draw Ruth Marlowe to them, before killing both the Ironworlder—Line Rohannan's only proof of Baligant's involvement—and the Swordwarden, and hiding the Sword once more.

Wizard logic. Baligant despised it, but with Baron Rohannan already in his hands, he could hardly afford to just let him go. So Baligant had left him in Amadis' hands but banished her from his presence to punish her, to deny her, to bring her crawling to him on her knees for what she must have—his kingmarked blood.

And she had not come.

It had been five days since he had learned of her malicious idiocy, and four days before that (when he had not known of it) since she had been slaked. The profligate employment of her power demanded refreshment at least once each phase of the moon. Nine days, and three days ago at most Amadis should have begun to beg him.

And she had not come.

He would not go to her—if the wizard had somehow found some way around their pact, she was no longer bound to preserve his life, and Baligant feared her unfettered power—but he must have counsel. There was only one place he could go.

Since the first day of her marriage to the Marchlord—an event that had occurred when Hermonicet was yet a child, years before Baligant had ever been born—Hermonicet the Fair had lived in her own place, her then lord's wedding gift to her, a tower crafted of magic, a single delicate spire the color of sea pearl that stood lone and solitary on the flat sea plain.

Baligant approached its gates alone. If she chose to deny him, he did not wish any servant present to see his shame. He rode a horse that was nearly as white as magic, richly and brightly draped, as if the color of its harness and its rider's clothing could by themselves bring high summer to the winter grayness of the fens.

It was by Hermonicet's aid that Baligant had become High King-Elect; Hermonicet loved him, Baligant told himself, but it was a feeble assertion at the best of times. He told himself that she could have chosen, could have supported any of the other candidates. In choosing him, must it not be true that she expressed her love?

No. A lifetime of being second best had stripped away all of his illusions. She did not love him. She had chosen him for purposes Baligant could not guess. But as long as she made him High King and participated in his vengeance against all those Morning Lords who had thought him not worth bothering with, he would accept her implicit bargain.

And play the lover.

The gates opened to him as he approached, and Baligant rode past the iridescent outer walls of his lady's nameless tower into its courtyard. No servitors waited to minister to him, only the ripple of unseen magics, as dense and complex as the tides of the sea. Magic filled the chamber with cool silver radiance, magic halted his horse and held it steady so that Baligant could dismount.

And when he had, and the beast had been led away to be tended by faceless, unseen hands, Baligant moved to the stair that led upward to the chamber where his lady waited, watching the sea. His spurs rang on the risers as he ascended, and he followed the spark of elflight that danced in the air before him, proof of his lady's favor.

The path to the rooms above never lay through the same rooms twice; magic indeed, though no one in all Chandrakar who spoke of

White Hermonicet spoke of her as having attained any strength in the Art Magical. For a moment Baligant wondered if Amadis served his lady as she did him, but he dismissed the notion. Still, a woman who could tame one wizard might tame another. . . .

Fruitless speculation.

At length Baligant reached a door that did not sweep open before him, and the glimmer in the air dissolved. He lifted one gauntleted hand and knocked, damning himself for his wistful hesitation. There was no love lost between them. She used him, nothing more. She did not love him.

But he had seen her face, and Baligant loved her.

The door opened, and he entered. This one chamber never changed; it was small and round and held two high-crowned windows, magic transmuting the harsh sea wind that blew through them to a clement swirling breath of salt air. Hermonicet sat before her mirror, slowly drawing an ivory comb through her hair.

This was the beauty that had maddened the Morning Lords, who for its possession had slaughtered one another for a hundred years. She raised her head and regarded Baligant through pale, storm-silver eyes, and he knew, with faint self-mocking despair, that he would do anything she asked to retain even this much of her regard, to have the chance merely to gaze upon that perfect elphen face.

"I give you good greeting, High King to be," Hermonicet said in a low musical voice. "Will you sit and take some refreshment?"

Baligant seated himself as close to her as he dared and gave her the gift he had brought—a rope of jewels whose beauty seemed dull and paltry beside her own. And by the time the unseen servants had brought wine and fruit, he had told Hermonicet the Fair of his predicament—that the Rohannan lord was held within Mourning's walls by Amadis, that somehow he had lost his power over the wizard.

"—and the Earthchild she used in the binding spell seeks him even now—him or the Sword, what does it matter? There is no one I may send after her to end her miserable life—no one I trust. . . ."

"And so you have come to me, to seek my poor woman's counsel," Hermonicet murmured, and Baligant could not tell if the words were meant in seriousness or jest. "Tell me, if you can, who accompanies the Ironworld mortal upon this rescue? For she is a stranger to our lands; whom shall she call upon for aid? Shall we see?"

Hermonicet passed a hand over the surface of her mirror, and though Baligant would have been willing to swear that it was as ordinary an object as any that lay within his lady's rooms, its surface now glowed and rippled like the surface of a lake, and images formed upon it that were no ordinary reflection: grass, trees, a road.

"The Eastern Road," Baligant said after a moment's reflection. Its width and the amount of traffic upon it told him that much, though of the knights and wagons upon the road none of the travelers resembled the Ironworld daughter Baligant feared.

"Yes," Hermonicet said. She leaned closer, and Baligant caught the faint perfume of civet and orange blossoms from her skin. He sat back, clenching his hands into fists. It would be so easy to cause her to laugh at him.

"There," his lady said.

A flash of white drew Baligant's attention back to the mirror. There on the road was a white horse, whiter than Baligant's own, magic-white. Upon its back rode an enormous man—a human man, Baligant realized after a moment, bull-huge, with hair like beaten gold and wearing a strange black and green armor.

Beside him rode a brown-haired human woman. She looked up—it was as if she looked directly into the mirror's searching eye—and Baligant knew that she was the woman they sought. Ruth Marlowe.

There were two others riding with Ruth Marlowe and the nameless paladin: an elfmaid and her human servant. Baligant dismissed the servant out of hand—the mud-born knew better than to interfere in the affairs of the Morning Lords—but the woman he knew.

"Floire Jausserande—the hopeful Cupbearer. What business does she have with the Ironworlder?"

"Perhaps she seeks the Cup of Morning Shadows." Hermonicet's voice was coolly amused.

The Cup, as Baligant recalled, had been severed by Amadis from its tanaiste-Cup, and as the Cup of Morning Shadows had been anchored to Chandrakar only by its shadow-Cup, it must by now have drifted far outside the borders of the land. Line Floire would never find it in time to present it; if Rohannan Lanval had not for some unaccountable reason sent his son, Rohannan Melior, in search of the Sword decades ago, Melior would not have it by him now—although, Baligant promised himself, the new Baron Rohannan would not have his bright toy for long.

But a scant year lay before the Kingmaking, and soon the panic would begin to spread among the Houses of the Twilight, as each Guardian sought his Treasure and found that it was lost. Each Line would hide its loss—a hundred years of war had bred little trust between baron and baron, earl and earl. Perhaps no one of them would know about the loss of any Treasure but his own until the very day of the Kingmaking, when Baligant would banish them all.

And then, with Amadis' help, he would recover the Treasures, and—

Hermonicet's hand upon his arm distracted Baligant from this pleasant train of thought. She gestured toward the mirror.

"But you see, my lord, the vast force arrayed against us: a girl-child of Floire and the human outlaw who is her companion (they would gladly slay one another if they only could), the soulless Ironworld daughter, and a paladin who knows not why he fights. Someone has meddled, to bring him here."

More interference that his wizard had not seen fit to warn him of! Baligant gritted his teeth, nettled, but Hermonicet merely raised her hand again, and once more the mirror was only a mirror. She smiled encouragingly at him, and Baligant felt his very bones melt for love of her.

"But if they choose to come, can Baligant High Prince be less gracious than to welcome them? Your wizard shall build a castle for their guesting and place the Rohannan lord and his Treasure within it, and when the others come they may seek him out, and afterward there will be no man living who may say what has befallen them." Hermonicet folded her hands in her lap and gazed at Baligant expectantly.

Use Rohannan Melior as bait to lure the Ironworld daughter and her protectors in—and that Floire brat who sought the Cup as well—and see that they did not leave? Such a plan had the virtue of simplicity. And no one would be surprised at the disappearance of either the Rohannan or the Floire Treasurekeeper . . . until it was too late.

There was only one problem. The wizard.

"But you have said, my lord, that my humble gift to you has grown strange and overproud. If you would but send her to me, my bridegroom, I shall remind her what a glory she finds in serving the most puissant prince that Chandrakar shall ever know."

Even as dazzled as he was, Baligant regarded his ladyfair with some doubt. In all his years of bitter intrigue and manipulation, he had never known Amadis to be interested in either service or reflected glory. "My lady—" he began.

"Send her to me," Hermonicet said huskily, leaning forward to brush his cheek with her lips. "I shall reason with her."

And there was nothing that Baligant could do but yield to her. It was, after all, only a small thing.

"Would you choose to fail me?" Hermonicet breathed.

The woman at her feet whimpered, pressing her body against the stones of the floor as if she were attempting to hide among them. Hot gold light bled from every pore of the human form she wore, taking power and pride with it.

"*. . . please . . .*" she moaned. One fine-boned hand was spread against the floor, and Hermonicet placed her slippered foot upon it, pressing down with all her weight. The jeweled net about Hermonicet's hair glittered in the soft silvery light of the room, as hard and unyielding as ice crystals against snow.

"I mean Baligant to become High King in this land, and he—and you—will break all the Treasures between you. Without the constraint of those forms, the power that makes Chandrakar manifest may be re-poured into a different vessel for my use alone. I shall become the embodiment of the Land, eternal as the Morning—and you, you tainted foolish creature, will not stop me." She ground her slipper against the hand beneath it, faintly irritated that it was not possible to cause her servant worse suffering. But though the terms of her pact were most elastic, they did not include the spilling of blood.

Still, Hermonicet's knowledge was extensive, and there were other methods by which to afflict. She was no Adept of the Wild Magic herself, but the one lone gift Hermonicet possessed had made all others unnecessary.

She could draw magic—all magic, any magic—into herself. And when she did this to a wizard, a creature whose very bones were made of magic . . .

The woman on the floor keened softly in her pain. The fabric that had laid smoothly over contours of vitality and power when she had entered the chamber now hung over gauntness and pain. Suppliant. Helpless. Drained.

It had cost Hermonicet a land's ransom in vows and promises and secret study to learn to trick and bind this most promising of the wizard Ophidias' apprentices into making her covenant with the Word prematurely. Half-trained and arrogant, Amadis had not been wary enough to conceal the secret of her power from one of the Bound-in-Time, and from that moment she had belonged to Hermonicet absolutely.

She could not even flee. If Amadis dared leave this land for any length of time, she would court discovery and punishment from the master she had betrayed. Until that moment when Hermonicet tasted that ultimate power which she craved, Amadis was bound to her utterly.

And afterward, she was expendable.

Reluctantly, Hermonicet relinquished her hold upon Amadis. She had taken enough of the Wizard's power to feel charged, vital, alive—a rapture that was a faint foretaste of what she would feel when the magic of an entire Morning Land was hers. And more vital, Amadis was drained to the point where she desperately needed the replenishment that (Hermonicet would see to it) only Baligant could give.

As for Rohannan Melior, Hermonicet had her own plans for the Morning Lord whose blood had been sufficient to satisfy Amadis' *geas*.

"Return to your master," Hermonicet told the wizard in an unyielding silver voice. "Convince him of your humility, of the need you have for him. I shall take possession of the young Baron Rohannan, and the Treasure he would guard so fiercely. And when the Ironworld daughter comes, I shall welcome her as well. Now go."

There was no protest. Amadis dragged herself from Hermonicet's chamber on her belly, and Hermonicet laughed.

Melior did not know how long he had languished at the mercy of the madwoman with the taste for his blood, but his delivery from that captivity was no sort of relief. He was no fool. He was far too inconvenient to be left alive.

The guards who came to Amadis' chamber to release him were terrified, though not of him. Melior had been kept in the wizard's own sanctum, and though its doors opened at a touch—proof enough that their entrance was permitted—the Wild Magic was danger itself. The guards barely dared to touch the locking pins of the hardened bronze shackles that were all that held Melior upright, and so he fell; first to dangle painfully by one hand, then to drop heavily to the cold stone floor. When they dragged him out, blood from a profusion of shallow unhealed wounds made a dark trail across the floor in his wake.

The men who handled him were not highborn knights to whom Melior could appeal for treatment according to the rules that governed prisoners and the arts of war. They were a sort much seen in the last years of the war—elphenborn who claimed no House, no family, and no honor, but who chose their master for his ability to pay and who would perform any task asked of them. Henchmen. Executioners. Melior did not understand why Baligant's wizard did not kill him herself, if that was her pleasure.

Once they had carried him down the flight of stairs that separated the wizard's chamber from the rest of the stronghold, they became more relaxed. The room they conveyed Melior to was obviously a barracks of some sort: cold and gloomy in the wintery chill, filled with the scent of burning candles, leather, oil, and metal. His captors dropped him with little ceremony onto a mat of crudely plaited rushes.

"What's that?" A voice whose source Melior could not see spoke.

"What does it look like, Rauf?" one of his keepers responded, and

Melior heard the movement and laughter of several men. He wished he could let go, slide into the deeper darkness where oblivion waited.

But he was the Swordwarden, and his Treasure was not in his hands. He did not have the luxury of dying now.

"Needs your services," the other guard added. "Come on, Raufy—we don't want him to die before we can deliver him to the White Ferret's mercy."

Melior painfully opened his eyes.

He was, as he had suspected, in a sort of guardroom. The room contained a table and chairs, and armor and weapons were racked along the walls; not the honest barracks where the King-Elect's guardsmen were lodged, but a makeshift accommodation, so that Baligant could keep his fell instruments of black policy beside him.

"Ho, he's not as dead as all that, Thib."

"Maybe we shouldn't—" the one called Thib said.

"Get out of my way," Rauf said, and added, "He might do better if you got him up off those stripes. Someone's a saucy hand with the cat; I wonder how *he* likes it for a change?"

Rough hands hauled Melior into a sitting position. He forced himself to keep his eyes open, holding to consciousness and learning all he could.

There were six of them, all in the identical motley well-used armor and badgeless surcoats that marked them for what they were more blatantly than any possible uniform could. Four were elves, a woman and three men, their tightly braided hair and hard, battle-scarred features marking them as veterans of many years of war. The woman wore a leather half-mask of the sort worn to conceal the ugliness of scars beyond the help of magic.

A fifth member of the company was human, with a human's ruddy skin. He had close-cropped hair the color of cherrywood coals, and his face was as hard as the rest, but he was young enough to have been born at the very end of the war. He stood a little behind the others, absently juggling a pair of throwing daggers and watching Melior, a merry mad light in his eyes and his expression feral.

The sixth—Rauf—knelt before him on the matting.

"Branded *and* flogged—what's your crime then, little lord? And cut up besides. If there were a Hiring Fair for the torturer, you'd be the showpiece." Rauf dragged open a pack as he spoke, not looking at Melior at all. In Rauf's features, human and elphen were subtly blended—Rauf was halfborn, belonging to neither world and scorned by both. "Get him a cup of wine at least, Thib."

"If I'd thought he was this lively . . ." Thib grumbled, moving over to the table. *"I'm* the one who needs the wine—wizards, by the Twelve; it will be dragons next, see if it isn't."

"Ah, Thib, don't they pay you enough for wizards?" the human cooed in fulsome mock sympathy, and the others laughed, in the easy comradeship of a shared joke.

Melior knew their kind better with each passing moment. They were what was left of a Free Company: fighters who, having lost their lord through some misfortune, declared no higher loyalty than to their sword-brethren. Some had found places in the Seven Houses again through marriage or service, but others could not—or chose not to—and continued instead to earn their bread in the New Peace in the only way they knew.

Melior opened his mouth, trying to rally his wits enough to speak. It did not seem that he was immediately about to die—or to be killed—but neither did he think that his companions bore him any good will.

"Save your breath," Rauf said briefly. The halfborn's eyes were pale green, and he looked at Melior as if he would much rather have looked away. He reached behind himself, taking the filled cup from Thib, and held it to Melior's lips.

Magic had kept Rohannan Melior alive in his captivity; now, outside the sphere of its influence, his injuries dragged at him with an ever-increasing weight, as though iron chains from the Last World itself were being slowly piled upon his body. He drank thirstily.

"Your lord will betray you," he said, when he could speak. Useless to even try, he knew, but he must make the effort.

"Evening Star has no lord," the elphen woman said, "and if he wants to sell us out, he'll have to catch us first."

"We've been betrayed by experts," Melior's other guard added with a bitter smile.

"I warned you," Rauf told Melior, and then, to the man behind him. "What are you to do with him, Thib? Give me another cup, will you?"

Thib grumbled but went to do Rauf's bidding; Rauf pulled a tiny bottle out of his pack and held it up to the light.

"Said we were to take him to *her,* in the other tower," Thib answered as he filled the cup. "And it didn't look when we took him down like he was going to live to get there, so . . ."

It took no great skill to sense the spreading reluctance and uneasiness that filled the mercenaries.

"And you didn't want to go anyway," the woman finished for him. "So I'll go, and Gryphon—and since her bloodstained ladyship won't even let him into the tower—"

Gryphon seemed to be the human with the daggers; at this remark both of them left his hands, to bury themselves in wood somewhere behind Melior's head. All that held Melior in this upright sitting position was the man behind him; he did not have enough strength to dare to try to move.

"Drink this," Rauf said, pouring the contents of his flask into a second cup of wine. "It'll make you strong enough to ride. It won't last forever, but by then you'll probably be dead anyway." Rauf smiled coldly.

Melior drank, and he felt deceptive strength flow into his limbs. He recognized the dose: This was a drug from far beyond Chandrakar's borders. Not magical, it gave the illusion of a true magical healing, but illusion was all it was. Its false glow would fade in an hour or two, and he would be in worse case than before.

But while it lasted, he would use what strength it lent him.

"I am Rohannan Melior of the House of the Silver Silences, Rohannan of Line Rohannan," Melior said. He pushed his blood-matted hair from his eyes and looked around at them all, then pushed himself to his feet. Half-healed injuries broke open to bleed again, and Melior could feel the hot pull of the whip-weals on his back and shoulders, but while the drug worked in him the pain of his injuries was a distant thing. "You must listen to me."

"Avelin, go get four horses. You and Gris come with us as far as the gate—this Morning Lord might think he's going to run," the woman said, as if Melior had not spoken.

"I am the Swordwarden I have been taken without cause and without hearing, just as Baligant will turn on any who oppose him. If the Twelve Treasures are lost to Chandrakar, what can save any of us, either of Earth or Air?"

"He speaks against our King to be," Gryphon said in tones of mock horror, walking past Melior to retrieve his knives. The elf Avelin walked with him and continued out the door.

"Child of Earth—" Melior began, turning toward Gryphon.

The woman in the half-mask grabbed Melior by the hair, jerking him back around to face her.

"Listen to me, Baron Rohannan—oh, yes, we know who you are; did you think we didn't?—there's none of us cares if Prince Baligant has all the Twelve under his seat cushion and wants to hold the Kingmaking tomorrow without any of you. It's nothing to us—this is a job, and until we leave it, we do as we're told."

"Even if it means wizards," Rauf commented, tossing the pack of medical supplies onto a bunk and leaning back against the wall beneath a torch. The flame gilded his skin, masking its earthborn coloration, but no disguise could allow him to pass for one of the Children of Air. He would be despised as both—and neither—belonging nowhere.

"How can you not care?" Melior demanded helplessly.

"I wouldn't," Gryphon said in a low voice.

"None of us cares any more who holds Chandrakar, Morning Lord. Let Baligant have the throne and White Hermonicet, and I hope he is as kind a husband to her as my own was to me when he rose to claim the throne because that White Ferret was the prize. He did this—" She released her hold on Melior's hair and pulled off her mask.

Across her face and cheek there was the blackened imprint of a hand, sunk through the flesh all the way to the bone. The flesh around it was pulled inward toward the spread shape of fingers and palm. One eye was destroyed, its socket sunken and fused. The other had narrowly escaped, and it glared now at Melior, daring him to pity her. Balefire: a middle spell of the High Magic whose effect could never be erased.

"I pledged to his worst enemy and rode out against him the next day."

She replaced the mask once more. It was cunningly fashioned, with glass and metal behind the blind eyesocket, impersonating what was no longer there.

"Told you," Gryphon breathed. "You got Elete mad." He slid his throwing knives back into their wrist sheaths and walked over to his bunk, beginning to put on his armor.

"Who presents his Line's Treasure at the Kingmaking and who doesn't makes no difference to us. We're the folk who'll be harrying you through the Gates when you fail; there's always work for us," Elete finished.

The sea air was bitter on his skin, but none of the mercenaries had offered Melior so much as a cloak. He rode barefoot and shirtless, the cut and charred rags of his breeches his only covering, at the center of a moving box of armed and armored, mounted warriors.

In the distance he could see the pale spire of the White Tower and knew they were taking him to Hermonicet. In its way, it was almost a relief. It meant that though his danger was greater than ever before, he would at least return to a world he knew.

He wished Baligant much joy of his hand-chosen hellhounds. They would pick his bones as quickly as those of any prey he set them on. Melior wondered if Baligant understood just how dispassionately they served him.

With the part of his mind that still believed that he would live, Melior brooded on the magnitude of the problem presented by groups such as this one composed of Elete and her friends. Elete had told no more than the simple truth: Houseless, lordless, they had no stake in Chandrakar's future. Unless the Seven Houses of the Twilight could find some place for them, Chandrakar was doomed, even if all twelve of the Treasurekeepers came with their Treasures to the Kingmaking.

And then they arrived at the White Tower.

· 10 ·

A Prince of Our Disorder

"SHE HAS THE Cloak," Mac said, staring at Margot from the door to the bedroom.

"You brought him back," Margot said in a dull voice. "I guess he must have remembered."

Margot's face had gone so white that Holly was afraid she'd faint. She dropped her purse to the floor with a thud and reached for the fastening of the Cloak around her neck. With quick angry jabs Margot unclasped it and then flung it toward Mac's feet. It landed halfway between the two of them with the heavy soft sound of a falling curtain.

"Here. Take it, if that's what it is. Enjoy," Margot said viciously.

Silence.

"Remembered what?" Carol asked in a small voice. She looked from Margot to Mac, her open round face worried.

"What is your patron's House, Child of Earth?" Mac said to Margot. She ignored him, walking across the room to the couch and sitting down heavily. She turned her head away from him, apparently obsessed with a bad knockoff of an engraving from a Renaissance herbal that hung on the wall.

"What's going on?" Holly's voice was an edgy whipcrack.

"It's been twenty-five years." To Holly's horror, Margot sounded as if she were about to cry.

"Margot? Marg?" Carol walked over to the couch and crouched

down in front of Margot, trying to make the other woman look at her. Carol took Margot's hand; it lay as lax and limp in hers as if it were a doll's.

"Margot? Please? You're scaring me," Carol pleaded.

"I said—" Holly began.

Mac walked into the room and picked up the cloak—or Cloak. He made a small sound of satisfaction as he swirled it around his shoulders. Holly was the only one looking at him; she saw the velvet surface of the Cloak ripple like an oil-slick, rings and bands of color spreading from the fabric where his fingers touched it out across the entire surface, until the garment he held in his hands was a rich deep green with a lining of old-gold tabby silk.

"It *is*," Holly said, interrupting herself. "It *is* that thing you're looking for!" She looked back toward Margot.

"Answer me, Child of Earth," Mac said, and there was a note of demand in his voice that Holly had never heard before.

"Amarmonde," Margot said, still not looking at him. Holly saw a tear roll down her cheek, but her voice was perfectly steady. "Line Amarmonde of the House of the Azure Stars holds the Cloak of Night and Daggers, as all once knew. Tell me, Morning Lord, who rules now in Chandrakar?"

"It was a long time ago," Margot said a few minutes later, clutching the empty glass. Holly had decided that emergency measures were called for and had opened the ruinously overpriced in room refrigerator/bar, poured two Bacardi miniatures and half a can of real Coke into a glass, and handed it to Margot. Margot had drunk it off as if it were water.

"I . . . it is said that Eirdois Baligant will be the choice of the Lords Temporal. Now tell me," Mac said, speaking out of that strange aura of authority, as if it were an even more magical cloak than the one he now wore. "How came you here—and where is your patron?"

"Dead," Margot said, still not looking at him. "Amarmonde Joldewyn is dead. She died on the High Road, a long time ago."

"Margot," Carol said, very gently, "do you mean you're from . . . somewhere else?"

Margot's eyes focused on her friend and she laughed harshly. "Oh, yes. My name was Marcet Castledaughter, and I was born in Domain Amarmonde in Canton Azure, in my lady's castle of Hoarfrost. I was her maidservant. She was Cloakward—Treasurekeeper, and the Twilight Houses were at war because we had no King. Oh, God, it all comes back so easily . . ." Margot put her face in her hands.

"And what became of your lady?" Makindeor demanded. "How is it that you are here with the Cloak, and she is dead?"

"I didn't kill her," Margot said, muffled.

She raised her head and looked at him for the first time. Her makeup was tear-blotched, the mascara smeared to make dark raccoon-rings beneath her hazel eyes. "I was a *child*, Morning Lord—she didn't confide her reasons to me. We left Hoarfrost in the dead of night with the Cloak; she used it to evade the patrols that her own liege lord had set; we were on the Iron Road before I even knew we'd passed the first Gate."

"She took her Treasure out of the Land in time of war?" Makindeor asked. "I find that hard to believe."

"If Margot says it's true, then it is," Holly said. She clenched her fists dangerously. "Leave it alone."

"And the rest, Child of Earth?" Makindeor said, his tone gentler this time.

"We rode," Margot said. "Always down—toward the Iron World. She'd brought me along in case she had to handle deathmetal and so I couldn't be tortured to say where she was once she'd gone. She was a kind mistress," Margot said, looking at Carol. "But I was a slave—her property. She could have done anything she wanted to with me, and no one would have lifted a finger to save me. I have never forgotten that. Could you reach me my purse?"

Carol got up to get it for her and brought it back, sitting down next to Margot with it. Margot dug through it until she found a packet of Kleenex. She wiped her eyes and blew her nose before resuming her story.

"I don't know how long we traveled. We never stopped in one place for very long, and every time we passed a Gate the seasons changed; I could never keep track. Afterward—once I was here—I tried to forget all of it, but then I started writing, and it surfaced in my books, so I guess you could say that no experience is ever wasted. And while we were on the Road, she died. I don't know *how* she died, or why—" Margot protested, in answer to Makindeor's unvoiced question. "We were sleeping in a trailhut, and she didn't wake up. She didn't wake up."

Margot stared off into space, her eyes fixed on the vista that existed only in memory.

"I didn't know what to do. I thought if someone found me there with her, they'd think *I* killed her, and I'd be hanged. I stayed there all day, but I couldn't face spending the night there with her body, so I drove my horse off and took hers. I took her cloak, too. It was pretty, and warmer than mine, and it didn't even begin to occur to me that she'd be *wearing* Amarmonde's Treasure as if it were just a piece of clothing. It didn't look the way it had when we'd left Castle Hoarfrost. I figured it out later, of course, but by then I was here." Margot shrugged, and wiped at her eyes again. "So color me stupid. I loved her. Maybe that's why I took it—to remember her. She was the only one who'd ever cared about me for any reason."

Carol put her arms around Margot, and Margot turned her face into Carol's shoulder. Holly came over to put her hand on Margot's back; the three of them formed a tight defensive grouping against outsiders.

Holly stared at Makindeor challengingly. The elf unclasped the Cloak from around his throat and took it off. He began to fold it carefully, making a smaller bundle of the bulky velvet than Holly would have believed possible.

"How did you come here to this place, Child of Earth?" Mac asked. "There was no word from Line Amarmonde that its Treasure was lost to them."

"Well they wouldn't say, would they?" Margot said, straightening up once more. Her cheeks were flushed now from the rum, and she stared at him defiantly. "They'd just try to find it, wouldn't they, and now you have instead, and you can take it back to them—but not me. You can't take me back. I'm staying here." Margot took a deep breath and sighed, then dutifully took up her tale once more.

"The Iron Road leads down—everyone knows that—and I guess by then we must have already been in the Border Lands. I stayed on the Road until it was gone. By then I was in West Lafayette, Indiana."

"What?" Holly said, for a moment thinking that her ears had betrayed her.

"West Lafayette," Margot repeated, a faint reluctant note of amusement in her voice. "You know, Purdue University, Barony of Rivenstar, Midrealm Dragons Rule, that sort of thing? Home of white socks and slide rules—at least it was back in the early sixties. An Ironrealm college town was a good place to end up—just about everybody thought I was an out-of-state student, and nobody compared notes. I learned enough to pass for an Ironworlder by auditing classes, and . . . I fit in. I picked up the name 'Reasoner' from some old news show. I liked it."

"But Margot," Carol said helplessly. "You told me you were *born* in Indiana!"

"I lied," Margot said simply. "Carol, I'm a *fantasy writer*—who was going to believe me if I said I'd come from Elfland? And . . . it just didn't come up in the conversation, okay? After enough time had passed—this was before I met either of you, and a *long* time before I sold my first book—I realized that I'd been pretty lucky. This is a human land, where nobody can say you're their property just because you happen to

have been born a member of the wrong race. Sure, there are places on
Earth that make Chandrakar look pretty good, but this isn't one of them.
I *like* it here. In real life, magic sucks, wizards are bastards, adventures
are scary, painful, and often fatal, and being chained in a dungeon has *no*
attractions at all. I like being warm and safe at night and having enough
to eat. I'll write about those other things all you like, but I don't ever want
to go back to living them." She looked almost pleadingly at Makindeor,
as if even now he had some power to compel her.

"Child of Earth, bide where you will; I will place no let or constraint
upon your freedom. I would promise to stand your blood-price before
House Azure, but I do not know how much time has passed there, nor
where my Line may now stand in relation to the Earl of Azure,"
Makindeor said, his voice oddly formal. There was something comforting
about such formality, as if he took this matter as seriously as Margot did.

"Don't worry," Margot said bitterly. "It'll come back to you. Are you
going to go home now?" she added hopefully.

"If I can." Makindeor's voice was doubtful. He stroked the Cloak
that he held and looked expectantly at Margot.

"You want me to *help a Morning Lord?*" Margot said in disbelief.
"Excuse me."

Margot got up quickly from the couch, her purse slung over her
shoulder, and walked past Makindeor to the bedroom. A moment later
the other three heard the bathroom door shut in the other room.

Carol looked at Holly.

"I guess this blows off the masquerade tonight, eh?" Holly said viva-
ciously, flopping down on the vacated couch. For some reason this whole
confession of Margot's struck her as bizarrely funny—in a very sick way,
of course. Poor Margot! "Now all we have to do is figure out how to get
out of the hotel without being arrested and killed—and figure out where
we can go after that, and—"

"Um," Carol said, "Could you excuse us for a moment, Mac?"

She went around the back of the couch and leaned over Holly, lowering her voice so Mac couldn't hear.

"Holly, have you been taking your meds lately?" Carol asked cautiously. "The lithium and stuff?"

Holly jerked away from the shorter woman, biting back an automatic
snarl of fury. She'd been feeling a pleasant sense of cheerful surreality
while Margot had been telling her unbelievable-but-obviously-incredibly-
true story, but Carol's question brought Holly back to mundane reality
with a swift, unwelcome impact.

"Is that the first thing that comes to your mind?" Holly snapped.
"Carol, I don't need a magic pill to know we're in serious trouble here.

They *shot* at me up there in Patroon County! I—" she stopped. Carol just looked at her steadily, concern in her warm gray eyes. *Get a grip, Hol.*

Carol was right. With iron self-control, Holly forced herself to face facts. Two little pills, one in the morning, one in the evening, ever since she was seventeen. Zoloft and Lithobid: It sounded like the title of an Elizabethan narrative poem. It was the price Holly Kendal paid for staying in the world. Not as bad as the Little Mermaid's. Better than Persephone's. Two little pills and a medical review every six months to see if her dosage needed to be adjusted; thirty minutes with her caseworker once a month and a MedAlert bracelet that she wore every moment of her life to make sure that her medication was never interrupted for any reason.

Two little pills that cut out all the highs and lows of life and made her . . . even, as much a normal person as a diabetic on insulin. Medication-dependent, but not—

Say it Holly. Not crazy. Not on a violent ward somewhere hopped up on Thorazine because nobody knows what's wrong. Not an outpatient covered with hesitation marks and taking a steadily increasing dosage of Prozac that just isn't working for some reason. Normal. Functional. In the world.

And the highs and lows that everyone else had and took for granted were something that Holly Kendal would never have. The sneaking curiosity about what it would be like just another of the insidious undermining temptations that Pendulum People had to learn to ignore. Surrendering to that coaxing inner voice would raise Holly to the heights of the angels in Paradise—then send her straight to Hell.

She felt herself begin to panic and sternly reined herself in. *Okay, Hol. Focus.* She knew that when a person broke her routine, there was always a chance of screwing up the meds. Usually she had a buddy she called if she expected things to get really hectic and there was a chance she'd forget or try to sabotage herself. But she hadn't been home, Rook didn't know to remind her, and the last three days had been more bizarre and traumatic than any others in most of her life.

Holly looked desperately toward Carol, trying to remember the last time she'd taken her dose. A couple of days shouldn't count much, should it? She was almost sure Carol was overreacting: Carol was such a mouse . . .

Friday at the airport while they were waiting for Margot—she'd taken them then and Carol had checked her. Saturday morning? Holly realized she didn't remember—she hadn't gone to bed Friday night at all; that might have been where things started to get strange. Saturday night? Sunday morning? Where had she been and what had she been doing? Holly put her face in her hands. Surely she must have gotten around to at least one round of pills in all that time.

But not this morning—that much she was sure of. Feeling angry and humiliated, Holly got up from the couch. She headed for her purse and rummaged around in it for the pharmacy bottles. When she got them out, Carol was standing behind her with the other half of the can of Coke, holding it out to her.

Holly shook the pills into her hand. *One for fun.* "Thanks, Carol," she said reluctantly. She tossed the pills onto the back of her tongue and chased them down with warm flat soda, ignoring the treacherous inner voice that told her she was fine, wonderful, great, cured at last—that she didn't need them, she *didn't,* all that was over and she didn't have to take her meds any more.

"Every day for the rest of your life," her therapist had said all those years ago. *"Without fail and without exception. You can't think of this any other way and survive."* Holly's therapist was bipolar, just as Holly was. Holly believed her. She had to.

She stood there, eyes closed, imagining she could already feel the chemical cocktail hitting her bloodstream, taking hold of her neurochemistry and exerting its leveling effect. Bringing Holly down from the heights.

It isn't fair, she thought with forlorn acceptance. Other people got to be giddy with happiness, aquiver with excitement, hysterical with joy. But not Holly Kendal. Never, ever, *ever* . . .

Margot came back out of the bathroom, her face scrubbed pink and new makeup painstakingly applied. She looked toward Holly, wary and puzzled and emotionally drained, but knowing something else was wrong. *This is all my fault,* Holly thought unhappily. If she'd never approached Mac, if she hadn't gone down that hall, if she'd turned him over to Hotel Security instead of bringing him back to her room.

There's just some learning experiences that drugs can't save you from, Holly-girl, Holly thought sarcastically.

"Hi, Margot," she said lamely.

"So," Margot said, "what's it going to be, then, eh?"

"This is a great time to be quoting the classics," Holly said with a wavery smile. She felt lightheaded and ill. "Mac? You've got the Cloak, you've got the Book—what's next?"

Someone tried the door.

All four of them—Holly, Mac, Carol, Margot—stared toward it, impelled by a sort of perverse fascination with disaster. There was the click of a key card being fitted into the electronic lock, and the door handle turned. Carol stared at it round-eyed, her hand over her mouth.

Nothing happened. A moment later, Holly realized why.

"The security bar," Holly whispered, pointing. She'd locked all of the locks when she, Carol, and Mac had come in, and had unlocked them again for Margot. But then she'd locked them again, fidgeting around. Now she blessed that impulse. The bad guys—or even the hotel maid—could have all the key cards in the world, and they still couldn't get in.

Carol pointed toward the window and mimed walking with her fingers. Holly realized she was right. They had to get out of here; the guy on the other side of the door knew that *someone* was in here if the bar was in place, even if he didn't know who. It was only a matter of time before he sent someone around to the window and bottled them up.

But the window?

Carol went over to the window—it was actually more of a glass door to nowhere—and began easing it open, trying to make as little noise as possible. As if he wanted to help conceal her actions, the person on the other side of the door started to knock loudly.

"You guys can't be serious," Holly said in an undertone. "We're on the fifth floor."

"True," Margot said, her voice equally soft, "but this is the Hotel Escher. The fifth floor is only two and a half stories up. And do you want to still be here when they finally get in?"

"No," Holly admitted, while wondering how someone of Margot's . . . Wagnerian build was going to get through the acrobatics that seemed called for to make their escape.

"Holly? Hey, Holly, let me in," the voice came through the door. "C'mon—it's Jack."

Holly shook her head at the others. Nobody she knew—but oh, so convincing. It would put almost anyone who heard it off their guard long enough to go over to the door and undo the deadbolt.

And then it would be all over.

Carol had the window open as far as it would go. She stepped out, leaning over the railing of the tiny shallow balcony. Margot began gathering their coats and purses together. She handled Mac's backpack as if it were a dead rat, but she did pick it up and hand it to him. He shoved the Cloak into it on top of the Book and shrugged the precious burden onto his back.

There was more rattling from the door and then a determined thump as the man outside threw his body against it. Margot handed Holly her Stone Mountain purse and Timberland down jacket and then began putting on her own coat.

Mac had followed Carol out onto the balcony. Inside the room Margot turned out the lights, and Holly blessed her friend's devious turn of mind—there was no sense advertising their presence by backlighting their escape.

Holly's eyes began to adjust to the dark. There was still a little light, from the lights in the parking lot, enough to see more of what they were doing than she actually wanted to. The balcony wasn't a real balcony, just a narrow ledge-with-railing, more for cosmetic purposes than anything else, although it was load-bearing. There was a quick consultation between Carol and Mac, and then Carol straddled the railing, working her way over it. Holly headed for the open window and peered out.

I just hope there's nobody in the room below us, Holly thought suddenly, remembering that when Frank Catalpano had called, he'd said he was in 455 on the floor below. But this was the Hotel Escher; Holly wasn't sure that 455 was anywhere near 555, vertically speaking. It might be on the other side of the building.

She hoped.

She wanted to look, to see if she saw lights from the floor below on the snow, but there wasn't room. *Oh, well, if there is someone down there, we can just try to convince them that this is live-action role-playing.*

Which it was in a sense, except that in this particular module, when your character died, you didn't get to come back as somebody else.

Now Carol was standing outside the railing, holding on tightly. Mac knelt on the narrow balcony and reached up through the bars to grasp Carol's wrists.

Carol let go of the railing and grasped the vertical bars. With Mac still holding her wrists—and supporting most of her weight—Carol kicked free of the balcony and slid down the bars. Mac went with her until he was bent almost double and Carol was hanging from his hands, her feet only a few feet above the balcony below. He released her and Carol fell the last of the distance, landing with a faint wince but apparently otherwise unharmed.

"Me next," Holly said, swinging her leg over the rail. Through the open window behind her she could hear the phone in their room ringing: four rings, then a stop as it went to voicemail, then four rings as someone tried again.

Mac dropped his backpack to Carol, and Holly followed it with her purse. The transfer went faster this time, with Carol below to grab Holly's legs and ease her down. Holly peered in through the window—dark and deserted—then out over the parking lot. She strained her eyes for lights or suspicious movements but saw nothing. The people who were hunting them would realize what the four of them had done soon—had they already figured it out? And even if Mac got them all out of the hotel, the four of them still had to get to Holly's car—and then where could they go?

Margot came next, with Mac handling her as if she weighed no more than Carol. She placed more trust in Mac's strength than either Carol or Holly had, kicking off from the balcony as though it were impossible for her to fall. But Holly, easing her down, felt the wild fluttering of Margot's heart as she hugged Margot against her tightly.

"I hate this," Margot hissed in her ear. *"Hate* it." Holly hugged her even tighter for a moment and then let her go.

It was crowded with the three of them wedged on the narrow fourth-floor balcony. There was a rumbling from the floor above—the window being shut—and then Mac clambered down among them, making the crowding even worse.

Holly looked over the side of the balcony. The even snowy surface of the ground was deceptively near, but the ground-floor rooms below them had concrete-lined light wells cut into the landscaping. They might be drifted full of snow now, but she still didn't relish jumping down into one of them.

"Come on, you guys," Carol pleaded.

Holly looked down again. Not a bad drop to the grass, but to get there she'd have to jump out, not down.

She felt Mac's hands on her waist.

"Can you fall?" he asked.

"Sure," Holly said. Every fighter learned that, early and often. "What are you thinking—and are you sure you're up to it?"

"I must be, must I not?" Mac said grimly. "Ready?"

"And I'll go get the car if you don't kill me," Holly muttered, and felt Mac laugh soundlessly behind her.

He lifted. Holly felt herself rising smoothly into the air. She balanced on the railing for a moment, then Mac heaved her outward as if she were a sack of grain.

There was one heartstopping glorious moment of flight, and then the false touchdown of hitting the snow, a feeling like rolling through soft wet feathers, and then Holly was staggering to her feet—damp and snow covered—and shaking herself off. She looked around. As far as she could tell, no one had seen her. She glanced at her watch: 5:30, and everyone inside the hotel would be concentrating on the upcoming masquerade.

Margot tossed Holly's purse down to her; it hit Holly's chest with the heavy definite impact of a football that contained two Chap-Sticks, a Snickers bar, a pair of bandage scissors, eight dollars in change, a book, a bottle of aspirin, and some smelling salts—in addition to Zoloft, Lithobid, a stethoscope, her wallet, and her keys. Holly staggered under the impact, almost losing her footing in the sloppy wet snow, then began wading toward the shoveled walkway.

Now all she had to do was get to the car and get back here.
That was all.

She tried to look inconspicuous as she walked around the side of the
hotel toward the parking at the front where Rosinante was. It would do
her no good to attract attention while getting her car; she still had to
swing back for the others. Her jeans were wet from the snow, generating
a burning uncomfortable cold that was rapidly turning to numbness.
Holly's mind automatically reviewed the symptoms of hypothermia and
frostbite. Now to get to her car, the faithful Rosinante, and get the lot of
them the hell out of here.

While there weren't many people wandering around outside the hotel, there were some; Holly waited, crouching in the shadow of the
bushes, until a flock of laughing talking fans exited the front door in the
direction of the parking lot. Holly drifted up behind them, following in
their wake. Fortunately, they seemed to be going in the right direction.

"Hey, did you find your friend?" It was Lenore, the gopher who'd
sold Holly her membership only a few hours earlier.

"Um . . . yeah," Holly said. "In fact, we're going out to dinner in
Elmsford now."

"Oh, that's good," Lenore said. "Be sure and get back in time for the
masquerade," she added, breaking off the conversation as her friends
found their cars.

My whole life is a masquerade, Holly thought bitterly. She continued
out to the edge of the lot, feeling exposed and vulnerable, like an animal
caught in a rifle sight. Hunted. Prey. When she reached the station
wagon, she had a fleeting wistful impulse just to jump in and take off,
going somewhere where none of this would ever find her again. The
notion vanished almost as she realized that it existed, and she carefully
unlocked all four doors of the Honda station wagon before sliding behind
the wheel and plugging the ignition key into the lock.

In her rearview mirror Holly could see the main entrance of the
hotel, lighted for night—and, standing outside it, peering into the parking
lot, a man in a dark suit—no sunglasses—his hand up as if it held a
walkie-talkie or cellular phone. There was no way he wasn't looking for
them.

*Oh, God, just let all of us get out of here and I promise to be good
forever,* Holly said, offering up the universal prayer. She started her car
and backed cautiously out of her space. She drove slowly around the edge
of the parking lot, hoping it made her look like a late arrival seeking a
parking spot. She turned left and slid smoothly around the side of the

building, her car's headlights giving her a false sense of security and vision.

She reached the balcony.

They weren't there.

For one hopeful moment Holly thought she'd just missed them or was looking toward the wrong windows. But the splodge she'd made landing in the snow was an unmistakable landmark. That was where they'd been.

The lights in the room were on.

She was almost sure Margot had turned them out, but could she have turned them back on for some reason before she came down? Had the others climbed back up?

Or had the villains arrived?

With no other choices, knowing that her headlights were marking her out for special notice, Holly drove doggedly on. She could not imagine what she was going to do if she did not find Mac and the others. She couldn't imagine leaving without them, and going back into the hotel seemed like another name for suicide. *Help . . . help . . . help . . .* Holly's mind prattled inanely. The station wagon glided on, as if its motion had nothing to do with her, as Holly drove toward the back of the hotel.

Margot was standing right under the light beside the service entrance, clutching her purse in front of her like a desperate commuter at a bus stop in Hell. Holly jammed on her brakes, the car skidding on a patch of packed snow that the snowplow had missed. Margot ran out to her, with the faintly painful-looking, mincing gate of a woman crossing uncertain ground in slick-soled dress pumps. Margot dragged open the passenger side door and fell into the car.

"By the dumpster," she said, gasping for breath. "He's using the Cloak."

"What were you *doing* there?" Holly demanded angrily. "Hanging out a sign?"

"One of us had to be where you'd see her," Margot said, "and Carol thought she might be able to bluff it if they caught her. Besides, my agent could probably get me out of any trouble," she added.

"Well, maybe," Holly said grudgingly. Margot's agent was Maggie Tanenbaum, widely reputed to devour two editors for breakfast every morning.

"There," Margot said, pointing.

The dumpsters were painted white, which helped. Holly slid up to them, slowing to a crawl and turning off her lights. She kept her eyes fixed on the road ahead, as if her not trying to see Carol and Mac would

automatically translate into their complete invisibility. She heard one of
the car doors open, and in the rearview mirror she saw a flash of paleness
as Carol clambered into the back seat.

"Go," Carol panted.

"Mac—" Holly protested.

"He's *in the car,*" Carol said urgently.

"Holly," Mac's disembodied voice said.

Cloak. Invisible. Holly drove off, heart racing. She resisted the urge to
floor it—Rosinante wouldn't do much over sixty anyway, and that was
going downhill.

"Lights," Margot reminded her, and Holly turned them on.

There can be no way they don't know my car, Holly thought suddenly.
They may be dim, but nobody's that dim. "Mac?" she said in a skittery,
quivery voice. *Oh, please, don't let me lose it now. Everyone's depending on
me. What does the Cloak do? What did he tell me? I can't remember . . .*
"Mac, tell me how to get out of here."

"Turn right," the disembodied voice commanded.

The back of the hotel was on her left; Holly was driving along the
long axis. Only a few cars were parked back here, mostly hotel employees'. On her right was piled snow, a band of scrub trees—and no road.

"I can't," she protested.

"Do it," Mac said inexorably. "Do you want to die?"

Margot grabbed the wheel and wrenched it toward herself. The car
veered right, and in its jouncing headlights Holly saw a gap between
snowplow-piled banks of snow. She slid the car between them, braking.

"Goddammit—don't you *ever*—" Holly said, and stopped, concentrating on her driving.

"Turn off your lights," Margot said tightly, and Holly did, slowing to a
crawl, driving as much by touch and feel now as by sight, as the branches
scraped wraithlike demanding fingers over the hood and doors and she
wondered if the next jolt would be the one that heralded the broken axle
that would strand them completely.

When she finally reached the parking lot beyond, it glowed serene
and peaceful beneath its security light, its unplowed surface an unbroken
sea of white.

"They are going to know for sure we've come through here," Holly
complained, stopping to rest for a moment before driving a tiny Japanese
car into several inches of unplowed snow. At least she didn't have to find
a way to get around another of those rucked-up walls of guck the plows
left. The parking lot hadn't been plowed at all—the building's employees
probably weren't expected back until New Year's.

"It will not matter what they know if we are gone," Mac said. "They watch the front—they have a description of your car and orders to follow you until they can force you off the road unobserved." Mac stopped talking.

"And?" Holly prompted.

"Never mind," Mac said. "They shall not find us."

" 'Oh, Holly, you are too much,' " Carol quoted sarcastically. "Do you think they're going to give you a parking ticket?"

"Oh." *No. It's just that nobody's ever really wanted to kill me before.* A soul-deep feeling of *resentment* began to kindle in her. It wasn't even fear; you resented bullies and hated them. You didn't respect and fear them. *Until they're actually pointing the gun at you.*

Holly shifted the car into gear and eased forward. Rosinante's front and rear wheels eased over the curb with two heart-stopping crunches, and Holly immediately felt all sense of traction vanish. She didn't dare go faster than two miles per hour for fear that the little car would simply go into a spin, and beneath the need to hold it steady Holly's frustration only grew stronger: Everything she did only made things worse. Even when they got out of the lot, where could they go?

This parking lot, like the hotel's, led directly onto a high-speed road. She didn't know which one it was or where it was going and she didn't care. Holly bumped over the last of the snow and was relieved to feel her front wheels bite roadway once more.

"Which way do we go now?" she asked Mac.

"I have no information on that," he said, and her spirits sank. There was a flicker in the rearview mirror and he appeared, a sorcerer in a dark cloak, his spiky saffron hair disarranged as he pushed the hood of the Cloak of Night and Daggers back.

"Well, can't you use that thing again?" Holly demanded irritably.

"Certainly," Mac replied. "If you want to drive back in the front entrance of the hotel, the Cloak will be within range again and we can learn all manner of wondrous things—"

His speech was cut short as Holly gunned the accelerator and shot out into a slightly-too-small gap in the Sunday evening traffic, Rosinante fishtailing as the little car zipped across two lanes of traffic.

"Fine," Holly said. "We're being chased by weirdos, one—two—of us are from way out of town, and *you're* out of ideas. I'll pick."

Brave words, but she'd never felt less brave. She felt helpless and angry and guilty—for the friends whose safety she'd endangered, for dragging up the secrets of Margot's past. The four of them had all been brave and clever and resourceful, and in her deepest thoughts, Holly didn't think it was going to do any of them any good at all.

"That is," she said a few beats later, "if somebody can tell me where we are now."

"I thought you said Corellians never got lost," Carol shot back with perfect timing, and Holly smiled. If they were all going to die, they could drive the opposition positively crazy first.

· 11 ·

Force Ten Minus Six

JUST AS ELETE predicted, Gryphon was not allowed to approach the White Tower very closely. While Baligant's mercenaries and their prisoner were still a good distance away, Gryphon's horse stopped dead and refused to go any farther, sweating and shaking its head.

Avelin and Grisegond reined up as well, and Melior continued forward with the masked elphenborn who seemed to act as the mercenaries' leader. Gryphon had called her Elete, but Melior knew that her true name was lost with her House, with the Morning Lord who had betrayed her.

He had no illusions about his chances of escape in this fell featureless wasteland whose only landmarks were the White Tower and Mourning, the stronghold of his enemy. His elphensight was blinded now by magic, as it had been blinded before by pain. But try as he might, even imagination could not tell Melior why Baligant had chosen to deliver him up to Hermonicet the Fair instead of slaying him at once.

White Hermonicet was the reason the Seven Houses of the Twilight had gone to war, for she had sworn she would wed no man but the High King, and every Earl and Baron had wished to be High King for no more reason than that. If Baligant had become High Prince and King-Elect, then perhaps Hermonicet had schemed to make it so. It was a logical hypothesis, but the thought still made Melior—who had never seen Hermonicet in his life—heart-heavy. Could it be? So beautiful, and yet so corrupt?

"Down," Elete ordered, and Melior dismounted. The long sea grass was cold and coarse beneath his bare feet, and the sea wind chilled his body.

"I'd pity you, Baron Rohannan, for what is going to happen to you now, but it's you and men like you that have given her all the power that she has."

Elete took his arm and dragged him toward the gates. They swung open before her. Elete flung him through the doorway with battle-hardened muscles. Beyond them all was darkness.

"We're supposed to break into *that?*" Fox said in disgust.

The land over which they rode was nominally a part of Domain Calogrenant in the Canton held by the Red Earl—Eirdois Ryence of the House of the Vermilion Shadows. These were the Eastern Marches, the territory at the very edge of Chandrakar, beyond which lay only the ocean and whatever Gates were upon the surface of the sea. Jausserande had volunteered that Calogrenant had been famous for its horses once, before the war.

The day was cloudy and overcast, raw and chill and promising winter. The wind was a monotonous thrust from the sea, constant and irritating. Their last night beneath a roof had been spent in Riptide, the principal castle of the Baron Calogrenant, whose Domain most closely edged the Eastern Marches. It had been a difficult and uncomfortable one for both Ruth and Philip, owing mostly to the unexpected presence of the Red Earl himself, an elflord who hated the members of House Silver only slightly more than he hated humans. Only the fact that Jausserande was one of the Treasurekeepers and Nic was obviously nobody to meddle with had gotten them out of Riptide unscathed, but Ruth and Philip had been forced to sleep in the scullery with Riptide's servants, who resented them as much as their masters had.

Knife fight, fleas, and all, those accommodations had still been superior to the ones they'd had since. The last three nights had been spent camping rough on the Marches themselves, under a steady damp wind that blew at their backs in the morning and their faces in the evening. Yesterday they had passed the broken remains of Calogrenant's eastern border markers, the Domain having claimed the Marches long since in a futile attempt to claim its tenant, Hermonicet the Fair. If they kept on, soon they would reach the edge of Chandrakar itself.

Drawn on by Ruth's tie to the Sword of Maiden's Tears, the four of them had ridden always eastward, through land that had flattened and opened and become at last plains covered with coarse salt-grass, stretching for miles. By now they had been traveling for nearly two weeks—which meant, Ruth calculated scrupulously, that Melior had been in enemy hands that long plus about a day. And now, ahead of them they could see for the first time what seemed to be their probable destination—a tower.

"That's the way to bet," Nic said easily in answer to Fox's remark. He looked at the tower, and then at Ruth. "Miss Marlowe?"

"This is the right direction," Ruth said grudgingly. "But that doesn't have to be it." *Oh, come on, Ruth, what else is there out here for it to be?*

In defiance of the laws of physics and extrapolated Bronze Age engineering skills, the tower was at least fifty stories tall. Black as coal, it reared up skyscraper-huge against the landscape, visible although they were at least two more days ride from reaching it. Beyond it, the flats stretched on up to heaven, gleaming and odorous with low tide.

There was a break in the cloud cover, and bars of sunlight lanced through, making a bridge between heaven and earth. As if its appearance had been planned as a commentary on their folly, the sunbeams struck the surface of the black tower, revealing a surface as unnaturally smooth and gleaming as the surface of a pool of oil.

"Give us all a break, Ruthie. Of course that's it. Do you see any other place around here that looks more like the lair of the Archfiend himself?" Fox asked.

"Will you stop treating this as a joke?" Ruth demanded irritably.

"Mordor is never a joke, Miss Marlowe," Nic Brightlaw said, "no matter what form it shows up in. We have to assume that they've already seen us and that we're going to go forward anyway and need to gain entrance to that. So what are our plans?"

I don't have any, Ruth thought miserably. She stared toward the castle. It was monstrous and gleaming and black, comparable to nothing in all her imagination. They would never get in there if whoever it belonged to didn't want them to get in.

"Well, okay. *I'm* daunted," Fox said mockingly. "Shall we just walk up and knock?"

"I shall demand entrance, by my Treasure," Jausserande said coolly. She rode to the front of the party, her black mare fresher than Philip or Ruth's horses and more spirited than Nic's blindingly white magic-bred steed. "Treasurekeepers are above all law, all quarrel, and may command support from any in Chandrakar."

Well, it worked at Riptide . . . She didn't look completely happy about doing it though, Ruth was pleased to see. Even Jausserande couldn't face something like this with equanimity.

"Lady Jausserande," Nic said, "it strikes me that, if we go by what your cousin had to say of him, Prince Baligant may not be all that eager to honor the old way of doing things."

"So you're screwed, Tink," Fox added helpfully.

"Perhaps," Jausserande said. "This is not Mourning, nor any stronghold I know, though Mourning and the White Ferret's tower both should lie here. Calogrenant did not speak of it, nor Ryence; perhaps Baligant does not lie within its walls at all.

"But think on this, should it fall out that he does. If Baligant No-House is the fell losel he is painted, he will not wish all his household to know it, nor the Earls by whose grace he will reign. He will not deny aid to the Cupbearer where any may see him do so. And recall also, I come here *only* because my pretty Fox has said Baligant may have the Cup of Morning Shadows. Should that be so, then perhaps he will choose to flaunt it before its rightful holder."

"But he might just kill you instead," Ruth protested.

"And will my fate be any prettier on the day of the Kingmaking, when I have failed all my line?" Jausserande snapped. "Here is where— you say—my cousin and the Sword abide. Here is where I must search for the Cup."

"Fox?" Ruth said helplessly.

In the weeks of travel, Fox's injuries had healed, until now he rode easily. He pushed back the hood of his traveling cloak, and a fugitive beam of sunlight brightened his flax-blond hair.

"Whistle up a squad of Merry Men to attack the place, you mean, Ruth? From where?" He looked around ostentatiously, at the miles of flat and empty grassland.

"Besides, we're a long way from Domain Rohannan. That was my power base—and my men were outlaws. You saw how much interest the solid citizens in Riptide had in following my suggestions." Fox shrugged, dismissing the idea. "They probably didn't even know I used to be famous."

In a small part of her mind, Ruth somehow doubted that. Everywhere they'd gone—even Riptide—she'd seen the way the humans looked at Fox as the elves ignored him. She thought his fame might have spread farther than he was willing to admit. But even if he could raise an army, even a thousand men could not breach that tower.

"So, Tink, what does the future say? Do you already know that we win?" Fox said. The magic that bound him to Jausserande gleamed at his throat.

For a moment Ruth didn't know what he was talking about, but then she remembered—the tricky, undependable elphensight, the ability the Morning Lords possessed to see a little way into the future. Melior had possessed it, Ruth remembered, though he'd never relied upon it. The gift's strength varied from person to person, and only to the High Adepts was it truly useful.

Jausserande looked toward Fox. "I know we ride all this day and tomorrow, so best we go." She dug her spurs into the black mare's sides and the animal trotted off. Fox shrugged and followed.

"After you, Miss Marlowe," Nic Brightlaw said.

Ruth looked at him beseechingly. "We're all going to die," she said plaintively. But she went.

"I've brought the prisoner." Elete's voice rang out. Melior passed his hands over his face, wondering why he could not see when she so obviously could. His hands were white shadows in the dimness, so he was not blind. He groped his way to his knees and then to his feet.

He should be able to see the doorway through which he had come, the dull autumn sunlight of the Marches, but there was nothing. He stretched out his hands—not blind, but somehow unable to understand what his eyes were telling him.

Elete took him by the arm and pulled him with her. He stumbled against the first of the steps; she waited impatiently as he found his footing. Her anger and bravado were gone as if they'd never been; Elete the mercenary moved like some emotionless automaton, doing her master's bidding and nothing more.

The stairs curved on and on, defying reason, and still the mist did not clear from before Melior's eyes. He could hear the scrape of Elete's boots on the stone and the small clinking of her armor, smell the scents of masonry and salt being slowly overlaid with the spices and perfumes of a noble hall, but he could not see beyond the shape of his own body.

At last the stairs ended. "Go on," Elete said. Melior heard the hissing of a sword drawn from its scabbard and then felt the sudden sharpness of her drawn sword at his back. "Go *on*," she repeated.

"Oh, don't hurt him," a sweet silken voice purred, and Melior felt a rush of trepidation. "But he's *filthy*," the voice added, sounding surprised.

"We were told to bring him at once, my lady," Elete said, her voice colorless. "He was as you see him now when he was taken from the wizard's chamber."

"How careless of her," the voice commented. The sword in Melior's back pressed deeper, and he took an unwilling step forward. "You have not healed him, have you?"

"No, my lady," Elete said, and Melior could hear the relief in her voice at having correctly guessed the voice's wishes. "It is only a drug from beyond the borders, else we could not have brought him under his own power."

"Very well," the silken voice said. "Send him in to me, and then you may go."

Elete seemed to realize that the sword was an insufficient motivation at the same moment Melior did. She jerked it up and away, the motion drawing a thin dark line across the weals on his back, and propelled him forward with one well-placed shove of her boot.

The floor beneath him dissolved away as if it were wet sand beneath the caress of a wave. Melior fell through air that reeked of magic, and as he fell he felt the touch of unseen servants upon his body. His skin tingled with the magic that washed over it to clean but not to heal—as if he were a body being washed and garbed for its burial.

Then he landed. And he could see.

The colors of the carpet that he crouched upon were jewel-bright by candlelight, and his impact had stirred a cloud of scent from the spices embedded in its weave. He could feel each separate brand and welt and cut like the imprint of a demon's kiss, and dark blood trickled down his bare forearm. His hair fell free and clean around his face like a silver curtain, and as he automatically wiped at the rilling blood with his fingers, he found he was garbed in a sleeveless robe of blood-violet hue, such as any lord might wear within his bedchamber.

Melior raised his head. Around him he could see the furnishings of a lady's chamber—here was the loom, there the mirror, tapestries were hung upon the walls and the windows were hinged and made of glass. It was a rich and comfortable apartment, one suited to the noble station of the widow of the Marchlord and the bride of the King-Elect.

Melior raised himself to his feet, levering himself up with the aid of a carved chair. The hem of the robe brushed his ankles, clinging gently to his body. The room was empty, and in its clutter of screens and tapestries he could see no door. He made his way to the window, searching for weapons, for some means of escape.

He reached the narrow window and looked out. This close to the ocean, the ground was as much sand as grass. The tower wall was perfectly sheer, a dizzying drop between the window and the ground. Even if he could manage to lever his body out through the window, the fall would kill him.

But perhaps that death would be a better thought than that of betraying his lady Ruth. How could Melior imagine he would not fall beneath Hermonicet's spell as so many others had, willing to do anything to gain her? He summoned up his dear lady's face as if it were a protection from evil: oval face and light blue eyes, straight light brown hair and serious expression, imperfect and human and loved. *Ruth. Heart twin.*

Once all the Morning Lords had felt such ties, in the days when they were newly come to Chandrakar. In those days a betrothal was not a matter of feasts and nuptial contracts but of the quest to find the one whose spirit was already linked to your own—to woo her and win her and prove the bond. In days such as those, Hermonicet's splendor could have done no damage.

The thought of his heart twin was a bitter weight. He had failed Ruth as he'd failed Chandrakar; he had promised his lady Ruth that he would make her safe, only to lead her into ambush on the High Road. He knew she was not dead—that was one thing he would always know, so long as she kept to the Lands Beyond the Morning—but beyond that, he did not even know where she was. She had saved his life half a dozen times, rendered him aid beyond his ability to repay, and all the service he had done her in return was to bring her Beyond the Morning and place her in mortal peril. He would give nearly anything he had to know her safe and secure once more. . . .

But he would not give the Sword. Beyond any other consideration, beyond even his lady, that duty came first. He must find the Sword of Maiden's Tears.

Find it? As his Ironworld friends would have it, who was he kidding? He knew exactly where it was. It hung within the wizard's chambers—he had seen it there. What he had to do was contrive some way to get it back.

"Do you find my hospitality so onerous then, Baron Rohannan, that you seek to leave it by any means?" the silvery voice of the castle's mistress said behind him.

Reluctantly Melior turned to face her. And though her beauty was all that the bards had sung and more, at first Melior did not even see Hermonicet the Fair because she was carrying the Sword of Maiden's Tears in her hands.

She held it before her like a lady in a *lais*, in the jeweled scabbard Line Rohannan had crafted for it, that was both boast and warning against the powerful magics that wreathed it. The crystal set in its pommel, the size of a man's heart, glowed with the merciless inner fire that was his lady Ruth's soul; it cast its many-colored light against Hermonicet's white throat and across her white bosom. Melior jerked the Sword from her hands, feeling deceptive relief at having it in his hands once more. Only then did he look at her face.

He was lost, spellbound. Hermonicet was all that the poets had named her. Her wide dreaming eyes were the cool silver of starlight and morning mist, and the diamond net that held her hair seemed dull against its lustre. To possess her was to occupy the gardens of Paradise, to wander in their beauty at will. The gems on the scabbard of the Sword of

Maiden's Tears cut into his hands as he clutched at it, while the savage lust for possession rioted through his blood.

She smiled, seeing the effect that she had on him, and Rohannan Melior of the House of Silver Silences despaired to know that other men had seen her. Beside Hermonicet, the Ironworlder Ruth Marlowe was nothing.

Ruth. My lady bright . . . The thought of his lady Ruth reminded Melior that once there had been a time before he had gazed on Hermonicet's beauty when he had loved Ruth, a love not built on a sudden dazzlement of form but on knowing her as she was, heart and soul, his heart twin, his dear imperfect human Ruth.

With an effort, Melior looked away from Hermonicet.

She tossed down the other thing she had brought—Ophidias' golden-scaled cloak that Melior must bestow upon the human bride he would choose for the wizard—and walked into the room. Melior could smell her fragrance, like a field of summer flowers in sunlight, and once more felt the temptation to yield his will to hers, to exhaust his life in service of her beauty as all the Seven Houses of the Twilight had in a hundred years of war.

"How could I consider leaving?" Melior answered caustically, "when I have been set upon, held prisoner, grievously used, and even now am being kept from leaving?"

It was not the answer she had expected, but if Hermonicet had hoped for some tale-singer's speech about how her beauty was payment for any privation, Melior reflected, she was doomed to disappointment. So long as he held Ruth before his mind's eye and remembered the bloody dowry Hermonicet had exacted in choosing her husband-elect, Melior could resist her enchantment.

Hermonicet crossed the room and seated herself upon a divan and gestured for Melior to join her. Unwillingly, holding the Sword before him like a talisman, he did as she indicated.

"But Lord Rohannan, no one keeps you from leaving. Neither I nor Lord Baligant knows quite how you came here, but be easy in your heart that we will give you every aid, for Eirdois Baligant was ever a friend of the Morning Lords," Hermonicet said in sweetly feigned sympathy.

Part of Melior wanted only to believe her, but somehow within his mind he could hear the raucous chorus of his Ironworld friends—Ruth, Michael, Philip, Jane, gallant Naomi—as they mocked Hermonicet's words and swore she lied. Baligant a friend to the Morning Lords? Before the war he had been a clerk in Rainouart's court, a nameless faceless nobody with neither land nor Line, his parentage a cryptic thing and his heart tuned to malice.

"Then give me a horse to replace the one your wizard slew, Lady Hermonicet, and I will be on my way," Melior said evenly.

If she had not expected his first answer, then twice did she not expect this one. For a moment her face showed only stunned surprise, and Melior would have laughed, had he dared to be so reckless. Instead, he tightened his grip upon the Sword's scabbard.

False tears glittered in Hermonicet's eyes. "Of course," she said, and her voice was low and husky. "After the evil welcome you have received, how can you trust my poor promises? Such evil has been said of me that surely some of it must be true," she added ruefully.

"No, Lady, it is not that," Melior found himself protesting. "It is only that—the Twilight Court meets, and I must go before it to take up my father's lands and duties."

"And to spread evil rumors of the King's ambition?" Hermonicet asked. Perfect tears, as bright and hard as the jewels in his sword, glittered in her storm-jewel eyes.

"No!" *Never would I harm you.* Melior opened his mouth to say the words aloud—and did not.

And you swore you'd hang him off your castle walls. It seemed to be Philip's voice that echoed now in Melior's mind, caustic and unforgiving. Philip, who knew Melior as even Ruth did not, as the merciless tool of Chandrakar's need.

"If the High Prince has evil ambition," Melior said, looking away from Hermonicet with an effort, "then it is a matter that must pass beyond rumor—and that before the Kingmaking."

He focused his gaze on the opulent litter of Hermonicet's solar, trying to concentrate on anything but her. He discovered himself wondering what she found to occupy her days here so far from vassal lands and court intrigue. Calogrenant held the Marches in her dead husband's place, and this slender tower filled with magic could contain little to occupy Hermonicet's administrative skills. Yet Melior had never heard— in the bygone war days when her interests were nearly as important to the Morning Lords as the disposition of their troops—that Hermonicet took any interest in either temporal studies or the pursuit of the Art Magical.

He felt the cool kiss of her hand upon his cheek; he turned, and once more he was drowning in the crystal pools of her eyes—an uncomfortable and deadly accurate comparison, he suddenly realized. Drown in those eyes, and Rohannan Melior would die to himself.

"You are wise beyond your years, Baron Rohannan. Truly the man who holds the Land must be beyond all reproach. Think on this: What if the High Prince—if the High King—were one whom all loved and trusted?" Hermonicet asked him. "Not this Baligant No-House, who will be High King at the sufferance of the Lords of Twilight, but one of whom they could truly say: 'Here stands the best of us all'? What would you say to that, Rohannan Melior?"

Melior reached for her hand. As he pulled it away from his face he saw his own hand, rilled and smudged with his blood, the ring that Ophidias had given him still upon its finger. As abruptly as if he had just awakened from a fever dream, it brought back to him the memory of what he'd suffered here, the memory that had been submerged by the strengthening drug Baligant's hellhounds had fed him and the sight of Hermonicet's beauty.

Melior got to his feet. *Ruth!* his heart mourned, and suddenly Hermonicet's fatal beauty was nothing.

"You are a faithless jade," he said to Hermonicet. "I have a sworn lady, and I will not set her aside for any man or woman's asking, nor for any prize. And you, also, are betrothed, lady—to the High Prince."

The stunned incredulity upon her face nearly rendered Hermonicet unbeautiful. "But . . . but . . ." she stammered. "I am to wed no one but the next High King. I have said it."

"And you think that gives you the right to choose who will occupy the high seat as well as your bed?" Melior said in scorn. *High King? I? For justice will I bring the land to war again—not for gain.*

He crossed the room to gather up Ophidias' cloak from the place that she had flung it. Its scales were cool and sharp beneath his fingers, and it seemed to weigh nothing at all in his hands. He swirled it around his shoulders, settling it into place. The Sword of Maiden's Tears in his hands was proof against any mortal foe; could he but get to the stables and saddle a horse before the elixir failed, he might even escape. Hermonicet had counted too much upon her beauty—but Melior was proof against that enchantment while his heart twin lived.

"Stop!" Hermonicet's voice rang out harshly.

Melior turned to look at her. Her beauty was as savage and implacable as a sword blade, but his lady Ruth was a puissant shield.

"So you would spurn me . . . the throne . . . all that you could gain . . . and prate to me of that mortal mud-born child you claim as your love? Very well, Baron Rohannan: I shall respect that." Hermonicet smiled, and her beauty was as terrible as that of dragons. "When she is dead, come back to me and I'll ask you again."

She rose to her feet, candle-slim and candle-bright, burning with cold and holy fire enough to make men lay all their homely pleasures of hearth and harvest, family and friend, at her feet for her to dance upon. Only now did he realize that he should have entreated her, pleaded with her—

though a small inner voice told him that any plea he might have made would only doom him.

"Do you care nothing for the Land?" Melior cried.

Hermonicet smiled, cool and fair. "I and the Land are one," she said. "How can you say you care for Chandrakar if you will not wed me?"

Melior took a step backward, denying her with his body as he had with his mind and heart. Hermonicet swirled her skirts around her as if she were any indignant gentlewoman disgusted with her cavalier's behavior and vanished through a door in the air.

He was alone.

Melior swept his gaze around the empty solar, searching for anything that could aid him. He did not believe he would simply walk from Hermonicet's tower in freedom, but for the sake of Ruth and the Treasure that he bore, he must try.

Keeping a wary eye on the empty room, Melior backed out through the door he had entered by. The corridor was equally deserted. And some uncountable time later, when the drug Rauf had given him had worn away and Melior lay upon the cold stone floor of the endless labyrinth, he realized that there was no escape from Hermonicet's tower. Escape was only another illusion, from a woman who was the mistress of illusion.

· 12 ·

A Legend Never Dies

"NO," HOLLY KENDAL said, very quietly.

Rosinante's headlights plainly revealed the long-cold scorch marks fanning out from the windows and door of Rook's trailer. Holly leaped from the car, already anticipating what she'd find but needing to see it anyway. She ran around the back of the trailer, heading for the kennel.

The Rottweilers lay on the floor of their runs, their bodies stiff and cold beneath a light dusting of snow. Blood had pooled and frozen beneath each corpse. A stitching of machine-gun bullets in a pattern familiar from movies and TV made a pattern across the shelters and along the trees beyond.

Holly forced herself to count the bodies. Gabriel, Lymond, Niccolo, Dolly, Gellis, Oonaugh. Six. Joletta must still be inside the trailer.

At least it's winter, Holly told herself with gallows practicality, and she went to finish her grisly task.

Mac and the others were still standing around the Honda when Holly returned to the front of the fire-bombed trailer. Margot stood as stiffly as if she were posing for a photo; she'd taken the opportunity to move as far away from Mac as she reasonably could. Carol and Mac stood huddled together like the proverbial babes in the wood; the snow that was still falling lightly had frosted the knit caps that both of them wore, giving the two blonds a fairy-tale ethereality.

"Somebody shot the dogs," Holly said shortly. "I'm going to go see what's in the trailer."

"I'll go with you," Carol said quickly. Holly shook her head.

"No. It's liable to be . . . pretty bad."

Whatever had been used to torch the trailer had burned fast and hot. Holly saw the familiar "alligator skin" charring of arson, and although some things had been melted and the surfaces of others crisped, the shapes of most of the objects in the trailer remained identifiable.

As she walked along, the floor bent and groaned beneath her weight; Holly stepped carefully. The acrid, poisonous smell of burnt plastics and synthetics hung on the cold smoky air, making her breathe shallowly. Despite her best efforts, the stench still scoured her throat; she couldn't stay here very long. But she had to know—had Rook been caught in the fire?

The Rottweiler bitch Joletta lay outstretched in the corner as if she had been stopped in midlunge, her carbonized body horribly recognizable despite the smashed skull that told Holly she had been dead long before the flames could have reached her. Holly investigated more closely, hating what she knew she'd find.

But though it was bad, it was not as bad as it could have been. Holly breathed a small prayer of reluctant thanks to whichever of the killers had taken the time to meticulously shoot each of the puppies before setting the fire. The huddled bodies nestled in the back of the whelping-box were mounds of ash, interspersed with the bright spangles of melted lead that were the bullets, but none of them had been burned alive.

She did not find Rook.

Holly searched quickly but thoroughly, digging through every possible place where someone drugged or wounded would go to hide from the fire. Increasing difficulty in breathing forced her to abandon the search before she was ready, but Holly already had to admit that even if she took the entire trailer apart, she would not find him here.

Rook was not anywhere in the trailer.

Outside, Holly sucked in deep lungfuls of the clean, icy, night air and promptly erupted into a spasm of coughing. Carol rushed forward to help her as Holly picked her way down the rickety metal steps that still hung precariously outside the trailer's door.

"Rook isn't in there," Holly said, when she could finally speak.

"Where is he?" Margot said, her voice sharp.

Holly shook her head. "I don't know. But he'd never let them shoot his dogs . . ." *If he was still alive.*

She shrugged helplessly, a feeling of hopelessness creeping over her. They—the mysterious people who had tortured Mac—had kidnapped Rook. He could never escape them. He was doomed. And so was Holly.

She'd committed murder, butchered a man in cold blood, and soon the police would track her down, take her and lock her up forever . . .

"So they've got him, or he wasn't even here when it happened and is still at large, or he got away from them and they did it while he was gone," Carol summarized briskly. "That gives you two good chances for him to be alive, Holly."

"I don't know what to do." Holly walked back to Rosinante and leaned against the side of the Honda.

"We still must hide the Book," Mac said suddenly.

The other three looked at him.

"I want to go home," Margot said implacably. "I want to go see my agent on Monday and my editor on Tuesday and then I want to go get on that big silver bird, pick up Longshot and Crusher from the vet in Indianapolis, and go *home.*"

"The Book is the key," Makindeor said pleadingly. "It is the Catalog for the Regalia, the Treasure that finds the rest—should it fall into unscrupulous hands, the damage it can do . . ."

"Won't come here. Won't matter here." Each word Margot spoke was flat and final.

"It already has, Margot." To Holly's mortified horror, she heard the sound of tears in her voice and felt the ever-present dread of flying out of balance, her equilibrium permanently awry. Despair—normal or not?— dragged at her like an undertow, promising an infinite future of mind-numbing pain. "Do you think these guys are just going to stop here and go away? They'll—"

With a supreme effort, Holly stopped herself. She hadn't told Rook she'd killed a man, and she wouldn't tell Margot and Carol either. The moment she did, they became accessories after the fact. She couldn't do that to them.

"They'll do bad things," Holly finally managed to say. "And I don't think they'll be terribly legal ones, either."

"They've already got my masquerade costume and my luggage," Margot said, as if that were the worst thing that could possibly happen. "And my laptop. My *next book* is on my laptop."

"Margot," Carol said in a strange voice, "You've got an agent now. Do you still put your home address on the first page of your manuscripts?"

"Of course I—" Margot began, and stopped as realization set in. "And my file of personal letters," she added, in a chastened voice. All anyone had to do was turn on Margot's laptop to find every place she might possibly run to.

"What are we going to do?" Holly said helplessly. "What are we going to do?"

"We must hide the *Book of Airts*. Now, while there is still time," Mac said insistently. "The Cloak of Night and Daggers will aid us—"

"What we have to do is get out of here," Carol said decisively. "Come on, everyone—back in the car. Margot, you drive."

"Why me?" Margot said, already moving around to the driver's side of the car.

"Because you aren't as tired as Holly is—and because, as they say on my planet, you could bluff the chrome off a trailer hitch," Carol said. "And my plan involves running and hiding until we can think things over, not getting arrested at the first roadblock."

"How?" Holly wailed, getting into the back seat beside Mac. "These guys are—They're—"

"Chill out, Hol. We just check into a motel," Margot said grimly. "And don't use plastic."

"We must hide the Book," Mac said. If she didn't still think of him as her patient, Holly would have been tempted to belt him one.

"You keep saying that," she said foggily. "Could you stop for a while?"

Wan morning light filtered through the curtains. Holly balanced gingerly on the edge of the bed, feeling as if her bones were filled with a mixture of lead and Jell-O. Groggy with lack of sleep and the aftermath of adrenaline, they'd finally checked into two adjoining rooms at a no-tell motel "somewhere between Albany and death," as Carol had phrased it. She'd slept, but she didn't feel rested.

What day was it now? Sunday? Monday? She'd lost track. Time for her meds, anyway. Holly began looking for her purse, wondering if she should fiddle with her dosages. If she only dared to call her doctor—

But if they were living in a world where that was possible, most of their other problems wouldn't exist either. And Holly was operating with a deadline none of the others had. She was only carrying enough medication for another ten days, and that was if she stuck to her regular maintenance dosage.

Once her meds were gone, her trick neurochemistry would have her riding the pendulum again within days, sliding her either into a reckless mania or a profound depression. Either emotional extreme would provoke behavior likely to get them all killed.

The connecting door creaked as Carol shoved it open. Holly could see light coming in through the front door of the other room. Margot must have gone in search of Diet Pepsi.

"Well," Carol said, "here we are. The Hotel Gigantic, somewhere on the Continent."

"Hiding the Book is important," Mac said. "I need your help."

"No you don't," Carol said seriously.

Holly rubbed her eyes, pulling her purse onto her knees. She tried to look on the bright side—she might be dead before she ran out of pills. The mattress teetered and creaked alarmingly at the movement, but Holly didn't care. Something about this conversation wasn't making any sense—she must still be tireder than she'd thought.

"If we help you hide it, we'll know where it is, too," Carol said seriously. "And we'd probably tell if they caught us."

"Margot wouldn't tell," Holly muttered rebelliously. "She's tough." She looked at the innocent-seeming little pill on the palm of her hand and wondered if she dared attempt to swallow it dry.

"Margot'll be back with sodas in a minute, Hol," Carol said. "So you see, Mac, only one person can know where it is, if it's that important."

"Can't he just take it with him?" Margot demanded, coming over to the door with an armful of cans that must have represented most of the contents of the no-brand soda machine. She set them down and walked off again to slam and lock the door.

Carol popped the lid on a can of grape soda and brought it over to Holly, who tossed back the pill and followed it with a slug of odd-tasting purple fizz. Sanity sold in doses.

"He *is* planning on leaving, isn't he?" Margot said belligerently, returning to Holly's room to resume the battle.

"I would not stay here for riches beyond imagining," Mac responded tartly, "and yes, I shall seek a Gate to the Iron Road as quickly as I may, but . . . I do not think I should bring the Book with me when I return."

"Whyever not?" Margot said archly, opening a soda of her own and leaning on the doorframe.

"Oh, Margot, stop copping attitude," Carol said. "It isn't Mac's fault he's here. There's some kind of trouble where you come from, isn't there?" she asked Mac.

Margot snorted. "Do you count a war?"

"I don't know," Mac said, frowning. "Although it might be more accurate to say 'more trouble' than 'trouble.' The land has been at war for decades, and the peace, I fear, is—or will not be—an easy one."

"So hide the Book and go home," Margot said mock-helpfully. "But count me out of the hiding part—*and* the going home part."

"So where's a good place to hide it without any of the rest of us knowing?" Carol said, more out of a desire to keep the peace than out of any interest in the answer.

"Where's a good place to hide a book?" Holly asked absently, taking another swig of horrible grape soda. *Breakfast,* her mind chanted obliviously. *I want breakfast.*

"With a bunch of other books?" Margot asked back.

"You went *here?*" Holly asked in disbelief, pulling Rosinante to a halt in the deserted parking lot.

Basingstoke College was a Seven Sisters wannabe founded in the nineteenth century by a local business man who'd possessed both a lucrative brewery and a suffragist wife. In the name of the latter, Melville St. Thomas Basingstoke had committed the former to erecting a collegiate monument to profligate expenditure and the gothic style—what might be termed Repentant Industrialist Gothic—upon the banks of the Hudson River.

The mandate of this miniature Oxford was higher education for ladies, and if the Board of Trustees couldn't find any ladies, it would enroll what it could get.

At least that was what Carol Goodchild said, and Carol, as she informed the others proudly, was Class of Eighty-mumble.

Basingstoke looked rather as if someone had Xeroxed the Cloisters and then dumped them in the middle of downtown Ippisiqua. Last week's snowfall had melted in the fickle December temperatures, and the campus lawns were that dejected shade of gray-yellow that only winter lawns can achieve.

"Everyone's got to be someplace," Carol pointed out. "And with the college closed for Christmas, this is a good place to be."

I could think of better places to be on Christmas Eve, Holly thought, getting out of the car and stretching. She was getting really tired of university libraries, even if it had been a brilliant idea, in Holly's humble opinion.

Mac was right: He needed their help to hide the *Book of Airts.* Carol was right: The more people who knew where it was hidden, the likelier it was to be found again.

It had been Margot who'd suggested that if Mac kept the Book hidden and told none of the rest of them at what point along their itinerary he'd hidden it, it would be nearly as hidden as if none of them had helped him at all. Trust Margot to come up with something that twisty and obvious.

"But what happens when you need to get it back?" Holly had asked over breakfast that first day. "Aren't you going to need it to crown this Urdu Belligerent guy king?"

"Indeed, if Eirdois Baligant is to be made High King, the Book will be needed," Mac had answered, "and that is all the more reason, my friend, that we must see that it is well-hidden now."

So they had skulked and hidden—and made a tour of every college library north of New York City. It began to seem to Holly as if there were a hundred colleges big and small scattered up and down the Hudson River, and by hook or crook they'd gotten into the libraries of every one. The State University of New York at Albany, stark and sere in the winter gales. SUNY New Paltz, SUNY Valhalla. Bard, Marist, Patroon Community College, Patroon Extension at Half Moon, Vassar, Marymount . . . Inside each one, Mac would leave them for a few minutes. Then he would return, and they would move on.

At first Holly had been sure she knew when Mac had hidden the Book, then she wasn't sure, and finally admitted that for all she knew he might still have it with him.

But Basingstoke College was their last stop. Basingstoke and the Ryerson. Ruth Marlowe, Carol's friend, worked at the Ryerson Public Library in Ippisiqua.

"I got to know her when we both worked at Brooklyn Public—she was just out of Columbia; it was an eighteen-month position, and, well, anyway—I just think she knows something about elves."

"*I* know something about elves. Precious little good does it do me," Margot had grumbled, but she'd agreed with the others that the best plan was simply to show up on Ruth's doorstep unannounced just as soon as they finished with Basingstoke.

Carol had been supposed to set up her visit from the convention (a delaying tactic that Holly had suspected of being a prelude to canceling it entirely), and all of them had been too spooked by what had happened to Rook to risk calling Ruth to warn her they were coming.

They'd just have to take their chances that Ruth *liked* elves.

The sky over Ippisiqua was leaden and overcast, promising snow but never quite delivering. Holly stood shivering in her new mall-bought clothes, one of a number of hit-and-run purchases financed by Margot's now suddenly understandable habit of carrying wodges of cash with her. If not for Margot's well-honed paranoia and Carol's intuitive understanding of the way law enforcement officers thought, Holly was certain they would have been caught a thousand times over.

What was she doing here? she wondered for the thousandth time. She ought to be at the SCA event—freezing her tail off, collecting new bruises, and having a ball. And Rook should be alive and free, to be there with her. Not knowing whether she should mourn him was the hardest part. He was just . . . gone.

Without turning around, Holly heard the opening and slamming of the other three doors as Carol, Makindeor, and Margot got out of the car. At least none of them who had jobs was late for work—but Holly was due back at the ambulance service next week, and Carol at her library in Idaho the week after. Though she'd called both Maggie and Sheila to make vague and somewhat garbled apologies, Margot had missed both her appointments in the city. It looked as though Prince Perigord and Azure Bowl were going to have to continue their quest for the Phoenix Throne without Margot's help for the time being.

But none of the others had Holly's particular deadline. And her time was fast running out.

No one stopped them as they crossed the Basingstoke campus, though Holly, at least, felt horribly exposed, as though she were crossing a firing range. From the way Mac was trying to look everywhere at once, Holly could tell he felt just as vulnerable out here as she did. She tried to force the apprehension to the back of her mind by focusing on immediate impressions.

Mac was wearing the Cloak of Night and Daggers, not that anyone could tell. (And not that its abilities did him any good in daylight.) Just as he'd said, the Cloak could change not only its aspect but its form, and to all appearances it was now an ankle-length black leather duster lined in indigo silk, making Makindeor—in jeans, turtleneck, and broad-brimmed hat—resemble a short Doc Holiday, except (of course) for the backpack. Which might or might not still contain the *Book of Airts*. Uneasy as she felt, Holly hoped it didn't.

"This is it," Carol said. Being the alumna, she must be presumed to know. "At least . . . I think it is," she added, destroying Holly's illusions.

The four of them stared up at the Basingstoke College Library in all its tripartite glory.

The main building was magnificently ornate in the High Gothic style, with spires, crenelations, buttresses, and the odd gargoyle, rather as if someone had washed Notre Dame Cathedral on the "hot" setting and it had shrunk. Its high narrow windows were dight with *faux* armigerousness and enough leaded mullioned panes to keep a battalion of antique dealers happy for a month.

The center section was flanked by what were obviously two later additions in which all concept of ornament, beauty, proportion, and form had been sacrificed to an unhealthy obsession with prestressed concrete. The new wings were not only ugly and glaringly out of place, they were *huge.*

"Well," Margot said. She cleared her throat, and tried again. "Well, at least we don't have to try to *find* a book in there."

The doors of the library were closed, the building dark. Basingstoke had closed promptly on Monday, December 4th and would not expect to see any of its student body until Twelfth Night at the earliest. Such were the benefits of higher education—the more you paid, the less you got.

"I guess," Carol said with a valiant attempt at nonchalance, "that they raised the building money they were after."

"They should have just razed the building," Margot said.

Mac looked at Carol expectantly. Carol smiled—it was an effort, after the past week, but she managed.

"It doesn't matter if it's locked. Mrs. Dean will be there."

"The Dean stays in the library over break?" Holly said.

"Not *the* Dean. *Mrs.* Dean. Come on," Carol said. She led the others around the side of the building and then in a larger detour around one of the modern wings. But soon enough she'd reached the back of the building and the inevitable staff entrance. Carol pounded on the back door with a gusto that suggested she'd discovered herself to be the entire rhythm section of an orchestra in the midst of committing *The 1812 Overture.*

It was a noise, Holly thought, calculated to rouse every campus cop from RPI to SUNY Valhalla.

But the door opened.

The woman who opened the door looked as if she'd appeared out of some Victorian engraving of a librarian. Barely five feet tall, she wore a long-sleeved midcalf-length dress in some dark flowered pattern. There was a paisley shawl around her shoulders, clasped firmly in place with an enormous jet and amber brooch. Her steel-gray hair was done up into a thick, hairpin-studded bun from which protruded a number of yellow #2 pencils, and she wore little wire-rimmed glasses that made her resemble drawings Holly had seen of Miss Manners.

"Yes?" the woman said, as coolly as if she were summoned to the library's back door by wild-eyed graduates and their friends every Christmas Eve.

"Mrs. Dean, it's me, Carol Falconer. Class of '82?"

"Oh, yes." The librarian smiled. "You married a Peter Goodchild a few years ago, didn't you? You sent me an invitation; I'm sorry I couldn't come but it was during the school year, you see."

"Pete's dead," Carol said starkly. "He died two years ago." The halt in the conversation was as abrupt as if she were a runner who had stumbled. Carol gathered herself together with a visible effort and plunged on. "Mrs. Dean, you told me if I ever needed anything—ever—I should come to you and you'd see what you could do. Well, I need something now. I need to get into the library with my friends. Not for long. Just for a few minutes."

"Come into the library? But, Carol, dear, the library's closed. It's Christmas Eve," Mrs. Dean said, as if Carol might not have noticed.

"I know," Carol said swiftly. "I don't want to check out a book. I just want to come inside—me and my friends."

"But, Carol, why?" Mrs. Dean asked, obviously bewildered.

"I can't tell you," Carol said. "It's because of . . . a book."

"Well, why didn't you say so?" Mrs. Dean said, opening the door and ushering them all inside.

Visiting the Basingstoke library on a deserted Christmas Eve was definitely one of the odder experiences of her life, Holly decided a few moments later.

The library was three stories tall, and in the fashion of an earlier day, the second and third floors were simply galleries around the back three walls. The great central space directly in front of the main entrance was one vast ecstatic leap into space, and the eye inevitably followed the bright ribbons of leaded glass upward from sill to crowning arch. Though the day was gloomy and overcast, it was still brighter outdoors than inside the library, and the contrast turned the sweep of the windows into silvery pillars of light. Holly stopped to look at them, completely entranced.

"Beautiful, aren't they? The library was the first structure to be finished when building on the campus began in the 1860s; Mr. Basingstoke sent to England and Boston for the original collection; it was open to the public until the Ryerson was built in—Carol! Where is that young man going?"

"He just needs to check something," Carol said, as Mac wandered purposefully off. "He won't hurt any of the books."

"Well, I shall have to examine his backpack when he returns. We've had to institute that rule since you were here," Mrs. Dean said severely.

"But—" Holly began, and stopped even before Carol shushed her. There was no way Holly intended to take on the task of explaining Mac, the *Book of Airts,* and the Men in Black to a college librarian who looked as if she was every bit as eccentric as any of the students.

Mrs. Dean swept the three of them with a minatory glance intended (apparently) to inoculate them against further transgressions and then moved off behind the charge desk. The swags of tinsel and the tiny plastic tree looked oddly out of place here, even though it was Christmas Eve.

"Well, this was a lucky break," Margot muttered to Carol and Holly. "How'd you know she'd be here, Carol?"

"Oh, that one was easy," Carol Goodchild—neé Falconer—said. "Mrs. Dean hasn't left this building in over twenty-five years.

"I don't know much more than that," Carol went on in a low voice, interpreting her companions' skeptical expressions as a demand for more information *right now*. "The seniors always let the freshmen think the place is haunted; then somebody manages to slip in, meet Mrs. Dean, and scare themselves to death. In my freshman year, it was me. She's the sweetest thing, and she knows the collection inside out. She just . . . doesn't leave."

"And nobody notices this perfectly normal-I-don't-think behavior?" Margot asked.

Carol shrugged. "I guess she has an apartment in the basement. I mean, the college has to know . . . don't they?"

Holly and Margot regarded her like judgmental owls. Carol's cheeks pinkened defensively. "Okay, so it sounds dumb. There're just some things you don't think about, okay?"

"Okay," Mac answered, coming up to them. Now the backpack was slung over one shoulder, as if he'd had to take it off, but it'd been that way at each one of their other stops. Holly couldn't fault him for consistency.

"Okay," Carol said. She turned to the front desk. "Mrs. Dean, we're ready to go, now. Thanks so much for letting us in."

"Not so fast," the diminutive librarian said. "Young man, I'll have to ask you to open your bag."

The four of them looked at each other. Mac's expression was unreadable, and finally he shrugged ever-so-slightly. Holly could see his point: The Ryerson was to have been their last stop. They'd been to at least a dozen academic libraries in the past week—one less wouldn't give their pursuers any significant advantage.

Mac walked over to the desk and unzipped the backpack, then, with a flourish, turned it inside out.

It was empty.

Holly released a lungful of air she hadn't known she'd been holding. At whatever point in their ramblings he'd actually stashed the *Book of Airts*, it was really gone now.

"Thanks again, Mrs. Dean, and Merry Christmas," Carol said a few moments later.

"Merry Christmas, Carol dear," Mrs. Dean said. "I'm so sorry to hear about Peter."

"Thank you," Carol said awkwardly. She gave Mrs. Dean an impulsive hug and then joined the others outside.

"Fine," said Margot briskly. "Now. Where's this Gate you say is somewhere around here?"

"Near here," Mac said, pulling out his glasses and putting them on. He peered through them. "According to the observations I have been able to make this week, the Wild Gate is definitely located somewhere within a league of here."

"Seven miles," Holly, who was as used to archaic measurements as any fantasy writer, groaned. "Can't you narrow it down any more than that, Mac?"

"Of course," Mac said, sounding faintly cross. "Drive in a circle for long enough and I can pinpoint it nearly exactly. Without that, all I can say is that there is a Wild Gate to the Morning Lands somewhere in Ippisiqua."

"Right," Holly muttered, striking off for the car at a pace the others had trouble matching. There was a Wild Gate in Ippisiqua. *Somewhere* in Ippisiqua. Having to take something like this seriously was bad enough for Holly's ability to keep a straight face, but hearing Gauvain Makindeor say a sentence like that out loud was worse: It was like hearing the stirring battle cry "the Wild Hunt is loose in . . . Toronto!" or discovering that the Seely and Unseely Courts were fighting for possession of Minneapolis. Elphame and Ippisiqua . . . it sounded like the title of an essay by Ursula K. LeGuin.

Still, if Mac said there was a Wild Gate in Ippisiqua, Holly supposed they'd better find it double quick.

Before somebody else did.

Frank Catalpano mounted the steps to Ruth Marlowe's apartment—one of six in a subdivided Victorian that had seen better days in a neighborhood that was far from the best in a city that didn't have any good ones—and rang the bell firmly. He already knew she wasn't home, but it was a good thing to go through the motions, even when you thought that was all they were. A few seconds later the master keys he carried had made short work of both the landlord's cheap lock and the "native New Yorker special" Marlowe had gotten installed. Frank was into the apartment faster than its legitimate tenant could have been.

As Frank had expected, the place was empty. Ruth Marlowe, it seemed, had found someplace to spend Christmas Eve. Frank wandered around the apartment, poking purposefully through the accumulated litter of living.

There wasn't much. Couch and chair, lamps and tables, amassed second-hand and embracing about as much of their new owner's personality as a safety-sealed bottle of aspirin. The living room smelled of winter damp and the inadequate efforts of an antique heating system. No pictures on the tables or walls, no knickknacks. Not even curtains to soften the blinds at the windows. No television, which struck Frank as a curious omission. Everyone had a television. What did Marlowe do at night when she came home from work—stare at the walls?

The kitchen was equally stark: teakettle and frying pan, a microwave that was obviously the only new thing in the apartment, a mismatched collection of thrift-shop mugs and a fresh out of the box Corelleware service for four. The table and chairs in the corner of the kitchen were another salvage job, belonging to the era of Donna Reed and June Cleaver. Frank checked the kitchen drawers. Most of them were empty; one held a muddle of cheap silverware. The shelves held tea and sugar and boxes of cookies and dry cereal. In the refrigerator was a half-empty bottle of wine, a quart of milk, and two six-packs of Diet Pepsi. The freezer held three ice cube trays and several cartons of frozen macaroni and cheese. Frank checked under the sink and found, as he expected, four unopened bottles of wine and a half-full bottle of Scotch. Not exactly the accent notes of gracious living. Martha Stewart would be disappointed in Marlowe.

If anyone was interested in his opinion, Frank Catalpano had seen safe houses with more personality. He'd known that Marlowe and her little buddies had been mixed up with the elfguy who'd come through two years ago—Rohannan Melior, the one Frank had gotten his hands on so briefly. If Information Management Services hadn't put a lid on it, the police would still be looking for the friend of Marlowe's who'd disappeared, Naomi Nasmyth. God knew her kendo teacher, Paul Robillard, had made enough of a fuss to keep any ordinary investigation front-burnered until the end of time.

After hushing that up, IMS had kept a long rein on the other four—too long. Philip LeStrange had come to work at Ryerson Public Library—and vanished—almost a year ago. Six months ago, Ruth Marlowe had taken his place. Frank had left Marlowe free to run after the decision had been made to shut down the loose ends on Project Sunwise, hoping that Gauvain Makindeor would run to her. Secretly, Frank had been sort of hoping that Marlowe would disappear too; once she had, he'd have the leverage to put the screws on the two remaining survivors. If he squeezed hard enough, he might even get Michael Peacock and Jane Greyson to give up the interdimensional transfer point that all the theory boys were sure was out there.

Not that Frank was supposed to know anything about that. No, Frank was just supposed to acquire runaway elves and tidy up loose ends.

Only the loose ends kept getting looser. It had been a week since his team had lost the others at the Science Fiction Convention. They'd counted on them acting like civilians and sticking around to argue and dither. They hadn't. And while Frank knew a number of interesting things about those three ladies by now, he didn't know where any of them was.

Holly Kendal had been the EMT who'd taken Rohannan Melior to Bellevue. When he'd disappeared from the secure ward, Frank had questioned her again. She'd denied knowing anything, but now Frank wasn't sure she'd been completely open with him. Makindeor had run to her as if he'd had printed directions—why?

Margot Reasoner wrote those silly slushy fantasies that women like Denise the space cadet bought by the pound. The interesting thing about Ms. Reasoner was that she hadn't existed before 1970, not as far as Frank's not inconsiderable resources could determine. So where had she been, if she hadn't been here?

Carol Falconer Goodchild was a superficially simple case: She'd worked with Ruth Marlowe at the Brooklyn Public Library and had met both Reasoner and Kendal there. When her policeman husband had been killed in the line of duty, Goodchild had run far and fast, ending up in Twisted River, Idaho. The only interesting thing about Goodchild was that Peter Goodchild had gone to school with Michael Peacock, who had later known Rohannan Melior.

The way all these people seemed to be connected together just below the surface was something that Frank found very interesting indeed. That, and the fact that the subjects *du jour*—Makindeor and his dysfunctional harem—seemed to be having no trouble at all in staying out of sight. If Kendal's car had turned up, Frank would have been willing to believe they'd moved out of state—but it hadn't, so he thought they were here. Somewhere.

He proceeded into the bedroom. It was, as he expected, a spartan little nun's cell. Single bed. Dresser. Mirror. Clothing that would have suited a backward twelve-year-old. And no evidence that Marlowe had entertained any recent company. Frank tossed the bathroom quickly—the only noteworthy thing was an up-to-date prescription for Halcion—and went back to the living room.

Marlowe wasn't here. No one else he was looking for was here. He didn't think any of them had been here, either. Frank dug a notebook out of his pocket and paged through it until he found the address he was looking for. Penny Canaday and Katy Battledore. One twenty seven and a half St. Thomas Close.

He'd try there next.

· 13 ·

Patriot Games

FOR THE REST of the day they headed toward the dark tower as fast as possible. The place in her mind where Melior's pain had burned so brightly had been replaced by a faint queasy numbness, puzzling and disturbing. The longer the tower loomed on the horizon, the more obsessed Ruth became with reaching it immediately, until, when Jausserande suggested a stop to hunt fresh meat for dinner, she could stand the delay no longer and hammered her heels into her mount's sides until the surprised animal had broken into a gallop.

It was Nic who caught up with her when her tired, stubborn horse had dropped back to a walk. Though the legs and bellies of the other three horses were crusted with mud, Nic's supernaturally white horse remained as unsullied as ever. It didn't even seem to be breathing hard.

"Give me your horse," Ruth said, when he reached her. The gelding she rode stopped when she let it, putting its head down to graze.

"I wouldn't if I could," Nic said evenly. "But I can't, since it seems to go with the paladin package. Why the sudden hurry?"

"This isn't just some walk in the park," Ruth snapped. She was furious, but her anger seemed thin and unconvincing, even to her. "Melior's in there, and—"

"And your arrival will not significantly improve his chances, unless there's something you haven't been telling us, Miss Marlowe," Nic Brightlaw observed.

Ruth turned in her saddle and looked back. Several hundred yards behind her she could see Fox and Jausserande, engaged in the elaborate equine ballet necessary to put up game here in the fenlands. Ruth saw the white flash of Jausserande's arm raised high over her head: Jausserande hunted with a sling, a wartime weapon, not a knightly one.

"I thought that at least *you* would understand about rescuing your friends," Ruth said before she thought.

There was a frisson of chill; it was as if the wind purling steadily over the marsh grass suddenly held its breath.

"I am possibly the world's greatest living authority on useless rescue missions," Nic said calmly, "but one has to get one's companions out of prison before one can properly go about the business of killing them. This much being obvious, it might be a nice gesture on our part to come up with a scheme that allows us to get both in and out alive—and to that end, we should conserve our travel rations and live off the land while we can."

Ruth's cheeks burned with humiliation. "I'm sorry," she said miserably.

Nic didn't answer, merely turning his horse and urging it into a walk. Ruth hauled at the reins until she'd gotten her horse's head up, and followed.

"I just can't see how we can get in," she offered a few minutes later, in a further attempt at apology.

"Oh, come now, Miss Marlowe," Nic chided absently. "They want us to go in; that part's going to be easy, unless I miss my guess. The hat trick is going to be getting out, getting out with your friend, and getting away."

When Ruth was roused just before dawn from her uneasy dreams of wandering in an endless maze (an improvement over dreaming about either the accident that had put her into a coma or the torture chamber in which Melior was being held, but not much of one), Nic was already up and dressed and testing his saddle's girthstrap. His horse glowed like the moon come to Earth, the brightest thing in the misty, chilly landscape.

"I'll see you on the other side," Nic said, swinging into the saddle.

"Fare you well, Ceiynt," Jausserande said. "Good hunting."

"Confusion to the enemy," Nic/Ceiynt returned. He turned his horse's head back the way they had come.

"Hey," Ruth said weakly. "What's going on?"

No one answered.

Nic's horse picked up speed: walk, trot, canter, and on into a gallop that made its body into a dwindling silvery arrow in the distance. At Ruth's back, Jausserande began feeding up the fire.

"They can see that for miles, you know," Fox pointed out.

"Do I care?" Jausserande demanded, her tone one of frayed patience. "We know where they are. They know where we are—and how many we are, and where we have come from, and where we are going. We know that they know, and they know we know it."

"We're a knowledgeable bunch of guys," Fox finished, turning Jausserande's circular assessment into a parody of a speech from one of James Goldman's plays.

"Why did Nic leave?" Ruth demanded, out of patience with both of them. The fire was small and pallid, but Ruth moved closer to it anyway. Her head hurt, her back hurt; a dinner of half burned, half raw rabbit followed by yet another night of sleeping on the ground wrapped in blankets did not make for a pleasant morning.

"Was it the hour? Was it the company?" Fox chanted absently, eyes fixed on the fire. He unwrapped some of the leftover rabbit and held it closer to the fire to inspect it. "What's for breakfast?" he asked rhetorically. "Burned bunny. Yum."

"Fox!" Ruth snapped.

"If you like not his prating now, perhaps I can school him to please you later," Jausserande said. She approached Ruth, a wineskin in her hand. "First—"

"Yeah, I know. 'First the thumbs.' Jesus, Tink, can't you even show a little originality?" Fox complained, as if it were not his death by torture that they spoke of.

"I shall, on the day," Jausserande said, with a fond cat-smile. "Count upon it, little Fox."

"I live for the moment," Fox assured her, and started to bite into the roast meat.

Ruth snatched it out of his hand and flung it into the fire. It fell with a soft impact, sending up a choking swirl of smoke, embers, and fine ash. Fox flung himself backward, landing himself inelegantly on his rump.

"Where's Nic going, *Philip?*" Ruth demanded, a vicious edge to her voice.

"To be our backup. To perform a flanking maneuver. To gather intelligence. Out for pizza. Pick one, Ruth. I guess he just thought it would be a nice gesture on our part if we all didn't get captured at once." Fox picked himself up and brushed at his clothes. "That was my breakfast," he complained plaintively.

"Have mine," Ruth offered poisonously. "And I hope you choke on it. Just when did you three decide that Nic should go live in his own personal Chuck Norris movie, and where was I while you discussed it?"

Fox understood the reference, Jausserande didn't, but their blank looks were identical.

"Someone had to," Fox said, as if it were so obvious that it went without saying. "I volunteered, of course, but—" he touched the gemstone at his throat, the bond that held him in Jausserande's presence more surely than any chains. "And Tinkerbelle wouldn't go, so that left Mr. Brightlaw."

"And we do not know if the link that binds you to my cousin runs two ways," Jausserande said, "so I took care that you did not hear our council. Even though you know it now, Ceiynt's magic will lay a decoy trail that may keep their main force away from us."

"Of course," Fox pointed out, selecting another piece of rabbit from their supplies and beginning to eat, "all they really have to do is wait for us to come up to the front door and knock and then cut all four of our throats with a kitchen knife. No Mel, no Sword, no proof. No problems."

Ruth turned her back on both of them. In the distance, beyond the tower, the sun was a pale salmon smear on the horizon, but the sky was already light. She turned in a half-circle. Nic was already gone; she couldn't even hear the hoofbeats of his horse. She turned back to the tower. Was Melior in there or only the Sword? Which was she following? Surely it was Melior—a sword couldn't bleed, couldn't hurt—but what if those images were only a trick, a spell . . . ?

"I *hate* magic," Ruth muttered under her breath. She hugged herself tightly, miserably aware that all they could do was go onward. "If you're through having quite this much fun, maybe we could get going?"

He did not know how long he lay on the floor of this blind labyrinth. He held the Sword of Maiden's Tears in its jeweled scabbard, and for a very long time that was all that Rohannan Melior truly knew. When at last he came back to himself, the fact that he still lay where he had fallen told him much that he would rather not have known.

With reluctant effort, Melior rolled over onto his back. Every mistreated muscle protested, and the scars of his flogging made a brief, distant fire. The effects of the potion Baligant's mercenaries had fed him were long since gone.

Darkness. Melior forced the elflight to his skin, pleased to see that this earliest magic had not deserted him. In the silvery light he could see the long corridor of black stone, curving as it followed—Melior conjectured—the outer wall of a tower. Further effort brought him to sit upright, to lean his back against the gently curving wall. The position made him lightheaded and dizzy; brilliance danced through Melior's vision that had no existence outside his debilitated mind, and the elflight died away, but he had already seen enough. This was not Mourning, the sea tower that the Lord of the Eastern Marches had built in order to watch over Hermonicet his bride, into which Baligant High Prince had moved to await his Kingmaking—and to watch over Hermonicet when she was his in turn. Nor did it seem to be Hermonicet's own white tower, with its ornate illusions and unseen servants. The walls were polished smooth, with no mark to show where the stones were joined together.

In Melior's own castle the walls would hold torches or baskets of burning cressets. There would be windows to let in the daylight, banners captured in battle and tapestries loomed by generations of Rohannan's ladies hung upon the walls. Signs of habitation, of family, of continuity.

This was another place entirely: a labyrinth crafted by an elegant and brutal magic foreign to both the High Adeptship and the Low—but a magic with which Melior was familiar. Copper and sunfire, roses and blood: This place was the creation of the wizard Amadis. It was a trap. And he was the bait.

Nobody had ever mentioned how much of life was just plain boredom, Ruth reflected sourly. She had been sure she'd expended her life's entire quota of boredom during the rehabilitation that followed her awakening from her coma eight years before, but that was a pallid transient thing in comparison to this endless ride. Nobody could be frightened or angry or nervous all the time, but the ability to be bored seemed to be endless. There was no drama or structure to the hours spent on horseback, and every instinct screamed out against the slow, steady march directly into the stronghold of the enemy.

Fox was riding ahead on her right. The hood of his cloak was pulled forward, his shoulders hunched against the eternal droning of the salt-scented wind. He rode with a boneless grace that Ruth envied; even with all the wonderful practice that she'd gotten lately, Ruth rode like a sack of potatoes, and she always seemed to be coming down just as her horse was going up.

She was cold. Her seat hurt from its endless application to the saddle. She'd be hungry except for the fact that the only things to eat were watered wine and undercooked rabbit. They'd been riding since dawn with only a few brief stops, moving at a steady ground-eating walk to spare horses that had worked hard yesterday and would be working tomorrow.

And the tower wasn't any closer. At least, it didn't seem to get any bigger, and in all this flatness there were no landmarks she could use to judge their progress. There wasn't even a road. Just the tower.

Which has to be magic, because let's face it, it's about the size of the Citicorp Tower and it looks like it's built right on the sand. So either there's just as much tower below ground—which I don't rule out—or this is some kind of stupid magic castle.

She sighed and tried to starve her imagination, to think of anything else, but it was difficult. When she brushed a wisp of hair back from her face with a gauntleted hand, she could not feel her face.

I want to stop. I want to go home. I want to do something else, dammit. And most of all, she didn't want to think about Melior, about finding him battered and maimed somewhere inside the tower, or worse—something she hadn't thought of until just now—finding instead that the tower wasn't her destination and that the trail led onward, across the sea.

"S'matter, Tink, elfish precognition letting you down?" Fox said.

Ruth gritted her teeth. Every time Fox took it into his head to start baiting Jausserande, Ruth knew it was going to end in a quarrel or, worse, a brawl. She'd stopped feeling sorry for Fox's bruises; apparently he wanted them. But without Nic here to separate the two of them, Ruth didn't know where it would end this time.

"Shut up, Fox," Jausserande said, but not as if she meant it to end anything.

There was a momentary silence. "Isn't it always the same?" Fox commiserated fulsomely. "Any time magic might actually be of some use, you point-ears have some reason it won't do any good. Is it that time of the month, Tink? Or are elves just not—"

"I said *shut up.*" There was an edge to Jausserande's voice that hadn't been there the time before.

"—capable of getting it up without the Twelve Shopping Opportunities of Chandrakar?" Fox finished, as if he hadn't heard her. The two of them were riding side by side, close enough that Jausserande could hear Fox clearly, even over the wind—and with the way her voice was rising with each exchange, he could certainly hear her.

Nic would have stopped them by now. Ruth wondered if she dared to try. All of them were cold, hungry, scared in varying degrees, and bored. A dangerous combination.

"You forget yourself, mud-born!" Jausserande snapped. She might never have been to the World of Iron, but after the last two weeks she understood Fox's idiom as well as she needed to.

"Any time you're tired of my company, I'll be happy to leave," Fox said. He'd promised Ruth to help her rescue Melior, and that was a promise he wouldn't break—but then, he could hardly expect Jausserande to take him up on his so-generous offer, could he?

"Do try," Jausserande suggested. "You owe me blood—"

"—and sweat, and tears, and pain—and every mud-born in this place whose neck you've ever stepped on has paid *that* debt in advance. And you can't stand the sight of us—"

Fox had raised his own voice now, which made the hairs on the back of Ruth's neck prickle warningly. In all their fights it was always Jausserande who lost her temper, not Fox.

"—because you know you've already lost; and when Baligant herds every fucking one of you wimp losers into death camps—"

Ruth's unconscious tightening of the reins pulled her horse to a halt. Fox reined up next as Jausserande dug spurs into her horse's sides, making it spring sideways and forward at the same time, her sword slithering from its scabbard with a singing hiss. Ruth saw its lackluster not-quite-iron blade flash suddenly bright in the dingy late afternoon light.

Fox shut up as if he'd been cued and spurred forward. Ruth clenched her eyes shut, expecting that the next sound she heard would be Fox's death scream. She heard a scream, but it was a quite different one.

"Go! Ruthie—go! Jesus, are you deaf?"

Ruth's eye snapped open. Fox was several yards ahead, standing in his stirrups and shouting at her. Jausserande was riding back the way they'd come.

Ruth looked back.

The sun was directly behind them now, a small silvery coin hanging in a colorless western sky. But on the grassland below, it was as if night had come early. A spreading darkness, dense and mobile as an oil spill, was moving over the grass toward them. The wind shifted, and a sound too faint for Ruth—but not Jausserande—to hear until now became audible over the wind: a moaning sound, low and muttering and bitter, as though the darkness that followed resented the effort of the chase.

"*Ruth!*" Fox's shout made her realize that she'd been staring, frozen, for the last several seconds. Jausserande was riding straight toward it, as though a bronze sword and an attitude could have some effect on something that covered a thousand yards of grass and . . . gibbered.

Ruth hammered her heels into her horse's flanks, gripping with her knees and kicking as if the animal were a defective soda machine. When Fox saw her horse begin to move, he turned his own around and began to gallop. Ruth, following Fox's example, crouched low on her horse's neck.

This was the pace Ruth had yearned to set yesterday, with speed and sheer battering sensation blotting out everything but fear. The horse's body surged between her legs; her full skirts cracked like a banner in the wind, and the random strands of mane that whipped her wind-numbed face stung like hot wires.

The tower appeared to be no closer.

Jausserande flashed by them on her hot-blooded mare, her hand beating the air as she flagged them down. It took a long time to understand what she wanted, and longer to convince the horse to do it. At last Ruth was reduced to dragging directly back on the reins, sawing them this way and that as if she were trying to take a sock away from a terrier, and the mare bounced to a sullen stop.

"Well?" Fox demanded. His face was reddened by the wind.

"Losels," Jausserande said, seeming to take no offense at his peremptory tone. She clucked to her sweating mare, and the animal moved forward at a slow walk. The other two followed. When Ruth looked back, the shadow was gone from the horizon.

"I thought that was just what you called us," Fox said, after a pause.

Jausserande turned toward him, smiling thinly. "It is what we call any nasty repellent vermin, mud-born—but here is where the name began."

"I don't understand," Ruth said. "What's a . . . losel?"

"They are small," Jausserande said. Her hands sketched a shape about six inches long in the air. "Black. Some say they were made what they are by magic; before the war began, it is said that they never swarmed, as they do now. I do not know what would be like them in your world. They eat what they can catch—mice, baby rabbits, eggs."

"Weasels," Fox said, and Ruth winced in agreement. Smaller than rats and far more savage—she had a faint children's book memory of mad red eyes and ivory needle teeth.

"Weasels, then," Jausserande agreed. "And sometimes losels swarm—like now. They gather in the thousands and migrate. And when they do, they eat anything in their path. There are thousands of them behind us now."

Fox looked back, just as Ruth had, but now there was nothing to see.

"Fire will turn them, but I don't dare set one. A grass fire could race over us and cook the losels' meat for them."

"I don't suppose there's any possibility of this being a coincidence?" Fox asked.

"Fox, losels live in the western Cantons, not the Eastern Marches," Jausserande said impatiently. "But as long as we keep moving, we'll be all right." There was a hollowness to her voice. Jausserande herself wasn't convinced of her words.

"Can we go around them?" Ruth asked nervously. "Let them pass us?"

"Go *where?*" Jausserande demanded. "The swarm is a mile wide, and it can change direction at whim! The tower is ahead of us—and its fell compass is the only shelter I can see. We'll walk the horses for half an hour, then lead them for the same, then run again. The more distance we can open between us and that which follows us, the better. They do not move very fast—but neither do they stop."

Jausserande spoke matter-of-factly, reminding Ruth of what Nic had told her, that Jausserande had grown up in war, a military commander at thirteen, a blooded fighter years before. And suddenly all of Fox's gibes about elvish precognition made sense.

"You knew this was coming!" Ruth burst out. "Both of you did!" And the quarrel that had frightened her so had been no quarrel—or mostly not—only a feint to draw an enemy whose nature they did not know.

"I knew something was coming," Jausserande said. "But I am no Adept, nor even so schooled as my cousin. I did not know what we would meet this day, only that it would be a lethal danger."

"Nic," Ruth breathed. Nic had left them that morning, heading in the direction the losels came from.

"He is behind them, or he is dead," Jausserande said harshly.

Jausserande and Philip were both wearing breeches and high hard riding boots; when it came time to walk the horses, they made much better progress through the waist-high grass than did Ruth in her heavy wool skirts and layers of petticoat. At least she'd had the sense to leave her cloak bundled on the saddle—it was one less thing to manage.

Her horse was as cranky and tired as she was, trying to step on her skirts when she let them hang, pulling at the reins to snatch mouthfuls of fodder when she paused to haul her skirts up again.

"Look," Fox finally said, after half an hour of this. "Let Ruth ride. She's just slowing us down, and we can't leave her."

"Thanks so much," Ruth muttered under her breath.

"We'll all ride," Jausserande said. She stared back the way they had come in a way that would have made Ruth nervous if she weren't already scared to death. Ruth looked back as well. There was nothing to see—and the lengthening shadows of sunset made it likely that even if there were something to see, they wouldn't see it.

It would be night soon. And tonight they wouldn't be able to stop to camp or to sleep. They'd just have to keep on going.

Jausserande shared a wineskin around, and then Fox helped Ruth clamber inelegantly up into the saddle. And they were off again.

Walk. Trot. Lead the horses for a while. Walk. Stop when they found a place for the horses to drink. Jausserande portioned out some of the grain they were carrying to the horses and badgered Ruth and Fox into eating as well. Then mount again, ride again, as sunset became twilight and then night. When it got too dark to see, Jausserande called a halt to the alternating gaits; they stayed mounted and rode on at a speed that was surely slower than the losels' progress. There was no moon, only a heavy overcast that made it seem as though the three of them were riding through some vast unlit sound stage.

Jausserande rode first, the elflight on her skin their only beacon. Fox rode last. Once Ruth had looked back and had seen the gem at his throat giving off a faint blue gleam.

Without stars or moon or wristwatch, time seemed to stretch on forever. No one spoke; grimly wedged in her saddle, Ruth had the nagging hallucination that they were not riding over the monotonous fens but through a lightless stone labyrinth, unending and impassable, in which they were trapped and through which they would wander forever. Melior was in there somewhere, blessedly free from his torturer but injured near to death, and there was nothing she could—

"—do, Tink. He's dead lame."

Fox's voice jarred Ruth awake. She sat up straight and looked around. Her horse had come to a stop. The glow that was Jausserande was behind her; in that faint illumination, Ruth could see that both Fox and Jausserande had dismounted and were standing by Fox's horse.

It was standing on three legs, one forefoot lifted. Every few minutes it would try to put the foot down and pick it up again.

"He isn't going anywhere," Fox said. "Hey, Ruth—you awake? Come over here—you're going to have to take my pack."

Ruth got her horse turned and walked it back to the others.

"What's wrong?" she asked, wanting to hear a different answer than the one she already had.

"In the parlance of our youth, my horse has a flat tire. Take this stuff, would you?" Fox slung his saddlebags over his shoulder and walked around Ruth's flank, beginning the process of transferring the contents of his bags to her own. Grain, dried fruits and nuts, sugar and salt. A couple of waterskins filled with a muddy brackish liquid Ruth thought she'd have to be a lot more desperate than she was now to be willing to drink.

"I can't find anything," Jausserande said in frustration, reaching for the horse's foot again. "No stone, no bruise."

" 'No service,' " Fox finished absently. He tied Ruth's packs closed and patted her horse on the rump, then walked back to his own and began removing the saddle.

"What are you doing?" Ruth said.

"He's lame. I can't ride him. How long until they get here?" This last was to Jausserande.

"A couple of hours." She didn't sound quite certain. "Around dawn."

"Might be all he needs is the rest," Fox said doubtfully. The saddle hit the ground with a dull crackle of broken grass; Fox held onto the bridle strap.

"And even a lame horse will run from a losel swarm," Jausserande said with dark humor. "But the advance line is too wide. Can you get him down?"

"Try," Fox said briefly.

"Here, Ruth—be of use," Jausserande snapped, thrusting the black mare's reins at Ruth.

Between coaxing and threats—and the fact that the animal was already tired and off-balance—Fox got it down and threw all his weight onto its neck before it could rise. Jausserande darted in like a mongoose, and Ruth saw the full flash of her sword in the elflight. Fox's horse kicked once and lay still.

Jausserande ran back to snatch the mare's reins from Ruth's gloved hand—the surviving two horses, unnerved by the smell of blood, had discovered surprising reserves of energy. She swung up into the saddle.

Ruth stared at her.

"I would not leave even Fox alive to losels," Jausserande said briefly. Fox finished wiping Jausserande's sword on the grass and joined them, handing the blade up to her without comment.

"Come on," Jausserande said. They turned the horses east again and went on.

As Jausserande had predicted, it was dawn when the losels found the dead horse. A wild, many-throated piping rose to a crescendo behind the exhausted travelers, loud enough to hear even this far distant. They reined in to listen; even Jausserande was beginning to look worried, and Ruth knew that her own face concealed nothing. Fox, on foot, looked bland as always—a little tireder, but that was all.

"It should slow them for a while. They'll fight, pick the body clean, eat their own dead," Jausserande said. "It's light enough now to move the horses faster. Come on."

The howling on the wind made Ruth's stomach hurt. The sound was as insistently unpleasant as fingernails dragged along a blackboard. The horses didn't like it either; Ruth could tell by the way her gelding's ears flickered and the black mare turned and sidled.

"I hope," said Fox nastily, "that you don't expect me to jog along at your stirrup like a good little mud-born."

Jausserande looked from Ruth to Fox, dispassionately assessing as the horses fussed. "You'll have to ride double—with Ruth."

Fox smirked, and went over to mount up behind Ruth as she struggled to hold her animal still. "Cheer up, Ruthie—it's not like we're engaged or anything."

"Don't call me Ruthie," she responded, trying to be witty if she couldn't be brave.

* * *

"Can't that thing go any faster?" Jausserande demanded.

"Not exhausted, underfed, and carrying double," Fox snarled back. Each time Jausserande had started to push the horses to a faster gait in order to gain the party a breathing space, the little mare had responded gallantly—and Ruth's gelding had not. The mare had more stamina, a better turn of speed. And now it mattered—and showed.

Ruth stood on a hummock of grass looking west. If you strained—if you had an overactive imagination—there was a thin black line just visible on the horizon. The losel swarm had spread into a wide crescent pattern, the black line of the swarm encroaching on left and right, half a mile distant but even at that far too close. The only safe direction was straight ahead.

Toward the tower.

If she hadn't been so tired, Ruth promised herself, she could have cared more about somebody besides herself. She ought to have been thinking of Melior; of Nic, who was probably dead; of Fox, whom she'd kept from running away when he'd had the chance. But all she could think of was that this slow danger wasn't *fair*. It wasn't fair, Ruth thought with the petulance of exhaustion, that they should be so terrifyingly harried toward the place they intended to go anyway. *We would have gone there—we would!* she told the invisible puppet master.

"All right," Jausserande said reluctantly. "I'll share out the last of the grain, then you come up with me, Fox."

"Yeah. Fine. Come on, Ruth—staring at it won't make it go away." Fox came over to her and took her arm.

"Why can't I feel anything?" Ruth said hopelessly to herself.

"Shock," Fox answered surprisingly. "Exhaustion, hunger, exposure. But cheer up—if you don't die out here, you'll have nightmares for years."

It was wonderful, Ruth reflected, what sort of things Fox felt were reassuring. She managed a smile as he led her back to where Jausserande had spread a blanket on the ground and was pouring grain out onto it in two piles.

"We have to find water," Jausserande sighed, pushing her hair back. "It's too bad we don't dare stop and look for it."

Ruth looked toward the tower. She thought it seemed closer, but she wasn't sure she trusted her eyesight any more. "What if they don't let us in?" Ruth asked.

"This's a fine time to bring that up," Fox muttered. Jausserande handed him two wineskins; he kept one and passed the other to Ruth. The horses had moved eagerly forward, devouring the heaped grain.

"Should they deny us, I'll risk the fire," Jausserande said. "The folk of Riptide at least will see it, and if those inside the black tower sally forth to put it out, we may be able to get in. But I surmise rather that they want us inside—this is only meant to keep us from thinking or doing anything but rushing straight into whatever trap they've laid."

"It's working," Fox said, putting the empty wineskin back in the gelding's pack. "Too bad they don't know that was our plan in the first place."

"And a pity that their herders may well kill us instead. Shut up and eat, little Fox," Jausserande said with rough comradeship. "I don't want to run for my life on an empty stomach."

They stuffed themselves hastily on what was left of their supplies, including the gaggingly sweet trail bars made of dried fruit, honey, and seeds, and Jausserande transferred everything she could possibly move from the mare to Ruth's gelding. Even with Ruth's horse carrying the blankets and the last of the food and water, Jausserande's mare would have the heavier load.

Fox put Ruth up into the saddle, and she prepared for another exhausting day of walk, trot, run.

Then it happened. Jausserande mounted, kicking her feet free of the stirrups to allow Fox to mount up behind her. She was leaning forward, tired and distracted; he was halfway astride—when the wind shifted, blowing from the losel swarm toward them. The wind brought a rank metallic scent that even human noses could smell.

The gelding flung up his head, nostrils flaring, and gathered himself to run. Ruth yanked back on the reins with all her strength, clinging desperately as her mount sidled and backed and fought the restraint.

But Jausserande's mare went wild. She went straight up, flinging Fox off and kicking out at the strange imbalance on her back. She slewed sideways, spinning around and coming down stiff legged, bouncing as if those legs were steel and springs instead of blood and bone. Without her feet in the stirrups, Jausserande had no hope of staying with her; the mare's saddle was empty in seconds, both of the riders down, and the mare began to run.

Despite Ruth's best efforts, the gelding took off after her; it took Ruth only a few seconds to realize that her horse had the right idea. Without at least two mounts, their chances out here went from slim to none. She had to catch the mare if she could.

Ruth gave the gelding his head, urging him on with every trick she'd learned, but the mare was a wing-heeled ghost, fleeing through the dawn as though she'd spent the last two weeks being pampered in her home stables. Soon she was only a rapidly diminishing speck on the bright horizon, and Ruth's own mount was laboring, more than willing to stop. She reined him in; his sides worked like a bellows and foam dripped from his mouth. The rank scent of horse sweat was even stronger than the smell of the sea.

Ruth sat in the saddle and felt frustration and despair batter her like physical, tangible things. They'd never catch Jausserande's horse. They couldn't keep ahead of the swarm on foot. They'd never reach the tower in time.

They were doomed.

Who says so?

Naomi's voice was so clear that for a moment Ruth was tempted to look around for her.

"Who says you're doomed? Everybody? Do you always believe what 'everybody' says? If everybody else was jumping off the Brooklyn Bridge, would you jump too?"

Ruth could almost see her—crisp, confident Naomi, who had never given up—never. Who had died rather than give up.

"That would depend on why they were jumping," Ruth said in answer. But the imagined dialogue had given her an emotional breathing space. *I can be doomed later,* she told herself, and she turned her horse back toward the others.

· 14 ·

Welcome to the Hotel Ippisiqua

"THE LIGHTS SHOULDN'T be on in there," Carol said.

It was 4:26 on Sunday, December 24th, the same day that Holly and her friends had visited the Basingstoke College Library. The snow that had been threatening all day had finally begun, the sullen pewter sky spitting grudging flakes of white at the earth below.

They'd taken Market Street on the way to Ruth Marlowe's apartment (mostly because Holly had gotten lost), and the sight of the Ryerson Memorial Public Library's Italian rococo glory blazing fully lit into the dusk had caused Holly to slow down, then to stop.

"Here," Mac said, peering through his glasses. "The lines converge here. But Holly, how did you know?"

"Ruth Marlowe works there," Holly said slowly.

"And Ruth knows about elves!" Carol announced, flinging her door open and running across the street.

Carol's persistent hammering on the glass of the front door finally gained someone's attention. By then the other three had joined her, leaving Rosinante safely parked in front of the War Memorial fountain across the street.

Even without Mac's insistence that this was their goal, Holly would have been able to figure out that something was wrong for herself. It was Christmas Eve. If you weren't a hotel or a restaurant, you were closed.

And a public library—impoverished almost by definition—certainly wouldn't close for the holiday and leave all lights burning.

The woman who approached the door in response to Carol's enthusiastic pounding bore a faint but determined resemblance to Mr. Greenjeans. She was wearing a set of grass-green Osh Kosh B'Gosh overalls with a white cotton shirt. Her long brown ponytail waggled as she shook her head at them, frowning and waving them away, and her brown eyes glowered.

"We're closed!" she shouted through the glass.

"Ruth!" Carol shouted back. "It's about Ruth Marlowe—do you know her?"

The name brought the woman in the green overalls all the way over to the door. She unlocked it, opening it a cautious crack.

"Ruth!" she said. "Have you seen her? Do you know where she is? We—"

She would have said more, but her gaze had drifted in automatic assessment from Carol's face to Mac's—where it stopped.

Holly glanced back over her shoulder and winced mentally.

Mac had taken off his large, Lamont Cranston slouch hat and was holding it in front of him. His face was as pearly-pale as that of any blighted knight in a Keats poem, and the pupils of his mismatched eyes had contracted to vertical slits in the light coming through the doorway. His haircut had been improved in random moments over the past several days until it was a short even crop—which did nothing to disguise his long pointed ears.

In short, he did *not* look like he came from around here.

Carol, seeing her chance, burrowed in past the woman at the door.

"Hey!" the woman in the overalls said.

"I'm really sorry about this," Holly said, following Carol and talking fast, "but this is really important and we really need to come inside and talk with you about it, because it's enormously important—"

"We need to find the Gate," Mac said.

"You're Margot Reasoner? I thought you'd be taller," Katy said.

Penny had introduced them to her clerk, Katy Battledore, whose five-foot-two-inches were combined with a mop of bright yellow curls and big brown eyes—and garnished with the voice of Lauren Bacall and the diction of a cigar-smoking carnival barker. Mac's otherworldly looks hadn't fazed her at all.

"I'll try to be," Margot promised solemnly. "Thanks so much for letting us in."

It was cold inside the Ryerson; Penny had turned off the lights in the front and retreated with the newcomers to the stacks where (hopefully) they would attract less attention from out-of-season library patrons.

"Well," Penny said, "I recognized you from *SF Chronicle*, and I guess an author doesn't need to steal a book—at least not from this collection. But you're sure you didn't see Ruth? Maybe outside?"

"Nope," Holly said. Carol shook her head.

"So if *they* don't have Ruth and Nic, who does?" Katy demanded suspiciously of Penny.

"Ruth really isn't here?" Carol said. She stopped, apparently at a loss for words. "When did you last see her?" Holly reflected, would make it sound as if Ruth Marlowe were a missing wristwatch.

"She came in with us—about half an hour ago," Penny said slowly. "Nic—he's the director—was answering a false alarm, and since we all work here and were having dinner together, we all came."

"You were answering a false alarm?" Margot said blankly.

"The machine goes off at random," Penny said vaguely. "But you always have to come in and reset it."

"And a perfectly good goose is sitting at home going to wrack and ruin in the oven. If I get my hands on Nicodemus Brightlaw, *I'll* cook his goose for him," Katy vowed sulfurously.

"Ruth couldn't have gotten out of the building," Penny said. "I locked us all in; it's a key lock, and only Nic and I and the head janitor have keys. So she couldn't get out, unless Nic let her out and left himself. But there's no reason for him to do that. And I've looked everywhere— biographies, local history, Children's Room. I even looked down in the Second File. They aren't here."

"They must have gone through the Gate to the Morning Lands," Mac said. "If they cannot have left and they are not here—then that is where they are."

"Welcome to the Second File," Penny Canaday said.

The basement of the Ryerson Memorial Library was, like the library, in Ippisiqua, New York, and (again, like the library) of an 1890s vintage. In the case of the basement, this meant that it was dug, unfinished, into the rocky bank of the Hudson River. It was cold, damp, and dirty, and infested with bats, squirrels, and heaven knew what else. The ceiling was low; the beams of the first floor supports were just scant inches above Penny's head.

"Where's the First File?" Margot asked.

"There's never a First File," Carol told her.

The Second File was illuminated in its entirety by one forty-watt bulb suspended in the middle of the space, giving the entire basement the indefinable air of a Ridley Scott movie. Piled tangles of ancient fixtures made inkblot shapes in the wan winter light from the high, narrow, and filth-opaqued windows at the back of the room.

"Here?" Holly said doubtfully.

"Here," Mac said. The lenses of his glasses gleamed with a faint illumination of their own in the dimness. "This is where it is," Mac said.

"The gate to Disneyland," Katy said.

"Elfland," Holly corrected.

Penny Canaday regarded him warily, still suspicious. She'd been ready to call the police and have them thrown out, but the fact that Carol was a librarian and Margot an author—and one Penny had read—had swayed her to their side, if only for the moment. But her better judgment was sure to surface soon.

Holly knew that if there were some way to get Mac home, that had to take first priority. But she also knew that every moment they spent here made it more likely that the people following would catch up to them somehow, and if somebody else died because of her, Holly didn't know if she could bear it. Every time she closed her eyes, she could see the face of the man she'd killed, as he lay shattered and dead in a pool of his own blood.

"I know it doesn't sound really plausible," Carol began, and stopped.

"It doesn't sound implausible," Margot growled. "It sounds barking mad. Unfortunately, it's true."

"There are Gates into and out of your world. All your legends speak of them. There is one here—a Wild Gate, one uncreated by the Adepts of the Nine Worlds and the Thousand Lands—a Gate not sensible to the control of magic," Makindeor said.

"And you think Ruth fell through it," Penny said.

"Ruth *knew* someone from . . . Beyond the Morning," Carol said.

Everyone—Holly, Margot, Mac, Penny, and Katy—stared at Carol. Carol's cheeks turned pink, giving her a resemblance to an embarrassed white mouse.

"She told me," Carol said reluctantly. "Well, a little—she'd had maybe a little too much to drink; I'd found out it was her birthday, and I'd dragged her out to dinner. She told me that there was—" Carol frowned, searching her memory while the others hung on her words raptly. "That she'd met someone who'd come from the Lands Beyond the Morning, and he'd had to go home again, on something called the Iron Road to Elphame, only she couldn't go."

Margot made a rude noise. "The Iron Road only leads down—to here. Going back costs . . ."

"Depending on the power of the Gate," Mac added absently. "By your leave, Lady Penny, may I try if the Gate is here? I can borrow from the Cloak's magic to do so," he added to Holly.

The courtly turn of phrase caught Penny by surprise. She gaped at Mac as if she meant to say something else and had forgotten what it was. "Yeah. Sure. Okay."

"What*ever,*" Katy added.

Mac walked away from the other five. He stopped in the farthest corner of the room, in front of what had been the back basement wall of the original library building before the 1923 addition: a wall of half-smoothed rock evened in places with plugs of brick and (now crumbling) mortar. Here where ceiling and wall made a mad rush at each other and met in a non-Euclidean tangle, there were rickety bookshelves against the wall, and a pile of hardbound *Life* magazines lay stacked in the middle of the floor, gathering more damp (if possible) than they would elsewhere. Behind them was the space on the bottom shelf they'd come from.

"Here," Mac said. He snapped his fingers, and a ball of elflight danced on his fingertips.

"He does that sometimes," Holly said to Penny.

"I know somebody just like him," Penny said.

The others crowded around to look, Margot hanging back as though she feared to be sucked into whatever it was.

"I don't see anything," Katy said.

Mac drew a deep breath, as though preparing for an enormous effort. He bent down, reaching out both hands as though he were about to pluck an imaginary thread up from the floor.

He pulled, straining against nothing they could see, and suddenly there was hot summer sunlight spilling into the room from the bottom of the bookshelf. Hot summer sunlight in the dead of winter, from a direction that ought to be solid rock.

"I think—I can—*open* it—farther—" Mac gasped. He pulled back and up, as if he were a mime opening a nonexistent window, and suddenly Reality tore in his hands like flawed photographic stock.

"Judith H. Crist," said Katy reverently.

The light spilling through the doorway was the brightest light in the basement. Here in Ippisiqua it was winter, cold and dark, but just the other side of the Wild Gate it was summer. They could see grass and trees, smell the heat and flowers. A path of white quartz pebbles began at the sharp cut between this world and that, curving onward out of sight. As the five women watched, a butterfly with bright metallic indigo wings fluttered through, then changed its mind and fluttered back again.

"Okay," Penny said. "I believe you." She took a step forward. Mac put a hand on her arm.

"It is a Wild Gate. I know not where it leads, save Beyond the Morning."

"And Ruth's there?" Penny said.

"Two Ironworlders have crossed this threshold within the last hour," Mac said, peering intently through his strange glasses at something none of the others could see. Penny took several steps backward, trying to find an angle that would let her see straight through the door.

"So how are you going to get them back?" Penny said. "I mean, Nic's the *director*—he can't just go running off to Middle Earth."

"Nic," Katy pointed out, "would be *happy* in Middle Earth." She looked at the others. "So that's *it?* We tell everybody they fell through a hole in the world?"

"I bet that's where Philip disappeared to," Penny said slowly. "I bet that's where *everyone* who's vanished from the Ryerson has disappeared to."

"Okay," said Holly. She felt curiously flat, without any emotions at all. "We've found it. So what do we do now?"

"I must go," Mac said, "to bring the Cloak to Chandrakar, and send someone back for the *Book of Airts*—though not through this Gate. I can promise you no more safety in the Morning Lands than there is for you here, but I will take any of you who wish to come. And there is one among you I truly need. Holly—come with me?" Mac stretched out his hand to Holly, who reached for it almost automatically.

Margot grabbed her, yanking her back.

"No!" Margot said. "If you want her to go with you, tell her all of it. Tell her that maybe she can't get back here ever; tell her that time changes when you're on the Iron Road, that the Iron World spins fastest, that if she gets back here at all, it's going to be years from now, and nobody's even going to know who she is."

"I would make a place for her in my world," Mac said softly.

"As a slave!" Margot snapped.

"As my friend," Mac answered. "She has done so much for me and for Chandrakar that it will take all the years I have left to repay the debt. And it would be my pleasure to try."

"Guys," Holly said, raising her voice slightly, "do you mind if I participate in this discussion? Mac, how long is that thing going to stay open?"

"We must go through as soon as we can. Those who follow us may have means of finding Gates just as the Adepts of my own world do, and this one is hard to miss." Makindeor took the sides of the opening in his hands and pulled them together. Summer vanished like the picture in an

old-fashioned TV picture tube: first a line, then a dot, then nothing was
there at all.

"Gee . . . just like on *Outer Limits,*" Katy breathed raptly.

"The Gate is still there," Mac explained. "And open. Only . . . not
as open. I will do what I can to seal it once we are through, but at the
moment this Gate is very . . . noticeable."

"Wait a minute," Penny said. "Back up to the part about how there
are people following you."

With the evidence of the Wild Gate before them, getting Penny and
Katy to believe the rest of the story wasn't as hard as it would have been
under other circumstances. Although they did leave out the part about
Margot having been born in Chandrakar—and Holly still didn't tell anyone that she'd killed somebody—among the four of them, taking turns
and interrupting one another frequently, they did cover almost everything
else that had happened since a week ago last Friday, when Holly had
picked up Mac wandering around the Hotel Escher.

"And that's the deal," Holly said, when they were done.

"I wish Nic were here," Penny said. "He always knows how to deal
with things like this."

Margot snorted eloquently. Holly shrugged. If she were telling the
truth—and she was—it wasn't her fault if the truth sounded silly.

Mac was standing near where the Gate had been, absently pulling
glowing trails of sunlight out of the air and weaving patterns with them.
Holly guessed he must be back in touch with his magic. He'd put his
glasses away into some pocket of the transformed Cloak that he wore; the
bright wash of sunlight on his face exposed all the ravages of torture and
drugs. It made it easy for Holly to think of him as her patient once
again—and to think about what he'd asked of her.

He'd asked her to go with him—to Chandrakar. Margot had implied
pretty heavily that it was a one-way trip. Should she go? Holly asked
herself. It was pretty clear she'd never get a second chance at something
like this. But if she went, there'd be no coming back. Was where she was
going better than where she'd been?

On the one hand, he did need her. This Gate wouldn't drop him out
in Chandrakar—just in a place he could reach Chandrakar from. He still
didn't have all his memory. Would what he didn't know kill him?

Should she go?

Abruptly, the face of the man she'd murdered rose up before her
mind's eye again. It was true that there'd been no word of the murder on
the news, but *someone* knew. And as long as she stayed, Holly's crime
could be used against her and her friends.

And Mac needed her.

"I'm going with you," Holly said suddenly, trying to sound so decisive that Margot wouldn't argue. "But there's a couple of things I need first. Penny, can you let me out to my car?"

Holly's camping equipment, her armor, and her sword had been sitting in Rosinante for the last week, packed in their nylon duffles. It took two trips, with everyone helping, to get everything in through the service entrance and down to the Second File.

Mac regarded it dubiously. "All this?" he asked.

"You said the Gate could take all six of us," Holly protested. All her bags together didn't even weigh as much as Carol—well, at least not *more* than Carol.

"But all of us are living things," Mac said. "Living things—natural things, and those within their aura of influence—feed any Gate and pass it easily."

Holly paused, thinking of what Lady Fantasy III and her plate armor had done to the magical protection field and the office building.

"So I can't take this stuff?" she said.

"Some of it," Mac said. "The important things at least—like your sword and armor."

The nice thing about Mac, Holly reflected, was that he shared her priorities.

"I don't think you should go at all," Margot said.

"I think someone needs to find Nic and Ruth," Penny said. "You'll do that, right?"

Mac opened his mouth to say something. "We'll do that," Holly said firmly, cutting him off before he could speak. "But you guys—are you really sure you're going to be all right here?"

That was the real question. It didn't matter that Margot wouldn't go back to Elfland at gunpoint; if by leaving them here Holly was leaving her friends in a danger she could avert, Holly didn't think she could do it.

"The Morning Lord and the Cloak will be gone," Margot said, "and the Gate will be sealed from the other side, which means it won't exist here any more. They can yell and kick, but they can't change that—and we don't know where the Book is, so we can tell them everything we know with a clear conscience. So I don't think they're going to want to cause any more loose ends, whoever they are, right? Besides, I'll call my agent."

Holly only hoped Margot's faith in the Maggie Tanenbaum Literary Agency wasn't misplaced.

"Nic gave me an emergency number to call," Penny Canaday said slowly. "I mean, for a *real* emergency. It's a Washington number. And I guess this is a real emergency."

"Wouldn't coming along be better?" Holly asked, vacillating.

"No," Margot said promptly.

"I guess I'm not the adventurous type," Carol said. "Sorry, Hol. Don't forget to write."

"Somebody's got to run the library," Penny said. "And make that phone call."

"What, and give up show biz?" Katy said.

"Okay." Holly sighed, and made her decision final. "It's just the two of us, then. Mac, help me go through this stuff and decide what I'm going to take. Other than my sword and armor."

"Considering what you spent on that stuff, I'm glad it's finally going to be practical," Margot said.

Mac felt that her garb would be more use than jeans and sneakers, so Holly made a pack of blankets, tunics, and field garb. Her good Bowie and her Shadowmaker dagger she bundled deep inside.

"Cold iron will come in useful over there," Margot said grimly. Mac shot her an oblique look.

"Her armor is iron—and her sword," he said mildly.

"Which should make you Elfland's version of The Terminator," Margot said.

"Oh, yeah?" Holly said vaguely, stuffing sealed bags of trail mix into belt pouches and sending Carol upstairs to fill her big water bottle from the drinking fountain. The two glass bottles of home-brewed mead she decided to take as they were, wrapped up good and put into the backpack Mac would carry.

Although her armor had been anachronistically designed to be worn primarily under field melee conditions and even marched in, Holly wasn't really sure how far she wanted to march in it. Still, Pennsic was a summer event and she managed, so she guessed she could survive in the summer beyond the door. She stripped off jeans and sweater and began to lace on the thick cotton padding she wore beneath the armor. She wrapped her braid around her head and wrapped a scarf around that—the first time she'd taken a head shot to some hairpins had been her last.

"You look like a ninja," Penny said.

"Oh, well, this isn't really period padding," Holly said, bashfully.

"Don't let her give you that maiden modesty routine," Margot said. "You're talking to the Martha Stewart of these current Middle Ages."

"Yeah, well, everybody's got to have a hobby," Holly said. She slid her feet into her boots and buckled them above the calf, then slid her sabatons, like strange armadillos, first over one shoe, then the other. Greaves, cuisses, poleyns over both knees, the fauld resting on her hips like post-punk panniers—armor went on from the ground up; that was one of the first things she'd ever learned about it.

She picked up the belly-and-back that were the heart of the armor and slipped into them as if they were some sort of odd sandwich board. The bright smears of lead from the gunman's bullets were still visible on the front, a grim reminder of might-have-been.

"That looks like somebody shot you," Penny said.

Margot and Carol looked at each other.

"Yeah, well—come on, Mac, buckle me in," Holly said hastily.

Mac took a step toward her and stopped.

"There's magic in the air," Margot said mockingly.

Mac turned on her, his expression angry. Holly thought he was going to snap at Margot, but he said nothing.

"Mac?" Holly said.

"You can't do it, can you?" Margot said.

Holly watched him keep hold on his temper and saw the effort it took him. "No, Child of Earth," he said. "I cannot."

"Could somebody close-caption this for the back-story impaired?" Katy asked.

"It's because it's steel—iron—cold iron—isn't it?" Carol said. She walked over to Holly and began tightening the buckles, then carefully lowered the gorget into place and locked it down.

Mac smiled ruefully. "In Chandrakar, as you know, we call it 'deathmetal.' Here in your magic-poor world it is only a matter of slow poisoning—a slight burn or even none at all if it is well-alloyed. But this close to an open Gate . . ." He shrugged. "The rules of my homeland apply."

"Oh," Holly said. There was a pause. "How am I going to get *out* of this armor, then, if you can't touch it?"

"He'll stick some human with the job," Margot said.

"You *will* need a squire," Makindeor said seriously.

Rerebraces, vambraces, coulters, and pauldrons—Carol helped Holly lock down the whole flexible architecture of the steel that covered her shoulders and arms. She was almost dressed save for the helm and gauntlets.

"Hand me my surcoat, would you? I want to wear it."

Margot picked up the surcoat with Holly's arms: on a field sable, a thistle proper with an owl pendant argent. She tossed it over Holly's head as if she were spreading a tablecloth on a table.

But it was Mac who brought Holly her swordbelt and her sword.

In the SCA's mock battles, Holly Kendal used what every other fighter used: rattan lightly padded and wrapped in duct tape (Q: What is the force that surrounds us, binds us, and holds the universe together? A: Duct tape.), and her swordbelt was designed to hold that sword in a cone-shaped leather holster. But the last time she'd worn this armor, she'd been carrying Lady Fantasy, and it was her steel sword in its scabbard that was laced into place on the leather swordbelt.

The sword's quartz counterweight gleamed in the dull chill winter light of the basement. Mac handled it as gingerly as if the sword were a red-hot bar of metal. He buckled the strap about Holly's waist as she settled the shoulder strap into place over her surcoat and then turned away to pick up her leather gauntlets and hand them to her.

"Thanks," Holly said awkwardly. She picked up her helm and fitted it into its locking collar. The world retreated to a blinkered distance, and she felt the familiar sense of pressure in her ears. She pushed up her visor. Carol handed her the steel gauntlets that would fit over her leather ones. Holly slipped them into the shoulder bag she'd emptied of all but essentials. Mac was going to have to be able to hold her hand to take her through, and he wouldn't be able to do that if she were wearing her steel gauntlets.

"Well," Penny said, "I guess this is it."

"Yeah," Katy growled. "So will you guys get the heck out of here so we can invite these nice people home for dinner? *Somebody's* got to eat that goose."

Mac picked up the pack and then turned to the bookshelf again. He traced a glowing line in the air, then pulled back as if there were a set of invisible double doors there.

The air swung open, and once more it was summer.

"We must go," Mac said. He held his hand out to Holly, wary of her armor. She put her gloved hand in his and followed as he led her toward the gate.

"Be careful!" Carol said. "Don't forget to write!"

"Carol, that's the—" Margot began, but Holly didn't hear the rest. She was gone, into the Morning Lands.

There was a bright flash when they passed through, and then only a fading afterimage of scrolls and angles in ornate golden fire. Then the Wild Gate faded away completely, leaving only mildew and *Life* magazines behind.

Penny took a deep breath and glanced around the library basement. "Well, that's that." She looked at her watch. "Five-thirty. Look—Margot, Carol. Our place isn't that far from here, and Katy's got goose with all the trimmings waiting. Why don't you come back to our place? Tomorrow's Christmas, after all."

"Sure," Margot said. "Thanks. I'll call Maggie on Monday, and everything'll be fine."

"You guys have been really great about all this," Carol said. "I'm sure they'll get Ruth and your friend Nic back. We'd better get this stuff cleaned up, and . . . oh."

The tone in Carol's voice made everyone turn and look at her. There, in the middle of the discarded camping equipment and half-empty duffels was the place where Holly had emptied her purse so she could carry her armor in it. And among the pile of discarded items from Holly's purse lay the small brown and white pharmacy bottles of Zoloft and Lithobid.

Frank Catalpano hunched down in the driver's seat of his car as he watched the small procession head up Market Street in the direction of 127½ St. Thomas Close. He risked a quick peek through his binoculars and recognized Carol Goodchild and Margot Reasoner. The other two were probably Penny Canaday and Katy Battledore, friends of Ruth Marlowe's. But Marlowe, Kendal, and Gauvain Makindeor were nowhere to be seen.

Frank hesitated, not liking the fact they'd split up. He hadn't bothered with backup, and now it was costing him.

He waited until they'd turned up St. Thomas Close before starting the engine and gave them another five minutes before he moved away from the curb. When he came around the corner, he found he'd timed it perfectly; Canaday was standing in the doorway, taking a last look up the street. She didn't give the moving car—obviously on its way to somewhere—a second glance as she went in and closed the door.

Frank circled the block once, but it looked as though they were in for the night. But where had they been, and were Marlowe, Kendal, and the elf still there?

Frank turned back the way he'd come. He thought he'd better see if he could turn up anything like a backtrail between here and Marlowe's apartment. The Ryerson might be a good place to start.

And then he'd be back.

· 15 ·

The Feast of Fools

THE GRAY SKY, the gray grass, and the gray fog of fatigue at the edges of Ruth's vision blurred into one endless uncaring universe. All their choices were gone; they walked for the rest of the day toward a tower that seemed to be a fixed and distant point. Jausserande led the horse. Somewhere around sunset the black wave of bodies was close enough to see once more.

Ruth stumbled onward with a robot-like endurance. Night fell, and no one mentioned stopping. Even a moment's rest would make it too easy to fall asleep, and once they had, they would wake to being eaten alive by the losel swarm.

A day, a night, and another day had already passed as they fled the losel swarm, and now the party traveled through another night without stopping. If they didn't get somewhere soon, they were going to drop in their tracks. This night was as dark as the last one had been, its darkness lending a hallucinatory unreality to their journey. At one point Ruth awoke from her torpor and found herself on horseback, riding without any memory of how she had come to be mounted. Even Jausserande showed signs of strain; she did not have the energy to maintain her elflight any longer, and without that illumination to guide them, all four of them—including the remaining horse—had to trust to Jausserande's superior night sight.

The horse stumbled to a stop. Fox, clinging to the stirrup, turned his face into its flank and stood motionless, unconscious on his feet.

"Ruth—are you awake?" Jausserande's voice came, low.

"Yes." Her throat was so dry that it ached when she tried to form words, and the consciousness of thirst was a constant pressure.

"Can you walk?" Jausserande came back to open one of the saddle packs. Ruth saw the pale oval of her face.

"Yes," Ruth said reluctantly.

Jausserande pulled out a fistful of trail bars and a waterskin. "Help me water him; then we have to put Fox up."

Ruth poured water into Jausserande's cupped hands as the gelding nuzzled at them. Afterward, he was willing—if not eager—to take the sweet feed.

"Poor beast," Jausserande said sadly, patting his neck. "You can't last much longer, can you, you sorry sack of bones?"

"How can you care what happens to him and still want to kill Fox?" Ruth asked. She felt as if she were drunk, or drugged—exhaustion and adrenaline and thirst had combined to produce the floating detachment that allowed her to ask such a question.

"Because Fox murdered Guiraut and this horse did not," Jausserande said shortly. But after she had finished with the horse, her voice and her hands were gentle as she forced Fox to mount. He lay across the horse's neck in a limp and alarming fashion.

"Don't faint again," Jausserande said to Ruth as she took the horse's head once more. "He can't carry both of you."

Ruth finally arranged to stay upright by looping her arm through the stirrup leather as if it were an old-fashioned subway strap, letting the gelding's stumbling motion pull her onward. The night seemed to go on forever; she felt oddly detached from her body, floating bodilessly down the river of night. It took her battered senses several minutes to realize they'd stopped again.

The thought of stopping made her weep. Why had they stopped? It was okay as long as they kept going; she could manage that. But they'd stopped, and she knew she couldn't start walking again. It was too much. No one should ask that of her.

With painful care, Ruth unwound her arm from the stirrup strap and staggered backward on unsteady feet. If she could only sleep . . .

"Ruth!" Jausserande's voice was a violent whisper. "Ruth!"

Ruth startled awake as she felt Fox's hands on her shoulders.

"What? What?" Ruth stammered, confused and unnerved and groggy all at once.

"It's okay," Fox said. He looked far more alert than Ruth would have under the same conditions, but there were dark circles under his eyes, and Ruth could see the shape of the skull beneath his skin.

"It is *not* okay," Jausserande said in an odd voice. "But we've reached it. We're here. At the tower."

"Is this . . . anyplace?" Holly said doubtfully.

She resisted the temptation to look behind her; the comprehension of what she had so casually done was seeping through her like an appalling mix of guilt and homesickness. Here. Now. Forever. She'd just walked away from her friends, her job, her *life* . . .

Some life. When her meds were gone, what had she been supposed to do—surrender? Or just wait for them to find her?

"No," Mac said seriously, "but as you Ironworlders say, you can get there from here."

Holly reached up and pulled off her helmet, blinking in the increased brightness. It was summer; the air smelled of heat and grass and flowers. They were in somebody's garden—at least, Holly had never been in any wilderness area where there were so many flowers. There were banks and bushes and stands of them all around her, a dozen kinds she didn't recognize, violet and yellow and orange and red.

They were standing on the same white path she'd seen through the Gate before; Holly scraped one of her sabatons over the surface and felt it give grittily. Sand. Hawaiian-beach-white sand.

What, no yellow brick?

She dropped her helmet into her shoulder bag and shrugged her shoulders, trying to settle the weight. The armor was already starting to heat up, even under her surcoat, and tiny beads of sweat had broken out on her forehead. She raised one leather-gauntleted hand to brush them away.

"Get there?" Holly asked. "Get where? Home?"

"I don't know." Mac shrugged off the backpack and then pulled off the black leather duster he was wearing. Beneath it he was wearing a baggy tunic of Holly's, denim Mongol pants, and Carol's spare sneakers. "Perhaps somewhere else would be better."

He shook out the duster; it stretched and billowed and *changed,* and when it settled again in his hands, Gauvain Makindeor was holding the Cloak of Night and Daggers as Holly had first seen it—a velvet cloak the deep indigo of the night sky in which jewel stars twinkled and shone. The inside of the cloak was lined in glossy silk charmeuse the color of a desert sunset. Mac settled it around his shoulders again and looked at the backpack.

"Well, *I'm* not going to carry it," Holly told him roundly. "But where are we going, if we aren't going home—to your home, I mean?" *And yours now, like it or not,* a tiny inner voice told her.

"We must go back to Chandrakar," Mac said, as though he was only just now reasoning it out. "I must find someone I can trust, to send to the Iron World for the *Book of Airts*. But . . ." He stopped again. Holly looked at him, worriedly. Intellectually, she knew that Mac had been a prisoner in a mental hospital a little over a week ago and that his memory was a chancy and intermittent thing. But it was frightening to know that, to have to depend on his memory anyway, and then to watch it fail.

"We will follow the trail of the Treasures to Chandrakar," Mac said after a moment. "The Cloak will call to them, like to like. Then all we need to do is to follow the Treasures to where they are gathered together, which will be at the High Seat, at Citadel, where we may lay all before the Twilight Court and restore to House Amarmonde its Treasure."

"Sounds good," Holly said. What it really sounded was far too easy. If Mac had hidden the *Book of Airts* rather than take it back to Chandrakar with him, things could not be as straightforward as just walking in and filing a report.

"Come, then," Mac said, and walked off down the path, Cloak billowing.

Holly stared down at the abandoned bundle, and sighed. And bent down, careful not to overbalance herself, and picked it up. Slinging it over her left shoulder along with the bits and pieces of her armor, she trudged after him.

Fortunately she did not have to walk far. Half an hour brought them to the main road, where Mac simply stopped and waited for someone to pass. They were in the Borders, he told Holly, and traffic here was heavy. And in fact a wagon stopped for them almost immediately to provide them—with many apologies for the lack of comfort for the lady knight—space in the back to ride. Holly, whose body told her it was late afternoon in winter, promptly fell asleep.

"Holly." She heard the voice from far off but saw no reason to wake up. The heavy restraint of her limbs told her she was sleeping in her armor again, so it must be Rook who was calling her. Well, he'd call again.

"Holly."

She was just about to wake up, and remember that it couldn't be Rook, when she was jerked sharply out of sleep by someone banging on her armor with a stick.

She sat up. Mac retreated carefully out of reach, the stick he'd used to wake her still in his hand.

"What?" Holly was not at her most gracious upon awakening, and she felt disoriented and jet-lagged. Her mental clock said it was the middle of the night, but her eyes told her it was late afternoon. Maybe neither one was right.

"We're here," Mac said.

"Chandrakar?" Holly said, sliding out down off the cart's tail and brushing wisps of straw from her surcoat. She resisted the impulse to stretch, which was nearly impossible in plate armor, and concentrated on limbering up instead. As she did, she looked around.

They'd reached the proverbial wide spot in the road. Zillions of the most enormous oak trees Holly had ever seen crowded close to the road on both sides. Where the cart had stopped, there was a pump and trough, and the carter was standing by the heads of his thirsty team as they drank from the filled container. Beyond them, farther from the road, was a low wooden building with a deep porch. It looked like an illustration from "The Opening of Kentucky in the 1700s" section of her grade school history book. A woman stood on the porch, looking toward them. She wore a cap, a smock, and an apron over the smock. When she saw Holly looking at her, she bobbed a curtsey.

Welcome to these current middle ages, Holly thought, staring uneasily. She didn't know why the appearance of the woman should make everything seem real when the cart and driver had not, but somehow it did.

"No. But we can reach the Iron Road from here," Mac told her. He waved to the driver, who stepped up to the driver's box and clucked to his team; the cart began to move off; Holly was jut fast enough to rescue the backpack.

"*You* carry it, this time," she demanded, setting it carefully at Mac's feet. She would have tossed it at him, but she remembered just in time that it contained two glass bottles of mead.

"Neither of us need do servants' work if I can find what I need here," Mac said. He turned away and walked toward the cabin.

As it turned out, he could not, but at least they settled the question of who carried the backpack.

Holly stared at the fat white pony. It was tied to the hitching post in front of the cottage and glared mistrustfully at her with the most beautiful blue eyes Holly had ever seen on any living thing. On its back was a packsaddle, the four wooden legs reaching heavenward like an inverted chair.

"Thelwell lives," Holly muttered, then: "Oh, come on now, Thing, it can't be that bad, can it?"

The pony shook its shaggy head, disagreeing.

"It can, indeed, be that bad," Mac assured her, setting the backpack into the center of the saddle and beginning to lash it down. "This was all the landlord had to sell, and it makes a poor bargain. The beast is enchanted: it can't even carry your armor."

"Oh, well," Holly said. To tell the truth, she felt safer in her armor than out of it and would just as soon wear it. "Enchanted how?" she asked dutifully. "And what's for lunch?"

"Bread and meat and hard cider. And if the tavern keeper knows any more about the pony, he did not tell it. Just do not touch it with iron, Holly; you might kill it or release something far less useful from its spell. He did say," Mac added, a puzzled tone in his voice, "that the Gates to the World of Iron are *closed*. That is why we found no horses here."

"I'm not that good a rider," Holly said conciliatingly. "But closed how? Why are they closed?"

"And who has closed them?" Mac said. "Leaving aside the matter of its impossibility. The Borders are like a sieve, Holly: That is their danger, that anything here might fall through to the Last World, the World of Iron. Long has sealing them been talked of, but it has never been done because to close all the ways between your world and the Border Lands, even temporarily, would require a Binding of such power . . ."

"Okay, I get the picture," said Holly, who didn't. The woman in the apron came through the door again, carrying a large wooden tray. She stared at Mac as if he were doing something astonishing, then bobbed another awkward curtsey and set the tray down upon the porch steps.

Mac seemed to disapprove of the rations, but Holly didn't; in her book there was nothing wrong with white bread and roast chicken, though she was careful not to drink too much of the cider. She ate standing. The armor was flexible enough that she could sit and even lie down in it, and she'd actually ridden horseback in it once, but getting down and up was a laborious process, and Mac couldn't help her to her feet. Getting out of her shell come bedtime was going to be an interesting process, all things considered.

She wondered where Margot and Carol were now and what they were doing. When she'd come through the Gate, had the World of Iron gone spinning off like a manic top, whirling them faster and faster through Time's dark pavilions—

Manic.

"Gotta take a pill," Holly muttered. She started digging through her purse, lifting the helm and gauntlets out and exposing the junk beneath.

It was odd, the things a person accumulated. She'd tossed out most of the deadwood, but here was her nursing pin and her wristwatch, a couple of candy bars, the issue of *Tournaments Illuminated* she'd gotten the day she left for HeliCon—why had she brought that?—a tube of cortisone cream, a bottle of Excedrin (both probably useful), some tea bags and restaurant sugar, a Swiss Army knife, the fake ID with her picture on it that she'd bought in the dealer's room, her cloak brooch with the blood-stones . . .

Her evening meds weren't there—or the morning ones either. She took everything out, then turned the bag upside down and shook it, but she already knew what she'd find. Nothing.

Fear mingled with a guilty sense of triumph. *Oh, Holly—be sensible!* her inner adult admonished. But what would the point of being sensible have been, really-really, when she'd only had a few days supply left any-way?

"Holly?" Mac asked.

"There's something I have to tell you," Holly said reluctantly. Why should this time be so hard, when she'd explained so many times over the years? "I left my meds—my pills—back on Earth."

"Medication," Mac said distastefully. "You won't need medication here. This is not your world, Holly."

"You don't understand," Holly said unwillingly. "I've got a . . . sick-ness." And was coming here with Makindeor just a flashy form of sui-cide? How could she have thought she could manage without her medica-tion? "It makes me . . ." she stopped, unable to say the word. She stared at Makindeor, willing him to understand.

"There is a warwolf that sleeps in your soul," Mac answered. "I understood that from the first moment I saw you, Holly Kendal. I *saw* it. But we are here in my own place now, and I can keep the wolf from waking. Or waken it," he added very softly as he turned to wrap up the remains of their meal in the cloth.

Keep the wolf from waking—the pendulum from swinging? Holly didn't think so. She took a deep breath against the enormity of what she'd done, trying to justify it at least to herself. She'd had to come. Maybe the pendulum couldn't follow her to Elfland. Maybe her brain had suddenly gone all right at last.

Maybe they'd both be dead before it could matter.

Holly led the pony, Mac led the way. She wondered when she'd start to feel different—how long she'd be up and how far "down" would be this time. Her heart beat nervously, and inside the leather gauntlets, her hands were damp.

It's okay, it's okay, it's okay— she repeated over and over to herself. *You were going to run out anyway.*

But in her own world she—or the MedAlert bracelet she still wore—could explain her problem. Here they'd probably try to exorcise her. She tried very hard not to care, knowing as she did that worrying was okay, a sign of health, that when the irrational optimism inevitably took over her mind, it would be too late for everything. She followed Mac down the road, and as evening shadows fell, Holly saw a light in the distance.

An oncoming train.

"The Iron Road," Mac said.

It was, Mac assured her, the greatest magic in all the Lands Beyond the Morning, but it didn't look like so much of a muchness to Holly. Of course it was beautiful—a white road that shone like the full moon—but it just sat there.

They'd turned off the road the cart had followed to follow the light through the trees until they came to it. On the far side of the Road the landscape changed profoundly: pine trees that were already black in the twilight, with mountains—still sunset colored—in the distance. The ground sloped sharply upward at the edge of the Iron Road; the Road itself was built along the bermed top of some interminable tumulus. The sides of the embankment were carved by runoff into branching riverine patterns, a homely and familiar decoration.

"So," said Holly, "what do we do now?" Her surcoat flapped about her knees in the evening breeze, but she couldn't feel it except on her face. The brief surge of energy she'd felt on awakening had faded, and she felt that stopping would be nice; she wasn't in trim for wearing her armor all day.

"Walk the Road to where the other Treasures lie," Mac answered. "It will not be long, Holly, and then Citadel will give both of us good guesting, and we will be home."

They walked beside the Road until they found a trail that led up onto it, and then they crossed onto the Road itself. Holly's armor sizzled as she passed from the mundane trail to the enchanted Road. She stared down at herself, more enchanted than appalled, as blue-violet fire raced over every inch of her armor, outlining each piece of it in splendor.

The pony set its heels on the other side of the invisible boundary line and refused to move.

Holly pulled. The pony pulled. Mac pushed, and got kicked at for his trouble.

"Yo, Rosinante II," Holly said. It seemed as if she could see her voice as well; the air shimmered with electricity, and every time she spoke it seemed to sparkle more brightly.

"You are an ungrateful animal," Mac told the pony. The pony simply set its ears back and closed its eyes, straining against the halter. Holly staggered half a step forward under the pressure.

Finally Mac unclasped the Cloak and draped it over the pony's head. Holly half expected the animal to vanish, as if this were a magician's trick, but it only shivered, and the tautness on the lead-rope relaxed.

"Pull," Mac said.

Holly pulled. The pony went docilely up onto the road. Mac followed—Holly had the fleeting impression of a subtle membrane sealing itself behind him—and took back his cloak. The pony flung up its head and glared in all directions, indignant at the trick.

Holly looked around. She felt the sense of stillness and solitude that only comes in the deepest part of the night, the sensation of standing on top of a high mountain, where the air was thin. Instead of simply coming from the road beneath her feet, as it had appeared before, the light seemed to be all around her, as if the air were made of diamonds.

"Don't lose your way," Mac said from behind her. Holly jumped, startled.

He walked on up the road a few paces ahead of her, to where she could see him. The Cloak of Night and Daggers was silvery-brilliant now, filling with an unfelt wind: a thing of aurora borealises and lightning, lined with a darkness so deep it hurt her eyes to look at it. Magic. The light from the Cloak and the Road gave Makindeor's face a harsh alien beauty, and his harlequin eyes flared with a hot red light.

"There are dangers to walking the Iron Road," Mac said. "It is easy to forget your purpose, to go where you do not wish, to lose your way and your self. Stay close to me."

Holly took a reluctant step forward. She didn't want to move at all. She wanted to stand right here, forever, and listen to the music of the night. But the pony moved up past her, pulling her along behind, and Makindeor waited expectantly.

"I guess . . ." Holly said, uncertainly.

"Come," said Mac. "Only a little way. The Road will take us to Chandrakar, and we will be home."

Your home, anyway, Holly thought.

But as things turned out, that wasn't exactly what happened either.

"This isn't it, is it?" Holly asked.

"No," Mac said briefly.

She looked behind her and did not see the road. All around the three of them—her, Mac, the pony Rosinante—there was nothing but a plain as flat as Kansas, covered with silvery-green grass that rippled in the wind. It was dawn (though they had not walked long enough for it to become dawn by any natural means), and above them seabirds hovered and banked. The sky was awash with light. The pony put its head down, unconcerned, and began to graze.

"It looks like the Eastern Marches," he said broodingly, "but why . . . ?" Mac fumbled in his belt pouch—hers, actually—for his glasses.

Holly turned slowly in a circle, looking about. It was hard for Holly to feel worried about having shown up in the wrong place when any place would have been equally strange. She'd never seen so much flat grass in her entire life. Then . . .

"Oh," she said.

"Oh, indeed," Mac said, looking in the same direction.

The black tower loomed to the east, monstrous against a bright line of sea. It cast a shadow at them like an accusing finger.

Holly stared down at the skeleton of the horse.

They'd been walking in this Land for about an hour, Holly judged: long enough for the sun to rise on a brightly colorless winter day, for her to decide she was *really* tired of walking, and for Mac to determine that no matter what else might be true, the largest collection of Treasures in the Land lay directly east of them—inside the tower.

And to stumble over the skeleton.

The bones were picked and jumbled—no, more than that: *polished* as clean as if they'd been boiled. There was no cartilage to hold them together; Holly reached down and picked up something that gleamed—a bar of hinged and jointed metal about six inches wide, made of . . . bronze? Whatever it was, it hadn't been here long enough to tarnish.

It was a horse's bit. The other scraps of metal she saw must also belong to the bridle, and once she saw that much, her eye was able to pick out the rest. Holly nudged what was left of the saddle with her foot. The leather was in tatters, the wooden saddletree beneath was gnawed, as if by rats. The gouges in the wood looked raw and new—whatever had happened, it had happened recently. There was a wisp of black horsehair caught beneath it. So much for the horse. She wondered what had happened to the rider.

Holly glanced back up at the tower, broodingly. It was as unbelievable-looking as a special effect: black as obsidian, smooth as glass, and huge. There might be anything inside—and hostile. Live-action role-playing wasn't turning out to be nearly as much fun as people always said it was.

"What did that?" she demanded of Mac.

"I don't know," he said simply. "I wish I knew whether this tower was supposed to be here at all. I remember—I think I remember—that this area was interdicted during the war because the tower of the Lady Hermonicet lies here, but surely this cannot be her place."

"Uh-huh," Holly said, not listening. She had the odd feeling that a storm was brewing. Though there wasn't a cloud anywhere in the sky, she had the odd unsettled feeling that comes of waiting for disaster. There was something out there.

"Listen," said Mac.

Holly listened, but she saw it before she heard it; a line of riders, approaching from the west.

"Mac? Are these the good guys?"

"I don't know." His voice was strained. "The sun has risen."

And the Cloak only worked at night.

The riders must have seen them, but they neither slowed down nor hailed the pair on foot. *Great armor. Great horses,* Holly thought automatically. *They look like the Näzgûl.* Black armor, breastplates and helms with chain mail, all beautifully matched. The coats of the horses gleamed. There must have been a dozen of them, armed with swords and pikes. The riders moved with the precision of a mounted drill team.

"Holly," Mac said. "We're going to have to fight. *You're* going to have to fight. I can stop the horses, but afterward it is up to you. Do you understand me?"

She turned to stare at him, shaking her head in bewilderment. Mac couldn't be serious.

"No," Holly said.

"Holly," Mac said in despairing tones. He turned back to the riders. They were only a few steps away now.

"——*!*" His shout bewildered Holly—it was the verbal equivalent of flash of lightning, abrupt and disorienting. Mac flung up his hands, and a bright spark flew from them to Holly's armor; he jerked back, shaking his hands and making sounds as if he'd been burned—but the oncoming riders stopped.

"Ah," Mac said in satisfaction. "So I have not yet lost all my skill."

The black riders' horses shied and plunged, going from a trot to a stand in seconds. Nothing their riders could do would move them.

"Kill the Adept first!" the captain shouted. One by one the riders began to dismount and move forward.

And Makindeor turned away from them, cupping a handful of air and tossing it into Holly's face.

She jerked back, startled. There'd been nothing in his hands, but it tingled on her skin like a handful of snowflakes. Doubt and fear faded away, and a cold gleeful anger took their place. She spared a moment to regret that she didn't have time to put on her helm and gauntlets, but she'd manage. Nobody was getting his hands on her patient while Holly Kendal was alive.

With one smooth pull she freed Lady Fantasy of her scabbard and fell into garde to face the first of the attackers. The steel gleamed in the sunlight like risen glory. A moment of purpose crackled between Holly and the attackers—an understanding that this was *real*. Then the pikeman closed, running forward, holding his weapon low to trip her.

This was her function, this was her calling. This was what she had been trained for. "Gotcha!" Holly cried, as the pikeman moved in on her. She parried the pike with an upswept blade, reversing her blow for a cut to the ribs that sheared through the bronze ring-mail her enemy wore as if it were smoke. Down he went, and Holly spun to face the next, putting a wall of steel between them and Mac.

They were well-trained, but she was better, as well as armed and armored with tempered steel. Cut high. Cut low. Blood turned the ground beneath her feet to mud as she swung Lady Fantasy in an edged dance of brilliant steel. Their weapons rang off Holly's armor with a stunning force that she would only feel later, and she laughed and shouted at them, taunting them to close and dance with her.

Until at last there were no more to face her, until she cut the last down from behind as he turned to run and stood over the body breathing like a blacksmith's bellows.

Until she heard the whining, whimpering sounds of an attack dog held back from the kill and knew that those sounds were coming from *her*.

Slowly, unwillingly, Holly came back to herself. Her head ached and she had a pounding weakness in every limb, as if she were recovering from a seizure.

Her sword was covered with something that looked like Welch's Grape Juice Concentrate. Elphen blood. Her armor was covered with it. She was wet to the elbows, wet and muddy to the knees. Her black surcoat hung in stiff sticky wet folds, her owl and thistle device almost obliterated with blood. She dripped and oozed and squished as though she'd been swimming in blood.

Holly shook blood from her leather gauntlet. It was cut across the back, and the steel showed through where she must have parried with her forearm. Sweat trickled itchily down inside her armor, and the air felt suddenly much colder. When she panted, she could taste the salt of the sea and smell the blood. Slowly she turned in a circle, looking around.

On the ground surrounding her, fallen in a circle a double swords-length wide, lay bodies. Seven—ten—she wasn't sure how many. All down. None moving.

"Mac?" Holly's voice was a rusty croak. She felt flat, drained, even sleepy, curiously uninvolved in the scene before her. As if this were only a movie.

"Here." It took her several minutes of work to focus her eyes enough to locate him. He was mounted on one of the fighters' horses, holding another by the reins.

"I'm all wet," Holly said plaintively. The sound of her own voice shocked her; it sounded drugged and childish and far from sane. "I killed them," she said, still trying to understand what had happened.

"I told you I could waken the wolf," said Mac somberly. "You are a great warrior, Holly Kendal. A *berserker.*"

· 16 ·

Smoke and Mirrors

I DO NOT want to go in there, Ruth Marlowe thought in a moment of crystal clarity.

It was night. The three of them stood beside the tower, huddled together as if for comfort, protected from the endless wind by the very massiveness of the structure. This close to its hugeness it looked more like a straight wall than a curved one, endless, cold, and black. There was no opening in it that Ruth could see.

"Honey, I'm home," Fox called. Jausserande rounded on him.

"Let's just get inside," Ruth said wearily, "before we're eaten alive."

"Is this the place?" Jausserande demanded.

"Does it matter?" Fox asked. "Unless you want to test your swimming skills against theirs—"

"Oh, shut up," Ruth said. She walked away from the other two around the side of the tower, and a few minutes later she was standing before the entrance to the black tower.

"This is a trap," Jausserande said, following her. The doorway was a darker dark than either the night or the tower, if that was possible, and none of them could see anything of the interior.

"So do we take the horse or not?" Fox said. Ruth muttered something profane and pushed past the other two before she could censor herself.

As soon as her foot touched the slick unnatural surface of the floor, Ruth knew this had been the worst mistake of her life, but by then it was too late to turn back. She slid forward like a hydroplaning Datsun, balanced upright for a brief moment, and then fell onto her stomach, still sliding forward. The floor was cold and glass-smooth beneath her fingers; a moment later she saw something white moving in its depths.

She recoiled with a squeak and so did the shadow. After a moment she realized it was the reflection of her own face.

"Are you okay?" Fox asked, kneeling beside her.

"It's getting lighter," Ruth said stupidly. She could see Fox's face clearly now.

Fox pointed upward and Ruth looked. They were in the middle of an enormous circular room, with walls so smooth she could see herself and her companions reflected in them as if in a mirror. All the way around the room a band of letter-like designs were engraved into the stone. They were the source of the light, glowing steadily brighter until the chamber was quite ordinarily bright. As the light strengthened, the floor beneath Ruth's hands became rougher, until she was able to regain her feet without difficulty. She looked around. It was large enough that being inside it shouldn't really bother her, but Ruth didn't like it, all the same.

"Water!"

Against one wall, carved of the same glassy black material as the rest of the tower, stood a watering trough. Water spewed from a gargoyle's mouth into the semicircular trough below. The horse stood before it, sucking noisily. Jausserande stood beside him, holding the weary horse's lead rope. As Ruth watched, she pulled him away from the water before he foundered, leading him back to the center of the room over his protests.

"All the Eumenides," Fox said. Ruth ignored him, staggering over to the fountain and bathing her face and hands in the icy stream. The water was as cold as if it flowed from the River Styx; it numbed her hands as she cupped them to drink, but nothing had ever tasted so wonderful. She stopped only when her stomach ached from the coldness and her teeth were chattering.

Fox drank and then went to rinse and fill the waterskins. Ruth looked around more carefully this time. The room was filled with archways, black on black. One, two, three—she turned around and around, losing count; were there eight doorways, or nine? Which one led to Melior—and which to the way out?

"You shouldn't have come after me," Ruth said. It was stupid, but she couldn't think of anything else to say.

"Yes," said Fox to Jausserande, ignoring Ruth, "I think this is definitely a trap."

"Now our lives are in your hands, Child of Earth," Jausserande said. "Lead us to the Sword."

Slowly Ruth began to circle the room. Which doorway led to Me-

lior—or didn't it matter which she chose? She felt damp and clammy—
except for her eyes, which were hot and dry. She closed them and tried to
think.

"Ruth. Wake up, Ruth."

She'd fallen asleep. But she was so tired . . . Ruth's cheeks flamed
in shame; here in the still silence, she could feel her tie to Melior clearly
once more. He was dying, and all she could think about was getting some
sleep—!

"Ruth. Beloved, do not grieve for me—"

She heard his voice. She started toward him. And realized she'd
never really been awake at all, as she fell from dream to dream, into
nightmare.

*She could smell gasoline and knew as clearly as if someone had told her
that the others—Jimmy and Kathy and Allen were dead. Ruth Marlowe held
her eyes tightly closed. If she opened them, something would start to hurt; she
knew it. And she didn't want to see what she had seen. A monster out of
myth, horrible and snakelike . . .*

*There was a wash of heat, of motion coming toward her face. She
struggled to open her eyes—to wake—to move—and could not. And as the
monster bent over her, and the wrenching, tearing pain began, Ruth Marlowe
realized she'd lost her last chance to escape.*

"Ruth!" Fox held her, calling her name. She flailed at him weakly,
remembering everything at last.

She had always been their pawn—the pawn of the magicians Beyond
the Morning who plotted to destroy the Twelve Treasures. They'd used
her just as Melior had said they had; they had reached into the World of
Iron and turned her life inside out. They'd wanted a soul, so they'd
arranged the crash that had killed her three closest friends and left her
floating in a comatose limbo for eight years while her soul wandered
Beyond the Morning.

They.

"Baligant," Ruth said aloud.

"Here?" Fox said. He actually sounded alarmed.

"Melior," Ruth said, trying to explain, but her words didn't make any
sense. "The dragon—"

"Give me some wine," Fox said over his shoulder, "she's raving."

"I hope so," Jausserande muttered. "Is there a cup, Fox? This is all
there is—I don't want her guzzling it."

"She's got one on her belt."

Ruth felt Fox's hands on her waist and batted at them irritably, trying to hold herself upright at the same time. Why couldn't he leave her alone?

"Here it—uh-oh," Fox said.

He held the tin cup that Ruth had taken from the Goblin Market in both hands. All three of them stared at it.

It was glowing as if it had been dipped in liquid neon, with the same chill magical light as the glyphs on the walls.

"This?" Ruth said.

"Looks familiar, doesn't it?" Fox said feebly.

It was a battered thing of discolored tin, the sort of thing Ruth'd seen at every inn she'd been to. Pitted and dented and thoroughly disreputable-looking, with a deep bowl set atop a crudely fashioned triangular base.

"How odd," Ruth said vaguely. "The glassware doesn't do that at home."

"The glassware at home isn't Chandrakar's own sacred Dixie Cup," Fox responded. His voice was hoarse with exhaustion and suprise. "Congratulations, Ruth—you've had the door-prize all along."

"A trick—it was a trick!" Jausserande shouted. Ruth heard the hiss of her drawn sword. "I'll kill you both—and you, Fox, slowly."

"Do and you lose it!" Fox said quickly. He pushed Ruth behind him, into the mouth of the corridor. "Ruth's the Cupbearer now—look, Tink!" Over his shoulder he spoke rapidly to Ruth. "Whatever you do, Ruthie, don't give it to her. It's like the Ruby Slippers—she can't take it away from you. You've got to give it freely."

It all made a sort of mad fairy-tale-logic sense. She, Ruth Marlowe, had the Cup of Morning Shadows, the Treasure for which Jausserande would do anything. And Jausserande could not take it from her. It must be given.

"No mud-born can wield the Treasures," Jausserande said.

"I used it before," Ruth said. She would have figured things out eventually, if everything hadn't been moving so fast. The Cup had let her heal Melior in the forest house. It had never done anything special for Ruth after that, so she hadn't realized what she had; but in the forest, she realized now, it had let Fox heal her sprained ankle.

Possibly he'd guessed—and being Fox, had said nothing.

"You are my cousin's leman," Jausserande raged. "Will you live untouched so that you may touch the Cup? So much for Rohannan's hopes! Give it to me now or watch as I cut your pretty Fox into a thousand screaming pieces." Jausserande took a menacing step forward.

"Live untouched so that you may touch the Cup . . ." That was why it

had stopped working for her. But Fox had used it. Ruth wondered if Fox knew what that said about him. "Touch him and I'll smash it!" Ruth said.

Jausserande froze where she stood. *So I* can *smash it.* Ruth felt the seductive lure of absolute power. She didn't like Jausserande very much, and now she could set any conditions she chose for transfer of ownership and Jausserande would meet them—for the Cup. She could demand that Jausserande pardon Fox or learn to love humans, or she could simply hold onto the Cup herself until the last possible moment, hoping she could put Melior's cousin through enough hell that she would be forced to learn wisdom and tolerance.

But how much would Jausserande learn through a promise that had been extorted from her at Cup-point? Ruth wondered sensibly. And anyway, things like that only worked out the way you wanted them to in pulp fiction.

"Any advice?" Ruth said to Fox.

"Smash it," Fox said.

Ruth shook her head. Fairy tales. This was all like something out of a fairy tale, and there was something in all of those old stories about elves, and gifts, and bargains. And besides, Ruth didn't have enough of a sadistic streak in her to want to play the farce out to the end. She tossed the Cup to Jausserande.

"Here. It's yours. Catch."

Jausserande snatched it out of the air, not even waiting for it to fall. In her hands the Cup flowed and changed, morphing and expanding until Jausserande held a jeweled chalice as long as her arm, its bell crusted with gemstones that each glistened with a bright particular fire. The Cup of Morning Shadows, revealed at last. There had never been a *tainaiste-*Cup, only the Cup itself, in disguise.

"That was stupid," Fox said in a weary voice.

Jausserande looked down at the Treasure in her hands, then up at Ruth. Her violet cat's-eyes welled with unashamed tears.

"I and all my Line owe you a great debt, Child of Earth."

"Melior," Ruth said.

Jausserande smiled. "Find the Sword," she whispered, and flung the Cup up into the air.

It hovered over Jausserande's head for a moment as they all stared at it—and then, as if it had chosen its direction, began to sail off down the corridor.

"Follow it!" Jausserande cried shrilly. Without waiting for a response from the other two, she swung into the saddle of their one remaining horse and drove it off down the corridor after the quickly retreating Cup.

"C'mon, Ruthie, let's all be lost together," Fox said, "it's more polite. And just remember—you owe me, too."

Ruth closed her hand until the seal ring that Fox had given her dug into her palm, and said nothing.

It wasn't difficult to follow Jausserande. The corridor branched, and soon enough Ruth and Fox were thoroughly disoriented, but the light was always visible, even if only as a faint reflection in the mirrored corridors.

As they stumbled along after Jausserande and the Cup, the light grew brighter, as if the sun were rising—bright enough to make the walls shine like silver.

"Yo! Tink!" Fox shouted. His voice echoed weirdly.

"Fox!" Jausserande shouted. Her voice sounded close by.

"Come on," said Fox.

"No," Ruth said, taking a step backward. The light was so bright now that her eyes were tearing; she turned her back to it instinctively, imagining that she could feel it on her skin, a sort of cold sunlight.

"All right, then," Fox said. "Stay here." He walked into the light. Ruth stood alone only a moment before groping after him. Melior was this way—he had to be.

Then why couldn't she feel him in her mind any more . . . ?

The corridor curved slightly. Ruth caught up to Fox easily; he was moving slowly, feeling his way. The hood of his cloak was pulled down over his face, and his eyes were tightly closed against the glare. The light was as bright as if the sun itself were present; Ruth could see the source through her closed eyelids, a brilliant upright bar with the Cup hovering at its apex and something as bright below. The Sword? Ruth winced, covering her closed eyes with her hands, but the light struck through her fingers, turning all the world red with green and purple moons waxing and fading behind her eyes.

"Turn it *off!*" Ruth shouted.

There was a clang as the Cup dropped at Jausserande's feet.

The lights went out.

"Gosh," said Fox perkily in the sudden darkness. "It's just like finding the Holy Grail, isn't it?"

Ruth groped blindly forward. She heard the jingle of the horse's tack and the sound of it shifting its feet on the hard floor, then her feet struck something soft. She knelt, feeling around for it.

Jausserande had sent the Cup of Morning Shadows after the Sword of Maiden's Tears—this was Melior. It *had* to be. She ran her hands over the body. Her fingertips rose and fell with the faint breathing. He was alive.

"Melior," Ruth said, and began to weep.

Her vision cleared slowly; when it had, Ruth could see that Melior lay unconscious in one of the tower's featureless corridors. The Sword of Maiden's Tears lay sheathed at his side, its baleful beauty muted in the faint and sourceless moonlike light that filled the corridor. Beside the Sword lay his cloak, the one he'd been wearing in the Goblin Market and at the forest house, the one made of brilliant scales the color of California poppies.

"Wizard-work," Jausserande said in distaste, fingering it. "Who is it meant for, I wonder?"

Who cares? Ruth thought. She looked warily at the Sword.

It was scabbarded, with the straps of its baldric curled about it and the dreaming opal pommel-weight as dark and colorless as glass. Melior lay as if he had fallen; when Ruth clutched at his hands, they were icy cold, and the wide welts from shackles on his wrists still oozed faintly. He wore a long robe of some color too dark to see in the dimness, belted at the waist with a sash of lighter-colored silk. She lifted the front of it away from his chest with trembling fingers, afraid of what she would see.

She wished she hadn't looked. The echoes of old pain, like the after-image of the brilliant light, stayed with her, making Ruth feel ill and shaky.

"Wake up," Ruth whispered.

Fox looked over her shoulder and untied the waistband of the robe that Melior wore. He pulled it all the way open, and Ruth winced away from the black bruises like holes in Melior's flesh, from the shiny raised rosettes of burns and the deep cuts that had bled dry but never healed. Rohannan Melior had been in his enemies' hands for a fortnight, and they had used his pain to draw Ruth to him.

"Don't think so," Fox said quietly.

It took Ruth a moment to realize what Fox meant. "No!" she said. "He's still alive! He's—"

"He's bleeding to death," Fox said brutally. "If not out here, then in there." He gestured at Melior's chest.

"You're just saying that," Ruth said desperately. "You hate him—you want him dead."

"I know what a dying man looks like," Fox said simply. "Or a dying elf, for that matter."

"The Cup can heal him," Ruth said, turning to Jausserande. "You know it can! *Do it!*"

Jausserande hesitated, looking down into the Cup. Ruth opened her mouth to speak again, but Fox put his hand on her arm and bent to speak directly into Ruth's ear.

"Don't push. She's never done this before. She doesn't have much magic," he said, in a voice lower than a whisper.

Ruth stared at Jausserande in dawning horror. Had she come all this way only to watch Melior die?

She had the Cup. She, Floire Jausserande of the House of the Silver Silences. This was the moment she'd yearned for since her sixteenth birthday. She had it. Line Floire's Treasure in Line Floire's hands once more.

Two months ago, and Guiraut would still be alive. One month ago, and she would not have seen Fox lose the *tainaiste*-Cup in the Vale of Stars. A fortnight—two weeks—ago, and she would not know what she knew now: that Melior had been right, and Baligant still plotted against the Seven Houses even though he had won the High King's seat.

And had Melior only died before they'd reached him, she would not be standing here now before two mud-born, about to dare the Cup's magic—and fail.

Heal him, Melior's Ironworld heart twin had said, but Jausserande knew that the Cup's power relied upon its bearer, and she knew that there was no health in her. She stared down into the golden bowl, while a soft inner voice urged her to take the Cup and the Sword and go. Line Rohannan would be grateful and would ask no questions about Baron Rohannan so long as Rohannan's Treasure was safe, and Jausserande would never be asked to wield the Cup again—only to present it at the Kingmaking, and secure her Line.

Let him die. At least let it be her choice and not her failure.

Jausserande glanced up and met Fox's eyes.

They were the odd pale blue of mud-born eyes, the opaque milky color of the winter sky. He watched her patiently, as if he knew what it was to be good at very many things and then be asked to do something else entirely. As if he knew what it was like to be so empty.

His eyes were not like Ceiynt's eyes. Ceiynt's eyes were dark and brilliant, almost an elphen blue. He had ridden into the losel swarm; all she had known was that danger followed them, and so she had sent him to deal with it. And he had gone, Ruth's champion, trusting Jausserande to care for her just as he would have. Leaving Ruth in her charge as if he believed she would—she *could*—honor even so implicit an oath. Believing that after so many years Jausserande could still nurture as well as destroy.

I killed my first man when I was twelve. She'd always said that, but it wasn't really true; almost from the time she'd learned to walk, she'd followed her nurse onto the battlefields, helping to finish the enemy wounded. Almost her first conscious memory was of watching the life-light fade from an enemy soldier's eyes. War had been her life, her guardianship of the Cup only another kind of war. To live chaste and inviolate was no hardship, Jausserande had felt. She had nothing left to give to a lover, to a family. There was no life in her. No life, no health, no healing.

Death, now, that was easy. She felt it flow through her fingertips, collecting in the bottom of the Cup; a sullen green-black fire, the color of death and pain and betrayal. All three of them could drink from it, and then . . .

No!

Pure self-interested terror drove the darkness away . . . for a moment. Was that all that was left of Floire Jausscrande of the House of the Silver Silences? A darkness that would grow darker still, until there was no light left anywhere?

The Cup was empty again, as if it had never begun to fill.

There must be something else left in her. Jausserande sought through all her memories for it, and all she could find was the thought that Ceiynt had trusted her to keep Ruth alive.

She clung to that thought, using it like a guiding-thread to lead her to others. Tiny, fleeting things. Her promise to Fox to spare his comrade's life. The pride she had felt in Guiraut's accomplishments.

Why couldn't you have lived? If Guiraut had lived, this would be so easy. He had always believed in her, in the bright honor that Jausserande herself had known was a matter of unmet temptation. With every breath she took, she mourned his death.

As Ruth would mourn Melior's. Before all politics and statecraft, there was this: If Melior died, Ruth would grieve.

There was so much pain in the world. It was such a small thing to end one grief before it began.

Jausserande let her mind fill with death once more, but this time she concentrated on the rage of the living left behind, on the unremitting pain that proceeded from that death. She let the fire of grief fill her, the denial of death and through it the denial of grief.

And the chalice filled once more, this time with life.

The pain of it was shocking and unexpected; her teachers had told Jausserande that strong magic was dangerous—what they hadn't told her was how much it *hurt*. The sides of the chalice burned her hands like deathmetal, and it took all her willpower to hold onto it. She took a step forward, staring down at her cousin's deathly still body. Fox and Ruth looked up at her, their ruddy human faces pale in the sapphire light of the chalice.

Jausserande hesitated, though the painful weight of the Cup of Morning Shadows grew heavier with each moment.

What if she were wrong? What if the Cup held only a different kind of death, not life?

She shrugged the thoughts away. To make any decision was more important than to make the best one. She had done all she could, given all that was in her. She tilted the Cup forward and began to pour.

Ruth yelped, lunging backward and landing in an inelegant supine sprawl. She'd been sure that thing was empty—and in her experience, anything that glowed that brightly was *not* good for you. And where had it come from? Jausserande hadn't even filled the Cup with anything that Ruth had seen in the first place.

"What are you—*oof!*"

Fox landed on top of her, all knees and elbows and smelling of horse. Ruth shoved him away and scrambled to her knees, staring.

Jausserande stood over Melior, pouring light into his body. It fell from the Cup like water, but it didn't splash or puddle. It just poured into him in a long glowing stream.

Then the Cup was empty. Jausserande took a step back, put her hand against the wall for support, and sat down. Ruth scrambled back to Melior's side. The burns were gone. The cuts were gone. He was whole. She gathered the whole warm living weight of his body into her arms and held him as tightly as if it were the only thing she needed to do for the rest of her life. He roused, weakly, and put his arms around her.

"Ruth," Melior whispered in wonderment. "You're here."

Ruth held him tighter and nodded, unable to speak.

"Yeah, well, I hope it's come to everybody's attention that we're still *in* this place," Fox pointed out.

Melior held Ruth away from him and stared at Fox.

"How came you here, Child of Earth?" he said.

"It's a long story," Ruth said weakly.

"I walked," Fox said.

"This is the losel outlaw Fox who haunts your woods, cousin, the murdering rogue who slew Guiraut and seeks your death as well," Jausserande announced from her seat on the floor.

"*Philip?*" Melior said in disbelief. "I have no quarrel with him."

"No," Fox said. "I didn't think you'd think so."

There was a brief pause.

"Whatever your grievance," Melior said, "I swear I will make good upon it. But you must tell me how it is that you have brought my lady Ruth to this unchancy place, for while she bides here, she is in mortal danger." He reached for the Sword and pulled it toward him. Ruth recoiled, and when she did, she saw Fox looking at her with a faint chill amusement.

Their stories were quickly told—Jausserande's, of following Ruth here on the faint hope that the Cup would be where the Sword was, Melior's, of being held prisoner first by a wizard of the Wild Magic and then by Hermonicet the Fair.

"The White Ferret!" Jausserande exclaimed. "But she has no magic—and she's stupid as a pig besides!"

"You are as harsh to anyone who is not a proven warrior," Melior pointed out mildly, "but I think the lady has proved her arts sufficiently in making this place—or causing its making—to warrant more respect from you. When she brought me before her, she offered to set me at her side in Baligant's place . . ."

"And you refused her?" Jausserande said incredulously.

Melior merely looked at Ruth, who found herself blushing furiously.

"Hermonicet's bad taste isn't proof that Baligant sabotaged your stupid Treasures," Fox pointed out.

Of course. How stupid. I'm his proof. It was stupid how much remembering it hurt; hadn't Melior proven to her, over and over, that Chandrakar and the Sword of Maiden's Tears came first? He'd do anything to keep them.

And she'd promised Fox she'd make him give them up.

Melior's signet ring—the token he had given to Fox back in the World of Iron, that Fox had given to Ruth here in Chandrakar burned coldly against her hand. Without Fox, nothing would have worked out the way it had. It was too late to unmake the bargain; he'd already paid his end.

Now it was up to her.

"So," said Ruth, her happiness suddenly gone. "What do we do now?"

"Leave," Jausserande said. "If we can."

"Bets?" asked Fox.

It should have been easy. The corridor curved, but there were no branchings that they might have taken coming here. When they passed a cross-corridor, Ruth realized they were lost.

"We're lost," she said.

"Fine," Fox snapped nastily. "If we're lost, that means we don't have to keep going. We can stop for the night—or day, or whatever—and go on being lost tomorrow." He put his back against the nearest wall and slid down it, pulling his hooded cloak around him like a cantankerous bat.

We've been up for two days—or is it three? Ruth realized. *I can't even think straight any more.* She didn't know whether they were going in the right direction or not, and she didn't care. All she knew was that she was so tired she wanted to cry.

Jausserande looked at Melior. "We did not come this way," she said uneasily. She looked hollow-eyed but vital, as if whatever power of the Cup had healed Melior had restored her strength as well.

Ruth closed her eyes, leaning against Melior not out of fondness but through default. She was so tired she didn't think she'd ever sleep again. "Didn't anybody think to bring breadcrumbs?" she muttered.

· 17 ·

Steel Crazy After All
These Years

BEING A BERSERKER, Holly thought, wasn't all that it was cracked up to be, especially when you were wrapped in bloody—though still untouchable by elves—armor.

Even though they'd moved several yards from the bodies, the black horse Makindeor had caught for her would not let her come close enough to mount. It backed away, ears laid flat and eyes rolling, until Mac's horse caught its nervous fear as well.

"It is no use, Holly," he finally said. "It is cold iron, and not the scent of blood, that repels them."

"But the pony—" Holly protested. She felt sweaty, nauseatingly filthy, and dangerously lightheaded.

"These are creatures of magic, partaking of the nature of their masters," Mac said.

"I don't care what they are!" Holly shouted. "I want my armor off and I want a bath and I don't want anybody trying to kill me! You *tricked* me, Makindeor Whatever-your-name-is, and—"

"Did you want to be dead?" Mac answered, equally hotly. "They would have killed us both! Why is this so hard for you Ironworlders to grasp? Surely you do not believe that everyone in your own place loves you, for I have seen enough violence there to make me doubt it!"

"You didn't tell me this place was worse," Holly said in a small voice. She knew she ought to care about who and what they were, but at the moment, she had other pressing matters on her mind. "Oh, Mac, I think I'm going to be sick."

She turned away from him and the horses, walking blindly. She got only a few feet before she fainted in her tracks, which at least solved the awkward problem of how to lie down in armor.

Someone was brushing her hair. It was a very odd sensation, to be lying on your back, in the grass, with someone brushing your hair. Holly opened her eyes. Mac knelt beside her, holding her hairbrush. She moved, trying to sit up.

"Wait a moment," Mac said. He turned away, putting on a set of gauntlets he'd scavenged from one of the men she'd killed, and gripped her above the elbow. Smoke curled up from the leather, and he winced slightly, but he managed to get her upright.

"Pretty bad?" Holly asked. Mac shrugged. She looked around.

Both the black horses were gone now. Mac had unpacked the pony and hobbled it; Holly lay on both their blankets. She couldn't imagine how he'd gotten her there; she weighed almost 180 pounds in her armor and he could barely touch her.

But he'd known to pull the locking-pins from her pauldrons so that they swiveled slightly forward, making it easier to lie on her back, and while she'd lain unconscious, he'd managed to remove her bloody surcoat, wipe away most of the spatters from her armor, brush her hair clean, and at least wipe Lady Fantasy dry. The sword lay naked beside her on the blanket, glinting dully in the sunlight, still smeared with the aftermath of her work. Holly shivered. She couldn't think about that now.

But she'd enjoyed it. With guilty unease, Holly remembered the unholy joy she'd felt when she'd faced those other men. It seemed as if what she had felt then had been the purest, most total emotion of her entire life, a happiness unshadowed even by anticipation.

"Some hero, eh?" Holly said.

"A great hero," Mac told her gravely. "But I fear that I have brought you into more danger than even your might can contest."

Holly frowned at him, puzzled.

"This is indeed Chandrakar, and it is the Eastern Marches, where the Lady Hermonicet has her place. But I do not see her tower, nor any landmark save the black tower. We are nowhere near . . . anywhere."

"Well, that's comprehensive," Holly agreed. "And those guys who attacked us?"

With a painful skill learned over many hours of attendance at automobile accidents and the other gruesome tragedies her profession encountered, Holly kept her mind away from what had just happened. What she'd just done. But she needed to know whether she was going to have to do it again.

"Wore livery of a great house, but I did not recognize the badge." Mac frowned. "Inconvenient."

He pulled off the gauntlets and looked around. Holly looked around. Tower and ocean and grass that went on flatly forever.

"There has been great magic here," Mac pronounced. He took out his glasses and settled them on his nose. "Do you not think it odd that carrion birds have not yet come to feast on the dead?" he asked matter-of-factly.

Holly swallowed hard. "Actually, I hadn't given it much thought," she said weakly.

Mac ran a few blades of grass through his fingers. "No insects in the earth, no mice . . . war has been here, and that recently, yet I would have sworn that I remembered a peace had been declared, and such artifice as this represents outlawed—"

"Help me up," Holly said quickly.

Mac looked at her, then over his shoulder, and pulled on his gloves once more. With Mac's help, Holly got to her knees, then, using him for balance as much as support, dragged herself to her feet.

"The locking pins—put them back." Mac hastened to obey her. "Where's the rest of my armor?" He'd taken her hair down, damn all bad timing. She grabbed her sword and jammed it into its scabbard and began hastily braiding her hair back up into its long thick plait.

And on the horizon, the bright spark that could have been sunlight on water—if the day weren't overcast and the ocean weren't the other way—continued moving toward them.

By the time Holly had her helm and gauntlets on, she could see that it was a lone horseman, riding *(a fiery horse with the speed of light)* the whitest horse she'd ever seen.

"Mac?" Holly said.

"I don't know," Makindeor said.

Holly looked behind her. The tower was at least a mile away and managed to look more threatening than one lone horseman, even if the last strangers they'd met had tried to kill them.

When she looked back the horseman was frighteningly close—as if he were riding a motorcycle, not a horse.

He was wearing armor that looked familiar to Holly and therefore bizarre in this fantasyland setting: a black helmet that looked like a cross between the old Wehrmacht coal scuttle and a football helmet, chrome-studded bracers on both arms, motorcycle boots . . . He wore a leather shirt stippled in camo brown and green and black that fit as tightly as

Superman's costume. The matching pants were tucked into the high black boots. If not for the horse, he would have been nearly invisible in the tall grass.

He closed the distance between them with frightening speed, pulling the horse to a stop less than a dozen feet away. Holly stared. Its coat was as white as swansdown, or ermine, and there wasn't a speck of mud on it. Its rider dismounted, pulling off his helmet.

"Hi," Nic Brightlaw said. "Come here often?"

"You're from Earth!" Holly said accusingly. Her voice echoed flatly inside her steel helm, and the padding pressed on her sinuses.

"Well, actually, I'm from New York State," the stranger said. He was a big man, as picture-beautiful as a cover model, with golden hair—*if you've only got one life to live, why not live it as a blond?* Holly thought irrelevantly—and blue eyes so intensely colored she could see their blueness from where she stood. And even his muscles had muscles.

"Did you fall through a bookcase recently?" Holly asked tentatively. "In Ippisiqua?"

"As a matter of fact, I did. Would you like to exchange life stories? It would be a great deal easier to talk to you if you didn't have a bucket over your head, by the way."

"You're that library director!" Holly said. She felt a vast feeling of relief and lowered Lady Fantasy until the sword's point was touching the ground. At least she wouldn't have to fight again.

"Your hat, Miss? It is 'Miss', isn't it?"

"Oh, sure." Holly slipped Lady Fantasy into her sheath and reached up to undo her helmet. "Holly Kendal. And you are?" she added, her voice slightly muffled as she pulled off her helmet.

"Ser—Nic Brightlaw. But you can call me 'Ceiynt,' Miss Kendal; it's the kind of name they use here."

Holly pulled off the helmet with a certain feeling of relief and shook her hair free. She saw Ceiynt's eyes widen slightly as the waist-length cinnamon braid tumbled free. *Jirel of Joiry rides again. You got a problem with that, white boy?*

"Saint Nic. Okay. Call me Holly." *Or call me Fiametta of the Danelaw.* She remembered Rook with a brief agonizing pang. This would have been an adventure she could love wholeheartedly if only she could have shared it with him.

Except that she wouldn't want anyone she loved to see what she'd become.

"So how is everyone back at the Ryerson?" Nic asked. "Have they found a replacement director yet?"

In an hour and a half? "How long do you think you've been here?" Holly said slowly.

Nic studied her face. "How long *have* I been gone?"

Automatically, Holly glanced down to where her watch ought to be. But it was in her purse, and it had stopped when she came through the Gate, anyway.

"It's Christmas Eve," Holly said.

"But—" The big man appeared to consider this. "I've been here for about four weeks, give or take a unicorn or two. And it's still the same day back home?"

"I guess so." Holly looked around. She'd gone from winter to summer and back again, walking from the borders of Fairyland to here. It was hard to keep track. "And . . . is Ruth Marlowe with you? Penny thought she was."

"I remember Penny."

The remark was just slightly off-kilter; if things had been calmer, Holly would have pursued it, or if Nic's next words hadn't claimed her entire attention.

"As for Miss Marlowe, I expect she's gone on ahead to make our reservation at the Mordor Hilton," Nic said, pointing directly at the black tower. "Assuming, of course, that she's not dead. I left them here two days ago," he added.

"That is where I must go also," Mac said. "Impossible as it is to believe, that tower is where the greatest concentration of the Treasures in all Chandrakar lies."

Fortunately Nic had no trouble with cold iron; the Ryerson Public Library's wandering director helped Holly check over her armor, making sure that all the parts she couldn't reach were buckled tight, and while he was resaddling the white pony—really more of a dirty beige, when you compared it to Nic's white horse—Holly rescued her damp and icky surcoat and rolled it tightly.

Mac had walked a little distance away. The Cloak of Night and Daggers undulated around him, billowing in the direction of the black tower, although there was no wind to blow it—and though if there were it would have been blowing in the other direction.

"You've got blood on your hands," Nic said, coming up behind Holly.

She flinched, looking down. She'd automatically rolled her black surcoat as tightly as she could; blood oozed between her fingers as she wrung it. Holly dropped it with a strangled sound and looked around for something to wipe her hands on, but there wasn't anything. She finally compromised by scrubbing her hands with a wad of grass.

"Care to tell me what happened here?" Nic asked. He gestured at the surcoat lying on the ground like a wet towel.

I'm bipolar and—in an unrelated incident—I kill people. No, that wouldn't work. Holly looked helplessly at Nic. "There were these guys," she began awkwardly.

"How many?" The question was abrupt but somehow dispassionate.

"Some," Holly said. "Over there." She pointed in what she hoped was the right direction.

He went to look, which surprised her, but Holly took the time to pick up the surcoat again and stuff it into her purse to add it to the pony's burden. Maybe it would dry before anything else got too messy. She couldn't bear to leave it behind.

The pony stared at her accusingly as she approached it, wary blue eyes gazing out from beneath a flaxen thatch of mane.

"Deal with it," Holly told the animal. She rummaged among the supplies still lying scattered on the grass, found her sword cleaning kit, and took out an oiled rag. Awkwardly, still standing, Holly began to clean Lady Fantasy.

"Seven with one blow. Impressive," Nic said when he got back. Holly didn't look up.

"It's easy when you're wearing steel and they're not," she said.

"It isn't easy at all," Nic corrected her. "I doubt I could kill anyone at all with a sword, and Uncle Sugar spent a lot of money teaching me to be dangerous."

Holly looked up at him.

"You did a good job," Nic said. "Did they hurt you?"

"They didn't even get close," Holly said forlornly. Lady Fantasy III was gleaming once more, and Holly slipped the blade back into her sheath.

"Be happy; pain hurts." Nic turned away and began gathering up the things she and Mac had brought from Ippisiqua, packing them onto the pony.

"What are we going to do when we get there?" Holly asked. She'd resigned herself to another hike through the tall grass, but at least this time Nic was leading the pony, not her.

"We will ring their doorbell very nicely and ask them if Ruth Marlowe can come out and play," Nic said, showing a lot of white teeth in a ferocious smile.

"What do you know of yon tower?" Mac asked, as casually as if people dropped "yon" into everyday conversation all the time. The quarterstave that Nic had carried across his horse's rump made Mac a perfectly good staff; carrying it, he looked like a picture of a magic-user in a book. "I do not—That is, I do not recall it being here before."

"It would be a little hard to miss," Holly observed. She craned her neck as far as she could in the armor, but she still could not see the top of the tower. It vanished into the clouds; the thing must be fifty stories tall.

"The Lady Jausserande didn't seem to feel it belonged in the neighborhood," Nic agreed. "But Miss Marlowe was of the opinion that her friend Melior—and possibly his sword—might be inside."

"Melior? Rohannan Melior? But Rohannan Lanval is the Swordbearer," Mac protested.

Nic shrugged. "Rohannan Melior. Sword of Maiden's Tears. The Cup of Morning Shadows, which Lady Jausserande was pretty keen on getting back—I have no idea if it's in there, though Fox did seem to be convinced it was."

"These names are strange to me," Makindeor groaned. "How much time has passed here while I lingered in the World of Iron?"

If ninety minutes there equaled three or four weeks here, several months must have passed here just since Friday night, and Mac had probably been in the bad guys' hands for a few months Earth-time at least.

It could have been years here in Chandrakar.

"What's the last thing you *do* remember?" Holly asked.

"The peace. There was a war when the Barons could not agree on who would be High King, but if my memory serves me, finally all of them came to settle on Eirdois Baligant of No House, though I heard that the House of the Vermilion Shadows, which holds the Mirror of Falling Souls as its sole Treasure, will claim him if he is to be High King."

"Generous of them," Nic commented. "Apparently they've already done it. According to Miss Marlowe, her boyfriend says that not only is this Baligant a done deal as the next King, he's involved in some kind of plot to arrange that the Treasures can't be handed over to him at the proper time."

"That's ridiculous—fever dreams!" Mac said. "If Baligant is High King, with the Lady Hermonicet to wife, what more can he possibly want?"

Holly had no idea, but in her experience there was always something. *Absolute power delights, and absolute power is absolutely delightful.* "So . . ." she said carefully. "What are your plans?"

"If Miss Marlowe went into that tower, I'm going in after her," Nic said.

"And some of the Treasures *are* there, so there I must go," Mac said, but Holly had already thought of something else.

"You said you came through the Ryerson with Ruth," Holly said to Nic. "So how come she's in there and you're out here?"

Nic smiled. "A little miscalculation. I'll tell you my story if you tell me yours."

It took them about half an hour to reach the tower, time enough for their stories to be told. Holly explained about Frank Catalpano and Information Management Systems, about how they'd held Makindeor prisoner and tortured him to make him read the *Book of Airts*. This time she even gritted her teeth and explained about the man she'd killed at the IMS offices.

"—and you'd think the police would have noticed, even if it was Christmas," she said inadequately, "but I never saw anything about it."

"These things happen," Nic said absently. "It sounds as if you stepped on some rather highly placed toes, Holly; but while we always knew that Christians in Action had ties to Never-Never Land, to discover they have ties to Middle Earth as well stretches credibility rather past the breaking point."

" 'Christians in Action'?" Holly asked, bewildered. It was such a normal conversation to be having—in Holly's opinion—that it made the tower and Mac's Treasure hunt seem even more unlikely.

"CIA," Nic said briefly. "Of course, things have probably changed a bit in the last eighteen years, but this still doesn't sound like a CIA package tour." He frowned. "Unless, of course, they're trying to overthrow your government?" he added politely to Mac.

Holly grinned, but Mac took the question at face value. "Someone from without the Land attempting to overset its rule? That would be a fell matter indeed—one that needs must be placed before the Emperor himself."

"Emperor?" Holly asked. "But I thought Baligant was part of the problem?"

"Baligant is to be High King, highest lord within Chandrakar. The Emperor is the overlord of *all* the Lands Beyond the Morning," Mac said. "It is an ill thing to have to consult him," he added darkly.

"God bless and keep the Czar—far away from me," Holly footnoted. "Anyway, whatever's going on back in the world isn't my problem any more, and Penny said she had a number she could call? Somewhere in Washington?"

The seemingly innocuous statement surprised Nic into a shout of laughter. "Lord! I'd forgotten about that. I must have given her Scruffy's number. I wonder when?" He shook his head, still smiling. "I hope she calls it. I really do." He shook his head again. "They deserve it."

His reaction comforted Holly; whoever "Scruffy" was, Nic obviously felt this person was more than a match for the CIA. Some of her anxiety about her friends eased.

"But to return to our information-swapping—and I don't see an entrance on this side of *chez* Mordor, so we may have to get creative in a few minutes, here—when Lady Jausserande warned me that there was something unfriendly on our tail, I thought that the only polite thing to do was go back and introduce myself . . ."

He'd ridden away from the others, expecting anything from another dragon to a giant in grass-green armor. What he found instead was a heavy, musky stench and a swarm of animals that covered the moors like a shroud of black velvet. He had no idea what he was looking at. Their voracious, deliberate progress suggested army ants, but they looked more like rats. Running ahead of them, like the foam that edged the wave, were the animals of the steppe. Nic watched as those that fell behind were devoured. He turned Shadowfax parallel to the advancing wave and began to gallop along it. How wide was the concentration of the animals? He didn't know how large an animal the swarm was willing to take on, but that was information he felt able to live without, all things considered.

The magic horse ran as it always did—swiftly, tirelessly—for enough miles to make Nic feel soberly respectful of the potential the swarm represented. He reached the edge. Though a few tendrils of the mass reached out toward him (Nic saw that the individual animals were actually quite small), whatever compulsion drove them was apparently great enough to override even the lure of the several hundred pounds of meat Nic and his magic horse represented. The wildlife of the grassland, flushed from cover by the black swarm, was fleeing due south, in a rustling carpet of life that parted around his horse's legs like a frantic living carpet. A few of the devourers started after them, but once they'd gone a few feet in the wrong direction they turned back to the forward-moving throng.

Interesting. And so unnatural that it was almost inevitable that this should be another premeditated attack.

Or was it—exactly—an attack? Nic looked back over his shoulder, toward the dark tower. Miss Marlowe and her companions were somewhere out there, heading in the direction of the tower, but going inside wasn't necessarily an inevitable consequence of arrival. And it had seemed to him that for the last several days, Miss Marlowe had been less sure than before of where Melior or his Sword—whichever of the two she

was really following—were. Without Miss Marlowe's assurance, he didn't
think the others would automatically try to enter the tower.

Unless they literally had no other choice.

Nic looked at the animals moving past him, as vast as a miniaturized
herd of buffalo and uncountable thousands strong. Though it hadn't attacked him, it was spreading itself wider as it moved, so that a front that
was five miles long would be twice that, if not more, by the time they
reached the others.

There was no way for the others to get around them. He turned
Shadowfax and set the magic horse to gallop.

"—By the time I circled the swarm and came back, they were gone. I
don't think they're dead; I've covered the territory pretty thoroughly and
the only skeletons I've seen were two horses. No matter what I did, I
couldn't get any closer to the tower, though—until now, when you
showed up. It seems rather coincidental, somehow."

Mac ignored the provocative remark. "There is no coincidence in
magic," he said. "You are meant to be here."

"I tend to hold the same opinion. But why should I burden you with
inessentials?"

"Especially," Mac said blandly, "when you do not particularly trust
us."

Nic smiled. "Especially then."

"We're here," Holly said.

There was no sidewalk, no ornamental bushes, not even a sign that
said "This Way to the Egress." The grass stopped and the tower started,
rising glistening and perpendicular from the ground. It was perfectly
seamless, gleaming as a mirror, and solidly black; Holly could see one elf,
one library director, one EMT, a magic horse, and a sullen pony reflected
in it, only slightly distorted by the curvature of the wall. Holly took off her
gauntlet and touched it. It was cold, but only as stone would be cold on
such a winter's day. It was the naturalness of it that was somehow unnatural, as if somewhere its creator was laughing at them all for being so
gullible.

"Mac?" Holly said. "What do you see through your glasses?"

"Nothing," Mac said, not bothering to put them on.

"Oh, come on!" Holly exclaimed. "What do you mean 'nothing'?"

Nic spurred his whiter-than-white horse around the side of the tower
and soon had disappeared beyond the curve.

"There is no tower here," Mac said.

"There's no way in," Nic said, returning.

" 'There's no way in, but it doesn't matter because it isn't there any-way'?" Holly said. "Not only is that stupid, it doesn't make sense."

"This—would be—a magic tower," Mac began pedantically. "Crafted by magic, just as the paladin's horse was bred by magic."

Holly looked at the white horse. It looked supernaturally clean and was faster than a Maserati, but other than that it looked like a perfectly normal horse to her.

" 'Would be'?" Nic asked.

"It isn't here," Mac said. "The Treasures are here, but the tower isn't."

"I think you'd better get those glasses fixed," muttered Holly. She rapped on the stone with her bare knuckles. It hurt. The sound was dull, without echo.

"Maybe you could interpret that remark," Nic said. "If this thing is some kind of illusion—"

"It would be a *magical* illusion," Mac said, "and it isn't. But my spectacles allow me to see more than just magic. With them, I can see all that something *is.*"

Holly thought back to that night in the diner when she'd tried on Mac's glasses, and what she'd seen. She'd seen the truth—about every-thing.

"Are you saying that when you put on your glasses and look through them—"

"The tower isn't there. Yes."

What could be so solid to the touch, have so little truth to it that Mac's glasses didn't see it, and contain no magic at all? Holly wondered. It was like some kind of nasty riddle—if they guessed the answer, could they gain entry to the tower?

Did they want to?

"Well my goodness." Nic's voice was flat, uninflected. "That *is* going to make it a little bit hard to get inside."

"Your mount will take you—but only you," Makindeor said.

Nic looked at him.

"It is a *magic* horse, Paladin," Makindeor said patiently. "It will take you where you want to go. If it is through that wall that you wish to go, you need only ride."

Nice work if you can get it, Holly thought.

"Leaving aside the question of—if that's true—why it didn't work three days ago, that does leave me with the problem of getting out with the others."

On his belt Nic wore a Bowie knife with a ten-inch blade. Mac stepped back as he pulled it. The blade was a wicked glitter in the sun. He crouched by the foundation, one hand on the wall, and began to dig at the foundation with the point.

Smoke rose up from the grass. Nic recoiled.

"What's happening?" Holly said. *Solid. No truth, no magic. No history—no past* . . .

"It's—" Nic broke off. "It doesn't like my knife very much, but every time I take the blade away it fills itself back in."

"Time," Holly said suddenly. "It's made out of Time."

Holly wasn't quite certain where she'd gotten the idea, but the moment she uttered the words she was certain she was right. Time was always now. Time was never anything but itself.

"Yes . . ." Mac said. "Yes, that would work—but by the Twelve, such a spell as this is not one lightly cast."

"Can you break it?" Nic and Holly said almost in unison. Mac didn't even hesitate.

"No. Such small skill in magic as I possess belongs to the High Art and no other—I am no wizard. I cannot say for certain that this even is an artifact of the Wild Magic, but wizards walk strange paths, and a wizard would know more of these things than I, or any Adept."

"That's useful," Holly muttered. How did you knock a hole in Time itself? This wasn't a question covered in nursing school.

"That sword of yours," Nic said suddenly. "What's it made of?"

"Steel," Holly answered, surprised. "High-carbon steel. She's very strong."

"Swing it at the wall, here," Nic said.

Holly put a hand protectively over her hilt. Lady Fantasy wouldn't shatter like one of those old Iron Age swords forged before the smiths had really understood how to temper a blade, but if Holly used her like a hammer it certainly wouldn't do her any good.

"Doesn't sound really practical to me," she said shortly.

"Look," Nic said, straightening up. He drove the Bowie at the wall, point first. The blade sank into the surface almost half an inch while the stone smoked and shimmered around it.

"We need something—iron—that will make a bigger dent in it than this knife. In fact, we need to chop a hole in it. If you can work from this side, I can work from the other."

Let's all give up and go home, Holly thought hopefully. "Does this sound reasonable to you?" she asked Mac.

"It will work," Nic said. "Look."

The bracer on his left arm was studded top and bottom with round metal balls. Nic pulled one loose, and Holly saw that it was a wicked little knife, almost an overgrown hat-pin, with a round ball to hold it by and a slender, deadly blade. With all his might, Nic rammed it into the wall. It sank in until only the steel ball was exposed, and all around it the wall smoked and morphed.

There were eight of the little knives on his bracers; Nic used them all, and when he was done, he'd outlined a crude arch in the wall.

"Hit it," Nic said again.

Without conscious volition, Holly drew her sword. "Clear!" she shouted, swinging the sword up and back. At the outermost corner of her mind there was the faint thought that the force Nic had described, the one that had herded Ruth Marlowe and the others into the black tower, wouldn't want them to meddle in its affairs and would certainly send someone to stop them soon.

"*Yah!*" Holly screamed at the top of her lungs, wound up, and swung.

She felt the familiar pull of muscles in her shoulders and her back as the sword traveled forward. She schooled herself not to check it, not to pull back at the last minute, but to let it deliver every ounce of force in her swing to the target.

It hit, meeting the dull resistance of something that was not flesh, not stone, but something queasily similar to both. Holly stared. The sword had sunk into the wall of the tower, into the center of the circle defined by Nic's knives.

"Wug?" she said intelligently. Smoke coiled out of the wall where the blade was imbedded, thick and slow and heavy as dry ice vapor. She wiggled it up and down; it looked so much as if it were simply cut off where it touched the wall that it was hard to believe that it wasn't simply broken.

"Push it." Ceiynt's voice startled her. She shoved the sword forward. It sank reluctantly deeper, as if she were bearing down into very soft wood.

"This is very weird," Holly said.

"Keep pushing."

Help, Holly thought to herself. This wasn't just very weird, this was beyond weird—sawing through a wall of Time with a beautiful but deeply ultramundane Stephen Mallison blade, in the company of an elphen magician and the Ryerson Public Library Director.

Nic added his weight to hers. The sword slid deeper, like cutting through fossil cheese. By now it was almost impossible for either one of them to see where it entered the wall: The white vapor was boiling out of the wall like cold steam every place that iron touched it.

"I don't suppose this stuff is unsafe to breathe?" Holly asked nervously.

"Do you want to live forever?" Nic asked, and the warwolf stirred faintly in the depths of Holly's soul in answer. No. She didn't want to live forever. *Stick-jocks, Stick-jocks wanna have fun,* Holly sang off-key in the broadcasting booth of her mind. *Weird Al Chrysostom rides again.*

Finally, after several minutes of shoving, Holly's sword was embedded into the tower wall all the way to the hilt.

"Now what?" Holly said, stepping back. She felt a little uneasy with her only means of defense so thoroughly out of commission, but Mac had apparently thought this was a good idea, and sooner or later you had to trust somebody, as the actress said to the bishop . . .

"Now, if I'm recollecting correctly, I try riding Shadowfax here through the wall and hope that sword of yours has made some mark on the other side."

It was like watching the set-up for the filming of one of the summer's big fantasy movies—without the camera and technical crew, of course. The sun was starting to set. White mist boiled from the side of the tower, spilling down the side and collecting around the base. A little way beyond it, Nic Brightlaw mounted his shining steed and prepared to ride through the tower wall itself.

"What if this doesn't work?" Holly found herself saying aloud. No one heard her.

Nic dug his heels into his horse, and it began to move forward. Holly admired the smoothness of the transitions, from walk to trot to flat out gallop. This must be going to work. No normal horse would run at top speed into a solid wall.

But maybe, if the horse was magic, it couldn't see the tower any more than Mac's glasses could.

That horrified thought uppermost in her mind, Holly shouted and waved, but her hail had no effect. The white horse coursed forward, as extended as a racehorse. Just before it reached the tower it gathered itself to leap, and soared with seeming slowness into the air, as if its weight and Nic's were nothing at all.

Holly blinked. The horse had vanished. She ran back toward the tower. "Mac! Mac? Did it work?"

Makindeor looked at her, the Cloak of Night and Daggers pulled tightly around him. "I hope so," he said.

Nic clung to the horse's back as the treacherous beast launched itself into the air. He hadn't been ready for that. He'd been too busy bracing himself for the possibility that he'd miscalculated and the two of them were about to go "splat" at roughly forty miles an hour. Instead, there was an effortless leap into the air—

—and all the lights went out.

His horse's hooves rang on stone as it landed, and there were a few hair-raising seconds while it scrabbled for traction. But then it stood steady, and Nic blinked his eyes.

He was somewhere as dark as the inside of a cave. He moved his fingers in front of his face and could not see them. He couldn't even see the horse, and making Shadowfax invisible took some darkness. He inhaled deeply and smelled cold stone and water. Somewhere not too far away he could hear water plashing, and the faint echoes it made encouraged him to think that he was in some sort of cave.

And not, as was also possible, blind.

His plan, once he'd gotten inside the tower, was to find the place where the sword blade was stuck into the wall and start cutting the Time away from this side, but now he wondered if that was even possible. He swung his arms out but touched nothing. And now, when the quarterstaff he'd carried across half the country would have come in really useful, it was on the other side of the wall.

"Any ideas, horse?" Nic asked. He heard it shake its head. It was a pity he hadn't gotten an owner's manual with it originally, since it seemed that the thing had a number of useful abilities that Ophidias hadn't bothered to mention to him when he'd swapped all the rest of his life for one month of unsupervised recreational activity in Middle Earth.

One month. Of which, if his makeshift calculations by the local moon were correct, he had something less than a week left. Only a few days to get Miss Marlowe settled down somewhere with her elvish boyfriend that was just a little safer than this tower.

Which meant being able to get himself in—apparently not a problem—and being able to get all of them out. Assuming always that they were here in the first place.

His eyes were beginning to adjust; there was a certain quality to the darkness now that hadn't been there before, a mosaic of darker and not so dark. And, off in the distance, something else entirely.

It might almost have been an afterimage, the faint purple patch that hung in space somewhere beyond his eyes, but he tried every trick he could think of to make it go away and it didn't. He wasn't sure he trusted the thought of riding the horse toward it, though; moving by touch, he dismounted from Shadowfax.

As he stood beside it, the thought occurred to Nic that this would be a good time to know he had a way to find his horse again. Moving by touch, Nic reached into his saddlebags and found the coil of long thin rope that he'd chosen from the supplies the wizard-firedrake had made available to him. He shook it out and then tied one end around his stirrup, this Otherworldly saddle not having come supplied with a convenient Western-style horn. At the moment he would have welcomed a manifestation of John Wayne to come and get all of them out of this. The Duke's side never lost.

His retreat secured, Nic began groping forward, paying the line out behind him and cursing the absence of the quarterstaff. There were a number of times that he lost sight of the elusive purple blotch in the darkness and had to wait for it to settle again.

The splotch seemed to be getting brighter; he closed the last few feet between him and it unerringly. The change in air currents told him he'd reached a wall; he reached out and brushed it with his fingers—cool, smooth. And in it, about shoulder height, a lighter patch, about the size of his palm. He touched it gingerly. Was it his imagination, or was the lighter patch faintly warmer than the stone around it?

He looped the end of the line around his wrist. He didn't know what was going to happen next, but he wanted to be able to get out of its way. Then he pulled the Bowie knife out of its sheath again and set its point at the center of the discoloration in the wall.

"What do we do if he doesn't come back?" Holly asked nervously. She'd returned to the wall and was clutching at her sword hilt, more out of tension than from any sense of purpose. White mist continued to boil from the wounds iron had made in it.

"Then we see if there's some other way of getting into the tower," Mac said. Holly sighed and studied the wall. There was a shallow but perceptible indentation in the wall now around each of the knives—largest around the sword—where the surface of the tower just seemed to be boiling away, but she doubted it would happen fast enough to do them any good.

There was a vibration along the blade of her sword.

"Hey!" Holly said, alarmed. The sensation came again; as though someone on the other side of the wall was tapping gently on the point of her sword. "There's something in here." She pulled on the sword hilt and then twisted it.

And the tower fell away around it.

Holly jerked her sword free and staggered back. Nic was standing in front of her a few feet away, his Bowie still clutched in his hand. When iron had met iron through the tower wall, it must have unraveled whatever sorcery had built the thing.

There was a hissing like sand; the surface before her face was all motion and shimmer, as if someone were emptying some heavenly sand-box filled from Maui's black sand beaches.

"You did it!" she heard Mac say, as if from a great distance. The sand mounded around her feet—not enough of it to have comprised the tower's vast bulk; it seemed to be trickling away through the earth itself, and she stepped back further. The shape of the tower was still there against the twilight sky, but now it was streaky and fading, as if the source from which the pouring had come had at last been emptied. First the height melted away, and then there was only a ring of wall, (on the other side of which she could see Nic, blinking owlishly at the daylight, and his white horse) then a mound of wall, then it was only sand, and at last the sand, like the sand of an hourglass, sank through the glass and vanished away.

"It's a dead-town," Mac said, in wonder. "It's the dead-dance of the East. But it has been hidden for a thousand years."

· 18 ·

The Dead Can Dance

THE DEAD-DANCE was as old as the land itself. Its twisting corridors and byways were part of the magic that set the borders of Chandrakar itself and brought it into being. There was a labyrinth in the center of the Morning; the Lands Beyond the Morning themselves formed a similar maze, with their Gates and interlocking borders, and a symbol of that complexity was the most potent binding of all: a knot of intention that could hold against any sending.

"Who—?" Mac stammered, seemingly at a loss for words.

Holly stared. What Mac called a dead-dance looked to her like a giant granite tiddlywink, gray and round and flat. Holly stepped up onto it.

"Holly!" Mac cried. She looked back at him. It wasn't as if this could be dangerous; nothing had happened to Nic when he'd gone into the tower.

"Be careful," Mac said, as if that were a much shorter version of what he'd originally intended. Holly shrugged.

"Looks like we're in. Why should this be so easy?" Holly asked him.

"Easy?" Mac looked at her in astonishment. "When entry requires a paladin bearing cold iron and another warrior with steel as well?"

When he put it that way, Holly did have to admit it sounded harder than it had seemed to be when they did it. But she still couldn't help wondering: If the mysterious *They* who were out to kill her and Mac and had kidnapped Ruth Marlowe had known about Nic, why had they set things up this way?

Habit? Habit can kill you.

"I don't see what either of us is looking for," Holly said, walking over to Nic. *Expect the unexpected. Trust no one. I'm not cut out for this.*

"Neither do I. There's some kind of design on this thing, but I'm not sure I can figure it out."

"Looks like a bull's eye," Holly said. There were various lines cut into the granite, some deep and some shallow. It was true that the most obvious marks were a series of concentric circles, but—

"What are these?"

A few feet to the left there was a circle about the size of a manhole cover sunk into the stone. It was set between two of the lines; there was another line above it about six inches away, then another six inches, then the grass began.

Holly stood over the circle. It was a hole leading somewhere; below its surface some sort of contents flashed and shimmered.

"Water?"

Nic knelt down and cupped up a palmful. He sniffed at it, then drank. "Water," he confirmed.

"And here's another one—whoa!" Holly reared back, from what seemed to be a bottomless pit from which a steady draft blew. "I wonder if that goes anywhere?" she said, turning away to the next one.

She walked toward the pit nearest the ocean; oddly enough, in this direction, the opening held fire. The heat it gave off was welcoming, a shimmering pillar of warmth.

The last of the pits contained nothing but glistening, freshly turned, dirt.

"Mac? Come look at this."

Makindeor stepped onto the dead-dance with the caution of a cat setting foot on snow. "I know what it is," he said testily. "It's a dead-dance, Holly, one of the four seals set on the land's making."

Have it your way, then: you heard a seal bark. Holly quoted Thurber to some purpose. "So tell us about it; this is not exactly a subject they covered in nursing school."

Mac brushed his hair back from his forehead. He was tired; after the week they'd had, they both were, and there seemed to be no rest or end in sight.

"Fire in the East, Water in the West. To the North, Air; to the South, Earth. I know that you Ironworlders have no magic, but what else would you expect to see here save the Four Elements at the Cardinal Points?"

"Driving directions?" Holly suggested hopefully.

"Perhaps these are," Nic said looking down. "If your friend would care to give his opinion?"

Holly walked back and stood beside Nic. There was another band of

symbols between the elements and the edge of the dance. There was one
directly above the spring: a Cup, shining as brightly as if it were inlaid
silver. Holly followed the band around; there weren't many symbols; two
between each pit, and one directly above it. Most of them looked wildly
unfamiliar to Holly.

"The Cup of Morning Shadows," said Mac, looking down. "And
here, beside it, the Cauldron of Beginning and the Harp of Making and
Unmaking: the Triad of Water. Here, at Air, is the Sword of Maiden's
Tears, then the Horse of Air and the Comb of Sight and Sorcery: the
Triad of Air. Fire: the Lance of Always Burning, the Mirror of Falling
Souls, the Cloak of Night and Daggers. Earth's Treasures are the Shield
of Virtue Triumphant, the *Book of Airts,* and the Crown of Reign and
Flowers."

It seemed weirdly familiar to Holly, like some sort of schizophrenic
Tarot deck. Sword and Lance and Cup and Shield she knew about; they
were the four Suits, what her witchy friends called the Four Elemental
Weapons. But . . . Mirror? *Comb?* What next—the Shopping Cart of
Power? The Gold Card of Terrific Bargains? Holly walked around the
perimeter, staring. Some of the symbols were obvious, some weren't.

The Lance and the Mirror were pretty easy to guess; the one between
them had to be the Cloak. "It's glowing," she observed.

"Because it's here?" Nic suggested. "The Sword and the Cup are lit
up, too."

"Yes," Mac said, considering the matter.

"So if they're here—where?" Holly said.

"In the dance," Mac said. "Will you walk it with me, Children of
Earth? I think we may find at least those Treasures if we do."

Every time we start out to do something, Holly thought broodingly, *we
end up doing something else.*

"Sure," Nic said mendaciously. "I haven't got anything better to do."

In the center of the dead-dance, a line crossed from one circle to
another, making a spiral shape. Mac gathered the three of them in the
center circle, staying as far away from Holly and her armor as he could
while keeping the three of them all together.

"Won't the iron get in the way?" Holly asked. "It blew up the tower."

"The tower wasn't a part of the dance. If it had been, do you think we
could have lost the location of the Great Seal for a millennium? No. The
dance is, and always has been, a labyrinth; I think the whole purpose of
the tower was to conceal the dance itself and to make sure that anyone
who entered the tower entered the labyrinth as well."

"And if we get in, are you sure we can get out?" Nic asked.

Mac didn't answer that one. He set his foot on the dark carving and began to walk.

Nic followed, then Holly. There was something weirdly familiar about this, almost a memory, but as far as she could remember, Holly'd never walked the Pattern in Amber, which was what this most reminded her of. If you walked Amber's Pattern, you might wind up anywhere.

She set one foot in front of the other, walking round and round. *Follow the yellow brick road . . .*

But the other magic, the older legend, told of a road that began with a spiral and led to your true heart's desire. *All I need is a pair of silver slippers,* Holly told herself, staring down at her feet.

She was concentrating so exactly on where she put her feet that for a while she didn't look up. The path widened beneath her feet; when she noticed that, she looked up and saw that the edges of the dance had receded into the distance, as if she had somehow shrunk. At its distant edge the white horse stood, the last bright thing in the gathering twilight. *Weirdness is happening,* a small delighted part of her mind caroled. *Hey— it's really magic! Merry Christmas!*

The walls began to rise, or the road to sink, and soon Holly was walking through a rut, then a trench, then a deep cut where the walls rose over her head and the only light came from Makindeor's shining body.

"We're in," Nic said.

In a chamber where the floor was inlaid with lines of silver that showed the gross geometries of the true world and its Gates, all lines led to the center of the room where a low black cube of glass supported an enormous alabaster bowl that was also webbed with silver. Amadis stared down into the pool of green fire collected within it and watched the ruin of all her hopes.

She was not in pain. She did not hunger. King's blood and roses her power must have, and when Hermonicet had returned her to him, Baligant had supplied these things without stint.

That he would starve her into ultimate agony later did not need to be said. She knew he would do it the moment he did not immediately need her power—and that because he needed it now, he met her needs.

Baligant was King to be—her magic said so; it had said so when she had seen him in Rainouart's funeral cortege. She had told her mistress, who had seen in Baligant the cat's-paw who would serve her plan. Hermonicet had set her war into motion and had placed Amadis—eventually—at his service, so that as the elphen Barons fought and Baligant rose in their councils, he could set her to steal away the Treasures that guarded Chandrakar. And so it had come to pass.

Baligant was High Prince, High King to be.

But Baron Rohannan's blood was sweet and filled with power . . .

Which meant either that there were *two* High Kings in the Land—impossible!—or that the sovereignty was even now passing from one to the other, as Baligant had not yet had the Kingmaking that would meld him irrevocably to the Land and the Treasures, and they to him. Before that time, the Land could choose another, though the Lords Temporal might still continue on their way and send their own choice and not the Land's to the Kingmaking. Once the ceremony had taken place, the confusion would end, but now, with Baligant chosen by the Children of Air, and Melior chosen by the Land, her magic did not care to choose between them. Slay Melior, and the Land, eternally patient, would choose again. Set Baligant on the High Seat, and the Land would be forced to abandon its own choice through the power of the Kingmaking.

The blood of the High King of the Land in his own Land was what she must have, and if she left Chandrakar, there were others who would find her, to summon her to judgment for the breaking of her oaths. There was no hope and no escape. She must serve Baligant until he died—or she did. Amadis gazed into her speculum again.

Hermonicet had taken sweet, sweet Melior from her, and Baligant, besotted, had let Hermonicet take the Sword of Maiden's Tears as well. Hermonicet had ordered that Amadis hide Melior away where no magic could find him—and so Amadis had.

She had hidden him inside one of the four Great Seals that bound Chandrakar into being. Each of the four was a magic so great that no lesser magic could be distinguished anywhere near it.

And then she had carefully placed a vast material tower atop the Seal, a tower that was as nonmagical as she could contrive and visible for at least a hundred miles, so that she could bring Ruth Marlowe to the Sword, as Baligant had commanded Amadis to do before Hermonicet had issued her own commands.

Ruth Marlowe of the Ironworld had come to Baron Rohannan, just as Amadis' lord Baligant had wanted, and so had come the Cup and the Cupbearer, which would please her master. And Amadis had sealed them all carefully inside and settled down to wait for Baligant to instruct her further.

But now things had gotten out of hand.

She did not object to the presence of the Cloak or the Cloak-warden—except that it indicated that the elaborate plot she had woven at Baligant's urging had come further unraveled—nor to his Earthchild berserker companion. But the paladin on his wizard-bred destrier disturbed her deeply, and when the paladin and the berserker had unmade her tower with thoughtless ease, Amadis began to fear.

A wizard's-man, with the stink of the Wild Magic on him. Who else dares to meddle here?

Amadis concentrated, but the patterns that a human would have called rational thought did not come naturally to her. What should she do here to serve the Design and the Word, and would that service be consistent with what her master commanded?

Baligant wanted the Treasures lost or hidden beyond retrieval by their Lines. They were hidden in the Seal, but they could be retrieved, providing someone knew they were there.

Baligant wanted Ruth Marlowe, Child of Earth, dead, so that her soul would flow completely into the Sword of Maiden's Tears and no proof would exist that Amadis, a wizard under Baligant's command, had tampered with the Treasures.

Amadis smiled to herself. She would kill Ruth Marlowe; that was simple enough. And if the others who were with her died too, there would be no one to say where these three of the Twelve Treasures lay.

The Cup of Morning Shadows, Jausserande assured them, could sustain them indefinitely; and though neither of the humans much liked the idea of drinking from it, Ruth had to admit that if it were a choice between drinking magic and dying of thirst, the magic would probably win every time.

She wasn't sure, however, what the point of surviving was if they were going to spend the rest of their lives underground, in the dark, in a maze. And she could have picked better people to spend eternity with than the outlaw Fox, an elfmaid who hated Ruth for no more reason than she was human, and Melior.

Whom Ruth loved, despite everything. Who said he loved her and said he'd use her for political expediency almost in the same breath. And though Ruth knew that they were talking about the safety and survival of an entire nation, and though the hero considered the heroine's comfort more important than the lives of uncounted thousands of people only in bad fiction, Ruth couldn't find it in her to find Melior's priorities admirable.

Right, maybe, but not admirable. And, to be brutally frank, she wasn't sure their love could survive the sacrifices Ruth was going to be asked—no, *forced*—to make for Melior's principles.

And on top of everything else, there was still the oath she'd sworn to Fox. A *binding* oath. She didn't know what would happen if she broke it.

Maybe she'd get lucky. Maybe they'd all die before she found out the answers to any of her questions.

"Are we anywhere yet?" Ruth asked hopefully.

"The same place we were the last time you asked. Lost," Fox said.

None of the four of them knew how long they'd been walking—long enough to know they were irredeemably lost and to finish the very last of their supplies. Ruth had slept, and so had Fox, but she doubted he felt any more rested than she did. The darkness made Ruth's eyes hurt, the balls of elflight that Jausserande and Melior spun out of nothing with such matter-of-factness made her uneasy, and Fox's studious noncommittalness was going to make her start screaming if he kept it up much longer. It was only now, when he was quiet, that she realized how much she missed his edgy banter with Jausserande—and realized how much he must hate Melior.

Any emotion that strong was worthy of a certain respect. Ruth, whose wizard-edited emotions were only pale ghosts of real ones, wondered how Fox managed to seem so calm, so normal, with such a depth of anger inside him and the thing he hated most close enough to touch.

Of course, Nic had seemed perfectly normal too, most of the time, Ruth thought. But it wasn't the same. Fox kept his emotions rigidly in check. Nic simply didn't have emotions anymore.

"Do you feel that?" Fox asked. "Fresh air."

"Yes!" Jausserande said quickly. "There must be an opening to the outside."

"But who has opened it?" Melior asked.

They never tell you that elves make great night-lights, Holly thought, staring at Makindeor's back. He was glowing as brightly as a 40-watt moonglobe, with a chill, misty radiance that illuminated the walls—black—and the ceiling—black and vaulted—and the floor, which, in surprising contrast to the walls and ceiling, was black. Her helm blinkered her peripheral vision, but few critters here would attack something in a steel lobster suit if everything she'd learned so far was true.

It only took one, though.

Their footsteps echoed off the walls, and so did every sound her armor made. Her metal gauntlets squeaked and rustled slightly as she moved her hand to touch Lady Fantasy's hilt again. She wished she weren't so noisy, but knights of old hadn't needed to worry about moving stealthily at all, and the only other time she'd tried to sneak around in this outfit was at the SCA's Pennsic War, in the Woods Battle, and she hadn't needed to be as stealthy as all that.

"You sound like the Tin Woodman," Nic Brightlaw said.

"I'm sorry all to hell," Holly said.

Talking was an effort. The brief surge of excitement she'd felt at Nic's arrival and at breaching the tower had faded, and she'd had to go back to living with herself—and the ghosts of the men she'd murdered. It was no good saying this was war, and kill or be killed, Holly was no soldier, carefully trained by her government to accept that sometimes it was okay to kill people. She was an ordinary civilian—a nurse—and down deep inside her, what she'd done *hurt.*

There was no use blaming Makindeor for it, either. He hadn't done anything to her the first time, back in Patroon County—she'd managed to kill that one all on her own. And the second time, here in Chandrakar, he'd only turned loose something she already was.

Berserker. Things like that always sounded much better in books. But this was reality—or something passing for it. She wasn't completely sure she could live with what she'd done, and it was starting to seem like too much of an effort to try. Mac was on his home turf here, and Saint Nic looked pretty dangerous; *he* could protect Mac. Assuming he had the least interest in doing that, of course . . .

"Quiet," Makindeor said. He came to a stop.

Ahead, the tunnels branched. *Two roads, both alike in dignity, in fair Elfland where we lay our scene,* Holly paraphrased irreverently. "Which way?" she said aloud.

Mac hesitated.

"Of course," Nic said, half-quoting, "people do go both ways."

"Oh, shut up," Holly groused under her breath, then: "Flip a coin? Split up? Turn back?"

"Splitting up would probably be a bad idea," Nic said. "We don't know what's waiting down here for us."

"There is something I must tell you about the Great Seals," Mac said, hesitantly.

Every time he says that, I have to resist the urge to clap my flippers together and bark, Holly thought mordantly.

"Go ahead," Nic said to Makindeor.

Mac drew a deep breath and furled the Cloak of Morning Shadows more tightly about himself. "I can find the other Treasures with the Cloak—Treasure calls to Treasure, if its Bearer wills it. But I believe the Cloak will follow the path of the making of the Great Seal to reach its fellows, and if they lie at its end, I cannot allow that. The Great Seal is woven as a knot—an endless knot, with no beginning and no ending. Do I unriddle the dead-dance with the Cloak, there is a chance that—by the power of the Treasure—I could unbind the Great Seal, and the Eastern

Marches would be open to anything that dares travel the Iron Road to reach it."

Holly resisted the urge to bang the side of her head. Too many years of endless paperback fantasy series and the SCA had made it hard for Holly to get a grip when faced with forsoothly language, whether what was being talked about was real or not.

"So if you let the Cloak go chasing after the others, and it follows the whole pattern of the Seal to find them, the Seal comes unraveled?" Nic said.

"There is that chance," Makindeor said.

"Oh, I don't care," Holly groaned, flinging herself back to rest against the wall. She preferred an adventure with a clear-cut objective at the best of times, and this was hardly that.

"I do," Nic said. "I should very much like the opportunity for a quiet chat with Miss Marlowe, just to assure myself that all is well. There must be some way to arrange that without causing too much fuss."

"The Cloak will find them, or it will not," Mac said. "There is no halfway-between, once I have set the *geas* upon it."

Psychic bloodhounds, details at eleven. "So why don't you just put it on a leash?" Holly said.

Melior at the head, holding the Sword of Maiden's Tears drawn and gleaming, Jausserande behind, the shining weight of the Cup an awkward weight in her hands, they had proceeded cautiously in the direction of the freshening breeze. Ruth followed Jausserande, and Fox brought up the rear. Jausserande had lent him her sword, which indicated to Ruth how much danger the two elves thought they were all in.

"Here we are," Fox said, walking half-turned to cover their backs. He was speaking mostly to himself, but Ruth could hear him. "The hardest metal, the strongest edge, that this culture can possibly produce without magic. *Bronze.*"

"There's something—" Melior said. He stopped.

Jausserande let out a breath of pure relief.

Ruth pushed forward, trying to see what they had seen. All she saw ahead was blackness, though the two elphenborn obviously thought there was nothing to fear.

"What—?" Ruth demanded. Then she saw the light radiating on the wall, and the movement of the long, swooping shadow.

If she'd been alone, or if either Melior or Jausserande had shown fear, Ruth might have been afraid. As it was, she merely watched in amazement as the bizarre procession hove into view.

The first thing she saw was a flying bundle of cloth straining toward them like a low-flying attack kite. It was cinched tight around the middle by a thin rope, and a glowing elf in a T-tunic, baggy jeans, and sneakers was hauling backward against the pull of the rope. Behind him was a walking suit of plate armor—casket helm, pigeon chest, and all—and behind that . . .

"Ceiynt!" Jausserande cried.

The glowing elf unleashed the flying laundry. It reached the Cup and the Sword and hovered between them, beginning its lethal heterodyne glow.

"Enough!" the elf in the sneakers cried. The glow ceased instantly, and the cloth dropped to the floor.

"Line Amarmonde," Jausserande said, looking at it.

"Chief Librarian," Melior said, looking at the elf in the sneakers. "How did you get here?"

"Now that the tower is gone, you would have found your way out eventually," Makindeor said. Everyone had been talking at once, sharing stories. Jausserande had even hugged Ceiynt, excitedly showing him her recovered Treasure. She looked much younger than she had before, Ruth realized, freed of the awful burden of failure.

"But I can take you directly to the opening—" Mac went on.

"No. I cannot allow that," the wizard Amadis said.

This was the face of Ruth's suppressed nightmares—monster or woman or warwasp in the Goblin Market, Ruth knew her. This was the creature who had destroyed Ruth's life.

"Magic . . ." Ruth whispered.

Amadis saw Ruth's face—saw that she knew her—and laughed, flinging up her arms. And the black stones of the Great Seal changed around them, and a tower grew in their place—a different tower, one made of stone. A tower with an objective reality, save for this one room which existed in a place that was no place and a time that was no time. A room made of magic and of a covenant with the Word.

"Now—" Amadis said.

"So you're a wizard, huh? Suck on this, then."

The voice was unmistakably female—and New York. Ruth watched as the armored figure drew her sword—and watched in disbelieving delight as the wizard-woman with a face like flowers and hair like blood flinched back from it.

"She can pull some pretty major stunts, but Cold Iron will kill her," Nic said quickly. He drew his Bowie. "So here we are again, Maleficent. What's on your mind?"

"Bargain with her," Fox said in an urgent undertone. "She's a wizard. They have to bargain."

Amadis' expression was one of unfeigned delight. "Would you bargain for favors? *You*, Fox?"

"Not me," Fox said hastily. "Her. Holly. For all of us, inclusive."

"Me?" Holly said, outraged.

"You haven't been here long enough to have made anybody any promises," Fox said. "That makes you strongest—if the iron jammies aren't enough. Just allow me to mention," Fox added evenly, "that wizards are very literal minded."

Holly glanced at the others. Ruth looked terrified, Melior grim. Saint Nic had no expression at all. Facing the wizard was like being in an episode of *Star Trek* that had a mad computer in it.

"You?" Amadis asked Holly. She looked even less human than she had a moment before, like a drawing, like a department store mannequin that had somehow gained the power of speech. "You will bargain with me? What will you bargain for? What will you bargain with?"

"I'll bargain—on behalf of all of us—for us," Holly said, playing for time. She didn't know how much help she was going to be allowed from the studio audience; at least in fairy tales, you didn't get much.

"Bargain, then." Amadis seemed to find the notion amusing. "I shall begin. One of you promises to stay to be my hound, and all the rest go free." She flung back her head and laughed.

Holly's heart sank. Here in this place where words had power, Amadis was demanding that one of them promise to stay behind and, in promising, bind him or herself more irrevocably than all the powers of the Wild Magic could bind them. Who could they sacrifice to this creature? How could they even imagine making such a choice?

And what would such a sacrifice render them vulnerable to?

"I accept your bargain." Nic Brightlaw stepped forward. "I promise to stay. That's what you asked. My promise. It's given." His white teeth glinted wolfishly. "I've broken every promise, every oath, every vow I ever made," Nic Brightlaw said. "My word can't hold me here. I promise to stay." He spread his arms wide. "Take me."

Amadis recoiled, an expression of fear on her face. Beyond the tower, all of them could suddenly sense the existence of a place of whiteness without brightness, a place so flat, so unnatural, so *fake*, that it was like having a blind spot everywhere you looked. Somehow it was here, just as the room was, both places existing simultaneously. Ruth reached out and took a fold of Melior's robe into her hand, just to feel something.

"I—You are promised to another," Amadis said, sounding oddly like an affronted Victorian maiden.

"But you didn't exempt any of us from volunteering," Nic said. "Fox said we were all part of the same group—so did Holly."

"Take him, or take none of us. You have made a false bargain, wizard," Makindeor said. He was wearing the Cloak once more.

"But I didn't mean . . ." Amadis faltered.

Her face contorted, as though beneath that perfect flower countenance there was something else trying to get out, something cruel and strange that did not have the shape of human bones. All of them heard a faint moan that seemed to rise up out of the very walls, as if—

—the wind were rising, preparing for a storm.

"It was night just a minute ago," Holly said, bewildered.

Ruth stared around. There was no tower. She couldn't even see it on the horizon. All she saw were black clouds boiling up along the shore. The wind flattened the grass, and in the distance Ruth could see two buildings: one a tall pale spire, still glistening even in the approaching storm, the other a more conventional castle.

"Ah, Holly, I would kiss you if I could," Mac said. "You made a wizard of the Wild Magic make a false bargain, something I never have seen. It let us go for shame of it."

"How could Baligant compel a *wizard?*" Jausserande asked in amazed dismay.

"It cannot matter as much as escaping her. That she has let us go does not mean she will not pursue us," Melior said. "You have startled her, nothing more."

The wind whipped up further. There was nothing else in sight—not Nic's horse, not Holly's pony, not even the horse Jausserande had ridden into the tower. All gone.

They were on foot, alone, and in the path of a gathering storm. And at any moment, Amadis would choose a new shape and attack them with it.

"What are we going to do now?" Holly said.

"Die?" Fox suggested.

"No," Nic said, and pointed.

Far off on the horizon there was a bright spark of white. And following it, a darkness broken by the flash of pennons and a sparkle of lances.

The household troops of the Red Earl, Eirdois Ryence of the House of the Vermilion Shadows, had arrived.

· 19 ·

Honor Bright

TOMORROW WAS THE last day of the Twilight Court, three days since the seven of them had escaped Amadis and the Black Tower.

Ruth Marlowe stood in the middle of what must by all accounts be considered a very grand bedchamber indeed. It was dominated by a canopied fourposter bed that ought by rights to have its own state capitol. The bed hangings were worked with gold and silver and sewn with gems. The walls were hung with tapestries. There was a fireplace big enough to roast a '57 Chevy in at one end of the room, surmounted by an intimidating display of used weapons. The entrance to the room was a massive set of ornately carved double doors, twenty feet high and yet in perfect proportion to the rest.

The entrance was guarded. Ever since the seven of them had been "rescued" from the Marches by the Earl of Vermilion's troops, Ruth Marlowe had gone very few places indeed without at least two guards. The only reason they were outside the doors and not inside the room was because this room had no windows.

It was very hard not to feel trapped, even though for the first time since she'd arrived Beyond the Morning, Ruth was—technically—safe, with an identity and a status and a place. She was clean, warm, fed—and extravagantly garbed in cramoise and argent, the colors of Line Rohannan. Her hair was held back by jeweled pins. She wore a necklace of rubies the size of cherries on steroids, and at dinner she'd been wearing half a dozen rings with even bigger stones set in them. She'd taken off the rings as soon as she'd gotten back here because they made her hands hurt, except for Melior's signet, Fox's gift, which she still wore as if it were a badge of . . . something.

Her hands weren't the only thing that hurt.

It was all right for the others, Ruth thought crossly. Melior, Makindeor, and Jausserande all belonged here, Holly Kendal was one of those SCA types who took to the place as though she were on her second honeymoon, Nic didn't seem to care what happened, and Fox . . .

She hadn't seen Fox at all—not since the first night of their rescue, when the Red Earl's Adepts had worked to open a Swan Road to Citadel.

A Swan Road, Ruth had discovered, was a way of getting from one known destination to another very fast—riding as swans flew, swift and direct. What Ruth remembered of the journey from Riptide to Citadel was riding pillion behind Melior with House Vermilion's troops all around them, down a highway of icy cloudcastles through a realm of blue light and arctic whistling wind, while the Adept who had cleared the way chanted out the landmarks and the horses ran like things demented. It was a strong and unsettling enchantment, and it had cut what would have been a month's travel to a day's, necessary because Melior *had* to reach Citadel before the Twilight Court rose from its month-long sitting.

Once they'd arrived, everyone had been very polite and very formal, and it was all very well to say now that she should have refused to be put off and demanded to know where Fox was, but when everyone from Nic to Melior had discouraged her from asking, it was hard to persist. Ruth was smart enough to know that making a fuss in public might do more harm than good, but she'd meant to demand answers from Melior as soon as they were alone together.

Only they never had been. In fact, since the seven of them had arrived at Citadel, Ruth had only seen the others at the formal banquets that stretched from afternoon into evening each day. There'd been no chance to speak privately with Melior, and by the time she'd realized what was going on . . .

. . . it was now. Here she was, locked up again. She'd just gotten back from the third damned banquet in as many days and sent the cream-faced elfmaid-in-waiting packing so that she could manage to have some time to think. Thinking was not something Ruth Marlowe had been terribly active at over the past several days. Or—why not admit it?—over the past several years. Or maybe even ever. But she'd better do some now.

Ruth glared around the lavish bedchamber as though it were a personal enemy and noticed that one of the tapestries was moving, billowing ever-so-slightly away from the wall, although there was no wind. A month ago she would have thought nothing of it. But a month ago people had not been trying to kill her.

Ruth looked around for a weapon and had just selected and hefted what weighed like a mostly gold candlestick set with tasteful plaques of carved lapis lazuli when Fox appeared from behind the tapestry.

She didn't need his warning gesture to keep her from crying out. Even someone stupider than Ruth Marlowe considered herself to be would have managed to learn something from experience by now.

"It's okay," Ruth said in a low voice, walking over to him. She was still holding the candlestick. "We're alone."

Fox relaxed slightly. Ruth inspected him closely for signs of ill-treatment. He still wore the same clothes Jausserande had given him at Black Bridge, though they were dirtier than they had been the last time Ruth had seen him, and his face and arms were smudged with fresh dust. There was something odd about him, but she couldn't quite put her finger on it just now. Ruth walked past him to the arras and looked behind it. As was typical in medieval castles, the tapestry hung several inches away from the wall. Behind it, a few feet above Ruth's head, there was a slit in the wall about three feet wide and eighteen inches high.

"Ventilation shaft," Fox said. "They lead all over the place in the central part of Citadel."

Ruth wished she hadn't seen it. It was easy enough to imagine things less congenial than Fox slithering through that slit to where Ruth waited helpless in her solitary bed.

"What are you doing here?" she demanded.

"I came to say goodbye. Give me back the ring."

"You came to—what?" Ruth spluttered.

"Give me back the ring," Fox repeated, patient and slow, as if he were talking to an idiot. "Give me the ring, and I'll give you back your promise."

Her promise. With a flash of guilt, Ruth realized that she'd nearly forgotten it—not that she'd had much of an opportunity yet to fulfil the oath she'd sworn. But now Fox was saying he would release her from her promise to make Melior give up everything he had—his lands, his guardianship of the Sword of Maiden's Tears. He'd paid out his side of the bargain—he'd gone with her—and now he was releasing her. But Fox making Ruth the instrument of his revenge had been the whole point of the bargain.

She hesitated. What did Fox really want? With a sudden flash of realization, Ruth realized that Fox wasn't wearing Jausserande's jewel around his throat any more. That was the difference.

"Which word didn't you understand?" Fox said sweetly.

"What a lovely evening we're having," Ruth said brittlely. "So nice of you to stop in. Do you care to take sherry? I'll ring for a footman."

Fox took a deep breath. "Just give me the goddamned ring, Ruthie. Maybe you don't understand. Promises are different here. You said you'd do something. The promise was sealed. If you don't do it now, and you don't let me give your promise back, things will just . . . happen. That's what magic is. It won't be up to me."

"And you know so much about magic," Ruth shot back at random. Fox looked disgusted.

"Just how do you think I got here, Ruthie—Swissair?"

He had a definite point, though the idea of that ultimate rationalist, Philip Leslie Lestrange, stooping—and successfully!—to magic gave Ruth a faint jolt.

"But I thought . . ." she began.

"I would love to discuss the politics of magical theory with you," Fox sighed, "I really would. But I'm supposed to be escaping, remember? So give me the ring and we can forget all about your stupid promise."

"You never could have escaped in the first place, could you?" Ruth said slowly. "Back in Black Bridge. I thought you were going to escape and I begged you not to. But you couldn't have gotten away, could you?"

Fox ran a hand over his hair, smearing the dust of the ventilation shaft through it and giving himself an oddly insubstantial appearance. "Maybe. I don't know. But whether I made it or not, every mud-born who'd so much as seen me would have been punished."

"So you do care about something besides yourself," Ruth said.

"Too many things to be a really successful terrorist," Fox said bitterly. "Now come on—" He held out his hand.

"Okay." The ring, which had been loose enough to fiddle with for weeks, now seemed to want to cling; Ruth worried at it savagely until at last it popped free. She dropped it into Fox's hand.

"I take back what I gave and give back what I took," Fox said in a formal tone. "Silver and gold unbind it, air and earth forget it." He put the ring back on his finger. "See you around." He turned back to the arras.

"No—wait! What's going on? Why are you escaping? Where are the others?" Ruth said.

"Like I knew," Fox replied. "I'm still under arrest; I've been locked up while everybody wrangled over who gets an outlaw of their very own. Rohannan and Floire can say they pardon me all they want, and it looks like Holly's friend Mac has enough pull with Line Gauvain to make them resign their claim, but none of that's enough when a mere mud-born dares to raise his hand against his puissant overlords. So—"

"What are you doing here?" Jausserande demanded from behind

Ruth. Ruth turned around, hefting the candlestick as she stifled a gasp of horror.

Jausserande closed the door quickly behind herself. She was dressed in even more splendor than Ruth was, in Line Floire's silver-and-violet, with full sweeping sleeves and full sweeping skirts. The Cup of Morning Shadows was appliqued in repeat on her skirts in blinding magical silver, and on her right shoulder she wore the same jeweled badge Ruth had seen Melior wearing: a replica of the Great Seal of Chandrakar, only with a cup in the center instead of a sword. "Haven't you escaped *yet?* What are you doing here?"

"Paying a social call," Fox snapped. "I was just going."

"Well, hurry," Jausserande said, equally crossly. "There's a horse waiting for you at the inn by the ford two miles west of here. They're all mud-born there," Jausserande couldn't quite keep the disparagement out of her voice, "so you ought to be safe enough."

"I know I know I know," Fox said, as if he'd heard it all before. "Wish me luck, Tink."

"I hope you die horribly," Jausserande said without heat. "Go on. The guards won't stay bribed forever—even if they don't know just what they've been bribed to overlook."

"I love you too," Fox said. He went behind the arras, followed by Ruth and Jausserande. When he jumped up to catch the lip of the ventilation shaft, Jausserande cupped her hands to make a step for him, and Fox wriggled the rest of the way out of sight.

Jausserande turned back to Ruth, brushing her hands clean.

"Just tell me what's going on," Ruth said. "Tell me you're not setting him up for something." Her hand felt curiously naked where the ring had been; she hoped nobody noticed it was gone and started to ask awkward questions.

"Setting him up?" Jausserande echoed blankly.

"Betraying him. You know. You and Fox hate each other—why should you help him escape?" And Fox hated Melior, but he'd released Ruth from a promise that would hurt him.

"Why not?" Jausserande said, moving over to one of the sideboards and rearranging the bowl of fruit there. "I am Cupbearer now—I may do as I please."

"And this pleases you?" Ruth asked. Jausserande turned back to her, eyes narrowed.

"I thought it would please *you,*" Jausserande said. "You gave me the Cup of Morning Shadows—you were Cupbearer, the Twelve alone know how—and you asked no repayment. There was no way to pardon him for what he had done, and his penalty would be death at the very least. So I have let him go. If he stays in Domain Rohannan, no one will hunt him very hard."

Go not to the elves for counsel, for they will say "Abort, Retry, Fail?" Holly Kendal had a button that said that, and Ruth thought it was good advice. She wasn't sure if elves, like Vulcans, never lied. She was pretty sure they never told the whole truth.

"It does please me. Thank you," Ruth said. She wondered if Fox would return the favor. She'd like to think he'd given up his plans for revenge, but she didn't think he had.

Jausserande turned back to the fruit. "Will you set down the candlestick, Lady Ruth? Or do you think I mean you harm?"

"I don't know if you do or not," Ruth answered. "What do you want, where are the others, and what's going on?"

"We are at Citadel, where the Twilight Court meets so that the Lords Temporal can put their grievances to rest short of war."

Jausserande grimaced slightly, as if there were some humor in this.

"Here your heart twin, Rohannan Melior of the House of the Silver Silences, comes to petition the gathered lords and his own overlord the Earl of Silver to confirm him as Baron Rohannan and head of Line Rohannan, lord of Domain Rohannan in Canton Silver, with all the castles, lands, and honors that were lately his father's, Rohannan Lanval of the House of the Silver Silences."

It was quite a mouthful, but Jausserande wasn't finished.

"Further, he seeks to lay before the lords in assembly his accusation against Baligant High Prince of House Vermilion, that Baligant has conspired with wizards to ravish the Treasures from their rightful bearers so that those Lines which hold them are attainted upon the day of the Kingmaking and cast out of the world forever. Last, he seeks Earl Silver's permission to wed, which Regordane Somhairle may grant, withhold, or choose to lay before the lords assembled for debate. This is Baron Rohannan's business with the Court.

"The others of our party are here at Citadel, as you are, all kept according to their station and degree. Ceiynt and the Ironworld berserker are our honored guests."

"Then why can't I see them?" Ruth demanded, before Jausserande could continue her exhaustive answer to Ruth's previous questions.

Jausserande turned away from the fruit and came closer, until she was standing face-to-face with Ruth. "Because we do not know who may try to kill you before tomorrow, or how, Ironworld girl. Melior would not show you even at High Table save that the Earl of Silver demands it, and my cousin seeks his grace. He has said you are troubled in mind and overset by your journey. Do we show you about, that hawk won't fly much longer. But now I am here to bring you to him privily so that he may speak to you of tomorrow."

Ruth's stomach lurched. That must mean that the moment she had dreaded and had found no way to avoid was nearly here—when Melior, the man she loved, would strip her soul naked in the middle of a room full of strangers to prove that Baligant had tampered with the Sword of Maiden's Tears. Would publicly call up a wizard to make it clear for anyone who cared to see that Ruth Marlowe's soul was spun out like taffy between herself and Melior's sword . . .

She took a reflexive step backward. She didn't know whether there was any way for her to talk Melior out of this, no matter how little she wanted to do it. And she didn't know how she'd feel about him afterward if he did it anyway—but it wasn't love in Ruth Marlowe's book if one person completely ignored what the other wanted. And even if she let him do it—which she probably would because the stakes were so very high—she wasn't really sure she wanted to take second place to anybody's love of country, no matter how civic-minded.

"Are you deaf, you mud-born mooncalf?" Jausserande demanded. "Come now to where my cousin bides—we do not have all the night and day before us!"

Holly Kendal stood alone in a gallery looking down at the Mother of All Revels. Globes of elflight hung in the air. The High Table was still there, as it had been during dinner, swathed in white linen, but now it was burdened with glittering *subtleties* made of marzipan and spun sugar and candied fruit. The other tables had been cleared away to make room for the dancing, and elves, a few humans, and some people who didn't look to Holly as if they were either one talked and laughed and drank and moved through the elaborate figures of court dances to the accompaniment of music played by musicians in one of the other galleries.

Holly didn't know any of the people or any of the dances, so she was watching from the gallery, well content. The sight before her eyes was beautiful, from the ornately carved stone walls to the several dozen banners hanging from the balconies. With new practice, Holly could pick out the violet and silver of Floire, with the Cup blazon added to the many quarterings of its device, and the crimson and silver of Line Rohannan, with the Sword. They shared a family resemblance deriving from the fact that they were two Lines of the same House. The ice-blue and green of Line Gauvain, with the Book in its lower right-hand corner—Mac's line— looked very different, although Holly supposed a mundane wouldn't be able to tell much difference among them at all.

She'd always said the SCA would come in handy some day.

Mac—Gauvain Makindeor of the House of the Crystal Wind, to give him his full and proper name—had been restored to his family, though in the few days since he and Holly had gotten here, his family physicians had not been able to penetrate the pall of electroshock-caused amnesia that still clouded his mind. With the confusion here relating to the Kingmaking, no one was quite sure when he'd vanished. His memories of Chandrakar were many years out of date; if he had spent all of his absence from here in the World of Iron, he would have had to have been there for more than a century. There might be no way for him to ever discover how he'd fallen out of Chandrakar into the World of Iron. Rohannan Melior had told Mac that the Borders were sealed, a fact that mattered to Holly only because she couldn't send her friends a message to tell them she was alive and well. Holly fingered the jewel at her throat, her attention on the pageantry and the sweet splendor of the music. This was Elf Hill, just as the legends said, and the price of a night spent here in revel was exile forever from the world she had known.

There were so many things she'd miss about the World of Iron, but Holly wasn't sorry she'd come. She looked down at the whirling dancers in their sparkling, jewel-colored costumes. Holly ran her thumb over the smooth cabochon of the single gemstone at her throat. She'd been paid in full for whatever they wanted of her.

She was free.

Other courtiers wore more opulent jewelry—Ruth Marlowe had worn a ruby necklace at the feast tonight that had left Holly's eyes popping with sheer disinterested envy—but Holly would not have traded what she wore for any of them.

On a thin gold chain about her throat she wore a stone about the size of a Jordan almond in a gold setting that allowed it to slide along the chain. The stone was clear as a drop of amber, bright honey gold and filled with dancing iridescent lights—and as long as she wore it, she was "even," free of manic highs and suicidal lows.

Makindeor's gift to her.

"Holly?"

Holly turned around in a graceful swish of skirts—her device was embroidered near the hem, in a repeating pattern of silver, green, and violet—to see Makindeor approaching her, two elaborate goblets in his hands. The lavish costume he wore reminded her faintly of the Italian Renaissance, with tight particolored leggings and small jeweled slippers. But the tunic with its jewelled hip belt was nothing that had ever been worn in Italy's sunny climes, at least not with those pants: tight ornamental undersleeves, two contrasting oversleeves, knots of ribbons at both shoulders and a deep sheer swag of material hanging from them behind.

A pair of gauntlets made of embroidered gauze—as ornamental and useless as a lady's fan—were tucked through his belt. In one ear he wore a drop earring that looked like a black opal, and there was a dusting of gold across his cheekbones and brow, looking like sunlight on snow.

I guess we're not in Kansas any more, Toto, Holly thought, smiling. She reached for one of the cups. "Is that for me?"

"Of course," Mac said. "Are you enjoying yourself?"

Holly's free hand moved automatically to touch the jewel at her throat. She thought she could even enjoy herself in a dungeon, as long as she wore this. She sipped from the cup. The contents were sweet and strange and tasted much more of herbs than any wine Holly was used to.

"So tomorrow's the big day, huh?" she said, leaning back against the balustrade.

"Tomorrow Line Rohannan makes its presentation," Mac agreed. "I have already spoken to Baron Gauvain, of my own line—it is as well that I resigned from the succession when I took the post of Chief Archivist, or things would be very awkward now—upon the matter of the World of Iron's aggression against us. And I have resigned my blood-claim upon the human outlaw Fox."

Holly must have looked as puzzled as she felt; Mac explained. "He admits that he killed Gauvain Guiraut, squire to Floire Jausserande. Guiraut was my grandson, three generations removed. I am the oldest living member of Line Gauvain in the direct line, so the blood-debt comes next to me."

"But you've resigned it." It made Holly feel odd to hear that Mac had great-great-great grandchildren, although she already knew that Morning Lords didn't die. It did make her wonder how old he was, though. "Don't you have any family left?"

"The Baron is my great-nephew, an elder brother or two, some nephews and cousins. My parents, my wife, my children all died long ago."

"So you're alone." Holly hadn't meant it to come out like that, as if she were trying to pair the two of them up like the animals in Noah's Ark. *The animals went in two by two, the elephant and the kangaroo . . .* "I mean—"

"I know what you mean, and it is true. In fact, I am in great disgrace, and not only for refusing lawful vengeance upon Guiraut. I have lost the *Book of Airts,* Holly, and that is a treason for which I cannot be lightly forgiven."

"But you know right where it is," Holly said, baffled.

"But is it still there—after how many weeks in the World of Iron? And young Melior says the Borders are sealed; I must try them myself, but I am afraid, from what we saw in Cockaigne, that he is right, and thus the Book is sealed beyond my reach. Yet I would not change what I did," Mac said somberly, as if he were trying to convince some absent person. "If the Book had been with me, I do not think the wizard Amadis would have been willing to bargain for our lives, and so be trapped. I think she would have killed us all."

Holly shuddered. She wasn't sure even iron armor and a steel sword would have been proof against the full fury of an enraged wizard. Only the Red Earl's arrival with his troops and the fact that Baligant, Amadis' master, didn't seem to want an open breach with his nobles had saved them, and Holly was acutely aware of how narrow the escape had been—and by how thin a thread their safety depended upon now.

"Which still leaves the musical question: What now? I just don't know where I fit in here, Mac—Makindeor."

"As my honored vadelet," Makindeor said seriously. "And—I hope—as my comrade and friend. I think we will all need friends in the days to come." His harlequin gaze left her, focusing on something unseen and disturbing.

Holly Kendal smiled. Whatever lay ahead, it would be an adventure, and Holly found herself looking forward to it.

On the battlements of Citadel, the autumn wind was an icy stream, cold as starlight turned to air. Jausserande stood leaning out between the crenelations. Her hair was braided into one long jewel-wrapped tail. It hung almost horizontal on the air, and her ermine-lined half-cape was plastered against her back by the force of the wind. Her hands and cheeks were numb. Jausserande didn't care.

"I thought I'd find you here," Ceiynt said.

She turned as he spoke. He was standing in the doorway that led to the stairs. When he was sure she saw him, he moved forward.

He was dressed all in blinding white: Chandrakar's acknowledgment that he was a paladin, a magic-charged, wizard-sent hero that it was much better not to meddle with, even if he was one of the Children of Earth. He came over to stand beside her. The icy night wind ruffled his coin-gold hair, tousling it over his forehead. "Is he out?" Ceiynt said.

"I've heard no outcry from the guards; he came to Citadel as my prisoner, so if he were found missing, I would have been told. He must be well away. I hate him!" Jausserande burst out passionately. "I hate him!"

"People die in war." Ceiynt's voice was unyielding. "Your squire was a casualty of war. You have to accept that and go on."

"I can't." Jausserande's voice was anguished. "Can you?"

Ceiynt looked directly at her. His blue eyes burned.

"There are things you can forgive and things you can't. When the enemy kills one of your men, you have to try to accept it. They're the enemy. That's their job. It's when you're sold out by your own side—when you die because your own commanders were too weak, too lazy, too *stupid* to make your death cost the enemy anything at all—that's when it's something that's never over."

Betrayed by her own. That, at least, was something Jausserande had never had to face—her Ravens had never been abandoned by their overlord, on or off the field. She put a hand on Ceiynt's arm. He smiled down at her, his expression brilliant with the ghost of ancient pain.

"Never mind, little girl. Miss Marlowe is united with her young man, Fox is out of trouble—for the moment—and all the rest will be over soon." He looked up at the moon.

Jausserande glanced up as well, judging the phase with expert opinion. Second night of the full moon tomorrow, the true full moon. "Over soon?" she asked, her question deceptively casual.

Ceiynt shrugged. "I told Miss Marlowe; I suppose she wasn't very forthcoming. I was lost, I was in bad shape, I met a wizard. He was a better bargainer than Amadis was."

"What did you promise him?" Jausserande said, a chill clutch of foreboding at her heart.

"Nothing much," Ceiynt said. "Nothing anybody's going to miss."

Ruth stood just inside the antechamber of Melior's rooms. Her ubiquitous guards stood just outside. Jausserande had brought her here and deserted her with the briskness of a postal worker delivering an Express Mail envelope.

The Baron-to-be kept great state. There was no bed in this room, and only one highly carved thronelike chair. Gryphons and sphinxes with gilded wings and jeweled eyes coiled about each other along the frame in eye-hurting complexity, and the seat cushion was adorned with far too much gold thread to look as if it would make a comfortable seat. The footstool that sat beside the chair like a faithful dog was equally gaudy.

For one brief shining moment Ruth wished she'd begged Fox to take her with him. At least living in the greenwood with a bunch of outlaws wouldn't leave her feeling so . . . inadequate.

Face it, Ruth: this is not *the sort of place you belong.*

Ruth wiped palms grown suddenly damp down the skirts of her dress and tried not to feel like an erring pupil summoned into the principal's presence. She *knew* Melior, even if she wasn't all that much in charity with him at the moment. She'd been to bed with the man, for heaven's sweet sake! This interview might be awkward and unpleasant, but it wasn't likely to be actively dangerous.

But she still wished it were over. Where was he? If he showed up with a gaggle of elphen courtiers, she wouldn't be able to stand it—she knew it.

The door opened, and Melior entered. He was dressed in red and silver, his clothing elaborately ornamented and jeweled until he looked like a Fabergé Easter egg. The Treasurekeeper badge on his shoulder looked almost stark by comparison. The first thing that Ruth looked for was the Sword of Maiden's Tears, and she felt a guilty pang of relief when she saw that he wasn't wearing it.

"Ruth," he said when he saw her.

Who did you expect, Dorothy Gale? "You sent for me," Ruth said aloud.

Melior grimaced. "Trust my cousin to put as bad a complexion on everything as possible. I only wanted to see you. To . . . talk. Before tomorrow."

"When you . . ." Ruth began, and could not continue.

Melior came and took her arm, and led her back through the door to the inner chamber. He closed the door behind them.

"When Ophidias unbinds you from the Sword," Melior finished for her. "And shows the Lords Temporal that Baligant has tampered with at least one of the Treasures."

Ruth looked away, unable to face him.

This must be where he stays when he's here, she thought with desperate irrelevancy. This inner room lacked both the chilly opulence of the chamber where Ruth was lodged and the off-putting extravagance of the antechamber. This was a rich room, but it was a place where somebody lived.

There was a curtained bed in one corner, its curtains looped back to reveal tumbled bed furs and a jumble of pillows. A merry fire burned in the fireplace carved of golden alabaster, and cherry light shone through the crystal eyes of the gilded salamanders on the firescreen. There was a standing desk tucked away in an alcove, with a closed book set upon its angled surface, and two more comfortable chairs stood angled to catch the fire's warmth, with a wine table poised between them.

Ruth chose not to be comforted.

"So," she said in a brittle voice. "What's this about?"

"I would speak to you," Melior repeated, "before we go before the High Court tomorrow." His voice was troubled, uncertain.

"What's there to say?" This would have been the place, if her oath were still binding, to demand that he leave the Sword and Chandrakar behind. Only Fox had released her from that, and if Fox could be so gracious, hating as he did, couldn't Ruth do better with what was left of love? "I mean—" She stopped again. "I feel as if I'm lost," Ruth complained.

"Oh, beloved." Melior came and put his arms around her from behind. Ruth let him, although the gesture made her feel prickly.

"Tomorrow you're going to do all sorts of magic—what then?" she said grudgingly.

"I pray that we do not go to war again," Melior said earnestly. "Though better war than Baligant to rule over us." He pressed his cheek against her hair—a rather lumpy proposition, with all the jewels, but apparently he didn't mind. "Yet when the High Court repudiates its choice of High King, they must choose another candidate, and Baligant High Prince is the only man they could agree on in over a century."

"Oh." The longer Ruth had been here, the more she had seen of the devastation a century of war had brought to Chandrakar—not only of the land itself, but of the souls of its people. Yet Melior spoke almost casually of more fighting. "Wouldn't it maybe be better to . . . ?" she asked hesitantly.

"To condone his evil?" Melior said, finishing her thought. "Never. If no one else will speak against him, I will stand alone. My Line will follow me."

Every time Ruth thought she understood him, Melior's thought patterns took off in this unexpected feudal direction. He spoke of starting a new civil war all by himself and assumed unquestioningly that his people would agree to follow him into revolt, just because he was the head of their Line and he said so. She shook her head, smiling painfully.

"I had rather not, you know," Melior said, "for all of us of Rohannan will die, should all the Seven Houses oppose us, and so brief a life is no life to offer you. But this will not come to pass—I am sure of it. I have the *proof*—they must see it and heed. The Cupbearer will speak for me as well."

"And your wizard." Ruth could not repress a shiver.

"He will not harm you—not while he expects me to find him a bride. And I have seen—" Melior hesitated. "I have seen our child, Ruth."

Ruth turned to face him, wide blue eyes serious. "You've seen our *what?*" she said.

"Our child. Naomi. In the Goblin Market, where she came to my aid. It was a great sorcery that she worked, and I saw her plain. She bore the Sword."

It was too much to take in, seeming improbable and faintly disrespectful to the dead all at once. And if Melior had seen this vision in the Goblin Market, then he'd seen it while he'd been poisoned and dying from Amadis' attack. Hallucinating, in fact.

"I'm sure that Goblin Market visions aren't admissible as evidence," Ruth muttered, resting her forehead against the unyielding lumpiness of Melior's jewel-covered chest.

"And it is true that I saw only what may be, not what is. But I would be a fool if I did not prepare for war as well as pray to avoid it, and so I beg you most humbly, Ruth Marlowe of the Ironworld—marry me now."

Ruth's mind had been elsewhere, on the harrowing events of the morrow. There was a long pause when Melior had finished speaking while her mind raced back to retrieve his last words and try to decide if she'd heard him correctly.

"What?" she finally said weakly.

"Tomorrow I am confirmed in my lands and given my father's titles. I have humbly petitioned the Earl of Silver, Rohannan's overlord, who is also the Regordane of Line Regordane, to marry, but he may not choose to speak in Council."

"These guys are going to do these things while you're saying that the king is a fink?" Ruth said skeptically.

Melior smiled grimly.

"Ah, but these matters come *first,* do you not see? And then, as Baron Rohannan, I have the right to speak before the Court instead of humbly petitioning it. The Lords Temporal would prefer not to grant so awkward a petition; rather they would confirm me in my titles and so keep themselves scatheless."

"My brain hurts," Ruth complained.

"We have all grown expert at diplomacy and betrayal since the war began," Melior said, a faint note of mockery in his voice. "I have spoken to many of the Lords Temporal in the last two days; I could tell you the temper of each Baron, which of the seven Earls is sure of his subjects, what alliances are contemplated and what old grudges still cry out for redress."

"Let's get back to this marriage thing," Ruth said.

"This marriage is a thing the Earl of Silver may not grant me, tomorrow or ever. I have been unable to discover his mind. And did he consent, the High King could overrule his choice—"

Ruth snorted derisively.

"But once we are wed, the Earl of Silver can only punish me, not set the marriage aside. And should Line Rohannan rise against the King-Elect tomorrow, I would that you had a place at my side—as my lady under the law as well as in my heart."

"Marry you," Ruth said, as witlessly as if she didn't love him, hadn't thought of it, hadn't expected it. "Are you sure you want to do something that radical? I mean, what if word gets around that Rohannan is consorting with known humans? And what about Nic? Or Holly? You can't marry—"

Melior kissed her. Ruth felt a flicker of passion in her attenuated soul, as quick and blinding as a lightning flash. She was possessed by the reckless self-destructive impulse to do what he wanted, to follow where he led. When she put her arms around him, the ornamentation of their clothes caught and slithered over each other; she tugged, and she heard something small and hard bounce to the floor.

"I will marry you if I must open the gates of Death to claim you," Melior said. "You are my heart twin; you are the only woman in all the Nine Worlds and the Thousand Lands Beyond the Morning I will ever love. Only say you will marry me, and we shall set the seal upon this here and now, and you will be my lady under law as well as in fact."

Ruth rested her cheek against his chest, feeling the gems on his doublet press into her cheek as Melior's arms tightened around her. But Ruth was not a reader of historical novels for nothing. Melior was urging marriage without his liege lord's consent, and the marriage of the nobility had never had much to do with romance. If Chandrakar was as feudal as it seemed, that sort of rebellion—marrying without his Earl's consent— could carry a very high price tag indeed. She didn't know how much she loved Melior or how much she'd love him after tomorrow, but she knew that she loved him enough to spare him this.

"I'll marry you with the Earl of Silver's consent—not without," Ruth said. Her voice seemed to come from somewhere outside her, distant and unyielding as the gems around her throat.

"My lady!" Melior dropped to one knee before her, clutching both her hands in his. "I beg you. You are my heart, but you are a stranger in my homeland. Let me give you a place here that all can understand and mantle you in Rohannan's protection."

His distress was evident, his desire enough to sway Ruth against her better judgment. But if what he was suggesting was so innocuous, he would not have brought her here secretly to arrange it at the very last minute.

"No," Ruth said again.

"You don't understand!" Melior burst out in frustration.

"Don't I?" Ruth's voice was kind, rather than scornful; she suspected she understood Melior's motives all too well. "You want to protect me. That's sweet, and heaven knows I need it. But there has to be some other way—or is somebody marrying Nic and Holly, too?"

Melior looked up at her from where he knelt. "Holly Kendal is liege-man to Gauvain Makindeor, under Line Gauvain and House Crystal's protection both. Nic Brightlaw is a paladin; he has his wizard's shelter, and our laws do not apply to him. But you, Ruth—"

"No." Ruth pulled her hands out of his and turned away.

"It isn't that I don't love you—I do." With an effort she kept herself from qualifying the simple statement. "And so I want you to do this right—or not at all. I'm not worth starting another war for. If the Earl won't come across, you can keep me in a labyrinth of roses, like the Fair Rosamund. Or something. And you don't *know* he won't say yes."

"You are worth a war—to me," Melior said quietly.

"No." Ruth turned back to him. *"No.* Don't you see—it would be so easy to let you take care of me. I've never done anything heroic in my entire life. All I've done is watch people die around me: Jimmy, Kathy, Allen, Naomi. They always say not to meddle in the affairs of wizards— but wizards have meddled in *my* affairs since I was eighteen years old. Now I'm over thirty—okay, I'll be thirty-three next May—and I'm tired of being everybody's pawn."

Ruth clenched her hands into fists. "Let me do something heroic for a change. Let me not drag you into a fight we can avoid."

"My gallant lady," Melior said.

He came toward her. Ruth stood her ground. Her heart was hammering in her chest with sheer nauseated tension—why did it seem that the only emotions she could feel were ugly ones?—but she vowed she would not back down.

Such a simple thing, a marriage. Hermonicet's marriage—or lack of it—had started a war that had spanned five human generations. Because of it, her wizard's meddling—or Baligant's wizard—had warped Ruth's entire life and killed Ruth's dearest friends. Whatever Ruth could do to frustrate those plans, she would gladly do. And that included not dragging Melior down in a tangle of messy romance.

Melior put his arms around her again, very gently.

"Then if you will not wed me, will you stay beside me until the day?"

"Yes." Ruth closed her eyes. "Yes, I will."

· 20 ·

In the Court of the Whirlwind

CITADEL, WHICH WAS the High King's seat, was set—so tradition had it—at an equal distance from all four of the Great Seals that fixed the borders of Chandrakar. It was built without stone or mortar, carved out of the living red granite itself, and was large enough to guest all the high nobility of Chandrakar simultaneously. It was to Citadel that the Twelve Treasures would be brought; it was here that the Kingmaking would take place, to seal the High King to the soul of the Land for as long as king and Land should endure together.

The heart of Citadel held three chambers, each named for its function: the High Court, where Adepts' affairs were transacted, the Twilight Court, where the Lords Temporal settled those matters of custom and politics that affected the entire land, and the King's Court, where the law was made by the High King and his advisors.

Of the High Court, no one unschooled in the Art Magical would speak. The King's Court had not met in well over a hundred years.

The Twilight Court was a circular chamber carved from the very heartstone of the tower. Doors pierced its walls all along its height, giving out into the ranks of carved seats that lined the chamber's walls in crescent arcs, rising tier upon tier toward the ceiling, as though the court's architect had planned for some future time when even so cyclopean a chamber would be filled. Even before the war, it had been a rare convocation that had seen more than the first three ranks of benches filled, but on this day the Twilight Court was filled beyond capacity—the seven Earls of the Seven Houses of Twilight, the Barons and Baronesses who ruled over the Lines within each house, the Counts and Countesses who held fee-lands of the Barons, the lordlings who were younger sons and daughters or well-married—every one of the Sons of the Morning and Daughters of the Twilight who could possibly manage to be in attendance here today was present.

Baligant was not here.

Ruth could only be grateful, all things considered. Flanked by guards in Rohannan livery, she stood on the topmost tier of seats. Jausserande and Nic stood beside her. Gauvain Makindeor was seated somewhere below, but Holly Kendal had not been allowed to attend at all, something that bothered Ruth much more than it had seemed to bother Holly.

Ruth shifted her weight and tried not to fidget. Both her hands nervously clutched at the carved stone railing before her, and she gazed down from three stories' height to the floor of the council chamber.

I'm going to be sick, Ruth thought with morbid dread. *I'm going to throw up, faint, and fall to my death.* She was glad that claustrophobia was her problem, not fear of heights. It was like being seated in the top tier of Madison Square Garden.

Far below, Melior stood in the center of a ring of seven fires, presenting himself and his claims to Line Rohannan to the Seven Houses of the Twilight. The Sword of Maiden's Tears was sheathed at his hip; he had brought his Treasure to the court, just as Jausserande had brought the Cup.

Other than the rather perfunctory firelight—the fires, Ruth gathered, were tokens, not meant to be very useful—the room was lit by the bodies of the inhabitants themselves.

Ruth found the unearthly radiance, the principal source of illumination in the gigantic chamber, unsettling. The elflight was somewhere around sixteenth or seventeenth on the list of things that disturbed her, a list that included Baligant's absence and the fact that she couldn't hear enough from this perch to know whether Melior was winning or not.

"What's he saying?" Ruth whispered to Jausserande. The sound of many voices rebounding from the stone walls made a sea-like sussuration that was a meaningless hash of noise to her human ears.

"Hush," Jausserande whispered back, leaning forward. "He has them—by the Twelve, why does Ryence not oppose him? Vermilion has no love for Silver—"

"What's *happening?*" Ruth demanded more urgently.

"They confirm him in Rohannan's lands: He is Lineholder and Baron." There was a pause as Jausserande strained to hear.

Far below, the Earl of Silver stepped out into the circle of fire to face
Melior. The two men looked tiny and distant as chesspieces. Melior first
set aside the Sword and knelt to do homage to his overlord, then took
up the Sword again so that the Earl could kneel to Melior as
Treasurekeeper. Then the Earl of Silver took his seat again, and this time
Melior sat down beside him. There was another pause.

"The Earl does not speak of the marriage," Jausserande said for
Ruth's benefit.

Good or bad? Ruth wondered nervously. Apparently the Earl of Silver had the choice of mentioning Melior's choice of bride to the other
Morning Lords or keeping the matter to himself, and he had chosen the
latter. Last night Melior had explained what he expected to happen today
in detail; what had taken place so far was almost ritual, stylized and
formal.

There might have been more argument against Melior's confirmation
if he hadn't shown up wearing the Sword of Maiden's Tears; the Morning
Lords' nearly superstitious reverence for the Treasures and their
Treasurekeepers had weighed heavily in Melior's favor.

"He does it—he speaks!" Jausserande muttered urgently. As Melior
stepped out from his place again and took a position in the center of the
seven fires, his cousin gripped Ruth's arm with her free hand; Ruth was
already in such an agony of tension she nearly didn't feel it.

Melior spoke, but Ruth only heard the sound of the first few words.
Then the chamber exploded into chaos, a battering wall of sound as
everyone—*everyone*—in the entire court tried to speak at once.

It was nearly half an hour before Melior could resume speaking. He
motioned to where the Ironworlders and Jausserande stood; Ruth felt the
gesture like a blow to the heart.

"It's time," Jausserande said. She started down the stairs to the floor
of the chamber.

Ruth followed, and Nic brought up the rear. Ruth's shoulder blades
crawled; if she died between now and the moment Melior summoned
Ophidias, Melior's proof would vanish. Ruth, gazing into the speculum of
her own death, wondered if she would still be *aware* once she was dead
and trapped within the Sword of Maiden's Tears like a fly in amber.

By the time she reached the floor, Ruth was filled with a vibrating
unreal sensation that had as much relation to stage fright as a firecracker
did to nuclear war.

"Rohannan pledges proof and offers wizards!" a scornful voice cried.
Ruth didn't see who it was. She concentrated on Melior, knowing that it
was odd to the point of deadly insult for her to be here at all.

"Rohannan offers truth!" Jausserande shouted back. "I speak now of my quest for the Cup of Morning Shadows. I sought it in the place appointed, passed to me by Floire Glorete, who had it from Floire Devisser, who set it there when Rainouart the Beautiful yet breathed. I sought it—and found it not, for it had been tampered with by the same malefactor whom Rohannan accuses!"

"Vermilion shares Floire's triumph in achieving its Treasure but finds it pathetic to see the Cupbearer bending truth to curry Rohannan favor."

This time Ruth did turn in the direction of the voice. The speaker was easy enough to spot: The Red Earl, the Earl of Vermilion, stood at his ringside seat and spoke in carrying tones. His harsh patrician features—Ruth knew them from her two visits to the Red Earl's castle—were softened almost to anonymity by the glowing nimbus that surrounded him, but Ruth had no difficulty in recognizing him. Vermilion was the House that had adopted Baligant once his star had risen, a House that had no love for Line Rohannan or its liege lord, the Earl of Silver. Or for humans.

"It was no action of the High Prince that withheld Floire's Treasure, but mud-born malice!" the Earl of Vermilion said.

There was a booming sound as the enormous double doors that were the official and ceremonial entrance to the court were flung open. They struck the walls with a deep reverberating tone that silenced even the undertone of speculation that filled the chamber. Ruth, Jausserande, Nic, and Melior all turned toward the portal.

Framed within that towering arch, Philip LeStrange—the outlaw Fox—stood in chains.

"It takes no more than this," the Red Earl said, gesturing as elphenborn in House Vermilion livery dragged Fox into the room. "The Earthchild malice of a brigand whom Rohannan softness has let flourish. Line Gauvain has felt the sting of Rohannan mercy this season; and if Rohannan may sully this place with mud-born, then Eirdois may do likewise. I can produce others of these outlaws who can bear witness under spell that it was the outlaw known as Fox who carried the Cup of Morning Shadows into the Vale of Stars, and Fox's hand that cast it away."

"Hathorne never could make up his mind to pick a side and stick to it," Fox said, loud enough for Ruth to hear. He looked remarkably composed for someone whose escape had gone so dreadfully wrong.

"Do you call me a liar, you cowardly eater of carrion?" Jausserande demanded of the Earl. Her hand went to her belt, seeking the sword she did not carry here. Melior placed a hand on her arm.

"Oh, Fox," Ruth groaned. Even she could see that any attempt to save him now would only make Melior's case look worse. But how could they abandon him?

"Bold words," the Red Earl sneered, "when the Cup renders you exempt from blood-insult."

"Rail against Floire how you will," Melior said, "I do not withdraw Rohannan's charge against the High Prince. And I say further that Baligant seeks the destruction of us all: He has tampered with the Sword of Maiden's Tears and I offer proof!" Melior threw the ring that would summon Ophidias into the nearest of the fires.

There was a moment's pause, as if the ring were an ice-cube deciding to melt, and then the fire fountained upward out of the bed of coals in a great unnatural arc. The flame boiled ceilingward, growing brighter all the while, and then spread, coalesced, and dulled.

"Who summons me?" the creature said.

Ruth stared. Melior had said "wizard." All of them had said "wizard." *This* was a dragon.

"Firedrake," Ophidias observed mildly.

If he'd actually been a dragon, perhaps Ophidias would not have been an especially large one. His throat and stomach were the pure hot gold of embers; his sides and back were the same color but slightly silvered, as if with a fine coating of ash. A pleasant warmth—at least at this distance—radiated from his skin in waves. He had a long serpentine neck, a long barbed whiplike tail, and vast webbed polydactyl wings whose golden opalescent membrane was the same shimmering poppy-gold of the jewel in the ring Melior had thrown into the fire.

The wizard's serpentine head was perhaps a yard long, more triangular than anything else. The fires in the room gleamed from its swooping chitinous planes and glittered in his pupilless golden eyes. It was not a face and a mouth shaped for human speech, but Ruth heard his voice clearly: a human, southern, cracker-barrel philosopher sort of a voice, as down-home and cognitively dissonant a cliché as Ruth had encountered yet in all the Lands Beyond the Morning.

"I summon you, wizard. This is the place and time appointed by me, and I charge you by the price I am sworn to pay to here unbind the Lady Ruth's soul from the Sword of Maiden's Tears, restore her soul to her entire, and make plain to all who watch here the one who performed the binding," Melior said.

This is it, Ruth thought.

"Very well, Child of Air; there's no need to shout. All you have asked, I shall perform, and because I have you will provide me a human bride who comes freely and of her own will to wed with me before the day that your firstborn son weds, or forfeit your line and all your hopes. Now bring me the woman," Ophidias said mildly.

The chamber was absolutely silent. Even Fox had nothing to say for himself. Ruth stood her ground as if she'd been bolted to it, wanting to cooperate but unable to. When Melior touched her arm to move her forward, she started painfully.

"Come along, Daughter of Earth. This won't hurt at all." The firedrake lifted one silky, glowing wing, inviting her to walk beneath, and summery heat wafted over her skin like a caress.

She supposed she shouldn't trust him, after all the things everyone here had said about wizards, but she did. Her heart slowed; it became easier to breathe, and after a few more seconds had passed, Ruth was able to walk forward, toward the serpent-wizard.

When she had passed beneath the canopy of its wing she felt safer, as though Ophidias could protect her from all the scheming and intrigue contained within the chamber of the Twilight Court. When Ruth looked up, she found herself almost nose-to-nose with Ophidias.

"A human bride?" Ruth asked.

"It's the usual sort of bargain. I've been feeling a certain lack around the cave. I'd hoped—But a wizard's hopes are foolish things, as your young man will surely tell you. Now turn out your pockets for me, daughter, and we'll see if we can start another war." The firedrake's voice was easy, amused.

War? "I don't have any—" *pockets in this dress* . . . Ruth finished mentally, dropping her hands to her sides and feeling the lumps along the hem.

The dress might have had pockets when she'd put it on this morning—if it had them, they'd been empty.

Not now. Ruth pulled her hands out of her pockets and opened them to reveal the litter of useless things she'd picked up in her travels: the golden embroidery scissors and the long gold-embroidered red ribbon with the bells that she'd bargained for in the Goblin Market; Nic's wristwatch (how had she gotten that?); and a ring, a silver magic ring with a golden stone that the dead man had been carrying back in the meadow where she met the unicorn, weeks and weeks ago.

"Ah," said Ophidias with satisfaction. "Everything we need, and you've brought it all with you."

Ruth stared down at the objects in her hands. "I'm sure this is all very symbolic," she began hesitantly.

"Take the scissors. Cut the ribbon. Throw the pieces into the fire," Ophidias ordered.

Feeling very silly, Ruth moved to comply. She slid the gleaming red ribbon between the shining golden blades of the scissors, and hesitated. The ribbon was so *very* red, the gold embroidery upon it so bright, that it seemed almost like wanton vandalism to cut it.

"Cut!" Ophidias commanded. Startled, Ruth squeezed the scissors shut.

She felt a piercing pang of *sensation*, as though something far inside her that was never meant to be handled had been touched in some way. Then the elusive discomfort was gone, to be replaced with a much more unequivocal awareness of being filled, or refilled, of some cold unnatural emptiness vanishing, an inner resonance restored. It was certainty, restlessness, determination.

It was her soul returning to its home.

Abruptly revolted, Ruth flung the scissors and the severed ribbon into the nearest fire. They vanished in a puff of brightness, magic unbound from the tyranny of form.

"And now . . ."

Ophidias raised his wing, unveiling Ruth to the Morning Lords. Colors seemed brighter, sharper; she turned toward Melior, catching his gaze and feeling her heart leap in response.

Heart twin. She hadn't quite understood what it meant until this moment. She took a step toward Melior, then another, and then his hands were warm and real in hers, and Ruth trembled with relief and gladness.

Ophidias continued to spread his wings, opening them, angling them backward until their extension formed twin arcs over his head. Wingtip and wingtip touched, and—sudden as a rediscovered memory—everyone in the Twilight Court knew all that Ruth knew about the binding.

"Amadis . . ." Ophidias' voice died away on a serpentine hiss. There was sorrow in it, and frost. "Throw the ring into the fire, Daughter of Earth."

Ruth looked down and realized with distaste that she was still clutching the ring with the golden stone between Melior's hands and hers. She pulled one hand free and tossed the ring into the fire.

As the flame had done for Ophidias' arrival, the blaze rose up in a firespout, dancing human-high above the coals. But that which was summoned now did not come willingly. The column of fire doubled over on itself, sinking down below the granite lip of the firepit only to rear up again as though something had thrust it away. Finally it settled, darkened—and became the form of the wizard Amadis.

"Child of Fire," Ophidias said.

Ruth clutched Melior's hands tighter. There was harsh grief in Ophidias' voice, and somehow there was fear in Amadis' unnaturally still countenance.

"Why did you flee from me?" the firedrake asked.

"I was called," Amadis said simply. "I serve."

"And who do you serve?" Ophidias asked, sounding as if he'd rather not.

"My master." Amadis' voice was remote, as inhuman as a robot's, or a doll's.

"Do you claim a master outside the Word?"

Melior's hands tightened on Ruth's. She caught his alarm through their bond, though she hardly needed that to tell her something crucial was taking place here—even if she wasn't quite sure what it was.

"I must," Amadis answered. "I am bound until the day of my release."

"What binds you, Firechild? What are you bound to do?" Ophidias asked reluctantly. The firedrake's wings fanned gently back and forth, sending waves of heat through the chamber.

Amadis hesitated. Her white feet were delicate as snowflakes upon the coals, and her copper fire hair lofted slightly away from her body with the waves of rising air; but it was as if something here pulled at the semblance of human form that she wore like a casual insult, and moment by moment Amadis lost her grasp of it.

There was a silent exchange of force between the two wizards, and finally Amadis spoke. "The blood of the High King binds me to ravish away the Twelve Treasures of Chandrakar, so that none of them may be brought forward on the day of the Kingmaking."

"Who binds you to this task?" Ophidias asked.

"It is Baligant, called Clerk Baligant, called Baligant No-House, called Eirdois Baligant of the House of the Vermilion Shadows, called Baligant High Prince, called High King-Elect, called groomsman of Hermonicet the Fair, who binds me to this task," Amadis said.

Everyone heard. Everyone knew that no wizard could lie. Their great delight was in tricking any of the Five Races who dealt with them by speaking nothing but the truth in a fashion so obscure that their victims never recognized their warnings until far too late. But Amadis had spoken with unambiguous clarity. Baligant commanded her. Baligant had tampered with the Sword of Maiden's Tears.

"Foolish child," Ophidias said. "You had only the least part of what I might have taught you, and in your haste to claim mastery made yourself prey to the Bound-in-Time. How many flawed bargains have you made—and how many more can you endure?"

"As many as I must," Amadis said. "Your power is greater than mine; release me to the place of my service, that I may work my master's will."

"That boon comes at a price," Ophidias said, and in his voice was the crackle of the devouring fire. "Surrender to me this form you wear, and go always in fire."

Amadis cried out in protest, but her shape was already shifting. The bright red-gold of her gown became the color of her skin, flowing to mingle with her hair as her form swirled and changed, dissolving in fire as if it were a sugar lump in water.

The salamander stood for a moment among the coals and then vanished.

"My part of our bargain is complete, Child of Air," Ophidias said. "Do not call upon me again until you have fulfilled yours."

Melior bowed.

Ophidias looked away, folding his wings against his sides and raising his head to scan the chamber. His head swiveled until his slanting golden eye was fixed on Nic. "And you, paladin—your sands are run."

"I'm ready." Nic's voice was as even as if he were discussing the weather.

He'd bargained with Ophidias. Ruth looked down at the watch in her hands. He'd said he'd swapped his *time* for the help he'd gotten. She knew he'd given up years of his past—had he bargained away his future as well?

"No!"

It was not Ruth who had cried out but Jausserande. Nic looked at her and shrugged. He took a step toward Ophidias.

"I said no!"

Jausserande grabbed Nic's arm and yanked. She would have had better luck shifting Ophidias. But moving him hadn't been her ambition. She leaped in front of him, holding Nic's Bowie knife.

His steel Bowie knife. Steel blade, steel pommel, steel quillons . . .

Even halfway across the room Ruth could smell the burning flesh. Fox shifted where he stood, his intentions unknown, and was yanked back into place by his elphen wardens.

"You shall not have him, wizard." Jausserande's voice was flat and steady, though tears of agony ran from her eyes and smoke curled between her fingers from where her flesh touched the iron tang of the blade. "Cold iron breaks all magic. It should kill you."

"Jausserande!" Melior cried. "In the name of reason, cousin—" He started forward, and stopped as Jausserande flashed the blade at him.

In the moment her attention was distracted, Nic jumped her. It was no contest; it was possible that Jausserande was stronger, but Nic was completely merciless in his attack. Seconds later, Jausserande lay sprawled on the floor, and Nic was sitting on her chest, prying her fingers open to get the knife.

"It will not have you! I'll kill you myself, first!" she snarled helplessly as he resheathed his knife at his belt.

"In some quarters I suppose that would be considered an induce-ment," he said.

Slowly Nic began to get to his feet. He looked from Jausserande to Ophidias. There was nothing in his face other than the unyielding inten-tion of keeping his word. Jausserande knelt upon the floor, her hand still smoking faintly, and stared at Nic as though he was her hope of grace.

Nic . . . and Jausserande? But I thought—She hates humans. Doesn't she? Ruth thought.

"If you do not go, paladin, who will go in your place?" Ophidias asked. He seemed genuinely interested in the answer, as if there were any other possibility.

Ruth looked down at the watch in her hand. Nic's timepiece—was it possible that, in some way, this was Nic's *time* as well?

Before she could decide what to do, Fox spoke. Somewhere he had learned that trick of projection that made his voice audible even across a chamber this size.

"I'll go," he said. This time he shrugged his guards off and stepped forward, wearing his chains as if they were some sort of theatrical grace-note to this absurd set piece.

"No!" This time Ruth did protest. "I won't lose both of you—" Not Philip and Naomi both.

"You never had me, Ruthie," Fox said, regaining some of his old cockiness. "You're just one of those sentimental pack-rat types. And per-sonally, I'd rather take my chances with Mister Lizard here than with that pack of prick-eared insider traders." He shrugged toward where the Red Earl sat. "Tampering with the Treasures—seems to be the new outdoor sport, doesn't it? Probably carries an even worse sentence than offing an elf."

Jausserande pulled herself unsteadily to her feet, off balance because she could not use her right hand.

Ophidias spread his wings and gazed at Fox. "So you will honor the bargain Nicodemus Brightlaw made with me?"

"Yeah," said Fox, looking up. His skin gleamed golden with the light radiating from Ophidias' body.

"Without knowing the terms?" the wizard asked.

"It doesn't matter a hell of a lot," Fox pointed out in the tone of voice that had always made Ruth long to smack him. "Whatever you do can't be worse than what they're going to do—and even if it is, I figure pissing them off is still worth something."

"And what of the clemency that Melior's lady Ruth would surely win you?" Ophidias asked.

"Look," said Fox, "could you just make up your mind? I don't get these noble impulses that often. But if you think anything Ruthie says about what a good boy I am is going to matter after Hathorne or whoever they've got is finished telling nothing but the truth, you're not a very bright wizard."

Fox shrugged in the direction of the Red Earl and then tried to fold his arms, but the fetters stopped him. Ruth glanced at Melior. He shook his head very slightly, his expression grim. No, even if Melior wished, there could be no pardon for the outlaw Fox. And the malice of House Vermilion would ensure that no second escape could be arranged.

"Take him," Jausserande urged the wizard. "Leave Ceiynt alone. He's nothing to you."

"Let it go, little girl," Nic said, low.

"Now, Cupbearer, how would you know what use I might have for a paladin?" the firedrake asked, amused.

"Nic!" Ruth hadn't meant it to be so loud, but her voice fell into a silence, and everyone heard. "Catch!" Ruth said, and threw the watch.

Ophidias' wings flared out, reflecting brightness as they unfurled. Nic's hand shot out, nearly skimming the coals as he snatched the flashing silver object out of the air. The moment his fingers touched it there was a soundless thunderclap: Nic Brightlaw stood transfixed, holding his wrist-watch in his hand.

"Someone has been meddling," Ophidias observed, but he didn't seem to be angry with Ruth.

"I . . . remember," Nic said aloud.

His words were nearly swallowed in the rumbling that came from the corridor outside. At first it had been almost below the threshold of audibility, and Ruth had subconsciously ascribed the sound to thunder—but who could possibly hear thunder in this room buried at the heart of the enormous castle?

But it was not thunder that broke in upon the tableau of wizard and paladin, outlaw and Treasurekeeper. It was a detachment of the garrison of Citadel itself, arriving on the run, armored and girded for war.

"My lords!" their leader said, faltering momentarily into silence at the sight of the firedrake. "My lords—Citadel is attacked: An army advances to besiege us!"

It was an hour later, and things had changed.

"You . . . idiot," Fox said to the man beside him. A farrier finished striking the bolts from his shackles, and Fox freed his wrists and stretched.

Raven regarded him with stubborn placidity. "We've a truce," he rumbled in his slow deep voice. "Highborn and us—they offered truce so I could come and talk to them."

"And you believed them," Fox said in disgust. "All they have to do is kill you, and who's going to care?"

"I will care," Melior said. Fox looked away and didn't quite spit.

"And I," Jausserande said, with honest reluctance. "We have offered truce and will abide by it. If this is war, let us fight it with honor."

It had not been, as some had feared, the High Prince's army on the road, or a preemptive breaking of the Twilight Court truce by one of the Morning Lords. The army upon the road had been . . . human.

Scarred infantry commanders, captains of horse. Outlaw, freeman, bonded farmer—the human vassals that the Morning Lords had used to fight their war, discarded and forgotten once the war was over. But *they* had not forgotten. And when they had been summoned, the skills honed over five human generations had made them a formidable army.

An army that Raven directed.

Raven had been Fox's lieutenant; before that, when he had been a free man, Raven had been a blacksmith. He had curling black hair and a thick black beard and an ugly twisted brand mark on one cheek. He was the largest man Ruth had ever seen. He made Nic Brightlaw look delicate, and Fox's head didn't even come to his shoulder.

Raven had come to bargain—Fox's life and freedom . . . for peace.

The council chamber had been cleared of all but the Earls and the more powerful Barons—and Ophidias, Ruth, Fox, and Nic. Perhaps fifty people now occupied its echoing amplitude, elphen nobles who knew what price war exacted and who had just been faced with crushing proof of their High King's malice toward them. Nobles who held the rule of Chandrakar in their hands and were now being forced to acknowledge human power for the first time.

"So this . . . rabble comes to demand their king?" the Red Earl sneered.

Ruth didn't think this particular social experiment was going to be a success, somehow.

"We will pay," Raven said. "All of us."

"Don't do this, Raven," Fox said in hopeless tones.

"What price will you set on your own lives? the Earl of the House of the Saffron Evenings asked with spurious kindness. "Outlawed men—or off your lands without permission—it is your own skins you should look to."

"We come for Fox," Raven repeated. "I must return by sundown with your answer."

There was a low muttering as the nobles conferred with one another.

What Fox had done had never touched most of them; his raids had been confined to Domain Rohannan, and until today most of them had not known that he existed.

But they knew now—and they knew more. They knew that Fox was a touchstone to draw the Children of Earth from field and hearth in every corner of Chandrakar, united into an army by the desire that one of their number should not feel the weight of elphen justice.

"Let me make a counterproposal," Fox said, as the stillness stretched.

Every eye in the room turned to him. There were those who might have tried to silence him save for the fact that the wizard Ophidias was still vividly present and Fox might, in some unknown fashion, enjoy the wizard's favor.

"You want to kill me. Fine. I can understand that."

("Don't push it, Fox," Ruth muttered under her breath.)

"And you want all these good people to go away and leave you to squabble in peace. That seems reasonable. Just give them some place to go—and you can have me."

"You do not know what you are saying," Jausserande said, looking appalled. Ruth saw the Red Earl smile with anticipation and longed to smash the expression from his face. She looked toward Ophidias.

Fox favored Jausserande with an insultingly sweet smile. "You don't think so, Tink? I'd say I've made a study of it—and you provided the optional extra credit assignment. I won't watch you prick-ears slaughter Raven and all the rest. This whole world belonged to them once—give them back a piece of it. I can make them leave peacefully."

Ruth, watching Raven's stubborn expression, wasn't as sure of that as Fox was. Revolutions were even harder to stop than they were to start, and any student of history knew that Chandrakar had most of the sociological playing pieces in place to manufacture a brutal dictatorship or a bloody revolution. Or both.

"A Free City for the mud-born?" Jausserande's voice was studiedly scornful. "They won't last a month. Give them the Vale of Stars, Cousin, for this paradise, do—and give Fox to me."

"Developing a taste for carrion at last, Cupbearer?" the Red Earl said. "Are you in such a hurry to resign your wardship over Floire's Treasure?"

The Cupbearer must live untouched to touch the Cup, Ruth remembered.

"Had I a taste for bestiality, I would mate with you, Ryence," Jausserande said coolly.

The Earl let her comment pass. "Give the little losel to me, and

Vermilion permits Floire to give away Rohannan lands to vermin as it wishes," he said.

"And I say that Vermilion has nothing to say about what transpires in Canton Silver," the Earl of Silver answered angrily.

Mother of mercy, they're going to fight over whether or not someone's said "Mother May I!" Ruth realized in dismay. Like feuding kindred, the Seven Houses were ready to brawl at the slightest provocation—and this was more than that.

"What Rohannan does on Rohannan lands is nothing to any man here," Melior said coldly.

"Do you swear to keep the peace of this city, Baron Rohannan?" the Earl of Silver said. "Consider the terms of your grant carefully; one handsbreadth outside it, Twilight justice must reign."

"Now *there's* an oxymoron," Fox muttered.

"Fox!" Raven protested.

Ruth caught Nic's eye and saw by the dark amusement in his expression that he'd deduced the same thing she had. For a man like Raven to interrupt his so-called betters was something the Morning Lords should take a lot more notice of than they would. It meant a change in the way humans saw elves—and would come to mean a change in the way elves would have to treat humans.

"We came for you, not for land," Raven said. "To bargain your life away like this—it isn't right."

"Land will be a lot more use to you than I'd ever be," Fox said. "And Ruth can help you run the place. It's a base, Raven—one they can't take away from you. Remember what I taught you, and some day there'll be Eight Houses of the Twilight—or more."

"*Me?*" said Ruth. She couldn't help anyone run a city. She couldn't even balance her checkbook.

"When the streets are paved with iron," the Red Earl mocked.

"You'll live long enough to see the day," Fox told him.

No! Ruth cried silently. No matter how twisted he'd become inside, she couldn't understand how Fox could willingly make such a bargain.

"There has been enough slaughter," the Earl of Silver said. "Since the loss in lands is Rohannan's alone, Silver allows the bargain and calls upon its fellows to uphold it. Set the bounds of your grant, Rohannan, and let the earthborn who cross it find their sanctuary there—but only in that moment, and not one span of ground before. I shall hold the outlaw for the High Justice under my own hand, the terms to be set between Silver and Crystal. Come here to me, Child of Earth." He held out his hand to Fox, his face grave.

Fox stepped forward. Raven grabbed him.

"Let me go, Raven," Fox said in an even voice. "You heard the man—and Mel will do it. You'll have a place, all of you. And it will really piss them off."

Considering how irritated she'd been with Fox's cool care-for-nothing affect, surely the spectacle of him throwing over his vendetta to trade his life for a gaggle of imperfect strangers and a handful of outlaws of whom he'd never spoken very highly should make her happier, Ruth reflected. But all she could feel was grief, and anger, and the resonance of the supplication circling within her brain: *Don't let this happen, don't let this happen, don't let this happen . . .*

"We do not give up our own for gain," Raven said. "I come for true justice—not to bargain. Fox has killed a man. We will pay a man's price to his kin—and no more than that."

This was open defiance, and every Morning Lord in the room finally knew it. "Kill them both," the Earl of Silver said quietly.

"Now just one high-faluting minute here, Children of Air."

It was Ophidias who spoke, and so there was self-conscious silence. Even Raven released his grip on Fox's shoulder.

"Now let's get all this straight. Rohannan promises a Free City for the Children of Earth in exchange for them going away now without a fuss. Since the next ruler of the line Rohannan and its lands will be half-blooded, that seems a satisfactory bargain to me, and thus I witness it, Earl of Silver. But I'm not sure it's reasonable that Rohannan pays and you get the outlaw. After all, there was another bargain pending before all this fuss started, and I think we ought to see how that works out before going any further with this."

There was a moment of aphasic silence.

"Oh. Right," Fox said. Ruth was insensibly relieved to hear the ragged tension in his voice—she'd been beginning to suspect he wasn't human. "My life for Mr. Brightlaw's. Fine with me if everything else the point-ears have agreed to stands."

"Oh, I think you can count on that," Ophidias said, amused. "But if you were to take the paladin's place, Child of Earth, I'd have your life, not his—and I have plans for his life."

"Maybe you ought to rethink them," Fox said promptly. "Since Ruthie just gave him his Time back, I don't think you've got a hold over him any more."

"Only as tenuous a hold as the credence that the earthborn give to the Word," Ophidias agreed, "but I think it's enough."

"Yes," Nic said simply. "I'm bought and paid for."

"Then pay now," Ophidias said. He rose to his feet and swept his wing down and out, shielding Nic from their sight and furling back, closing and closing until Nic Brightlaw's presence was only a trick of the light, and then suddenly the mind accepted that he was gone and the chamber empty of paladins.

It had all happened so fast that Ruth didn't have time to brace herself for it. A sob caught in her throat, and Melior held her close, his expression coldly daring any of his peers to say a word.

Jausserande made a sound low in her throat, like one who has received a mortal wound and has only barely realized it.

"Buck up, Tink. It only gets worse," Fox said.

"Then the bargain is done, wizard," the Earl of Silver said into the silence. "And if it pleases you, you may leave the justice of the Land in our hands."

"But it doesn't," Ophidias said. "Or, rather, it almost does—but not quite. The bargains are done, but I'm always receptive to gifts," the firedrake said meaningfully.

Ruth saw Fox hesitate, weighing the chance of making more trouble against the possibility of the House of the Silver Silences overturning Rohannan's bargain.

"Forget that," Ruth said, stepping away from Melior. *And standing on my own two feet for once,* she thought with bleak literalist humor.

"You can't have him either. Everybody who has a right to Philip's stupid life has filed a quitclaim. And no matter what anybody says—or can be made to say with half-truths—he didn't hide the Cup, he got it back. He killed someone, but Raven's right—he shouldn't have to pay more for that than an elf would. And nobody has a right to own his life but him."

"That hurts, Ruthie," Fox said quietly.

"You deserve it," Ruth said simply.

"All right, you've convinced me," Ophidias said promptly. "The boy goes free. Isn't that right, Somhairle?"

Regordane Somhairle, the Earl of Silver, looked from Ruth to Ophidias. His face was dark with glittering fury. "The . . . bargain," he said, as if the words strangled him, "stands. Get from my sight, Rohannan lord, and take your mud-born cattle with you. If I see you between today's sunset and next year's Court, your lands and your life are forfeit. You will find your taxes heavy in the spring."

Had they won? Ruth wasn't sure.

"And what of Baligant?" Melior said. "He has betrayed you all— what of your Treasures?"

Jausserande closed her eyes as if in prayer.

The feverish tension broke in jeers and catcalls. The Earl of Silver deliberately turned his back on Melior.

"What of them? Line Eirdois holds the Mirror of Falling Souls, just as it always has," Eirdois Ryence, the Earl of Vermilion, said silkily.

"Gauvain has lost the Book!" someone called from the back.

"But it was *Gauvain* that lost it—not wizard meddling," the Red Earl answered promptly.

Melior prepared to argue.

"Cousin, I beg you by your Sword—provoke them *later,*" Jausserande said under the cover of renewed argument.

"We have only the wizard's word that it acted at the High Prince's command," Vermilion said. "I counsel the Bearers to look to their charges, as Eirdois defends its own—and we will send to Mourning to hear Baligant High Prince's response to the charges that Rohannan lays against him." Ryence smiled, and Ruth saw the faces around him relax in approval, even though the Earl's explanation had made no sense even to her.

"In the name of sanity—" Melior began, as the hum of discussion— of acceptance—rose to fill the room.

Fox moved then, jerking free of Raven and shoving Melior hard in the chest.

"You owe me," Fox said viciously. "More than you can *ever* repay. So get your butt the fuck out of here and take Ruthie and those poor suckers outside with you."

Jausserande, too, shoved Melior toward the door, then turned back to bully Fox and Raven ahead of her. Looking back over her shoulder as she followed Melior out, Ruth would nearly have sworn that she saw a smile of satisfaction on Ophidias' face.

What did the wizard gain from all this? Did Ophidias want war? If that was what he wanted, he hadn't gotten it—Melior had gambled that the accusation and the proof would be enough to make the Twilight Court rise up against Baligant, but after all it had cost to bring them before the Morning Lords, even proof hadn't been enough. The Morning Lords were tired of war.

They would not fight.

"They will not fight," Melior said again, bewildered astonishment in his voice.

Behind Melior's hastily assembled baggage train marched those members of Raven's ragtag army who had not simply slipped away to their own homesteads once Fox's freedom had been gained. Fox rode with them; Ruth wasn't sure whether he was happy with the way things had turned out or was plotting a new chapter in his own vendetta. Maybe the Free City would keep him out of trouble; those who were not with them now would spread the word of the Free City in the Vale of Stars. And the city would grow.

"They'll fight," Jausserande said grimly. "We are sure of Cloak, Cup, and Sword, three Treasures only—Ryence lies as easily as breath, and it is Baligant's own heir who is said to hold the Mirror. Come, Cousin, do you think after what you have shown them our fellow Bearers do aught but fly to their charges?"

Melior shook his head. "But they do not condemn Baligant for his treachery. And soon it will be too late," Melior said despairingly. "Even if all of the Twelve are recovered, it will be too late."

"Then we shall fight again—for the Land itself, and not the heat of a woman's bed," Jausserande predicted.

And everything will change. But not slowly, and not easily. Ruth sighed, almost content, even in the face of such a turbulent future. Ruth was going home—to Dawnheart, in Domain Rohannan. Home. For the first time in her adult life, Ruth Marlowe was all in one place, with a future to build.

And hadn't Ophidias implied that her children would inherit in Domain Rohannan?

Wizards only told the truth.

· Epilogue ·

Black Knight's Endgame

NEITHER MARGOT NOR Carol thought they could possibly eat a thing when they got back to Penny and Katy's house. The departure of Holly for Elfland and the possibly involuntary disappearance of Ruth and Nic was still completely unreal to the other four, and after a couple of glasses of Katy's homemade *athol brose,* it seemed even more so.

But with the arrival of the roast goose—seemingly none the worse for its prolonged wait—and all the trimmings, Margot and Carol both recovered their appetites enough to do Katy's cooking a certain amount of justice. An hour later, replete to groaning but with plum pudding still in the offing, Carol was helping Katy clear away the remains when there was a jarring crash from the back of the house. Everything shook.

Margot gave a startled yelp—more of indignation than anything else—and dropped the dish she was holding. It bounced once, then settled to the linoleum and shattered into shards.

"What was that?" Penny said, already on the run toward it.

"*Who* is that?" Margot said in reverential tones a few minutes later.

"That's Nic," Katy said.

"You're back," Penny said, in faintly poleaxed tones.

Nicodemus Brightlaw, Director of the Ryerson Memorial Public Library in Ippisiqua, New York, got slowly to his feet. He stared around Penny's bedroom in bewilderment, then down at the near-black three-piece wool suit, white button-down Oxford shirt, and anonymous burgundy tie.

"I'm back," he said, equally blankly. "And it's still . . . ?"

"Christmas," Penny said. "Christmas Eve."

"Oh blesséd spirits," Nic said, giddily. "All three in one night. God bless us every one. But I'm afraid Miss Marlowe isn't going to be joining us for dinner."

"She isn't dead, is she?" Katy asked. "And it's leftovers now, anyway: We ate it."

"Not dead," Nic said, ignoring the specter of leftovers. "Miss Marlowe is . . . home, I guess you'd say. With the gentleman who proposes to marry her as soon as all the fuss dies down."

"But what happened?" Penny demanded. "Where did you go? Was it Elfland? Did you see Holly and Mac? What about—"

"Who sent you back *here?*" Margot said, cutting directly to the chase.

Nic smiled faintly. "Well you see, ladies—and I'm afraid I haven't quite been introduced all around . . ."

"Margot Leigh Reasoner," Margot said.

"Carol Goodchild. We're friends of Holly's. And we know who you are, Mr. Brightlaw."

"Well any friend of Holly Kendal's, as the saying goes," Nic said mildly. "And if I can trouble you for some dinner, Katy, I'll tell you more or less what happened. You see, there was this wizard . . ."

Nic draped an arm around Penny's shoulder. Penny was grinning in a joyful relieved fashion that made everyone feel that Christmas had come early, at least for one person there.

In a straggly drove, the party made for the dining room of Katy and Penny's Victorian house—and stopped.

There was a man with a gun in the dining room.

The silence that followed was so profound that the ticking of the antique schoolroom clock on the wall became the loudest sound in the room. Through the open door to the kitchen, cheerful yellow light shone down on white tile and sparkling green-and-white checkerboard linoleum, and it was a universe as far off and unattainable as the Lands Beyond the Morning.

"Good evening, Mr. Brightlaw," Frank Catalpano said. "I didn't see you come in." The gun he held in his gloved hand looked large and cold, and it was pointed unwaveringly at Nic's stomach. "You can call me Frank. I have an interest in some mutual acquaintances."

"Damn," Margot said irritatedly.

Moving slowly, Nic disentangled himself from Penny and stepped sideways.

"Don't try it," Frank advised kindly. "I've read your jacket, but that was a long time ago. All I want is a little assistance."

"You were after us at the hotel," Carol said. Frank bowed slightly, not taking his eyes off Nic. Behind him, the long oval of the dining room table was still half-cluttered with the remains of the dinner dishes. It did not seem possible to the four women that this could still be part of the same day.

"This is *those* guys?" Katy said, sounding more impressed than scared.

Penny put a hand on her arm, as if Katy might try to rush forward and disarm the man. "Nic, Holly told us all about these people; they're—"

"Where is Gauvain Makindeor of the House of the Crystal Wind?" Frank asked, cutting her off.

There was a long pause. Frank seemed to sigh. "Very well. Miss Goodchild, would you come over here please?"

Carol shifted uneasily. Nic put up a hand to stop her.

"Why not just tell me what you want . . . Frank?" Nic said. "I'm sure we can come to some sort of accommodation, don't you think?"

Frank smiled thinly. "In no particular order, I'd like Gauvain Makindeor and a book he has in his possession. I'd also like to know where Ruth Marlowe and Holly Kendal are."

"Well," said Nic blandly, "the last time I saw the three of them, they were before the Twilight Court of Chandrakar, so I suppose that's where your book is, too."

Frank's eyes flickered. Nic took a step forward. Very deliberately, Frank pointed the gun at Margot. Nic stopped.

"I'm afraid that isn't the right answer," Frank said. "I think all of you are going to have to come with me."

"No," Nic Brightlaw said.

Frank looked at him. "I'm afraid I'll have to insist."

"Sorry," Nic said, shrugging slightly. "I don't care which alphabet agency you work for. Nobody here is going with you today or any day. The three people you mentioned are far beyond your reach; you're welcome to hunt for them as long as you like, but these people are under my protection, Mr. Catalpano."

The gun barrel jerked an inch to the side and back again, a nervous tic.

"You see, I have some idea of what you want. These women aren't of any use to you at all. And if you don't back off, I'm afraid I'm going to have to kill you."

The words were said with such mild matter-of-factness that it took the four women several seconds to realize what had been said.

This is not happening, Penny said to herself. She tried to remember that only a few hours ago she and Katy had been about to sit down to Christmas Eve dinner with Nic and Ruth. She vowed that if she got out of here alive, one of the first things she was going to do was smash the alarm system at the Ryerson.

"You can't protect them forever," Frank Catalpano said. "You'll find I have powerful friends."

"And you might be surprised at what kind of favors I can call in," Nic answered blandly. "And I don't imagine your people like surprises very much. Be reasonable, Mr. Catalpano. Makindeor and Miss Marlowe are gone, and your people are going to have to look somewhere else for your extraterrestrial bolt-hole. That's the bottom line. So just walk away and leave the ladies alone, because if any of them ever gets so much as a parking ticket—"

"Skip the idle chatter," Frank interrupted, flipping his coat back to put his gun away. "You're right. They aren't worth taking in. But you've made a powerful enemy here tonight, Mr. Nicodemus Brightlaw."

"So have you." Nic's smile widened, brilliant with heartless threat. "So have you."